Nightwings

Old Earth has reached its Third Cycle, a tired planet basking in the faded glories of a lost civilisation. Long ago it had been great – but the pride and greed of its rulers had brought about a terrible downfall. And now, far out in space, an alien race prepares to conquer.

A Time of Changes

On a colony world that forbids emotional sharing, where even the mention of the word 'I' is taboo, an Earthman arrives with a self-baring drug. In his own words, princeling Kinnall Darival recounts his awakening, beginning with the greatest of heresies: 'I am Kinnall Darival and I mean to tell you all about myself.'

Lord Valentine's Castle

On the immense world of Majipoor, Valentine, an itinerant juggler, comes to realise that he is in fact his namesake: Lord Valentine, the Coronal – his body and throne stolen by a usurper. Across this giant world, Valentine sets out on a quest to win back his throne – and discover which of his enemies has the power to vanquish him so utterly from not just his throne, but from his very life ...

Also By Robert Silverberg

Robert Silverberg

SF GATEWAY OMNIBUS

NIGHTWINGS
A TIME OF CHANGES
LORD VALENTINE'S CASTLE

GOLLANCZ

LONDON

This omnibus copyright © Robert Silverberg 2013
Nightwings copyright © Robert Silverberg 1969
A Time of Changes copyright © Robert Silverberg 1971
Lord Valentine's Castle copyright © Robert Silverberg 1980
Introduction copyright © SFE Ltd 2013

First published in Great Britain in 2013 by
Gollancz
An imprint of the Orion Publishing Group
Orion House, 5 Upper St Martin's Lane,
London WC2H 9EA

An Hachette UK Company

A CIP catalogue record for this book
is available from the British Library

ISBN 978 0 575 12903 0

1 3 5 7 9 10 8 6 4 2

Typeset by Input Data Services Ltd, Bridgwater, Somerset

Printed and bound by CPI Group (UK) Ltd, Croydon, CR0 4YY

The Orion Publishing Group's policy is to use papers
that are natural, renewable and recyclable products and
made from wood grown in sustainable forests. The logging
and manufacturing processes are expected to conform to
the environmental regulations of the country of origin.

www.orionbooks.co.uk
www.gollancz.co.uk

CONTENTS

ENTER THE SF GATEWAY . . .

Towards the end of 2011, in conjunction with the celebration of fifty years of coherent, continuous science fiction and fantasy publishing, Gollancz launched the SF Gateway.

Over a decade after launching the landmark SF Masterworks series, we realised that the realities of commercial publishing are such that even the Masterworks could only ever scratch the surface of an author's career. Vast troves of classic SF & Fantasy were almost certainly destined never again to see print. Until very recently, this meant that anyone interested in reading any of those books would have been confined to scouring second-hand bookshops. The advent of digital publishing changed that paradigm for ever.

Embracing the future even as we honour the past, Gollancz launched the SF Gateway with a view to utilising the technology that now exists to make available, for the first time, the entire backlists of an incredibly wide range of classic and modern SF and fantasy authors. Our plan, at its simplest, was – and still is! – to use this technology to build on the success of the SF and Fantasy Masterworks series and to go even further.

The SF Gateway was designed to be the new home of classic Science Fiction & Fantasy – the most comprehensive electronic library of classic SFF titles ever assembled. The programme has been extremely well received and we've been very happy with the results. So happy, in fact, that we've decided to complete the circle and return a selection of our titles to print, in these omnibus editions.

We hope you enjoy this selection. And we hope that you'll want to explore more of the classic SF and fantasy we have available. These are wonderful books you're holding in your hand, but you'll find much, much more ... through the SF Gateway.

www.sfgateway.com

INTRODUCTION

from The Encyclopedia of Science Ficton

Robert Silverberg (1935–) is a US writer, and the extremely prolific author of more than one hundred SF books, a large number of nonfiction books (not always under his own name) and a great deal of other work, including an estimated two hundred erotic novels as Don Elliott and other undisclosed pseudonyms; he has also edited or co-edited more than seventy anthologies.

He began to write while studying for his BA at Columbia University, where he continued an involvement in SF Fandom; his first professionally published story was 'Gorgon Planet' for *Nebula* in February 1954, though his first actual sale was 'The Sacred River' for Lilith Lorraine's little magazine *The Avalonian* in 1952; his first novel, a Young Adult tale, was *Revolt on Alpha C* (1955). By 1956 he had begun to publish prolifically – forty-nine SF stories in that year alone, work whose obvious quality immediately won him a Hugo as Most Promising New Author – and continued to specialize in the Genre SF that had shaped him for three more years. He worked for the Ziff-Davis stable, producing wordage at assembly-line speed for *Amazing Stories* and *Fantastic*, and was a prolific contributor to such magazines as *Science Fiction Adventures* and *Super-Science Fiction*, using many different names. For part of this time Randall Garrett was a partner in this 'fiction factory'; they wrote in collaboration as Robert Randall, Gordon Aghill and Ralph Burke (Silverberg also used the Burke pseudonym on solo work). The most important pseudonyms which Silverberg used exclusively were Calvin M. Knox and David Osborne.

Early stories by Silverberg writing solo have appeared in various collections, though he has never allowed the whole of this early material to be gathered together in any of his various retrospective assemblies, which include *In the Beginning: Tales from the Pulp Era* (2006) and various volumes incorporated into either the first or the second of two recent sequences both published under the same series surtitle, The Collected Short Stories of Robert Silverberg.

The most notable full-length fictions from Silverberg's early period are *Master of Life and Death* (1957), a novel dealing with institutionalized measures to combat Overpopulation, *Invaders from Earth* (1958), a drama of political corruption involved with the Colonization of Ganymede, and *Recalled to Life* (1962), which investigates the social response to a method of reviving the newly dead. The Nidor series, which he wrote with Garrett as Robert Randall – *The Shrouded Planet* (1957) and *The Dawning Light* (1959) – interestingly depicts an Invasion of Aliens planning Uplift activities from the view of the affected Nidorians: the aliens turn out to be us. Tales like *Stepsons of Terra* (1958) or *Invaders from Earth* (1958) or *The Seed of Earth* (1962) or *The Silent Invaders* (1963) or *The Planet Killers* (1958) are demonstrably competent, but just as demonstrably routine; and the bibliographical maze – created through title changes, revisions and repackagings, and pseudonym switches – seems at times almost deliberately confusing. The majority of the SF books he published 1960–1966 were rewritten from work originally done in 1957–1959, though the Regan sequence comprising *Regan's Planet* (1964) and *World's Fair, 1992* (1970) was original work; the second volume interestingly locates the eponymous exposition on a space station.

Despite the occasional exceptions, however, Silverberg virtually abandoned SF for some years after as the magazine market began to shrink in 1959. His output had been prodigious to this point, but somewhat mechanical, except for a handful of nonfiction books – notably *The Golden Dream* (1967) and *Mound-Builders of Ancient America* (1968) – which were painstakingly researched and carefully written. He would never write fiction again at this rate.

A new phase of Silverberg's career, in which for the first time he brought the full range of his skills and intellect to bear on SF, began around 1967 and ended in the mid-1970s. Along with the sixty or so stories written during this period, the twenty-three novels published in these years comprise (with few routine exceptions) the creative and career *summa* of perhaps the most concentratedly intelligent and controlled writer the field had yet seen. There is no easy default Silverberg story from this period to point to as exemplary, as his story-types are so various and superficially dissimilar: perhaps the closest it is possible to come is to suggest that that default story – 'Schwartz Between the Galaxies' (1974) is representative – depicts a man of flattened affect and solitary soul who is enmeshed in a world of great present complexity but whose sense of that world is fatally retrospective, vitiating his sense of Identity. With only occasional exceptions, whatever happens in a tale or novel of the great years *happens too late*.

Titles of significance from the late 1960s include *Thorns* (1967), a stylized novel of alienation and psychic Vampirism, and *Hawksbill Station* (1968), in which political exiles are sent back in time to a Cambrian Prison camp. *The Masks of Time* (1968) describes a visit by an enigmatic time traveller to the world of 1999. *The Man in the Maze* (1969) is a dramatization of the problems of alienation, based on the Greek myth of Philoctetes, the hero who is needed for his skill with the bow, but whose festering wound makes him repulsive; both wound and bow are here represented by an involuntary Telepathic broadcast which, though repellent, offers the key to a First Contact problem. *Nightwings* (1969) is a lyrical account of the conquest of a senescent Earth by Aliens, which culminates with the rebirth of its hero. *Up the Line* (1969) is a clever Time-Travel and Time-Paradox story, a flamboyant Time Opera featuring a 'Time Courier' at odds with the Time Police authorities who monitor his behaviour. *Downward to the Earth* (1970) is a story of repentance and rebirth, with calculated echoes of Joseph Conrad's *Heart of Darkness* and strong religious imagery – Silverberg homaged Conrad again in the much later *The Secret Sharer* (1988). *Tower of Glass* (1970) also makes use of religious imagery in its study of the obsessional construction of a new 'Tower of Babel' and the struggle of an Android race to win emancipation. *A Time of Changes* (1971) describes a society in which selfhood is a cardinal sin. *Son of Man* (1971) is a surreal evolutionary fantasy of the Far Future. *The World Inside* (1971), set in a Dystopian Keep known as an Urbmon, is a study of life under conditions of high population density. *The Second Trip* (1972) is an intense psychological novel describing the predicaments of a telepathic girl and a man whose Identity has been newly created in the body of an 'erased' criminal. *The Book of Skulls* (1971) is a painstaking analysis of relationships among four young men on a competitive quest for Immortality. Two of the finest novels from this period are told within a wholly realized New York frame. *Dying Inside* (1972), set almost wholly in Manhattan, is a brilliant study in which a telepath's gradual loss of his power works as a telling analogue of his loss of creative joy; given its readily assimilable metaphorical structure, the novel has unsurprisingly gained more widespread attention than some others from this period, and has been better appreciated outside the field than (see below) within. And *The Stochastic Man* (1975) is a complementary study, almost as intense, of a man developing the power to foresee the future.

The last novel composed during this extraordinary period, *Shadrach in the Furnace* (1976), concerns the predicament of the personal physician of a future dictator who finds his Identity in jeopardy. Silverberg then quit writing for four years, ostensibly because of his disenchantment with the functioning of the SF marketplace, where his books seemed to him to be suffering 'assassination' as they were allowed to go out of print after a few months; sheer exhaustion may also have been a factor. In view of the sustained quality of this astonishing burst of creativity, it is perhaps surprising that only one of these full-length works won a major award in America – *A Time of Changes* (1971), which gained a Nebula. Several excellent novels, most notably *Dying Inside*, went unrewarded, perhaps because the voters found them too intense and too uncompromising both in their depictions of anguish and desperation, and in the sense they convey that all stories that might be told are stories that have already been told. In any case, Silverberg's ensuing silence may have had something to do with the field's lack of response to these years of unremitting high-quality creative work.

Silverberg did, however, win awards for several shorter pieces: the novella *Nightwings* won a Hugo; and Nebulas went to 'Passengers' (1968), a story about people who temporarily lose control of their bodies to alien invaders, 'Good News from the Vatican' (1971), about the election of the first Robot pope, and the brilliant novella *Born with the Dead* (1988), about relationships between the living and the beneficiaries of a scientific technique guaranteeing life after death. The novella 'The Feast of St Dionysus' (1973), about the experience of religious ecstasy, won a Jupiter award. In addition to his award-winners Silverberg published almost unfailingly excellent stories during this second phase of his career. Particularly notable are 'To See the Invisible Man' (1963), 'Sundance' (1969), and 'In Entropy's Jaws' (1971). The most elaborate presentation of this body of work, accompanied by informative author's notes, appears in *The Collected Stories of Robert Silverberg: Volume Three: Something Wild is Loose 1969–72* (2008) and *The Collected Stories of Robert Silverberg: Volume Four: Trips 1972–73* (2009). The thirty tales assembled in these two volumes, plus a few slightly earlier stories from the late 1960s, comprise a *summa* of the art of the short story in SF: observant of thematic and narrative traditions of the field; open to the innovations of twentieth-century literature in general; inherently innovative; all unmistakably from the same intense pen.

At the end of the 1970s Silverberg returned to writing with the first of the Majipoor sequence, *Lord Valentine's Castle* (1980), a polished and – significantly marking the new phase – luxuriantly expansive if at points rather leisurely Science Fantasy which won a Locus Award for best fantasy novel; it is set on the world of Majipoor, where he also set the shorter pieces collected in *Majipoor Chronicles* (1982). Later titles include *Valentine Pontifex* (1983), a sequel to the first tale, plus with *The Mountains of Majipoor* (1995), *Sorcerers of Majipoor* (1997), *Lord Prestimion* (1999) and *The King of Dreams* (2001). Almost all of Silverberg's work of the 1980s was in the same relaxed vein: the psychological intensity of his mid-period work was toned down, and much of his SF was evidently pitched towards what he considered to be the demands of the market. His work of this period was commercially successful, but the full-length SF sometimes seemed rather mechanical, though the historical fantasies *Lord of Darkness* (1983) and *Gilgamesh the King* (1984) appear to have been projects dearer to his heart. The gypsy king in *Star of Gypsies* (1986), waiting in self-imposed exile for his one-time followers to realize how badly they need him, might be reckoned an ironic self-portrait. Some of the best works of this third phase of Silverberg's career are novellas, most notably *Sailing to Byzantium* (1985), winner of a 1985 Nebula and *The*

Secret Sharer (1988). Silverberg also won Hugo awards in this period for the novella 'Gilgamesh in the Outback' (1986), which was a sequel to *Gilgamesh the King* and was integrated into *To the Land of the Living* (1989), and the novelette 'Enter a Soldier. Later, Enter Another' (1989).

More recent work includes the unfinished New Springtime trilogy about the repopulation of Earth by various races (not including humans) after a future ice age, comprising *At Winter's End* (1988) and *The Queen of Springtime* (1989). Singletons of interest include *The Face of the Waters* (1991), a novel about diasporan humans living as exiles on a watery world after the destruction of Earth; *Hot Sky at Midnight* (1994), a tale which, set in the early years of the twenty-first century, is told in a tone of searingly bleak pessimism that was increasingly to be encountered in SF writers in their late prime as the millennium approached; and *Roma Eterna* (2003), an Alternate History in which the Roman empire has endured, seemingly endlessly. Much of his short fiction of this period is assembled in various volumes of the two sequences of collected stories identically surtitled The Collected Stories of Robert Silverberg; but some significant later fiction – like the novella 'Hot Times in Magma City' (1995), in which Los Angeles has been transformed by geological Disasters – remain uncollected.

Silverberg was president of the Science Fiction Writers of America 1967–1968. *The Magazine of Fantasy & Science Fiction* published a special issue devoted to him in April 1974. An autobiographical essay appeared in *Hell's Cartographers* (1975) edited by Brian W. Aldiss and Harry Harrison. For more than half a century, his productivity has seemed almost superhuman, and his abrupt metamorphosis from a writer of standardized pulp fiction into a prose artist was an accomplishment unparalleled within the field. He was elected to the Science Fiction Hall of Fame in 1999, and in 2004 received the SFWA Grand Master Award. In the early twenty-first century, he remains one of the most imaginative and versatile writers ever to have been involved with Genre SF, which he was instrumental in transforming after about 1970. His relegation to the sidelines by the American literary establishment is scandalous.

No three novels out of Silverberg's enormous oeuvre can truly encapsulate his astonishing career, but the three chosen here go as far as possible to give a sense of the professional skill and emotional commitment he invested in all of his mature work. *Nightwings* is set in an ornately complex Far Future time, when Genetic Engineering has multiplied Homo sapiens's options, though internecine savageries demand a healing; which the protagonist hopes to offer through old wisdom and new telepathy. (This tale, written immediately after Silverberg's house burned to the ground, passionately seeks for a way to redeem time past.) *A Time of Changes*, which deserved its Nebula Award, again probes the nature of alienation. Set on a colony planet settled by a diseased puritan culture which prohibits self-assertion, the tale comprises the autobiography of a rebel who hopes to unite his fellows through a telepathic drug. (His arguments for doing this are directly contradicted in the later *Dying Inside*.) *Lord Valentine's Castle* (the novel that marked Silverberg's return, refreshed after four years' silence) is a long loving leisurely gift to the reader, who will not be surprised that the book's amnesiacal protagonist will come upon his heritage: which is the entire huge world of Majipoor, and the throne. Each of these books differs radically; but deep inside they are identical: because each of them is about human beings learning how to join hands.

For a more detailed version of the above, see Robert Silverberg's author entry in *The Encyclopedia of Science Fiction*: http://sf-encyclopedia.com/entry/silverberg_robert

Some terms above are capitalised when they would not normally be so rendered; this indicates that the terms represent discrete entries in *The Encyclopedia of Science Fiction*.

NIGHTWINGS

For Harlan,
to remind him of open windows,
the currents of the Delaware River,
quarters with two heads,
and other pitfalls.

PART I

Nightwings

1

Roum is a city built on seven hills. They say it was a capital of man in one of the earlier cycles. I did not know of that, for my guild was Watching, not Remembering; but yet as I had my first glimpse of Roum, coming upon it from the south at twilight, I could see that in former days it must have been of great significance. Even now it was a mighty city of many thousands of Souls.

Its bony towers stood out sharply against the dusk. Lights glimmered appealingly. On my left hand the sky was ablaze with splendor as the sun relinquished possession; streaming bands of azure and violet and crimson folded and writhed about one another in the nightly dance that brings the darkness. To my right, blackness had already come. I attempted to find the seven hills, and failed, and still I knew that this was that Roum of majesty toward which all roads are bent, and I felt awe and deep respect for the works of our bygone fathers.

We rested by the long straight road, looking up at Roum. I said, 'It is a goodly city. We will find employment there.'

Beside me, Avluela fluttered her lacy wings. 'And food?' she asked in her high fluty voice. 'And shelter? And wine?'

'Those too,' I said. 'All of those.'

'How long have we been walking, Watcher?' she asked.

'Two days. Three nights.'

'If I had been flying, it would have been more swift.'

'For you,' I said. 'You would have left us far behind and never Seen us again. Is that your desire?'

She came close to me and rubbed the rough fabric of my sleeve, and then she pressed herself at me the way a flirting cat might do. Her wings unfolded into two broad sheets of gossamer through which I could still see the sunset and the evening lights, blurred, distorted, magical. I sensed the fragrance of her midnight hair. I put my arms to her and embraced her slender, boyish body.

She said, 'You know it is my desire to remain with you always, Watcher. Always!'

'Yes, Avluela.'

'Will we be happy in Roum?'

'We will be happy,' I said, and released her.

'Shall we go into Roum now?'

'I think we should wait for Gormon,' I said, shaking my head. 'He'll be back soon from his explorations.' I did not want to tell her of my weariness. She was only a child, seventeen summers old; what did she know of weariness or of age? And I was old. Not as old as Roum, but old enough.

'While we wait,' she said, 'may I fly?'

'Fly, yes.'

I squatted beside our cart and warmed my hands at the throbbing generator while Avluela prepared to fly. First she removed her garments, for her wings have little strength and she cannot lift such extra baggage. Lithely, deftly, she peeled the glassy bubbles from her tiny feet and wriggled free of her crimson jacket and of her soft furry leggings. The vanishing light in the west sparkled over her slim form. Like all Fliers, she carried no surplus body tissue: her breasts were mere bumps, her buttocks flat, her thighs so spindly that there was a span of inches between them when she stood. Could she have weighed more than a quintal? I doubt it. Looking at her, I felt, as always, gross and earthbound, a thing of loathsome flesh, and yet I am not a heavy man.

By the roadside she genuflected knuckles to the ground, head bowed to knees, as she said whatever ritual it is that the Fliers say. Her back was to me. Her delicate wings fluttered, filled with life, rose about her like a cloak whipped up by the breeze. I could not comprehend how such wings could possibly lift even so slight a form as Avluela's. They were not hawk-like but butterfly-wings, veined and transparent, marked here and there with blotches of pigment, ebony and turquoise and scarlet. A sturdy ligament joined them to the two flat pads of muscle beneath her sharp shoulderblades; but what she did not have was the massive breastbone of a flying creature, the bands of corded muscle needed for flight. Oh, I know that Fliers use more than muscle to get aloft, that there are mystical disciplines in their mystery. Even so, I, who was of the Watchers, remained skeptical of the more fantastic guilds.

Avluela finished her words. She rose; she caught the breeze with her wings; she ascended several feet. There she remained, suspended between earth and sky, while her wings beat frantically. It was not yet night, and Avluela's wings were merely nightwings. By day she could not fly, for the terrible pressure of the solar wind would hurl her to the ground. Now, midway between dusk and dark, it was still not the best time for her to go up. I saw her thrust toward the east by the remnant of light in the sky. Her arms as well as her wings thrashed; her small pointed face was grim with concentration; on her thin lips were the words of her guild. She doubled her body and shot it out, head going one way, rump the other; and abruptly she hovered horizontally, looking groundward, her wings thrashing against the air. *Up, Avluela! Up!*

Up it was, as by will alone she conquered the vestige of light that still glowed.

With pleasure I surveyed her naked form against the darkness. I could see her clearly, for a Watcher's eyes are keen. She was five times her own height in the air, now, and her wings spread to their full expanse, so that the towers of Roum were in partial eclipse for me. She waved. I threw her a kiss and offered words of love. Watchers do not marry, nor do they engender children, but yet Avluela was as a daughter to me, and I took pride in her flight. We had travelled together a year, now, since we had first met in Agupt, and it was as though I had known her all my life. From her I drew a renewal of strength. I do not know what it was she drew from me: security, knowledge, a continuity with the days before her birth. I hoped only that she loved me as I loved her.

Now she was far aloft. She wheeled, soared, dived, pirouetted, danced. Her long black hair streamed from her scalp. Her body seemed only an incidental appendage to those two great wings which glistened and throbbed and gleamed in the night. Up she rose, glorying in her freedom from gravity, making me feel all the more leaden-footed; and like some slender rocket she shot abruptly away in the direction of Roum. I saw the soles of her feet, the tips of her wings; then I saw her no more.

I sighed. I thrust my hands into the pits of my arms to keep them warm. How is it that I felt a winter chill while the girl Avluela could soar joyously bare through the sky?

It was the twelfth of the twenty hours, and time once again for me to do the Watching. I went to the cart, opened my cases, prepared the instruments. Some of the dial covers were yellowed and faded; the indicator needles had lost their luminous coating; sea stains defaced the instrument housings, a relic of the time that pirates had assailed me in Earth Ocean. The worn and cracked levers and nodes responded easily to my touch as I entered the preliminaries. First one prays for a pure and perceptive mind; then one creates the affinity with one's instruments; then one does the actual Watching, searching the starry heavens for the enemies of man. Such was my skill and my craft. I grasped handles and knobs, thrust things from my mind, prepared myself to become an extension of my cabinet of devices.

I was only just past my threshold and into the first phase of Watchfulness when a deep and resonant voice behind me said, 'Well, Watcher, how goes it?'

I sagged against the cart. There is a physical pain in being wrenched so unexpectedly from one's work. For a moment I felt claws clutching at my heart. My face grew hot; my eyes would not focus; the saliva drained from my throat. As soon as I could, I took the proper protective measures to ease the metabolic drain, and severed myself from my instruments. Hiding my trembling as much as possible, I turned round.

Gormon, the other member of our little band, had appeared and stood jauntily beside me. He was grinning, amused at my distress, but I could not feel angry with him. One does not show anger at a guildless person no matter what the provocation.

Tightly, with effort, I said, 'Did you spend your time rewardingly?'

'Very. Where's Avluela?'

I pointed heavenward. Gormon nodded.

'What have you found?' I asked.

'That this city is definitely Roum.'

'There never was doubt of that.'

'For me there was. But now I have proof.'

'Yes?'

'In the overpocket. Look!'

From his tunic he drew his overpocket, set it on the pavement beside me, and expanded it so that he could insert his hands into its mouth. Grunting a little, he began to pull something heavy from the pouch – something of white stone – a long marble column, I now saw, fluted, pocked with age.

'From a temple of Imperial Roum!' Gormon exulted.

'You shouldn't have taken that.'

'Wait!' he cried, and reached into the overpocket once more. He took from it a handful of circular metal plaques and scattered them jingling at my feet. 'Coins! Money! Look at them, Watcher! The faces of the Caesars!'

'Of whom?'

'The ancient rulers. Don't you know your history of past cycles?'

I peered at him curiously. 'You claim to have no guild, Gormon. Could it be you are a Rememberer and are concealing it from me?'

'Look at my face, Watcher. Could I belong to any guild? Would a Changeling be taken?'

'True enough,' I said, eying the golden hue of him, the thick waxen skin, the red-pupiled eyes, the jagged mouth. Gormon had been weaned on teratogenetic drugs; he was a monster, handsome in his way, but a monster nevertheless, a Changeling, outside the laws and customs of man as they are practised in the Third Cycle of civilization. And there is no guild of Changelings.

'There's more,' Gormon said. The overpocket was infinitely capacious, the contents of a world, if need be, could be stuffed into its shriveled gray maw, and still it would be no longer than a man's hand. Gormon took from it bits of machinery, reading spools, an angular thing of brown metal that might have been an ancient tool, three squares of shining glass, five slips of paper – *paper!* – and a host of other relics of antiquity. 'See?' he said. 'A fruitful

8

stroll, Watcher! And not just random booty. Everything recorded, every-thing labeled, stratum, estimated age, position when *in situ*. Here we have many thousands of years of Roum.'

'Should you have taken these things?' I asked doubtfully.

'Why not? Who is to miss them? Who of this cycle cares for the past?'

'The Rememberers.'

'They don't need solid objects to help them do their work.'

'Why do you want these things, though?'

'The past interests me, Watcher. In my guildless way I have my scholarly pursuits. Is that wrong? May not even a monstrosity seek knowledge?'

'Certainly, certainly. Seek what you wish. Fulfill yourself in your own way. This is Roum. At dawn we enter. I hope to find employment here.'

'You may have difficulties.'

'How so?'

'There are many Watchers already in Roum, no doubt. There will be little need for your services.'

'I'll seek the favour of the Prince of Roum,' I said.

'The Prince of Roum is a hard and cold and cruel man.'

'You know of him?'

Gormon shrugged. 'Somewhat.' He began to stuff his artifacts back in the overpocket. 'Take your chances with him, Watcher. What other choice do you have?'

'None,' I said, and Gormon laughed, and I did not.

He busied himself with his ransacked loot of the past. I found myself deeply depressed by his words. He seemed so sure of himself in an uncertain world, this guildless one, this mutated monster, this man of inhuman look; how could he be so cool, so casual? He lived without concern for calamity and mocked those who admitted to fear. Gormon had been traveling with us for nine days, now, since we had met him in the ancient city beneath the volcano to the south by the edge of the sea. I had not suggested that he join us; he had invited himself along, and at Avluela's bidding I accepted. The roads are dark and cold at this time of year, and dangerous beasts of many species abound, and an old man journeying with a girl might well consider taking with him a brawny one like Gormon. Yet there times I wished he had not come with us, and this was one.

Slowly I walked back to my equipment.

Gormon said, as though first realizing it, 'Did I interrupt you at your Watching?'

I said mildly, 'You did.'

'Sorry. Go and start again. I'll leave you in peace.' And he gave me his dazzling lopsided smile, so full of charm that it took the curse off the easy arrogance of his words.

I touched the knobs, made contact with the nodes, monitored the dials. But I did not enter Watchfulness, for I remained aware of Gormon's presence and fearful that he would break into my concentration once again at a painful moment, despite his promise. At length I looked away from the apparatus. Gormon stood at the far side of the road, craning his neck for some sight of Avluela. The moment I turned to him he became aware of me.

'Something wrong, Watcher?'

'No. The moment's not propitious for my work. I'll wait.'

'Tell me,' he said. 'When Earth's enemies really do come from the stars, will your machines let you know it?'

'I trust they will.'

'And then?'

'Then I notify the Defenders.'

'After which your life's work is over?'

'Perhaps,' I said.

'Why a whole guild of you, though? Why not one master center where the Watch is kept? Why a bunch of itinerant Watchers drifting from place to place?'

'The more vectors of detection,' I said, 'the greater the chance of early awareness of the invasion.'

'Then an individual Watcher might well turn his machines on and not see anything, with an invader already here.'

'It could happen. And so we practice redundancy.'

'You carry it to an extreme, I sometimes think.' Gormon laughed. 'Do you actually believe an invasion is coming?'

'I do,' I said stiffly. 'Else my life was a waste.'

'And why should the star people want Earth? What do we have besides the remnants of old empires? What would they do with miserable Roum? With Perris? With Jorslem? Rotting cities! Idiot princes! Come, Watcher, admit it: the invasion's a myth, and you go through meaningless motions four times a day. Eh?'

'It is my craft and my science to Watch. It is yours to jeer. Each of us to our speciality, Gormon.'

'Forgive me,' he said with mock humility. 'Go, then, and Watch.'

'I shall.'

Angrily I turned back to my cabinet of instruments, determined now to ignore any interruption, no matter how brutal. The stars were out; I gazed at the glowing constellations, and automatically my mind registered the many worlds. Let us Watch, I thought. Let us keep our vigil despite the mockers.

I entered full Watchfulness.

I clung to the grips and permitted the surge of power to rush through me. I cast my mind to the heavens and searched for hostile entities. What ecstasy! What incredible splendor! I who had never left this small planet roved the black spaces of the void, glided from star to burning star, saw the planets spinning like tops. Faces stared back at me as I journeyed, some without eyes, some with many eyes, all the complexity of the many-peopled galaxy accessible to me. I spied out possible concentrations of inimicable force. I inspected drilling grounds and military encampments. I sought four times daily for all my adult life, for the invaders who had been promised us, the conquerors who at the end of days were destined to seize our tattered world.

I found nothing, and when I came up from my trance, sweaty and drained, I saw Avluela descending.

Feather-light she landed. Gormon called to her, and she ran, bare, her little breasts quivering, and he enfolded her smallness in his powerful arms, and they embraced, not passionately but joyously. When he released her she turned to me.

'Roum,' she gasped. *'Roum!'*

'You saw it?'

'Everything! Thousands of people! Lights! Boulevards! A market! Broken buildings many cycles old! Oh, Watcher, how wonderful Roum is!'

'Your flight was a good one, then,' I said.

'A miracle!'

'Tomorrow we go to dwell in Roum.'

'No, Watcher, tonight, tonight!' She was girlishly eager, her face bright with excitement. 'It's just a short journey more! Look, it's just over there!'

'We should rest first,' I said 'We do not want to arrive weary in Roum.'

'We can rest when we get there,' Avluela answered 'Come! Pack everything! You've done your Watching, haven't you?'

'Yes. Yes.'

'Then let's go. To Roum! To Roum!'

I looked in appeal at Gormon. Night had come; it was time to make camp, to have our few hours of sleep.

For once Gormon sided with me. He said to Avluela. 'The Watcher's right. We can all use some rest. We'll go on into Roum at dawn.'

Avluela pouted. She looked more like a child than ever. Her wings drooped, her underdeveloped body slumped. Petulantly she closed her wings until they were mere fist-sized humps on her back, and picked up the garments she had scattered on the road. She dressed while we made camp. I distributed food tablets; we entered our receptacles; I fell into troubled sleep and dreamed of Avluela limned against the crumbling moon, and Gormon flying beside her. Two hours before dawn I arose and performed my first watch of the new day, while they still slept. Then I roused them, and we went onward toward the fabled imperial city, onward toward Roum.

2

The morning's light was bright and harsh, as though this were some young world newly created. The road was all but empty; people do not travel much in these latter days unless, like me, they are wanderers by habit and profession. Occasionally we stepped aside to let a chariot of some member of the guild of Masters go by, drawn by a dozen expressionless neuters harnessed in series. Four such vehicles went by in the first two hours of the day, each shuttered and sealed to hide the Master's proud features from the gaze of such common folk as we. Several rollerwagons laden with produce passed us, and a number of floaters soared overhead. Generally we had the road to ourselves, however.

The environs of Roum showed vestiges of antiquity: isolated columns, the fragments of an aqueduct transporting nothing from nowhere to nowhere, the portals of a vanished temple. That was the oldest Roum we saw, but there were accretions of the later Roums of subsequent cycles: the huts of peasants, the domes of power drains, the hulls of dwelling-towers. Infrequently we met with the burned-out shell of some ancient airship. Gormon examined everything, taking samples from time to time. Avluela looked, wide-eyed, saying nothing. We walked on, until the walls of the city loomed before us.

They were of a blue glossy stone, neatly joined, rising to a height of perhaps eight men. Our road pierced the wall through a corbeled arch; the gate stood open. As we approached the gate a figure came toward us; he was hooded, masked, a man of extraordinary height wearing the somber garb of the guild of Pilgrims. One does not approach such a person oneself, but one heeds him if he beckons. The Pilgrim beckoned.

Through his speaking grille he said, 'Where from?'

'The south. I lived in Agupt awhile, then crossed Land Bridge to Talya,' I replied.

'Where bound?'

'Roum, awhile.'

'How goes the Watch?'

'As customary.'

'You have a place to stay in Roum?' the Pilgrim asked.

I shook my head. 'We trust to the kindness of the Will.'

'The Will is not always kind,' said the Pilgrim absently. 'Nor is there much need of Watchers in Roum. Why do you travel with a Flier?'

'For company's sake. And because she is young and needs protection.'

'Who is the other one?'

'He is guildless, a Changeling.'

'So I can see. But why is he with you?'

'He is strong and I am old, and so we travel together. Where are you bound, Pilgrim?'

'Jorslem. Is there another destination for my guild?'

I conceded the point with a shrug.

The Pilgrim said, 'Why do you not come to Jorslem with me?'

'My road lies north now. Jorslem is in the south, close by Agrup.'

'You have been to Agrup and not to Jorslem?' he said, puzzled.

'Yes. The time was not ready for me to see Jorslem.'

'Come now. We will walk together on the road, Watcher, and we will talk of the old times and of the times to come, and I will assist you in your Watching, and you will assist me in my communions with the Will. Is it agreed?'

It was a temptation. Before my eyes flashed the image of Jorslem the Golden, its holy buildings and shrines, its places of renewal where the old are made young, its spires, its tabernacles. Even though I am a man set in his ways, I was willing at the moment to abandon Roum and go with the Pilgrim to Jorslem.

I said, 'And my companions—'

'Leave them. It is forbidden for me to travel with the guildless, and I do not wish to travel with a female. You and I, Watcher, will go to Jorslem together.'

Avluela, who had been standing to one side frowning through all this colloquy, shot me a look of sudden terror.

'I will not abandon them,' I said.

'Then I go to Jorslem alone,' said the Pilgrim. Out of his robe stretched a bony hand, the fingers long and white and steady. I touched my fingers reverently to the tips of his, and the Pilgrim said, 'Let the Will give you mercy, friend Watcher. And when you reach Jorslem, search for me.'

He moved on down the road without further conversation.

Gormon said to me, 'You would have gone with him, wouldn't you?'

'I considered it.'

'What could you find in Jorslem that isn't here? That's a holy city and so is this. Here you can rest awhile. You're in no shape for more walking now.'

'You may be right,' I conceded, and with the last of my energy I strode toward the gate of Roum.

Watchful eyes scanned us from slots in the wall. When we were at midpoint in the gate, a fat, pockmarked Sentinel with sagging jowls halted us and asked our business in Roum. I stated my guild and purpose, and he gave a snort of disgust.

'Go elsewhere, Watcher! We need only useful men here.'

'Watching has its uses,' I said mildly.

'No doubt. No doubt.' He squinted at Avluela. 'Who's this? Watchers are celibates, no?'

'She is nothing more than a traveling companion.'

The Sentinel guffawed coarsely. 'It's a route you travel often, I wager! Not that there's much to her. What is she, thirteen, fourteen? Come here, child. Let me check you for contraband.' He ran his hands quickly over her, scowling as he felt her breasts, then raising an eyebrow as he encountered the mounds of her wings below her shoulders. 'What's this? What's this? More in back than in front! A Flier, are you? Very dirty business, Fliers consorting with foul old Watchers.' He chuckled and put his hand on Avluela's body in a way that sent Gormon starting forward in fury, murder in his fire-circled eyes. I caught him in time and grasped his wrist with all my strength, holding him back lest he ruin the three of us by an attack on the Sentinel. He tugged at me, nearly pulling me over; then he grew calm and subsided, icily watching as the fat one finished checking Avluela for 'contraband.'

At length the Sentinel turned in distaste to Gormon and said, 'What kind of thing are you?'

'Guildless, your mercy,' Gormon said in sharp tones. 'The humble and worthless product of teratogenesis, and yet nevertheless a free man who desires entry to Roum.'

'Do we need more monsters here?'

'I eat little and work hard.'

'You'd work harder still if you were neutered,' said the Sentinel.

Gormon glowered. I said, 'May we have entry?'

'A moment.' The Sentinel donned his thinking cap and narrowed his eyes as he transmitted a message to the memory tanks. His face tensed with the effort; then it went slack, and moments later came the reply. We could not hear the transaction at all; but from his disappointed look, it appeared evident that no reason had been found to refuse us admission to Roum.

'Go on in,' he said. 'The three of you. Quickly!'

We passed beyond the gate.

Gormon said, 'I could have split him open with a blow.'

'And be neutered by nightfall. A little patience, and we've come into Roum.'

'The way he handled her—!'

'You have a very possessive attitude toward Avluela,' I said. 'Remember that she's a Flier, and not sexually available to the guildless.'

Gormon ignored my thrust. 'She arouses me no more than you do, Watcher. But it pains me to see her treated that way. I would have killed him if you hadn't held me back.'

Avluela said, 'Where shall we stay, now that we're in Roum?'

'First let me find the headquarters of my guild,' I said. 'I'll register at the Watchers' Inn. After that, perhaps we'll hunt up the Fliers' Lodge for a meal.'

'And then,' said Gormon drily, 'we'll go to the Guildless Gutter and beg for coppers.'

'I pity you because you are a Changeling,' I told him, 'but I find it ungraceful of you to pity yourself. Come.'

We walked up a cobbled, winding street away from the gate and into Roum itself. We were in the outer ring of the city, a residential section of low, squat houses topped by the unwielding bulk of defense installations. Within lay the shining towers we had seen from the fields the night before; the remnant of ancient Roum carefully preserved across ten thousand years or more; the market, the factory zone, the communications hump, the temples of the Will, the memory tanks, the sleepers' refuges, the outworlders' brothels, the government buildings, the headquarters of the various guilds.

At the corner, beside a Second Cycle building with walls of rubbery texture, I found a public thinking cap and slipped it on my forehead. At once my thoughts raced down the conduit until they came to the interface that gave them access to one of the storage brains of a memory tank. I pierced the interface and saw the wrinkled brain itself, a pale gray against the deep green of its housing. A Rememberer once told me that, in cycles past, men built machines to do their thinking for them, although these machines were hellishly expensive and required vast amounts of space and drank power gluttonously. That was not the worst of our forefathers' follies; but why build artificial brains when death each day liberates scores of splendid natural ones to hook into the memory tanks? Was it that they lacked the knowledge to use them? I find that hard to believe.

I gave the brain my guild identification and asked the coordinates of our inn. Instantly I received them, and we set out, Avluela on one side of me, Gormon on the other, myself wheeling as always the cart in which my instruments resided.

The city was crowded. I had not seen such throngs in sleepy, heat-fevered Agupt, nor at any other point on my northward journey. The streets were full of Pilgrims, secretive and masked. Jostling through them went busy Rememberers and glum Merchants and now and then the litter of a Master. Avluela saw a number of Fliers, but was barred by the tenets of her guild from greeting them until she had undergone her ritual purification. I regret to say that I spied many Watchers, all of whom looked upon me disdainfully and without welcome. I noted a good many Defenders and ample representation of such lesser guilds as Vendors, Servitors, Manufactories, Scribes, Communicants, and Transporters. Naturally, a host of neuters went silently about their humble business, and numerous outworlders of all descriptions flocked the streets, most of them probably tourists, some here to do what business could be done with the sullen, poverty-blighted people of Earth. I noticed many Changelings limping furtively through the crowd, not one of them as proud of bearing as Gormon beside me. He was unique among his kind; the others, dappled and piebald and asymmetrical, limbless or overlimbed, deformed in a thousand imaginative and artistic ways, were slinkers, squinters, shufflers, hissers, creepers; they were cutpurses, brain-drainers, organ-peddlers, repentance-mongers, gleam-buyers, but none held himself upright as though he thought he were a man.

The guidance of the brain was exact, and in less than an hour of walking we arrived at the Watchers' Inn. I left Gormon and Avluela outside and wheeled my cart within.

Perhaps a dozen members of my guild lounged in the main hall. I gave them the customary sign, and they returned it languidly. Were these the guardians on whom Earth's safety depended? Simpletons and weaklings!

'Where may I register?' I asked.

'New? Where from?'

'Agupt was my last place of registry.'

'Should have stayed there. No need of Watchers here.'

'Where may I register?' I asked again.

A foppish youngster indicated a screen in the rear of the great room. I went to it, pressed my fingertips against it, was interrogated, and gave my name, which a Watcher must utter only to another Watcher and only within the precincts of an inn. A panel shot open, and a puffy-eyed man who wore the Watcher emblem on his right cheek and not on the left, signifying his high rank in the guild, spoke my name and said, 'You should have known better than to come to Roum. We're over our quota.'

'I claim lodging and employment nonetheless.'

'A man with your sense of humor should have been born into the guild of Clowns,' he said.

'I see no joke.'

'Under laws promulgated by our guild in the most recent session, an inn is under no obligation to take new lodgers once it has reached its assigned capacity. We are at our assigned capacity. Farewell, my friend.'

I was aghast. 'I know of no such regulation! This is incredible! For a guild to turn away a member from its own inn – when he arrives footsore and numb! A man of my age, having crossed Land Bridge out of Agupt, here as a stranger and hungry in Roum—'

'Why did you not check with us first?'

'I had no idea it would be necessary.'

'The new regulations—'

'May the Will shrivel the new regulations!' I shouted. 'I demand lodging! To turn away one who has Watched since before you were born—'

'Easy, brother, easy.'

'Surely you have some corner where I can sleep – some crumbs to let me eat—'

Even as my tone had changed from bluster to supplication, his expression softened from indifference to mere disdain. 'We have no room. We have no food. These are hard times for our guild, you know. There is talk that we will be disbanded altogether, as a useless luxury, a drain upon the Will's resources. We are very limited in our abilities. Because Roum has a surplus of Watchers, we are all on short rations as it is, and if we admit you our rations will be all the shorter.'

'But where will I go? What shall I do?'

'I advise you,' he said blandly, 'to throw yourself upon the mercy of the Prince of Roum.'

3

Outside, I told that to Gormon, and he doubled with laughter, guffawing so furiously that the striations on his lean cheeks blazed like bloody stripes. 'The mercy of the Prince of Roum!' he repeated. 'The mercy – of the Prince of Roum—'

'It is customary for the unfortunate to seek the aid of the local ruler,' I said coldly.

'The Prince of Roum knows no mercy,' Gormon told me. 'The Prince of Roum will feed you your own limbs to ease your hunger!'

'Perhaps,' Avluela put in, 'we should try to find the Fliers' Lodge. They'll feed us there.'

'Not Gormon,' I observed. 'We have obligations to one another.'

'We could bring food out to him,' she said.

'I prefer to visit the court first,' I insisted. 'Let us make sure of our status. Afterwards we can improvise living arrangements, if we must.'

She yielded, and we made our way to the palace of the Prince of Roum, a massive building fronted by a colossal column-ringed plaza, on the far side of the river that splits the city. In the plaza we were accosted by mendicants of many sorts, some not even Earthborn; something with ropy tendrils and a corrugated, noseless face thrust itself at me and jabbered for alms until Gormon pushed it away, and moments later a second creature, equally strange, its skin pocked with luminescent craters and its limbs studded with eyes, embraced my knees and pleaded in the name of the Will for my mercy. 'I am only a poor Watcher,' I said, indicating my cart, 'and am here to gain mercy myself.' But the being persisted, sobbing out its misfortunes in a blurred, feathery voice, and in the end, to Gormon's immense disgust, I dropped a few food tablets into the shelf-like pouch on its chest. Then we muscled on toward the doors of the palace. At the portico a more horrid sight presented itself: a maimed Flier, fragile limbs bent and twisted, one wing half unfolded and severely cropped, the other missing altogether. The Flier rushed upon Avluela, called her by a name not hers, moistened her leggings with tears so copious that the fur of them matted and stained. 'Sponsor me to the lodge,' he appealed. 'They have turned me away because I am crippled, but if you sponsor me—' Avlueva explained that she could do nothing, that she was a stranger to this lodge. The broken Flier would not release her, and Gormon with great delicacy lifted him like the bundle of dry bones that he was and set him aside. We stepped up onto the portico and at once were confronted by a trio of soft-faced neuters, who asked our business and admitted us quickly to the next line of barrier, which was manned by a pair of wizened Indexers. Speaking in unison, they queried us.

'We seek audience,' I said. 'A matter of mercy.'

'The day of audience is four days hence,' said the Indexer on the right. 'We will enter your request on the rolls.'

'We have no place to sleep!' Avluela burst out. 'We are hungry! We—'

I hushed her. Gormon, meanwhile, was groping in the mouth of his overpocket. Bright things glimmered in his hand; pieces of gold, the eternal metal, stamped with hawk-nosed, bearded faces. He had found them grubbing in the ruins. He tossed one coin to the Indexer who had refused us. The man snapped it from the air, rubbed his thumb roughly across its shining obverse, and dropped it instantly into a fold of his garment. The second Indexer waited expectantly. Smiling, Gormon gave him his coin.

'Perhaps,' I said, 'we can arrange for a special audience within.'

'Perhaps you can,' said one of the Indexers. 'Go through.'

And so we passed into the nave of the palace itself and stood in the great, echoing space, looking down the central aisle toward the shielded throne-chamber at the apse. There were more beggars in here – licensed ones holding hereditary concessions – and also throngs of Pilgrims, Communicants, Rememberers, Musicians, Scribes, and Indexers. I heard muttered prayers; I smelled the scent of spicy incense; I felt the vibration of subterranean gongs. In cycles past, this building had been a shrine of one of the old religions – the Christers, Gormon told me, making me suspect once more that he was a Rememberer masquerading as a Changeling – and it still maintained something of its holy character even though it served as Roum's seat of secular government. But how were we to get to see the Prince? To my left I saw a small ornate chapel which a line of prosperous-looking Merchants and Landholders was slowly entering. Peering past them, I noted three skulls mounted on an interrogation fixture – memory-tank input – and beside them, a burly Scribe. Telling Gormon and Avluela to wait for me in the aisle, I joined the line.

It moved infrequently, and nearly an hour passed before I reached the interrogation fixture. The skulls glared sightlessly at me; within their sealed crania, nutrient fluids bubbled and gurgled, caring for the dead, yet still functional, brains whose billion billion synaptic units now served as incomparable mnemonic devices. The Scribe seemed aghast to find a Watcher in this line, but before he could challenge me I blurted, 'I come as a stranger to claim the Prince's mercy. I and my companions are without lodging. My own guild has turned me away. What shall I do? How may I gain an audience?'

'Come back in four days.'

'I've slept on the road for more days than that. Now I must rest more easily.'

'A public inn—'

'But I am guilded!' I protested. 'The public inns would not admit me while my guild maintains an inn here, and my guild refuses me because of some new regulation, and you see my predicament?'

In a wearied voice the Scribe said, 'You may have application for a special audience. It will be denied, but you may apply.'

'Where?'

'Here. State your purpose.'

I identified myself to the skulls by my public designation, listed the names and status of my two companions, and explained my case. All this was absorbed and transmitted to the ranks of brains mounted somewhere in the depths of the city, and when I was done the Scribe said, 'If the application is approved, you will be notified.'

'Meanwhile where shall I stay?'

'Close to the palace, I would suggest.'

I understood. I could join that legion of unfortunates packing the plaza. How many of them had requested some special favor of the Prince and were still there, months or years later, waiting to be summoned to the Presence? Sleeping on stone, begging for crusts, living in foolish hope!

But I had exhausted my avenues. I returned to Gormon and Avluela, told them of the situation, and suggested that we now attempt to hunt whatever accommodations we could. Gormon, guildless, was welcome at any of the squalid public inns maintained for his kind; Avluela could probably find residence at her own guild's lodge; only I would have to sleep in the streets – and not for the first time. But I hoped that we would not have to separate.

I had come to think of us as a family, strange thought though that was for a Watcher.

As we moved toward the exit, my timepiece told me softly that the hour of Watching had come round again. It was my obligation and my privilege to tend to my Watching wherever I might be, regardless of the circumstances, whenever my hour came round; and so I halted, opened the cart, activated the equipment. Gormon and Avluela stood beside me. I saw smirks and open mockery on the faces of those who passed in and out of the palace; Watching was not held in very high repute, for we had Watched so long, and the promised enemy had never come. Yet one has one's duties, comic though they may seem to others. What is a hollow ritual to some is a life's work to others. Doggedly I forced myself into a state of Watchfulness. The world melted away from me, and I plunged into the heavens. The familiar joy engulfed me; and I searched the familiar places, and some that were not so familiar, my amplified mind leaping through the galaxies in wild swoops. Was an armada massing? Were troops drilling for the conquest of Earth? Four times a day I Watched, and the other members of my guild did the same, each at slightly different hours, so that no moment went by without some vigilant mind on guard. I do not believe that that was a foolish calling.

When I came up from my trance, a brazen voice was crying, '—for the Prince of Roum! Make way for the Prince of Roum!'

I blinked and caught my breath and fought to shake off the last strands of my concentration. A gilded palanquin borne by a phalanx of neuters had emerged from the rear of the palace and was proceeding down the nave toward me. Four men in the elegant costumes and brilliant masks of the guild of Masters flanked the litter, and it was preceded by a trio of Changelings, squat and broad, whose throats were so modified to imitate the sounding-boxes of bullfrogs; they emitted a trumpet like boom of majestic sound as they advanced. It struck me as most strange that a prince would admit Changelings to his service, even ones as gifted as these.

My cart was blocking the progress of this magnificent procession, and hastily I struggled to close it and move it aside before the parade swept down upon me. Age and fear made my fingers tremble, and I could not make the sealings properly; while I fumbled in increasing clumsiness, the strutting Changelings drew so close that the blare of their throats was deafening, and Gormon attempted to aid me, forcing me to hiss at him that it is forbidden for anyone not of my guild to touch the equipment. I pushed him away; and an instant later a vanguard of neuters descended on me and prepared to scourge me from the spot with sparkling whips. 'In the Will's name,' I cried, 'I am a Watcher.'

And in antiphonal response came the deep, calm, enormous reply, 'Let him be. He is a Watcher.'

All motion ceased. The Prince of Roum had spoken.

The neuters drew back. The Changelings halted their music. The bearers of the palanquin eased it to the floor. All those in the nave of the palace had pulled back, save only Gormon and Avluela and myself. The shimmering chain-curtains of the palanquin parted. Two of the Masters hurried forward and thrust their hands through the sonic barrier within, offering aid to their monarch. The barrier died away with a whimpering buzz.

The Prince of Roum appeared.

He was so young! He was nothing more than a boy, his hair full and dark, his face unlined. But he had been born to rule, and for all his youth he was as commanding as anyone I had ever seen. His lips were thin and tightly compressed; his aquiline nose was sharp and aggressive; his eyes, deep and cold, were infinite pools. He wore the jeweled garments of the guild of Dominators, but incised on his cheek was the double-barred cross of the Defenders, and around his neck he carried the dark shawl of the Rememberers. A Dominator may enrol in as many guilds as he pleases, and it would be a strange thing for a Dominator not also to be a Defender; but it startled me to find this prince a Rememberer as well. That is not normally a guild for the fierce.

He looked at me with little interest and said, 'You choose an odd place to do your Watching, old man.'

'The hour chose the place, sire,' I replied. 'I was here, and my duty compelled me. I had no way of knowing that you were about to come forth.'

'Your Watching found no enemies?'

'None, sire.'

I was about to press my luck, to take advantage of the unexpected appearance of the Prince to beg for his aid; but his interest in me died like a guttering candle as I stood there, and I did not dare call to him when his head had turned. He eyed Gormon a long moment, frowning and tugging at his chin. Then his gaze fell on Avluela. His eyes brightened. His jaw muscles flickered. His delicate nostrils widened. 'Come up here, little Flier,' he said, beckoning. 'Are you this Watcher's friend?'

She nodded, terrified.

The Prince held out a hand to her and grasped; she floated up onto the palanquin, and with a grin so evil it seemed a parody of wickedness, the young Dominator drew her through the curtain. Instantly a pair of Masters restored the sonic barrier, but the procession did not move on. I stood mute. Gormon beside me was frozen, his powerful body rigid as a rod. I wheeled my cart to a less conspicuous place. Long moments passed. The courtiers remained silent, discreetly looking away from the palanquin.

At length the curtain parted once more. Avluela came stumbling out, her face pale, her eyes blinking rapidly. She seemed dazed. Streaks of sweat gleamed on her cheeks. She nearly fell, and a neuter caught her and swung her down to floor level. Beneath her jacket her wings were partly erect, giving her a hunchbacked look and telling me that she was in great emotional distress. In ragged sliding steps she came to us, quivering, wordless; she darted a glance at me and flung herself against Gormon's broad chest.

The bearers lifted the palanquin. The Prince of Roum went out from his palace.

When he was gone, Avluela stammered hoarsely, 'The Prince has granted us lodging in the royal hostelry!'

4

The hostelkeepers, of course, would not believe us.

Guests of the Prince were housed in the royal hostelry, which was to the rear of the palace in a small garden of frostflowers and blossoming ferns. The usual inhabitants of such a hostelry were Masters and an occasional Dominator; sometimes a particularly important Rememberer on an errand of research would win a niche there, or some highly placed Defender visiting for purposes of strategic planning. To house a Flier in a royal hostelry was distinctly odd; to admit a Watcher was unlikely; to take in a Changeling or some other guildless person was improbable beyond comprehension. When we presented ourselves, therefore, we were met by Servitors whose attitude was at first one of high humor at our joke, then of irritation, finally of scorn. 'Get away,' they told us ultimately. 'Scum! Rabble!'

Avluela said in a grave voice, 'The Prince has granted us lodging here, and you may not refuse us.'

'Away! Away!'

One snaggle-toothed Servitor produced a neural truncheon and brandished it in Gormon's face, passing a foul remark about his guildlessness. Gormon slapped the truncheon from the man's grasp, oblivious to the painful sting, and kicked him in the gut, so that he coiled and fell over, puking. Instantly a throng of neuters came rushing from within the hostelry. Gormon seized another of the Servitors and hurled him into the midst of them, turning them into a muddled mob. Wild shouts and angry cursing cries attracted the attention of a venerable Scribe who waddled to the door, bellowed for silence, and interrogated us. 'That's easily checked,' he said, when Avluela had told the story. To a Servitor he said contemptuously, 'Send a think to the Indexers, fast!'

In time the confusion was untangled and we were admitted. We were given separate but adjoining rooms. I had never known such luxury before, and perhaps never shall again. The rooms were long, high and deep. One entered them through telescopic pits keyed to one's own thermal output, to assure privacy. Lights glowed at the resident's merest nod, for hanging from ceiling globes and nestling in cupolas on the walls were spicules of slave-light from one of the Brightstar worlds, trained through suffering to obey such commands. The windows came and went at the dweller's whim; when not in use, they were concealed by streamers of quasi-sentient outworld gauzes, which not only were decorative in their own right, but which functioned as monitors to produce delightful scents according to requisitioned patterns. The rooms were equipped with individual thinking caps connected to the main memory banks. They likewise had conduits that summoned Servitors, Scribes, Indexers, or Musicians as required. Of course, a man of my own humble guild would not deign to make use of other human beings that way, out of fear of their glowering resentment; but in any case I had little need of them.

I did not ask of Avluela what had occurred in the Prince's palanquin to bring us such bounty. I could well imagine, as could Gormon, whose barely suppressed inner rage was eloquent of his never-admitted love for my pale, slender little Flier.

We settled in. I placed my cart beside the window, draped it with gauzes, and left it in readiness for my next period of Watching. I cleaned my body of grime while entities mounted in the wall sang me to peace. Later I ate. Afterwards Avluela came to me, refreshed and relaxed, and sat beside me in my room as we talked of our experiences. Gormon did not appear for hours. I thought that perhaps he had left this hostelry altogether, finding the atmosphere too rarefied for him, and had sought company among his own guildless kind. But at twilight, Avluela and I walked in the cloistered courtyard of the hostelry and mounted a ramp to watch the stars emerge in Roum's sky, and Gormon was there. With him was a lanky and emaciated man in a Rememberer's shawl; they were talking in low tones.

Gormon nodded to me and said, 'Watcher, meet my new friend.'

The emaciated one fingered his shawl. 'I am the Rememberer Basil,' he intoned, in a voice as thin as a fresco that has been peeled from its wall. 'I have come from Perris to delve into the mysteries of Roum. I shall be here many years.'

'The Rememberer has fine stories to tell,' said Gormon. 'He is among the foremost of his guild. As you approached, he was describing to me the techniques by which the past is revealed. They drive a trench through the strata of Third Cycle deposits, you see, and with vacuum cores they lift the molecules of earth to lay bare the ancient layers.'

'We have found,' Basil said, 'the catacombs of Imperial Roum, and the rubble of the Time of Sweeping, the books inscribed on slivers of white metal, written toward the close of the Second Cycle, All these go to Perris for examination and classification and decipherment; then they return. Does the past interest you, Watcher?'

'To some extent.' I smiled. 'This Changeling here shows much more fascination for it. I sometimes suspect his authenticity. Would you recognize a Rememberer in disguise?'

Basil scrutinized Gormon; he lingered over the bizarre features, the excessively muscular frame. 'He is no Rememberer,' he said at length. 'But I agree that he has antiquarian interests. He has asked me many profound questions.'

'Such as?'

'He wishes to know the origin of Guilds. He asks the name of the genetic surgeon who crafted the first true-breeding Fliers. He wonders why there are Changelings, and if they are truly under the curse of the Will.'

'And do you have answers for these?' I asked.

'For some,' said Basil. 'For some.'

'The origin of guilds?'

'To give structure and meaning to a society that has suffered defeat and destruction,' said the Rememberer. 'At the end of the Second Cycle all was in flux. No man knew his rank nor his purpose. Through our world strode haughty outworlders who looked upon us all as worthless. It was necessary to establish fixed frames of reference by which one man might know his value beside another. So the first guilds appeared: Dominators, Masters, Merchants, Landholders, Vendors and Servitors. Then came Scribes, Musicians, Clowns and Transporters. Afterwards Indexers became necessary, and then Watchers and Defenders. When the Years of Magic gave us Fliers and Changelings, those guilds were added, and then the guildless ones, the neuters, were produced, so that—'

'But surely the Changelings are guildless too!' said Avluela.

The Rememberer looked at her for the first time. 'Who are you, child?'

'Avluela of the Fliers. I travel with this Watcher and this Changeling.'

Basil said, 'As I have been telling the Changeling here, in the early days his kind was guilded. The guild was dissolved a thousand years ago by the order of the Council of Dominators after an attempt by a disreputable Changeling faction to seize control of the holy places of Jorslem, and since that time Changelings have been guildless, ranking only above neuters.'

'I never knew that,' I said.

'You are no Rememberer,' said Basil smugly. 'It is our craft to uncover the past.'

'True. True.'

Gormon said, 'And today, how many guilds are there?'

Discomfited, Basil replied vaguely, 'At least a hundred, my friend. Some quite small; some are local. I am concerned only with the original guilds and their immediate successors; what has happened in the past few hundred years is in the province of others. Shall I requisition an information for you?'

'Never mind,' Gormon said. 'It was only an idle question.'

'Your curiosity is well developed,' said the Rememberer.

'I find the world and all it contains extremely fascinating. Is this sinful?'

'It is strange,' said Basil. 'The guildless rarely look beyond their own horizons.'

A Servitor appeared. With a mixture of awe and contempt he genuflected before Avluela and said, 'The Prince has returned. He desires your company in the palace at this time.'

Terror glimmered in Avluela's eyes. But to refuse was inconceivable. 'Shall I come with you?' she asked.

'Please. You must be robed and perfumed. He wishes you to come to him with your wings open, as well.'

Avluela nodded. The Servitor led her away.

We remained on the ramp a while longer; the Rememberer Basil talked of the old days of Roum, and I listened, and Gormon peered into the gathering darkness. Eventually, his throat dry, the Rememberer excused himself and moved solemnly away. A few moments later, in the courtyard below us, a door opened and Avluela emerged, walking as though she were of the guild of Somnambulists, not of Fliers. She was nude under transparent draperies, and her fragile body gleamed ghostly in the starbeams. Her wings were spread and fluttered slowly in a sombre systole and diastole. One Servitor grasped each of her elbows: they seemed to be propelling her toward the palace as though she were but a dreamed facsimile of herself and not a real woman.

'Fly, Avluela, fly,' Gormon growled. 'Escape while you can!'

She disappeared into a side entrance of the palace.

The Changeling looked at me. 'She has sold herself to the Prince to provide lodging for us.'

'So it seems.'

'I could smash down that palace!'

'You love her?'

'It should be obvious.'

'Cure yourself,' I advised. 'You are an unusual man, but still a Flier is not for you. Particularly a Flier who has shared the bed of the Prince of Roum.'

'She goes from my arms to his.'

I was staggered. 'You've known her?'

'More than once,' he said, smiling sadly. 'At the moment of ecstasy her wings thrash like leaves in a storm.'

I gripped the railing of the ramp so that I would not tumble into the courtyard. The stars whirled overhead; the old moon and its two blank-faced consorts leaped and bobbed. I was shaken without fully understanding the cause of my emotion. Was it wrath that Gormon had dared to violate a canon of the law? Was it a manifestation of those pseudo-parental feelings I had toward Avluela? Or was it mere envy of Gormon for daring to commit a sin beyond my capacity, though not beyond my desires?

I said, 'They could burn your brain for that. They could mince your soul. And now you make me an accessory.'

'What of it? That Prince commands, and he gets – but others have been there before him. I had to tell someone.'

'Enough. Enough.'

'Will we see her again?'

'Princes tire quickly of their women. A few days, perhaps a single night – then he will throw her back to us. And perhaps then we shall have to leave this hostelry.' I sighed. 'At least we'll have known it a few nights more than we deserved.'

'Where will you go then?' Gormon asked.

'I will stay in Roum a while.'

'Even if you sleep in the streets? There does not seem to be much demand for Watchers here.'

'I'll manage,' I said. 'Then I may go toward Perris.'

'To learn from the Rememberers?'

'To see Perris. What of you? What do you want in Roum?'

'Avluela.'

'Stop that talk!'

'Very well,' he said, and his smile was bitter. 'But I will stay here until the Prince is through with her. Then she will be mine, and we'll find ways to survive. The guildless are resourceful. They have to be. Maybe we'll scrounge lodgings in Roum awhile, and then follow you to Perris. If you're willing to travel with monsters and faithless Fliers.'

I shrugged. 'We'll see about that when the time comes.'

'Have you ever been in the company if a Changeling before?'

'Not often. Not for long.'

'I'm honored.' He drummed on the parapet. 'Don't cast me off, Watcher. I have a reason for wanting to stay with you.'

'Which is?'

'To see your face on the day your machines tell you that the invasion of Earth has begun.'

I let myself sag forward, shoulders drooping. 'You'll stay with me a long time, then.'

'Don't you believe the invasion is coming?'

26

'Some day. Not soon.'

Gormon chuckled. 'You're wrong. It's almost here.'

'You don't amuse me.'

'What is it, Watcher? Have you lost your faith? It's been known for a thousand years: another race covets Earth and owns it by treaty, and will some day come to collect. That much was decided at the end of the Second Cycle.'

'I know all that, and I am no Rememberer.' Then I turned to him and spoke words I never thought I would say aloud. 'For twice your lifetime, Changeling, I've listened to the stars and done my Watching. Something done that often loses meaning. Say your own name ten thousand times and it will be an empty sound. I have Watched, and Watched well, and in the dark hours of the night I sometimes think I Watch for nothing, that I have wasted my life. There is a pleasure in Watching, but perhaps there is no real purpose.'

His hand encircled my wrist. 'Your confession is as shocking as mine. Keep your faith, Watcher. The invasion comes!'

'How could you possibly know?'

'The guildless also have their skills.'

The conversation troubled me. I said, 'Is it painful to be guildless?'

'One grows reconciled. And there are certain freedoms to compensate for the lack of status. I may speak freely to all.'

'I notice.'

'I move freely. I am always sure of food and lodging, though the food may be rotten and the lodging poor. Women are attracted to me despite all prohibitions. Because of them, perhaps. I am untroubled by ambitions.'

'Never desire to rise above your rank?'

'Never.'

'You might have been happier as a Rememberer.'

'I am happy now. I can have a Rememberer's pleasures without his responsibility.'

'How smug you are!' I cried. 'To make a virtue of guildlessness!'

'How else does one endure the weight of the Will?' He looked towards the palace. 'The humble rise. The mighty fall. Take this as prophecy, Watcher: that lusty Prince in there will know more of life before summer comes. I'll rip out his eyes for taking Avluela!'

'Strong words. You bubble with treason tonight.'

'Take it as prophecy.'

'You can't get close to him,' I said. Then, irritated for taking his foolishness seriously, I added, 'And why blame him? He only does as princes do. Blame the girl for going to him. She might have refused.'

'And lost her wings. Or died. No, she had no choice. I do!' In a sudden, terrible gesture the Changeling held out thumb and forefinger, double-jointed, long-nailed, and plunged them into imagined eyes. 'Wait,' he said. 'You'll see!'

In the courtyard two Chronomancers appeared, set up the apparatus of their guild, and lit tapers by which to read the shape of tomorrow. A sickly odor of pallid smoke rose to my nostrils. I had now lost further desire to speak with the Changeling.

'It grows late,' I said. 'I need rest, and soon I must do my Watching.'

'Watch carefully,' Gormon told me.

5

At night in my chamber I performed my fourth and last Watch of that long day, and for the first time in my life I detected an anomaly. I could not interpret it. It was an obscure sensation, a mingling of tastes and sounds, a feeling of being in contact with some colossal mass. Worried, I clung to my instruments far longer than usual, but perceived no more clearly at the end of my seance than at its commencement.

Afterward I wondered about my obligations.

Watchers are trained from childhood to be swift to sound the alarm; and the alarm must be sounded when the Watcher judges the world in peril. Was I now obliged to notify the Defenders? Four times in my life the alarm had been given, on each occasion in error; and each Watcher who had thus touched off a false mobilization had suffered a fearful loss of status. One had contributed his brain to the memory banks; one had become a neuter out of shame; one had smashed his instruments and gone to live among the guildless; and one, vainly attempting to continue in his profession, had discovered himself mocked by all his comrades. I saw no virtue in scorning one who had delivered a false alarm, for was it not preferable for a Watcher to cry out too soon than not at all? But those were the customs of our guild, and I was constrained by them.

I evaluated my position and decided that I did not have valid grounds for an alarm.

I reflected that Gormon had placed suggestive ideas in my mind that evening. I might possibly be reacting only to his jeering talk of imminent invasions.

I could not act. I dared not jeopardize my standing by hasty outcry. I mistrusted my own emotional state.

I gave no alarm.

Seething, confused, my soul boiling, I closed my cart and let myself sink into a drugged sleep.

At dawn I woke and rushed to the window, expecting to find invaders in the streets. But all was still; a winter grayness hung over the courtyard, and sleepy Servitors pushed passive neuters about. Uneasily I did my first Watching of the day, and to my relief the strangeness of the night before did not return, although I had it in mind that my sensitivity is always greater at night than upon arising.

I ate and went to the courtyard. Gormon and Avluela were already there. She looked fatigued and downcast, depleted by her night with the Prince of Roum, but I said nothing to her about it. Gormon, slouching disdainfully against a wall embellished with the shells of radiant mollusks, said to me, 'Did your Watching go well?'

'Well enough.'

'What of the day?'

'Out to roam Roum,' I said. 'Will you come? Avluela? Gormon?'

'Surely,' he said, and she gave a faint nod; and, like the tourists we were, we set off to inspect the splendid city of Roum.

Gormon acted as our guide to the jumbled pasts of Roum, belying his claim never to have been here before. As well as any Rememberer he described the things we saw as we walked the winding streets. All the scattered levels of thousands of years were exposed. We saw the power domes of the Second Cycle, and the Colosseum where at an unimaginably early date man and beast contended like jungle creatures. In the broken hull of that building of horrors Gormon told us of the savagery of that unimaginably ancient time. 'They fought,' he said, 'naked before huge throngs. With bare hands men challenged beasts called lions, great hairy cats with swollen heads; and when the lion lay in its gore, the victor turned to the Prince of Roum and asked to be pardoned for whatever crime it was that had cast him into the arena. And if he had fought well, the Prince made a gesture with his hand, and the man was freed.' Gormon made the gesture for us: a thumb upraised and jerked backward over the right shoulder several times. 'But if the man had shown cowardice, or if the lion had distinguished itself in the manner of its dying, the Prince made another gesture, and the man was condemned to be slain by a second beast.' Gormon showed us that gesture too: the middle finger jutting upward from a clenched fist and lifted in a short sharp thrust.

'How are these things known?' Avluela asked, but Gormon pretended not to hear her.

We saw the line of fusion-pylons built early in the Third Cycle to draw energy from the world's core; they were still functioning, although stained and corroded. We saw the shattered stump of a Second Cycle weather machine, still a mighty column at least twenty men high. We saw a hill on which white marble relics of First Cycle Roum sprouted like pale clumps of winter deathflowers. Penetrating toward the inner part of the city, we came upon the embankment of defensive amplifiers waiting in readiness to hurl the full impact of the Will against invaders. We viewed a market where visitors from the stars haggled with peasants for excavated fragments of antiquity. Gormon strode into the crowd and made several purchases. We came to a flesh-house for travelers from afar, where one could buy anything from quasi-life to mounds of passion-ice. We ate at a small restaurant by the edge of the River Tver, where guildless ones were served without ceremony, and at Gormon's insistence we dined on mounds of a soft doughy substance and drank a tart yellow wine, local specialities.

Afterward we passed through a covered arcade in whose many aisles plump Vendors peddled star-goods, costly trinkets from Afreek, and the flimsy constructs of the local Manufactories. Just beyond we emerged in a plaza that contained a fountain in the shape of a boat, and to the rear of this rose a flight of cracked and battered stone-stairs ascending to a zone of rubble and weeds. Gormon beckoned, and we scrambled into this dismal area, then passed rapidly through it to a place where a sumptuous palace, by its looks early Second Cycle or even First, brooded over a sloping vegetated hill.

'They say this is the center of the world,' Gormon declared. 'In Jorslem one finds another place that also claims the honor. They mark the spot here by a map.'

'How can the world have one center,' Avluela asked, 'when it is round?'

Gormon laughed. We went in. Within, in wintry darkness, there stood a colossal jeweled globe lit by some inner glow.

'Here is your world,' said Gormon, gesturing grandly.

'Oh!' Avluela gasped. 'Everything! Everything is here!'

The map was a masterpiece of craftsmanship. It showed natural contours and elevations, its seas seemed deep liquid pools, its deserts were so parched as to make thirst spring in one's mouth, its cities swirled with vigor and life. I beheld the continents, Eyrop, Afreek, Ais, Stralya. I saw the vastness of Earth Ocean. I traversed the golden span of Land Bridge, which I had crossed so toilfully on foot not long before. Avluela rushed forward and pointed to Roum, to Agupt, to Jorslem, to Perris. She tapped the globe at the high mountains north of Hind and said softly, 'This is where I was born, where the ice lives, where the mountains touch the moons. Here is where the Fliers have their kingdom.' She ran a finger westward toward Fars and beyond it into the terrible Arban Desert, and on to Agupt. 'This is where I flew. By night, when I left my girlhood. We all must fly, and I flew here. A hundred times I thought I would die. Here, here in the desert, sand in my throat as I flew, sand beating against my wings – I was forced down, I lay

30

naked on the hot sand for days, and another Flier saw me, he came down to me and pitied me, and lifted me up, and when I was aloft my strength returned, and we flew on toward Agupt. And he died over the sea, his life stopped though he was young and strong, and he fell down into the sea, and I flew down to be with him, and the water was hot even at night. I drifted and morning came, and I saw the living stones growing like trees in the water, and the fish of many colors, and they came to him and pecked at his flesh as he floated with his wings outspread on the water, and I left him, I thrust him down to rest there, and I rose, and I flew on to Agupt, alone, frightened, and there I met you, Watcher.' Timidly she smiled at me. 'Show us the place where you were young, Watcher.'

Painfully, for I was suddenly stiff at the knees, I hobbled to the far side of the globe. Avluela followed me; Gormon hung back, as though not interested at all. I pointed to the scattered islands rising in two long strips from Earth Ocean – the remnants of the Lost Continents.

'Here,' I said, indicating my native island in the west. 'I was born here.'

'So far away!' Avluela cried.

'And so long ago,' I said. 'In the middle of the Second Cycle, it sometimes seems to me.'

'No! That is not possible!' But she looked at me as though it might have been true that I was thousands of years old.

I smiled and touched her satiny cheek. 'It only seems that way to me,' I said.

'When did you leave home?'

'When I was twice your age,' I said. 'I came first to here—' I indicated the eastern group of islands. 'I spent a dozen years as a Watcher on Palash. Then the Will moved me to cross Earth Ocean to Afreek. I came. I lived awhile in the hot countries. I went on to Agupt. I met a certain small Flier.' Falling silent, I looked a long while at the islands that had been my home, and within my mind my image changed from the gaunt and eroded thing I now had become, and I saw myself young and well-fleshed, climbing the green mountains and swimming in the chill sea, doing my Watching at the rim of a white beach hammered by surf.

While I brooded Avluela turned away from me to Gormon and said, 'Now you. Show us where you came from, Changeling!'

Gormon shrugged. 'The place does not appear to be on this globe.'

'But that's *impossible!*'

'Is it?' he asked.

She pressed him, but he evaded her, and we passed through a side exit and into the streets of Roum.

I was growing tired, but Avluela hungered for this city and wished to devour it all in an afternoon, and so we went on through a maze of interlocking streets, through a zone of sparkling mansions of Masters and Merchants, and through a foul den of Servitors and Vendors that extended into subterranean catacombs, and to a place where Clowns and Musicians resorted, and to another where the guild of Somnambulists offered its doubtful wares. A bloated female Somnambulist begged us to come inside and buy the truth that comes with trances, and Avluela urged us to go, but Gormon shook his head and I smiled, and we moved on. Now we were at the edge of a park close to the city's core. Here the citizens of Roum promenaded with an energy rarely seen in hot Agupt, and we joined the parade.

'Look there!' 'Avluela said. 'How bright it is!'

She pointed toward the shining arc of a dimensional sphere enclosing some relic of the ancient city; shading my eyes, I could make out a weathered stone wall within, and a knot of people. Gormon said, 'It is the Mouth of Truth.'

'What is that?' Avluela asked.

'Come. See.'

A line progressed into the sphere. We joined it and soon were at the tip of the interior, peering at the timeless region just across the threshold. Why this relic and so few others had been accorded such special protection I did not know, and I asked Gormon, whose knowledge was so unaccountably as profound as any Rememberer's, and he replied, 'Because this is the realm of certainty, where what one says is absolutely congruent with what actually is the case.'

'I don't understand,' said Avluela.

'It is impossible to lie in this place,' Gormon told her. 'Can you imagine any relic more worthy of protection?' He stepped across the entry duct, blurring as he did so, and I followed him quickly within. Avluela hesitated. It was a long moment before she entered; pausing a moment on the very threshold, she seemed buffeted by the wind that blew along the line of demarcation between the outer world and the pocket universe in which we stood.

An inner compartment held the Mouth of Truth itself. The line extended toward it, and a solemn Indexer was controlling the flow of entry to the tabernacle. It was a while before we three were permitted to go in. We found ourselves before the ferocious head of a monster in high relief, affixed to an ancient wall pockmarked by time. The monster's jaws gaped; the open mouth was a dark and sinister hole. Gormon nodded, inspecting it, as though he seemed pleased to find it exactly as he had thought it would be.

'What do we do?' Avluela asked.

Gormon said, 'Watcher, put your right hand into the Mouth of Truth.'

Frowning, I complied.

'Now,' Said Gormon, 'one of us asks a question. You must answer it. If you speak anything but the truth, the mouth will close and sever your hand.'

'No!' Avluela cried.

I stared uneasily at the stone jaws rimming my wrist. A Watcher without both his hands is a man without a craft; in Second Cycle days one might have obtained a prosthesis more artful than one's original hand, but the Second Cycle had long ago been concluded, and such niceties were not to be purchased on Earth nowadays.

'How is such a thing possible?' I asked.

'The Will is unusually strong in these precincts,' Gormon replied. 'It distinguishes sternly between truth and untruth. To the rear of this wall sleeps a trio of Somnambulists through whom the Will speaks, and they control the Mouth. Do you fear the Will, Watcher?'

'I fear my own tongue.'

'Be brave. Never has a lie been told before this wall. Never has a hand been lost.'

'Go ahead, then,' I said. 'Who will ask me a question?'

'I,' said Gormon. 'Tell me, Watcher: all pretense aside, would you say that a life spent in Watching has been a life spent wisely?'

I was silent a long moment, rotating my thoughts, eyeing the jaws.

At length I said, 'To devote oneself to vigilance on behalf of one's fellow man is perhaps the noblest purpose one can serve.'

'Careful!' Gormon cried in alarm.

'I am not finished,' I said.

'Go on.'

'But to devote oneself to vigilance when the enemy is an imaginary one is idle, and to congratulate oneself for looking long and well for a foe that is not coming is foolish and sinful. My life has been a waste.'

The jaws of the Mouth of Truth did not quiver.

I removed my hand. I stared at it as though it had newly sprouted from my wrist. I felt suddenly several cycles old. Avluela, her eyes wide, her hands to her lips, seemed shocked by what I had said. My own words appeared to hang congealed in the air before the hideous idol.

'Spoken honestly,' said Gormon, 'although without much mercy for yourself. You judge yourself too harshly, Watcher.'

'I spoke to save my hand,' I said. 'Would you have had me lie?'

He smiled. To Avluela the Changeling said, 'Now it's your turn.'

Visibly frightened, the little Flier approached the Mouth. Her dainty hand trembled as she inserted it between the slabs of cold stone. I fought back an urge to rush toward her and pull her free of that devilish grimacing head.

'Who will question her? I asked.

'I,' said Gormon.

Avluela's wings stirred faintly beneath her garments. Her face grew pale; her nostrils flickered; her upper lip slid over the lower one. She stood slouched against the wall and stared in horror at the termination of her arm. Outside the chamber vague faces peered at us; lips moved in what no doubt were expressions of impatience over our lengthy visit to the Mouth; but we heard nothing. The atmosphere around us was warm and clammy, with a musty tang like that which would come from a well that was driven through the structure of Time.

Gormon said slowly, 'This night past you allowed your body to be possessed by the Prince of Roum. Before that, you granted yourself to the Changeling Gormon, although such liaisons are forbidden by custom and law. Much prior to that you were the mate of a Flier, now deceased. You may have had other men, but I know nothing of them, and for the purposes of my question they are not relevant. Tell me this, Avluela: which of the three gave you the most intense physical pleasure, which of the three aroused your deepest emotions, and which of the three would you choose as a mate?'

I wanted to protest that the Changeling had asked her three questions, not one, and so had taken unfair advantage. But I had no chance to speak, because Avluela replied unfalteringly, hand wedged deep into the Mouth of Truth, 'The Prince of Roum gave me greater pleasure of the body than I had ever known before, but he is cold and cruel, and I despise him. My dead Flier I loved more deeply than any person before or since, but he was weak, and I would not have wanted a weakling as a mate. You, Gormon, seem almost a stranger to me even now, and I feel that I know neither your body nor your soul, and yet, though the gulf between us is wide, it is you with whom I would spend my days to come.'

She drew her hand from the Mouth of Truth.

'Well spoken!' said Gormon, though the accuracy of her words had clearly wounded as well as pleased him. 'Suddenly you find eloquence, eh, when the circumstances demand it. And now the turn is mine to risk my hand.'

He neared the Mouth. I said, 'You have asked the first two questions. Do you wish to finish the job and ask the third as well?'

'Hardly,' he said, He made a negligent gesture with his free hand. 'Put your heads together and agree on a joint question.'

Avluela and I conferred. With uncharacteristic forwardness she proposed a question; and since it was the one I would have asked, I accepted it and told her to ask it.

She said, 'When we stood before the globe of the world, Gormon, I asked you to show me the place where you were born, and you said you were unable to find it on the map. That seemed most strange. Tell me now: are you what you say you are, a Changeling who wanders the world?'

He replied. 'I am not.'

In a sense he had satisfied the question as Avluela had phrased it; but it went without saying that his reply was inadequate, and he kept his hand in the Mouth of Truth as he continued, 'I did not show my birthplace to you on the globe because I was born nowhere on this globe, but on a world of a star I must not name. I am no Changeling in your meaning of the word, though by some definitions I am, for my body is somewhat disguised, and on my own world I wear a different flesh. I have lived here ten years.'

'What was your purpose in coming to Earth?' I asked.

'I am obliged only to answer one question,' said Gormon. Then he smiled. 'But I give you the answer anyway: I was sent to Earth in the capacity of a military observer, to prepare the way for the invasion for which you have Watched so long and in which you have ceased to believe, and which will be upon you in a matter now of some hours.'

'Lies!' I bellowed. '*Lies!*'

Gormon laughed. And drew his hand from the Mouth of Truth, intact, unharmed.

6

Numb with confusion, I fled with my cart of instruments from that gleaming sphere and emerged into a street suddenly cold and dark. Night had come with winter's swiftness; it was almost the ninth hour, and almost the time for me to Watch once more.

Gormon's mockery thundered in my brain. He had arranged everything: he had maneuvered us in to the Mouth of Truth; he had wrung a confession of lost faith from me and a confession of a different sort from Avluela; he had mercilessly volunteered information he need not have revealed, spoken words calculated to split me to the core.

Was the Mouth of Truth a fraud? Could Gormon lie and emerge unscathed?

Never since I first took up my tasks had I Watched at anything but the appointed hours. This was a time of crumbling realities; I could not wait for the ninth hour to come round; crouching in the windy street, I opened my cart, readied my equipment, and sank like a diver into Watchfulness.

My amplified consciousness roared toward the stars.

Godlike I roamed infinity. I felt the rush of the solar wind, but I was no Flier to be hurled to destruction by that pressure, and I soared past it, beyond the reach of those angry particles of light, into the blackness at the edge of the sun's dominion. Down upon me there beat a different pressure.

Starships coming near.

Not the tourist lines bringing sightseers to gape at our diminished world. Not the registered mercantile transport vessels, nor the scoopships that collect the interstellar vapors, nor the resort craft on their hyperbolic orbits.

These were military craft, dark, alien, menacing. I could not tell their number; I knew only that they sped Earthward at many lights, nudging a cone of deflected energies before them; and it was that cone that I had sensed, that I had felt also the night before, booming into my mind through my instruments, engulfing me like a cube of crystal through which stress patterns play and shine.

All my life I had Watched for this.

I had been trained to sense it. I had prayed that I never would sense it, and then in my emptiness I had prayed that I *would* sense it, and then I had ceased to believe in it. And then by grace of the Changeling Gormon, I had sensed it after all, Watching ahead of my hour, crouching in a cold Roumish street just outside the Mouth of Truth.

In his training, a Watcher is instructed to break from his Watchfulness as soon as his observations are confirmed by a careful check, so that he can sound the alarm. Obediently I made my check by shifting from one channel to another to another, triangulating and still picking up that foreboding sensation of titanic force rushing upon Earth at unimaginable speed.

Either I was deceived, or the invasion was come. But I could not shake from my trance to give the alarm.

Lingeringly, lovingly, I drank in the sensory data for what seemed like hours. I fondled my equipment; I drained from it the total affirmation of faith that my readings gave me. Dimly I warned myself that I was wasting vital time, that it was my duty to leave this lewd caressing of destiny to summon the Defenders.

And at last I burst free from Watchfulness and returned to the world I was guarding.

Avluela was beside me; she was dazed, terrified, her knuckles to her teeth, her eyes blank,

'Watcher! Watcher, do you hear me? What's happening? What's going to happen?'

'The invasion,' I said. 'How long was I under?'

'About half a minute. I don't know. Your eyes were closed. I thought you were dead.'

'Gormon was speaking the truth! The *invasion* is almost here. Where is he? Where did he go?'

'He vanished as we came away from that place with the Mouth,' Avluela whispered. 'Watcher, I'm frightened. I feel everything collapsing. I have to fly – I can't stay down here now!'

'Wait,' I said, clutching at her and missing her arm. 'Don't go now. First I have to give the alarm, and then—'

But she was already stripping off her clothing. Bare to the waist, her pale body gleamed in the evening light, while about us people were rushing to and fro in ignorance of all that was about to occur. I wanted to keep Avluela beside me, but I could delay no longer in giving the alarm, and I turned away from her, back to my care.

As though caught up in a dream born of overripe longings I reached for the node that I had never used, the one that would send forth a planet wide alert to the Defenders.

Had the alarm already been given? Had some other Watcher sensed what I had sensed, and less paralyzed by bewilderment and doubt, performed a Watcher's final task?

No. No. For then I would be hearing the sirens' shriek reverberating from the orbiting loudspeakers above the city.

I touched the node. From the corner of my eye I saw Avluela, free of her encumbrances now, kneeling to say her Words, filling her tender wings with strength. In a moment she would be in the air, beyond my grasp.

With a single swift tug I activated the alarm.

In that instant I became aware of a burly figure striding toward us. Gormon, I thought: and as I rose from my equipment I reached out to him; I wanted to seize him and hold him fast. But he who approached was not Gormon but some officious dough-faced Servitor who said to Avluela, 'Go easy, Flier, let your wings drop. The Prince of Roum sends me to bring you to his presence.'

He grappled with her. Her little breasts heaved; her eyes flashed anger at him.

'Let go of me! I'm going to fly!'

'The Prince of Roum summons you,' the Servitor said, enclosing her in his heavy arms.

'The Prince of Roum will have other distractions tonight,' I said. 'He'll have no need of her.'

As I spoke the sirens began to sing from the skies.

The Servitor released her. His mouth worked noiselessly for an instant; he made one of the protective gestures of the Will; he looked skyward and grunted, 'The alarm! Who gave the alarm? You, old Watcher?'

Figures rushed about insanely in the streets.

Avluela, freed, sped past me – on foot, her wings but half-furled – and was swallowed up in the surging throng. Over the terrifying sound of the sirens came booming messages from the public annunciators, giving in-structions for defense and safety. A lanky man with the mark of the guild of Defenders upon his cheek rushed to me, shouted words too incoherent to be understood, and sped on down the street. The world seemed to have gone mad.

Only I remained calm. I looked to the skies, half-expecting to see the invaders' black ships already hovering above the towers of Roum. But I saw nothing except the hovering nightlights and the other objects one might expect overhead.

'Gormon?' I called. 'Avluela?'

I was alone.

A strange emptiness swept over me. I had given the alarm; the invaders were on their way; I had lost my occupation. There was no need of Watchers now. Almost lovingly I touched the worn cart that had been my companion for so many years. I ran my fingers over its stained and pitted instruments; and then I looked away, abandoning it, and went down the dark streets cart-less, burdenless, a man whose life had found and lost meaning in the same instant. And about me raged chaos.

7

It was understood that when the moment of Earth's final battle arrived, all guilds would be mobilized, the Watchers alone exempted. We who had manned the perimeter of defense for so long had no part in the strategy of combat; we were discharged by the giving of a true alarm. Now it was the time of the guild of Defenders to show its capabilities. They had planned for half a cycle what they would do in time of war. What plans would they call forth now? What deeds would they direct?

My only concern was to return to the royal hostelry and wait out the crisis. It was hopeless to think of finding Avluela, and I pummeled myself savagely for having let her slip away, naked and without a protector, in that confused moment. Where would she go? Who would shield her?

A fellow Watcher, pulling his cart madly along, nearly collided with me. 'Careful!' I snapped. He looked up, breathless, stunned. 'Is it true?' he asked. 'The alarm?'

'Can't you hear?'

'But is it real?'

I pointed to his cart. 'You know how to find that out.'

'They say the man who gave the alarm was drunk, an old fool who was turned away from the inn yesterday.'

'It could be so,' I admitted.

'But if the alarm is real—!'

Smiling, I said, 'If it is, now we all may rest. Good day to you, Watcher.'

'Your cart! Where's your cart?' he shouted at me.

But I had moved past him, toward the mighty carven stone pillar of some relic of Imperial Roum.

Ancient images were carved on that pillar; battles and victories, foreign monarchs marched in the chains of disgrace through the streets of Roum, triumphant eagles celebrating imperial grandeur. In my strange new calmness I stood awhile before the column of stone and admired its elegant engravings. Toward me rushed a frenzied figure whom I recognized as the Rememberer Basil; I hailed him, saying, 'How timely you come! Do me the kindness of explaining these images, Rememberer. They fascinate me, and my curiosity is aroused.'

'Are you insane? Can't you hear the alarm?'

'I gave the alarm, Rememberer.'

'Flee, then! Invaders come! We must fight!'

'Not I. Basil. Now my time is over. Tell me of these images. These beaten kings, these broken emperors. Surely a man of your years will not be doing battle.'

'All are mobilized now!'

'All but Watchers,' I said. 'Take a moment. Yearning for the past is born in me. Gormon has vanished; be my guide to these lost cycles.'

The Rememberer shook his head wildly, circled around me, and tried to get away. Hoping to seize his skinny arm and pin him to the spot, I made a lunge at him, but he eluded me and I caught only his dark shawl, which pulled free and came loose in my hands. Then he was gone, his spindly limbs pumping madly as he fled down the street and left my view. I shrugged and examined the shawl I had so unexpectedly acquired. It was shot through with glimmering threads of metal arranged in intricate patterns that teased the eye: it seemed to me that each strand disappeared into the weave of the fabric, only to appear at some improbable point, like the lineage of dynasties unexpectedly revived in distant cities. The workmanship was superb. Idly I draped the shawl about my shoulders.

I walked on.

My legs, which had been on the verge of failing me earlier in the day, now served me well. With renewed youthfulness I made my way through the chaotic city, finding no difficulties in choosing my route. I headed for the river, then crossed it and, on the Tver's far side, sought the palace of the Prince. The night had deepened, for most lights were extinguished under the mobilization orders; and from time to time a dull boom signaled the explosion of a screening bomb overhead, liberating clouds of murk that shielded the city from most forms of long-range scrutiny. There were fewer pedestrians in the streets. The sirens still cried out. Atop the buildings the defense installations were going into action; I heard the bleeping sounds of repellors warming up, and I saw long spidery arms of amplification booms swinging from tower to tower as they linked for maximum output. I had no doubt now that the invasion actually was coming. My own instruments might have been fouled by inner confusion, but they would not have proceeded this far with the mobilization if the initial report had not been confirmed by the findings of hundreds of other members of my guild.

As I neared the palace a pair of breathless Rememberers sped toward me, their shawls flapping behind them. They called to me in words I did not comprehend – some code of their guild, I realized, recollecting that I wore Basil's shawl. I could not reply, and they rushed upon me, still gabbling; and switching to the language of ordinary men they said, 'What is the matter with you? To your post! We must record! We must comment! We must observe!'

'You mistake me,' I said mildly. 'I keep this shawl only for your brother Basil, who left it in my care. I have no post to guard at this time.'

'A Watcher,' they cried in unison, and cursed me separately, and ran on. I laughed and went to the palace.

Its gates stood open. The neuters who had guarded the outer portals had gone, as were the two Indexers who had stood just within the door. The beggars that had thronged the vast plaza had jostled their way into the building itself to seek shelter; this had awakened the anger of the licensed hereditary mendicants whose customary stations were in that part of the building, and they had fallen upon the inflowing refugees with fury and unexpected strength. I saw cripples lashing out with their crutches held as clubs; I saw blind men landing blows with suspicious accuracy; meek penitents were wielding a variety of weapons ranging from stilettos to sonic pistols. Holding myself aloof from this shameless spectacle, I penetrated to the inner recesses of the palace and peered into chapels where I saw Pilgrims beseeching the blessings of the Will, and Communicants desperately seeking spiritual guidance as to the outcome of the coming conflict.

Abruptly I heard the blare of trumpets and cries of, 'Make way! Make way!'

A file of sturdy Servitors marched into the palace, striding toward the Prince's chambers in the apse. Several of them held a struggling, kicking, frantic figure with half-unfolded wings: Avluela! I called out to her, but my voice died in the din, nor could I reach her. The Servitors shoved me aside. The procession vanished into the princely chambers. I caught a final glimpse of the little Flier, pale and small in the grip of her captors, and then she was gone once more.

I seized a bumbling neuter who had been moving uncertainly in the wake of the Servitors.

'That Flier! Why was she brought here?'

'Ha – he – they—'

'Tell me!'

'The Prince – his woman – in his chariot – he – he – they – the invaders—'

I pushed the flabby creature aside and rushed toward the apse. A brazen wall ten times my own height confronted me. I pounded on it. 'Avluela!' I shouted hoarsely. '*Av ... lu ... ela ...!*'

I was neither thrust away nor admitted. I was ignored. The bedlam at the western doors of the palace had extended itself now to the nave and aisles, and as the ragged beggars boiled toward me I executed a quick turn and found myself passing through one of the side doors of the palace.

Suspended and passive, I stood in the courtyard that led to the royal hostelry. A strange electricity crackled in the air. I assumed it was an emanation from one of Roum's defense installations, some kind of beam designed to screen the city from attack. But an instant later I realized that it presaged the actual arrival of the invaders.

Starships blazed in the heavens.

When I had perceived them in my Watching they had appeared black against the infinite blackness, but now they burned with the radiance of suns. A stream of bright, hard, jewel-like globes bedecked the sky; they were ranged side by side, stretching from east to west in a continuous band, filling all the celestial arch, and as they erupted simultaneously into being it seemed to me that I heard the crash and throb of an invisible symphony heralding the arrival of the conquerors of Earth.

I do not know how far above me the starships were, nor how many of them hovered there, not any of the details of their design. I know only that in sudden massive majesty they were there, and that if I had been a Defender my soul would have withered instantly at the sight.

Across the heavens shot light of many hues. The battle had been joined. I could not comprehend the actions of our warriors, and I was equally baffled by the maneuvers of those who had come to take possession of our history-crusted but time-diminished planet. To my shame I felt not only out of the struggle but above the struggle, as though this was no quarrel of mine. I wanted Avluela beside me, and she was somewhere within the depths of the palace of the Prince of Roum. Even Gormon would have been a comfort now, Gormon the Changeling, Gormon the spy, Gormon the monstrous betrayer of our world.

Gigantic amplified voices bellowed, 'Make way for the Prince of Roum! The Prince of Roum leads the Defenders in the battle for the fatherworld!'

From the palace emerged a shining vehicle the shape of a teardrop, in whose bright-metaled roof a transparent sheet had been mounted so that all the populace could see and take heart in the presence of the ruler. At the controls of the vehicle sat the Prince of Roum, proudly erect, his cruel, youthful features fixed in harsh determination; and beside him, robed like an empress, I beheld the slight figure of the Flier Avluela. She seemed in a trance.

The royal chariot soared upward and was lost in the darkness.

It seemed to me that a second vehicle appeared and followed its path, and that the Prince's reappeared, and that the two flew in tight circles, apparently locked in combat. Clouds of blue sparks wrapped both chariots now; and then they swung high and far and were lost to me behind one of the hills of Roum.

Was the battle now raging all over the planet? Was Perris in jeopardy, and holy Jorslem, and even the sleepy isles of the Lost Continents? Did starships hover everywhere? I did not know. I perceived events in only one small segment of the sky over Roum, and even there my awareness of what was taking place was dim, uncertain, and ill-informed. There were momentary flashes of light in which I saw battalions of Fliers streaming across the sky; and then darkness returned as though a velvet shroud had been hurled over the city. I saw the great machines of our defense firing in fitful bursts from the tops of our towers; and yet I saw the starships untouched, unharmed, unmoved above. The courtyard in which I stood was deserted, but in the distance I heard voices, full of fear and foreboding, shouting in tinny tones that might have been the screeching of birds. Occasionally there came a booming sound that rocked all the city. Once a platoon of Somnambulists was driven past where I was; in the plaza fronting the palace I observed what appeared to be an array of Clowns unfolding some sort of sparkling netting of a military look; by one flash of lightning I was able to see a trio of Rememberers making copious notes of all that elapsed as they soared aloft on the gravity plate. It seemed – I was not sure – that the vehicle of the Prince of Roum returned, speeding across the sky with its pursuer clinging close. 'Avluela,' I whispered, as the twin dots of light left my sight. Were the starships disgorging troops? Did colossal pylons of force spiral down from those orbiting brightnesses to touch the surface of the Earth? Why had the Prince seized Avluela? Where was Gormon? What were our Defenders doing? Why were the enemy ships not blasted from the sky?

Rooted to the ancient cobbles of the courtyard, I observed the cosmic battle in total lack of understanding throughout the long night.

Dawn came. Strands of pale light looped from tower to tower. I touched fingers to my eyes, realizing that I must have slept while standing. Perhaps I should apply for membership in the guild of Somnambulists, I told myself lightly. I put my hands to the Rememberer's shawl about my shoulders and wondered how I managed to acquire it, and the answer came.

I looked toward the sky.

The alien starships were gone. I saw only the ordinary morning sky, gray with pinkness breaking through. I felt the jolt of compulsion and looked about for my cart, and reminded myself that I need do no more Watching, and I felt more empty than one would ordinarily feel at such an hour.

Was the battle over?

Had the enemy been vanquished?

Were the ships of the invaders blasted from the sky and lying in charred ruin outside Roum?

All was silent. I heard no more celestial symphonies. Then out of the eerie stillness there came a new sound, a rumbling noise as of wheeled vehicles passing through the streets of the city. And the invisible Musicians played one final note, deep and resonant, which trailed away jaggedly as though every string had been broken at once.

Over the speakers used for public announcements came quiet words.

'Roum is fallen. Roum is fallen.'

8

The royal hostelry was untended. Neuters and members of the servant guilds all had fled. Defenders, Masters, and Dominators must have perished honorably in combat. Basil the Rememberer was nowhere about; likewise none of his brethren. I went to my room, cleansed and refreshed and fed myself, gathered my few possessions, and bade farewell to the luxuries I had known so briefly. I regretted that I had had such a short time to visit Roum; but at least Gormon had been a most excellent guide, and I had seen a great deal.

Now I proposed to move on.

It did not seem prudent to remain in a conquered city. My room's thinking cap did not respond to my queries, and so I did not know what the extent of the defeat was, here or in other regions, but it was evident to me that Roum at least had passed from human control, and I wished to depart quickly. I weighed the thought of going to Jorslem, as that tall Pilgrim had suggested upon my entry into Roum; but then I reflected and chose a westward route, toward Perris, which not only was closer but held the headquarters of the Rememberers. My own occupation had been destroyed; but on this first morning of Earth's conquest I felt a sudden powerful and strange yearning to offer myself humbly to the Rememberers and seek with them knowledge of our more glittering yesterdays.

At midday I left the hostelry. I walked first to the palace, which still stood open. The beggars lay strewn about, some drugged, some sleeping, most dead; from the crude manner of their death I saw that they must have slain one another in their panic and frenzy. A despondent-looking Indexer squatted beside the three skulls of the interrogation fixture in the chapel. As I entered he said, 'No use. The brains do not reply.'

'How goes it with the Prince of Roum?'

'Dead. The invaders shot him from the sky.'

'A young Flier rode beside him. What do you know of her?'

'Nothing. Dead, I suppose.'

'And the city?'

'Fallen. Invaders are everywhere.'

'Killing?'

'Not even looting,' the Indexer said. 'They are most gentle. They have *collected* us.'

'In Roum alone, or everywhere?'

The man shrugged. He began to rock rhythmically back and forth. I let him be, and walked deeper into the palace. To my surprise, the imperial chambers of the Prince were unsealed. I went within; I was awed by the sumptuous luxury of the hangings, the draperies, the lights, the furnishings. I passed from room to room, coming at last to the royal bed, whose coverlet was the flesh of a colossal bivalve of the planet of another star, and as the shell yawned for me I touched the infinitely soft fabric under which the Prince of Roum had lain, and I recalled that Avluela too had lain here, and if I had been a younger man I would have wept.

I left the palace and slowly crossed the plaza to begin my journey toward Perris.

As I departed I had my first glimpse of our conquerors. A vehicle of alien design drew up at the plaza's rim and perhaps a dozen figures emerged. They might almost have been human. They were tall and broad, deep-chested, as Gormon had been, and only the extreme length of their arms marked them instantly as alien. Their skins were of strange texture, and if I had been closer I suspect I would have seen eyes and lips and nostrils that were not of a human design. Taking no notice of me, they crossed the plaza, walking in a curiously loose-jointed loping way that reminded me irresistibly of Gormon's stride, and entered the Palace. They seemed neither swaggering nor belligerent.

Sightseers. Majestic Roum once more exerted its magnetism upon strangers.

Leaving our new masters to their amusement, I walked off, toward the outskirts of the city. The bleakness of eternal winter crept into my soul. I wondered: did I feel sorrow that Roum had fallen? Or did I mourn the loss of Avluela? Or was it only that I now had missed three successive

Watchings, and like an addict I was experiencing the pangs of withdrawal?

It was all of these that pained me, I decided. But mostly the last.

No one was abroad in the city as I made for the gates. Fear of the new masters kept the Roumish in hiding, I supposed. From time to time one of the alien vehicles hummed past, but I was unmolested. I came to the city's western gate in the late afternoon. It was open, revealing to me a gentle rising hill on whose breast rose trees with dark green crowns. I passed through and saw, a short distance beyond the gate, the figure of a Pilgrim who was shuffling slowly away from the city.

I overtook him easily.

His faltering, uncertain walk seemed strange to me, for not even his thick brown robes could hide the strength and youth of his body; he stood erect, his shoulders square and his back straight, and yet he walked with the hesitating, trembling step of an old man. When I drew abreast of him and peered under his hood I understood, for affixed to the bronze mask all Pilgrims wear was a reverberator, such as is used by blind men to warn them of obstacles and hazards. He became aware of me and said, 'I am a sightless Pilgrim. I pray you do not molest me.'

It was not a Pilgrim's voice. It was a strong and harsh and imperious voice.

I replied, 'I molest no one. I am a Watcher who has lost his occupation this night past.'

'Many occupations were lost this night past, Watcher.'

'Surely not a Pilgrim's.'

'No,' he said. 'Not a Pilgrim's.'

'Where are you bound?'

'Away from Roum.'

'No particular destination?'

'No,' the Pilgrim said. 'None. I will wander.'

'Perhaps we should wander together,' I said, for it is accounted good luck to travel with a Pilgrim, and, shorn of my Flier and my Changeling, I would otherwise have traveled alone. 'My destination is Perris. Will you come?'

'There as well as anywhere else,' he said bitterly. 'Yes. We will go to Perris together. But what business does a Watcher have there?'

'A Watcher has no business anywhere. I go to Perris to offer myself in service to the Rememberers.'

'Ah,' he said. 'I was of that guild too, but it was only honorary.'

'With Earth fallen, I wish to learn more of Earth in its prime.'

'Is all Earth fallen, then, and not only Roum?'

'I think it is so,' I said.

'Ah,' replied the Pilgrim. 'Ah!'

He fell silent and we went onward. I gave him my arm, and now he shuffled no longer, but moved with a young man's brisk stride. From time to time he uttered what might have been a sigh or a smothered sob. When I asked him details of his Pilgrimage, he answered obliquely or not at all. When we were an hour's journey outside Roum, and already amid forests, he said suddenly, 'This mask gives me pain. Will you help me adjust it?'

To my amazement he began to remove it. I gasped, for it is forbidden for a Pilgrim to reveal his face. Had he forgotten that I was not sightless too?

As the mask came away he said, 'You will not welcome this sight.'

The bronze grillwork slipped down from his forehead, and I saw first eyes that had been newly blinded, gaping holes where no surgeon's knife, but possibly thrusting fingers, had penetrated, and then the sharp regal nose, and finally the quirked, taut lips of the Prince of Roum.

'Your Majesty!' I cried.

Trails of dried blood ran down his cheeks. About the raw sockets themselves were smears of ointment. He felt little pain, I suppose, for he had killed it with those green smears, but the pain that burst through me was real and potent.

'Majesty no longer,' he said. 'Help me with the mask!' His hands trembled as he held it forth. 'These flanges must be widened. They press cruelly at my cheeks. Here – here—'

Quickly I made the adjustments, so that I would not have to see his ruined face for long.

He replaced the mask. 'I am a Pilgrim now,' he said quietly. 'Roum is without its Prince. Betray me if you wish, Watcher; otherwise help me to Perris; and if ever I regain my power you will be well rewarded.'

'I am no betrayer,' I told him.

In silence we continued. I had no way of making small talk with such a man. It would be a somber journey for us to Perris; but I was committed now to be his guide. I thought of Gormon and how well he had kept his vows. I thought too of Avluela, and a hundred times the words leaped to my tongue to ask the fallen Prince how his consort the Flier had fared in the night of defeat, and I did not ask.

Twilight gathered, but the sun still gleamed golden-red before us in the west. And suddenly I halted and made a hoarse sound of surprise deep in my throat, as a shadow passed overhead.

High above me Avluela soared. Her skin was stained by the colors of the sunset, and her wings were spread to their fullest, radiant with every hue of the spectrum. She was already at least the height of a hundred men above the ground, and still climbing, and to her I must have been only a speck among the trees.

'What is it?' the Prince asked. 'What do you see?'

'Nothing.'

'Tell me what you see!'

I could not deceive him. 'I see a Flier, your Majesty. A slim girl far aloft.'

'Then the night must have come.'

'No,' I said. 'The sun is still above the horizon.'

'How can that be? She can only have nightwings. The sun would hurl her to the ground.'

I hesitated. I could not bring myself to explain how it was that Avluela flew by day, though she had only nightwings. I could not tell the Prince of Roum that beside her, wingless, flew the invader Gormon, effortlessly moving through the air, his arms about her thin shoulders, steadying her, supporting her, helping her resist the pressure of the solar wind. I could not tell him that his nemesis flew with the last of his consorts above his head.

'Well?' he demanded. 'How does she fly by day?'

'I do not know,' I said. 'It is a mystery to me. There are many things nowadays I can no longer understand.'

The Prince appeared to accept that 'Yes, Watcher. Many things none of us can understand.'

He fell once more into silence. I yearned to call out to Avluela, but I knew she could not and would not hear me, and so I walked on toward the sunset, toward Perris, leading the blind Prince. And over us Avluela and Gormon sped onward, limned sharply against the day's last glow, until they climbed so high they were lost to my sight.

PART II

Among The Rememberers

1

To journey with a fallen Prince is no easy thing. His eyes were gone, but not his pride; blinding had taught him no humility. He wore the robes and mask of a Pilgrim, but there was no piety in his soul and little grace. Behind his mask he still knew himself to be the Prince of Roum.

I was all his court now, as we walked the road to Perris in early spring-time. I led him along the right roads; I amused him at his command with stories of my wanderings; I nursed him through moods of sulky bitterness. In return I got very little except the assurance that I would eat regularly. No one denies food to a Pilgrim, and in each village on our way we stopped in inns, where he was fed and I, as his companion, also was given meals. Once, early in our travels, he erred and haughtily told an innkeeper, 'See that you feed my servant as well!' The blinded Prince could not see that look of shocked disbelief – for what would a Pilgrim be doing with a servant? – but I smiled at the innkeeper, and winked, and tapped my forehead, and the man understood and served us both without discussion. Afterward I explained the error to the Prince, and thereafter he spoke of me as his companion. Yet I knew that to him I was nothing but a servant.

The weather was fair. Eyrop was growing warm as the year turned. Slender willows and poplars were greening beside the road, though much of the way out of Roum was planted with lavish star-trees imported during the gaudy days of the Second Cycle, and their blue-bladed leaves had resisted our puny Eyropan winter. The birds, too, were coming back from their season across the sea in Afreek. They sparkled overhead, singing, discussing among themselves the change of masters in the world. 'They mock me,' said the Prince one dawn. 'They sing to me and defy me to see their brightness!'

Oh, he was bitter, and with good reason. He, who had had so much and lost all, had a good deal to lament. For me, the defeat of Earth meant only an end to habits. Otherwise all was the same: no longer need I keep my Watch, but I still wandered the face of the world, alone even when, as now, I had a companion.

I wondered if the Prince knew why he had been blinded. I wondered if, in the moment of his triumph, Gormon had explained to the Prince that it was as elemental a matter as jealousy over a woman that had cost him his eyes.

'You took Avluela,' Gormon might have said. 'You saw a little Flier, and you thought she'd amuse you. And you said, here, girl, come to my bed. Not thinking of her as a person. Not thinking she might prefer others. Thinking only as a Prince of Roum might think – imperiously. Here, Prince!'

—and the quick, forked thrust of long-tipped fingers—

But I dared not ask. That much awe remained in me for this fallen monarch. To penetrate his privacy, to strike up a conversation with him about his mishaps as though he were an ordinary companion of the road – no, I could not. I spoke when I was spoken to. I offered conversation upon command. Otherwise I kept my silence, like a good commoner in the presence of royalty.

Each day we had our reminders that the Prince of Roum was royalty no longer.

Overhead flew the invaders, sometimes in floaters or other chariots, sometimes under their own power. Traffic was heavy. They were taking inventory of their world. Their shadows passed over us, tiny eclipses, and I looked up to see our new masters and oddly felt no anger at them, only relief that Earth's long vigil was over. For the Prince it was different. He always seemed to know when some invader passed above, and he clenched his fists, and scowled, and whispered black curses. Did his optic nerves still somehow record the movements of shadows? Or were his remaining senses so sharpened by the loss of one that he could detect the imperceptible humming of a floater and sniff the skins of the soaring invaders? I did not ask. I asked so little.

Sometimes at night, when he thought I slept, he sobbed. I pitied him then. He was so young to lose what he had, after all. I learned in those dark hours that even the sobs of a Prince are not those of ordinary men. He sobbed defiantly, belligerently, angrily. But yet he sobbed.

Much of the time he seemed stoic, resigned to his losses. He put one foot before the other and walked on briskly beside me, every step taking him farther from his great city of Roum, nearer to Perris. At other times, though, it seemed I could look through the bronze grillwork of his mask to see the curdled soul within. His pent-up rage took petty outlets. He mocked me for my age, for my low rank, for the emptiness of my life's purpose now that the invasion for which I had Watched had come. He toyed with me.

'Tell me your name, Watcher!'

'It is forbidden, Majesty.'

'Old laws are now repealed. Come on, man, we have months to travel together. Can I go on calling you Watcher all that time?'

'It is the custom of my guild.'

'The custom of mine,' he said, 'is to give orders and have them obeyed. Your name!'

'Not even the guild of Dominators can have a Watcher's name without due cause and a guildmaster's writ.'

He spat. 'What a jackal you are, to defy me when I'm like this! If we were in my palace now you'd never dare!'

'In your palace, Majesty, you would not make this unjust demand on me before your court. Dominators have obligations too. One of them is to respect the ways of lesser guilds.'

'He lectures me,' said the Prince. Irritably he threw himself down beside the road. Stretching against the grassy slope, he leaned back, touched one of the star-trees, snapped off a row of blades, clenched them in his hand so that they must have pricked his palm painfully. I stood beside him. A heavy land-vehicle rumbled by, the first we had seen on that empty road this morning. Within it were invaders. Some of them waved to us. After a long while the Prince said in a lighter, almost wheedling tone, 'My name is Enric. Now tell me yours.'

'I beg you to let me be, Majesty.'

'But you have my name! It is just as forbidden for me to give mine as you yours!'

'I did not ask yours,' I said firmly.

In the end I did not give him my name. It was a small enough victory, to refuse such information to a powerless Prince, but in a thousand little ways he made me pay for it. He nagged, chivvied, teased, cursed, and berated me. He spoke with contempt of my guild. He demanded menial services of me. I lubricated his metal mask; I sponged ointment into his ruined eyes; I did other things too humiliating to recall. And so we stumbled along the highway to Perris, the empty old man and the emptied young man, full of hatred for one another, and yet bound by the needs and the duties of wayfarers.

It was a difficult time. I had to cope with his changing moods as he soared to cosmic rapture over his plans for redeeming conquered Earth, and as he sank to abysses upon his realization that the conquest was final. I had to protect him from his own rashness in the villages, where he sometimes behaved as though he were still Prince of Roum, ordering folk about, slapping them even, in a way that was unbecoming to a holy man. Worse yet, I had to minister to his lusts, buying him women who came to him in darkness, unaware that they were dealing with one who claimed to be a Pilgrim. As a Pilgrim he was a fraud, for he did not carry the starstone with which Pilgrims make communion with the Will. Somehow I got him past all of these crises, even the time when we encountered on the road another Pilgrim, a genuine one. This was a formidable and disputatious old man full of theological quibbles. 'Come and talk with me of the immanence of the Will,' he said to the Prince, and the Prince, whose patience was frayed that afternoon, replied obscenely. I kicked the princely shin in a surreptitious way, and to the shocked Pilgrim I said, 'Our friend is unwell today. Last night he held communion with the Will and received a revelation that unsettled his mind.

I pray you, let us go on, and give him no talk of holiness until he is himself once more.'

With such improvisations I managed our journey.

As the weather warmed, the Prince's attitude mellowed. Perhaps he was growing reconciled to his catastrophe, or possibly, in the prison of his light-less skull, he was teaching himself new tactics for meeting his changed existence. He talked almost idly of himself, his downfall, his humiliation. He spoke of the power that had been his in terms that said unmistakably that he had no illusions about ever recapturing it. He talked of his wealth, his women, his jewels, his strange machines, his Changelings and Musicians and Servitors, the Masters and even fellow Dominators who had knelt to him. I will not say that at any time I liked him, but at least at these times I recognized a suffering human being behind his impassive mask.

He even recognized in me a human being. I know it cost him much.

He said, 'The trouble with power, Watcher, is that it cuts you off from people. People become things. Take yourself. To me, you were nothing but a machine that walked around Watching for invaders. I suppose you had dreams, ambitions, angers, all the rest, but I saw you as a dried-up old man without any independent existence outside of your guild function. Now I see much more by seeing nothing.'

'What do you see?'

'You were young once, Watcher. You had a town you loved. A family. A girl, even. You chose, or had chosen for you, a guild, you went into apprenticeship, you struggled, your head ached you, your belly griped you, there were many dark moments when you wondered what it was all about, what it was for. And you saw us ride by, Masters, Dominators, and it was like comets going past. Yet here we are together, cast up by the tides on the road to Perris. And which of us is happier now?'

'I am beyond happiness or sorrow,' I said.

'Is that the truth? Is that the truth? Or is it a line you hide behind? Tell me, Watcher: I know your guild forbids you to marry, but have you ever loved?'

'Sometimes.'

'And are you beyond that now?'

'I am old,' I said evasively.

'But you could love. You could love. You're released from your guild vows now, eh? You could take a bride.'

I laughed. 'Who'd have me?'

'Don't speak that way. You're not that old. You have strengths. You've seen the world, you understand it. Why, in Perris you could find yourself some wench who—' He paused. 'Were you ever tempted, while you still were under your vows?'

Just then a Flier passed overhead. She was a woman of middle years, struggling a little in the sky, for some daylight remained to press on her wings. I felt a pang, and I wanted to tell the Prince: yes, yes, I was tempted, there was a little Flier not long ago, a girl, a child, Avluela; and in my way I loved her, though I never touched her; and I love her still.

I said nothing to Prince Enric.

I looked, though, at that Flier, freer than I because she had wings, and in the warmth of that spring evening I felt the chill of desolation enfolding me.

'Is it far to Perris?' the Prince asked.

'We will walk, and one day we will get there.'

'And then?'

'For me an apprenticeship in the guild of Rememberers, and a new life. For you?'

'I hope to find friends there,' he said.

We walked on, long hours each day. There were those who went by and offered us rides, but we refused, for at the checkpoints the invaders would be seeking such wandering nobility as the Prince. We walked a tunnel miles long under sky-storming mountains sheathed in ice, and we entered a flat land of farming peasants, and we paused by awakening rivers to cool our toes. Golden summer burst upon us. We moved through the world but were not of it; we listened to no news of the conquest, although it was obvious that the invaders had taken full possession. In small vehicles they hovered everywhere, seeing our world that now was theirs.

I did the bidding of the Prince in all ways, including the unpleasant ones. I attempted to make his life less bleak. I gave him a sensation of being still a ruler – albeit of only one useless old Watcher. I taught him, too, how best to masquerade as a Pilgrim. From what little I knew I gave him postures, phrases, prayers. It was obvious that he had spent little time in contact with the Will while he reigned. Now he pretended faith, but it was insincere, part of his camouflage.

In a town called Dijon, he said, 'Here I will purchase eyes.'

Not true eyes. The secret of making such replacements perished in the Second Cycle. Out among the more fortunate stars any miracle is available for a price, but our Earth is a neglected world in a backwater of the universe. The Prince might have got out there in the days before conquest to purchase new sight, but now the best that was available to him was a way of distinguishing light from dark. Even that would give him a rudiment of sight; at present he had no other guidance than the reverberator that warned him of obstacles in his path. How did he know, though, that in Dijon he would find a craftsman with the necessary skills? And with what would he meet the cost?

He said, 'The man here is a brother of one of my Scribes. He is of the guild of Artificers, and I often bought his work in Roum. He'll have eyes for me.'

'And the cost?'

'I am not entirely without resources.'

We stopped in a field of gnarled cork-trees, and the Prince undid his robes. Indicating a place in the fleshy part of his thigh, he said, 'I carry a reserve here for emergencies. Give me your blade!' I handed it to him, and he seized the handle and pressed the stud that brought forth the cool, keen beam of light. With his left hand he felt his thigh, surveying for the exact place; then, stretching the flesh between two fingers, he made a surgically precise cut two inches long. He did not bleed, nor was there a sign that he felt pain. I watched in bewilderment as he slipped his fingers into the cut, spread its edges, and seemed to grope as if in a sack. He tossed my blade back to me.

Treasures tumbled from his thigh.

'Watch that nothing is lost,' he ordered me.

To the grass there fell seven sparkling jewels of alien origin, a small and artful celestial globe, five golden coins of Imperial Roum of cycles past, a ring set with a glowing dab of quasi-life, a flask of some unknown perfume, a group of miniature musical instruments done in precious woods and metals, eight statuettes of regal-looking men, and more. I scooped these wonders into a dazzling heap.

'An overpocket,' the Prince said coolly, 'which a skilled Surgeon implanted in my flesh. I anticipated a time of crisis in which I might need to leave the palace hurriedly. Into it I stuffed what I could; there is much more where these came from. Tell me, tell me what I have taken out!'

I gave him the full inventory. He listened tensely to the end, and I knew that he had kept count of all that had poured forth, and was testing my honesty. When I was done, he nodded, pleased. 'Take the globe,' he said, 'and the ring, and the two brightest jewels. Hide them in your pouch. The rest goes back within.' He spread the lips of the incision, and one by one I dropped the glories inside, where they joined who knew what splendid things lying in another dimension, the outlet from which was embedded in the Prince. He might have half the contents of the palace tucked away in his thigh. At the end he pressed the cut together, and it healed without a trace of a mark as I watched. He robed himself.

In town we quickly located the shop of Bordo the Artificer. He was a squat man with a speckled face, a grizzled beard, a tic in one eye, and a flat coarse nose, but his fingers were as delicate as a woman's. His shop was a dark place with dusty wooden shelves and small windows; it could have been a building ten thousand years old. A few elegant items were on display. Most were not. He looked at us guardedly, obviously baffled that a Watcher and a Pilgrim should come to him.

At the Prince's prodding I said, 'My friend needs eyes.'

'I make a device, yes. But it is expensive, and it takes many months to prepare. Beyond the means of any Pilgrim.'

I laid one jewel on the weathered counter. 'We have means.'

Shaken, Bordo snatched up the jewel, turned it this way and that, saw alien fires glowing at its heart.

'If you come back when the leaves are falling—'

'You have no eyes in stock?' I asked.

He smiled. 'I get few calls for such things. We keep a small inventory.'

I put down the celestial globe. Bordo recognized it as the work of a master, and his jaw sagged. He put it in one palm and tugged at his beard with the other hand. I let him look at it long enough to fall in love with it, and then I took it back and said, 'Autumn is too long to wait. We will have to go else-where. Perris, perhaps.' I caught the Prince's elbow, and we shuffled toward the door.

'Stop!' Bordo cried. 'At least let me check! Perhaps I have a pair some-where—' And he began to rummage furiously in overpockets mounted in the rear wall.

He had eyes in stock, of course, and I haggled a bit on the price, and we settled for the globe, the ring, and one jewel. The Prince was silent through-out the transaction. I insisted on immediate installation and Bordo, nod-ding excitedly, shut his shop, slipped on a thinking cap, and summoned a sallow-faced Surgeon. Shortly the preliminaries of the operation were under way. The Prince lay on a pallet in a sealed and sterile room. He removed his reverberator and then his mask; and as those sharp features came into view, Bordo – who had been to the court of Roum – grunted in amazement and began to say something. My foot descended heavily on his. Bordo swallowed his words; and the Surgeon, unaware, began tranquilly to swab the ruined sockets.

The eyes were pearl-gray spheres, smaller than real eyes and broken by transverse slits. What mechanism was within I do not know, but from their rear projected tiny golden connections to fasten to the nerves. The Prince slept through the early part of the task, while I stood guard and Bordo assisted the Surgeon. Then it was necessary to awaken him. His face con-vulsed in pain, but it was so quickly mastered that Bordo muttered a prayer at this display of determination.

'Some light here,' said the Surgeon.

Bordo nudged a drifting globe closer. The Prince said, 'Yes, yes, I see the difference.'

'We must test. We must adjust,' the Surgeon said.

Bordo went outside. I followed. The man was trembling, and his face was green with fear.

'Will you kill us now?' he asked.

'Of course not.'

'I recognized—'

'You recognized a poor Pilgrim,' I said, 'who has suffered a terrible misfortune while on his journey. No more. Nothing else.'

I examined Bordo's stock awhile. Then the Surgeon and his patient emerged. The Prince now bore the pearly spheres in his sockets, with a meniscus of false flesh about them to insure a tight fit. He looked more machine than man, with those dead things beneath his brows, and as he moved his head the slits widened, narrowed, widened again, silently, stealthily. 'Look,' he said, and walked across the room, indicating objects, even naming them. I knew that he saw as though through a thick veil, but at least he saw, in a fashion. He masked himself again and by nightfall we were gone from Dijon.

The Prince seemed almost buoyant. But what he had in his skull was a poor substitute for what Gormon had ripped from him, and soon enough he knew it. That night, as we slept on stale cots in a Pilgrim's hostelry, the Prince cried out in wordless sounds of fury, and by the shifting light of the true moon and the two false ones I saw his arms rise, his fingers curl, his nails strike at an imagined enemy, and strike again, and again.

2

It was summer's end when we finally reached Perris. We came into the city from the south, walking a broad, resilient highway bordered by ancient trees, amid a fine shower of rain. Gusts of wind blew shriveled leaves about us. That night of terror on which we both had fled conquered Roum now seemed almost a dream; we were toughened by a spring and summer of walking, and the gray towers of Perris seemed to hold out promise of new beginnings. I suspected that we deceived ourselves, for what did the world hold for a shattered Prince who saw only shadows, and a Watcher long past his proper years?

This was a darker city than Roum. Even in late winter, Roum had had clear skies and bright sunlight. Perris seemed perpetually clouded over, buildings and environment both somber. Even the city walls were ash-gray, and they had no sheen. The gate stood wide. Beside it there lounged a small, sullen man in the garb of the guild of Sentinels, who made no move to challenge us as we approached. I looked at him questioningly. He shook his head.

'Go in, Watcher.'

'Without a check?'

'You haven't heard? All cities were declared free six nights ago. Order of the invaders. Gates are never closed now. Half the Sentinels have no work.'

'I thought the invaders were searching for enemies,' I said. 'The former nobility.'

'They have their checkpoints elsewhere, and no Sentinels are used. The city is free. Go in. Go in.'

As we went in, I said, 'Then why are you here?'

'It was my post for forty years,' the Sentinel said. 'Where should I go?'

I made the sign that told him I shared his sorrow, and the Prince and I entered Perris.

'Five times I came to Perris by the southern gate,' said the Prince. 'Always by chariot, with my Changelings walking before me and making music in their throats. We proceeded to the river, past the ancient buildings and monuments, on to the palace of the Comt of Perris. And by night we danced on gravity plates high above the city, and there were ballets of Fliers, and from the Tower of Perris there was performed an aurora for us. And the wine, the red wine of Perris, the women in their saucy gowns, the red-tipped breasts, the sweet thighs! We bathed in wine, Watcher.' He pointed vaguely. 'Is that the Tower of Perris?'

'I think it is the ruin of this city's weather machine,' I said.

'A weather machine would be a vertical column. What I see rises from a wide base to a slender summit, as does the Tower of Perris.'

'What I see,' I said gently, 'is a vertical column, at least thirty men high, ending in a rough break. The Tower would not be this close to the southern gate, would it?'

'No,' said the Prince, and muttered a foulness. 'The weather machine it is, then. These eyes of Bordo's don't see so clearly for me, eh? I deceive myself, Watcher. I deceive myself. Find a thinking cap and see if the Comt has fled.'

I stared a moment longer at the truncated pillar of the weather machine, that fantastic device which had brought such grief upon the world in the Second Cycle. I tried to penetrate its sleek, almost oily marble sides, to see the coiling intestines of mysterious devices that had been capable of sinking whole continents, that long ago had transformed my homeland in the west from a mountainous country to a chain of islands. Then I turned away, donned a public cap, asked for the Comt, got the answer I expected, and demanded to know the locations of places where we might find lodging.

The Prince said, 'Well?'

'The Comt of Perris was slain during the conquest along with all his sons. His dynasty is extinguished, his title is abolished, his palace has been transformed into a museum by the invaders. The rest of the Perrisian nobility is dead or has taken flight. I'll find a place for you at the lodge of Pilgrims.'

'No. Take me with you to the Rememberers.'

'Is that the guild you seek now?'

He gestured impatiently. 'No, fool! But how can I stay alone in a strange city, with all my friends gone? What would I say to true Pilgrims in their hostelry? I'll stay with you. The Rememberers can hardly turn away a blind Pilgrim.'

He gave me no choice. And so he accompanied me to the Hall of Rememberers.

We had to cross half the city, and it took us nearly the whole day. Perris seemed to me to be in disarray. The coming of the invaders had upset the structure of our society, liberating from their tasks great blocs of people, in some cases whole guilds. I saw dozens of my fellow Watchers in the streets, some still dragging about with them their cases of instruments, others, like me, freed of that burden and scarcely knowing what to do with their hands. My guildmates looked glum and hollow; many of them were dull-eyed with carousing, now that all discipline was shattered. Then there were Sentinels, aimless and dispirited because they had nothing to guard, and Defenders, cowed and dazed at the ending of defense. I saw no Masters and of course no Dominators, but many unemployed Clowns, Musicians, Scribes, and other court functionaries drifted randomly. Also there were hordes of dull neuters, their nearly mindless bodies slumped from unfamiliar disuse. Only Vendors and Somnambulists seemed to be carrying on business as usual.

The invaders were very much in evidence. In twos and threes they strolled on every street, long-limbed beings whose hands dangled nearly to their knees; their eyelids were heavy, their nostrils were hidden in filtration pouches, their lips were full and, when not apart, joined almost seamlessly. Most of them were dressed in identical robes of a deep, rich green, perhaps a uniform of military occupation; a few carried weapons of an oddly primitive kind, great heavy things slung across their backs, probably more for display than for self-defense. They seemed generally relaxed as they moved among us – genial conquerors, self-confident and proud, fearing no molestation from the defeated populace. Yet the tact that they never walked alone argued that they felt an inner wariness. I could not find it in me to resent their presence, nor even the implied arrogance of their possessive glances at the ancient monuments of Perris; yet the Prince of Roum, to whom all figures were merely upright bars of dark gray against a field of light gray, instinctively sensed their nearness to him and reacted with quick hostile intakes of breath.

Also there were many more outworld visitors than usual, star-beings of a hundred kinds, some able to breathe our air, others going about in hermetic globes or little pyramid-shaped breathing-boxes or contour suits. It was nothing new to see such strangers on Earth, of course, but the sheer quantity of them was astonishing. They were everywhere, prowling into the houses of Earth's old religion, buying shining models of the Tower of Perris from Vendors at street corners, clambering precariously into the upper levels of the walkways, peering into occupied dwellings, snapping images, exchanging currency with furtive hucksters, flirting with Fliers and Somnambulists, risking their lives at our restaurants, moving in shepherded groups from sight to sight. It was as though our invaders had passed the word through the galaxies: SEE OLD EARTH NOW. UNDER NEW MANAGEMENT.

At least our beggars were flourishing. The outworld ones fared poorly at the hands of the alien almsgivers, but those who were Earthborn did well, except for the Changelings, who could not be recognized as native stock. I saw several of these mutants, disgruntled at being refused, turn on other beggars who had had better luck and beat them to the ground, while image-snappers recorded the scene for the delight of galactic stay-at-homes.

We came in time to the Hall of Rememberers.

It was an imposing building, as well it might be, housing as it did all our planet's past. It rose to an enormous height on the southern bank of the Senn, just opposite the equally massive palace of the Comt. But the dwelling of the deposed Comt was an ancient building, truly ancient, of the First Cycle even, a long, involuted structure of gray stone with a green metal roof in the traditional Perrisian style, while the Hall of Rememberers was a shaft of polished whiteness, its surface unbroken by windows, about which there coiled from summit to base a golden helix of burnished metal that bore inscribed on it the history of mankind. The upper coils of the helix were blank. At a distance I could read nothing, and I wondered whether the Rememberers had taken the trouble to inscribe upon their building the tale of Earth's final defeat. Later I learned that they had not – that the story, in fact, terminated at the end of the Second Cycle, leaving untold much for which little pleasure was felt.

Night was falling now. And Perris, which had looked so dreary in the clouded and drizzly day, came to beauty like a dowager returning from Jorslem with her youth and voluptuousness restored. The City's lights cast a soft but dazzling radiance that magically illuminated the old gray buildings, turning angles hazy, hiding antiquity's grime, blurring ugliness into poetry. The Comt's palace was transformed from a heavy thing of sprawling bulk into an airy fable. The Tower of Perris, spotlighted against the dusk, loomed above us to the east like a giant gaunt spider, but a spider of grace and charm. The whiteness of the Hall of Rememberers was now intolerably beautiful, and the helical coil of history no longer seemed to wind to the summit, but plunged directly into one's heart. The Fliers of Perris were abroad at this hour, taking their ease above us in a graceful ballet, their filmy wings spread wide to catch the light from below, their slender bodies trailing at an angle to the horizon. How they soared, these genetically altered children of

Earth, these fortunate members of a guild that demands only that its members find pleasure in life! They shed beauty upon the groundlings like little moons. They were joined in their airborne dance by invaders, flying in some method unknown to me, their lengthy limbs drawn close to their bodies. I noticed that the Fliers showed no distaste for those who had come to share their sport, but rather appeared to welcome the outworlders, allowing them places in the dance.

Higher, on the backdrop of the sky itself, whirled the two false moons, blank and burnished, skimming from west to east; and blobs of disciplined light swirled in mid-atmosphere in what I supposed was a customary Perisian diversion; and speakers floating beneath the clouds showered us with sparkling music I heard the laughter of girls from somewhere; I scented bubbling wine. If this is Perris conquered, I wondered, what must Perris free have been like?

'Are we at the Hall of Rememberers?' asked Prince Enric testily.

'This is it, yes,' I replied. 'A tower of white.'

'I know what it looks like, idiot! But now – I see less well after dark – that building there?'

'You point to the palace of the Comt, Majesty.'

'There, then.'

'Yes.'

'Why have we not gone in?'

'I am seeing Perris,' I said. 'I have never known such beauty. Roum is attractive too, in a different way. Roum is an emperor; Perris is a courtesan.'

'You talk poetry, you shriveled old man!'

'I feel my age dropping away. I could dance in the streets now. This city sings to me.'

'Go in. Go in. We are here to see the Rememberers. Let it sing to you later.'

I sighed and guided him toward the entrance to the great hall. We passed up a walkway of some black glossy stone, while beams of light played down on us, scanning us and recording us. A monstrous ebon door, five men wide and ten men high, proved to be only a projected illusion, for as we neared it I sensed the depth of it, saw its vaulted interior, and knew it for a deception. I felt a vague warmth and tasted a strange perfume as we passed through it.

Within was a mammoth antechamber nearly as awesome as the grand inner space of the palace of the Prince of Roum. All was white, the stone glowing with an inner radiance that bathed everything in brilliance. To right and left, heavy doorways led to inner wings. Although night had come, many individuals were clustered about access banks mounted on the rear wall of the antechamber, where screens and caps gave them contact with the massive files of the guild of Rememberers. I noticed with interest that many of those who had come here with questions about mankind's past were invaders.

Our footsteps crackled on the tiled floor as we crossed it.

I saw no actual Rememberers, and so I went to an access bank, put on a thinking cap, and notified the embalmed brain to which it was connected that I sought the Rememberer Basil, he whom I had met briefly in Roum.

'What is your business with him?'

'I bring with me his shawl, which he left in my care when he fled Roum.'

'The Rememberer Basil has returned to Roum to complete his research, by permission of the conqueror. I will send to you another member of the guild to receive the shawl.'

We did not have long to wait. We stood together near the rear of the ante-chamber, and I contemplated the spectacle of the invaders who had so much to learn, and in moments there came to us a thick-set, dour-faced man some years younger than myself, but yet not young, who wore about his broad shoulders the ceremonial shawl of his guild.

'I am the Rememberer Elegro,' he announced portentously.

'I bring you Basil's shawl.'

'Come. Follow.'

He had emerged from an imperceptible place in the wall where a Sliding block turned on pivots. Now he slid it once more and rapidly went down a passageway. I called out to him that my companion was blind and could not match his pace, and the Rememberer Elegro halted, looking visibly im-patient. His downcurving mouth twitched, and he buried his short fingers in the deep black curls of his beard. When we had caught up with him he moved on less swiftly. We pursued an infinity of passageways and ended in Elegro's domicile, somewhere high in the tower.

The room was dark but amply furnished with screens, caps, scribing equipment, voice-boxes, and other aids to scholarship. The walls were hung with a purple-black fabric, evidently alive, for its marginal folds rippled in pulsating rhythms. Three drifting globes gave less than ample light.

'The shawl,' he said.

I produced it from my pouch. It had amused me to wear it for a while in those first confused days of the conquest – after all, Basil had left it in my hands when he fled down the street, and I had not meant to wrest it from him, but he obviously had cared little for its loss – but shortly I had put it away, since it bred confusion for a man in Watcher's garb to wear a Remem-berer's shawl. Elegro took it from me curtly and unfolded it, scrutinizing it as though looking for lice.

'How did you get this?'

'Basil and I encountered one another in the street during the actual moment of the invasion. He was highly agitated. I attempted to restrain him and he ran past me, leaving me still grasping his shawl.'

'He told a different story.'

'I regret if I have compromised him,' I said.

'At any rate, you have returned his shawl. I'll communicate the news to Roum tonight. Are you expecting a reward for delivering it?'

'Yes.'

Displeased, Elegro said, 'Which is?'

'To be allowed to come among the Rememberers as an apprentice.'

He looked startled. 'You have a guild!'

'To be a Watcher in these days is to be guildless. For what should I watch? I am released from my vows.'

'Perhaps. But you are old to be trying a new guild.'

'Not *too* old.'

'Ours is a difficult one.'

'I am willing to work hard. I desire to learn. In my old age curiosity is born in me.'

'Become a Pilgrim like your friend here. See the world.'

'I have seen the world. Now I wish to join the Rememberers and learn of the past.'

'You can dial an information below. Our access banks are open to you, Watcher.'

'It is not the same. Enroll me.'

'Apprentice yourself to the Indexers,' Elegro suggested. 'The work is similar, but not so demanding.'

'I claim apprenticeship here.'

Elegro sighed heavily. He steepled his fingers, bowed his head, quirked his lips. This was plainly unique to him. While he pondered, an inner door opened and a female Rememberer entered the room, carrying a small turquoise music-sphere cradled in both her hands. She took four paces and halted, obviously surprised that Elegro was entertaining visitors.

She made a nod of apology and said, 'I will return later.'

'Stay,' said the Rememberer. To myself and the Prince he said, 'My wife. The Rememberer Olmayne.' To his wife he said, 'These are travelers newly come from Roum. They have delivered Basil's shawl. The Watcher now asks apprenticeship in our guild. What do you advise?'

The Rememberer Olmayne's white brow furrowed. She put down her music-sphere in a dark crystal vase; the sphere was unintentionally activated as she did so, and it offered us a dozen shimmering notes before she switched it off. Then she contemplated us, and I her. She was notably younger than her husband, who was of middle years, while she seemed to be hardly past first bloom. Yet there was a strength about her that argued for greater maturity. Perhaps, I thought, she had been to Jorslem to renew her youth; but in that case it was odd that her husband had not done the same, unless he prized his look of age. She was surely attractive. Her face was broad, with a high forehead, pronounced cheekbones, a wide, sensual mouth, a jutting chin. Her hair was lustrous black, contrasting most vividly with the pallor of her skin. Such white skin is a rarity among us, though now I know that it was more common in ancient times, when the breed was different. Avluela, my lovely little Flier, had displayed that same combination of black and white, but there the resemblance ended, for Avluela was all fragility, and the Rememberer Olmayne was strength itself. Below her long slender neck her body blossomed into well-set shoulders, high breasts, firm legs. Her posture was regal.

She studied us at length, until I could scarcely meet the level gaze of her widely spaced dark eyes. Ultimately she said, 'Does the Watcher regard himself as qualified to become one of us?'

The question appeared aimed at anyone in the chamber who cared to reply. I hesitated; Elegro did likewise; and at length it was the Prince of Roum who replied in his voice of command, 'The Watcher is qualified to enter your guild.'

'And who are you?' Olmayne demanded.

Instantly the Prince adopted a more accommodating tone. 'A miserable blind Pilgrim, milady, who has wandered here on foot from Roum, in this man's company. If I am any judge, you could do worse than admit him as an apprentice.'

Elegro said, 'And yourself? What plans have you?'

'I wish only refuge here,' said the Prince. 'I am tired of roaming and there is much thinking I must do. Perhaps you could allow me to carry out small tasks here. I would not want to be separated from my companion.'

To me Olmayne said, 'We will confer on your case. If there is approval, you will be given the tests. I will be your sponsor.'

'Olmayne!' blurted Elegro in unmistakable amazement.

She smiled serenely at us all.

A family quarrel appeared on the verge; but it was averted, and the Rememberers offered us hospitality, juices, sharper beverages, a night's lodging. We dined apart from them in one section of their suite, while other Rememberers were summoned to consider my irregular application. The Prince seemed in strange agitation; he bolted down his food, spilled a flask of wine, fumbled with his eating utensils, put his fingers again and again to his gray metallic eyeballs as though trying to scratch an itch upon the lobes of his brain.

At length he said in a low, urgent voice, 'Describe her to me!'

I did so, in detail, coloring and shading my words to draw him the most vivid pictures I could.

'She is beautiful, you say?'

'I believe so. You know that at my age one must work from abstract notions, not from the flow of the glands.'

'Her voice arouses me,' said the Prince. 'She has power. She is queenly. She *must* be beautiful; there'd be no justice if her body failed to match the voice.'

'She is,' I said heavily, 'another man's wife, and the giver of hospitality.'

I remembered a day in Roum when the Prince's palanquin had come forth from the palace, and the Prince had spied Avluela, and ordered her to him, drawing her through the curtain to make use of her. A Dominator may command lesser folk that way; but a Pilgrim may not, and I feared Prince Enric's schemes now. He dabbed at his eyes again. His facial muscles worked.

'Promise me you'll not start trouble with her,' I said.

The corner of his mouth jerked in what must have been the beginning of an angry retort, quickly stifled. With effort he said, 'You misjudge me, old man. I'll abide by the laws of hospitality here. Be a good man and get me more wine, eh?'

I thumbed the serving niche and obtained a second flask. It was strong red wine, not the golden stuff of Roum. I poured; we drank; the flask was swiftly empty. I grasped it along its lines of polarity and gave it the proper twist, and it popped and was gone like a bubble. Moments later the Rememberer Olmayne entered. She had changed her garments; earlier she had worn an afternoon gown of dull hue and coarse fabric, but now she was garbed in a sheer scarlet robe fastened between her breasts. It revealed to me the planes and shadows of her body, and it surprised me to see that she had chosen to retain a navel. It broke the smooth downward sweep of her belly in an effect so carefully calculated to arouse that it nearly incited even me.

She said complacently, 'Your application has been approved under my sponsorship. The tests will be administered tonight. If you succeed, you will be pledged to our division.' Her eyes twinkled in sudden mischief. 'My husband, you should know, is most displeased. But my husband's displeasure is not a thing to be feared. Come with me, both of you.'

She stretched forth her hands, taking mine, taking the Prince's. Her fingers were cool. I throbbed with an inner fever and marveled at this sign of new youth that arose within me – not even by virtue of the waters of the house of renewal in sacred Jorslem.

'Come,' said Olmayne, and led us to the place of test.

3

And so I passed into the guild of Rememberers.

The tests were perfunctory. Olmayne brought us to a circular room somewhere near the summit of the great tower. Its curving walls were inlaid with rare woods of many hues, and shining benches rose from the floor, and in the center of all was a helix the height of a man, inscribed with letters too small to be read. Half a dozen Rememberers lounged about, plainly there only by Olmayne's whim, and not in the slightest interested in this old and shabby Watcher whom she had so unaccountably sponsored.

A thinking cap was offered me. A scratchy voice asked me a dozen questions through the cap, probing for my typical responses, querying me on biographical details. I gave my guild identification so that they could contact the local guildmaster, check my *bona fides,* and obtain my release. Ordinarily one could not win release from a Watcher's vows, but these were not ordinary times, and I knew my guild was shattered.

Within an hour all was done. Olmayne herself placed the shawl over my shoulders.

'You'll be given sleeping quarters near our suite,' she said. 'You'll have to surrender your Watcher garb, though your friend may remain in Pilgrim's clothes. Your training will begin after a probationary period. Meanwhile you have full access to any of our memory tanks. You realize, of course, that it will be ten years or more before you can win full admission to the guild.'

'I realize that,' I said.

'Your name now will be Tomis,' Olmayne told me. 'Not yet the Rememberer Tomis, but Tomis of the Rememberers. There is a difference. Your past name no longer matters.'

The Prince and I were conducted to the small room we would share. It was a humble enough place, but yet it had facilities for washing, outlets for thinking caps and other information devices, and a food vent. Prince Enric went about the room, touching things, learning the geography. Cabinets, beds, chairs, storage units, and other furniture popped in and out of the walls as he blundered onto the controls. Eventually he was satisfied; not blundering now, he activated a bed, and a sheaf of brightness glided from a slot. He stretched out.

'Tell me something, Tomis of the Rememberers.'

'Yes?'

'To satisfy curiosity that eats me. What was your name in previous life?'

'It does not matter now.'

'No vows bind you to secrecy. Will you thwart me still?'

'Old habit binds me,' I said. 'For twice your lifetime I was conditioned never to speak my name except lawfully.'

'Speak it now.'

'Wuellig,' I said.

It was strangely liberating to commit that act. My former name seemed to hover in the air before my lips; to dart from the room like a jewelbird released from its captivity; to soar, to turn sharply, to strike a wall and shiver to pieces with a light, tinkling sound. I trembled, 'Wuellig,' I said again. 'My name was Wuellig.'

'Wuellig no more.'

'Tomis of the Rememberers.'

And we both laughed until it hurt, and the blinded Prince swung himself to his feet and slapped his hand against mine in high good fellowship, and we shouted my name and his and mine again and again, like small boys who suddenly have learned the words of power and have discovered at last how little power those words really have.

Thus I took up my new life among the Rememberers.

For some time to come I did not leave the Hall of Rememberers at all. My days and nights were completely occupied, and I remained a stranger to Perris without. The Prince, too, though his time was not as fully taken up, stayed in the building almost always, going out only when boredom or fury overtook him. Occasionally the Rememberer Olmayne went with him, or he with her, so that he would not be alone in his darkness; but I know that on occasion he left the building by himself, defiantly intending to show that, even sightless, he could cope with the challenges of the city.

My waking hours were divided among these activities:

+ Primary orientations.
+ Menial duties of an apprentice.
+ Private researches.

Not unexpectedly, I found myself much older than the other apprentices then in residence. Most were youngsters, the children of Rememberers themselves; they looked upon me in bafflement, unable to comprehend having such an ancient for a schoolmate. There were a few fairly mature apprentices, those who had found a vocation for Remembering midway in life, but none approaching my age. Hence I had little social contact with my fellows in training.

For a part of each day we learned the techniques by which the Rememberers recapture Earth's past. I was shown wide-eyed through the laboratories where analysis of field specimens is performed; I saw the detectors which, by pinpointing the decay of a few atoms, give an age to an artifact; I watched as beams of many-colored light lancing from a ringed outlet turned a sliver of wood to ash and caused it to give up its secrets; I saw the very images of past events peeled from inanimate substance. We leave our imprint where we go: the particles of light rebound from our faces, and the photonic flux nails them to the environment. From which the Rememberers strip them, categorize them, fix them. I entered a room where a phantasmagoria of faces drifted on a greasy blue mist: vanished kings and guildmasters, lost dukes, heroes of ancient days. I beheld cold-eyed technicians prodding history from handfuls of charred matter. I saw damp lumps of trash give up tales of revolutions and assassinations, of cultural change, of the discarding of mores.

Then I was instructed superficially in the techniques of the field. Through cunning simulation I was shown Rememberers at work with vacuum cores digging through the mounds of the great ruined cities of Afreek and Ais. I participated vicariously in the undersea quest for the remnants of the civilizations of the Lost Continents; teams of Rememberers entered translucent, teardrop-shaped vehicles like blobs of green gelatin and sped into the depths of Earth Ocean, down and down to the slime-crusted prairies of the former land and with dancing beams of violet force, they drilled through muck and girders to find buried truths. I watched the gatherers of shards, the diggers of shadows, the collectors of molecular films. One of the best of the orientation experiences they provided was a sequence in which truly heroic Rememberers excavated a weather machine in lower Afreek, baring the base of the titanic thing, lifting it on power pulls from the soil, an extraction so mighty that the earth itself seemed to shriek when it was done. High aloft they floated the ponderous relic of Second Cycle folly, while shawled experts prodded in its root-place to learn how the column had been erected in the first instance. My eyes throbbed at the spectacle.

I emerged from the sessions with an overwhelming awe for this guild I had chosen. Individual Rememberers whom I had known had struck me generally as pompous, disdainful, haughty, or merely aloof; I did not find them charming. Yet is the whole greater than the sum of its parts, and I saw such men as Basil and Elegro, so vacant, so absent from ordinary human concerns, so disinterested, as part of a colossal effort to win back from eternity our brilliant yesterdays. This research into lost time was magnificent, the only proper substitute for mankind's former activities; having lost our present and our future, we had of necessity to bend all our endeavors to the past, which no one could take from us if only we were vigilant enough.

For many days I absorbed the details of this effort, every stage of the work from the collection of specks of dust in the field through their treatment and analysis in the laboratory to the highest endeavor of all, synthesis and interpretation, which was carried out by senior Rememberers on the highest level of this building. I was given but a glimpse of those sages: withered and dry, old enough to be grandfathers to me, white heads bent forward, thin lips droning comments and interpretations, quibbles and corrections. Some of them, I was told in a hushed whisper, had been renewed at Jorslem two and three times apiece, and now were beyond renewal and in their final great age.

Next we were introduced to the memory tanks where the Rememberers store their findings, and from which are dispensed informations for the benefit of the curious.

As a Watcher I had had little curiosity and less interest in visiting memory tanks. Certainly I had never seen anything like this, for the tanks of the Rememberers were no mere three-brain or five-brain storage units, but mammoth installations with a hundred brains or more hooked in series. The room to which they took us – one of dozens beneath the building, I learned – was an oblong chamber, deep but not high, in which brain cases were arrayed in rows of nine that faded into shadowed depths. Perspective played odd tricks; I was not sure if there were ten rows or fifty, and the sight of those bleached domes was overpoweringly immense.

'Are these the brains of former Rememberers?' I asked.

The guide replied, 'Some of them are. But there's no necessity to use only Rememberers. Any normal human brain will do; even a Servitor has more storage capacity than you'd believe. We have no need for redundancy in our circuits, and so we can use the full resources of each brain.'

I tried to peer through the heavy block of sleekness that protected the memory tanks from harm. I said, 'What is recorded in this particular room?'

'The names of dwellers in Afreek in Second Cycle times, and as much personal data about each as we have so far recovered. Also, since these cells are not fully charged, we have temporarily stored in them certain geographical details concerning the Lost Continents, and information pertaining to the creation of Land Bridge.'

'Can such information be easily transferred from temporary storage to permanent?' I asked.

'Easily, yes. Everything is electromagnetic here. Our facts are aggregates of charges; we shift them from brain to brain by reversing polarities.'

'What if there were an electrical failure?' I demanded. 'You say you have no redundancy here. Is there no possibility of losing data through some accident?'

'None,' said the guide smoothly. 'We have a series of fallback devices to insure continuity of power. And by using organic tissue for our storage cells, we have the best assurance of safety of all: for the brains themselves will retain their data in the event of a power interruption. It would be taxing but not impossible to recapture their contents.'

'During the invasion,' I said, 'were difficulties experienced?'

'We are under the protection of the invaders, who regard our work as vital to their own interests.'

Not long afterward, at a general convocation of the Rememberers, we apprentices were permitted to look on from a balcony of the guildhall; below us, in full majesty, were the guild members, shawls in place, Elegro and Olmayne among them. On a dais that bore the helical symbol was Chancellor Kenishal of the Rememberers, an austere and commanding figure, and beside him was an even more conspicuous personage who was of the species that had conquered Earth. Kenishal spoke briefly. The resonance of his voice did not entirely conceal ths hollowness of his words; like all administrators everywhere, he gushed platitudes, praising himself by implication as he congratulated his guild for its notable work. Then he introduced the invader.

The alien stretched forth his arms until they seemed to touch the walls of the auditorium.

'I am Manrule Seven,' he said quietly. 'I am Procurator of Perris, with particular responsibility for the guild of Rememberers. My purpose here today is to confirm the decree of the provisional occupational government. You Remembers are to go totally unhampered in your work. You are to have free access to all sites on this planet or on any other planet or on any other world that may have bearing on your mastery of the past of this planet. All files are to remain open to you, except those pertaining to the organization of the conquest itself. Chancellor Kenishal has informed me that the conquest lies outside the scope of your present research in any case, so no hardship will be worked. We of the occupying government are aware of the value of the work of your guild. The history of this planet is of great significance, and we wish your efforts continued.'

'To make Earth a better tourist attraction,' said the Prince of Roum bitterly at my side.

Manrule Seven went on, 'The Chancellor has requested me to inform you of one administrative change that will necessarily follow from the occupied status of your planet. In the past, all disputes among you were settled by the courts of your own guild, with Chancellor Kenishal having the highest right of appeal. For the sake of efficient administration it now becomes mandatory for us to impose our jurisdiction over that of the guild. Therefore the Chancellor will transfer to us those litigations which he feels no longer fall into his sphere of authority.'

The Rememberers gasped. There was a sudden shifting of postures and exchanging of glances on the floor below.

'The Chancellor's abdicating!' blurted an apprentice near me.

'What choice does he have, fool?' another whispered harshly.

The meeting broke up in some confusion. Rememberers flooded into the hallways, gesticulating, debating, expostulating. One venerable wearer of the shawl was so shaken that he crouched down and began to make the series of stabilizer responses, heedless of the throng. The tide swept over us apprentices, forcing us back. I attempted to protect the Prince, fearing that he would be thrown to the floor and trampled; but we were swept apart and I lost sight of him for minutes. When I saw him again he stood with the Rememberer Olmayne. Her face was flushed, her eyes were bright; she was speaking rapidly, and the Prince was listening. His hand clung to her elbow as if for support.

4

After the conclusion of the early period of orientations, I was given trivial tasks. Chiefly I was asked to do things that in an earlier time would have been performed wholly by machine: for example, to monitor the feed lines that oozed nutrients into the brain-boxes of the memory tanks. For several hours each day I walked through the narrow corridor of the inspection panels, searching for clogged lines. It had been so devised that when a line became blocked, a stress pattern was created the length of the clear tubing that contained it, and beams of a special polarised light illuminated that pattern for benefit of the inspector. I did my humble task, now and again finding a blockage, and I did other little jobs as befitted my status of apprenticeship.

However, I also had the opportunity to pursue my own investigations into the events of my planet's past.

Sometimes one does not learn the value of things until they are lost. For a lifetime I served as a Watcher, striving to give early warning of a promised invasion of Earth, while caring little who might wish to invade us, or why. For a lifetime I realised dimly that Earth had known grander days than those of the Third Cycle into which I had been born, and yet I sought no knowledge of what those days had been like and of the reasons of our present diminished condition. Only when the starships of the invaders blossomed in the sky did I feel a sudden hunger to know of that lost past. Now, as the most elderly of apprentices, I, Tomis of the Rememberers, rummaged through the archives of vanished time.

Any citizen has the right to go to a public thinking cap and requisition an information from the Rememberers on any given subject. Nothing is concealed. But the Rememberers volunteer no aid; you must know how to ask, which means you must know what to ask. Item by item you must seek your facts. It is useful for those who must know, say, the long-term patterns of climate in Agupt, or the symbols of the crystallisation disease, or the limitations in the charter of one of the guilds; but it is no help at all to the man who wishes knowledge of the larger questions. One would need to requisition a thousand informations merely to make a beginning. The expense would be great; few would bother.

As an apprentice Rememberer I had full access to all data. More important, I had access to the indexes. The Indexers are a guild subsidiary to the Rememberers, a donkey-guild of drudges who record and classify that which they often do not understand; the end product of their toil serves the greater guild, but the indexes are not open to all. Without them one scarcely is able to cope with the problems of research. I will not summarise the stages by which I came by my knowledge – the hours spent shuffling through interwoven corridors, the rebuffs, the bewilderments, the throbbing of the brain. As a foolish novice I was at the mercy of pranksters, and many a fellow apprentice, even a guild member or two, led me astray for the sheer wicked joy of it. But I learned which routes to follow, how to set up sequences of questions, how to follow a path of references higher and higher until the truth bursts dazzingly upon one. With persistence rather than with great intellect I wrung from the files of the Rememberers a coherent tale of the downfall of man.

This:

There was a time in ages past when life on Earth was brutal and primitive. We call this time the First Cycle. I do not speak of the period before civilisation, that time of grunting and hairiness, of caves and stone tools. We consider the First Cycle to have commenced when man first learned to record information and to control environment. This occurred in Agupt and Sumir. By our way of reckoning the First Cycle commenced some 40,000 years ago – however, we are uncertain of its true length in its own terms, since the span of the year was altered at the end of the Second Cycle, and we have been unable thus far to determine how long, in previous eras, it took for our world to circle its sun. Somewhat longer than at present, perhaps.

The First Cycle was the time of Imperial Roum and of the first flowering of Jorslem. Eyrop remained savage long after Ais and parts of Afreek were civilised. In the west, two great continents occupied much of Earth Ocean, and these too were held by savages.

It is understood that in this cycle mankind had no contact with other worlds or stars. Such solitude is difficult to comprehend, but yet so it occurred. Mankind had no way of creating light except through fire; he could not cure his ills; life was not susceptible to renewal. It was a time without comforts, a gay time, harsh in its simplicity. Death came early; one barely had time to scatter a few sons about, and one was carried off. One lived with fear, but mostly not fear, of real things.

The soul recoils from such an era. But yet it is true that in the First Cycle magnificent cities were founded – Roum, Perris, Atin, Jorslem – and splendid deeds were accomplished. One stands in awe of those ancestors, foul-smelling (no doubt), illiterate, without machines, and still capable of coming to terms with their universe and to some extent of mastering it.

War and grief were constant throughout the First Cycle.

Destruction and creation were nearly simultaneous. Flames ate man's most glorious cities. Chaos threatened always to engulf order. How could men have endured such conditions for thousands of years?

Towards the close of the First Cycle much of the primitivism was out-grown. At last sources of power were accessible to man; there was the be-ginning of true transportation; communications over distances became possible; many inventions transformed the world in a short time. Methods of making war kept pace with the technological growth in other directions; but total catastrophe was averted, although several times it appeared to have arrived. It was during the final phase of the cycle that the Lost Continents were colonised, also Stralya, and that first contact was made with the ad-joining planets of our solar system.

The transition from First Cycle to Second is arbitarily fixed at the point when man first encountered intelligent beings from distant worlds. This, the Rememberers now believe, took place less than fifty generations after the First Cycle folk had mastered electronic and nuclear energy. Thus we may rightly say that the early people of Earth stumbled headlong from savagery to galactic contact – or, perhaps, that they crossed that gap in a few quick strides.

This too is cause for pride. For if the First Cycle was great despite its hand-icaps, the Second Cycle knew of no handicaps and achieved miracles.

In this epoch mankind spread out to the stars, and the stars came to mankind. Earth was a market for goods of all worlds. Wonders were com-monplace. One might hope to live for hundreds of years; eyes, hearts, lungs, kidneys were replaced as easily as shoes; the air was pure, no man went hungry, war was forgotten. Machines of every sort served man. But the machines were not enough, and so the Second Cycle folk bred men who were machines, or machines who were men: creatures that were genetically human, but were born artificially, and were treated with drugs that pre-vented the permanent storing of memories. These creatures, analogous to our neuters, were capable of performing an efficient day's work, but were unable to build up that permanent body of experiences, memories, expec-tations, and abilities that is the mark of a human soul. Millions of such not-quite humans handled the duller tasks of the day, freeing others for lives of glistening fulfilment. After the creation of the subhumans came the creation of the superanimals who, through biochemical manipulation of the brain, were able to carry out tasks once beyond the capacity of their species: dogs, cats, mice, and cattle were enrolled in the labour force, while certain high primates received functions formerly reserved for humans. Through this exploitation of the environment to the fullest, man created a paradise on Earth.

The spirit of man soared to the loftiest peak it had known. Poets, scholars, and scientists made splendid contributions. Shining cities sprawled across the land. The population was enormous, and even so, there was ample room for all, with no shortage of resources. One could indulge one's whims to any extent; there was much experimentation with genetic surgery and with mutagenetic and teratogenetic drugs, so that the human species adopted many new forms. There was, however, nothing yet like the variant forms of our cycle.

Across the sky in stately procession moved space stations serving every imaginable need. It was at this time that the two new moons were built, although the Rememberers have not yet determined whether their purpose was functional or esthetic. The auroras that now appear each night in the sky may have been installed at this time, although some factions of Rememberers argue that the presence of temperate-zone auroras began with the geophysical upheavals that heralded the close of the cycle.

It was, at any rate, the finest of times to be alive.

'See earth and die,' was the watchword of the outworlders. No one making the galactic grand tour dared pass up this planet of miracles. We welcomed the strangers, accepted their compliments and their money, made them comfortable in the ways they preferred, and proudly displayed our greatnesses.

The Prince of Roum can testify that it is the fate of the mighty eventually to be humbled, and also that the higher one reaches for splendour, the more catastrophic one's downfall is apt to be. After some thousands of years of glories beyond my capacity to comprehend, the fortunate ones of the Second Cycle over reached themselves and committed two misdeeds, one born of foolish arrogance, the other born of excessive confidence. Earth is paying yet for those overreachings.

The effects of the first were slow to be felt. It was a function of Earth's attitude toward the other species of the galaxy, which had shifted during the Second Cycle from awe to matter-of-fact acceptance to contempt. At the beginning of the cycle, brash and naive Earth had erupted into a galaxy already peopled by advanced races that long had been in contact with one another. This could well have produced a soul-crushing trauma, but instead it generated an aggressive urge to excel and surpass. And so it happened that

Earthmen quickly came to look upon most of the galactics as equals, and then, as progress continued on Earth, as inferiors. This bred the easy habit of contempt for the backward.

Thus it was proposed to establish 'study compounds' on Earth for specimens of inferior races. These compounds would reproduce the natural habitat of the races and would be accessible to scholars wishing to observe the life-processes of these races. However, the expense of collecting and maintaining the specimens was such that it quickly became necessary to open the compounds to the public at large, for purposes of amusement. These supposedly scientific compounds were, in fact, zoos for other intelligent species.

At the outset only the truly alien beings were collected, those so remote from human biological or psychological norms that there was little danger of regarding them as 'people.' A many-limbed being that dwells in a tank of methane under high pressure does not strike a sympathetic response from those likely to object to the captivity of intelligent creatures. If that methane-dweller happens to have a complex civilization of a sort uniquely fitted to its environment, it can be argued that it is all the more important to duplicate that environment on Earth so that one can study so strange a civilization. Therefore the early compounds contained only the bizarre. The collectors were limited, also, to taking creatures who had not attained the stage of galactic travel themselves. It would not have been good form to kidnap life-forms whose relatives were among the interstellar tourists on whom our world's economy had come so heavily to depend.

The success of the first compounds led to the demand for the formation of others. Less critical standards were imposed; not merely the utterly alien and grotesque were collected, but samplings of any sort of galactic life not in a position to register diplomatic protests. And, as the audacity of our ancestors increased, so did the restrictions on collection loosen, until there were samplings from a thousand worlds on Earth, including some whose civilizations were older and more intricate than our own.

The archives of the Rememberers show that the expansion of our compounds stirred some agitation in many parts of the universe. We were denounced as marauders, kidnappers, and pirates; committees were formed to criticize our wanton disregard for the rights of sentient beings; Earthmen travelling to other planets were occasionally beset by mobs of hostile life-forms demanding that we free the prisoners of the compounds at once. However, these protesters were only a minority – most galactics kept an uncomfortable silence about our compounds. They regretted the barbarity of them, and nevertheless made a point of touring them when they visited Earth. Where else, after all, could one see hundreds of life-forms, culled from every part of the universe, in a few days? Our compounds were a major attraction, one of the wonders of the cosmos. By silent conspiracy our neighbors in the galaxy winked at the amorality of the basic concept in order to share the pleasure of inspecting the prisoners.

There is in the archives of the Rememberers a memory-tank entry of a visit to a compound area. It is one of the oldest visual records possessed by the guild, and I obtained a look at it only with great difficulty and upon the direct intercession of the Rememberer Olmayne. Despite the use of a double filter in the cap, one sees the scene only blurredly; but yet it is clear enough. Behind a curved shield of a transparent material are fifty or more beings of an unnamed world. Their bodies are pyramidial, with dark blue surfaces and pink visual areas at each vertex; they walk upon short, thick legs; they have one pair of grasping limbs on each face. Though it is risky to attempt to interpret the inner feelings of extraterrestrial beings, one can clearly sense a mood of utter despair in these creatures. Through the murky green gases of their environment they move slowly, numbly, without animation. Several have joined tips in what must be communication. One appears newly dead. Two are bowed to the ground like tumbled toys, but their limbs move in what perhaps is prayer. It is a dismal scene. Later, I discovered other such records in neglected corners of the building. They taught me much.

For more than a thousand Second Cycle years the growth of these compounds continued unchecked, until it came to seem logical and natural to all except the victims that Earth should practice these cruelties in the name of science. Then, upon a distant world not previously visited by Earthmen, there were discovered certain beings of a primitive kind, comparable perhaps to Earthmen in early First Cycle days. These beings were roughly humanoid in form, undeniably intelligent, and fiercely savage. At the loss of several Earthborn lives, a collecting team acquired a breeding colony of these people and transported them to Earth to be placed in a compound.

This was the first of the Second Cycle's two fatal errors.

At the time of the kidnapping, the beings of this other world – which is never named in the records, but known only by the code designation H362 – were in no position to protest or to take punitive steps. But shortly they were visited by emissaries from certain other worlds aligned politically against Earth. Under the guidance of these emissaries, the beings of H362 requested the return of their people. Earth refused, citing the long precedent of interstellar condonement of the compounds. Lengthy diplomatic representations followed, in the course of which Earth simply reaffirmed its right to have acted in such a fashion.

The people of H362 responded with threats. 'One day,' they said, 'we will cause you to regret this. We will invade and conquer your planet, set free all the inhabitants of the compounds, and turn Earth itself into a gigantic compound for its own people.'

Under the circumstances this appeared quite amusing.

Little more was heard of the outraged inhabitants of H362 over the next few millennia. They were progressing rapidly, in their distant part of the universe, but since by all calculations it would take them a cosmic period to pose any menace to Earth, they were ignored. How could one fear spear-wielding savages?

Earth addressed itself to a new challenge: full control of the planetary climate.

Weather modification had been practiced on a small scale since late First Cycle. Clouds holding potential rain could be induced to release it; fogs could be dispelled; hail could be made less destructive. Certain steps were taken toward reducing the polar ice packs and toward making deserts more fruitful. However, these measurers were strictly local and, with few exceptions, had no lasting effects on environment.

The Second Cycle endeavor involved the erection of enormous columns at more than one hundred locations around the globe. We do not know the heights of these columns, since none has survived intact and the specifications are lost, but it is thought that they equaled or exceeded the highest buildings previously constructed, and perhaps attained altitudes of two miles or more. Within these columns was equipment which was designed, among other things, to effect displacements of the poles of Earth's magnetic field.

As we understand the aim of the weather machines, it was to modify the planet's geography according to a carefully conceived plan arising from the division of what we call Earth Ocean into a number of large bodies. Although interconnected, these suboceans were considered to have individual existences since along most of their boundary region they were cut off from the rest of Earth Ocean by land masses. In the northern Lost Continent (known as Usa-amrik) in the west and the proximity of Usa-amrik to Eyrop in the east left only narrow straits through which the polar waters could mingle with those of the warmer oceans flanking the Lost Continents.

Manipulation of magnetic forces produced a libration of Earth on its orbit, calculated to break up the north polar ice pack and permit the cold water trapped by this pack to come in contact with warmer water from elsewhere. By removing the northern ice pack and thus exposing the northern ocean to evaporation, precipitation would be greatly increased there. To prevent this precipitation from falling in the north as snow, additional manipulations were to be induced to change the pattern of the prevailing westerly winds which carried precipitation over temperate areas. A natural conduit was to be established that would bring the precipitation of the polar region to areas in lower latitudes lacking in proper moisture.

There was much more to the plan than this. Our knowledge of the details is hazy. We are aware of schemes to shift ocean currents by causing land subsidence or emergence, of proposals to deflect solar heat from the tropics to the poles, and of other rearrangements. The details are unimportant. What is significant to us are the consequences of this grandiose plan.

After a period of preparation lasting centuries and after absorbing more effort and wealth than any other project in human history, the weather machines were put into operation.

The result was devastation.

The disastrous experiment in planetary alteration resulted in a shifting of the geographical poles, a lengthy period of glacial conditions throughout most of the northern hemisphere, the unexpected submergence of Usa-amrik and Sud-amrik, its neighbor, the creation of Land Bridge joining Afreek and Eyrop, and the near destruction of human civilization. These upheavals did not take place with great speed. Evidently the project went smoothly for the first several centuries; the polar ice thawed, and the corresponding rise in sea levels was dealt with by constructing fusion evaporators – small suns, in effect – at selected oceanic points. Only slowly did it become clear that the weather machines were bringing about architectonic changes in the crust of Earth. These, unlike the climatic changes, proved irreversible.

It was a time of furious storms followed by unending droughts; of the loss of hundreds of millions of lives; of the disruption of all communications; of panicky mass migrations out of the doomed continents. Chaos triumphed. The splendid civilization of the Second Cycle was shattered. The compounds of alien life were destroyed.

For the sake of saving what remained of its population, several of the most powerful galactic races took command of our planet. They established energy pylons to stabilize Earth's axial wobble; they dismantled those weather machines that had not been destroyed by the planetary convulsions; they fed the hungry, clothed the naked, and offered reconstruction loans. For us it was a Time of Sweeping, when all the structures and conventions of society were expunged. No longer masters in our own world, we accepted the charity of strangers and crept pitifully about.

Yet, because we were still the same race we had been, we recovered to some extent. We had squandered our planet's capital and so could never again be anything but bankrupts and paupers, but in a humbler way we entered into our Third Cycle. Certain scientific techniques of earlier days still remained to us. Others were devised, working generally on different principles. Our guilds were formed to give order to society: Dominators, Master, Merchants, and the rest. The Rememberers strove to salvage what could be pulled from the wreck of the past.

Our debts to our rescuers were enormous. As bankrupts, we had no way of repaying those debts; we hoped instead for a quitclaim, a statement of absolution. Negotiations to that effect were already under way when an unexpected intervention occurred. The inhabitants of H362 approached the committee of Earth's receivers and offered to reimburse them for their expenses — in return for an assignment of all rights and claims in Earth to H362.

It was done.

H362 now regarded itself the owner by treaty of our world. It served notice to the universe at large that it reserved the right to take possession at any future date. As well it might, since at that time H362 was still incapable of interstellar travel. Thereafter, though, H362 was deemed legal possessor of the assets of Earth, as purchaser in bankruptcy.

No one failed to realize that this was H362's way of fulfilling its threat to 'turn Earth itself into a gigantic compound,' as revenge for the injury inflicted by our collecting team long before.

On Earth, Third Cycle society constituted itself along the lines it now holds, with its rigid stratification of guilds. The threat of H362 was taken seriously, for ours was a chastened world that sneered at no menace, however slight; and a guild of Watchers was devised to scan the skies for attackers. Defenders and all the rest followed. In some small ways we demonstrated our old flair for imagination, particularly in the Years of Magic, when a fanciful impulse created the self-perpetuating mutant guild of Fliers, a parallel guild of Swimmers, of whom little is heard nowadays, and several other varieties, including a troublesome and unpredictable guild of Changelings whose genetic characteristics were highly erratic.

The Watchers watched. The Dominators ruled. The Fliers soared. Life went on, year after year, in Eyrop and in Ais, in Stralya, in Afreek, in the scattered islands that were the only remnants of the Lost Continents of Usa-amrik and Sud-amrik. The vow of H362 receded into mythology, but yet we remained vigilant. And far across the cosmos our enemies gathered strength, attaining some measure of the power that had been ours in our Second Cycle. They never forgot the day when their kinsmen had been held captive in our compounds.

In a night of terror they came to us. Now they are our masters, and their vow is fulfilled, their claim asserted.

All this, and much more, I learned as I burrowed in the accumulated knowledge of the guild of Rememberers.

5

Meanwhile the former Prince of Roum was wantonly abusing the hospitality of our co-sponsorer, the Rememberer Elegro. I should have been aware of what was going on, for I knew the Prince and his ways better than any other man in Perris. But I was too busy in the archives, learning of the past. While I explored the details of the Second Cycle's protoplasm files and regeneration nodules, its time-wind blowers and its photonic-flue fixers, Prince Enric was seducing the Rememberer Olmayne.

Like most seductions, I imagine that this was no great contest of wills. Olmayne was a woman of sensuality, whose attitude toward her husband was affectionate but patronizing. She regarded Elegro openly as ineffectual, a bumbler; and Elegro, whose haughtiness and stern mien did not conceal his underlying weakness of purpose, seemed to merit her disdain. What kind of marriage they had was not my business to observe, but clearly she was the stronger, and just as clearly he could not meet her demands.

Then, too, why had Olmayne agreed to sponsor us into her guild?

Surely not out of any desire for a tattered old Watcher. It must have been the wish to know more of the strange and oddly commanding blind Pilgrim who was that Watcher's companion. From the very first, then, Olmayne must have been drawn to Prince Enric; and he, naturally, would need little encouragement to accept the gift she offered.

Possibly they were lovers almost from the moment of our arrival in the Hall of Rememberers.

I went my way, and Elegro went his, and Olmayne and Prince Enric went theirs, and summer gave way to autumn and autumn to winter. I excavated the records with passionate impatience. Never before had I known such involvement, such intensity of curiosity. Without benefit of a visit to Jorslem I felt renewed. I saw the Prince infrequently, and our meetings were generally silent; it was not my place to question him about his doings, and he felt no wish to volunteer information to me.

Occasionally I thought of my former life, and of my travels from place to place, and of the Flier Avluela who was now, I supposed, the consort of one of our conquerors. How did the false Changeling Gormon style himself, now that he had emerged from his disguise and owned himself to be one of those from H362? Earthking Nine? Oceanlord Five? Overman Three? Wherever he was, he must feel satisfaction, I thought, at the total success of the conquest of Earth.

Toward winter's end I learned of the affair between the Rememberer

Olmayne and Prince Enric of Roum. I picked up whispered gossip in the apprentice quarters first; then I noticed the smiles on the faces of other Rememberers when Elegro and Olmayne were about; lastly, I observed the behavior of the Prince and Olmayne toward one another. It was obvious. Those touchings of hand to hand, those sly exchanges of catchwords and private phrases – what else could they mean?'

Among the Rememberers the marriage vow is regarded solemnly. As with Fliers, mating is for life, and one is not supposed to betray one's partner as Olmayne was doing. When one is married to a fellow Rememberer – a custom in the guild, but not universal – the union is all the more sacred.

What revenge would Elegro take when in time he learned the truth?

It happened that I was present when the situation at last crystallized into conflict. It was a night in earliest spring. I had worked long and hard in the deepest pits of the memory tanks, prying forth data that no one had bothered with since it had first been stored; and, with my head aswim with images of chaos, I walked through the glow of the Perris night, seeking fresh air. I strolled along the Senn and was accosted by an agent for a Somnambulist, who offered to sell me insight into the world of dreams. I came upon a lone Pilgrim at his devotions before a temple of flesh. I watched a pair of young Fliers in passage overhead, and shed a self-pitying tear or two. I was halted by a starborn tourist in breathing mask and jeweled tunic; he put his cratered red face close to mine and vented hallucinations in my nostrils. At length I returned to the Hall of Rememberers and went to the suite of my sponsors to pay my respects before retiring.

Olmayne and Elegro were there. So, too, was Prince Enric. Olmayne admitted me with a quick gesture of one fingertip, but took no further notice of me, nor did the others. Elegro was tensely pacing the floor, stomping about so vehemently that the delicate life-forms of the carpet folded and unfolded their petals in wild agitation.. 'A Pilgrim!' Elegro cried. 'If it had been some trash of a Vendor, it would only be humiliating. But a Pilgrim? That makes it monstrous!'

Prince Enric stood with arms folded, body motionless. It was impossible to detect the expression beneath his mask of Pilgrimage, but he appeared wholly calm.

Elegro said, 'Will you deny that you have been tampering with the sanctity of my pairing?'

'I deny nothing. I assert nothing.'

'And you?' Elegro demanded, whirling on his lady. 'Speak truth, Olmayne! For once, speak truth! What of the stories they tell of you and this Pilgrim?'

'I have heard no stories,' said Olmayne sweetly.

'That he shares your bed! That you taste potions together! That you travel to ecstasy together!'

Olmayne's smile did not waver. Her broad face was tranquil. To me she looked more beautiful than ever.

Elegro tugged in anguish at the strands of his shawl. His dour, bearded face darkened in wrath and exasperation. His hand slipped within his tunic and emerged with the tiny glossy bead of a vision capsule, which he thrust forth toward the guilty pair on the palm of his hand.

'Why should I waste breath?' he asked. 'Everything is here. The full record in the photonic flux. You have been under surveillance. Did either of you think anything could be hidden here, of all places? You, Olmayne, a Rememberer, how could you think so?'

Olmayne examined the capsule from a distance, as though it were a primed implosion bomb. With distaste she said, 'How like you to spy on us, Elegro. Did it give you great pleasure to watch us in our joy?'

'Beast!' he cried.

Pocketing the capsule, he advanced toward the motionless Prince. Elegro's face was now contorted with righteous wrath. Standing at arm's length from the Prince he declared icily, 'You will be punished to the fullest for this impiety. You will be stripped of your Pilgrim's robes and delivered up to the fate reserved for monsters. The Will shall consume your soul!'

Prince Enric replied, 'Curb your tongue.'

'Curb my tongue? Who are you to speak that way? A Pilgrim who lusts for the wife of his host – who doubly violates holiness – who drips lies and sanctimony at the same moment?' Elegro frothed. His iciness was gone. Now he ranted in nearly incoherent frenzy, displaying his interior weakness by his lack of self-control. We three stood frozen, astounded by his torrent of words, and at last the stasis broke when the Rememberer, carried away by the tide of his own indignation, seized the Prince by the shoulders and began violently to shake him.

'Filth,' Enric bellowed, 'you may not put your hands to me!'

With a double thrust of his fists against Elegro's chest he hurled the Rememberer reeling backward across the room. Elegro crashed into a suspension cradle and sent a flank of watery artifacts tumbling; three flasks of scintillating fluids shivered and spilled their contents; the carpet set up a shrill cry of pained protest. Gasping, stunned, Elegro pressed a hand to his breast and looked to us for assistance.

'Physical assault—' Elegro wheezed. 'A shameful crime!'

'The first assault was your doing,' Olmayne reminded her husband.

Pointing trembling fingers, Elegro muttered, 'For this there can be no forgiveness, Pilgrim!'

'Call me Pilgrim no longer,' Enric said. His hands went to the grillwork of his mask. Olmayne cried out, trying to prevent him; but in his anger the Prince knew no check. He hurled the mask to the floor and stood with his harsh face terribly exposed, the cruel features hawk-lean, the gray mechanical spheres in his eyesockets masking the depths of his fury. 'I am the Prince of Roum,' he announced in a voice of thunder. 'Down and abase! Down and abase! Quick, Rememberer, the three prostrations and five abasements!'

Elegro appeared to crumble. He peered in disbelief; then he sagged, and in a kind of reflex of amazement he performed a ritual obeisance before his wife's seducer. It was the first time since the fall of Roum that the Prince had asserted his former status, and the pleasure of it was so evident on his ravaged face that even the blank eyeballs appeared to glow in regal pride.

'Out,' the Prince ordered. 'Leave us.'

Elegro fled.

I remained, astounded, staggered. The Prince nodded courteously to me. 'Would you pardon us, old friend, and grant us some moments of privacy?'

6

A weak man can be put to rout by a surprise attack, but afterward he pauses, reconsiders, and hatches schemes. So was it with the Rememberer Elegro. Driven from his own suite by the unmasking of the Prince of Roum, he grew calm and crafty once he was out of that terrifying presence. Later that same night, as I settled into my sleeping cradle and debated aiding slumber with a drug, Elegro summoned me to his research cell on a lower level of the building.

There he sat amid the paraphernalia of his guild: reels and spools, data-flakes, capsules, caps, a quartet of series-linked skulls, a row of output screens, a small ornamental helix, all the symbology of the gatherers of information. In his hands he grasped a tension-draining crystal from one of the Cloud-worlds; its milky interior was rapidly tingeing with sepia as it pulled anxieties from his spirit. He pretended a look of stern authority, as if forgetting that I had seen him exposed in his spinelessness.

He said, 'Were you aware of this man's identity when you came with him to Perris?'

'Yes.'

'You said nothing about it.'

'I was never asked.'

'Do you know what a risk you have exposed all of us to, by causing us unknowingly to harbor a Dominator?'

'We are Earthmen,' I said. 'Do we not still acknowledge the authority of the Dominators?'

'Not since the conquest. By decree of the invaders all former governments are dissolved and their leaders subject to arrest.'

'But surely we should resist such an order!'

The Rememberer Elegro regarded me quizzically. 'Is it a Rememberer's function to meddle in politics? Tomis, we obey the government in power, whichever it may be and however it may have taken control. We conduct no resistance activities here.'

'I see.'

'Therefore we must rid ourselves at once of this dangerous fugitive. Tomis, I instruct you to go at once to occupation headquarters and inform Manrule Seven that we have captured the Prince of Roum and hold him here for pickup.'

'*I* should go?' I blurted. 'Why send an old man as a messenger in the night? An ordinary thinking-cap transmission would be enough!'

'Too risky. Strangers may intercept cap communications. It would not go well for our guild if this were spread about. This has to be a personal communication.'

'But to choose an unimportant apprentice to carry it – it seems strange.'

'There are only two of us who know,' said Elegro. 'I will not go. Therefore you must.'

'With no introduction to Manrule Seven I will never be admitted.'

'Inform his aides that you have information leading to the apprehension of the Prince of Roum. You'll be heard.'

'Am I to mention your name?'

'If necessary. You may say that the Prince is being held prisoner in my quarters with the cooperation of my wife.'

I nearly laughed at that. But I held a straight face before this cowardly Rememberer, who did not even dare to go himself and denounce the man who had cuckolded him.

'Ultimately,' I said, 'the Prince will become aware of what we have done. Is it right of you to ask me to betray a man who was my companion for so many months?'

'It is not a matter of betrayal. It is a matter of obligations to the government.'

'I feel no obligation to this government. My loyalties are to the guild of Dominators. Which is why I gave assistance to the Prince of Roum in his moment of peril.'

'For that,' said Elegro, 'your own life could be forfeit to our conquerors. Your only expiation is to admit your error and cooperate in bringing about his arrest. Go. Now.'

In a long and tolerant life I have never despised anyone so vehemently as I did the Rememberer Elegro at that moment.

Yet I saw that I was faced with few choices, none of them palatable. Elegro wished his undoer punished, but lacked the courage to report him himself; therefore I must give over to the conquering authorities one whom I had sheltered and assisted, and for whom I felt a responsibility. If I refused, Elegro would perhaps hand me to the invaders for punishment myself, as an accessory to the Prince's escape from Roum; or he might take vengeance against me within the machinery of the guild of Rememberers. If I obliged Elegro, though, I would have a stain on my conscience forever, and in the event of a restoration of the power of the Dominators I would have much to answer for.

As I weighed the possibilities, I triply cursed the Rememberer Elegro's faithless wife and her invertebrate husband.

I hesitated a bit. Elegro offered more persuasion, threatening to arraign me before the guild on such charges as unlawfully gaining access to secret files and improperly introducing into guild precincts a proscribed fugitive. He threatened to cut me off forever from the information pool. He spoke vaguely of vengeance.

In the end I told him I would go to the invaders' headquarters and do his bidding. I had by then conceived a betrayal that would – I hoped – cancel the betrayal Elegro was enforcing on me.

Dawn was near when I left the building. The air was mild and sweet; a low mist hung over the streets of Perris, giving them a gentle shimmer. No moons were in sight In the deserted streets I felt uneasy, although I told myself that no one would care to do harm to an aged Rememberer; but I was armed only with a small blade, and I feared bandits.

My route lay on one of the pedestrian ramps. I panted a bit at the steep incline, but when I had attained the proper level I was more secure, since here there were patrol nodes at frequent intervals, and here, too, were some other late-night strollers. I passed a spectral figure garbed in white satin through which alien features peered: a revenant, a ghostly inhabitant of a planet of the Bull, where reincarnation is the custom and no man goes about installed in his own original body. I passed three female beings of a Swan planet who giggled at me and asked if I had seen males of their species, since the time of conjugation was upon them. I passed a pair of Changelings who eyed me speculatively, decided I had nothing on me worth robbing, and moved on, their piebald dewlaps jiggling and their radiant skins flashing like beacons.

At last I came to the squat octagonal building occupied by the Procurator of Perris.

It was indifferently guarded. The invaders appeared confident that we were incapable of mounting a counter-assault against them, and quite likely they were right; a planet which can be conquered between darkness and dawn is not going to launch a plausible resistance afterwards. Around the building rose the pale glow of a protective scanner. There was a tinge of ozone in the air. In the wide plaza across the way, Merchants were setting up their market for the morning; I saw barrels of spices being unloaded by brawny Servitors, and dark sausages carried by files of neuters. I stepped through the scanner beam and an invader emerged to challenge me.

I explained that I carried urgent news for Manrule Seven, and in short order, with amazingly little consultation of intermediaries, I was ushered into the Procurator's presence.

The invader had furnished his office simply but in good style. It was decked entirely with Earthmade objects: a drapery from Afreek weave, two alabaster pots from ancient Agupt, a marble statuette that might have been early Roumish, and a dark Talyan vase in which a few wilting deathflowers languished. When I entered, he seemed preoccupied with several message-cubes; as I had heard, the invaders did most of their work in the dark hours, and it did not surprise me to find him so busy now. After a moment he looked up and said, 'What is it, old man? What's this about a fugitive Dominator?'

'The Prince of Roum,' I said. 'I know of his location.'

At once his cold eyes sparkled with interest. He ran his many-fingered hands across his desk, on which were mounted the emblems of several of our guilds, Transporters and Rememberers and Defenders and Clowns, among others. 'Go on,' he said.

'The Prince is in this city. He is in a specific place and has no way of escaping from it.'

'And you are here to inform me of his location?'

'No,' I said. 'I'm here to buy his liberty.'

Manrule Seven seemed perplexed. 'There are times when you humans baffle me. You say you've captured this runaway Dominator, and I assume that you want to sell him to us, but you say you want to *buy* him. Why bother coming to us? Is this a joke?'

'Will you permit an explanation?'

He brooded into the mirrored top of his desk while I told him in a compressed way of my journey from Roum with the blinded Prince, of our arrival at the Hall of Rememberers, of Prince Enric's seduction of Olmayne, and of Elegro's petty, fuming desire for vengeance. I made it clear that I had come to the invaders only under duress and that it was not my intention to betray the Prince into their hands. Then I said, 'I realize that all Dominators are forfeit to you. Yet this one has already paid a high price for his freedom. I ask you to notify the Rememberers that the Prince of Roum is under amnesty, and to permit him to continue on as a Pilgrim to Jorslem. In that way Elegro will lose power over him.'

'What is it that you offer us,' asked Manrule Seven, 'in return for this amnesty for your Prince?'

'I have done research in the memory tanks of the Rememberers.'

'And?'

'I have found that for which your people have been seeking.'

Manrule Seven studied me with care. 'How would you have any idea of what we seek?'

'There is in the deepest part of the Hall of Rememberers,' I said quietly, 'an image recording of the compound in which your kidnapped ancestors lived while they were prisoners on Earth. It shows their sufferings in poignant detail. It is a superb justification for the conquest of Earth by H362.'

'Impossible! There's no such document!'

From the intensity of the invader's reaction, I knew that I had stung him in the vulnerable place.

He went on, 'We've searched your files thoroughly. There's only one recording of compound life, and it doesn't show our people. It shows a non-humanoid pyramid-shaped race, probably from one of the Anchor worlds.'

'I have seen that one,' I told him. 'There are others. I spent many hours searching for them, out of hunger to know of our past injustices.'

'The indexes—'

'—are sometimes incomplete. I found this recording only by accident. The Rememberers themselves have no idea it's there. I'll lead you to it – if you agree to leave the Prince of Roum unmolested.'

The Procurator was silent a moment. At length he said, 'You puzzle me. I am unable to make out if you are a scoundrel or a man of the highest virtue.'

'I know where true loyalty lies.'

'To betray the secrets of your guild, though—'

'I am no Rememberer, only an apprentice, formerly a Watcher. I would not have you harm the Prince at the wish of a cuckolded fool. The Prince is in his hands; only you can obtain his release now. And so I must offer you this document.'

'Which the Rememberers have carefully deleted from their indexes, so it will not fall into our hands.'

'Which the Rememberers have carelessly misplaced and forgotten.'

'I doubt it,' said Manrule Seven. 'They are not careless folk. They hid that recording; and by giving it to us, are you not betraying all your world? Making yourself a collaborator with the hated enemy?'

I shrugged. 'I am interested in having the Prince of Roum made free. Other means and ends are of no concern to me. The location of the document is yours in exchange for the grant of amnesty.'

The invader displayed what might have been his equivalent of a smile. 'It is not in our best interests to allow members of the former guild of

Dominators to remain at large. Your position is precarious, do you see? I could extract the document's location from you by force – and still have the Prince as well.'

'So you could,' I agreed. 'I take that risk. I assume a certain basic honor among people who came to avenge an ancient crime. I am in your power, and the whereabouts of file document is in my mind, yours for the picking.'

Now he laughed in an unmistakable show of good humor.

'Wait a moment,' he said. He spoke a few words of his own language into an amber communication device, and shortly a second member of his species entered the office, I recognized him instantly, although he was shorn of some of the flamboyant disguise he had worn when he traveled with me as Gormon, the supposed Changeling. He offered the ambivalent smile of his kind and said, 'I greet you, Watcher.'

'And I greet you, Gormon.'

'My name now is Victorious Thirteen.'

'I now am called Tomis of the Rememberers,' I said.

Manrule Seven remarked, 'When did you two become such fast friends?'

'In the time of the conquest,' said Victorious Thirteen. 'While performing my duties as an advance scout, I encountered this man in Talya and journeyed with him to Roum. But we were companions, in truth, and not friends.'

I trembled. 'Where is the Flier Avluela?'

'In Pars, I believe,' he said offhandedly. 'She spoke of returning to Hind, to the place of her people.'

'You loved her only a short while, then?'

'We were more companions than lovers,' said the invader. 'It was a passing thing for us.'

'For you, maybe,' I said.

'For us.'

'And for this passing thing you stole a man's eyes?'

He who had been Gormon shrugged. 'I did that to teach a proud creature a lesson in pride.'

'You said at the time that your motive was jealousy,' I reminded him. 'You claimed to act out of love.'

Victorious Thirteen appeared to lose interest in me. To Manrule Seven he said, 'Why is this man here? Why have you summoned me?'

'The Prince of Roum is in Perris,' said Manrule Seven.

Victorious Thirteen registered sudden surprise.

Manrule Seven went on, 'He is a Prisoner of the Rememberers. This man offers a strange bargain. You know the Prince better than any of us; I ask your advice.'

The Procurator sketched the outlines of the situation. He who had been Gormon listened thoughtfully, saying nothing. At the end, Manrule Seven said, 'The problem is this: shall we give amnesty to a proscribed Dominator?'

'He is blind,' said Victorious Thirteen. 'His power is gone. His followers are scattered. His spirit may be unbroken, but he presents no danger to us. I say accept the bargain.'

'There are administrative risks in exempting a Dominator from arrest,' Manrule Seven pointed out. 'Nevertheless, I agree. We undertake the deal.' To me he said, 'Tell us the location of the document we desire.'

'Arrange the liberation of the Prince of Roum first,' I said calmly.

Both invaders displayed amusement. 'Fair enough,' said Manrule Seven. 'But look: how can we be certain that you'll keep your word? Anything might happen to you in the next hour while we're freeing the Prince.'

'A suggestion,' put in Victorious Thirteen. 'This is not so much a matter of mutual mistrust as it is one of timing. Tomis, why not record the document's location on a six hour delay cube? We'll prime the cube so that it will release its information only if within that six hours the Prince of Roum himself, and no one else, commands it to do so. If we haven't found and freed the Prince in that time, the cube will destruct. If we do release the Prince, the cube will give us the information, even if – ah – something should have happened to you in the interval.'

'You cover all contingencies,' I said.

'Are we agreed?' Manrule Seven asked.

'We are agreed,' I said.

They brought me a cube and placed me under a privacy screen while I inscribed on its glossy surface the rack number and sequence equations of the document I had discovered. Moments passed; the cube everted itself and the information vanished into its opaque depths. I offered it to them.

Thus did I betray my Earthborn heritage and perform a service for our conquerors, out of loyalty to a blinded wife-stealing Prince.

7

Dawn had come by this time. I did not accompany the invaders to the Hall of Rememberers; it was no business of mine to oversee the intricate events that must ensue, and I preferred to be elsewhere. A fine drizzle was falling as I turned down the gray streets that bordered the dark Senn. The time-less river, its surface stippled by the drops, swept unwearingly against stone arches of First Cycle antiquity, bridges spanning uncountable millennia, survivors from an era when the only problems of mankind were of his own making. Morning engulfed the city. Through an old and ineradicable reflex I searched for my instruments so that I could do my Watching, and had to remind myself that that was far behind me now. The Watchers were disbanded, the enemy had come, and old Wuellig, now Tomis of the Rememberers, had sold himself to mankind's foes.

In the shadow of a twin-steepled religious house of the ancient Christers I let myself be enticed into the booth of a Somnambulist. This guild is not one with which I have often had dealings; in my way I am wary of charlatans, and charlatans are abundant in our time. The Somnambulist, in a state of trance, claims to see what has been, what is, and what will be. I know something of trances myself, for as a Watcher I entered such a state four times each day; but a Watcher with pride in his craft must necessarily despise the tawdry ethics of those who use second sight for gain, as Somnambulists do.

However, while among the Rememberers I had learned, to my surprise, that Somnambulists frequently were consulted to aid in unearthing some site of ancient times, and that they had served the Rememberers well. Though still skeptical, I was willing to be instructed. And, at the moment, I needed a shelter from the storm that was breaking over the Hall of Rememberers.

A dainty, mincing figure garbed in blade greeted me with a mocking bow as I entered the low-roofed booth.

'I am Samit of the Somnambulists,' he said in a high, whining voice. 'I offer you welcome and good tidings. Behold my companion, the Somnambulist Murta.'

The Somnambulist Murta was a robust woman in lacy robes. Her face was heavy with flesh, deep rings of darkness surrounded her eyes, a trace of mustache lined her upper lip. Somnambulists work their trade in teams, one to do the huckstering, one to perform; most teams were man and wife, as was this. My mind rebelled at the thought of the embrace of the flesh-mountain Murta and the miniature-man Samit, but it was no concern of mine. I took my seat as Samit indicated. On a table nearby I saw some food tablets of several colors; I had interrupted this family's breakfast. Murta, deep in trance, wandered the room with ponderous strides, now and again grazing some article of furniture in a gentle way. Some Somnambulists, it is said, waken only two or three hours of the twenty, simply to take meals and relieve bodily needs; there are some who ostensibly live in continuous trance and are fed and cared for by acolytes.

I scarcely listened as Samit of the Somnambulists delivered his sales-talk in rapid, feverish bursts of ritualized word-clusters. It was pitched to the ignorant; Somnambulists do much of their trade with Servitors and Clowns and other menials. At length, seemingly sensing my impatience, he cut short his extolling of the Somnambulist Murta's abilities and asked me what it was I wished to know.

'Surely the Somnambulist already is aware of that,' I said.

'You wish a general analysis?'

'I want to know of the fate of those about me. I wish particularly for the Somnambulist's concentration to center on events now occurring in the Hall of Rememberers.'

Samit tapped long fingernails against the smooth table and shot a glaring look at the cow like Murta. 'Are you in contact with the truth?' he asked her.

Her reply was a long feathery sigh wrenched from the core of all the quivering meat of her.

'What do you see?' he asked her.

She began to mutter thickly. Somnambulists speak in a language not otherwise used by mankind; it is a harsh thing of edgy sounds, which some claim is descended from an ancient tongue of Agupt. I know nothing of that. To me it sounded incoherent, fragmentary, impossible to hold meaning. Samit listened a while, then nodded in satisfaction and extended his palm to me.

'There is a great deal,' he said.

We discussed the fee, bargained briefly, came to a settlement. 'Go on,' I told him. 'Interpret the truth.'

Cautiously he began, 'There are outworlders involved in this, and also several members of the guild of Rememberers.' I was silent, giving him no encouragement. 'They are drawn together in a difficult quarrel. A man without eyes is at the heart of it'

I sat upright with a jolt.

Samit smiled in cool triumph. 'The man without eyes has fallen from greatness. He is Earth, shall we say, broken by conquerors? Now he is near the end of his time. He seeks to restore his former condition, but he knows it is impossible. He has caused a Rememberer to violate an oath. To their guildhall have come several of the conquerors to – to chastise him? No. No. To free him from captivity. Shall I continue?'

'Quickly!'

'You have received all that you have paid for.'

I scowled. This was extortion; but yet the Somnambulist had clearly seen the truth. I had learned nothing here that I did not already know, but that was sufficient to tell me I might learn more. I added to my fee.

Samit closed his fist on my coins and conferred once more with Murta. She spoke at length, in some agitation, whirling several times, colliding violently with a musty divan.

Samit said, 'The man without eyes has come between a man and his wife. The outraged husband seeks punishment; the outworlders will thwart that. The outworlders seek hidden truths; they will find them, with a traitor's help. The man without eyes seeks freedom and power; he will find peace. The stained wife seeks amusement; she will find hardship.'

'And I?' I said into an obstinate and expensive silence. 'You say nothing of me!'

'You will leave Perris soon, in the same manner as you entered it. You will not leave alone. You will not leave in your present guild.'

'What will be my destination?'

'You know that as well as we do, so why waste your money to tell you?'

He fell silent again.

'Tell me what will befall me as I journey to Jorslem,' I said.

'You could not afford such information. Futures become costly. I advise you to settle for what you now know.'

'I have some questions about what has already been said.'

'We do not clarify at any price.'

He grinned. I felt the force of his contempt. The Somnambulist Murta, still bumbling about the room, groaned and belched. The powers with whom she was in contact appeared to impart new information to her; she whimpered, shivered, made a blurred chuckling sound. Samit spoke to her in their language. She replied at length. He peered at me. 'At no cost,' he said, 'a final information. Your life is in no danger, but your spirit is. It would be well if you made your peace with the Will as quickly as possible. Recover your moral orientation. Remember your true loyalties. Atone for well-intentioned sins. I can say no more.'

Indeed Murta stirred and seemed to wake. Great slabs of flesh jiggled in her face and body as the convulsion of leaving the trance came over her. Her eyes opened, but I saw only whites, a terrible sight. Her thick lips twitched to reveal crumbling teeth. Samit beckoned me out with quick brushing gestures of his tiny hands. I fled into a dark, rain-drenched morning.

Hurriedly I returned to the Hall of Rememberers, arriving there out of breath, with a red spike of pain behind my breastbone. I paused a while outside the superb building to recover my strength. Floaters passed overhead, leaving the guildhall from an upper level. My courage nearly failed me. But in the end I entered the hall and ascended to the level of the suite of Elegro and Olmayne.

A knot of agitated Rememberers filled the hall. A buzz of whispered comment drifted toward me. I pressed forward; and a man whom I recognized as high in the councils of the guild held up a hand and said, 'What business do you have here, apprentice?'

'I am Tomis, who was sponsored by the Rememberer Olmayne. My chamber is close to here.'

'Tomis!' a voice cried.

I was seized and thrust ahead into the familiar suite, now a scene of devastation.

A dozen Rememberers stood about, fingering their shawls in distress. I recognized among them the taut and elegant figure of Chancellor Kenishal, his gray eyes now dull with despair. Beneath a coverlet to the left of the entrance lay a crumpled figure in the robes of a Pilgrim: the Prince of Roum, dead in his own pooled blood. His gleaming mask, now stained, lay beside him. At the opposite side of the room, slumped against an ornate credenza containing Second Cycle artifacts of great beauty, was the Rememberer Elegro, seemingly asleep, looking furious and surprised both at once. His throat was transfixed by a single slender dart. To the rear, with burly Rememberers flanking her, stood the Rememberer Olmayne looking wild and disheveled. Her scarlet robe was torn in front and revealed high white breasts; her black hair tumbled in disorder; her satiny skin glistened with perpiration. She appeared lost in a dream far from these present surroundings.

'What has happened here?' I asked.

'Murder twice over,' said Chancellor Kenishal in a broken voice. He advanced toward me: a tall, haggard man, white-haired, an uncontrollable tic working in the lid of one eye. 'When did you last see these people alive, apprentice?'

'In the night.'

'How did you come to be here?'

'A visit, no more.'

'Was there a disturbance?'

'A quarrel between the Rememberer Elegro and the Pilgrim, yes,' I admitted.

'Over what?' asked the Chancellor thinly.

I looked uneasily at Olmayne, but she saw nothing and heard less.

'Over her,' I said.

I heard snickerings from the other Rememberers. They nudged each other, nodded, even smiled; I had confirmed the scandal. The Chancellor grew more solemn.

He indicated the body of the Prince.

'This was your companion when you entered Perris,' he said. 'Did you know of his true identity?'

I moistened my lips. 'I had suspicions.'

'That he was—'

'The fugitive Prince of Roum,' I said. I did not dare attempt subterfuges now; my status was precarious.

More nods, more nudges. Chancellor Kenishal said, 'This man was subject to arrest. It was not your place to conceal your knowledge of his identity.'

I remained mute.

The Chancellor went on, 'You have been absent from this hall for some hours. Tell us of your activities after leaving the suite of Elegro and Olmayne.'

'I called upon the Procurator Manrule Seven,' I said.

Sensation.

'For what purpose?'

'To inform the Procurator,' I said, 'that the Prince of Roum had been apprehended and was now in the suite of a Rememberer. I did this at the instruction of the Rememberer Elegro. After delivering my information I walked the streets several hours for no particular end, and returned here to find – to find—'

'To find everything in chaos,' said Chancellor Kenishal. 'The Procurator was here at dawn. He visited this suite; both Elegro and the Prince must still have been alive at that time. Then he went into our archives and removed – and removed – material of the highest sensitivity – the highest sensitivity – removed – material not believed to be accessible to – the highest sensitivity—' The Chancellor faltered. Like some intricate machine smitten with instant rust, he slowed his motions, emitted rasping sounds, appeared to be on the verge of systematic breakdown. Several high Rememberers rushed to his aid; one thrust a drug against his arm. In moments the Chancellor appeared to recover. 'These murders occurred after the Procurator departed from the building,' he said. 'The Rememberer Olmayne has been unable to give us information concerning them. Perhaps you, apprentice, know something of value.'

'I was not present. Two Somnambulists near the Senn will testify that I was with them at the time the crimes were committed.'

Someone guffawed at my mention of Somnambulists. Let them; I was not seeking to retrieve dignity at a time like this. I knew that I was in peril.

The Chancellor said slowly, 'You will go to your chamber, apprentice, and you will remain there to await full interrogation. Afterwards you will leave the building and be gone from Perris within twenty hours. By virtue of my authority I declare you expelled from the guild of Rememberers.'

Forewarned as I had been by Samit, I was nevertheless stunned.

'*Expelled?* Why?'

'We can no longer trust you. Too many mysteries surround you. You bring us a Prince and conceal your suspicions; you are present at murderous quarrels; you visit a Procurator in the middle of the night. You may even have helped to bring about the calamitous loss suffered by our archive this morning. We have no desire for men of enigmas here. We sever our relationship with you.' The Chancellor waved his hand in a grand sweep. 'To your chamber now, to await interrogation, and then go!'

I was rushed from the room. As the entrance pit closed behind me, I looked back and saw the Chancellor, his face ashen, topple into the arms of his associates, while in the same instant the Rememberer Olmayne broke from her freeze and fell to the floor, screaming.

8

Alone in my chamber, I spent a long while gathering together my posses-sions, though I owned little. The morning was well along before a Remem-berer whom I did not know came to me; he carried interrogation equipment. I eyed it uneasily, thinking that all would be up with me if the Rememberers found proof that it was I who had betrayed the location of that compound record to the invaders. Already they suspected me of it; the Chancellor had hesitated to make the accusation only because it must have seemed odd to him that an apprentice such as myself would have cared to make a private search of the guild archive.

Fortune rode with me. My interrogator was concerned only with the de-tails of the slaying; and once he had determined that I knew nothing on that subject, he let me be, warning me to depart from the hall within the allotted time. I told him I would do so.

But first I needed rest. I had had none that night; and so I drank a three-hour draught and settled into soothing sleep. When I awakened a figure stood beside me: the Rememberer Olmayne.

She appeared to have aged greatly since the previous evening. She was dressed in a single chaste tunic of a sombre color, and she wore neither orna-ment nor decoration. Her features were rigidly set. I mastered my surprise at finding her there, and sat up, mumbling an apology for my delay in ac-knowledging her presence.

'Be at ease,' she said gently. 'Have I broken your sleep?'

'I had my full hours.'

'I have had none. But there will be time for sleep later. We owe each other explanations, Tomis.'

'Yes.' I rose uncertainly. 'Are you well? I saw you earlier, and you seemed lost in trance.'

'They have given me medicines,' she replied.

'Tell me what you can about last night.'

Her eyelids slid momentarily closed. 'You were there when Elegro chal-lenged us and was cast out by the Prince. Some hours later, Elegro returned. With him were the Procurator of Perris and several other invaders. Elegro appeared to be in a mood of great jubiliation. The Procurator produced a cube and commanded the Prince to put his hand to it. The Prince balked, but Manrule Seven persuaded him finally to cooperate. When he had touched the cube, the Procurator and Elegro departed, leaving the Prince and myself together again, neither of us comprehending what had happened. Guards were posted to prevent the Prince from leaving. Not long afterward the Procurator and Elegro returned. Now Elegro seemed subdued and even confused, while the Procurator was clearly exhilarated. In our room the Procurator announced that amnesty had been granted to the former Prince of Roum, and that no man was to harm him. There-upon all of the invaders departed.'

'Proceed.'

Olmayne spoke as though a Somnambulist. 'Elegro did not appear to comprehend what had occurred. He cried out that treason had been done; he screamed that he had been betrayed. An angry scene followed. Elegro was womanish in his fury; the Prince grew more haughty; each ordered the other to leave the suite. The quarrel became so violent that the carpet itself began to die. The petals drooped; the little mouths gaped. The climax came swiftly. Elegro seized a weapon and threatened to use it if the Prince did not leave at once. The Prince misjudged Elegro's temper, thought he was bluffing, and came forward as if to throw Elegro out. Elegro slew the Prince. An instant later I grasped a dart from our rack of artifacts and hurled it into Elegro's throat. The dart bore poison; he died at once. I summoned others, and I remember no more.'

'A strange night,' I said.

'Too strange. Tell me now, Tomis: why did the Procurator come, and why did he not take the Prince into custody?'

I said, 'The Procurator came because I asked him to, under the orders of your late husband. The Procurator did not arrest the Prince because the Prince's liberty had been purchased.'

'At what price?'

'The price of a man's shame,' I said.

'You speak a riddle.'

'The truth dishonors me. I beg you not to press me for it.'

'The Chancellor spoke of a document that had been taken by the Procurator—'

'It has to do with that,' I confessed, and Olmayne looked toward the floor and asked no further questions.

I said ultimately, 'You have committed a murder, then. What will your punishment be?'

'The crime was committed in passion and fear,' she replied. 'There will be no penalty of the civil administration. But I am expelled from my guild for my adultery and my act of violence.'

'I offer my regrets.'

'And I am commanded to undertake the Pilgrimage to Jorslem to purify my soul. I must leave within the day, or my life is forfeit to the guild.'

'I too am expelled,' I told her. 'And I too am bound at last for Jorslem, though of my own choosing.'

'May we travel together?'

My hesitation betrayed me. I had journeyed here with a blind Prince; I cared very little to depart with a murderous and guildless woman. Perhaps the time had come to travel alone. Yet the Somnambulist had said I would have a companion.

Olmayne said smoothly, 'You lack enthusiasm. Perhaps I can create some in you.' She opened her tunic. I saw mounted between the snowy hills of her breasts a gray pouch. She was tempting me not with her flesh but with an overpocket. 'In this,' she said, 'is all that the Prince of Roum carried in his thigh. He showed me those treasures, and I removed them from his body as he lay dead in my room. Also there are certain objects of my own. I am not without resources. We will travel comfortably. Well?'

'I find it hard to refuse.'

'Be ready in two hours.'

'I am ready now,' I said.

'Wait, then.'

She left me to myself. Nearly two hours later she returned, clad now in the mask and robes of a Pilgrim. Over her arm she held a second set of Pilgrim's gear, which she offered to me. Yes: I was guildless now, and it was an unsafe way to travel. I would go, then, as a Pilgrim to Jorslem. I donned the unfamiliar gear. We gathered our possessions.

'I have notified the guild of Pilgrims,' she declared as we left the Hall of Rememberers. 'We are fully registered. Later today we may hope to receive our starstones. How does the mask feel, Tomis?'

'Snug.'

'As it should be.'

Our route out of Perris took us across the great plaza before the ancient gray holy building of the old creed. A crowd had gathered; I saw invaders at the center of the group. Beggars made the profitable orbit about it. They ignored us, for no one begs from a Pilgrim; but I collared one rascal with a gouged face and said, 'What ceremony is taking place here?'

'Funeral of the Prince of Roum,' he said. 'By order of the Procurator. State funeral with all the trimmings. They're making a real festival out of it.'

'Why hold such an event in Perris?' I asked. 'How did the Prince die?'

'Look, ask somebody else. I got work to do.'

He wriggled free and scrambled on to work the crowd.

'Shall we attend the funeral?' I asked Olmayne.

'Best not to.'

'As you wish.'

We moved toward the massive stone bridge that spanned the Senn. Behind us, a brilliant blue glow arose as the pyre of the dead Prince was kindled. That pyre lit the way for us as we made our slow way through the night, eastward to Jorslem.

PART III

The Road To Jorslem

1

Our world was now truly theirs. All the way across Eyrop I could see that the invaders had taken everything, and we belonged to them as beasts in a barnyard belong to the farmer.

They were everywhere, like fleshy weeds taking root after a strange storm. They walked with cool confidence, as if telling us by the sleekness of their movements that the Will had withdrawn favor from us and conferred it upon them. They were not cruel to us, and yet they drained us of vitality by their mere presence among us. Our sun, our moons, our museums of ancient relics, our ruins of former cycles, our cities, our palaces, our future, our present, and our past had all undergone a transfer of tide. Our lives now lacked meaning.

At night the blaze of the stars mocked us. All the universe looked down on our shame.

The cold wind of winter told us that for our sins our freedom had been lost. The bright heat of summer told us that for our pride we had been humbled.

Through a changed world we moved, stripped of our past selves. I, who had roved the stars each day now had lost that pleasure. Now, bound for Jorslem, I found cool comfort in the hope that as a Pilgrim I might gain redemption and renewal in that holy city. Olmayne and I repeated each night the rituals of our Pilgrimage toward that end:

'We yield to the Will.'

'We yield to the Will.'

'In all things great and small.'

'In all things great and small.'

'And ask forgiveness.'

'And ask forgiveness.'

'For sins actual and potential.'

'For sins actual and potential.'

'And pray for understanding and repose.'

'And pray for understanding and repose.'

'Through all our days until redemption comes.'

'Through all our days until redemption comes.'

Thus we spoke the words. Saying them, we clutched the cool polished spheres of starstone, icy as frostflowers, and made communion with the

Will. And so we journeyed Jorslemward in this world that no longer was owned by man.

2

It was at the Talyan approach to Land Bridge that Olmayne first used her cruelty on me. Olmayne was cruel by first nature; I had had ample proof of that in Perris; and yet we had been Pilgrims together for many months, traveling from Perris eastward over the mountains and down the length of Talya to the Bridge, and she had kept her claws sheathed. Until this place.

The occasion was our halting by a company of invaders coming north from Afreek. There were perhaps twenty of them, tall and harsh-faced, proud of being masters of conquered Earth. They rode in a gleaming covered vehicle of their own manufacture, long and narrow, with thick sand-colored treads and small windows. We could see the vehicle from far away, raising a cloud of dust as it neared us.

This was a hot time of year. The sky itself was the color of sand, and it was streaked with folded sheets of heat-radiation – glowing and terrible energy streams of turquoise and gold.

Perhaps fifty of us stood beside the road, with the land of Talya at our backs and the continent of Afreek before us. We were a varied group: some Pilgrims, like Olmayne and myself, making the trek toward the holy city of Jorslem, but also a random mix of the rootless, men and women who floated from continent to continent for lack of other purpose. I counted in the band five former Watchers, and also several Indexers, a Sentinel, a pair of Communicants, a Scribe, and even a few Changelings. We gathered into a straggling assembly awarding the road by default to the invaders.

Land Bridge is not wide, and the road will not allow many to use it at any time. Yet in normal times the flow of traffic had always gone in both directions at once. Here, today, we feared to go forward while invaders were this close, and so we remained clustered timidly, watching our conquerors approach.

One of the Changelings detached himself from the others of his kind and moved toward me. He was small of stature for that breed, but wide through the shoulders; his skin seemed much too tight for his frame; his eyes were large and green-rimmed; his hair grew in thick widely spaced pedestal-like clumps, and his nose was barely perceptible, so that his nostrils appeared to sprout from his upper lip. Despite this he was less grotesque than most

Changelings appear. His expression was solemn, but had a hint of bizarre playfulness lurking somewhere.

He said in a voice that was little more than a feathery whisper. 'Do you think we'll be delayed long, Pilgrims?'

In former times one did not address a Pilgrim unsolicited – especially if one happened to be a Changeling. Such customs meant nothing to me, but Olmayne drew back with a hiss of distaste.

I said, 'We will wait here until our masters allow us to pass. Is there any choice?'

'None, friend, none.'

At that *friend,* Olmayne hissed again and glowered at the little Changeling. He turned to her, and his anger showed, for suddenly six parallel bands of scarlet pigment blazed brightly beneath the glossy skin of his cheeks. But his only overt response to her was a courteous bow. He said, 'I introduce myself. I am Bernalt, naturally guildless, a native of Nayrub in Deeper Afreek. I do not inquire after your names, Pilgrims. Are you bound for Jorslem?'

'Yes,' I said, as Olmayne swung about to present her back. 'And you? Home to Nayrub after travels?'

'No,' said Bernalt. 'I go to Jorslem also.'

Instantly I felt cold and hostile, my initial response to the Changeling's suave charm fading at once. I had had a Changeling, false though he turned out to be, as a traveling companion before; he too had been charming, but I wanted no more like him. Edgily, distantly, I said, 'May I ask what business a Changeling might have in Jorslem?'

He detected the chill in my tone, and his huge eyes registered sorrow. 'We too are permitted to visit the holy city, I remind you. Even our kind. Do you fear that Changelings will once again seize the shrine of renewal, as we did a thousand years ago before we were cast down into guildlessness?' He laughed harshly. 'I threaten no one, Pilgrim. I am hideous of face, but not dangerous. May the Will grant you what you seek. Pilgrim.' He made a gesture of respect and went back to the other Changelings.

Furious, Olmayne spun round on me.

'Why do you talk to such beastly creatures?'

'The man approached me. He was merely being friendly. We are all cast together here, Olmayne, and—'

'*Man. Man!* You call a Changeling a man?'

'They *are* human, Olmayne.'

'Just barely. Tomis, I loathe such monsters. My flesh creeps to have them near me. If I could, I'd banish them from this world!'

'Where is the serene tolerance a Rememberer must cultivate?'

She flamed at the mockery in my voice. 'We are not required to love

Changelings, Tomis. They are one of the curses laid upon our planet – parodies of humanity, enemies of truth and beauty. I despise them!'

It was not a unique attitude. But I had no time to reproach Olmayne for her intolerance; the vehicle of the invaders was drawing near. I hoped we might resume our journey once it went by. It slowed and halted, however, and several of the invaders came out. They walked unhurriedly toward us, their long arms dangling like slack ropes.

'Who is the leader here?' asked one of them.

No one replied, for we were independent of one another in our travel.

The invader said impatiently, after a moment, 'No leader? No leader? Very well, all of you, listen. The road must be cleared. A convoy is coming through. Go back to Palerm and wait until tomorrow.'

'But I must be in Agupt by—' the Scribe began.

'Land Bridge is closed today,' said the invader. 'Go back to Palerm.'

His voice was calm. The invaders are never peremptory, never overbearing. They have the poise and assurance of those who are secure possessors.

The Scribe shivered, his jowls swinging, and said no more.

Several of the others by the side of the road looked as if they wished to protest. The Sentinel turned away and spat. A man who boldly wore the mark of the shattered guild of Defenders in his cheek clenched his fists and plainly fought back a surge of fury. The Changelings whispered to one another. Bernalt smiled bitterly at me and shrugged.

Go back to Palerm? Waste a day's march in this heat? For what? For what?

The invader gestured casually, telling us to disperse.

Now it was that Olmayne was unkind to me. In a low voice she said, 'Explain to them, Tomis, that you are in the pay of the Procurator of Perris, and they will let the two of us pass.'

Her dark eyes glittered with mockery and contempt.

My shoulders sagged as if she had loaded ten years on me. 'Why did you say such a thing?' I asked.

'It's hot. I'm tired. It's idiotic of them to send us back to Palerm.'

'I agree. But I can do nothing. Why do you hurt me?'

'Does the truth hurt that much?'

'I am no collaborator, Olmayne.'

She laughed. 'You say that so well! But you are, Tomis, you are! You sold them the documents.'

'To save the Prince, your lover,' I reminded her.

'You dealt with the invaders, though. No matter what your motive was, that fact remains.'

'Stop it, Olmayne.'

'Now you give me orders?'

'Olmayne—'

'Go up to them, Tomis. Tell them who you are, make them let us go ahead.'

'The convoys would run us down on the road. In any case I have no influence with invaders. I am not the Procurator's man.'

'I'll die before I go back to Palerm!'

'Die, then,' I said wearily, and turned my back on her.

'Traitor! Treacherous old fool! Coward!'

I pretended to ignore her, but I felt the fire of her words. There was no falsehood in them, only malice. I *had* dealt with the conquerors, I *had* betrayed the guild that sheltered me, I *had* violated the code that calls for sullen passivity as our only way of protest for Earth's defeat. All true; yet it was unfair for her to reproach me with it. I had given no thought to higher matters of patriotism when I broke my trust; I was trying only to save a man to whom I felt bound, a man moreover with whom she was in love. It was loathsome of Olmayne to tax me with treason now, to torment my conscience, merely because of a petty rage at the heat and dust of the road.

But this woman had coldly slain her own husband. Why should she not be malicious in trifles as well?

The invaders had their way; we abandoned the road and straggled back to Palerm, a dismal, sizzling, sleepy town. That evening, as if to console us, five Fliers passing information overhead took a fancy to the town, and in the moonless night they came again and again through the sky, three men and two women, ghostly and slender and beautiful. I stood watching them for more than an hour, until my soul itself seemed lifted from me and into the air to join them. Their great shimmering wings scarcely hid the starlight; their pale angular bodies moved in graceful arcs, arms held pressed close to sides, legs together, backs gently curved. The sight of these five stirred my memories of Avluela and left me tingling with troublesome emotions.

The Fliers made their last pass and were gone. The false moons entered the sky soon afterward. I went into our hostelry then, and shortly Olmayne asked admittance to my room.

She looked contrite. She carried a squat octagonal flask of green wine, not a Talyan brew but something from an outworld, no doubt purchased at great price.

'Will you forgive me, Tomis?' she asked. 'Here. I know you like these wines.'

'I would rather not have had those words before, and not have the wine now,' I told her.

'My temper grows short in the heat. I'm sorry, Tomis. I said a stupid and tactless thing.'

I forgave her, in hope of a smoother journey thereafter, and we drank most of the wine, and then she went to her own room nearby to sleep. Pilgrims must live chaste lives – not that Olmayne would ever have bedded with such a withered old fossil as I, but the commandments of our adopted guild prevented the question from arising.

For a long while I lay awake beneath a lash of guilt. In her impatience and wrath Olmayne had stung me at my vulnerable place: I was a betrayer of mankind. I wrestled with the issue almost to dawn.

– What had I done?

I had revealed to our conquerors a certain document.

– Did the invaders have a moral right to the document?

It told of the shameful treatment they had had at the hands of our ancestors.

– What, then, was wrong about giving it to them?

One does not aid one's conquerors even when they are morally superior to one.

– Is a small treason a serious thing?

There are no small treasons.

– Perhaps the complexity of the matter should be investigated. I did not act out of love of the enemy, but to aid a friend.

Nevertheless I collaborated with our foes.

– This obstinate self-laceration smacks of sinful pride.

But I feel my guilt. I drown in shame.

In this unprofitable way I consumed the night. When the day brightened, I rose and looked skyward and begged the Will to help me find redemption in the waters of the house of renewal in Jorslem, at the end of my Pilgrimage. Then I went to awaken Olmayne.

3

Land bridge was open on this day, and we joined the throng that was crossing over out of Talya into Afreek. It was the second time I had traveled Land Bridge, for the year before – it seemed so much farther in the past – I had come the other way, out of Agupt and bound for Roum.

There are two main routes for Pilgrims from Eyrop to Jorslem. The northern route involves going through the Dark Lands east of Talya, taking the ferry at Stanbool, and skirting the western coast of the continent of Ais to Jorslem. It was the route I would have preferred since, of all the world's great cities, old Stanbool is the one I have never visited. But Olmayne had been there to do research in the days when she was a Rememberer, and disliked the place; and so we took the southern route – across Land Bridge into Afreek and along the shore of the great Lake Medit, through

Agupt and the fringes of the Arban Desert and up to Jorslem.

A true Pilgrim travels only by foot. It was not an idea that had much appeal to Olmayne, and though we walked a great deal, we rode whenever we could. She was shameless in commandeering transportation. On only the second day of our journey she had gotten us a ride from a rich Merchant bound for the coast; the man had no intention of sharing his sumptuous vehicle with anyone, but he could not resist the sensuality of Olmayne's deep, musical voice, even though it issued from the sexless grillwork of a Pilgrim's mask.

The Merchant traveled in style. For him the conquest of Earth might never have happened, nor even all the long centuries of Third Cycle decline. His self-primed landcar was four times the length of a man and wide enough to house five people in comfort; and it shielded its riders against the outer world as effectively as a womb. There was no direct vision, only a series of screens revealing upon command what lay outside. The temperature never varied from a chosen norm. Spigots supplied liquers and stronger things; food tablets were available; pressure couches insulated travelers against the irregularities of the road. For illumination, there was slavelight keyed to the Merchant's whims. Beside the main couch sat a thinking cap, but I never learned whether the Merchant carried a pickled brain for his private use in the depths of the landcar, or enjoyed some sort of remote contact with the memory tanks of the cities through which he passed.

He was a man of pomp and bulk, clearly a savourer of his own flesh. Deep olive skin, with a thick pompadour of well-oiled black hair and somber, scrutinizing eyes, he rejoiced in his solidity and in his control of an uncertain environment. He dealt, we learned, in foodstuffs of other worlds; he bartered our poor manufacturers for the delicacies of the starborn ones. Now he was en route to Marsay to examine a cargo of hallucinatory insects newly come in from one of the Belt planets.

'You like the car?' he asked, seeing our awe. Olmayne, no stranger to ease herself, was peering at the dense inner mantle of diamonded brocade in obvious amazement. 'It was owned by the Comt of Perris,' he went on. 'Yes, I mean it, the Comt himself. They turned his palace into a museum, you know.'

'I know,' Olmayne said softly.

'This was his chariot. It was supposed to be part of the museum, but I bought it off a crooked invader. You didn't know they had crooked ones too, eh?' The Merchant's robust laughter caused the sensitive mantle on the walls of the car to recoil in disdain. 'This one was the Procurator's boy friend. Yes, they've got *those,* too. He was looking for a certain fancy root that grows on a planet of the Fishes, something to give his virility a little boost, you know, and he learned that I controlled the whole supply here, and so we were able to work out a little deal. Of course, I had to have the car adapted, a little. The Comt kept four neuters up front and powered the engine right off their metabolisms, you understand, running the thing on thermal differentials. Well, that's a fine way to power a car, if you're a Comt, but it uses up a lot of neuters through the year, and I felt I'd be overreaching my status if I tried anything like that. It might get me into trouble with the invaders, too. So I had the drive compartment stripped down and replaced with a standard heavy-duty rollerwagon engine – a really subtle job – and there you are. You're lucky to be in here. It's only that you're Pilgrims. Ordinarily I don't let folks come inside, on account of them feeling envy, and envious folks are dangerous to a man who's made something out of his life. Yet the Will brought you two to me. Heading for Jorslem, eh?'

'Yes,' Olmayne said.

'Me too, but not yet! Not just yet, thank you!' He patted his middle. 'I'll be there, you can bet on it, when I feel ready for renewal, but that's a good way off, the Will willing! You two been Pilgriming long?'

'No,' Olmayne said.

'A lot of folks went Pilgriming after the conquest, I guess. Well, I don't blame 'em. We each adapt in our own ways to changing times. Say, you carrying those little stones the Pilgrims carry?'

'Yes,' Olmayne said.

'Mind if I see one? Always been fascinated by the things. There was this trader from one of the Darkstar worlds – little skinny bastard with skin like oozing tar – he offered me ten quintals of the things. Said they were genuine, gave you the real communion, just like the Pilgrims had. I told him no, I wasn't going to fool with the Will. Some things you don't do, even for profit. But afterward I wished I'd kept one as a souvenir. I never even touched one.' He stretched a hand toward Olmayne. 'Can I see?'

'We may not let others handle the starstone,' I said.

'I wouldn't tell anybody you let me!'

'It is forbidden.'

'Look, it's private in here, the most private place on Earth, and—'

'Please. What you ask is impossible.'

His face darkened, and I thought for a moment he would halt the car and order us out, which would have caused me no grief. My hand slipped into my pouch to finger the frigid starstone sphere that I had been given at the outset of my Pilgrimage. The touch of my fingertips brought faint resonances of the communion-trance to me, and I shivered in pleasure. He must not have it, I swore. But the crisis passed without incident. The Merchant, having tested us and found resistance, did not choose to press the matter.

We sped onward toward Marsay.

He was not a likeable man, but he had a certain gross charm, and we were rarely offended by his words. Olmayne, who after all was a fastidious woman and had lived most of her years in the glossy seclusion of the Hall of Rememberers, found him harder to take than I; my intolerances have been well blunted by a lifetime of wandering. But even Olmayne seemed to find him amusing when he boasted of his wealth and influence, when he told of the women who waited for him on many worlds, when he catalogued his homes and his trophies and the guildmasters who sought his counsel, when he bragged of friendships with former Masters and Dominators. He talked almost wholly of himself and rarely of us, for which we were thankful; once he asked how it was that a male Pilgrim and a female Pilgrim were traveling together, implying that we must be lovers; we admitted that the arrangement was slightly irregular and went on to another theme, and I think he remained persuaded of our unchastity. His bawdy guesses mattered not at all to me nor, I believe, to Olmayne. We had more serious guilts as our burdens.

Our Merchant's life seemed enviably undisrupted by the fall of our planet: he was as rich as ever, as comfortable, as free to move about. But even he felt occasionally irked by the presence of the invaders, as we found out by night not far from Marsay, when we were stopped at a checkpoint on the road.

Spy-eye scanners saw us coming, gave a signal to the spinnerets, and a golden spiderweb spurted into being from one shoulder of the highway to the other. The land-car's sensors detected it and instantly signaled us to a halt. The screens showed a dozen pale human faces clustered outside.

'Bandits?' Olmayne asked.

'Worse,' said the Merchant. 'Traitors.' He scowled and turned to his communicator horn. 'What is it?' he demanded.

'Get out for inspection.'

'By whose writ?'

'The Procurator of Marsay,' came the reply.

It was an ugly thing to behold: human beings acting as road-agents for the invaders. But it was inevitable that we should have begun to drift into their civil service, since work was scarce, especially for those who had been in the defensive guilds. The Merchant began the complicated process of unsealing his car. He was stormy-faced with rage, but he was stymied, unable to pass the checkpoint's web. 'I go armed,' he whispered to us. 'Wait inside and fear nothing.'

He got out and engaged in a lengthy discussion, of which we could hear nothing, with the highway guards. At length some impasse must have forced recourse to higher authority, for three invaders abruptly appeared, waved their hired collaborators away, and surrounded the Merchant. His demeanor changed; his face grew oily and sly, his hands moved rapidly in eloquent gestures, his eyes glistened. He led the three interrogators to the car, opened it, and showed them his two passengers, ourselves. The invaders appeared puzzled by the sight of Pilgrims amid such opulence, but they did not ask us to step out. After some further conversation the Merchant rejoined us and sealed the car; the web was dissolved; we sped onward toward Marsay.

As we gained velocity he muttered curses and said, 'Do you know how I'd handle that long-armed filth? All we need is a coordinated plan. A night of knives: every ten Earthmen make themselves responsible for taking out one invader. We'd get them all.'

'Why has no one organized such a movement?' I asked.

'It's the job of the Defenders, and half of them are dead, and the other half's in the pay of *them*. It's not my place to set up a resistance movement. But that's how it should be done. Guerrilla action: sneak up behind 'em, give 'em the knife. Quick. Good old First Cycle methods; they've never lost their value.'

'More invaders would come,' Olmayne said morosely.

'Treat 'em the same way!'

'They would retaliate with fire. They would destroy our world,' she said.

'These invaders pretend to be civilized, more civilized than ourselves,' the Merchant replied. 'Such barbarity would give them a bad name on a million worlds. No, they wouldn't come with fire. They'd just get tired of having to conquer us over and over, of losing so many men. And they'd go away, and we'd be free again.'

'Without having won redemption for our ancient sins,' I said.

'What's that, old man? What's that?'

'Never mind.'

'I suppose you wouldn't join them, either of you, if we struck back at them?'

I said, 'In former life I was a Watcher, and I devoted myself to the protection of this planet against them. I am no more fond of our masters than you are, and no less eager to see them depart. But your plan is not only impractical: it is also morally valueless. Mere bloody resistance would thwart the scheme the Will has devised for us. We must earn our freedom in a nobler way. We were not given this ordeal simply so that we might have practice in slitting throats.'

He looked at me with contempt and snorted. 'I should have remembered. I'm talking to Pilgrims. All right. Forget it all. I wasn't serious, anyway. Maybe you like the world the way it is, for all I know.'

'I do not,' I said.

He glanced at Olmayne. So did I, for I half-expected her to tell the Merchant that I had already done my bit of collaborating with our conquerors. But Olmayne fortunately was silent on that topic, as she would be for some months more, until that unhappy day by the approach to Land Bridge when, in her impatience, she taunted me with my sole fall from grace.

We left our benefactor in Marsay, spent the night in a Pilgrim hostelry, and set out on foot along the coast the next morning. And so we traveled, Olmayne and I, through pleasant lands swarming with invaders; now we walked, now we rode some peasant's rollerwagon, once even we were the guests of touring conquerors. We gave Roum a wide berth when we entered Talya, and turned south. And so we came to Land Bridge, and met delay, and had our frosty moment of bickering, and then were permitted to go on across that narrow tongue of sandy ground that links the lake-sundered continents. And so we crossed into Afreek, at last.

4

Our first night on the other side, after our long and dusty crossing, we tumbled into a grimy inn near the lake's edge. It was a square whitewashed stone building, practically windowless and arranged around a cool inner courtyard. Most of its clientele appeared to be Pilgrims, but there were some members of other guilds, chiefly Vendors and Transporters. At a room near the turning of the building there stayed a Rememberer, whom Olmayne avoided even though she did not know him; she simply did not wish to be reminded of her former guild.

Among those who took lodging there was the Changeling Bernalt. Under the new laws of the invaders, Changelings might stay at any public inn, not merely those set aside for their special use; yet it seemed a little strange to see him here. We passed in the corridor. Bernalt gave me a tentative smile, as though about to speak again, but the smile died and the glow left his eyes. He appeared to realize I was not ready to accept his friendship. Or perhaps he merely recalled that Pilgrims, by the laws of their guild, were not supposed to have much to do with guildless ones. That law still stood.

Olmayne and I had a greasy meal of soups and stews. Afterward I saw her to her room and began to wish her good night when she said, 'Wait. We'll do our communion together.'

'I've been seen coming into your room,' I pointed out. 'There will be whispering if I stay long.'

'We'll go to yours, then!'

Olmayne peered into the hall. All clear: she seized my wrist, and we rushed toward my chamber, across the way. Closing and sealing the warped door, she said, 'Your starstone, now!'

I took the stone from its hiding place in my robe, and she produced hers, and our hands closed upon them.

During this time of Pilgrimage I had found the starstone a great comfort. Many seasons now had passed since I had last entered a Watcher's trance, but I was not yet reconciled entirely to the breaking of my old habit; the starstone provided a kind of substitute for the swooping ecstasy I had known in Watching.

Starstones come from one of the outer worlds – I could not tell you which – and may be had only by application to the guild. The stone itself determines whether one may be a Pilgrim, for it will burn the hand of one whom it considers unworthy to don the robe. They say that without exception every person who has enrolled in the guild of Pilgrims has shown uneasiness as the stone was offered to him for the first time.

'When they gave you yours,' Olmayne asked, 'were you worried?'

'Of course.'

'So was I.'

We waited for the stones to overwhelm us. I gripped mine tightly. Dark, shining, more smooth than glass, it glowed in my grasp like a pellet of ice, and I felt myself becoming attuned to the power of the Will.

First came a heightened perception of my surroundings. Every crack in the walls of this ancient inn seemed now a valley. The soft wail of the wind outside rose to a keen pitch. In the dim glow of the room's lamp I saw colors beyond the spectrum.

The quality of the experience the starstone offered was altogether different from that given by my instruments of Watching. That, too, was a transcending of self. When in a state of Watchfulness I was capable of leaving my Earth-bound identity and soaring at infinite speed over infinite range, perceiving all, and this is as close to godhood as a man is likely to come. The starstone provided none of the highly specific data that a Watcher's trance yielded. In the full spell I could see nothing, nor could I identify my surroundings. I knew only that when I let myself be drawn into the stone's effect, I was engulfed by something far larger than myself, that I was in direct contact with the matrix of the universe.

Call it communion with the Will.

From a great distance I heard Olmayne say, 'Do you believe what some people say of these stones? That there is no communion, that it's all an electrical deception?'

'I have no theory about that,' I said. 'I am less interested in causes than in effects.'

Skeptics say that the starstones are nothing more than amplifying loops which bounce a man's own brain-waves back into his mind; the awesome oceanic entity with which one comes in contact, these scoffers hold, is merely the thunderous recycling oscillation of a single shuttling electrical pulse beneath the roof of the Pilgrim's own skull. Perhaps.

Olmayne extended the hand that gripped her stone. She said, 'When you were among the Rememberers, Tomis, did you study the history of early religion? All through time, man has sought union with the infinite. Many religions – not all! – have held forth the hope of such a divine merging.'

'And there were drugs, too,' I murmured.

'Certain drugs, yes, cherished for their ability to bring the taker momentarily to a sensation of oneness with the universe. These starstones, Tomis, are only the latest in a long sequence of devices for overcoming the greatest of human curses, that, is, the confinement of each individual soul within a single body. Our terrible isolation from one another and from the Will itself is more than most races of the universe would be able to bear. It seems unique to humanity.'

Her voice grew feathery and vague. She said much more, speaking to me out of the wisdom she had learned with the Rememberers, but her meaning eluded me; I was always quicker to enter communion than she, because of my training as a Watcher, and often her final words did not register.

That night as on other nights I seized my stone and felt the chill and closed my eyes, and heard the distant tolling of a mighty gong, the lapping of waves on an unknown beach, the whisper of the wind in an alien forest. And felt a summons. And yielded. And entered the state of communion. And gave myself up to the Will.

And slipped down through the layers of my life, through my youth and middle years, my wanderings, my old loves, my torments, my joys, my troubled later years, my treasons, my insufficiencies, my griefs, my imperfections.

And freed myself of myself. And shed my selfness. And merged. And became one of thousands of Pilgrims, not merely Olmayne nearby, but others trekking the mountains of Hind and the sands of Arba, Pilgrims at their devotions in Ais and Palash and Strayla, Pilgrims moving toward Jorslem on the journey that some complete in months, some in years, and some never at all. And shared with all of them the instant of submergence into the Will. And saw in the darkness a deep purple glow on the horizon – which grew in intensity until it became an all-encompassing red brilliance. And went into it, though unworthy, unclean, flesh-trapped, accepting fully the communion offered and wishing no other state of being than this divorce from self.

And was purified.

And wakened alone.

5

I knew Afreek well. When still a young man I had settled in the continent's dark heart for many years. Out of restlessness I had left, finally, going as far north as Agupt, where the antique relics of First Cycle days have survived better than anywhere else. In those days antiquity held no interest for me, however. I did my Watching and went about from place to place, since a Watcher does not need to have a fixed station; and chance brought me in contact with Avluela just as I was ready to roam again, and so I left Agupt for Roum and then Perris.

Now I had come back with Olmayne. We kept close to the coast and avoided the sandy inland wastes. As Pilgrims we were immune from most of the hazards of travel: we would never go hungry or without shelter, even in a place where no lodge for our guild existed, and all owed us respect. Olmayne's great beauty might have been a hazard to her, traveling as she was with no escort other than a shriveled old man, but behind the mask and robe of a Pilgrim she was safe. We unmasked only rarely, and never where we might be seen.

I had no illusions about my importance to Olmayne. To her I was merely part of the equipment of a journey – someone to help her in her communions and rituals, to arrange for lodgings, to smooth her way for her. That role suited me. She was, I knew, a dangerous woman, given to strange whims and unpredictable fancies. I wanted no entanglements with her.

She lacked a Pilgrim's purity. Even though she had passed the test of the starstone, she had not triumphed – as a Pilgrim must – over her own flesh. She slipped off, sometimes, for half a night or longer, and I pictured her lying maskless in some alley gasping in a Servitor's arms. That was her affair entirely; I never spoke of her absences upon her return.

Within our lodgings, too, she was careless of her virtue. We never shared a room – no Pilgrim hostelry would permit it – but we usually had adjoining ones, and she summoned me to hers or came to mine whenever the mood took her. Often as not she was unclothed; she attained the height of the grotesque one night in Agupt when I found her wearing only her mask, all her gleaming white flesh belying the intent of the bronze grillwork that hid her face. Only once did it seem to occur to her that I might ever have been young enough to feel desire. She looked my scrawny, shrunken body over and said, 'How will you look, I wonder, when you've been renewed in Jorslem? I'm trying to picture you young, Tomis. Will you give me pleasure then?'

'I gave pleasure in my time,' I said obliquely.

Olmayne disliked the heat and dryness of Agupt. We traveled mainly by night and clung to our hostelries by day. The roads were crowded at all hours. The press of Pilgrims towards Jorslem was extraordinarily heavy, it appeared. Olmayne and I speculated on how long it might take us to gain access to the waters at such a time.

'You've never been renewed before?' she asked.

'Never.'

'Nor I. They say they don't admit all who come.'

'Renewal is a privilege, not a right,' I said. 'Many are turned away.'

'I understand also,' said Olmayne, 'that not all who enter the waters are successfully renewed.'

'I know little of this.'

'Some grow older instead of younger. Some grow young too fast, and perish. There are risks.'

'Would you not take those risks?'

She laughed. 'Only a fool would hesitate.'

'You are in no need of renewal at this time,' I pointed out. 'You were sent to Jorslem for the good of your soul, not that of your body, as I recall.'

'I'll tend to my soul as well, when I'm in Jorslem.'

'But you talk as if the house of renewal is the only shrine you mean to visit.'

'It's the important one,' she said. She rose, flexing her supple body voluptuously. 'True, I have atoning to do. But do you think I've come all the way to Jorslem just for the sake of my spirit?'

'I have,' I pointed out.

'*You!* You're old and withered! You'd better look after your spirit – and your flesh as well. I wouldn't mind shedding some age, though. I won't have them take off much. Eight, ten years, that's all. The years I wasted with that fool Elegro. I don't need a full renewal. You're right: I'm still in my prime.' Her face clouded. 'If the city is full of Pilgrims, maybe they won't let me into the house of renewal at all! They'll say I'm too young – tell me to come back in forty or fifty years – Tomis, would they do that to me?'

'It is hard for me to say.'

She trembled. 'They'll let *you* in. You're a walking corpse already – they have to renew you! But me – Tomis, I won't let them turn me away! If I have to pull Jorslem down stone by stone, I'll get in somehow!'

I wondered privately if her soul were in fit condition for one who poses as a candidate for renewal. Humility is recommended when one becomes a Pilgrim. But I had no wish to feel Olmayne's fury, and I kept my silence. Perhaps they would admit her to renewal despite her flaws. I had concerns of my own. It was vanity that drove Olmayne; my goals were different. I had wandered long and done much, not all of it virtuous; I needed a cleansing of my conscience in the holy city more, perhaps, than I did a lessening of my years.

Or was it only vanity for me to think so?

6

Several days eastward of that place, as Olmayne and I walked through a parched countryside, village children chattering in fear and excitement rushed upon us.

'Please, come, come!' they cried. 'Pilgrims, come!'

Olmayne looked bewildered and irritated as they plucked at her robes. 'What are they saying, Tomis? I can't get through their damnable Aguptan accents!'

'They want us to help,' I said. I listened to their shouts. 'In their village,' I told Olmayne, 'there is an outbreak of the crystallization disease. They wish us to seek the mercies of the Will upon the sufferers.'

Olmayne drew back. I imagined the disdainful wince behind her mask. She flicked out her hands, trying to keep the children from touching her. To me she said, 'We can't go there!'

'We must.'

'We're in a hurry! Jorslem's crowded; I don't want to waste time in some dreary village.'

'They need us, Olmayne.'

'Are we Surgeons?'

'We are Pilgrims,' I said quietly. 'The benefits we gain from that carry certain obligations. If we are entitled to the hospitality of all we meet, we must also place our souls at the free disposal of the humble. Come.'

'I won't go!'

'How will that sound in Jorslem, when you give an accounting of yourself, Olmayne?'

'It's a hideous disease. What if we get it?'

'Is that what troubles you? Trust in the Will! How can you expect renewal if your soul is so deficient in grace?'

'May you rot, Tomis,' she said in a low voice. 'When did you become so pious? You're doing this deliberately, because of what I said to you by Land Bridge. In a stupid moment I taunted you, and now you're willing to expose us both to a ghastly afflction for your revenge. Don't do it, Tomis!'

I ignored her accusation. 'The children are growing agitated, Olmayne.

Will you wait here for me, or will you go to the next village and wait in the hostelry there?'

'Don't leave me alone in the middle of nowhere!'

'I have to go to the sick ones,' I said.

In the end she accompanied me – I think not out of any suddenly conceived desire to be of help, but rather out of fear that her selfish refusal might somehow be held against her in Jorslem. We came shortly to the village, which was small and decayed, for Agupt lies in a terrible hot sleep and changes little with the millennia. The contrast with the busy cities farther to the south in Afreek – cities that prosper on the output of luxuries from their great Manufactories – is vast.

Shivering with heat, we followed the children to the houses of sickness.

The crystallization disease is an unlovely gift from the stars. Not many afflictions of outworlders affect the Earth-born; but from the worlds of the Spear came this ailment, carried by alien tourists, and the disease has settled among us. If it had come during the glorious days of the Second Cycle we might have eradicated it in a day; but our skills are dulled now, and no year has been without its outbreak. Olmayne was plainly terrified as we entered the first of the day huts where the victims were kept.

There is no hope for one who has contracted this disease. One merely hopes that the healthy will be spared; and fortunately it is not a highly contagious disease. It works insidiously, transmitted in an unknown way, often failing to pass from husband to wife and leaping instead to the far side of a city, to another land entirely, perhaps. The first symptom is a scaliness of the skin; itch, flakes upon the clothing, inflammation. There follows a weakness in the bones as the calcium is dissolved. One grows limp and rubbery, but this is still an early phase. Soon the outer tissues harden. Thick, opaque membranes form on the surface of the eyes; the nostrils may close and seal; the skin grows coarse and pebbled. In this phase prophecy is common. The sufferer partakes of the skills of a Somnambulist, and utters oracles. The soul may wander, separating from the body for hours at a time, although the life-processes continue. Next, within twenty days after the onset of the disease, the crystallization occurs. While the skeletal structure dissolves, the skin splits and cracks, forming shining crystals in rigid geometrical patterns. The victim is quite beautiful at this time and takes on the appearance of a replica of himself in precious gems. The crystals glow with rich inner lights, violet and green and red; their sharp facets adopt new alignments from hour to hour; the slightest illumination in the room causes the sufferer to give off brilliant glittering reflections that dazzle and delight the eye. All this time the internal body is changing, as if some strange chrysalis is forming. Miraculously the organs sustain life throughout every transformation, although in the crystalline phase the victim is no longer able to communicate with others and possibly is unaware of the changes in himself. Ultimately the metamorphosis reaches the vital organs, and the process fails. The alien infestation is unable to reshape those organs without killing its host. The crisis is swift: a brief convulsion, a final discharge of energy along the nervous system of the crystallized one, and there is a quick arching of the body, accompanied by the delicate tinkling sounds of shivering glass, and then all is over. On the planet to which this is native, crystallization is not a disease but an actual metamorphosis, the result of thousands of years of evolution toward a symbiotic relationship. Unfortunately, among the Earthborn, the evolutionary preparation did not take place, and the agent of change invariably brings its subject to a fatal outcome.

Since the process is irreversible, Olmayne and I could do nothing of real value here except offer consolation to these ignorant and frightened people. I saw at once that the disease had seized this village some time ago. There were people in all stages, from the first rash to the ultimate crystallization. They were arranged in the hut according to the intensity of their infestation. To my left was a somber row of new victims, fully conscious and morbidly scratching their arms as they contemplated the horrors that awaited them. Along the rear wall were five pallets on which lay villagers in the coarse-skinned and prophetic phase. To my right were those in varying degrees of crystallization, and up front, the diadem of the lot, was one who clearly was in his last hours of life. His body, encrusted with false emeralds and rubies and opals, shimmered in almost painful beauty; he scarcely moved; within that shell of wondrous color he was lost in some dream of ecstasy, finding at the end of his days more passion, more delight, than he could ever have known in all his harsh peasant years.

Olmayne shied back from the door.

'It's horrible,' she whispered. 'I won't go in!'

'We must. We are under an obligation.'

'I never wanted to be a Pilgrim!'

'You wanted atonement,' I reminded her. 'It must be earned.'

'We'll catch the disease!'

'The Will can reach us anywhere to infect us with this, Olmayne. It strikes at random. The danger is no greater for us inside this building than it is in Perris.'

'Why, then, are so many in this one village smitten?'

'This village has earned the displeasure of the Will.'

'How neatly you serve up the mysticism, Tomis,' she said bitterly. 'I misjudged you. I thought you were a sensible man. This fatalism of yours is ugly.'

'I watched my world conquered,' I said. 'I beheld the Prince of Roum destroyed. Calamities breed such attitudes as I now have. Let us go in, Olmayne.'

We entered, Olmayne still reluctant. Now fear assailed me, but I concealed it. I had been almost smug in my piety while arguing with the lovely Rememberer woman who was my companion, but I could not deny the sudden seething of fright.

I forced myself to be tranquil.

There are redemptions and redemptions, I told myself. If this disease is to be the source of mine, I will abide by the Will.

Perhaps Olmayne came to some such decision too, as we went in, or maybe her own sense of the dramatic forced her into the unwanted role of the lady of mercy. She made the rounds with me. We passed from pallet to pallet, heads bowed, starstones in our hands. We said words. We smiled when the newly sick begged for reassurance. We offered prayers. Olmayne paused before one girl in the secondary phase, whose eyes already were filming over with horny tissue, and knelt and touched her starstone to the girl's scaly cheek. The girl spoke in oracles, but unhappily not in any language we understood.

At last we came to the terminal case, he who had grown his own superb sarcophagus. Somehow I felt purged of fear, and so too was Olmayne, for we stood a long while before this grotesque sight, silent, and then she whispered, 'How terrible! How wonderful! How beautiful!'

Three more huts similar to this one awaited us.

The villagers clustered at the doorways. As we emerged from each building in turn, the healthy ones fell down about us, clutching at the hems of our robes, stridently demanding that we intercede for them with the Will. We spoke such words as seemed appropriate and not too insincere. Those within the huts received our words blankly, as if they already realized there was no chance for them; those outside, still untouched by the disease, clung to every syllable. The headman of the village – only an acting headman; the true chief lay crystallized – thanked us again and again, as though we had done something real. At least we had given comfort, which is not to be despised.

When we came forth from the last of the sickhouses, we saw a slight figure watching us from a distance: the Changeling Bernalt. Olmayne nudged me.

'That creature has been following us, Tomis. All the way from Land Bridge!'

'He travels to Jorslem also.'

'Yes, but why should he stop here? Why in this awful place?'

'Hush, Olmayne. Be civil to him now.'

'To a *Changeling?*'

Bernalt approached. The mutated one was clad in a soft white robe that blunted the strangeness of his appearance. He nodded sadly toward the village and said, 'A great tragedy. The Will lies heavily on this place.'

He explained that he had arrived here several days ago and had met a friend from his native city of Nayrub. I assumed he meant a Changeling, but no, Bernalt's friend was a Surgeon, he said, who had halted here to do what he could for the afflicted villagers. The idea of a friendship between a Changeling and a Surgeon seemed a bit odd to me, and positively contemptible to Olmayne, who did not trouble to hide her loathing of Bernalt.

A partly crystallized figure staggered from one of the huts, gnarled hands clutching. Bernalt went forward and gently guided it back within. Returning to us, he said, 'There are times one is actually glad one is a Changeling. That disease does not affect us, you know.' His eyes acquired a sudden glitter. 'Am I forcing myself on you, Pilgrims? You seem like stone behind your masks. I mean no harm; shall I withdraw?'

'Of course not,' I said, meaning the opposite. His company disturbed me; perhaps the ordinary disdain for Changelings was a contagion that had at last reached me. 'Stay awhile. I would ask you to travel with us to Jorslem, but you know it is forbidden for us.'

'Certainly. I quite understand.' He was coolly polite, but the seething bitterness in him was close to the surface. Most Changelings are such degraded bestial things that they are incapable of knowing how detested they are by normal guilded men and women; but Bernalt clearly was gifted with the torment of comprehension. He smiled, and then he pointed. 'My friend is here.'

Three figures approached. One was Bernalt's Surgeon, a slender man, dark-skinned, soft-voiced, with weary eyes and sparse yellow hair. With him were an official of the invaders and another outworlder from a different planet 'I had heard that two Pilgrims were summoned to this place,' said the invader. 'I am grateful for the comfort you may have brought these sufferers. I am Earthclaim Nineteen; this district is under my administration. Will you be my guests at dinner this night?'

I was doubtful of taking an invader's hospitality, and Olmayne's sudden clenching of her fist over her starstone told me that she also hesitated. Earthclaim Nineteen seemed eager for our acceptance. He was not as tall as most of his kind, and his malproportioned arms reached below his knees. Under the blazing Aguptan sun his thick waxy skin acquired a high gloss, although he did not perspire.

Into a long, tense, and awkward silence the Surgeon inserted: 'No need to hold back. In this village we all are brothers. Join us tonight, will you?'

We did. Earthclaim Nineteen occupied a villa by the shore of Lake Medit; in the clear light of late afternoon I thought I could detect Land Bridge jutting forward to my left, and even Eyrop at the far side of the lake. We were waited upon by members of the guild of Servitors who brought us cool drinks on the patio. The invader had a large staff, all Earthborn; to me it was another sign that our conquest had become institutionalized and was wholly accepted by the bulk of the populace. Until long after dusk we talked, lingering over drinks even as the writhing auroras danced into view to herald the night. Bernalt the Changeling remained apart, though, perhaps ill at ease in our presence. Olmayne too was moody and withdrawn; a mingled depression and exaltation had settled over her in the stricken village, and the presence of Bernalt at the dinner party had reinforced her silence, for she had no idea how to be polite in the presence of a Changeling. The invader, our host, was charming and attentive, and tried to bring her forth from her bleakness. I had seen charming conquerors before. I had traveled with one who had posed as the Earthborn Changeling Gormon in the days just before the conquest. This one, Earthclaim Nineteen, had been a poet on his native world in those days. I said, 'It seems unlikely that one of your inclinations would care to be part of a military occupation.'

'All experiences strengthen the art,' said Earthclaim Nineteen. 'I seek to expand myself. In any case I am not a warrior but an administrator. Is it so strange that a poet can be an administrator, or an administrator a poet?' He laughed. 'Among your many guilds, there is no guild of Poets. Why?'

'There are Communicants,' I said. 'They serve your muse.'

'But in a religious way. They are interpreters of the Will, not of their own souls.'

'The two are indistinguishable. The verses they make are divinely inspired, but rise from the hearts of their makers,' I said.

Earthclaim Nineteen looked unconvinced. 'You may argue that all poetry is at bottom religious, I suppose. But this stuff of your Communicants is too limited in scope. It deals only with acquiescence to the Will.'

'A paradox,' said Olmayne. 'The Will encompasses everything, and yet you say that our Communicants' scope is limited.'

'There are other themes for poetry besides immersion in the Will, my friends. The love of person for person, the joy of defending one's home, the wonder of standing naked beneath the fiery stars—' The invader laughed. 'Can it be that Earth fell so swiftly because its only poets were poets of acquiescence to destiny?'

'Earth fell,' said the Surgeon, 'because the Will required us to atone for the sin our ancestors committed when they treated your ancestors like beasts. The quality of our poetry had nothing to do with it.'

'The Will decreed that you would lose to us by way of punishment, eh? But if the Will is omnipotent, it must have decreed the sin of your ancestors that made the punishment necessary. Eh? Eh? The Will playing games with itself. You see the difficulty of believing in a divine force that determines all events? Where is the element of choice that makes suffering meaningful? To force you into a sin, and then to require you to endure as atonement, seems to me an empty exercise. Forgive my blasphemy.'

The Surgeon said, 'You misunderstand. All that has happened on this planet is part of a process of moral instruction. The Will does not shape every event great or small; it provides the raw material of events, and allows us to follow such patterns as we desire.'

'Example?'

'The Will imbued the Earthborn with skills and knowledge. During the First Cycle we rose from savagery in little time; in the Second Cycle we attained greatness. In our moment of greatness we grew swollen with pride, choosing to exceed our limitations. We imprisoned intelligent creatures of other worlds under the pretense of "study," when we acted really out of an arrogant desire for amusement, and we toyed with our world's climate until oceans joined and continents sank and our old civilization was destroyed. Thus the Will instructed us in the boundaries of human ambition.'

'I dislike that dark philosophy even more,' said Earthclaim Nineteen. 'T—'

'Let me finish,' said the Surgeon. 'The collapse of Second Cycle Earth was our punishment. The defeat of Third Cycle Earth by you folk from the stars is a completion of that earlier punishment, but also the beginning of a new phase. You are the instruments of our redemption. By inflicting on us the final humiliation of conquest, you bring us to the bottom of our trough; now we renew our souls, now we begin to rise, tested by adversities.'

I stared in sudden amazement at this Surgeon, who was uttering ideas that been stirring in me all along the road to Jorslem, ideas of redemption both personal and planetary. I had paid little attention to the Surgeon before.

'Permit me a statement,' Bernalt said suddenly, his first words in hours.

We looked at him. The pigmented bands in his face were ablaze, marking his emotion.

He said, nodding to the Surgeon, 'My friend, you speak of redemption for the Earthborn. Do you mean all Earthborn, or only the guilded ones?'

'All Earthborn, of course,' said the Surgeon mildly. 'Are we not all equally conquered?'

'We are not equal in other things, though. Can there be redemption for a planet that keeps millions of its people thrust into guildlessness? I speak of my own folk, of course. We sinned long ago when we thought we were striking out against those who had created us as monsters. We strove to take Jorslem from you; and for this we were punished, and our punishment has lasted for a thousand years. We are still outcasts, are we not? Where has our hope of redemption been? Can you guilded ones consider yourself purified and made virtuous by your recent suffering, when you still step on us?'

The Surgeon looked dismayed. 'You speak rashly, Bernalt. I know that

Changelings have a grievance. But you know as well as I that the time of deliverance is at hand. In the days to come no Earthborn one will scorn you, and you will stand beside us when we regain our freedom.'

Bernalt peered at the floor. 'Forgive me, my friend. Of course, of course, you speak the truth. I was carried away. The heat – this splendid wine – how foolishly I spoke!'

Earthclaim Nineteen said, 'Are you telling me that a resistance movement is forming that will shortly drive us from your planet?'

'I speak only in abstract terms,' said the Surgeon.

'I think your resistance movement will be purely abstract too,' the invader replied easily. 'Forgive me, but I see little strength in a planet that could be conquered in a single night. We expect our occupation of Earth to be a long one and to meet little opposition. In the months that we have been here there has been no sign of increasing hostility to us. Quite the contrary: we are increasingly accepted among you.'

'It is part of a process,' said the Surgeon. 'As a poet, you should understand that words carry meanings of many kinds. We do not need to overthrow our alien masters in order to be free of them. Is that poetic enough for you?'

'Splendid,' said Earthclaim Nineteen, getting to his feet. 'Shall we go to dinner now?'

7

There was no way to return to the subject. A philosophical discussion at the dinner table is difficult to sustain; and our host did not seem comfortable with this analysis of Earth's destinies. Swiftly he discovered that Olmayne had been a Rememberer before turning Pilgrim, and thereafter directed his words to her, questioning her on our history and our early poetry. Like most invaders he had a fierce curiosity concerning our past. Olmayne gradually came out of the silence that gripped her, and spoke at length about her re-searches in Perris. She talked with great familiarity of our hidden past, with Earthclaim Nineteen occasionally inserting an intelligent and informed question; meanwhile we dined on delicacies of a number of worlds, perhaps imported by the same fat, insensitive Merchant who had driven us from Perris to Marsay; the villa was cool and the Servitors attentive; that miser-able plague-stricken peasant village half an hour's walk away might well have been in some other galaxy, so remote was it from our discourse now.

When we left the villa in the morning, the Surgeon asked permission to join our Pilgrimage. 'There is nothing further I can do here,' he explained. 'At the outbreak of the disease I came up from my home in Nayrub, and I've been here many days, more to console than to cure, of course. Now I am called to Jorslem. However, if it violates your vows to have company on the road—'

'By all means come with us,' I said.

'There will be one other companion,' the Surgeon told us.

He meant the third person who had met us at the village: the outworlder, an enigma, yet to say a word in our presence. This being was a flattened spike-shaped creature somewhat taller than a man and mounted on a jointed tripod of angular legs; it place of origin was in the Golden Spiral; its skin was rough and bright red in hue, and vertical rows of glassy oval eyes descended on three sides from the top of its tapered head. I had never seen such a creature before. It had come to Earth, according to the Surgeon, on a data-gathering mission, and had already roamed much of Ais and Stralya. Now it was touring the lands on the margin of Lake Medit; and after seeing Jorslem it would depart for the great cities of Eyrop. Solemn, unsettling in its perpetual watchfulness, never blinking its many eyes nor offering a comment on what those eyes beheld, it seemed more like some odd machine, some information-intake for a memory tank, than a living creature. But it was harmless enough to let it come with us to the holy city.

The Surgeon bade farewell to his Changeling friend, who went on alone ahead of us, and paid a final call on the crystallized village. We stayed back, since there was no point in our going. When he returned, his face was somber. 'Four new cases,' he said. 'This entire village will perish. There has never been an outbreak of this kind before on Earth – so concentrated an epidemic'

'Something new, then?' I asked. 'Will it spread everywhere?'

'Who knows? No one in the adjoining village has caught it. The pattern is unfamiliar: a single village wholly devastated and nowhere else besides; These people see it as divine retribution for unknown sins.'

'What could peasants have done,' I asked, 'that would bring the wrath of the Will so harshly upon them?'

'They are asking that too,' said the Surgeon.

Olmayne said, 'If there are new cases, our visit yesterday was useless. We risked ourselves and did them no good.'

'Wrong,' the Surgeon told her. 'These cases were already incubating when we arrived. We may hope that the disease will not spread to those who still were in full health.'

He did not seem confident of that.

Olmayne examined herself from day to day for symptoms of the disease, but none appeared. She gave the Surgeon much trouble on that score, bothering him for opinions concerning real or fancied blemishes of her skin, embarrassing him by removing her mask in his presence so that he could determine that some speck on her cheek was not the first trace of crystallization.

The Surgeon took all this in good grace, for, while the outworld being was merely a cipher plodding alongside us, the Surgeon was a man of depth, patience and sophistication. He was native to Afreek, and had been dedicated to his guild at birth by his father, since healing was the family tradition. Traveling widely, he had seen most of our world and had forgotten little of what he had seen. He spoke to us of Roum and Perris, of the frostflower fields of Stralya, of my own birthplace in the western island group of the Lost Continents. He questioned us tactfully about our starstones and the effects they produced – I could see he hungered to try the stone himself, but that of course was forbidden to one who had not declared himself a Pilgrim – and when he learned that in former life I had been a Watcher, he asked me a great deal concerning the instruments by which I had scanned the heavens, wishing to know what it was I perceived and how I imagined the perception was accomplished. I spoke to him as fully as I could on these matters, though in truth I knew little.

Usually we kept on the green strip of fertile land bordering the lake, but once, at the Surgeon's insistence, we detoured into the choking desert to see something that he promised would be of interest. He would not tell us what it was. We were at this point traveling in hired rollerwagons, open on top, and sharp winds blew gusts of sand in our faces. Sand adhered briefly to the outworlder's eyes, I saw; and I saw how efficiently it flushed each eye with a flood of blue tears every few moments. The rest of us huddled in our garments, heads down, whenever the wind arose.

'We are here,' the Surgeon announced finally. 'When I traveled with my father I first visited this place long ago. We will go inside – and then you, the former Rememberer, will tell us where we are.'

It was a building two stories high made of bricks of white glass. The doors appeared sealed, but they gave at the slightest pressure. Lights glowed into life the moment we entered.

In long aisles, lightly strewn with sand, were tables on which instruments were mounted. Nothing was comprehensible to me. There were devices shaped like hands, into which one's own hand could be inserted; conduits led from the strange metal gloves to shining closed cabinets, and arrangements of mirrors transmitted images from the interiors of those cabinets to giant screens overhead. The Surgeon placed his hands in the gloves and moved his fingers; the screens brightened, and I saw images of tiny needles moving through shallow arcs. He went to other machines and released dribbles of unknown fluids; he touched small buttons and produced musical sounds; he moved freely through a laboratory of wonders, clearly ancient, which seemed still in order and awaiting the return of its users.

Olmayne was ecstatic. She followed the Surgeon from aisle to aisle, handling everything.

'Well, Rememberer?' he asked finally. 'What is this?'

'A Surgery,' she said in lowered voice. 'A Surgery of the Years of Magic!'

'Exactly! Splendid!' He seemed in an oddly excited state. 'We could make dazzling monsters here! We could work miracles! Fliers, Swimmers, Changelings, Twiners, Burners, Climbers – invent your own guilds, shape men to your whims! This was the place!'

Olmayne said, 'These Surgeries have been described to me. There are six of them left, are there not, one in northern Eyrop, one on Palash, one here, one far to the south in Deeper Afreek, one in western Ais—' She faltered.

'And one in Hind, the greatest of all!' said the Surgeon.

'Yes, of course, Hind! The home of the Fliers!'

Their awe was contagious. I said, 'This was where the shapes of men were changed? How was it done?'

The Surgeon shrugged. 'The art is lost. The Years of Magic were long ago, old man.'

'Yes, yes, I know. But surely if the equipment survives, we could guess how—'

'With these knives,' said the Surgeon, 'we cut into the fabric of the unborn, editing the human seed. The Surgeon placed his hands here – he manipulated – and within that incubator the knives did their work. Out of this came Fliers and all the rest. The forms bred true. Some are extinct today, but our Fliers and our Changelings owe their heritage to some such building, as this. The Changelings, of course, were the Surgeons' mistakes. They should not have been permitted to live.'

'I thought that these monsters were the products of teratogenic drugs given to them when they still were within the womb,' I said. 'You tell me now that Changelings were made by Surgeons. Which is so?'

'Both,' he replied. 'All Changelings today are descended from the flaws and errors committed by the Surgeons of the Years of Magic. Yet mothers in that unhappy group often enhance the monstrousness of their children with drugs, so that they will be more marketable. It is an ugly tribe not merely in looks. Small wonder that their guild was dissolved and they were thrust outside society. We—'

Something bright flew through the air, missing his face by less than a hand's breadth. He dropped to the floor and shouted to us to take cover. As I fell I saw a second missile fly toward us. The outworld being, still observing all phenomena, studied it impassively in the moment of life that remained to it. Then the weapon struck two thirds of the way up the outworlder's body and severed it instantly. Other missiles followed, clattering against the wall behind us. I saw our attackers: a band of Changelings, fierce, hideous. We were unarmed. They moved toward us. I readied myself to die.

From the doorway a voice cried out: a familiar voice, using the thick and unfamiliar words of the language Changelings speak among themselves. Instantly the assault ceased. Those who menaced us turned toward the door. The Changeling Bernalt entered.

'I saw your vehicle,' he said. 'I thought you might be here, and perhaps in trouble. It seems I came in time.'

'Not altogether,' said the Surgeon. He indicated the fallen outworlder, which was beyond all aid. 'But why this attack?'

Bernalt gestured. '*They* will tell you.'

We looked at the five Changelings who had ambushed us. They were not of the educated, civilized sort such as Bernalt, nor were any two of them of the same styles; each was a twisted, hunched mockery of the human form, one with ropy tendrils descending from his chin, one with a face that was a featureless void, another whose ears were giant cups, and so forth. From the one closest to us, a creature with small platforms jutting from his skin in a thousand places, we learned why we had been assaulted. In a brutal Aguptan dialect he told us that we had profaned a temple sacred to Changelings. 'We keep out of Jorslem,' he told us. 'Why must you come here?'

Of course he was right. We asked forgiveness as sincerely as we could, and the Surgeon explained that he had visited this place long ago and it had not been a temple then. That seemed to soothe the Changeling, who admitted that only in recent years had his kind used it as a shrine. He was soothed even more when Olmayne opened the overpocket fastened between her breasts and offered a few glittering gold coins, part of the treasure she had brought with her from Perris. The bizarre and deformed beings were satisfied at that and allowed us to leave the building. We would have taken the dead outworlder with us, but during our parley with the Changelings the body had nearly vanished, nothing but a faint gray streak remaining on the sandy floor to tell us where it had fallen. 'A mortuary enzyme,' the Surgeon explained. 'Triggered by interruption of the life processes.'

Others of this community of desert-dwelling Changelings were lurking about outside the building as we came forth. They were a tribe of nightmares, with skin of every texture and color, facial features arranged at random, all kinds of genetic improvisations of organs and bodily accessories. Bernalt himself, although their brother, seemed appalled by their monstrousness. They looked at him with awe. At the sight of us some of them fondled the throwing weapons at their hips, but a sharp command from Bernalt prevented any trouble.

He said, 'I regret the treatment you received and the death of the outworlder. But of course it is risky to enter a place that is sacred to backward and violent people.'

'We had no idea,' the Surgeon said. 'We never would have gone in if we had realized—'

'Of course. Of course.' Was there something patronizing about Bernalt's soft, civilized tones? 'Well, again I bid you farewell.'

I blurted suddenly, 'No. Travel with us to Jorslem! It's ridiculous for us to go separately to the same place.'

Olmayne gasped. Even the Surgeon seemed amazed. Only Bernalt remained calm. He said, 'You forget, friend, that it is improper for Pilgrims to journey with the guildless. Besides, I am here to worship at this shrine, and it will take me a while. I would not wish to delay you.' His hand reached out to mine. Then he moved away, entering the ancient Surgery. Scores of his fellow Changelings rushed in after him. I was grateful to Bernalt for his tact; my impulsive offer of companionship, though sincerely meant, had been impossible for him to accept.

We boarded our rollerwagons. In a moment we heard a dreadful sound: a discordant Changeling hymn in praise of I dare not think what deity, a scraping, grinding, screeching song as misshapen as those who uttered it.

'The beasts,' Olmayne muttered. 'A sacred shrine! A Changeling temple! How loathsome! They might have killed us all, Tomis. How can such monsters have a religion?'

I made no reply. The Surgeon looked at Olmayne sadly and shook his head as though distressed by so little charity on the part of one who claimed to be a Pilgrim.

'They also are human,' he said.

At the next town along our route we reported the star-born being's death to the occupying authorities. Then, saddened and silent, we three survivors continued onward to the place where the coastline trends north rather than east. We were leaving sleepy Agupt behind and entering now into the borders of the land in which holy Jorslem lies.

8

The city of Jorslem sits some good distance inland from Lake Medit on a cool plateau guarded by a ring of low, barren, rock-strewn mountains. All my life, it seemed, had been but a preparation for my first glimpse of this golden city, whose image I knew so well. Hence when I saw its spires and parapets rising in the east, I felt not so much awe as a sense of homecoming.

A winding road took us down through the encircling hills to the city, whose wall was made of squared blocks of a fine stone, dark pink-gold in color. The houses and shrines, too, were of this stone. Groves of trees bordered the road, nor were they star-trees, but native products of Earth, as was fitting to this, the oldest of man's cities, older than Roum, older than Perris, its roots deep in the First Cycle,

The invaders, shrewdly, had not meddled with Jorslem's administration. The city remained under the governorship of the Guildmaster of Pilgrims, and even an invader was required to seek the Guildmaster's permission to enter. Of course, this was strictly a matter of form; the Pilgrim Guildmaster, like the Chancellor of the Rememberers and other such officials, was in truth a puppet subject to our conqueror's wishes. But that harsh fact was kept concealed. The invaders had left our holy city as a city apart, and we would not see them swaggering in armed teams through Jorslem's streets.

At the outer wall we formally requested entry from the Sentinel guarding the gate. Though elsewhere most Sentinels were now unemployed – since cities stood open by command of our masters – this man was in full guild array and calmly insisted on thorough procedure. Olmayne and I, as Pilgrims, were entitled to automatic access to Jorslem; yet he made us produce our starstones as evidence that we came by our robes and masks honestly, and then donned a thinking cap to check our names with the archives of our guild. In time we met approval. The Surgeon, our companion, had an easier time; he had applied in advance for entry while in Afreek, and after a moment to check his identity he was admitted.

Within the walls everything had the aspect of great antiquity. Jorslem alone of the world's cities still preserves much of its First Cycle architecture: not merely broken columns and ruined aqueducts, as in Roum, but whole streets, covered arcades, towers, boulevards, that have lasted through every upheaval our world has seen. And so once we passed into the city we wandered in wonder through its strangeness, down streets paved with cobbled stones, into narrow alleys cluttered with children and beggars, across markets fragrant with spices. After an hour of this we felt it was time to seek lodgings, and here it was necessary for us to part company with the Surgeon, since he was ineligible to stay at a Pilgrim hostelry, and it would have been costly and foolish for us to stay anywhere else. We saw him to the inn where he had previously booked a room. I thanked him for his good companionship on our journey, and he thanked us just as gravely and expressed the hope that he would see us again in Jorslem in the days to come. Then Olmayne and I took leave of him and rented quarters in one of the numerous places catering to the Pilgrim trade.

The city exists solely to serve Pilgrims and casual tourists, and so it is really one vast hostelry; robed Pilgrims are as common in Jorslem's streets as Fliers in Hind. We settled and rested awhile; then we dined and afterward walked along a broad street from which we could see, to the east, Jorslem's inner and most sacred district. There is a city within a city here. The most ancient part, so small it can be traversed in less than an hour on foot, is wrapped in a high wall of its own. Therein lie shrines revered by Earth's former religions: the Christers, the Hebers, the Mislams. The place where the god of the Christers died is said to be there, but this may be a distortion wrought by time, since what kind of god is it that dies? On a high place in one corner of the Old City stands a gilded dome sacred to the Mislams, which is carefully tended by the common folk of Jorslem. And to the fore part of that high place are the huge gray blocks of a stone wall worshipped by the Hebers. These things remain, but the ideas behind them are lost; never while I was among the Rememberers did I meet any scholar who could explain the merit of worshipping a wall or a gilded dome. Yet the old records assure us that these three First Cycle creeds were of great depth and richness.

In the Old City, also, is a Second Cycle place that was of much more immediate interest to Olmayne and myself. As we stared through the darkness at the holy precincts Olmayne said, 'We should make application tomorrow at the house of renewal.'

'I agree. I long now to give up some of my years.'

'Will they accept me, Tomis?'

'Speculating on it is idle,' I told her. 'We will go, and we will apply, and your question will be answered.'

She said something further, but I did not hear her words, for at that moment three Fliers passed above me, heading east. One was male, two female; they flew naked, according to the custom of their guild; and the Flier in the center of the group was a slim, fragile girl, mere bones and wings, moving with a grace that was exceptional even for her airy kind.

'*Avluela!*' I gasped.

The trio of Fliers disappeared beyond the parapets of the Old City. Stunned, shaken, I clung to a tree for support and struggled for breath.

'Tomis?' Olmayne said. 'Tomis, are you ill?'

'I know it was Avluela. They said she had gone back to Hind, but no, that was Avluela! How could I mistake her?'

'You've said that about every Flier you've seen since leaving Perris,' said Olmayne coldly.

'But this time I'm certain! Where is a thinking cap? I must check with the Fliers' Lodge at once!'

Olmayne's hand rested on my arm. 'It's late, Tomis. You act feverish. Why this excitement over your skinny Flier, anyway? What did she mean to you?'

'She—'

I halted, unable to put my meaning in words. Olmayne knew the story of my journey up out of Agupt with the girl, how as a celibate old Watcher I had conceived a kind of parental fondness for her, how I had perhaps felt something more powerful than that, how I had lost her to the false Changeling Gormon, and how *he* in turn had lost her to the Prince of Roum. But yet what was Avluela to me? Why did a glimpse of someone who merely might have been Avluela send me into this paroxysm of confusion? I chased symbols in my turbulent mind and found no answers.

'Come back to the inn and rest,' Olmayne said. 'Tomorrow we must seek renewal.'

First, though, I donned a cap and made contact with the Fliers' Lodge. My thoughts slipped through the shielding interface to the storage brain of the guild registry; I asked and received the answer I had sought. Avluela of the Fliers was indeed now a resident in Jorslem. 'Take this message for her,' I said. 'The Watcher she knew in Roum now is here as a Pilgrim, and wishes to meet her outside the house of renewal at midday tomorrow.'

With that done, I accompanied Olmayne to our lodgings. She seemed sullen and aloof; and when she unmasked in my room her face appeared rigid with – jealousy? Yes. To Olmayne all men were vassals, even one so shriveled and worn as I; and she loathed it that another woman could kindle such a flame in me. When I drew forth my starstone, Olmayne at first would not join me in communion. Only when I began the rituals did she submit. But I was so tense that night I was unable to make the merging with the Will, nor could she achieve it; and thus we faced one another glumly for half an hour, and abandoned the attempt, and parted for the night.

9

One must go by one's self to the house of renewal. At dawn I awoke, made a brief and more successful communion, and set out unbreakfasted, without Olmayne. In half an hour I stood before the golden wall of the Old City; in half an hour more I had finished my crossing of the inner city's tangled lanes. Passing before that gray wall so dear to the ancient Hebers, I went up onto the high place; I passed near the gilded dome of the vanished Mislams and, turning to the left, followed the stream of Pilgrims which already at this early hour was proceeding to the house of renewal.

This house is a Second Cycle building, for it was then that the renewal process was conceived; and of all that era's science, only renewal has come down to us approximately as it must have been practiced in that time. Like those other few Second Cycle structures that survive, the house of renewal is supple and sleek, architecturally understated, with deft curves and smooth textures; it is without windows; it bears no external ornament whatever. There are many doors. I placed myself before the easternmost entrance, and in an hour's time I was admitted.

Just inside the entrance I was greeted by a green-robed member of the guild of Renewers – the first member of this guild I had ever seen. Renewers are recruited entirely from Pilgrims who are willing to make it their life's work to remain in Jorslem and aid others toward renewal. Their guild is under the same administration as the Pilgrims; a single guildmaster directs the destinies of both; even the garb is the same except for color. In effect Pilgrims and Renewers are of one guild and represent different phases of the same affiliation. But a distinction is always drawn.

The Renewer's voice was light and cheerful. 'Welcome to this house, Pilgrim. Who are you, where are you from?'

'I am the Pilgrim Tomis, formerly Tomis of the Rememberers, and prior to that a Watcher, born to the name Wuellig. I am native to the Lost Continents and have traveled widely both before and after beginning my Pilgrimage.'

'What do you seek here?'

'Renewal. Redemption.'

'May the Will grant your wishes,' said the Renewer. 'Come with me.'

I was led through a close, dimly lit passage into a small stone cell. The Renewer instructed me to remove my mask, enter into a state of communion, and wait. I freed myself from the bronze grillwork and clasped my starstone tightly. The familiar sensations of communion stole over me, but no union with the Will took place; rather, I felt a specific link forming with the mind of another human being. Although mystified, I offered no resistance.

Something probed my soul. Everything was drawn forth and laid out as if for inspection on the floor of the cell: my acts of selfishness and of cowardice, my flaws and failings, my doubts, my despairs, above all the most shameful of my acts, the selling of the Rememberers' document to the invader overlord. I beheld these things and knew that I was unworthy of renewal. In this house one might extend one's lifetime two or three times over; but why should the Renewers offer such benefits to anyone as lacking in merit as I?

I remained a long while in contemplation of my faults. Then the contact broke, and a different Renewer, a man of remarkable stature, entered the cell.

'The mercy of the Will is upon you, friend,' he said, reaching forth fingers of extraordinary length to touch the tips of mine.

When I heard that deep voice and saw those white fingers, I knew that I was in the presence of a man I had met briefly before, as I stood outside the gates of Roum in the season before the conquest of Earth. He had been a Pilgrim then, and he had invited me to join him on his journey to Jorslem, but I had declined, for Roum had beckoned to me.

'Was your Pilgrimage an easy one?' I asked.

'It was a valuable one,' he replied. 'And you? You are a Watcher no longer, I see.'

'I am in my third guild this year.'

'With one more yet to come,' he said.

'Am I to join you in the Renewers, then?'

'I did not mean that guild, friend Tomis. But we can talk more of that when your years are fewer. You have been approved for renewal, I rejoice to tell you.'

'Despite my sins?'

'Because of your sins, such that they are. At dawn tomorrow you enter the first of the renewal tanks. I will be your guide through your second birth. I am the Renewer Talmit. Go, now, and ask for me when you return.'

'One question—'

'Yes?'

'I made my Pilgrimage together with a woman, Olmayne, formerly a Re-memberer of Perris. Can you tell me if she has been approved for renewal as well?'

'I know nothing of this Olmayne.'

'She's not a good woman,' I said. 'She is vain, imperious, and cruel. But yet I think she is not beyond saving. Can you do anything to help her?'

'I have no influence in such things,' Talmit said. 'She must face interrogation like everyone else. I can tell you this, though: virtue is not the only criterion for renewal.'

He showed me from the building. Cold sunlight illuminated the city. I was drained and depleted, too empty even to feel cheered that I had qualified for renewal. It was midday; I remembered my appointment with Avluela; I circled the house of renewal in rising anxiety. Would she come?

She was waiting by the front of the building, beside a glittering monument from Second Cycle days. Crimson jacket, furry leggings, glass bubbles on her feet, telltale humps on her back: from afar I could make her out to be a Flier. 'Avluela!' I called.

She whirled. She looked pale, thin, even younger than when I had last seen her. Her eyes searched my face, once again masked, and for a moment she was bewildered.

'Watcher?' she said. 'Watcher, is, that you?'

'Call me Tomis now,' I told her. 'But I am the same man you knew in Agupt and Roum.'

'Watcher! Oh, Watcher! *Tomis.*' She clung to me. 'How long it's been! So much has happened!' She sparkled now, and, the paleness fled her cheeks. 'Come, let's find an inn, a place to sit and talk! How did you discover me here?'

'Through your guild. I saw you overhead last night.'

'I came here in the winter. I was in Pars for a while, halfway back to Hind, and then I changed my mind. There could be no going home. Now I live near Jorslem and I help with—' She cut her sentence sharply off. 'Have you won renewal, Tomis?'

We descended from the high place into a humbler part of the inner city. 'Yes,' I said, 'I am to be made younger. My guide is the Renewer Talmit – we met him as a Pilgrim outside Roum, do you remember?'

She had forgotten that. We seated ourselves at an open-air patio adjoining an inn, and Servitors brought us food and wine. Her gaiety was infectious; I felt renewed just to be with her. She spoke of those final cataclysmic days in Roum, when she had been taken into the palace of the Prince as a concubine; and she told me of that terrible moment when Gormon the Changeling defeated the Prince of Roum on the evening of the conquest – announcing himself as no Changeling but an invader in disguise, and taking from the Prince at once his throne, his concubine, and his vision.

'Did the Prince die?' she asked.

'Yes, but not of his blinding.' I told her how that proud man had fled Roum disguised as a Pilgrim, and how I had accompanied him to Perris, and how, while we were among the Rememberers, he had involved himself with Olmayne, and had been slain by Olmayne's husband, whose life was there upon taken by his wife. 'I also saw Gormon in Perris,' I said. 'He goes by the name of Victorious Thirteen now. He is high in the councils of the invaders.'

Avluela smiled. 'Gormon and I were together only a short while after the conquest. He wanted to tour Eyrop; I flew with him to Donsk and Sved, and there he lost interest in me. It was then that I felt I must go home to Hind, but later I changed my mind. When does your renewal begin?'

'At dawn.'

'Oh, Tomis, how will it be when you are a young man? Did you know that I loved you? All the time we traveled, all while I was sharing Gormon's bed and consorting with the Prince, you were the one I wanted! But of course you were a Watcher, and it was impossible. Besides, you were so old. Now you no longer Watch, and soon you will no longer be old, and—' Her hand rested on mine. 'I should never have left your side. We both would have been spared much suffering.'

'We learn, from suffering,' I said.

'Yes. Yes. I see that. How long will your renewal take?'

'The usual time, whatever that may be.'

'After that, what will you do? What guild will you choose? You can't be a Watcher, not now.'

'No, nor a Rememberer either. My guide Talmit spoke of some other guild, which he would not name, and assumed that I would enroll in it when I was done with renewal. I supposed he thought I'd stay here and join the Renewers, but he said it was another guild.'

'Not the Renewers,' said Avluela. She leaned close. 'The Redeemers,' she whispered.

'Redeemers? That is a guild I do not know.'

'It is newly founded.'

'No new guild has been established in more than a—'

'This is the guild Talmit meant. You would be a desirable member. The skills you developed when you were a Watcher make you exceptionally useful.'

'Redeemers,' I said, probing the mystery. '*Redeemers*. What does this guild do?'

Avluela smiled jauntily. 'It rescues troubled souls and saves unhappy worlds. But this is no time to talk of it. Finish your business in Jorslem, and everything will become clear.' We rose. Her lips brushed mine. 'This is the last time I'll see you as an old man. It will be strange, Tomis, when you're renewed!'

She left me then.

Toward evening I returned I to my lodging. Olmayne was not in her room. A Servitor told me that she had been out all day. I waited until it was late; then I made my communion and slept, and at dawn I paused outside her door. It was sealed. I hurried to the house of renewal.

10

The renewer Talmit met me within the entrance and conducted me down a corridor of green tile to the first renewal tank. 'The Pilgrim Olmayne,' he informed me, 'has been accepted for renewal and will come here later this day.' This was the last reference to the affairs of another human being that I was to hear for some time. Talmit showed me into a small low room, close and humid, lit by dim blobs of slavelight and smelling faintly of crushed deathflower blossoms. My robe and my mask were taken from me, and the Renewer covered my head with a fine golden-green mesh of some flimsy metal, through which he sent a current; and when he removed the mesh, my hair was gone, my head was as glossy as the tiled walls. 'It makes insertion of the electrodes simpler,' Talmit explained. 'You may enter the tank, now.'

A gentle ramp led me down into the tank, which was a tub of no great size. I felt the warm soft slipperiness of mud beneath my feet, and Talmit nodded and told me it irradiated regenerative mud, which would stimulate the increase of cell division that was to bring about my renewal, and I accepted it. I stretched out on the floor of the tank with only my head above the shimmering dark violet fluid that it contained. The mud cradled and caressed my tired body. Talmit loomed above me, holding what seemed to be a mass of entangled copper wires, but as he pressed the wires to my bare scalp they opened as of their own accord and their tips sought my skull and burrowed down through skin and bone into the hidden wrinkled grayness. I felt nothing more than tiny prickling sensations. 'The electrodes,' Talmit explained, 'seek out the centers of aging within your brain; we transmit signals that will induce a reversal of the normal processes of decay, and your brain will lose its perception of the direction of the flow of time. Your body thus will become more receptive to the stimulation it receives from the environment of the renewal tank. Close your eyes.' Over my face he placed a breathing mask. He gave me a gentle shove, and the back of my head slipped from the edge of the tank, so that I floated out into the middle. The warmth increased. I dimly heard bubbling sounds. I imagined black sulfurous bubbles coming up from the mud and through the fluid in which I floated; I imagined that the fluid had turned the color of mud. Adrift in a tideless sea I lay, distantly aware that a current was passing over the electrodes, that something was tickling my brain, that I was engulfed in mud and in what could well have been an amniotic fluid. From far away came the deep voice of the Renewer Talmit summoning me to youth, drawing me back across the decades, unreeling time for me. There was a taste of salt in my mouth. Again I was crossing Earth Ocean, beset by pirates, defending my Watching equipment against their jeers and thrusts. Again I stood beneath the hot Aguptan sun meeting Avluela for the first time. I lived once more on Palash. I returned to the place of my birth in the western isles of the Lost Continents, in what formerly had been Usa-amrik. I watched Roum fall a second time. Fragments of memories swam through my softening brain. There was no sequence, no rational unrolling of events. I was a child. I was a weary ancient. I was among the Rememberers. I visited the Somnambulists. I saw the Prince of Roum attempt to purchase eyes from an Artificer in Dijon. I bargained with the Procurator of Perris. I gripped the handles of my instruments and entered Watchfulness. I ate sweet things from a far-off world; I drew into my nostrils the perfume of springtime on Palash; I shivered in an old man's private winter; I swam in a surging sea, buoyant and happy;

I sang; I wept; I resisted temptation; I yielded to temptations; I quarreled with Olmayne; I embraced Avluela; I experienced a flickering succession of nights and days as my biological clock moved in strange rhythms of reversal and acceleration. Illusions beset me. It rained fire from the sky; time rushed in several directions; I grew small and then enormous. I heard voices speaking in shades of scarlet and turquoise. Jagged music sparkled on the mountains. The sound of my drumming heartbeats was rough and fiery. I was trapped between strokes of my brain-piston, arms pressed to my sides so that I would occupy as little space as possible as it rammed itself home again and again and again. The stars throbbed, contracted, melted. Avluela said gently, 'We earn a second youth time through the indulgent, benevolent impulses of the Will and through the performance of individual good works.' Olmayne said, 'How sleek I get!' Talmit said, 'These oscillations of perception signify only the dissolution of the wish toward self-destruction that lies at the heart of the aging process.' Gormon said, 'These perceptions of oscillation signify only the self-destruction of the wish toward dissolution that lies at the aging process of the heart.' The Procurator Manrule Seven said, 'We have been sent to this world as the devices of your purgation. We are instruments of the Will.' Earthclaim Nineteen said, 'On the other hand, permit me to disagree. The intersection of Earth's destinies and ours is purely accidental.' My eyelids turned to stone. The small creatures comprising my lungs began to flower. My skin sloughed off, revealing strands of muscle clinging to bone. Olmayne said, 'My pores grow smaller. My flesh grows tight. My breasts grow small.' Avluela said, 'Afterwards you will fly with us, Tomis.' The Prince of Roum covered his eyes with his hands. The towers of Roum swayed in the winds of the sun. I snatched a shawl from a passing Rememberer. Clowns wept in the streets of Perris. Talmit said, 'Awaken, now, Tomis, come up from it, open your eyes.'

'I am young again,' I said.

'Your renewal has only begun,' he said.

I could no longer move. Attendants seized me and swathed me in porous wrappings, and placed me on a rolling car, and took me to a second tank, much larger, in which dozens of people floated, each in a dreamy seclusion from the others. Their naked skulls were festooned with electrodes; their eyes were covered with pink tape; their hands were peacefully joined on their chests. Into this tank I went, and there were no illusions here, only a long slumber unbroken by dreams. This time I awakened to the sounds of a rushing tide, and found myself passing feet first through a constricted conduit into a sealed tank, where I breathed only fluid, and where I remained something more than a minute and something less than a century, while layers of skin were peeling from my soul. It was slow, taxing work. The Surgeons worked at a distance, their hands thrust into gloves that controlled the tiny flaying-knives, and they flensed me of evil with flick after flick after flick of the little blades, cutting out guilt and sorrow, jealousy and rage, greed, lust, and impatience.

When they were done with me they opened the lid of the tank and lifted me out. I was unable to stand unaided. They attached instruments to my limbs that kneaded and massaged my muscles, restoring the tone. I walked again. I looked down at my bare body, strong and taut-fleshed and vigorous. Talmit came to me and threw a handful of mirror-dust into the air so that I could see myself; and as the tiny particles cohered, I peered at my gleaming reflection.

'No,' I said. 'You have the face wrong. I didn't look like that. The nose was sharper – the lips weren't so full – the hair not such a deep black—'

'We have worked from the records of the guild of Watchers, Tomis. You are more exactly a replica of your early self than your own memory realizes.'

'Can that be?'

'If you prefer, we can shape you to fit your self-conceptions and not reality. But, it would be a frivolous thing to do, and it would take much time.'

'No,' I said. 'It hardly matters.'

He agreed. He informed me that I would have to remain in the house of renewal a while longer, until I was fully adapted to my new self. I was given the neutral clothes of a guildless one to wear, for I was without affiliation now; my status as Pilgrim had ended with my renewal, and I might now opt for any guild that would admit me once I left the house. 'How long did my renewal last?' I asked Talmit as I dressed. He replied, 'You came here in summer. Now it is winter. We do not work swiftly.'

'And how fares my companion Olmayne?'

'We failed with her.'

'I don't understand.'

'Would you like to see her?' Talmit asked.

'Yes,' I said, thinking that he would bring me to Olmayne's tank. I stood on a ramp looking down into a sealed container; Talmit indicated a fiber telescope, and I peered into its staring eye and beheld Olmayne. Or rather, what I was asked to believe was Olmayne. A naked girl-child of about eleven, smooth-skinned and breastless, lay curled up in the tank, knees drawn close to the flat chest, thumb thrust in mouth. At first I did not understand. Then the child stirred, and I recognized the embryonic features of the regal Olmayne I had known: the wide mouth, the strong chin, the sharp, strong cheekbones. A dull shock of horror rippled through me, and I said to Talmit, 'What is this?'

'When the soul is too badly stained, Tomis, we must dig deep to cleanse it. Your Olmayne was a difficult case. We should not have attempted her; but she was insistent, and there were some indications that we might succeed with her. Those indications were in error, as you can see.'

'But what happened to her?'

'The renewal entered the irreversible stage before we could achieve a purging of her poisons,' Talmit said.

'You went too far? You made her too young?'

'As you can see. Yes.'

'What will you do? Why don't you get her out of there and let her grow up again?'

'You should listen more carefully, Tomis. I said the renewal is irreversible.'

'Irreversible?'

'She is lost in childhood's dreams. Each day she grows years younger. The inner clock whirls uncontrollably. Her body shrinks; her brain grows smooth. She enters babyhood shortly. She will never awaken.'

'And at the end—' I looked away. 'What then? A sperm and an egg, separating in the tank?'

'The retrogression will not go that far. She will die in infancy. Many are lost this way.'

'She spoke of the risks of renewal,' I said.

'Yet she insisted on our taking her. Her soul was dark, Tomis. She lived only for herself. She came to Jorslem to be cleansed, and now she has been cleansed, and she is at peace with the Will. Did you love her?'

'Never. Not for an instant.'

'Then what have you lost?'

'A segment of my past, perhaps.' I put my eye to the telescope again and beheld Olmayne, innocent now, restored to virginity, sexless, cleansed. At peace with the Will. I searched her oddly altered yet familiar face for an insight into her dreams. Had she known what was befalling her, as she tumbled helplessly into youthfulness? Had she cried out in anguish and frustration when she felt her life slipping away? Had there been a final flare of the old imperious Olmayne before she sank into this unwanted purity? The child in the tank was smiling. The supple little body uncoiled, then drew more tightly into a huddled ball. Olmayne was at peace with the Will. Suddenly, as though Talmit had spread another mirror in the air, I looked into my own new self, and saw what had been done for me, and knew that I had been granted another life with the proviso that I make something more of it than I had of my first one, and I felt humbled, and pledged myself to serve the Will, and I was engulfed in joy that came in mighty waves, like the surging tides of Earth Ocean, and I said farewell to Olmayne, and asked Talmit to take me to another place.

11

And Avluela came to me in my room in the house of renewal, and we both were frightened when we met. The jacket she wore left her bunched-up wings bare; they seemed hardly under her control at all, but fluttered nervously, starting to open a short way, their gossamer tips expanding in little quivering flickers. Her eyes were large and solemn; her face looked more lean and pointed than ever. We stared in silence at one another a long while; my skin grew warm, my vision hazy; I felt the churning of inner forces that had not pulled at me in decades, and I feared them even as I welcomed them.

'Tomis?' she said finally, and I nodded.

She touched my shoulders, my arms, my lips. And I put my fingers to her wrists, her flanks, and then, hesitantly, to the shallow bowls of her breasts. Like two who had lost their sight we learned each other by touch. We were strangers. That withered old Watcher she had known and perhaps loved had gone, banished for the next fifty years or more, and in his place stood someone mysteriously transformed, unknown, unmet. The old Watcher had been a sort of father to her; what was this guildless young Tomis supposed to be? And what was she to me, a daughter no longer? I did not know myself of myself. I was alien to my sleek, taut skin. I was perplexed and delighted by the juices that now flowed, by the throbbings and swellings that I had nearly forgotten.

'Your eyes are the same,' she said. 'I would always know you by your eyes.'

'What have you done these many months, Avluela?'

'I have been flying every night. I flew to Agupt and deep into Afreek. Then I returned and flew to Stanbool. When it gets dark, I go aloft. Do you know, Tomis, I feel truly alive only when I'm up there?'

'You are of the Fliers. It is in the nature of your guild to feel that way.'

'One day we'll fly side by side, Tomis.'

I laughed at that. 'The old Surgeries are closed, Avluela. They work wonders here, but they can't transform me into a Flier. One must be born with wings.'

'One doesn't need wings to fly.'

'I know. The invaders lift themselves without the help of wings. I saw you, one day soon after Roum fell – you and Gormon in the sky together—' I shook my head. 'But I am no invader either.'

'You will fly with me, Tomis. We'll go aloft, and not only by night, even though my wings are merely nightwings. In bright sunlight we'll soar together.'

Her fantasy pleased me. I gathered her into my arms, and she was cool and fragile against me, and my own body pulsed with new heat. For a while we talked no more of flying, though I drew back from taking what she offered at that moment, and was content merely to caress her. One does not awaken in a single lunge.

Later we walked through the corridors, passing others who were newly renewed, and we went into the great central room whose ceiling admitted the winter sunlight, and studied each other by that changing pale light, and walked, and talked again. I leaned a bit on her arm, for I did not have all my strength yet, and so in a sense it was as it had been for us in the past, the girl helping the old dodderer along. When she saw me back to my room, I said, 'Before I was renewed, you told me of a new guild of Redeemers. I—'

'There is time for that later,' she said, displeased.

In my room we embraced, and abruptly I felt the full fire of the renewed leap up within me, so that I feared I might consume her cool slim body. But it is a fire that does not consume – it only kindles its counterpart in others. In her ecstasy her wings unfolded until I was wrapped in their silken softness. And as I gave myself to the violence of joy, I knew I would not need again to lean on her arm.

We ceased to be strangers; we ceased to feel fear with one another. She came to me each day at my exercise time, and I walked with her, matching her stride for stride. And the fire burned even higher and more brightly for us.

Talmit was with me frequently too. He showed me the arts of using my renewed body, and helped me successfully grow youthful. I declined his invitation to view Olmayne once more. One day he told me that her retrogression had come to its end. I felt no sorrow over that, just a curious brief emptiness that soon passed.

'You will leave here soon,' the Renewer said. 'Are you ready?'

'I think so.'

'Have you given much thought to your destination after this house?'

'I must seek a new guild, I know.'

'Many guilds would have you, Tomis. But which do you want?'

'The guild in which I would be most useful to mankind,' I said. 'I owe the Will a life.'

Talmit said, 'Has the Flier girl spoken to you of the possibilities before you?'

'She mentioned a newly founded guild.'

'Did she give it a name?'

'The guild of Redeemers.'

'What do you know of it?'

'Very little,' I said.

'Do you wish to know more?'

'If there is more to know.'

'I am of the guild of Redeemers,' Talmit said. 'So is the Flier Avluela.'

'You both are already guilded! How can you belong to more than one guild? Only the Dominators were permitted such freedom; and they—'

'Tomis, the guild of Redeemers accepts members from all other guilds. It is the supreme guild, as the guild of Dominators once was. In its ranks are Rememberers and Scribes, Indexers, Servitors, Fliers, Landholders, Somnambulists, Surgeons, Clowns, Merchants, Vendors. There are Changelings as well, and—'

'Changelings?' I gasped. 'They are outside all guilds, by law! How can a guild embrace Changelings?'

'This is the guild of Redeemers. Even Changelings may win redemption, Tomis.'

Chastened, I said, 'Even Changelings, yes. But how strange it is to think of such a guild!'

'Would you despise a guild that embraces Changelings?'

'I find this guild difficult to comprehend.'

'Understanding will come at the proper time.'

'When is the proper time?'

'The day you leave this place,' said Talmit.

That day arrived shortly. Avluela came to fetch me. I stepped forth uncertainly into Jorslem's springtime to complete the ritual of renewal. Talmit had instructed her on how to guide me. She took me through the city to the holy places, so that I could worship at each of the shrines. I knelt at the wall of the Hebers and at the gilded dome of the Mislams; then I went down into the lower part of the city, through the marketplace, to the gray, dark, ill-fashioned building covering the place where the god of the Christers is said to have died; then I went to the spring of knowledge and the fountain of the Will, and from there to the guild-house of the guild of Pilgrims to surrender my mask and robes and starstone, and thence to the wall of the Old City. At each of these places I offered myself to the Will with words I had waited long to speak. Pilgrims and ordinary citizens of Jorslem gathered at a respectful distance; they knew that I had been lately renewed and hoped that some emanation from my new youthful body would bring them good fortune. At last my obligations were fulfilled. I was a free man in full health, able now to choose the quality of the life I wished to lead.

Avluela said, 'Will you come with me to the Redeemers now?'

'Where will we find them? In Jorslem?'

'In Jorslem, yes. A meeting will convene in an hour's time for the purpose of welcoming you into membership.'

From her tunic she drew something small and gleaming, which I recognized in bewilderment as a starstone. 'What are you doing with that?' I asked. 'Only Pilgrims—'

'Put your hand over mine,' she said, extending a fist in which the starstone was clenched.

I obeyed. Her small pinched face grew rigid with concentration for a moment. Then she relaxed. She put the starstone away.

'Avluela, what—?'

'A signal to the guild,' she said gently. 'A notice to them to gather now that you are on your way.'

'How did you get that stone?'

'Come with me,' she said. 'Oh, Tomis, if only we could fly there! But it is not far. We meet almost in the shadow of the house of renewal. Come, Tomis. Come!'

12

There was no light in the room. Avluela led me into the subterranean blackness, and told me that I had reached the guildhall of the Redeemers, and left me standing by myself. 'Don't move,' she cautioned.

I sensed the presence of others in the room about me. But I heard nothing and saw nothing.

Something was thrust toward me.

Avluela said, 'Put out your hands. What do you feel?'

I touched a small square cabinet resting, perhaps, on a metal framework. Along its face were familiar dials and levers. My groping hands found handles rising from the cabinet's upper surface. At once it was as though all my renewal had been undone, and the conquest of Earth canceled as well: I was a Watcher again, for surely this was a Watcher's equipment!

I said, 'It is not the same cabinet I once had. But it is not greatly different.'

'Have you forgotten your skills, Tomis?'

'I think they remain with me even now.'

'Use the machine, then,' said Avluela. 'Do your Watching once more, and tell me what you see.'

Easily and happily I slipped into the old attitudes. I performed the preliminary rituals quickly, clearing my mind of doubts and frictions. It was surprisingly simple to bring myself into a spirit of Watchfulness; I had not attempted it since the night Earth fell, and yet it seemed to me that I was able to enter the state more rapidly than in the old days.

Now I grasped the handles. How strange they were! They did not terminate in the grips to which I was accustomed: rather, something cool and hard was mounted at the tip of each handle. A gem of some kind, perhaps. Possibly even a starstone, I realized. My hands closed over the twin coolnesses. I felt a moment of apprehension, even of raw fear. Then I regained the necessary tranquillity, and my soul flooded into the device before me, and I began to Watch.

In my Watchfulness I did not soar to the stars, as I had in the old days. Although I perceived, my perception was limited to the immediate surroundings of my room. Eyes closed, body hunched in trance, I reached out and came first to Avluela; she was near me, almost upon me. I saw her plainly. She smiled; she nodded; her eyes were aglow.

—I love you.

—Yes, Tomis. And we will be together always.

—I have never felt so close to another person.

—In this guild we are all close, all the time. We are the Redeemers, Tomis. We are new. Nothing like this has been on Earth before.

—How am I speaking to you, Avluela?

—Your mind speaks to mine through the machine. And some day the machine will not be needed.

—And then we will fly together?

—Long before then, Tomis.

The starstones grew warm in my hands. I clearly perceived the instrument, now: a Watcher's cabinet, but with certain modifications, among them the starstones mounted on the handles. And I looked beyond Avluela and saw other faces, ones that I knew. The austere figure of the Renewer Talmit was to my left. Beside him stood the Surgeon with whom I had journey to Jorslem, with the Changeling Bernalt at his elbow, and now at last I knew what business it was that had brought these men of Nayrub to the holy city. The others I did not recognize; but there were two Fliers, and a Rememberer grasping his shawl, and a woman Servitor, and others. And I saw them all by an inner light for the room was as dark as it had been when I entered it. Not only did I see them, but I touched them, mind to mind.

The mind I touched first was Bernalt's. I met it easily though fearfully, drew back, met it again. He greeted me and welcomed me. I realized then, that only if I could look upon a Changeling as my brother could I, and Earth itself, win the sought-for redemption. For until we were truly one people, how could we earn an end to our punishment?

I tried to enter Bernalt's mind but I was afraid. How could I hide those prejudices, those petty contempts, those conditioned reflexes with which we unavoidably think of Changelings?

'Hide nothing,' he counseled. 'Those things are no secret to me. Give them up now and join me.'

I struggled. I cast out demons. I summoned up the memory of the moment outside the Changeling shrine, after Bernalt had saved us, when I had invited him to journey with us. How had I felt then toward him? Had I regarded him, at least for a moment, as a brother?

I amplified that moment of gratitude and companionship. I let it swell, and blaze, and it obliterated the encrustations of scorn and empty distain; and I saw the human soul beneath the strange Changeling surface, and I broke through that surface and found the path to redemption. He drew me toward his mind.

I joined Bernalt, and he enrolled me in his guild. I was of the Redeemers now.

Through my mind rolled a voice, and I did not know whether I heard the resonant boom of Talmit, or the dry ironic tone of the Surgeon, or Bernalt's controlled murmur, or Avluela's soft whisper, for it was all these voices at once, and others, and they said:

'When all mankind is enrolled in our guild, we will be conquered no longer. When each of us is part of every other one of us, our sufferings will end. There is no need for us to struggle against our conquerors, for we will absorb them, once we are all Redeemed. Enter us, Tomis who was the Watcher Wuellig.'

And I entered.

And I became the Surgeon and the Flier and the Renewer and the Changeling and the Servitor and the rest. And they became me. And so long as my hands gripped the starstones we were of one soul and one mind. This was not the merging of communion, in which a Pilgrim sinks anonymously into the Will, but rather a union of self and self, maintaining independence within a larger dependence. It was the keen perception one gets from Watching coupled with the submergence in a larger entity that one gets from communion, and I knew this was something wholly new on Earth, not merely the founding of a new guild but the initiation of a new cycle of human existence, the birth of the Fourth Cycle upon this defeated planet.

The voice said, 'Tomis, we will Redeem those in greatest need first. We will go into Agupt, into the desert where miserable Changelings huddle in an ancient building that they worship, and we will take them into us and make them clean again. We will go on, to the west, to a pitiful village smitten by the crystallization disease, and we will reach the souls of the villagers and free them from taint, and the crystallization will cease and their bodies will be healed. And we will go on beyond Agupt, to all the lands of the world, and find those who are without guilds, and those who are without hope, and those who are without tomorrows, and we will give them life and purpose again. And a time will come when all Earth is Redeemed.'

They put a vision before me of a transformed planet, and of the harsh-faced invaders yielding peacefully to us and begging to be incorporated into that new thing that had germinated in the midst of their conquest. They showed me an Earth that had been purged of its ancient sins.

Then I felt it was time to withdraw my hands from the machine I grasped, and I withdrew my hands.

The vision ebbed. The glow faded. But yet I was no longer alone in my skull, for some contact lingered, and the room ceased to be dark.

'How did this happen?' I asked. 'When did this begin?'

'In the days after the conquest,' said Talmit, 'we asked ourselves why we had fallen so easily, and how we could lift ourselves above what we had been. We saw that our guilds had not provided enough of a structure for our lives, that some closer union was our way to redemption. We had the starstones; we had the instruments of Watching; all that remained was to fuse them.'

The Surgeon said, 'You will be important to us, Tomis, because you understand how to throw your mind forth. We seek former Watchers. They are the nucleus of our guild. Once your soul roved the stars to search out mankind's enemies; now it will roam the Earth to bring mankind together.'

Avluela said, 'You will help me to fly, Tomis, even by day. And you will fly beside me.'

'When do you leave?' I asked.

'Now,' she said. 'I go to Agupt, to the temple of the Changelings, to offer them what we have to offer. And all of us will join to give me strength, and that strength will be focused through you, Tomis.' Her hands touched mine. Her lips brushed mine. 'The life of Earth begins again, now, this year, this new cycle. Oh, Tomis, we are all reborn!'

13

I remained alone in the room. The others scattered. Avluela went above, into the street. I put my hands to the mounted starstones, and I saw her as clearly as though she stood beside me. She was preparing herself for flight. First she put off her clothing, and her bare body glistened in the afternoon sun. Her little body seemed impossibly delicate; a strong wind would shatter her, I thought. Then she knelt, bowed, made her ritual. She spoke to herself, yet I heard her words, the words Fliers say as they ready themselves to leave the ground. All guilds are one in this new guild; we have no secrets from one another; there are no mysteries. And as she beseeched the favor of the Will and the support of all her kind, my prayers joined with hers.

She rose and let her wings unfold. Some passers-by looked oddly at her, not because there was anything unusual about the sight of a naked Flier in the streets of Jorslem, but because the sunlight was so strong and her transparent wings, so lightly stained with pigment, were evidently nightwings, incapable of withstanding the pressure of the solar wind.

'I love you,' we said to her, and our hands ran lightly over her satiny skin in a brief caress.

Her nostrils flickered in delight. Her small girl-child's breasts became agitated. Her wings now were fully spread, and they gleamed wonderously in the sunlight.

'Now we fly to Agupt,' she murmured, 'to Redeem the Changelings and make them one with us. Tomis, will you come with me?'

'I will be with you,' we said, and I gripped the starstones tightly and crouched over my cabinet of instruments in the dark room beneath the place where she stood. 'We will fly together, Avluela.'

'Up then,' she said, and we said, 'Up.'

Her wings beat, curving to take the wind, and we felt her struggling in the first moment, and we gave her the strength she needed, and she took it as it poured from us through me to her, and we rose high. The spires and parapets of Jorslem the golden grew small, and the city became a pink dot in the green hills, and Avluela's throbbing wings thrust her swiftly westward, toward the setting sun, toward the land of Agupt. Her ecstasy swept through us all. 'See, Tomis, how wonderful it is, far above everything? Do you feel it?'

'I feel it,' I whispered. 'The cool wind against bare flesh – the wind in my hair – we drift on the currents, we coast, we soar, Avluela, we soar!'

To Agupt. To the sunset.

We looked down at sparkling Lake Medit. In the distance somewhere was Land Bridge. To the north, Eyrop. To the south, Afreek. Far ahead, beyond Earth Ocean, lay my homeland. Later I would return there, flying westward with Avluela, bringing the good news of Earth's transformation.

From this height one could not tell that our world had ever been conquered. One saw only the beauty of the colors of the land and the sea, not the checkpoints of the invaders.

Those checkpoints would not long endure. We would conquer our conquerors, not with weapons but with love; and as the Redemption of Earth became universal we would welcome into our new self even the beings who had seized our planet.

'I knew that some day you would fly beside me, Tomis,' said Avluela.

In my dark room I sent new surges of power through her wings.

She hovered over the desert. The old Surgery, the Changeling shrine, would soon be in sight. I grieved that we would have to come down. I wished we could stay aloft forever, Avluela and I.

'We will, Tomis, we will!' she told me. 'Nothing can separate us now! You believe that, don't you, Tomis?'

'Yes,' we said, 'I believe that.' And we guided her down through the darkening sky.

A TIME OF CHANGES

For Terry and Carol Carr

INTRODUCTION

Somebody once wrote, so I am told, a novel that contains no word that uses the letter 'e.' When I first heard about it, the idea gave me the shivers; for writing novels is hard enough work using one's free range of vocabulary, and tossing in a handicap like that is enough to guarantee a case of terminal hiccups, at the very least. Spare me from the urge to attempt such stunts, I prayed.

And then, years later, I found myself embarked on a novel in which it was forbidden for any character to refer to himself in the first person.

I had been working on it for a week or so, struggling against the strange constraint of avoiding the vertical pronoun, when I remembered that 'e'-less novel. I broke into a sweat and wondered how I would ever get to the other end of my book with my sanity reasonably intact; and then I took a deep breath, told myself that I was writing my book this way neither as a stunt nor as an act of penance, and got back to work. And eventually finished the novel and had it published and won a Nebula award for it as the best science fiction book of 1971, and lived happily ever after, and I'll never ask of myself a similar exercise again.

The purpose of avoiding the use of 'I' in *A Time of Changes* is not to show my own cleverness, of course, but to represent, by a grammatical approximation in an equivalent language, the linguistic practices of an extraterrestrial culture so repressed, so enchained by rigorous self-effacement, that all references to self are taboo and must be handled euphemistically. It was not a particularly original notion – there are existing cultures on our own world, notably among the Eskimo, where first person singular is considered improper usage – but I thought it was reasonably new to science fiction. In this I was wrong, naturally. (Absolutely new ideas in science fiction are a lot less common than is generally suspected. I mean altogether new ideas, not merely ingenious variants on familiar ones; the last one of these I can think of is Bob Shaw's 'slow glass' concept, and that was a dozen years ago. It will probably turn out that something much like slow glass figures in an 1883 Jules Verne novel, anyway.)

My central situation in *A Time of Changes* had at least one well-known previous use – in a book that I had read in 1953 and long since forgotten. This was Ayn Rand's *Anthem*, a short novel first published in 1946 and dedicated to Rand's usual theme, 'The world is perishing from an orgy of self-sacrificing.' In the dystopian world of *Anthem* the collective society has triumphed, and the first person singular pronoun has been abolished; the narrator speaks of himself as 'we,' as does everyone else in that society, but eventually he discovers the Unspeakable Word and launches a revolution intended to restore the sacred rights of the individual ego. This is not quite what I was doing in *A Time of Changes,* where the problem is not all-engulfing collectivist socialism but rather a dour, ritualized, formalized pseudo-modesty that conceals ferocious *macho* self-assertiveness. But the narrative effect is the same. Rand's character and mine struggle toward liberation of self, moving through grammatical thickets, hers speaking of himself as 'we' and mine speaking of himself as 'one,' and there is a similar rigid courtliness to the style. What struck me as eerie, though, was the similarity between Rand's opening lines and my own. When I rediscovered *Anthem* in 1972, almost twenty years after I had last read or thought of it, and several years after I had written *A Time of Changes,* this, to my astonishment, was its opening paragraph:

It is a sin to write this. It is a sin to think words no others think and to put them down upon a paper no others are to see. It is base and evil. It is as if we were speaking alone to no ears but our own. And we know well that there is no transgression blacker than to do or think alone. We have broken the laws. The laws say that men may not write unless the Council of Vocations bid them so. May we be forgiven! (. . .)

It is dark here. The flame of the candle stands still in the air. Nothing moves in this tunnel save our hand on the paper. We are alone here under the earth. It is a fearful word, alone. The laws say that none among men may be alone, ever and at any time, for this is the great transgression and the root of all evil. But we have broken many laws. And now there is nothing here save our one body, and it is strange to see only two legs stretched on the ground, and on the wall before us the shadow of our one head.

Now look at the opening page of *A Time of Changes.* The resemblance is startling – Rand's narrator alone in a tunnel, mine in a desert shack, each beginning his tale by speaking of transgressions against a rigid society. I had forgotten even the existence of her book when I began my own, and unless you would argue that whatever we read is permanently recorded in some cerebral niche and is apt to come floating to consciousness at any time subsequent, the similarity can only be considered coincidence, but a strange one. (The rest of my book is scarcely at all like Rand's – thank goodness.)

I wrote *A Time of Changes* in the summer of 1970, and it was, I suppose, my response to all that had happened in the last few years of the 1960s, that time of changes for so many of us. I had been as rigid and controlled as anyone else in the old pre-Beatle, pre-psychedelic, pre-revolutionary world of the Eisenhower years, and I had been rocked by transformations in the crazy decade that followed, transformations that had altered my attitude toward life, my way of dress, my work, and just about everything else. In 1970 I hovered emotionally and spiritually somewhere between New York and California, between the old life and the new, and I oscillated uncertainly, not yet having opted fully for California; and *A Time of Changes* is the record of that inner upheaval, altered by the metaphors of science fiction but thoroughly recognizable for what lay behind them. (Some of my more straight friends misunderstood the book, thinking it was merely a tract urging wider and wilder use of psychedelic drugs. That wasn't my intention at all, but it was hard to convince them.)

The novel was serialized in *Galaxy Science Fiction,* my main magazine publisher at that time, and early in 1971 was published in a hardcover edition by the Science Fiction Book Club, with the first paperback edition appearing that summer. In April of 1972 the members of the Science Fiction Writers of America awarded it a Nebula as best novel of the year – and, a few days after I had begun my new existence in the San Francisco area, I flew down to the awards ceremony in Los Angeles to collect my handsome lucite trophy. There was something deliciously appropriate, I think, about being handed a Nebula for *A Time of Changes* the very week that I had broken from my old confined life in New York to breathe the fresher, stranger air of California.

—Robert Silverberg
Oakland, California
May 1978

1

I am Kinnall Darival and I mean to tell you all about myself.

That statement is so strange to me that it screams in my eyes. I look at it on the page, and I recognize the hand as my own – narrow upright red letters on the coarse gray sheet – and I see my name, and I hear in my mind the echoes of the brain-impulse that hatched those words. *I am Kinnall Darival and I mean to tell you all about myself.* Incredible.

This is to be what the Earthman Schweiz would call an autobiography. Which means an account of one's self and deeds, written by one's self. It is not a literary form that we understand on our world – I must invent my own method of narrative, for I have no precedents to guide me. But this is as it should be. On this my planet I stand alone, now. In a sense, I have invented a new way of life; I can surely invent a new sort of literature. They have always told me I have a gift for words.

So I find myself in a clapboard shack in the Burnt Lowlands, writing obscenities as I wait for death, and praising myself for my literary gifts.

I am Kinnall Darival.

Obscene! Obscene! Already on this one sheet I have used the pronoun 'I' close to twenty times, it seems. While also casually dropping such words as 'my,' 'me,' 'myself,' more often than I care to count. A torrent of shamelessness. I I I I I. If I exposed my manhood in the Stone Chapel of Manneran on Naming Day, I would be doing nothing so foul as I am doing here. I could almost laugh. Kinnall Darival practicing a solitary vice. In this miserable lonely place he massages his stinking ego and shrieks offensive pronouns into the hot wind, hoping they will sail on the gusts and soil his fellow men. He sets down sentence after sentence in the naked syntax of madness. He would, if he could, seize you by the wrist and pour cascades of filth into your unwilling ear. And why? Is proud Darival in fact insane? Has his sturdy spirit entirely collapsed under the gnawing of mindsnakes? Is nothing left but the shell of him, sitting in this dreary hut, obsessively titillating himself with disreputable language, muttering 'I' and 'me' and 'my' and 'myself,' blearily threatening to reveal the intimacies of his soul?

No. It is Darival who is sane and all of you who are sick, and though I know how mad that sounds, I will let it stand. I am no lunatic muttering filth to wring a feeble pleasure from a chilly universe. I have passed through a time of changes, and I have been healed of the sickness that affects those who inhabit my world, and in writing what I intend to write I hope to heal you as well, though I know you are on your way into the Burnt Lowlands to slay me for my hopes.

So be it.

I am Kinnall Darival and I mean to tell you all about myself.

2

Lingering vestiges of the customs against which I rebel still plague me. Perhaps you can begin to comprehend what an effort it is for me to frame my sentences in this style, to twist my verbs around in order to fit the first-person construction. I have been writing ten minutes and my body is covered with sweat, not the hot sweat of the burning air about me but the dank, clammy sweat of mental struggle. I know the style I must use, but the muscles of my arm rebel against me, and fight to put down the words in the old fashion, saying, *One has been writing for ten minutes and one's body is covered with sweat,* saying, *One has passed through a time of changes, and he has been healed of the sickness that affects those who inhabit his world.* I suppose that much of what I have written could have been phrased in the old way, and no harm done; but I do battle against the self-effacing grammar of my world, and if I must, I will joust with my own muscles for the right to arrange my words according to my present manner of philosophy.

In any case, however my former habits trick me into misconstructing my sentences, my meaning will blaze through the screen of words. I may say, 'I am Kinnall Darival and I mean to tell you all about myself,' or I may say, 'One's name is Kinnall Darival and he means to tell you all about himself,' but there is no real difference. Either way, the content of Kinnall Darival's statement is – by your standards, by the standards I would destroy – disgusting, contemptible, obscene.

3

Also I am troubled, at least in these early pages, by the identity of my audience. I assume, because I must, that I will have readers. But who are they? Who are you? Men and women of my native planet, perhaps, furtively turning my pages by torchlight, dreading the knock at the door. Or maybe otherworlders, reading for amusement, scanning my book for the insight it may give into an alien and repellent society. I have no idea. I can establish no easy relationship with you, my unknown reader. When I first conceived my plan of setting down my soul on paper, I thought it would be simple, a mere confessional, nothing but an extended session with an imaginary drainer who would listen endlessly and at last give me absolution. But now I realize I must take another approach. If you are not of my world, or if you are of my world but not of my time, you may find much here that is incomprehensible.

Therefore I must explain. Possibly I will explain too much, and drive you off by pounding you with the obvious. Forgive me if I instruct you in what you already know. Forgive me if my tone and mode of attack show lapses of consistency and I seem to be addressing myself to someone else. For you will not hold still for me, my unknown reader. You wear many faces for me. Now I see the crooked nose of Jidd the drainer, and now the suave smile of my bondbrother Noim Condorit, and now the silkiness of my bondsister Halum, and now you become the tempter Schweiz of pitiful Earth, and now you are my son's son's son's son's son, not to be born for a cluster of years and eager to know what manner of man your ancestor was, and now you are some stranger of a different planet, to whom we of Borthan are grotesque, mysterious, and baffling. I do not know you, and so I will be clumsy in my attempts to talk to you.

But, by Salla's Gate, before I am done you will know me, as no man of Borthan has ever been known by others before!

4

I am a man of middle years. Thirty times since the day of my birth has Borthan traveled around our golden-green sun, and on our world a man is considered old if he has lived through fifty such circuits, while the most ancient man of whom I ever heard died just short of his eightieth. From this you may be able to calculate our spans in terms of yours, if otherworlder you happen to be. The Earthman Schweiz claimed an age of forty-three years by his planet's reckoning, yet he seemed no older than I.

My body is strong. Here I shall commit a double sin, for not only shall I speak of myself without shame, but I shall show pride and pleasure in my physical self. I am tall: a woman of normal height reaches barely to the lower vault of my chest. My hair is dark and long, falling to my shoulders. Lately streaks of gray have appeared in it, and likewise in my beard, which is full and thick, covering much of my face. My nose is prominent and straight, with a wide bridge and large nostrils; my lips are fleshy and give me, so it is said, a look of sensuality; my eyes are deep brown and are set somewhat far apart in my skull. They have, I am given to understand, the appearance of the eyes of one that has been accustomed all his life to commanding other men.

My back is broad and my chest is deep. A dense mat of coarse dark hair grows nearly everywhere on me. My arms are long. My hands are large. My muscles are well developed and stand out prominently beneath my skin. I move gracefully for a man my size, with smooth coordination; I excel in sports, and when I was younger I hurled the feathered shaft the entire length of Manneran Stadium, a feat that had never been achieved until then.

Most women find me attractive – all but those who prefer a flimsier, more scholarly looking sort of man and are frightened of strength and size and virility. Certainly the political power I have held in my time has helped to bring many partners to my couch, but no doubt they were drawn to me as much by the look of my body as by anything more subtle. Most of them have been disappointed in me. Bulging muscles and a hairy hide do not a skilled lover make, nor is a massive genital member such as mine any guarantee of ecstasy. I am no champion of copulation. See: I hide nothing from you. There is in me a certain constitutional impatience that expresses itself outwardly only during the carnal act; when I enter a woman I find myself swiftly swept away, and rarely can I sustain the deed until her pleasure comes. To no one, not even a drainer, have I confessed this failing before, nor did I ever expect that I would. But a good many women of Borthan have learned of this my great flaw in the most immediate possible way, to their cost, and doubtless some of them, embittered, have circulated the news in order that they might enjoy a scratchy joke at my expense. So I place it on the record here, for perspective's sake. I would not have you think of me as a hairy mighty giant without also your knowing how often my flesh has betrayed my lusts. Possibly this failing of mine was among the forces that shaped my destinies toward this day in the Burnt Lowlands, and you should know of that.

5

My father was hereditary septarch of the province of Salla on our eastern coast. My mother was daughter of a septarch of Glin; he met her on a diplomatic mission, and their mating was, it was said, ordained from the moment they beheld one another. The first child born to them was my brother Stirron, now septarch in Salla in our father's place. I followed two years later; there were three more after me, all of them girls. Two of these still live. My youngest sister was slain by raiders from Glin some twenty moontimes ago.

I knew my father poorly. On Borthan everyone is a stranger to everyone, but one's father is customarily less remote from one than others; not so with the old septarch. Between us lay an impenetrable wall of formality. In addressing him we used the same formulas of respect that subjects employed. His smiles were so infrequent that I think I can recall each one. Once, and it was unforgettable, he took me up beside him on his rough-hewn blackwood throne, and let me touch the ancient yellow cushion, and called me fondly by my child-name; it was the day my mother died. Otherwise he ignored me. I feared and loved him, and crouched trembling behind pillars in his court to watch him dispense justice, thinking that if he saw me there he would have me destroyed, and yet unable to deprive myself of the sight of my father in his majesty.

He was, oddly, a man of slender body and modest height, over whom my brother and I towered even when we were boys. But there was a terrible strength of will in him that led him to surmount every challenge. Once in my childhood there came some ambassador to the septarchy, a hulking sun-blackened westerner who stands in my memory no smaller than Kongoroi Mountain; probably he was as tall and broad as I am now. At feasting-time the ambassador let too much blue wine down his throat, and said, before my father and his courtiers and his family, 'One would show his strength to the men of Salla, to whom he may be able to teach something of wrestling.'

'There is one here,' my father replied in sudden fury, 'to whom, perhaps, nothing need be taught.'

'Let him be produced,' the huge westerner said, rising and peeling back his cloak. But my father, smiling – and the sight of that smile made his courtiers quake – told the boastful stranger it would not be fair to make him compete while his mind was fogged with wine, and this of course maddened the ambassador beyond words. The musicians came in then to ease the tension, but the anger of our visitor did not subside, and, after an hour, when the drunkenness had lifted somewhat from him, he demanded again to meet my father's champion. No man of Salla, said our guest, would be able to withstand his might.

Whereupon the septarch said, 'I will wrestle you myself.'

That night my brother and I were sitting at the far end of the long table, among the women. Down from the throne-end came the stunning word 'I' in my father's voice, and an instant later came 'myself.' These were obscenities that Stirron and I had often whispered, sniggering, in the darkness of our bedchamber, but we had never imagined we would hear them hurled forth in the feasting-hall from the septarch's own lips. In our shock we reacted differently, Stirron jerking convulsively and knocking over his goblet, myself letting loose a half-suppressed shrill giggle of embarrassment and delight that earned me an instant slap from a lady-in-waiting. My laughter was merely the mask for my inner horror. I could barely believe that my father knew those words, let alone that he would say them before this august company. *I will wrestle you myself.* And while the reverberations of the forbidden forms of speech still dizzied me, my father swiftly stepped forward, dropping his cloak, and faced the great hulk of an ambassador, and closed with him, and caught him by one elbow and one haunch in a deft Sallan hold, and sent him almost immediately toppling to the polished floor of gray stone. The ambassador uttered a terrible cry, for one of his legs was sticking strangely out at a frightening angle from his hip, and in pain and humiliation he pounded the flat of his hand again and again against the floor. Perhaps diplomacy is practiced in more sophisticated ways now in the palace of my brother Stirron.

The septarch died when I was twelve and just coming into the first rush of my manhood. I was near his side when death took him. To escape the time of rains in Salla he would go each year to hunt the hornfowl in the Burnt Lowlands, in the very district where now I hide and wait. I had never gone with him, but on this occasion I was permitted to accompany the hunting party, for now I was a young prince and must learn the skills of my class. Stirron, as a future septarch, had other skills to master; he remained behind as regent in our father's absence from the capital. Under a bleak and heavy sky bowed with rainclouds the expedition of some twenty groundcars rolled westward out of Salla City and through the flat, sodden, winter-bare countryside. The rains were merciless that year, knifing away the precious sparse topsoil and laying bare the rocky bones of our province. Everywhere the farmers were repairing their dikes, but to no avail; I could see the swollen rivers running yellow-brown with Salla's lost wealth, and I nearly wept to think of such treasure being carried into the sea. As we came into West Salla, the narrow road began to climb the foothills of the Huishtor range, and soon we were in drier, colder country, where the skies gave snow and not rain, and the trees were mere bundles of sticks against the blinding whiteness. Up we went into the Huishtors, following the Kongoroi road. The countryfolk came out to chant welcomes to the septarch as he passed. Now the naked mountains stood like purple teeth ripping the gray sky, and even in our sealed groundcars we shivered, although the beauty of this tempestuous place took my mind from my discomforts. Here great flat shields of striated tawny rock flanked the rugged road, and there was scarcely any soil at all, nor did trees or shrubs grow except in sheltered places. We could look back and see all of Salla like its own map below us, the whiteness of the western districts, the dark clutter of the populous eastern shore, everything diminished, unreal. I had never been this far from home before. Though we were now deep into the uplands, midway, as it were, between sea and sky, the inner peaks of the Huishtors still lay before us, and to my eye they formed an unbroken wall of stone spanning the continent from north to south. Their snow-crowned summits jutted raggedly from that continuous lofty breastworks of bare rock; were we supposed to go over the top, or would there be some way through? I knew of Salla's Gate, and that our route lay toward it, but somehow the gate seemed mere myth to me at that moment.

Up and up and up we rode, until the generators of our groundcars were gasping in the frosty air, and we were compelled to pause frequently to defrost the power conduits, and our heads whirled from shortness of oxygen. Each night we rested at one of the camps maintained for the use of traveling septarchs, but the accommodations were far from regal, and at one, where the entire staff of servants had perished some weeks before in a snowslide, it was necessary for us to dig our way through mounds of ice in order to enter. We were all of us in the party men of the nobility, and all of us wielded shovels except the septarch himself, for whom manual labor would have been sinful. Because I was one of the biggest and strongest of the men, I dug more vigorously than anyone, and because I was young and rash, I strained myself beyond my strength, collapsing over my shovel and lying half dead in the snow for an hour until I was noticed. My father came to me while they were treating me, and smiled one of his rare smiles; just then I believed it was a gesture of affection, and it greatly sped my recovery, but afterward I came to see it was more likely a sign of his contempt.

That smile buoyed me through the remainder of our ascent of the Huishtors. No longer did I fret about getting over the mountains, for I knew that I would, and on the far side my father and I would hunt the hornfowl in the Burnt Lowlands, going out together, guarding one another from peril, collaborating ultimately on the tracking and on the kill, knowing a closeness that had never existed between us in my childhood. I talked of that one night to my bondbrother Noim Condorit, who rode with me in my groundcar, and who was the only person in the universe to whom I could say such things. 'One hopes to be chosen for the septarch's own hunt-group,' I said. 'One has reason to think that one will be asked. And an end made to the distance between father and son.'

'You dream,' said Noim Condorit. 'You live in fantasies.'

'One could wish,' I replied, 'for warmer encouragement from one's bondbrother.'

Noim was ever a pessimist; I took his dourness in stride, and counted the days to Salla's Gate. When we reached it, I was unprepared for the splendor of the place. All morning and half an afternoon we had been following a thirty-degree grade up the broad breast of Kongoroi Mountain, shrouded in the shadow of the great double summit. It seemed to me we would climb forever and still have Kongoroi looming over us. Then our caravan swung around to the left, car after car disappearing behind a snowy pylon on the flank of the road, and our car's turn came, and when we had turned the corner, I beheld an astonishing sight: a wide break in the mountain wall, as if some cosmic hand had pried away one corner of Kongoroi. Through the gap came daylight in a glittering burst. This was Salla's Gate, the miraculous pass across which our ancestors came when first they entered our province, so many hundreds of years back, after their wanderings in the Burnt Lowlands. We plunged joyously into it, riding two and even three cars abreast over the hardpacked snow, and before we made camp for the night we were able to see the strange splendor of the Burnt Lowlands spread out astonishingly below us.

All the next day and the one that followed we rode the switchbacks down Kongoroi's western slope, creeping at a comical pace along a road that had little room to spare for us: a careless twitch of the stick and one's car would tumble into an infinite abyss. There was no snow on this face of the Huishtors, and the raw sunpounded rock had a numbing, oppressive look. Ahead everything was red soil. Down into the desert we went, quitting winter and entering a stifling world where every breath tingled in the lungs, where dry winds lifted the ground in clouds, where odd twisted-looking beasts scampered in terror from our oncoming cavalcade. On the sixth day we reached the hunting-grounds, a place of ragged escarpments far below sea level. I am no more than an hour's ride from that place now. Here the hornfowl have their nests; all day long they range the baking plains, seeking meat, and at twilight they return, collapsing groundward in weird spiraling flight to enter their all but inaccessible burrows.

In the dividing of personnel I was one of thirteen chosen for the septarch's companions. 'One shares your joy,' Noim told me solemnly, and there were tears in his eyes as well as in mine, for he knew what pain my father's coldness had brought me. At daybreak the hunt-groups set out, nine of them, in nine directions.

To take a hornfowl near its nest is deemed shameful. The bird returning is usually laden with meat for its young, and it therefore is clumsy and vulnerable, shorn of all its grace and power. Killing one as it plummets is no great task, but only a craven selfbarer would attempt it. *(Selfbarer!* See how my own pen mocks me! I, who have bared more self than any ten men of Borthan, still unconsciously use the term as a word of abuse! But let it stand.) I mean to say that the virtue in hunting lies in the perils and difficulties of the chase, not in the taking of the trophy, and we hunt the hornfowl as a challenge to our skills, not for its dismal flesh.

Thus hunters go into the open Lowlands, where even in winter the sun is devastating, where there are no trees to give shade or streams to ease the thirst. They spread out, one man here, two men there, taking up stations in that trackless expanse of barren red soil, offering themselves as the hornfowl's prey. The bird cruises at inconceivable heights, soaring so far overhead that it can be seen only as a black scratch in the brilliant dome of the sky; it takes the keenest vision to detect one, though a hornfowl's wingspread is twice the length of a man's body. From its lofty place the hornfowl scans the desert for incautious beasts. Nothing, no matter how small, escapes its glossy eyes; and when it detects good quarry, it comes down through the turbulent air until it hovers house-high above the ground. Now it commences its killing-flight, flying low, launching itself on a series of savage circles, spinning a death-knot around its still unsuspecting victim. The first swing may sweep over the equivalent of half a province's area, but each successive circuit is tighter and tighter, while acceleration mounts, until ultimately the hornfowl has made itself a frightful engine of death that comes roaring in from the horizon at nightmarish velocity. Now the quarry learns the truth, but it is knowledge not held for long: the rustle of mighty wings, the hiss of a slim powerful form cleaving the hot sluggish air, and then the single long deadly spear sprouting from the bird's bony forehead finds its mark, and the victim falls, enfolded in the black fluttering wings. The hunter hopes to bring down his hornfowl while it cruises, almost at the limits of human sight; he carries a weapon designed for long-range shooting, and the test is in the aim, whether he can calculate the interplay of trajectories at such vast distances. The peril of hunting hornfowl is this, that one never knows if one is the hunter or the hunted, for a hornfowl on its killing-flight cannot be seen until it strikes its stroke.

So I went forth. So I stood from dawn to midday. The sun worked its will on my winter-pale skin, such of it as I dared to expose; most of me was swaddled in hunting clothes of soft crimson leather, within which I boiled. I sipped from my canteen no more often than survival demanded, for I imagined that the eyes of my comrades were upon me and I would reveal no weaknesses to them. We were arrayed in a double hexagon with my father alone between the two groups. Chance had it that I drew the point of my hexagon closest to him, but it was more than a feathered shaft's toss from his place to mine, and all the morning long the septarch and I exchanged not a syllable. He stood with feet planted firm, watching the skies, his weapon at ready. If he drank at all as he waited, I did not see him do it. I too studied the skies, until my eyes ached for it, until I felt twin strands of hot light drilling my brain and hammering against the back wall of my skull. More than once I imagined I saw the dark splinter of a hornfowl's shape drifting into view up there, and once in sweaty haste I came to the verge of raising my gun to it, which would have brought me shame, for one must not shoot until one has established priority of sighting by crying one's claim. I did not fire, and when I blinked and opened my eyes, I saw nothing in the sky. The hornfowl seemed to be elsewhere that morning.

At noon my father gave a signal, and we spread farther apart over the plain, maintaining our formation. Perhaps the hornfowl found us too closely clustered, and were staying away. My new position lay atop a low earthen mound, in the form almost of a woman's breast, and fear took hold of me as I took up my place on it. I supposed myself to be terribly exposed and in imminent peril of hornfowl attack. As fright crept through my spirit, I became convinced that a hornfowl was even now flying its fatal circuits around my hammock, and that at any moment its lance would pierce my kidneys while I gazed stupidly at the metallic sky. The premonition grew so strong that I had to struggle to hold my ground; I shivered, I stole wary peeks over my shoulders, I clenched the stock of my gun for comfort, I strained my ears for the sound of my enemy's approach, hoping to whirl and fire before I was speared. For this cowardice I reproached myself severely, even offering thanks that Stirron had been born before me, since obviously I was unfit to succeed to the septarchy. I reminded myself that not in three years had a hunter been killed in this way. I asked myself if it was plausible that I should die so young, on my first hunt, when there were others like my father who had hunted for thirty seasons and gone unscathed. I demanded to know why I felt this overwhelming fear, when all my tutors had labored to teach me that the self is a void and concern for one's person a wicked sin. Was not my father in equal jeopardy, far across the sun-smitten plain? And had he not much more than I to lose, being a septarch and a prime septarch at that, while I was only a boy? In this way I cudgelled the fear from my damp soul, and studied the sky without regard for the spear that might be aimed at my back, and in minutes my former fretting seemed an absurdity to me. I would stand here for days, if need be, unafraid. At once I had the reward of this triumph over self: against the shimmering fierceness of the sky I made out a dark floating form, a notch in the heavens, and this time it was no illusion, for my youthful eyes spied wings and horn. Did the others see it? Was the bird mine to attempt? If I made the kill, would the septarch pound my back and call me his best son? All was silence from the other hunters.

'One cries claim!' I shouted jubilantly, and lifted my weapon, and eyed the sight, remembering what I had been taught, to let the inner mind make the calculations, to aim and fire in one swift impulse before the intellect, by quibbling, could spoil the intuition's command.

And in the instant before I sent my bolt aloft there came a ghastly outcry from my left, and I fired without aiming at all, turning in the same instant toward my father's place, and seeing him half hidden beneath the madly flapping form of another hornfowl that had gored him from spine to belly. The air about them was clouded with red sand as the monster's wings furiously slapped the ground; the bird was struggling to take off, but a hornfowl cannot lift a man's weight, though this does not prevent them from attacking us. I ran to aid the septarch. He still was shouting, and I saw his hands clutching for the hornfowl's scrawny throat, but now there was a liquid quality about his cries, a bubbling tone, and when I reached the scene – I was the first one there – he lay sprawled and quiet, with the bird still rammed through him and covering his body like a black cloak. My blade was out; I slashed the hornfowl's neck as if it were a length of hose, kicked the carcass aside, began to wrench desperately at the demonic head mounted so hideously upon the septarch's upturned back. Now the others came; they pulled me away; someone seized me by the shoulders and shook me until my fit was past. When I turned to them again, they closed their ranks, to keep me from seeing my father's corpse, and then, to my dismay, they dropped to their knees before me to do homage.

But of course it was Stirron and not I who became septarch in Salla. His crowning was a grand event, for, young though he was, he would be the prime septarch of the province. Salla's six other septarchs came to the capital – only on such an occasion were they ever to be found at once in the same city – and for a time everything was feasting and banners and the blare of trumpets. Stirron was at the center of it all, and I on the margins, which was as it should be, though it left me feeling more like a stableboy than a prince. Once he was enthroned, Stirron offered me titles and land and power, but he did not really expect me to accept, and I did not. Unless a septarch is a weakling, his younger brothers had best not stay nearby to help him rule, for such help is not desired often. I had had no living uncles on my father's side of the family, and I did not care to have Stirron's sons be able to make the same statement; therefore I took myself quickly from Salla once the time of mourning was ended.

I went to Glin, my mother's land. There, however, things were unsatisfactory for me, and after a few years I moved on to the steamy province of

Manneran, where I won my wife and sired my sons and became a prince in more than name, and lived happily and sturdily until my time of changes began.

6

Perhaps I should set down some words concerning my world's geography.

There are five continents on our planet of Borthan. In this hemisphere there are two, Velada Borthan and Sumara Borthan, which is to say, the Northern World and the Southern World. It is a long sea journey from any shore of these continents to the continents of the opposite hemisphere, which have been named merely Umbis, Dabis, Tibis, that is, One, Two, Three.

Of those three distant lands I can tell you very little. They first were explored some seven hundred years ago by a septarch of Glin, who laid down his life for his curiosity, and there have not been five seeking-parties to them in all the time since. No human folk dwell in that hemisphere. Umbis is said to be largely like the Burnt Lowlands, but worse, with golden flames bursting from the tormented land in many places. Dabis is jungles and fever-ridden swamps, and someday will be full of our people hoping to prove manhood, for I understand it is thick with dangerous beasts. Tibis is covered with ice.

We are not a race afflicted with the wanderlust. I myself was never a voyager until circumstances made me one. Though the blood of the ancient Earthmen flows in our veins, and they were wanderers whose demons drove them out to prowl the stars, we of Borthan stay close to home. Even I who am somewhat different from my comrades in my way of thinking never hungered to see the snowfields of Tibis or the marshes of Dabis, except perhaps when I was a child and eager to gobble all the universe. Among us it is considered a great thing merely to journey from Salla to Glin, and rare indeed is the man who has crossed the continent, let alone ventured to Sumara Borthan, as I have done.

As I have done.

Velada Borthan is the home of our civilization. The mapmakers' art reveals it to be a large squarish landmass with rounded corners. Two great V-shaped indentations puncture its periphery: along the northern coast, midway between the eastern and western corners, there is the Polar Gulf, and, due south on the opposite coast, there is the Gulf of Sumar. Between those two bodies of water lie the Lowlands, a trough that spans the entire continent from north to south. No point in the Lowlands rises higher above sea level than the height of five men, and there are many places, notably in the Burnt Lowlands, that are far below sea level.

There is a folktale we tell our children concerning the shape of Velada Borthan. We say that the great iceworm Hrungir, born in the waters of the North Polar Sea, stirred and woke one day in sudden appetite, and began to nibble at the northern shore of Velada Borthan. The worm chewed for a thousand thousand years, until it had eaten out the Polar Gulf. Then, its voracity having made it somewhat ill, it crawled up on the land to rest and digest what it had devoured. Uneasy at the stomach, Hrungir wriggled southward, causing the land to sink beneath its vast weight and the mountains to rise, in compensation, to the east and west of its resting-place. The worm rested longest in the Burnt Lowlands, which accordingly were depressed more deeply than any other region. In time the worm's appetite revived, and it resumed its southward crawl, coming at last to a place where a range of mountains running from east to west barred its advance. Then it chewed the mountains, creating Stroin Gap, and proceeded toward our southern coast. In another fit of hunger the worm bit out the Gulf of Sumar. The waters of the Strait of Sumar rushed in to fill the place where the land had been, and the rising tide carried Hrungir to the continent of Sumara Borthan, where now the iceworm lives, coiled beneath the volcano Vashnir and emitting poisonous fumes. So the fable goes.

The long narrow basin that we think of as Hrungir's track is divided into three districts. At the northern end we have the Frozen Lowlands, a place of perpetual ice where no man is ever seen. Legend has it that the air is so dry and cold that a single breath will turn a man's lungs to leather. The polar influence reaches only a short distance into our continent, however. South of the Frozen Lowlands lie the immense Burnt Lowlands, which are almost totally without water, and on which the full fury of our sun constantly falls. Our two towering north-south mountain ranges prevent a drop of rain from entering the Burnt Lowlands, nor do any rivers or streams reach it. The soil is bright red, with occasional yellow streaks, and this we blame on the heat of Hrungir's belly, though our geologists tell another tale. Small plants live in the Burnt Lowlands, taking their nourishment from I know not where, and there are many kinds of beasts, all of them strange, deformed, and unpleasant. At the southern end of the Burnt Lowlands there is a deep east-west valley, several days' journey in breadth, and on its far side lies the small district known as the Wet Lowlands. Northerly breezes coming off the Gulf of Sumar carry moisture through Stroin Gap; these winds meet the fierce hot blasts out of the Burnt Lowlands and are forced to drop their burden not far above the Gap, creating a land of dense, lush vegetation. Never do the water-laden breezes from the south succeed in getting north of the Wet Lowlands to bathe the zone of red soil. The Frozen Lowlands, as I have said, go forever unvisited, and the Burnt Lowlands are entered only by hunters and those who must travel between the eastern and western coasts, but the Wet Lowlands are populated by several thousand farmers, who raise exotic fruits for the city folk. I am told that the constant rain rots their souls, that they have no form of government, and that our customs of self-denial are imperfectly observed. I would be among them now, to discover their nature at first hand, if only I could slip through the cordon that my enemies have set up to the south of this place.

The Lowlands are flanked by two immense mountain ranges: the Huishtors in the east, the Threishtors in the west. These mountains begin on Velada Borthan's northern coast, virtually at the shores of the North Polar Sea, and march southward, gradually curving inland; the two ranges would join not far from the Gulf of Sumar if they were not separated by Stroin Gap. They are so high that they intercept all winds. Therefore their inland slopes are barren, but the slopes facing the oceans enjoy fertility.

Mankind in Velada Borthan has carved out its domain in the two coastal strips, between the oceans and the mountains. In most places the land is at best marginal, so that we are hard put to have all the food we need, and life is a constant struggle against hunger. Often one wonders why our ancestors, when they came to this planet so many generations ago, chose Velada Borthan as their settling-place; the farming would have been far easier in the neighboring continent of Sumara Borthan, and even swampy Dabis might have offered more cheer. The explanation we are given is that our forefathers were stern, diligent folk who relished challenge, and feared to let their children dwell in a place where life might be insufficiently harsh. Velada Borthan's coasts were neither uninhabitable nor unduly comfortable; therefore they suited the purposes. I believe this to be true, for certainly the chief heritage we have from those ancient ones is the notion that comfort is sin and ease is wickedness. My bondbrother Noim, though, once remarked that the first settlers chose Velada Borthan because that was where their starship happened to come down, and, having hauled themselves across all the immensities of space, they lacked the energy to travel onward even one more continent in quest of a better home. I doubt it, but the slyness of the idea is characteristic of my bondbrother's taste for irony.

The firstcomers planted their initial settlement on the western coast, at the place we call Threish, that is, the place of the Covenant. They multiplied rapidly, and, because they were a stubborn and quarrelsome tribe, they splintered early, this group and that going off to live apart. Thus the nine western provinces came into being. To this day there are bitter border disputes among them.

In time the limited resources of the west were exhausted, and emigrants sought the eastern coast. We had no air transport then, not that we have a great deal now; we are not a mechanically minded people, and we lack natural resources to serve as fuel. Thus they went east by groundcar, or whatever served as groundcars then. The three Threishtor passes were discovered, and the bold ones bravely entered the Burnt Lowlands. We sing long mythic epics of the hardships of these crossings. Getting over the Threishtors into the Lowlands was difficult, but getting out on the far side was close to impossible, for there is only one route over the Huishtors out of the red-soil country fit for humans, and that is by way of Salla's Gate, the finding of which was no small task. But they found it and poured through, and established my land of Salla. When the quarreling came, a good many went north and founded Glin, and later others went south to settle in holy Manneran. For a thousand years it was sufficient to have but three provinces in the east, until in a new quarrel the small but prosperous maritime kingdom of Krell carved itself out of a corner of Glin and a corner of Salla.

There also were some folk who could not abide life in Velada Borthan at all, and put to sea from Manneran, sailing off to settle in Sumara Borthan. But one need not speak of them in a geography lesson; I will have much to say of Sumara Borthan and its people when I have begun to explain the changes that entered my life.

7

This cabin where I hide myself now is a shabby thing. Its clapboard walls were indifferently put together to begin with, and now are crazed, so that gaps yawn at the joins and no angle is true. The desert wind passes through here unhindered; my page bears a light coating of red soil, my clothes are caked with it, even my hair has a red tinge. Lowlands creatures crawl freely in with me: I see two of them moving about the earthen floor now, a many-legged gray thing the size of my thumb and a sluggish two-tailed serpent not so long as my foot. For hours they have circled one another idly, as though they wish to be mortal foes but cannot decide which of them is to eat the other. Dry companions for a parched time.

I should not mock this place, though. Someone troubled to drag its makings here, in order that weary hunters might have shelter in this inhospitable land. Someone put it together, doubtless with more love than skill, and left it here for me, and it serves me well. Perhaps it is no fit home for a septarch's son, but I have known my share of palaces, and I no longer need stone walls and groined ceilings. It is peaceful here. I am far from the fishmongers and the drainers and the wine-peddlers and all those others whose songs of commerce clang in the streets of cities. A man can think; a man can look within his soul, and find those things that have been the shaping of him, and draw them forth, and examine them, and come to know himself. In this our world we are forbidden by custom to make our souls known to others, yes, but why has no one before me observed that that same custom, without intending it, keeps us from coming to know ourselves? For nearly all my life I kept the proper social walls between myself and others, and not till the walls were down did I see I had walled myself away from myself as well. But here in the Burnt Lowlands I have had time to contemplate these matters and to arrive at understanding. This is not the place I would have chosen for myself, but I am not unhappy here.

I do not think they will find me for some while yet.

Now it is too dark in here to write. I will stand by the cabin door and watch the night come rolling across the Lowlands toward the Huishtors. Perhaps there will be hornfowl drifting through the dusk, heading home from an empty hunt. The stars will blaze. Schweiz once tried to show me the sun of Earth from a mountaintop in Sumara Borthan, and insisted he could see it, and begged me to squint along the line of his pointing hand, but I think he was playing a game with me. I think that that sun may not be seen at all from our sector of the galaxy. Schweiz played many a game with me when we traveled together, and perhaps he will play more such games one day, if ever we meet again, if still he lives.

8

Last night in a dream my bondsister Halum Helalam came to me.

With her there can never be more games, and only through the slippery-walled tunnel of dreams is she apt to reach me. Therefore while I slept she glowed in my mind more brightly than any star that lights this desert, but waking brought me sadness and shame, and the memory of my loss of her who is irreplaceable.

Halum of my dream wore only a light filmy veil through which her small rosy-tipped breasts showed, and her slim thighs, and her flat belly, the belly of an unchilded woman. It was not the way she often dressed in life, especially when paying a call on her bondbrother, but this was the Halum of my dream, made wanton by my lonely and troubled soul. Her smile was warm and tender and her dark shining eyes glistened with love.

In dreams one's mind lives on many levels. On one level of mine I was a detached observer, floating in a haze of moonlight somewhere near the roof of my hut, looking down upon my own sleeping body. On another level I lay asleep. The dream-self that slept did not perceive Halum's presence, but the dream-self that watched was aware of her, and I, the true dreamer, was aware of them both, and also aware that all I saw was coming to me in a vision. But inevitably there was some mingling of these levels of reality, so that I could not be sure who was the dreamer and who the dreamed, nor was I certain that the Halum who stood before me in such radiance was a creature of my fantasy rather than the living Halum I once had known.

'Kinnall,' she whispered, and in my dream I imagined that my sleeping dream-self awoke, propping himself upon his elbows, with Halum kneeling close beside his cot. She leaned forward until her breasts brushed the shaggy chest of that man who was I, and touched her lips to mine in a flick of a caress, and said, 'You look so weary, Kinnall.'

'You should not have come here.'

'One was needed. One came.'

'It is not right. To enter the Burnt Lowlands alone, to seek out one who has brought you only harm—'

'The bond that links one to you is sacred.'

'You've suffered enough for that bond, Halum.'

'One has not suffered at all,' she said, and kissed my sweaty forehead. 'How *you* must suffer, hiding in this dismal oven!'

'It is no more than one has earned,' I said.

Even in my dream I spoke to Halum in the polite grammatical form. I had never found it easy to use the first person with her; certainly I never used it before my changes, and afterward, when no reason remained for me to be so chaste with her, I still could not. My soul and my heart had yearned to say 'I' to Halum, and my tongue and lips were padlocked by propriety.

She said, 'You deserve so much more than this place. You must come forth from exile. You must guide us, Kinnall, toward a new Covenant, a Covenant of love, of trust in one another.'

'One fears he has been a failure as a prophet. One doubts the value of continuing such efforts.'

'It was all so strange to you, so new!' she said. 'But you were able to change, Kinnall, and to bring changes to others—'

'To bring grief to others and to oneself.'

'No. No. What you tried to do was right. How can you give up now? How can you resign yourself to death? There's a world out there in need of being freed, Kinnall!'

'One is trapped in this place. One's capture is inevitable.'

'The desert is wide. You can slip away from them.'

'The desert is wide, but the gates are few, and all of them are watched. There's no escape.'

She shook her head, and smiled, and pressed her hands urgently against my hips, and said, in a voice thick with hope, 'I will lead you to safety. Come with me, Kinnall.'

The sound of that *I* and the *me* that followed it, out of Halum's imagined mouth, fell upon my dreaming soul like a rainfall of rusted spikes, and the shock of hearing those obscenities in her sweet voice nearly awakened me. This thing I tell you to make it clear that I am not fully converted to my own changed way of life, that the reflexes of my upbringing still govern me in the deepest corners of my soul. In dreams we reveal our true selves, and my reaction of numb dismay to the words that I had placed (for who else could have done it?) in the dream-Halum's mouth told me a great deal about my innermost attitudes. What happened next was also revealing, though far less subtle. To urge me from my cot Halum's hands slipped over my body, working their way through the tangled thatch over my gut, and her cool fingers seized the stiffened rod of my sex. Instantly my heart thundered and my seed spurted, and the ground heaved as though the Lowlands were splitting apart, and Halum uttered a little cry of fear. I reached for her, but she was growing indistinct and insubstantial, and in one terrible convulsion of the planet I lost sight of her and she was gone. And there was so much I had wanted to say to her, so many things I had meant to ask. I woke, coming up through the levels of my dream. I found myself alone in the hut, of course, sticky-skinned with my outpourings and sickened by the villainies that my shameful mind, allowed to roam the night unfettered, had concocted.

'*Halum!*' I cried. 'Halum, Halum, Halum!'

My voice made the cabin quiver, but she did not return. And slowly my sleep-fogged mind grasped the truth, that the Halum who had visited me had been unreal.

We of Borthan do not take such visions lightly, however. I rose, and went from my cabin into the darkness outside, and walked about, scuffing at the warm sand with my bare toes as I struggled to excuse my inventions to myself. Slowly I calmed. Slowly I came to equilibrium. Yet I sat by my doorstep unsleeping for hours, until dawn's first green fingers crept upon me.

Beyond doubt you will agree with me that a man who has been apart from women some time, living under the tensions I have known since my flight into the Burnt Lowlands, will occasionally experience such sexual eruptions in his sleep, nor is there anything unnatural about them. I must maintain also, though I have little enough evidence to prove it, that many men of Borthan find themselves giving way in slumber to expressions of desire for their bondsisters, simply because such desires are so rigidly repressed in the waking time. And further, although Halum and I enjoyed intimacies of soul far beyond those which men customarily enjoy with their bondsisters, never once did I seek her physically, nor did such a union ever occur. Take this on faith, if you will: in these pages I tell you so much that is discreditable to me, making no attempt to conceal that which is shameful, that if I had violated Halum's bond I would tell you that as well. So you must believe that it was not a deed I did. You may not hold me guilty of sins committed in dreams.

Nevertheless I held myself guilty through the waning of the night and into this morning, and only as I purge myself now by putting the incident on paper does the darkness lift from my spirit. I think what has really troubled me these past few hours is not so much my sordid little sexual fantasy, for which even my enemies would probably forgive me, as it is my belief that I am responsible for Halum's death, for which I am unable to forgive myself.

9

Possibly I should say that every man of Borthan, and by the same token every woman, is sworn at birth or soon thereafter to a bondsister and bondbrother. No member of any such tripling may be blood-kin to any other. The bondings are arranged soon after a child is conceived, and often are the subject of intricate negotiation, since one's bondbrother and bondsister are customarily closer to one than one's own family-by-blood; hence a father owes it to his child to make the bondings with care.

Because I was to be a septarch's second son, arranging my bondings was a matter of high circumstance. It might have been good democracy, but poor sense, to bond me to a peasant's child, for one must be reared on the same social plane as one's bond-kin if any profit is to come from the relationship. On the other hand I could not be bonded to the kin of some other septarch, since fate might one day elevate me to my father's throne, and a septarch must not be tangled in ties of bonding to the royal house of another district lest he find his freedom of decision circumscribed. Thus it was necessary to make bondings for me with the children of nobility but not of royalty.

The project was handled by my father's bondbrother, Ulman Kotril; it was the last aid he ever gave my father, for he was slain by bandits from Krell not long after my birth. To find a bondsister for me, Ulman Kotril went down into Manneran and obtained bonding with the unborn child of Segvord Helalam, High Justice of the Port. It had been determined that Helalam's child was to be female; hence my father's bondbrother returned to Salla and completed the tripling by compacting with Luinn Condorit, a general of the northern patrol, for his coming son.

Noim, Halum, and I were born all the same week, and my father himself performed the service of bonding. (We were known by our child-names then, of course, but I ignore that here to simplify things.) The ceremony took place in the septarch's palace, with proxies standing in for Noim and Halum; later, when we were old enough to travel, we repledged our bonds in each other's presence, I going to Manneran to be bonded to Halum. Thereafter we were only infrequently apart. Segvord Helalam had no objection to letting his daughter be raised in Salla, for he hoped she would strike a glittering marriage with some prince at my father's court. In this he was to be disappointed, for Halum went unmarried, and, for all I know, virgin, to her grave.

This scheme of bondings allows us a small escape from the constricting solitude in which we of Borthan are expected to live. You must know by now – even if you who read this be a stranger to our planet – that it has long been forbidden by custom for us to open our souls to others. To talk excessively of oneself, so our forefathers believed, leads inevitably to self-indulgence, self-pity, and self-corruption; therefore we are trained to keep ourselves to ourselves, and, so that the prisoning bands of custom may be all the more steely, we are prohibited even from using such words as 'I' or 'me' in polite discourse. If we have problems, we settle them in silence; if we have ambitions, we fulfill them without advertising our hopes; if we have desires, we pursue them in a selfless and impersonal way. To these harsh rules only two exceptions are made. We may speak our hearts freely to our drainers, who are religious functionaries and mere hirelings; and we may, within limits, open ourselves to our bond-kin. These are the rules of the Covenant.

It is permissible to confide almost anything to a bondsister or a bond-brother, but we are taught to observe etiquette in going about it. For example, proper people consider it improper to speak in the first person even to one's bond-kin. It is not done, ever. No matter how intimate a confession we make, we must couch it in acceptable grammar, not in the vulgarities of a common selfbarer.

(In our idiom a *selfbarer* is one who exposes himself to others, by which is meant that he exposes his soul, not his flesh. It is deemed a coarse act and is punished by social ostracism, or worse. Selfbarers use the censured pronouns of the gutter vocabulary, as I have done throughout what you now read. Although one is allowed to *bare* one's *self* to one's bond-kin, one is not a *selfbarer* unless one does it in tawdry blurtings of 'I' and 'me.')

Also we are taught to observe reciprocity in our dealings with bond-kin. That is, we may not overload them with our woes, while failing to ease them of their own burdens. This is plain civility: the relationship depends on mutuality, and we may make use of them only if we are careful to let them make use of us. Children are often one-sided in their dealings with bond-kin; one may dominate his bondbrother, and chatter endlessly at him without pausing to heed the other's woes. But such things usually come into balance early. It is an unpardonable breach of propriety to show insufficent concern for one's bond-kin; I know no one, not even the weakest and most slovenly among us, who is guilty of that sin.

Of all the prohibitions having to do with bonding the most severe is the one against physical relationships with our bond-kin. In sexual matters we are generally quite free, only we dare not do this one thing. This struck at me most painfully. Not that I yearned for Noim, for that has never been my path, nor is it a common one among us; but Halum was my soul's desire, and neither as wife nor as mistress could she ever comfort me. Long hours we sat up together, her hand in mine, telling one another things we could tell no one else, and how easy it would have been for me to draw her close, and part her garments, and slip my throbbing flesh inside hers. I would not attempt it. My conditioning held firm; and, as I hope to survive long enough to tell you, even after Schweiz and his potion had changed my soul, still did I respect the sanctity of Halum's body, although I was able to enter her in other ways. But I will not deny my desire for her. Nor can I forget the shock I felt when I learned in boyhood that of all Borthan's women only Halum, my beloved Halum, was denied to me.

I was extraordinarily close to Halum in every but the physical way, and she was for me the ideal bondsister: open, giving, loving, serene, radiant, adaptable. Not only was she beautiful – creamy-skinned, dark-eyed and dark of hair, slender and graceful – but also she was remarkable within herself, for her soul was gentle and sleek and supple, a wondrous mixture of purity and wisdom. Thinking of her, I see the image of a forest glade in the mountains, with black-needled evergreen trees rising close together like shadowy swords springing from a bed of newly fallen snow, and a sparkling stream dancing between sun-spattered boulders, everything clean and untainted and self-contained. Sometimes when I was with her I felt impossibly thick and clumsy, a hulking lumbering mountain of dull meat, with an ugly hairy body and stupid ponderous muscles; but Halum had the skill of showing me, with a word, with a laugh, with a wink, that I was being unjust to myself when I let the sight of her lightness and gaiety lead me to wish I was woman-soft and woman-airy.

On the other side I was equally close to Noim. He was my foil in many ways: slender where I am burly, crafty where I am direct, cautious and calculating where I am rash, bleak of outlook where I am sunny. With him as with Halum I frequently felt awkward, not really in any bodily sense (for, as I have told you, I move well for a man my size) but in my inward nature.

Noim, more mercurial than I, livelier, quicker of wit, seemed to leap and cavort where I merely plodded, and yet the prevailing pessimism of his spirit made him appear deeper than I as well as more buoyant. To give myself credit, Noim looked with envy on me just as I did on him. He was jealous of my great strength, and furthermore he confessed that he felt mean-souled and petty when he peered into my eyes. 'One sees simplicity and power there,' he admitted, 'and one is aware that one often cheats, that one is lazy, that one breaks faith, that one does a dozen wicked things daily, and none of these things is any more natural to you than dining on your own flesh.'

You must understand that Halum and Noim were no bond-kin to one another, and were linked only by way of their common relationship to me. Noim had a bondsister of his own, a certain Thirga, and Halum was bonded to a girl of Manneran, Nald by name. Through such ties the Covenant creates a chain that clasps our society together, for Thirga had a bondsister too, and Nald a bondbrother, and each of them was bonded in turn on the other side, and so on and so on to form a vast if not infinite series. Obviously one comes in contact often with the bond-kin of his own bond-kin, though one is not free to assume with them the same privileges one has with those of his own bonding; I frequently saw Noim's Thirga and Halum's Nald, just as Halum saw my Noim and Noim saw my Halum, but there was never anything more than nodding friendship between me and Thirga or me and Nald, while Noim and Halum took to each other with immediate warmth. Indeed I suspected for a time that they might marry one another, which would have been uncommon but not illegal. Noim, though, perceived that it would disturb me if my bondbrother shared my bondsister's bed, and took care not to let the friendship ripen into love of that sort.

Halum now sleeps forever under a stone in Manneran, and Noim has become a stranger to me, perhaps even an enemy to me, and the red sand of the Burnt Lowlands blows in my face as I set down these lines.

10

After my brother Stirron became septarch in Salla, I went, as you know, to the province of Glin. I will not say that I *fled* to Glin, for no one openly compelled me to leave my native land; but call my departure a deed of tact. I left in order to spare Stirron the eventual embarrassment of putting me to death, which would have weighed badly upon his soul. One province cannot hold safely the two sons of a late septarch.

Glin was my choice because it is customary for exiles from Salla to go to Glin, and also because my mother's family held wealth and power there. I thought, wrongly as it turned out, that I might gain some advantage from that connection.

I was about three moontimes short of the age of thirteen when I took my leave of Salla. Among us that is the threshold of manhood; I had reached almost my present height, though I was much more slender and far less strong than I would soon become, and my beard had only lately begun to grow full. I knew something of history and government, something of the arts of warfare, something of the skills of hunting, and I had had some training in the practice of the law. Already I had bedded at least a dozen girls, and three times I had known, briefly, the tempests of unhappy love. I had kept the Covenant all my life; my soul was clean and I was at peace with our gods and with my forefathers. In my own eyes at that time I must have seemed hearty, adventurous, capable, honorable, and resilient, with all the world spread before me like a shining highway, and the future mine for the shaping. The perspective of thirty years tells me that that young man who left Salla then was also naïve, gullible, romantic, over-earnest, and conventional and clumsy of mind: quite an ordinary youth, in fact, who might have been skinning seapups in some fishing village had he not had the great good fortune to be born a prince.

The season of my going was early autumn, after a springtime when all Salla had mourned my father and a summer when all Salla had hailed my brother. The harvest had been poor – nothing odd in Salla, where the fields yield pebbles and stones more graciously than they do crops – and Salla City was choked with bankrupt husbandmen, hoping to catch some largess from the new septarch. A dull hot haze hung over the capital day after day, and above it lay the first of autumn's heavy clouds, floating in on schedule from the eastern sea. The streets were dusty; the trees had begun to drop their leaves early, even the majestic firethorns outside the septarch's palace; the dung of the farmers' beasts clogged the gutters. These were poor omens for Salla at the beginning of a septarch's reign, and to me it seemed like a wise season for getting out. Even this early Stirron's temper was fraying and unlucky councillors of state were going off to dungeons. I was still cherished at court, coddled and complimented, plied with fur cloaks and promises of baronies in the mountains, but for how long, how long? Just now Stirron was troubled with guilt that he had inherited the throne and I had nothing, and so he treated me softly, but let the dry summer give way to a bitter winter of famine and the scales might shift; envying me my freedom from responsibility, he might well turn on me. I had studied the annals of royal houses well. Such things had happened before.

Therefore I readied myself for a hasty exit. Only Noim and Halum knew

179

of my plans. I gathered those few of my possessions that I had no wish to abandon, such things as a ring of ceremony bequeathed by my father, a favorite hunting jerkin of yellow leather, and a double-cameo amulet bearing the portraits of my bondsister and bondbrother; all my books I relinquished, for one can get more books wherever one goes, and I did not even take the hornfowl spear, my trophy of my father's death-day, that hung in my palace bedchamber. There was to my name a fairly large amount of money, and this I handled in what I believed was a shrewd manner. It was all on deposit in the Royal Salla Bank. First I transferred the bulk of my funds to the six lesser provincial banks, over the course of many days. These new accounts were held jointly with Halum and Noim. Halum then proceeded to make withdrawals, asking that the money be paid into the Commercial and Seafarers Bank of Manneran, for the account of her father Segvord Helalam. If we were detected in this transfer, Halum was to declare that her father had undergone financial reverses and had requested a loan of short duration. Once my assets were safely on deposit in Manneran, Halum asked her father to transfer the money again, this time to an account in my name in the Covenant Bank of Glin. In this zigzag way I got my cash from Salla to Glin without arousing the suspicions of our Treasury officials, who might wonder why a prince of the realm was shipping his patrimony to our rival province of the north. The fatal flaw in all this was that if the Treasury became disturbed about the flow of capital to Manneran, questioned Halum, and then made inquiries of her father, the truth would emerge that Segvord prospered and had had no need of the 'loan,' which would have led to further questions and, probably, to my exposure. But my maneuvers went unnoticed.

Lastly I went before my brother to ask his permission to leave the capital, as courtly etiquette required.

This was a tense affair, for honor would not let me lie to Stirron, yet I dared not tell him the truth. Long hours I spent with Noim, first, rehearsing my deceptions. I was a slow pupil in chicanery; Noim spat, he cursed, he wept, he slapped his hands together, as time and again he slipped through my guard with a probing question. 'You were not meant to be a liar,' he told me in despair.

'No,' I agreed, 'this one never was meant to be a liar.'

Stirron received me in the northern robing chamber, a dark and somber room of rough stone walls and narrow windows, used mainly for audiences with village chieftains. He meant no offense by it, I think; it was merely where he happened to be when I sent in my equerry with word that I wished a meeting. It was late afternoon; a thin greasy rain was falling outside; in some far tower of the palace a carillonneur was instructing apprentices, and leaden bell-tones, scandalously awry, came humming through the drafty walls. Stirron was formally dressed: a bulky gray robe of stormshield furs, tight red woolen leggings, high boots of green leather. The sword of the Covenant was at his side, the heavy glittering pendant of office pressed against his breast, rings of title cluttered his fingers, and if memory does not deceive me, he wore yet another token of power around his right forearm. Only the crown itself was missing from his regalia. I had seen Stirron garbed this way often enough of late, at ceremonies and meetings of state, but to find him so enveloped in insignia on an ordinary afternoon struck me as almost comical. Was he so insecure that he needed to load himself with such stuff constantly, to reassure himself that he was indeed septarch? Did he feel that he had to impress his younger brother? Or did he, childlike, take pleasure in these ornaments for pleasure's own sake? No matter which, some flaw in Stirron's character was revealed, some inner foolishness. It astounded me that I could find him amusing rather than awesome. Perhaps the genesis of my ultimate rebellion lies in that moment when I walked in on Stirron in all his splendor and had to fight to hold my laughter back.

Half a year in the septarchy had left its mark on him. His face was gray and his left eyelid drooped, I suppose from exhaustion. He held his lips tightly compressed and stood in a rigid way with one shoulder higher than the other. Though only two years separated us in age, I felt myself a boy beside him, and marveled how the cares of office can etch a young man's visage. It seemed centuries since Stirron and I had laughed together in our bedchambers, and whispered all the forbidden words, and bared our ripening bodies to one another to make the edgy comparisons of adolescence. Now I offered formal obeisance to my weary royal brother, crossing my arms over my breast and flexing my knees and bowing my head as I murmured, 'Lord Septarch, long life be yours.'

Stirron was man enough to deflect my formality with a brotherly grin. He gave me a proper acknowledgment of my greeting, yes, arms raised and palms turned out, but then he turned it into an embrace, swiftly crossing the room and seizing me. Yet there was something artificial about his gesture, as though he had been studying how to show warmth to his brother, and quickly I was released. He wandered away from me, eyeing a nearby window, and his first words to me were, 'A beastly day. A brutal year.'

'The crown lies heavy, Lord Septarch?'

'You have leave to call your brother by his name.'

'The strains show in you, Stirron. Perhaps you take Salla's problems too closely to heart.'

'The people starve,' he said. 'Shall one pretend that is a trifling thing?'

'The people have always starved, year upon year,' I said. 'But if the septarch drains his soul in worry over them—'

'Enough, Kinnall. You presume.' Nothing brotherly about the tone now; he was hard put to hide his irritation with me. He was plainly angered that

I had so much as noticed his fatigue, though it was he who had begun our talk with lamenting. The conversation had veered too far toward the intimate. The condition of Stirron's nerves was no affair of mine: it was not my place to comfort him, he had a bondbrother for that. My attempted kindness had been improper and inappropriate. 'What do you seek here?' he asked roughly.

'The lord septarch's leave to go from the capital.'

He whirled away from the window and glared at me. His eyes, dull and sluggish until this moment, grew bright and harsh, and flickered disturbingly from side to side. 'To go? To go where?'

'One wishes to accompany one's bondbrother Noim to the northern frontier,' I said as smoothly as I could manage. 'Noim pays a call on the headquarters of his father, General Luinn Condorit, whom he has not seen this year since your lordship's coronation, and one is asked to travel northward with him, for bondlove and friendship.'

'When would you go?'

'Three days hence, if it please the septarch.'

'And for how long a stay?' Stirron was virtually barking these questions at me.

'Until the first snow of winter falls.'

'Too long. Too long.'

'One might be absent then a shorter span,' I said.

'Must you go at all, though?'

My right leg quivered shamefully at the knee. I struggled to be calm. 'Stirron, consider that one has not left Salla City for so much as an entire day since you assumed the throne. Consider that one cannot justly ask one's bondbrother to journey uncomforted through the northern hills.'

'Consider that you are the heir to the prime septarchy of Salla,' Stirron said, 'and that if misfortune comes to your brother while you are in the north, our dynasty is lost.'

The coldness of his voice, and the ferocity with which he had questioned me a moment earlier, threw me into panic. Would he oppose my going? My fevered mind invented a dozen reasons for his hostility. He knew of my transfers of funds, and had concluded I was about to defect to Glin; or he imagined that Noim and I, and Noim's father with his troops, would stir up an insurrection in the north, the aim being to place me on the throne; or he had already resolved to arrest and destroy me, but the time was not yet ripe for it, and he wished not to let me get far before he could pounce; or – but I need not multiply hypotheses. We are a suspicious people on Borthan, and no one is less trusting than one who wears a crown. If Stirron would not release me from the capital, and it appeared that he would not, then I must sneak away, and I might not succeed at that.

I said, 'No misfortunes are probable, Stirron, and even so, it would be no large task to return from the north if something befell you. Do you fear usurpation so seriously?'

'One fears everything, Kinnall, and leaves little to chance.'

He proceeded then to lecture me on necessary caution, and on the ambitions of those who surrounded the throne, naming a few lords as possible traitors whom I would have placed among the pillars of the realm. As he spoke, going far beyond the strictures of the Covenant in exposing his uncertainties to me, I saw with amazement what a tortured, terrified man my brother had become in this short time of septarchy; and I realized, too, that I was not going to be granted my leave. He went on and on, fidgeting as he spoke, rubbing his talismans of authority, several times picking up his scepter from where it lay on an ancient wood-topped table, walking to the window and coming back from it, pitching his voice now low and now high as though searching for the best septarchical resonances. I was frightened for him. He was a man of my own considerable size, and at that time much thicker in body and greater in strength than I, and all my life I had worshiped him and modeled myself upon him; and here he was corroded with terror and committing the sin of *telling me about it.* Had just these few moontimes of supreme power brought Stirron to this collapse? Was the loneliness of the septarchy that awful for him? On Borthan we are born lonely, and lonely we live, and lonely we die; why should wearing a crown be so much more difficult than bearing the burdens we inflict upon ourselves each day? Stirron told me of assassins' plots and of revolution brewing among the farmers who thronged the town, and even hinted that our father's death had been no accident. I tried to persuade myself that hornfowl could be trained to slay a particular man in a group of thirteen men, and would not swallow the notion. It appeared that royal responsibilities had driven Stirron mad. I was reminded of a duke some years back who displeased my father, and was sent for half a year to a dungeon, and tortured each day that the sun could be seen. He had entered prison a sturdy and vigorous figure, and when he emerged he was so ruined that he befouled his own clothes with his dung, and did not know it. How soon would Stirron be brought to that? Perhaps it was just as well, I thought, that he was refusing me permission to go away, for it might be better that I remain at the capital, ready to take his place if he crumbled beyond repair.

But he amazed me at the finish of his rambling oration; for it had taken him clear across the room, to an alcove hung with dangling silver chains, and at the end, suddenly bunching the chains and yanking a dozen of them from their mountings, he swung round to face me and cried hoarsely, 'Give your pledge, Kinnall, that you will come back from the north in time to attend the royal wedding!'

I was doubly pronged. For the last several minutes I had begun to make plans on the basis of staying in Salla City; now I found I could depart after all, and was not sure I should, in view of Stirron's deterioration. And then too he demanded from me a promise of swift return, and how could I give the septarch such a promise without lying to him, a sin I was not prepared to commit? So far all that I had told him was the truth, though only part of the truth; I *did* plan to travel north with Noim to visit his father, I *would* remain in northern Salla until winter's first snow. How though could I set a date for my coming back to the capital?

My brother was due to marry, forty days hence, the youngest daughter of Bryggil, septarch of Salla's southeastern district. It was a cunning match. So far as the traditional order of primacy went, Bryggil stood seventh and lowest in the hierarchy of Salla's septarchs, but he was the oldest, the cleverest, and the most respected of the seven, now that my father was gone. To combine Bryggil's shrewdness and stature with the prestige that accrued to Stirron by virtue of his rank as prime septarch would be to cement the dynasty of our family to the throne. And no doubt sons would shortly come marching out of Bryggil's daughter's loins, relieving me of my position as heir apparent; her fertility must have passed the necessary tests, and of Stirron's there could be no question, since he had already scattered a litter of bastards all over Salla. I would have certain ceremonial roles to play at the wedding as brother to the septarch.

I had wholly forgotten the wedding. If I skipped out of Salla before it came about, I would wound my brother in a way that saddened me. But if I stayed here, with Stirron in this unstable state, I had no guarantee of being a free man when the nuptial day arrived, or even of still owning my head. Nor was there any sense in going north with Noim if I bound myself to return in forty days. It was a hard choice: to postpone my departure and run the risks of my brother's royal whims, or to leave now, knowing I was taking on myself the stain of breaking a pledge to my septarch.

The Covenant teaches us that we should welcome dilemmas, for it toughens character to grapple with the insoluble and find a solution. In this instance events made a mockery of the Covenant's lofty moral teachings. As I hesitated in anguish, Stirron's telephone summoned him; he snatched its handpiece, jabbed at the scrambler, and listened to five minutes of gibberish, his face darkening and his eyes growing fiery. At length he broke the contact and peered up at me as though I were a stranger to him. 'They are eating the flesh of the newly dead in Spoksa,' he muttered. 'On the slopes of the Kongoroi they dance to demons in hopes of finding food. Insanity! Insanity!' He clenched his fists and strode to the window, and thrust his face to it, and closed his eyes, and I think forgot my presence for a time. Again the telephone asked for him. Stirron jerked back like one who has been stabbed, and started toward the machine. Noticing me standing frozen near the door, he fluttered his hands impatiently at me and said, 'Go, will you? Off with your bondbrother, wherever you go. This province! This famine! Father, father, father!' He seized the handpiece. I started to offer a genuflection of parting, and Stirron furiously waved me from the room, sending me unpledged and unchecked toward the borders of his realm.

11

Noim and I set forth three days afterward, just the two of us and a small contingent of servants. The weather was bad, for summer's dryness had given way not merely to the thick dreary gray clouds of autumn but to a foresampling of winter's heavy rains. 'You'll be dead of the mildew before you see Glin,' Halum told us cheerfully. 'If you don't drown in the mud of the Grand Salla Highway.'

She stayed with us, at Noim's house, on the eve of our departure, sleeping chastely apart in the little chamber just under the roof, and joined us for breakfast as we made ready to go. I had never seen her looking lovelier; that morning she wore a bloom of shimmering beauty that cut through the murk of the drizzly dawn like a torch in a cave. Perhaps what enhanced her so greatly then was that she was about to pass from my life for an unknown length of time, and, conscious of my self-inflicted loss, I magnified her attractiveness. She was clad in a gown of delicate golden chainmesh, beneath which only a gossamer wrap concealed her naked form, and her body, shifting this way and that under its flimsy coverings, aroused in me thoughts that left me drenched in shame. Halum then was in the ripeness of early womanhood, and had been for several years; it had already begun to puzzle me that she remained unwed. Though she and Noim and I were of the same age, she had leaped free of childhood before us, as girls will do, and I had come to think of her as older than the two of us, because for a year she had had breasts and the monthly flow, while Noim and I were still without hair on cheek or body. And while we had caught up to her in physical maturity, she was still more adult in her bearing than my bondbrother or I, her voice more smoothly modulated, her manner more poised, and it was impossible for me to shake off that notion that she was senior sister to us. Who soon must accept some suitor, lest she become overripe and sour in her maidenhood; I was suddenly certain that Halum would marry while I was off hiding in Glin, and the thought of some sweaty stranger planting babies between her thighs so sickened me that I turned away from her at the table, and lurched to the window to gulp the humid air into my throbbing lungs.

'Are you unwell?' Halum asked.

'One feels a certain tension, bondsister.'

'Surely there's no danger. The septarch's permission has been granted for you to go north.'

'There is no document to show it,' Noim pointed out.

'You are a septarch's son!' Halum cried. 'What guardian of the roads would dare to trifle with you?'

'Exactly,' I said. 'There is no cause for fear. One feels only a sense of uncertainty. One is beginning a new life, Halum.' I forced a faint smile. 'The time of going must be here.'

'Stay a while longer,' Halum begged.

But we did not. The servants waited in the street. The groundcars were ready. Halum embraced us, clasping Noim first, then me, for I was the one who would not be returning, and that called for a longer farewell. When she came into my arms I was stunned by the intensity with which she offered herself: her lips to my lips, her belly to my belly, her breasts crushed against my chest. On tiptoes she strained to press her body into mine, and for a moment I felt her trembling, until I began myself to tremble. It was not a sisterly kiss and certainly not a bondsisterly kiss; it was the passionate kiss of a bride sending her young husband off to a war from which she knows there is no coming back. I was singed by Halum's sudden fire. I felt as though a veil had been ripped away and some Halum I had not known before had flung herself against me, one who burned with the needs of the flesh, one who did not mind revealing her forbidden hunger for a bondbrother's body. Or did I imagine those things in her? It seemed to me that for a single protracted instant Halum repressed nothing and allowed her arms and lips to tell me the truth about her feelings; but I could not respond in kind – I had trained myself too well in the proper attitudes toward one's bondsister – and I was distant and cool as I clasped her. I may even have thrust her back a little, shocked by her forwardness. And, as I say, there may have been no forwardness at all except in my overwrought mind, but only legitimate grief at a parting. In any event the intensity went quickly from Halum; her embrace slackened and she released me, and she appeared downcast and chilled, as if I had rebuffed her cruelly by being so prim when she was giving so much.

'Come now,' Noim said impatiently, and, trying somehow to rescue the situation, I lifted Halum's hand and touched my palm lightly to her cool palm, and smiled an awkward smile, and she smiled even more awkwardly, and perhaps we would have said a stumbling word or two, but Noim caught me by the elbow and stolidly led me outside to begin my journey away from my homeland.

12

I insisted on opening myself to a drainer before leaving Salla City. I had not planned on doing so, and it irritated Noim that I took the time for it; but an uncontrollable yearning for the comforts of religion rose up in me as we neared the outskirts of the capital.

We had been traveling almost an hour. The rain had thickened, and gusty winds slammed it against the windscreens of our groundcars, so that cautious driving was in order. The cobbled streets were slippery. Noim drove one of the cars, I sitting sullenly beside him; the other, with our servants, followed close behind. The morning was young and the city still slept. Each passing street was a surgery to me, for a segment of my life was ripped off by it: there goes the palace compound, there go the spires of the House of Justice, there the university's great gray blocky buildings, there the godhouse where my royal father brought me into the Covenant, there the Museum of Mankind that I visited so often with my mother to stare at the treasures from the stars. Circling through the fine residential district that borders the Skangen Canal, I even spied the ornate townhouse of the Duke of Kongoroi, on whose handsome daughter's silken bedsheets I had left my virginity in a clammy puddle, not too many years before. In this city I had lived all my life, and I might never see it again; my yesterdays were washing away, like the topsoil of Salla's sad farms under the knives of the winter rains. Since boyhood I had known that one day my brother would be septarch and this city would cease to have a place for me, but yet I had denied that to myself, saying, 'It will not happen soon, perhaps it will not happen at all.' And my father lay dead in his firethorn coffin, and my brother crouched beneath the awful weight of his crown, and I was fleeing from Salla before my life had fairly begun, and such a mood of self-pity came over me that I did not dare even to speak to Noim, though what is a bondbrother for if not to ease one's soul? And when we were driving through the ramshackle streets of Salla Old Town, not far from the city walls, I spied a dilapidated godhouse and said to Noim, 'Pull up at the corner here. One must go within to empty himself.'

Noim, fretful, did not want to spare the time, and made as if to drive on. 'Would you deny one the godright?' I asked him hotly, and only then, simmering and cross, did he halt the car and back it up to let me out by the godhouse.

Its façade was worn and peeling. An inscription beside the door was illegible. The pavement before it was cracked and tilted. Salla Old Town has a pedigree of more than a thousand years; some of its buildings have been continuously inhabited since the founding of the city, though most are in ruins, for the life of that district ended, in effect, when one of the medieval septarchs chose to move his court to our present palace atop Skangen Hill, much to the south. At night Salla Old Town comes alive with pleasure-seekers, who guzzle the blue wine in cellar cabarets, but at this misty hour it was a grim place. Blank stone walls faced me from every building: we have a fashion of making mere slits serve for windows in Salla, but here they carried it to an extreme. I wondered if the godhouse could have a scanning machine in working order to watch my approach. Yes, as it happened. When I neared the godhouse door, it swung partly open, and a scrawny man in drainer's robes looked out. He was ugly, of course. Who ever saw a handsome drainer? It is a profession for the ill-favored. This one had greenish skin, heavily pocked, and a rubbery snout of a nose, and a dimness in one eye: standard for his trade. He gave me a fishy stare and, by his wariness, seemed to be regretting having opened the door.

'The peace of all gods be on you,' I said. 'Here is one in need of your craft.'

He eyed my costly costume, my leather jerkin and my heavy jewelry, and studied the size and swagger of me, and evidently concluded I was some young bully of the aristocracy out to stir trouble in the slums. 'It is too early in the day,' he said uneasily. 'You come too soon for comfort.'

'You would not refuse a sufferer!'

'It is too early.'

'Come, come, let one in. A troubled soul stands here.'

He yielded, as I knew he must, and with many a twitch of his long-nosed face he admitted me. Within there was the reek of rot. The old woodwork was impregnated with the damp, the draperies were moldering, the furniture had been gnawed by insects. The lighting was dim. The drainer's wife, as ugly as the drainer himself, skulked about. He led me to his chapel, a small sweaty room off the living-quarters, and left me kneeling by the cracked and yellowing mirror while he lit the candles. He robed himself and finally came to me where I knelt.

He named his fee. I gasped.

'Too much by half,' I said.

He reduced it by a fifth. When I still refused, he told me to find my priesting elsewhere, but I would not rise, and, grudgingly, he brought the price of his services down another notch. Still it was probably five times what he charged the folk of Salla Old Town for the same benefit, but he knew I had money, and, thinking of Noim fuming in the car, I could not bring myself to haggle.

'Done,' I said.

Next he brought me the contract. I have said that we of Borthan are suspicious people; have I indicated how we rely on contracts? A man's word is merely bad air. Before a soldier beds a whore they come to the terms of their bargain and scrawl it on paper. The drainer gave me a standard form, promising me that all I said would be held in strictest confidence, the drainer merely acting as intermediary between me and the god of my choice, and I for my part pledging that I would hold the drainer to no liability for the knowledge he would have of me, that I would not call him as witness in a lawsuit or make him my alibi in some prosecution, et cetera, et cetera. I signed. He signed. We exchanged copies and I gave him his money.

'Which god would you have preside here?' he asked.

'The god who protects travelers,' I told him. We do not call our gods aloud by their names.

He lit a candle of the appropriate color – pink – and put it beside the mirror. By that it was understood that the chosen god would accept my words.

'Behold your face,' the drainer said. 'Put your eyes to your eyes.'

I stared at the mirror. Since we shun vanity, it is not usual to examine one's face except on these occasions of religion.

'Open now your soul,' the drainer commanded. 'Let your griefs and dreams and hungers and sorrows emerge.'

'A septarch's son it is who flees his homeland,' I began, and at once the drainer jerked to attention, impaled by my news. Though I did not take my eyes from the mirror, I guessed that he was scrabbling around to look at the contract and see who it was that had signed it. 'Fear of his brother,' I continued, 'leads him to go abroad, but yet he is sore of soul as he departs.'

I went on in that vein for some while. The drainer made the usual interjections every time I faltered, prying words out of me in his craft's cunning way, and shortly there was no need for such midwifery, for the words gushed freely. I told him how close I had come to lying to Stirron; I confessed that I would miss the royal wedding and give my brother injury thereby; I admitted several small sins of self-esteem, such as anyone commits daily.

The drainer listened.

We pay them to listen and to do nothing but listen, until we are drained and healed. Such is our holy communion, that we lift these toads from the mud, and set them up in their godhouses, and buy their patience with our money. It is permitted under the Covenant to say anything to a drainer, even if it is drivel, even if it is a shameful catalog of throttled lusts and hidden filth. We may bore a drainer as we have no right to bore our bond-kin, for it is the drainer's obligation by contract to sit with the patience of the hills as we speak of ourselves. We need not worry what the drainer's problems may be, nor what he thinks of us, nor whether he would be happier doing something else. He has a calling and he takes his fee, and he must serve those who have need of him. There was a time when I felt it was a miraculously fine scheme, to give us drainers in order that we might rid our hearts of pain. Too much of my life was gone before I realized that to open oneself to a drainer is no more comforting than to make love to one's own hand: there are better ways of loving, there are happier ways of opening.

But I did not know that then, and I squatted by the mirror, getting the best healing that money could buy. Whatever residue of wrongness was in my soul came forth, syllable smoothly following syllable, the way sweet liquor will flow when one taps the thorny flanks of the gnarled and repellent-looking flesh-trees that grow by the Gulf of Sumar. As I spoke the candles caught me in their spell, and by the flickering of them I was drawn into the curved surface of the mirror so that I was drawn out of myself; the drainer was a mere blur in the darkness, unreal, unimportant, and I spoke now directly to the god of travelers, who would heal me and send me on my way. And I believed that this was so. I will not say that I imagined a literal godplace where our deities sit on call to serve us, but I had then an abstract and metaphorical understanding of our religion by which it seemed to me, in its way, as real as my right arm.

My flow of words halted and the drainer made no attempt to renew the outpour. He murmured the phrases of absolution. I was done. He snuffed the godcandle between two fingers and rose to doff his robes. Still I knelt, weak and quivering from my draining, lost in reveries. I felt cleansed and purified, stripped of my soul's grit and debris, and, in the music of that moment, was only dimly aware of the squalor about me. The chapel was a place of magic and the drainer was aflame with divine beauty.

'Up,' he said, nudging me with the tip of his sandal. 'Out. Off about your journeys.'

The sound of his splintery voice doused all the wonder. I stood up, shaking my head to cure it of its new lightness, while the drainer half pushed me into the corridor. He was no longer afraid of me, that ugly little man, even though I might be a septarch's son and could kill him with one wad of my spittle, for I had told him of my cowardice, of my forbidden hunger for Halum, of all the cheapnesses of my spirit, and that knowledge reduced me in his eyes: no man newly drained can awe his drainer.

The rain was even worse when I left the building. Noim sat scowling in the car, his forehead pressed to the steering-stick. He looked up and tapped his wrist to tell me I had dallied too long at the godhouse.

'Feel better now that your bladder's empty?' he asked.

'What?'

'That is, did you have a good soul-pissing in there?'

'A foul phrase, Noim.'

'One grows blasphemous when his patience is extended too far.'

He kicked the starter and we rolled forward. Shortly we were at the ancient walls of Salla City, by the noble tower-bedecked opening known as Glin Door, which was guarded by four sour-faced and sleepy warriors in dripping uniforms. They paid no heed to us. Noim drove through the gate and past a sign welcoming us to the Grand Salla Highway. Salla City dwindled swiftly behind us; northward we rushed toward Glin.

13

The Grand Salla Highway passes through one of our best farming districts, the rich and fertile Plain of Nand, which each spring receives a gift of topsoil stripped from the skin of West Salla by our busy streams. At that time the septarch of the Nand district was a notorious coinclutcher, and thanks to his penury the highway was in poor repair there, so, as Halum had predicted in jest, we were hard put to wallow through the mud that clogged the road. It was good to finish with Nand and enter North Salla, where the land is a mixture of rock and sand and the people live on weeds and on scuttling things that they take from the sea. Groundcars are unusual sights in North Salla, and twice we were stoned by hungry and sullen townsfolk, who found our mere passage through their unhappy place an insult. But at least the road was free of mud.

Noim's father's troops were stationed in extreme North Salla, on the lower bank of the River Huish. This is the grandest of Velada Borthan's rivers. It begins as a hundred trifling brooks trickling down the eastern slopes of the Huishtors in the northern part of West Salla; these brooks merge in the foothills to become a swift stream, gray and turbulent, that rushes through a narrow granite canyon marked by six great steplike plunges. Emerging from those wild cascades onto its alluvial plain, the Huish proceeds more serenely on a northeastern course toward the sea, growing wider and wider in the flatlands, and splitting ultimately so that, at its broad delta, it gives itself to the ocean through eight mouths. In its rapid western reaches the Huish forms the boundary between Salla and Glin; at its placid easternmost end it divides Glin from Krell.

For all its length the great river is unbridged, and one might think little need exists to fortify its banks against invaders from the far side. But many times in Salla's history have the men of Glin crossed the Huish by boat to make war, and just as many times have we of Salla gone to ravage Glin; nor is the record of neighborliness between Glin and Krell any happier. So all along the Huish sprout military outposts, and generals like Luinn Condorit consume their lives studying the riverfogs for glimpses of the enemy.

I stayed a short while at Noim's father's camp. The general was not much like Noim, being a large-featured, heavy man whose face, eroded by time and frustration, was like a contour map of bouldery North Salla. Not once in fifteen years had there been any significant clash along the border he guarded, and I think that idleness had chilled his soul: he said little, scowled often, turned every statement into a bitter grumble, and retreated speedily from conversation into private dreams. They must have been dreams of war; no doubt he could not glance at the river without wishing that it swarmed with the landing-craft of Glin. Since men like him surely patrol the Glin side of the river as well, it is a wonder that the border guards do not trespass on one another out of sheer boredom, every few years, and embroil our provinces in pointless conflict.

A dull time we had of it there. Noim was bound by filial ties to call upon his father, but they had nothing to say to one another, and the general was a stranger to me. I had told Stirron I would stay with Noim's father until the first snow of winter fell, and I was true to that, yet luckily it was no lengthy visit I made; winter comes early in the north. On my fifth day there white sprinkles fluttered down and I was released from my self-imposed pledge.

Ferries, shuttling between terminals in three places, link Salla to Glin except when there is war. Noim drove me to the nearest terminal one black dawn, and solemnly we embraced and made our farewells. I said I would send my address, when I had one in Glin, so that he could keep me informed of doings in Salla. He promised to look after Halum. We talked vaguely of when he and she and I would meet again; perhaps they would visit me in Glin next year, perhaps we would all three go on holiday in Manneran. We made these plans with little conviction in our voices.

'This day of parting should never have come,' Noim said.

'Partings lead only to reunions,' I told him jauntily.

'Perhaps you could have come to some understanding with your brother, Kinnall—'

'There was never hope of that.'

'Stirron has spoken warmly of you. Is he then insincere?'

'He means his warmth, just now. But it would not be long before it became inconvenient for him to have a brother dwelling by his side, and then embarrassing, and then impossible. A septarch sleeps best when there is no potential rival of the royal blood close at hand.'

The ferry beckoned me with a bellow of its horn.

I clasped Noim's arm and we made farewells again, hurriedly. The last thing I said to him was, 'When you see the septarch, tell him that his brother loves him.' Then I went aboard.

The crossing was too quick. Less than an hour and I found myself on the alien soil of Glin. The immigration officials examined me brusquely, but they thawed at the sight of my passport, bright red to denote my place in the nobility, with a golden stripe to show that I was of the septarch's family. At once I had my visa, good for an indefinite stay. Such officials are a gossipy sort; beyond question they were on the telephone the instant I left them, sending word to their government that a prince of Salla was in the land, and I suppose that not much later that bit of information was in the hands of Salla's diplomatic representatives in Glin, who would relay it to my brother for his displeasure.

Across the way from the customs shed I came upon a branch of the Covenant Bank of Glin, and changed my Salla money for the currency of the northerners. With my new funds I hired a driver to take me to the capital city, which they call Glain, half a day's journey north of the border.

The road was narrow and winding, and traversed a bleak countryside where winter's touch had long ago pulled the leaves from the trees. Dirty snow was banked high. Glin is a frosty province. It was settled by men of a puritan nature, who found the living too easy in Salla, and felt that if they remained there, they might be tempted away from the Covenant; failing to reform our forefathers into greater piety, they left, crossing the Huish by rafts to hack out a livelihood in the north. Hard folk for a hard land; however poor the farming is in Salla, it is twice as unrewarding in Glin, and they live there mainly by fishing, by manufacturing, by the jugglements of commercial dealings, and by piracy. But that my mother had sprung from Glin, I would never have chosen it for my place of exile. Not that I gained anything from my family ties.

14

Nightfall saw me in Glain. A walled city it is, like Salla's capital, but otherwise not much like it. Salla City has grace and power; its buildings are made of great blocks of substantial stone, black basalt and rosy granite quarried in the mountains, and its streets are wide and sweeping, affording noble vistas and splendid promenades. Apart from our custom of letting narrow slits stand in place of true windows, Salla City is an open, inviting place, the architecture of which announces to the world the boldness and self-sufficiency of its citizens. But that dismal Glain! Oh!

Glain is fashioned of scruffy yellow brick, here and there trimmed with miserable poor pink sandstone that rubs to particles at a finger's nudge. It has no streets, only alleyways; the houses jostle one another as if afraid that some interloper may try to slip between them if they relax their guard. An avenue in Glain would not impress a gutter in Salla. And the architects of Glain have created a city fit only for a nation of drainers, since everything is lopsided, awry, uneven, and coarse. My brother, who had once been to Glain on a diplomatic errand, had described the place to me, but I put his harsh words off to mere patriotic prejudice; now I saw that Stirron had been too kind.

Nor were the folk of Glain more lovely than their city. On a world where suspicion and secrecy are godly virtues, one expects to find charm in short supply; yet I found the Glainish virtuous beyond all necessity. Dark clothes, dark frowns, dark souls, closed and shrunken hearts. Their speech itself displays their constipation of spirit. The language of Glin is the same as that of Salla, though the northerners have pronounced accents, clipping their syllables and shifting their vowels. That did not disturb me, but their syntax of self-effacement did. My driver, who was not a city man and therefore seemed almost friendly, left me at a hostelry where he thought I would have kind treatment, and I entered and said, 'One would have a room for tonight, and for some days beyond this one, perhaps.' The innkeeper stared balefully at me as if I had said, '*I* would have a room,' or something equally filthy. Later I discovered that even our usual polite circumlocution seems too vain for a northerner; I should not have said, 'One would have a room,' but rather, 'Is there a room to be had?' At a restaurant it is wrong to say, 'One will dine on thus and thus,' but rather, 'These are the dishes that have been chosen.' And so on and so on, twisting everything into a cumbersome passive form to avoid the sin of acknowledging one's own existence.

For my ignorance the innkeeper gave me his meanest room, and charged me twice the usual tariff. By my speech I had branded myself a man of Salla; why should he be courteous? But in signing the contract for my night's lodgings I had to show him my passport, which made him gasp when he saw that he was host to a visiting prince; he softened more than a little, asking me if I would have wine sent to my room, or maybe a buxom Glainish wench. I took the wine but declined the wench, for I was very young and overly frightened of the diseases that might lurk in foreign loins. That night I sat alone in my room, watching snowflakes drowning in a murky canal below my window, and feeling more isolated from humanity than ever before, ever since.

15

Over a week passed before I found the courage to call upon my mother's kin. I strolled the city for hours every day, keeping my cloak wrapped close against the winds and marveling at the ugliness of all I beheld, people and structures. I located the embassy of Salla, and lurked outside it, not wishing to go in but merely cherishing the link to my homeland that the squat grim building provided. I bought heaps of cheaply printed books and read far into the night to learn something of my adopted province: there was a history of Glin, and a guidebook to the city of Glain, and an interminable epic poem dealing with the founding of the first settlements north of the Huish, and much else. I dissolved my loneliness in wine – not the wine of Glin, for none is made there, but rather the good sweet golden wine of Manneran, that they import in giant casks. I slept poorly. One night I dreamed that Stirron had died of a fit and a search was being made for me. Several times in my sleep I saw the hornfowl strike my father dead; this is a dream that still haunts me, coming twice or thrice a year. I wrote long letters to Halum and Noim, and tore them up, for they stank of self-pity. I wrote one to Stirron, begging him to forgive me for fleeing, and tore that up too. When all else failed, I asked the innkeeper for a wench. He sent me a skinny girl a year or two older than I, with odd large breasts that dangled like inflated rubber bags. 'It is said you are a prince of Salla,' she declared coyly, lying down and parting her thighs. Without replying I covered her and thrust myself into her, and the size of my organ made her squeal with fear and pleasure both, and she wriggled her hips so fiercely that my seed burst from me within half a moment. I was angered at myself for that, and turned my wrath on her, pulling free and shouting, 'Who told you to start moving? I wasn't ready to have you move! I didn't want you to!' She ran from my room still naked, terrified more, I think, by my obscenities than by my wrath. I had never said 'I' in front of a woman before. But she was only a whore, after all. I soaped myself for an hour afterward. In my naïveté I feared that the innkeeper would evict me for speaking so vulgarly to her, but he said nothing. Even in Glin, one need not be polite to whores.

I realized that there had been a strange pleasure in shouting those words at her. I yielded to curious reveries of fantasy, in which I imagined the big-breasted slut naked on my bed, while I stood over her crying, 'I! I! I! I! I!' Such daydreams had the power to make my maleness stand tall. I considered going to a drainer to get rid of the dirty notion, but instead, two nights later, I asked the innkeeper for another wench, and with each jab of my body I silently cried, 'I! Me! I! Me!'

Thus I spent my patrimony in the capital of puritan Glin, wenching and drinking and loitering. When the stench of my own idleness offended me, I put down my timidity and went to see my Glainish relatives.

My mother had been a daughter of a prime septarch of Glin; he was dead, as was his son and successor; now his son's son, Truis, my mother's nephew, held the throne. It seemed too forward to me to go seeking preferment from my royal cousin directly. Truis of Glin would have to weigh matters of state as well as matters of kinship, and might not want to aid the runaway brother of Salla's prime septarch, lest it lead him into friction with Stirron. But I had an aunt, Nioll, my mother's younger sister, who had often been in Salla City in my mother's lifetime, and who had held me fondly when I was a babe; would she not help me?

She had married power to power. Her husband was the Marquis of Huish, who held great influence at the septarch's court, and also – for in Glin it is not thought unseemly for the nobility to dabble in commerce – controlled his province's wealthiest factor-house. These factor-houses are something akin to banks, but of another species; they lend money to brigands and merchants and lords of industry, only at ruinous rates, and always taking a slice of ownership in any enterprise they aid; thus they insinuate their tentacles into a hundred organizations and attain immense leverage in economic matters. In Salla the factor-houses were forbidden a century ago, but in Glin they thrive almost as a second government. I had no love for the system, but I preferred joining it to begging.

Some inquiries at the inn gained me directions to the palace of the marquis. By Glainish standards it was an imposing structure of three interlocking wings beside a mirror-smooth artificial lake, in the aristocrats' sector of the city. I made no attempt to talk my way inside; I had come prepared with a note, informing the marquise that her nephew Kinnall, the septarch's son of Salla, was in Glain and wished the favor of an audience; he could be found at such-and-such a hostelry. I returned to my lodgings and waited, and on the third day the innkeeper, popeyed with awe, came to my room to tell me I had a visitor in the livery of the Marquis of Huish. Nioll had sent a car for me; I was taken to her palace, which was far more lavish within than without, and she received me in a great hall cunningly paneled with mirrors set at angles to other mirrors to create an illusion of infinity.

She had aged greatly in the six or seven years since I had last seen her, but my amazement at her white hair and furrowed face was swallowed up in her astonishment over my transformation from tiny child to hulking man in so short a time. We embraced in the style of Glin, fingertips to fingertips; she offered condolences on the death of my father, and apologies for not having attended Stirron's coronation; then she asked me what brought me to Glin, and I explained, and she showed no surprise. Did I propose to dwell permanently here? I did, I said. And how would I support myself? By working in the factor-house of her husband, I explained, if such a position could be procured for me. She did not act as though she found my ambition unreasonable, but merely asked if I had any skills that might recommend me to the marquis. To this I replied that I had been trained in the lawcodes of Salla (not mentioning how incomplete my training was) and might be of value in the factor-houses's dealings with that province; also, I said, I had connections of bonding to Segvord Helalam, High Justice of the Port of Manneran, and could serve the firm well in its Manneran business; lastly, I remarked, I was young and strong and ambitious, and would place myself wholly in the service of the factor-house's interests, for our mutual advantage. These statements seemed to sit smoothly with my aunt, and she promised to gain for me an interview with the marquis himself. I left her palace much pleased with my prospects.

Several days later came word to the hostelry that I should present myself at the offices of the factor-house. My appointment, however, was not with the Marquis of Huish; rather, I was to see one of his executives, a certain Sisgar. I should have taken that as an omen. This man was smooth to the point of oiliness, with a beardless face and no eyebrows and a bald head that looked as if it had been waxed, and a dark green robe that was at once properly austere and subtly ostentatious. He questioned me briefly about my training and experience, discovering in some ten queries that I had had little of the former and none of the latter; but he exposed my failings in a gentle and amiable way, and I assumed that despite my ignorance, my high birth and kinship to the marquise would gain me a post. Alas for complacency! I had begun to hatch a dream of climbing to great responsibilities in this factor-house when I caught with only half an ear the words of Sisgar, telling me, 'Times are hard, as surely your grace comprehands, and it is unfortunate that you come to us at a time when retrenching is necessary. The advantages of giving you employment are many, yet the problems are extreme. The marquis wishes you to know that your offer of service was greatly appreciated, and it is his hope to bring you into the firm when economic conditions permit.' With many bows and a pleasant smile of dismissal he drove me from his office, and I was on the street before I realized how thoroughly I had been destroyed. They could give me nothing, not even a fifth assistant clerkship in some village office! How was this possible? I nearly rushed back within, planning to cry, 'This is a mistake, you deal with your septarch's cousin here, you reject the nephew of the marquise!' But they knew those things, and yet they shut their doors to me. When I telephoned my aunt to express my shock, I was told she had gone abroad, to pass the winter in leafy Manneran.

16

Eventually what had occurred became clear to me. My aunt had spoken of me to the marquis, and the marquis had conferred with the septarch Truis, who, concluding that it might embarrass him with Stirron to allow me any kind of employ, instructed the marquis to turn me away. In my fury I thought of going straight to Truis to protest, but I saw the futility of that soon enough, and since my protector Nioll had plainly gone out of Glin to shake herself free of me, I knew there was no hope in that direction. I was alone in Glain with the winter coming on, and no position in this alien place, and my lofty birth worse than useless to me.

Harder blows followed.

Presenting myself at the Covenant Bank of Glin one morning to withdraw funds for living expenses, I learned that my account had been sequestered at the request of the Grand Treasurer of Salla, who was investigating the possibility of an illegal transfer of capital out of that province. By blustering and waving my royal passport about, I managed to break loose enough money for seven days' food and lodging, but the rest of my savings was lost to me, for I had no stomach for the kind of appeals and maneuvers that might free it.

Next I was visited at my hostelry by a diplomat of Salla, a jackal of an undersecretary who reminded me, with many a genuflection and formula of respect, that my brother's wedding would shortly take place and I was expected to return and serve as ring-linker. Knowing that I would never leave Salla City again if ever I gave myself into Stirron's hands, I explained that urgent business required me to remain in Glain during the season of the nuptials, and asked that my deep regrets be conveyed to the septarch. The undersecretary received this with professional grace, but it was not hard for me to detect the savage gleam of pleasure beneath his outer mask: I was buying me trouble, he was telling himself, and he would gladly help me close the contract.

On the fourth day thereafter my innkeeper came to tell me that I could no longer stay at the hostelry, for my passport had been revoked and I had no legal status in Glin.

This was an impossibility. A royal passport such as I carried is granted for life, and is valid in every province of Velada Borthan except in times of war, and there was no war at the moment between Salla and Glin. The innkeeper shrugged away my words; he showed me his notice from the police, ordering him to evict his illegal alien, and he suggested that if I had objections I should take the matter up with the appropriate bureau of the Glinish civil service, for it was beyond his scope. I regarded filing such an appeal as unwise. My eviction had not come about by accident, and should I appear at any government office, I was likely to find myself arrested and hustled across the Huish into Stirron's grasp forthwith.

Seeing such an arrest as the most probable next development, I wondered how to elude the government agents. Now I sorely felt the absence of my bondbrother and bondsister, for where else could I turn for help and advice? Nowhere in Glin was there anyone to whom I might say, 'One is frightened, one is in grave peril, one asks assistance of you.' Everyone's soul was walled against me by stony custom. In all the world were only two whom I could regard as confidants, and they were far away. I must find my own salvation.

I would go into hiding, I decided. The innkeeper granted me a few hours to prepare myself. I shaved my beard, traded my royal cloak for the dim rags of another lodger nearly my height, and arranged the pawn of my ring of ceremony. My remaining possessions I bundled together to serve as a hump on my back, and I hobbled out of the hostelry doubled up, with one eye sealed shut and my mouth twisted far around to one side. Whether it was a disguise that could have fooled anyone, I cannot say; but no one waited to arrest me, and thus uglified I walked out of Glain under a cold, thin rain that soon turned to snow.

17

Outside the city's northwestern gate (for it was there my feet had taken me) a heavy truck came rumbling by me, and its treads rolled through a pool of half-frozen slush, spraying me liberally. I halted to scrape the chilly stuff from my leggings; the truck halted too, and the driver clambered down, exclaiming, 'There is cause for apology here. It was not intended to douse you so!'

This courtesy so astounded me that I stood to my full height, and let the distortions slip from my features. Evidently the driver had thought me a feeble, bent old man; he showed amazement at my transformation, and laughed aloud. I knew not what to say. Into my gaping silence he declared, 'There is room for one to ride, if you have the need or the whim.'

Into my mind sprang a bright fantasy: he would drive me toward the coast, where I would sign on aboard a merchant vessel bound for Manneran, and in that happy tropical land I would throw myself on the mercies of my bondsister's father, escaping all this harassment.

'Where are you bound?' I asked.

'Westward, into the mountains.'

So much for Manneran. I accepted the ride all the same. He offered me no contract of defined liabilities, but I let that pass. For some minutes we did not speak; I was content to listen to the slap of the treads on the snowy road, and think of the distance growing between myself and the police of Glain.

'Outlander, are you?' he said at length.

'Indeed.' Fearing that some alarm might be out for a man of Salla, I chose belatedly to adopt the soft slurred speech of southern folk, that I had learned from Halum, hoping he would come to believe that I had not spoken first to him with Sallan accents. 'You travel with a native of Manneran, who finds your winter a strange and burdensome thing.'

'What brought you north?' he asked.

'The settlement of one's mother's estate. She was a woman of Glain.'

'Did the lawyers treat you well, then?'

'Her money melted in their hands, leaving nothing.'

'The usual story. You're short of cash, eh?'

'Destitute,' I admitted.

'Well, well, one understands your situation, for one has been there oneself. Perhaps something can be done for you.'

I realized from his phrasing, from his failure to use the Glinish passive construction, that he too must be an outlander. Swinging round to face him, I said, 'Is one right that you likewise are from elsewhere?'

'This is true.'

'Your accent is unfamiliar. Some western province?'

'Oh, no, no.'

'Not Salla, then?'

'Manneran,' he said, and burst into hearty laughter, and covered my shame and confusion by telling me, 'You do the accent well, friend. But you needn't make the effort longer.'

'One hears no Manneran in your voice,' I mumbled.

'One has lived long in Glin,' he said, 'and one's voice is a soup of inflections.'

I had not fooled him for a moment, but he made no attempt to penetrate my identity, and seemed not to care who I might be or where I came from. We talked easily a while. He told me that he owned a lumber mill in western Glin, midway up the flanks of the Huishtors where the tall yellow-needled honey-trees grow; before we had driven much farther along he was offering me a job as a logger in his camp. The pay was poor, he said, but one breathed clean air there, and government officials were never seen, and such things as passports and certificates of status did not matter.

Of course I accepted. His camp was beautifully situated, above a sparkling mountain lake which never froze, for it was fed by a warm spring whose source was said to be deep beneath the Burnt Lowlands. Tremendous ice-topped Huishtor peaks hung above us, and not far away was Glin Gate, the pass through which one goes from Glin to the Burnt Lowlands, crossing a bitter corner of the Frozen Lowlands on the way. He had a hundred men in his employ, rough and foul-mouthed, forever shouting 'I' and 'me' without shame, but they were honest and hardworking men, and I had never been close to their sort before. My plan was to stay there through the winter, saving my pay, and go off to Manneran when I had earned the price of my passage. Some news of the outer world reached the camp from time to time, though, and I learned in this way that the Glinish authorities were seeking a certain young prince of Salla, who was believed to have gone insane and was wandering somewhere in Glin; the septarch Stirron urgently wished the unhappy young man to be returned to his homeland for the medical care he so desperately needed. Suspecting that the roads and ports would be watched, I extended my stay in the mountains through the spring, and, my caution deepening, I stayed the summer also. In the end I spent something more than a year there.

It was a year that changed me greatly. We worked hard, felling the huge trees in all weathers, stripping them of boughs, feeding them to the mill, a long tiring day and a chilly one, but plenty of hot wine at night, and every tenth day a platoon of women brought in from a nearby town to amuse us. My weight increased by half again, all of it hard muscle, and I grew taller until I surpassed the tallest logger in the camp, and they made jokes about my size. My beard came in full and the planes of my face changed as the plumpness of youth went from me. The loggers I found more likable than the courtiers among whom all my prior days had been passed. Few of them were able even to read, and of polite etiquette they knew nothing, but they were cheerful and easy-spirited men, at home in their own bodies. I would not have you think that because they talked in 'I' and 'me' they were open-hearted and given to sharing of confidences; they kept the Covenant in that respect, and might even have been more secretive than educated folk about certain things. Yet they seemed more sunny of soul than those who speak in passives and impersonal pronouns, and perhaps my stay among them planted in me that seed of subversion, that understanding of the Covenant's basic wrongness, which the Earthman Schweiz later guided into full flowering.

I told them nothing of my rank and origin. They could see for themselves, by the smoothness of my skin, that I had not done much hard labor in my life, and my way of speaking marked me as an educated man, if not necessarily one of high birth. But I offered no revelations of my past, and none were sought. All I said was that I came from Salla since my accent marked me as Sallan anyway; they granted me the privacy of my history. My employer, I think, guessed early that I must be the fugitive prince whom Stirron sought, but he never queried me about that. For the first time in my life, then, I had an identity apart from my royal status. I ceased to be Lord Kinnall, the septarch's second son, and was only Darival, the big logger from Salla.

From that transformation I learned much. I had never played one of your swaggering, bullying young nobles; being a second son instills a certain humility even in an aristocrat. Yet I could not help feeling set apart from ordinary men. I was waited on, bowed to, served, and pampered; men spoke softly to me and made formal gestures of respect, even when I was a child. I was, after all, the son of a septarch, that is to say a king, for septarchs are hereditary rulers and thus are part of mankind's procession of kings, a line that goes back to the dawn of human settlement on Borthan and beyond, back across the stars to Earth itself, to the lost and forgotten dynasties of her ancient nations, ultimately to the masked and painted chieftains enthroned in prehistoric caves. And I was part of that line, a man of royal blood, somehow superior by circumstance of birth. But in this logging camp in the mountains I came to understand that kings are nothing but men set high. The gods do not anoint them, but rather the will of men, and men can strip them of their lofty rank; if Stirron were to be cast down by insurrection, and in his place that loathsome drainer from Salla Old Town became septarch, would not the drainer then enter that mystic procession of kings, and Stirron be relegated to the dust? And would not that drainer's sons become blood-proud, even as I had been, although their father had been nothing for most of his life, and their grandfather less than that? I know, I know, the sages would say that the kiss of the gods had fallen upon that drainer, elevating him and all his progeny and making them forever sacred, yet as I felled trees on the slopes of the Huishtors I saw kingship with clearer eyes, and, having been cast down by events myself, I realized that I was no more than a man among men, and always had been. What I would make of myself depended on my natural gifts and ambitions, not upon the accident of rank.

So rewarding was that knowledge, and the altered sense of self it brought me, that my stay in the mountains ceased to seem like an exile, but more like a vacation. My dreams of fleeing to a soft life in Manneran left me, and, even after I had saved more than enough to pay my passage to that land, I found myself with no impulse to move onward. It was not entirely fear of arrest that kept me among the loggers, but also a love of the crisp clear cold Huishtor air, and of my arduous new craft, and of the rough but genuine men among whom I dwelled. Therefore I stayed on, through summer and into autumn, and welcomed the coming of a new winter, and gave no thought to going.

I might be there yet, only I was forced into flight. One woeful winter afternoon, with the sky like iron and the threat of a blizzard over us like a fist, they brought the whores up from town for our regularly appointed night of frolic, and this time there was among them a newcomer whose voice announced her place of birth to be Salla. I heard her instantly as the women came cavorting into our hall of sport, and would have crept away, but she spied me and gasped and cried out on the spot: 'Look you there! For sure that is our vanished prince!'

I laughed and tried to persuade everyone that she was drunk or mad, but my scarlet cheeks gave me the lie, and the loggers peered at me in a new way. A prince? A prince? Was it so? They whispered to one another, nudging and winking. Recognizing my peril, I claimed the woman for my own use and drew her aside, and when we were alone, I insisted to her she was mistaken: I am no prince, I said, but only a common logger. She would not have it. 'The Lord Kinnall marched in the septarch's funeral procession,' she said, 'and this one beheld him, with these eyes. And you are he!' The more I protested, the more convinced she was. There was no shifting her mind. Even when I embraced her, she was so awe-smitten at opening herself to a septarch's son that her loins remained dry, and I injured her in entering her.

Late that night, when the revelry had ended, my employer came to me, solemn and uneasy. 'One of the girls has made strange talk about you this evening,' he said. 'If the talk is true, you are endangered, for when she returns to her village she'll spread the news, and the police will be here soon enough.'

'Must one flee, then?' I asked.

'The choice is yours. Alarms still are out for this prince; if you are he, no one here can protect you against the authorities.'

'Then one must flee. At daybreak—'

'Now,' he said. 'While the girl still lies here asleep.'

He pressed money of Glin into my hand, over and beyond what he owed me in current wages; I gathered my few belongings, and we went outside together. The night was moonless and the winter wind was savage. By starlight I saw the glitter of lightly falling snow. My employer silently drove me down the slope, past the foothills village from which the whores came, and out along a back-country road which we followed for some hours. When dawn met us we were in south-central Glin, not overly far from the River Huish. He halted, at last, in a village that proclaimed itself to be Klaek, a winter-bound place of small stone cottages bordering on broad snowy fields. Leaving me in the truck, he entered the first of the cottages, emerging after a moment accompanied by a wizened man who poured forth a torrent of instructions and gesticulations; with the aid of this guidance we found our way to the place my employer was seeking, the cottage of a certain farmer named Stumwil. This Stumwil was a fair-haired man of about my own height, with washed-out blue eyes and an apologetic smile. Maybe he was some kinsman of my employer's, or, more probably, he owed him a debt – I never asked. In any case the farmer readily agreed to my employer's request, and accepted me as a lodger. My employer embraced me and drove off into the gathering snow; I saw him never again. I hope the gods were kind to him, as he was to me.

18

The cottage was one large room, divided by flimsy curtains into areas. Stumwil put up a new curtain, gave me straw for my mattress, and I had my living quarters. There were seven of us under that roof: Stumwil and myself, and Stumwil's wife, a weary wench who I could have been persuaded was his mother, and three of their children – two boys some years short of manhood and a girl in mid-adolescence – and the bondsister of the girl, who was lodging with them that year. They were sunny, innocent, trusting folk. Though they knew nothing about me, they all instantly adopted me as a member of the family, some unknown uncle unexpectedly returned from far voyaging. I was not prepared for the easy way they accepted me, and credited it at first to some net of obligation in which my former employer had bound them to me, but no: they were kindly by nature, unquestioning, unsuspicious. I took my meals at their table; I sat among them by their fire; I joined in their games. Every fifth night Stumwil filled a huge dented tub with hot water for the entire family, and I bathed with them, two or three of us in the tub at once, though it disturbed me inwardly to rub up against the plump bare bodies of Stumwil's daughter and her friend. I suppose I could have had the daughter or the bondsister if I had cared to, but I kept back from them, thinking such a seduction would be a breach of hospitality. Later, when I understood more about peasants, I realized that it was my abstinence that had been a breach of hospitality, for the girls were of age and surely willing, and I had disdained them. But I saw that only after I had left Stumwill's place. Those girls now have adult children of their own. I suppose by this time they have forgiven me for my lack of gallantry.

I paid a fee for my lodging, and I helped also with the chores, though in winter there was little to do except shovel snow and feed the fire. None of them showed curiosity about my identity or history. They asked me no questions, and I believe that no questions ever passed through their minds.

Nor did the other townspeople pry, though they gave me the scrutiny any stranger would receive.

Newspapers occasionally reached this village, and those that did went from hand to hand until all had read them, when they were placed on deposit at the wineshop at the head of the main village thoroughfare. I consulted them there, a file of stained and tattered scraps, and learned what I could of the events of the past year. I found that my brother Stirron's wedding had taken place on schedule, with appropriate regal pomp; his lean, troubled face looked up out of a blurry, grease-splotched bit of old paper, and beside him was his radiant bride, but I could not make out her features. There was tension between Glin and Krell over fishing rights in a disputed coastal area, and men had died in border skirmishes. I pitied General Condorit, whose patrol sector was at the opposite end of the boundary, almost, from the Krell-Glin line, and who therefore must have missed the fun of somehow involving Salla in the shooting. A sea monster, golden-scaled and sinuous, more than ten times the length of a man's body, had been sighted in the Gulf of Sumar by a party of Mannerangi fishermen, who had sworn a mighty oath in the Stone Chapel as to the authenticity of their vision. The prime septarch of Threish, a bloody old brigand if the tales they tell of him are true, had abdicated, and was dwelling in a godhouse in the western mountains not far from Stroin Gap, serving as a drainer for pilgrims bound to Manneran. Such was the news. I found no mention of myself. Perhaps Stirron had lost interest in having me seized and returned to Salla.

It might therefore be safe for me to try to leave Glin.

Eager as I was to get out of that frosty province, where my own kin rebuffed me and only strangers showed me love, two things held me back. For one, I meant to stay with Stumwil until I could help him with his spring planting, in return for his kindness to me. For another, I would not set forth undrained on so dangerous a journey, lest in some mishap my spirit go to the gods still full of poisons. This village of Klaek had no drainer of its own, but depended for its solace on itinerant drainers who passed now and then through the countryside. In the winter these wanderers rarely came by, and so perforce I had gone undrained since the late summer, when a member of that profession had visited the logging camp. I felt the need.

There came a late-winter snow, a storm of wonders that coated every branch with a fiery skin of ice, and immediately thereafter there came a thaw. The world melted. Klaek was surrounded by oceans of mud. A drainer driving a battered and ancient groundcar came to us through this slippery sea and set up shop in an old shack, doing fine business among the villagers. I went to him on the fifth day of his visit, when the lines were shorter, and unburdened myself for two hours, sparing him nothing, neither the truth about my identity nor my subversive new philosophy of kingship nor the usual grimy little repressed lusts and prides. It was more of a dose, evidently, than a country drainer expected to receive, and he seemed to puff and swell as I poured out my words; at the end he was shaking as much as I, and could barely speak. I wondered where it was that drainers went to unload all the sins and sorrows they absorbed from their clients. They are forbidden to talk to ordinary men of anything they have learned in the confessional; did they therefore have drainer-drainers, servants of the servants, to whom they might deliver that which they could not mention to anyone else? I did not see how a drainer could carry such a bundle of sadnesses for long unaided, as he got from any dozen of his customers in a day's listening.

With my soul cleansed, I had only to wait for planting-time, and it was not long in coming. The growing season in Glin is short; they get their seeds into the ground before winter's grip has fully slipped, so that they can catch every ray of spring sunlight. Stumwil waited until he felt certain that the thaw would not be followed by one last tumult of snow, and then, with the land still a sucking quagmire, he and his family went out into the fields to plant breadseed and spiceflower and blueglobe.

The custom was to go naked to the planting. On the first morning I looked out of Stumwil's cottage and beheld the neighbors on all sides walking bare toward the furrows, children and parents and grandparents stripped to the skin with sacks of seed slung over their shoulders – a procession of knobby knees, sagging bellies, dried-out breasts, wrinkled buttocks, illuminated here and there by the smooth, firm bodies of the young. Thinking I was in some waking dream, I looked around and saw Stumwil and his wife and their daughter already disrobed, and beckoning to me to do the same. They took their sacks and left the cottage. The two young sons scampered after them, leaving me with the bondsister of Stumwil's daughter, who had overslept and had just appeared. She shucked her garments too; a supple saucy body she had, with small high dark-nippled breasts and slender well-muscled thighs. As I dropped my clothes I asked her, 'Why is it done to be naked outdoors in such a cold time?'

'The mud gives cause for slipping,' she explained, 'and it is easier to wash raw skin than garments.'

There was truth enough in that, for the planting was a comic show, with peasants skidding in the tricky muck every tenth step they took. Down they went, landing on hip or haunch and coming up smeared with brown; it was a matter of skill to grasp the neck of one's seed-sack as one toppled, so that no precious seeds would be scattered. I fell like the rest, learning the knack of it quickly, and indeed there was pleasure in slipping, for the mud had a voluptuous oozy feel to it. So we marched on, staggering and lurching, slapping flesh to mud again and again, laughing, singing, pressing our seeds into the cold soft soil, and not one of us but was covered from scalp to tail with muck within minutes. I shivered miserably at the outset, but soon I was warmed by laughter and tripping, and when the day's work was done, we stood around shamelessly naked in front of Stumwil's cottage and doused one another with buckets of water to clean ourselves. By then it seemed reasonable to me that they should prefer to expose their skins rather than their clothing to such a day's labor, but in fact the girl's explanation was incorrect; I learned from Stumwil later that week that the nakedness was a religious matter, a sign of humility before the gods of the crops, and nothing else.

Eight days it took to finish the planting. On the ninth, wishing Stumwil and his people a hearty harvest, I took my leave of the village of Klaek, and began my journey to the coast.

19

A neighbor of Stumwil's took me eastward the first day in his cart. I walked most of the second, begged a ride on the third and fourth, and walked again on the fifth and sixth. The air was cool but the crackle of spring was in it, as buds unfolded and birds returned. I bypassed the city of Glain, which might have been dangerous for me, and without any events that I can clearly recall I made my way swiftly to Biumar, Glin's main seaport and second most populous city.

It was a handsomer place than Glain, though hardly beautiful: a greasy gray sprawl of an oversized town, backed up against a gray and menacing ocean. On my first day there I learned that all passenger service between Glin and the southern provinces had been suspended three moontimes before, owing to the dangerous activities of pirates operating out of Krell, for Glin and Krell were now engaged in an undeclared war. The only way I could reach Manneran, it seemed, was overland via Salla, and I hardly wished to do that. I was resourceful, though. I found myself a room in a tavern near the docks and spent a few days picking up maritime gossip. Passenger service might be suspended, but commercial seafaring, I discovered, was not, since the prosperity of Glin depended upon it; convoys of merchant vessels, heavily armed, went forth on regular schedules. A limping seaman who stayed in the same tavern told me, when blue wine of Salla had oiled him sufficiently, that a merchant convoy of this sort would leave in a week's time, and that he had a berth aboard one of the ships. I considered drugging him on the eve of sailing and borrowing his identity, as is done in pirate tales for children, but a less dramatic method suggested itself to me: I bought his shipping-papers. The sum I offered him was more than he would have earned by shipping out to Manneran and back, so he was happy to take my money and let me go in his place. We spent a long drunken night conferring about his duties on the ship, for I knew nothing of seamanship. At the coming of dawn I still knew nothing, but I saw ways I could bluff a minimal sort of competence.

I went unchallenged on board the vessel, a low-slung air-powered craft heavily laden with Glinish goods. The checking of papers was perfunctory. I picked up my cabin assignment, installed myself, reported for duty. About half the jobs they asked me to do, over the first few days, I managed to carry out reasonably well by imitation and experiment; the other things I merely muddled with, and soon my fellow sailors recognized me for a bungler, but they kept knowledge of that from the officers. A kind of loyalty prevailed in the lower ranks. Once again I saw that my dark view of mankind had been overly colored by my boyhood among aristocrats; these sailors, like the loggers, like the farmers, had a kind of hearty fellowship among themselves that I had never found among those more strict to the Covenant. They did for me the jobs I could not do myself, and I relieved them of dull work that was within my narrow skills, and all went well. I swabbed decks, cleaned filters, and spent endless hours manning the guns against pirate attacks. But we got past Krell's dreaded pirate coast without incident, and slipped easily down the coast of Salla, which already was green with spring.

Our first port of call was Cofalon, Salla's chief seaport, for five days of selling and buying. I was alarmed at this, for I had not known we planned to halt anywhere in my homeland. I thought at first to announce myself ill and hide belowdecks all our time in Cofalon; but then I rejected the scheme as cowardly, telling myself that a man must test himself frequently against risk, if he would keep his manhood. So I boldly went wenching and wining in town with my shipmates, trusting that time had sufficiently changed my face, and that no one would expect to find Lord Stirron's missing brother in a sailor's rough clothes in such a town as this. My gamble succeeded: I went unvexed the full five days. From newspapers and careful overhearing I learned all I could about events in Salla in the year and a half since my leaving. Stirron, I gathered, was popularly held to be a good ruler. He had brought the province through its winter of famine by purchasing surplus food from Manneran on favorable terms, and our farms had since then had better fortune. Taxes had been cut. The people were content. Stirron's wife had been delivered of a son, the Lord Dariv, who now was heir to the prime septarchy, and another son was on the way. As for the Lord Kinnall, brother to the septarch, nothing was said of him; he was forgotten as though he had never been.

We made other stops here and there down the coast, several in southern Salla, several in northern Manneran. And in good time we came to that great seaport at the southeastern corner of our continent, the holy city of Manneran, capital of the province that bears the same name. It was in Manneran that my life would begin anew.

20

Manneran the province was favored by the gods. The air is mild and sweet, filled all the year through with the fragrance of flowers. Winter does not reach so far south, and the Mannerangi, when they would see snow, go as tourists to the Huishtor peaks and gape at the strange cold coating of whiteness that passes for water in other lands. The warm sea that borders Manneran on east and south yields food enough to feed half the continent, and to the southwest there is the Gulf of Sumar as well, with further bounty. War has rarely touched Manneran, protected as it is by a shield of mountains and water from the peoples of the western lands, and separated from its neighbor to the north, Salla, by the immense torrent of the River Woyn. Now and again we have attempted to invade Manneran by sea, but never with any conviction that we would be successful, nor has there been any success; when Salla engages seriously in war, the foe is always Glin.

Manneran the city must also have enjoyed special divine blessings. Its site is the finest natural harbor in all Velada Borthan, a deep-cut bay framed by two opposing fingers of land, jutting toward one another in such a way that no breakwaters are needed there, and ships sit easily at anchor. This harbor is one mighty source of the province's prosperity. It constitutes the chief link between the eastern and western provinces, for there is little landborne commerce across the continent by way of the Burnt Lowlands, and since our world lacks natural fuels, so far as we know, airborne traffic is never likely to amount to much here. So ships of the nine western provinces travel eastward through the Strait of Sumar to the port of Manneran, and ships from Manneran make regular calls on the western coast. The Mannerangi then retail western goods to Salla, Glin, and Krell in their own vessels, reaping the usual profits of go-betweens. The harbor of Manneran is the only place on our world where men of all thirteen provinces mingle and where all thirteen flags may be seen at once; and this busy commerce spills an unending flow of wealth into the coffers of the Mannerangi. In addition, their inland districts are rich in fertility, even up to the Huishtor slopes, which in their latitudes are unfrozen except at the summits. The farms of Manneran have two or three harvests a year, and, by way of Stroin Gap, the Mannerangi have access to the Wet Lowlands and all the strange and valuable fruits and spices produced there. Small wonder, then, that those who love luxuries seek their fortunes in Manneran.

As if all this good fortune were not enough, the Mannerangi have persuaded the world that they live in the holiest spot on Borthan, and multiply their revenues by maintaining sacred shrines as magnets for pilgrims. One might think that Threish, on the western coast, where our ancestors first settled and the Covenant was drawn up, would put itself forward as a place of pilgrimage second to none. Indeed, there is some sort of shrine in Threish, and westerners too poor to travel to Manneran visit it. But Manneran has established itself as the holy of holies. The youngest of all our provinces, too, except only the breakaway kingdom of Krell; yet by a show of inner conviction and energetic advertisement has Manneran managed to make itself sacred. There is irony in this, for the Mannerangi hold more loosely to the Covenant than any of us in the thirteen provinces; their tropical life has softened them somewhat, and they open their souls to one another to a degree that would get them ostracized as selfbarers in Glin or Salla. Still, they have the Stone Chapel, where miracles are reliably reported to have occurred, where the gods supposedly came forth in the flesh only seven hundred years ago, and it is everyone's hope to have his child receive his adult name in the Stone Chapel on Naming Day. From all over the continent they come for that festival, to the vast profit of the Mannerangi hotelkeepers. Why, I was named in the Stone Chapel myself.

21

When we were docked in Manneran and the longshoremen were at work unloading our cargo, I collected my pay and left ship to enter town. At the foot of the pier I paused to pick up a shore pass from the Mannerangi immigration officials. 'How long will you be in town?' I was asked, and blandly I replied that I meant to stay among them for three days, although my real intent was to settle for the rest of my years in this place.

Twice before had I been in Manneran: once just out of my infancy, to be bonded to Halum, and once when I was seven, for my Naming Day. My memories of the city amounted to nothing more than vague and random patterns of colors: the pale pink and green and blue tones of the buildings, the dark green masses of the heavy vegetation, the black solemn interior of the Stone Chapel. As I walked away from the waterfront those colors bombarded me again, and glowing images out of my childhood shimmered before my dazzled eyes. Manneran is not built of stone, as our northern cities are, but rather of a kind of artificial plaster, which they paint in light pastel hues, so that every wall and façade sings joyfully, and billows like a curtain in the sunlight. The day was a bright one, and the beams of light bounced gaily about, setting the streets ablaze and forcing me to shade my eyes. I was stunned also by the complexity of the streets. Mannerangi architects rely greatly on ornament; the buildings are decked with ornate ironwork balconies, fanciful scrollings, flamboyant rooftiles, gaudy window-draperies, so that the northern eye beholds at first glance a monstrous baffling clutter, which resolves itself only gradually into a vista of elegance and grace and proportion. Everywhere, too, there are plants: trees lining both sides of each street, vines cascading from window boxes, flowers bursting forth in curbside gardens, and the hint of lush vegetation in the sheltered courtyards of the houses. The effect is refined and sophisticated, an interplay of jungle profusion and disciplined urban textures. Manneran is an extraordinary city, subtle, sensuous, languorous, overripe.

My childhood recollections did not prepare me for the heat. A steamy haze enveloped the streets. The air was wet and heavy. I felt I could almost touch the heat, could seize it and grasp it, could wring it like water from the atmosphere. It was raining heat and I was drenched in it. I was clad in a coarse, heavy gray uniform, the usual wintertime issue aboard a Glinish merchant ship, and this was a sweltering spring morning in Manneran; two dozen paces in that stifling humidity and I was ready to rip off my chafing clothes and go naked.

A telephone directory gave me the address of Segvord Helalam, my bondsister's father. I hired a taxi and went there. Helalam lived just outside the city, in a cool leafy suburb of grand homes and glistening lakes; a high brick wall shielded his house from the view of passersby. I rang at the gate and waited to be scanned. My taxi waited too, as if the driver knew certainly that I would be turned away. A voice within the house, some butler, no doubt, queried me over the scanner line and I replied, 'Kinnall Darival of Salla, bondbrother to the daughter of the High Justice Helalam, wishes to call upon the father of his bondsister.'

'The Lord Kinnall is dead,' I was informed coldly, 'and so you are some impostor.'

I rang again. 'Scan this, and judge if he be dead,' I said, holding up to the machine's eye my royal passport, which I had kept so long concealed. 'This is Kinnall Darival before you, and it will not go well with you if you deny him access to the High Justice!'

'Passports may be stolen. Passports may be forged.'

'Open the gate!'

There was no reply. A third time I rang, and this time the unseen butler told me that the police would be summoned unless I departed at once. My taxi driver, parked just across the road, coughed politely. I had not reckoned on any of this. Would I have to go back to town, and take lodgings, and write Segvord Helalam for an appointment, and offer evidence that I still lived?

By good fortune I was spared those bothers. A sumptuous black ground-car drew up, of a kind used generally only by the highest aristocracy, and from it stepped Segvord Helalam, High Justice of the Port of Manneran. He was then at the height of his career, and he carried himself with kingly grace: a short man, but well constructed, with a fine head, a florid face, a noble mane of white hair, a look of strength and purpose. His eyes, an intense blue, were capable of flashing fire, and his nose was an imperial beak, but he canceled all his look of ferocity with a warm, ready smile. He was recognized in Manneran as a man of wisdom and temperance. I went immediately toward him, with a glad cry of 'Bondfather!' Swinging about, he stared at me in bewilderment, and two large young men who had been with him in his groundcar placed themselves between the High Justice and myself as though they believed me to be an assassin.

'Your bodyguard may relax,' I said. 'Are you unable to recognize Kinnall of Salla?'

'The Lord Kinnall died last year,' Segvord replied quickly.

'That comes as grievous news to Kinnall himself,' I said. I drew myself tall, resuming princely mien for the first time since my sad exit from the city of Glain, and gestured at the High Justice's protectors with such fury that they gave ground, slipping off to the side. Segvord studied me carefully. He had last seen me at my brother's coronation; two years had gone by since then, and the last softness of childhood had been stripped from me. My year of felling logs showed in the contours of my frame, and my winter among the farmers had weathered my face, and my weeks as a sailor had left me grimy and unkempt, with tangled hair and a shaggy beard. Segvord's gaze cut gradually through these transformations until he was convinced of my identity; then suddenly he rushed at me, embracing me with such fervor that I nearly lost my footing in surprise. He cried my name, and I cried his; then the gate was opening, and he was hurrying me within, and the lofty cream-colored mansion loomed before me, the goal of all my wanderings and turmoil.

22

I was conducted to a pretty chamber and told that it was to be mine, and two servant-girls came to me, plucking off my sweaty seaman's garb; they led me, giggling all the while, to a huge tiled tub, and bathed and perfumed me, and cropped my hair and beard somewhat, and let me pinch and tumble them a bit. They brought me clothes of fine fabric, of a sort I had not worn since my days as royalty, all sheer and white and flowing and cool. And they offered me jewelry, a triple ring set with – I later learned – a sliver of the Stone Chapel's floor, and also a gleaming pendant, a tree-crystal from the land of Threish, on a leather thong. At length, after several hours of polishing, I was deemed fit to present to the High Justice. Segvord received me in the room he called his study, which actually was a great hall worthy of a septarch's palace, in which he sat enthroned even as a ruler would. I recall feeling some annoyance at his pretensions, for not only was he not royal, but he was of the lower aristocracy of Manneran, who had been of no stature whatever until his appointment to high office had put him on the road to fame and wealth.

I asked at once after my bondsister Halum.

'She fares well,' he said, 'though her soul was darkened by the tidings of your supposed death.'

'Where is she now?'

'On holiday, in the Sumar Gulf, on an island where we have another home.'

I felt a chill. 'Has she married?'

'To the regret of all who love her, she has not.'

'Is there anyone, though?'

'No,' Segvord said. 'She seems to prefer chastity. Of course, she is very young. When she returns, Kinnall, perhaps you could speak to her, pointing out that she might think now about making a match, for now she might have some fair lord, while in a few years' time there will be new maidens ahead of her in line.'

'How soon will she be back from this island?'

'At any moment,' said the High Justice. 'How amazed she will be to find you here!'

I asked him concerning my death. He replied that word had come, two years earlier, that I was mad and had wandered, helpless and deluded, into Glin. Segvord smiled as though to tell me that he knew right well why I had left Salla, and that there had been nothing of insanity about my motives.

'Then,' he said, 'there were reports that the Lord Stirron had sent agents into Glin after you, so that you could be brought back for treatment. Halum feared greatly for your safety at that time. And lastly, this summer past, one of your brother's ministers gave it out that you had gone roaming in the Glinish Huishtors in the pit of winter, and had been lost in the snows, in a blizzard no man could have survived.'

'But of course the Lord Kinnall's body was not recovered in the warm months of the year gone by, and was left to wither in the Huishtors, instead of being brought back to Salla for a proper burial.'

'There was no news of finding the body, no.'

'Then obviously,' I said, 'the Lord Kinnall's body awakened in the springtime, and trekked about on a ghostly parade, and went its way southward, and now at last has presented itself on the doorstep of the High Justice of the Port of Manneran.'

Segvord laughed. 'A healthy ghost!'

'A weary one, as well.'

'What befell you in Glin?'

'A cold time in more ways than one.' I told him of my snubbing at the hands of my mother's kin, of my stay in the mountains, and all the rest. When he had heard that, he wished to know what my plans were in Manneran; to this I replied that I had no plans other than to find some honorable enterprise, and succeed in it, and marry, and settle down, for Salla was closed to me and Glin held no temptations. Segvord nodded gravely. There was, he said, a clerkship open at this very moment in his office. The job carried little pay and less prestige, and it was absurd to ask a prince of Salla's royal line to accept it, but still it was clean work, with a fine chance of advancement, and it might serve to give me a foothold while I acclimated myself to the Mannerangi way of life. Since I had had some such opportunity in mind all along, I told him at once that I would gladly enter his employ, with no heed to my royal blood, since all that was behind me now, done with, and imaginary besides. 'What one makes of himself here,' I said soberly, 'will depend wholly on his merits, not on the circumstances of rank and influence.' Which was, of course, pure piffle: instead of trading on my high birth, I would instead here make capital out of being bondbrother to the High Justice of the Port's daughter, a connection that had come to me because of my high birth alone, and where was the effect of merit in any of that?

23

The searchers are getting closer to me all the time. Yesterday, while on a long walk through this zone of the Burnt Lowlands, I found, well south of here, the fresh track of a groundcar impressed deep in the dry and fragile crust of the red sand. And this morning, idly strolling in the place where the hornfowl gather – drawn there by some suicidal impulse, maybe? – I heard a droning in the sky, and looked up to see a plane of the Sallan military passing overhead. One does not often see sky-vehicles here. It swooped and circled, hornfowl-fashion, but I huddled under a twisted erosion-knoll, and I think I went unnoticed.

I might be mistaken about these intrusions: the groundcar just some hunting party casually passing through the region, the plane merely out on a training flight. But I think not. If there are hunters here, it is I they hunt. The net will close about me. I must try to write more quickly, and be more concise; too much of what I need to say is yet untold, and I fear being interrupted before I am done. Stirron, let me be for just a few more weeks!

24

The High Justice of the Port is one of Manneran's supreme officials. He holds jurisdiction over all commercial affairs in the capital; if there are disputes between merchants, they are tried in his court, and by treaty he has authority over the nationals of every province, so that a seacaptain of Glin or Krell, a Sallan or a westerner, when hailed before the High Justice, is subject to his verdicts with no rights of appeal to the courts of his homeland. This is the High Justice's ancient function, but if he were nothing but an arbiter of mercantile squabbles he would hardly have the grandeur that he does. However, over the centuries other responsibilities have fallen to him. He alone regulates the flow of foreign shipping into the harbor of Manneran, granting trade permits for so many Glinish vessels a year, so many from Threish, so many from Salla. The prosperity of a dozen provinces is subject to his decisions. Therefore he is courted by septarchs, flooded with gifts, buried in kindnesses and praise, in the hope that he will allow this land or that an extra ship in the year to come. The High Justice, then, is the economic filter of Velada Borthan, opening and closing commercial outlets as he pleases; he does this not by whim but by consideration of the ebb and flow of wealth across the continent, and it is impossible to overestimate his importance in our society.

The office is not hereditary, but the appointment is for life, and a High Justice can be removed only through intricate and well-nigh impracticable impeachment procedures. Thus it comes to pass that a vigorous High Justice, such as Segvord Helalam, can become more powerful in Manneran than the prime septarch himself. The septarchy of Manneran is in decay in any case; two of the seven seats have gone unfilled for the past hundred years or more, and the occupants of the remaining five have ceded so much of their authority to civil servants that they are little more than ceremonial figures. The prime septarch still has some shreds of majesty, but he must consult with the High Justice of the Port on all matters of economic concern, and the High Justice has entangled himself so inextricably in the machinery of Manneran's government that it is difficult to say truly who is the ruler and who the civil servant.

On my third day in Manneran, Segvord took me to his courthouse to contract me into my job. I who was raised in a palace was awed to see the headquarters of the Port Justiciary; what amazed me was not its opulence (for it had none) but its great size. I beheld a broad yellow-colored brick structure, four stories high, squat and massive, that seemed to run the entire length of the waterfront two blocks inland from the piers. Within it at worn desks in high-ceilinged offices were armies of drudging clerks, shuffling papers and stamping receipts, and my soul quivered at the thought that this was how I was to spend my days. Segvord led me on an endless march through the building, receiving the homage of the workers as he passed their dank and sweaty offices; he paused here and there to greet someone, to glance casually at some half-written report, to study a board on which, apparently, the movements of every vessel within three days' journey of Manneran were being charted. At length we entered a noble suite of rooms, far from the bustle and hurry I had just seen. Here the High Justice himself presided. Showing me a cool and splendidly furnished room adjoining his own chamber, Segvord told me that this was where I would work.

The contract I signed was like a drainer's: I pledged myself to reveal nothing of what I might learn in the course of my duties, on pain of terrible penalties. For its part the Port Justiciary promised me lifetime employment, steady increases of salary, and various other privileges of a kind princes do not normally worry about.

Quickly I discovered that I was to be no humble inkstained clerk. As Segvord had warned me, my pay was low and my rank in the bureaucracy almost nonexistent, but my responsibilities proved to be great ones; in effect,

I was his private secretary. All confidential reports intended for the High Justice's eyes would cross my desk first. My task was to discard those that were of no importance and to prepare abridgments of the others, all but those I deemed to be of the highest pertinence, which went to him complete. If the High Justice is the economic filter of Velada Borthan, I was to be the filter's filter, for he would read only what I wished him to read, and make his decisions on the basis of what I gave him. Once this was clear to me I knew that Segvord had placed me on the path to great power in Manneran.

25

Impatiently I awaited Halum's return from her isle in the Gulf of Sumar. Neither bondsister nor bondbrother had I had for over two years, and drainers could not take their place; I ached to sit up late at night with Halum or Noim, as in the old days, opening self to self. Noim was somewhere in Salla, I supposed, but I knew not where, and Halum, though she was said to be due back imminently from holidaying, did not appear in my first week in Manneran, nor the second. During the third, I left the Justiciary office early one day, feeling ill from the humidity and the tensions of mastering my new role, and was driven to Segvord's estate. Entering the central courtyard on my way to my room, I caught sight of a tall, slender girl at the far end, plucking from a vine a golden flower for her dark glossy hair. I could not see her face, but from her figure and bearing I had no doubt of her, and joyfully I cried, 'Halum!' and rushed across the courtyard. She turned frowning to me, halting me in mid-rush. Her brow was furrowed and her lips were tight together; her gaze was chilly and remote. What did that cold glance mean? Her face was Halum's face – dark eyes, fine slim proud nose, firm chin, bold cheekbones – and yet her face was strange to me. Could two years have changed my bondsister so greatly? The main differences between the Halum I remembered and the woman I saw were subtle ones, differences of expression, a tilt of the eyebrows, a flicker of the nostrils, a quirking of the mouth, as though the whole soul itself within her had altered. Also there were some minor differences of feature, I saw as I drew nearer, but these could be ascribed to the passing of time or to the faults of my memory. My heart sped and my fingers trembled and an odd heat of confusion spread across my shoulders and back. I would have gone to her and embraced her, but suddenly I feared her in her transformations.

'Halum?' I said uncertainly, hoarse-voiced, dry-throated.

'She is not yet here.' A voice like falling snow, deeper than Halum's, more resonant, colder.

I was stunned. Like enough to Halum to be her twin! I knew of only one sister to Halum, then still a child, not yet sprouting her breasts. It was not possible for her to have concealed from me all her life a twin, or a sister somewhat older. But the resemblance was extraordinary and disturbing. I have read that on old Earth they had ways of making artificial beings out of chemicals, that could deceive even a mother or a lover with the likeness to some real person, and I could well have been persuaded that moment that the process had come down to us, across the centuries, across the gulf of night, and that this false Halum before me was a devilishly clever synthetic image of my true bondsister.

I said, 'Forgive this foolish error. One mistook you for Halum.'

'It happens often.'

'Are you some kin of hers?'

'Daughter to the brother of the High Justice Segvord.'

She gave her name as Loimel Helalam. Never had Halum spoken to me of this cousin, or if she had, I had no recollection of it. How odd that she had hidden from me the existence of this mirror-Halum in Manneran! I told her my name, and Loimel recognized it as that of Halum's bondbrother, of whom she had evidently heard a good deal; she softened her stance a little, and some of the chill that was about her now thawed. For my part I was over the shock of finding the supposed Halum to be another, and I was beginning to warm to Loimel, for she was beautiful and desirable, and – unlike Halum herself! – available. I could by looking at her out of one eye pretend to myself that she was indeed Halum, and I even managed to deceive myself into accepting her voice as my bondsister's. Together we strolled the courtyard, talking. I learned that Halum would come home this evening and that Loimel was here to arrange a hearty reception for her; I learned also some things about Loimel, for, in the injudicious fashion of many Mannerangi, she guarded her privacy less sternly than a northerner would. She told me her age: a year older than Halum (and I also). She told me she was unmarried, having recently terminated an unpromising engagement to a prince of an old but unfortunately impoverished family of Mannerangi nobility. She explained her resemblance to Halum by saying that her mother and Halum's were cousins, as well as her father being brother to Halum's, and five minutes later, when we walked arm in arm, she hinted scandalously that in fact the High Justice had invaded his elder brother's bridal couch long ago, so that she was properly half-sister to Halum, not cousin. And she told me much more.

I could think only of Halum, Halum, Halum, Halum. This Loimel existed for me solely as a reflection of my bondsister. An hour after we first met, Loimel and I were together in my bedroom, and when her gown had dropped from her I told myself that Halum's skin must be creamy as this, that Halum's breasts must be much like these, that Halum's thighs could be no less smooth, that Halum's nipples would also turn to turrets when a man's thumbs brushed their tips. Then I lay naked beside Loimel and made her ready for taking with many cunning caresses; soon she gasped and pumped her hips and cried out, and I covered her with my body, but an instant before I would have thrust myself into her the thought came coldly to me, *Why, this is forbidden, to have one's bondsister,* and my weapon went limp as a length of rope. It was only a momentary embarrassment: looking down at her face, I told myself brusquely that this was Loimel and not Halum who waited for my thrust, and my manhood revived, and our bodies joined. But another humiliation awaited me. In the moment of entering her my traitor mind said to me, *You cleave Halum's flesh,* and my traitor body responded with an instantaneous explosion of my passions. How intricately our loins are linked to our minds, and how tricky a thing it is when we embrace a woman while pretending she is another! I sank down on Loimel in shame and disgust, hiding my face in the pillow; but she, gripped by urgent needs, thrashed about against me until I found new vigor, and this time I carried her to the ecstasy she sought.

That evening my bondsister Halum at last returned from her holiday in the Gulf of Sumar, and wept with happy surprise to see me alive and in Manneran. When she stood beside Loimel I was all the more amazed by their near twinship: Halum's waist was more slender, Loimel's bosom deeper, but one finds these variations even in true sisters, and in most ways of the body Halum and her cousin seemed to have been stamped from the same mold. Yet I was struck by a profound and subtle difference also, most visible in the eyes, through which, as the poem says, there shines the inner light of the soul. The radiance that came from Halum was tender and gentle and mild, like the first soft beams of sunlight drifting through a summer morning's mist; Loimel's eyes gave a colder, harsher glow, that of a sullen winter afternoon. As I looked from one girl to the other, I formed a quick intuitive judgment: *Halum is pure love, and Loimel is pure self.* But I recoiled from that verdict the instant it was born. I did not know Loimel; I had not found her thus far to be anything but open and giving; I had no right to disparage her in that way.

The two years had not aged Halum so much as burnished her, and she had come to the full radiance of her beauty. She was deeply tanned, and in her short white sheath she seemed like a bronzed statue of herself; the planes of her face were more angular than they had been, giving her a delicate look of almost boyish charm; she moved with floating grace. The house was full of strangers for this her homecoming party, and after our first embrace she was swept away from me, and I was left with Loimel. But toward the end of the evening I claimed my bondright and took Halum away to my chamber, saying, 'There is two years' talking to do.' Thoughts tumbled chaotically in my mind: how could I tell her all that had happened to me, how could I learn from her what she had done, all in the first rush of words? I could not arrange my thinking. We sat down facing one another at a prim distance, Halum on the couch where only a few hours before I had coupled with her cousin, pretending then to myself that she was Halum. A tense smile passed between us. 'Where can one begin?' I said, and Halum, at the same instant, said the same words. That made us laugh and dissolved the tension. And then I heard my own voice asking, without preamble, whether Halum thought that Loimel would accept me as her husband.

26

Loimel and I were married by Segvord Helalam in the Stone Chapel at the crest of the summer, after months of preparatory rituals and purifications. We made these observances by request of Loimel's father, a man of great devoutness. For his sake we undertook a rigorous series of drainings, and day after day I knelt and yielded up the full contents of my soul to a certain Jidd, the best-known and most costly drainer in Manneran. When this was done Loimel and I went on pilgrimage to the nine shrines of Manneran, and I squandered my slender salary on candles and incense. We even performed the archaic ceremony known as the Showing, in which she and I stepped out on a secluded beach one dawn, chaperoned by Halum and Segvord, and, screened from their eyes by an elaborate canopy, formally disclosed our nakedness to one another, so that neither of us could say afterward that we had gone into marriage concealing defects from the other.

The rite of union was a grand event, with musicians and singers. My bondbrother Noim, summoned from Salla, stood up as pledgeman for me, and did the ringlinking. Manneran's prime septarch, a waxen old man, attended the wedding, as did most of the local nobility. The gifts we received were of immense value. Among them was a golden bowl inlaid with strange gems, manufactured on some other world, and sent to us by my brother Stirron, along with a cordial message expressing regret that affairs of state required him to remain in Salla. Since I had snubbed his wedding, it was no surprise for him to snub mine. What did surprise me was the friendly tone of his letter. Making no reference to the circumstances of my disappearance from Salla, but offering thanks that the rumor of my death had proven false, Stirron gave me his blessing and asked me to come with my bride for a ceremonial visit to his capital as soon as we were able. Apparently he had learned that I meant to settle permanently in Manneran, and so would be no rival for his throne; therefore he could think of me warmly again.

I often wondered, and after all these years still do wonder, why Loimel accepted me. She had just turned down a prince of her own realm because he was poor: here was I, also a prince, but an exiled one, and even poorer. Why take me? For my charm in wooing? I had little of that; I was still young and thick-tongued. For my prospects of wealth and power? At that time those prospects seemed feeble indeed. For my physical appeal? Certainly I had some of that, but Loimel was too shrewd to marry just for broad shoulders and powerful muscles; besides, in our very first embrace I had shown her my inadequacies as a lover, and rarely did I improve on that bungled performance in the couplings that followed. I concluded, finally, that there were two reasons why Loimel took me. First, that she was lonely and troubled after the breakup of her other trothing, and, seeking the first harbor that presented itself, went to me, since I was strong and attractive and of royal blood. Second, that Loimel envied Halum in all things, and knew that by marrying me she would gain possession of the one thing Halum could never have.

My own motive for seeking Loimel's hand needs no deep probing to uncover. It was Halum I loved; Loimel was Halum's image; Halum was denied me, therefore I took Loimel. Beholding Loimel, I was free to think I beheld Halum. Embracing Loimel, I might tell myself I embraced Halum. When I offered myself to Loimel as husband, I felt no particular love for her, and had reason to think I might not even like her; yet I was driven to her as the nearest proxy to my true desire.

Marriages contracted for such reasons as Loimel's and mine do not often fare well. Ours thrived poorly; we began as strangers and grew ever more distant the longer we shared a bed. In truth I had married a secret fantasy, not a woman. But we must conduct our marriages in the world of reality, and in that world my wife was Loimel.

27

Meanwhile in my office at the Port Justiciary I struggled to do the job my bondfather had given me. Each day a formidable stack of reports and memoranda reached my desk; each day I tried to decide which must go before the High Justice and which were to be ignored. At first, naturally, I had no grounds for judgment. Segvord helped me, though, as did several of the senior officials of the Justiciary, who rightly saw that they had more to gain by serving me than by trying to block my inevitable rise. I took readily to the nature of my work, and before the full heat of summer was upon Manneran I was operating confidently, as if I had spent the last twenty years at this task.

Most of the material submitted for the guidance of the High Justice was nonsense. I learned swiftly to detect that sort by a quick scanning, often by looking at just a single page. The style in which it was written told me much: I found that a man who cannot phrase his thoughts cleanly on paper probably has no thoughts worth notice. The style is the man. If the prose is heavy-footed and sluggish, so too, in all likelihood, is the mind of its author, and then what are his insights into the operations of the Port Justiciary worth? A coarse and common mind offers coarse and common perceptions. I had to do a great deal of writing myself, summarizing and condensing the reports of middling value, and whatever I have learned of the literary art may be traced to my years in the service of the High Justice. My style too reflects the man, for I know myself to be earnest, solemn, fond of courtly gestures, and given to communicating more perhaps than others really want to know; all these traits I find in my own prose. It has its faults, yet am I pleased with it: I have my faults, yet am I pleased with me.

Before long I realized that the most powerful man in Manneran was a puppet whose strings I controlled. I decided which cases the High Justice should handle, I chose the applications for special favor that he would read, I gave him the capsuled commentaries on which his verdicts were based. Segvord had not accidentally allowed me to attain such power. It was necessary for someone to perform the screening duties I now handled, and until my coming to Manneran the job had been done by a committee of three, all ambitious to hold Segvord's title some day. Fearing those men, Segvord had arranged to promote them to positions of greater splendor but lesser responsibilities. Then he slid me into their place. His only son had died in boyhood; all his patronage therefore fell upon me. Out of love of Halum he had coolly chosen to make a homeless Sallan prince one of the dominant figures of Manneran.

It was widely understood, by others long before by me, how important I was going to be. Those princes at my wedding had not been there out of respect for Loimel's family, but to curry favor with me. The soft words from Stirron were meant to insure I would show no hostility to Salla in my decision-making. Doubtless my royal cousin Truis of Glin now was wondering uneasily if I knew that it was his doing that the doors of his province had closed in my face; he too sent a fine gift for my marriage-day. Nor did the flow of gifts cease with the nuptial ceremony. Constantly there came to me handsome things from those whose interests were bound up in the doings of the Port Justiciary. In Salla we would call such gifts by their rightful name, which is *bribes;* but Segvord assured me that in Manneran there was no harm in accepting them, so long as I did not let them interfere with my objectivity of judgment. Now I realized how, on the modest salary of a judge, Segvord had come to live in such princely style. In truth I did try to put all this bribery from my mind while at my official duties, and weigh each case on its merits alone.

So I found my place in Manneran. I mastered the secrets of the Port Justiciary, developed a feel for the rhythms of maritime commerce, and served the High Justice ably. I moved among princes and judges and men of wealth. I purchased a small but sumptuous house close by Segvord's, and soon had the builders out to increase its size. I worshipped, as only the mighty do, at the Stone Chapel itself, and went to the celebrated Jidd for my drainings. I was taken into a select athletic society, and displayed my skills with the feathered shaft in Manneran Stadium. When I visited Salla with my bride the springtime after our wedding, Stirron received me as if I were a Mannerangi septarch, parading me through the capital before a cheering multitude and feasting me royally at the palace. He said not a word to me about my flight from Salla, but was wholly amiable in a reserved and distant fashion. My first son, who was born that autumn, I named for him.

Two other sons followed, Noim and Kinnall, and daughters named Halum and Loimel. The boys were straightbodied and strong; the girls promised to show the beauty of their namesakes. I took great pleasure in heading a family. I longed for the time when I could have my sons with me hunting in the Burnt Lowlands, or shooting the rapids of the River Woyn; meanwhile I went hunting without them, and the spears of many hornfowl came to decorate my home.

Loimel, as I have said, remained a stranger to me. One does not expect to penetrate the soul of one's wife as deeply as that of one's bondsister, but nevertheless, despite the customs of self-containment we observe, one expects to develop a certain communion with someone one lives with. I never penetrated anything of Loimel's except her body. The warmth and openness she had showed me at our first meeting vanished swiftly, and she became as aloof as any coldbelly wife of Glin. Once in the heat of lovemaking I used 'I' to her, as I sometimes did with whores, and she slapped me and twisted her hips to cast me from her loins. We drifted apart. She had her life, mine; after a time we made no attempt to reach across the gulf to one another. She spent her time at music, bathing, sunsleeping, and piety, and I at hunting, gaming, rearing my sons, and doing my work. She took lovers and I took mistresses. It was a frosty marriage. We scarcely ever quarreled; we were not close enough even for that.

Noim and Halum were with me much of the time. They were great comforts to me.

At the Justiciary my authority and responsibility grew year by year. I was not promoted from my position as clerk to the High Justice, nor did my salary increase by any large extent; yet all of Manneran knew that I was the one who governed Segvord's decisions, and I enjoyed a lordly income of 'gifts.' Gradually Segvord withdrew from most of his duties, leaving them to me. He spent weeks at a time on his island retreat in the Gulf of Sumar, while I initialed and stamped documents in his name. In my twenty-fourth year, which was his fiftieth, he gave up his office altogether. Since I was not a Mannerangi by birth, it was impossible for me to become High Justice in his place; but Segvord arranged for the appointment of an amiable nonentity as his successor, one Noldo Kalimol, with the understanding that Kalimol would retain me in my place of power.

You would be right to assume that my life in Manneran was one of ease and security, of wealth and authority. Week flowed serenely into week, and, though perfect happiness is given to no man, I had few reasons for discontent. The failings of my marriage I accepted placidly, since deep love between man and wife is not often encountered in our kind of society; as for my other sorrow, my hopeless love for Halum, I kept it buried deep within me, and when it rose painfully close to the surface of my soul I soothed myself by a visit to the drainer Jidd. I might have gone on uneventfully in that fashion to the end of my days, but for the arrival in my life of Schweiz the Earthman.

28

Earthmen come rarely to Borthan. Before Schweiz, I had seen only two, both in the days when my father held the septarchy. The first was a tall redbearded man who visited Salla when I was about five years old; he was a traveler who wandered from world to world for his own amusement, and had just crossed the Burnt Lowlands alone and on foot. I remember studying his face with intense concentration, searching for the marks of his otherworldly origin – an extra eye, perhaps, horns, tendrils, fangs.

He had none of these, of course, and so I openly doubted his story of having come from Earth. Stirron, with the benefit of two years' more schooling than I, was the one who told me, in a jeering tone, that all the worlds of the heavens, including our own, had been settled by people from Earth, which was why an Earthman looked just like any of us. Nevertheless, when a second Earthman showed up at court a few years later, I still searched for fangs and tendrils. This one was a husky, cheerful man with light brown skin, a scientist making a collection of our native wildlife for some university in a far part of the galaxy. My father took him out into the Burnt Lowlands to get hornfowl; I begged to go along, and was whipped for my nagging.

I dreamed of Earth. I looked it up in books and saw a picture of a blue planet with many continents, and a huge pockmarked moon going around it, and I thought, this is where we all came from. This is the beginning of everything. I read of the kingdoms and nations of old Earth, the wars and devastation, the monuments, the tragedies. The going-forth into space, the attainment of the stars. There was a time when I even imagined I was an Earthman myself, born on that ancient planet of wonders, and brought to Borthan in babyhood to be exchanged for a septarch's true son. I told myself that when I grew up I would travel to Earth and walk through cities ten thousand years old, retracing the line of migration that had led my forefathers' forefathers from Earth to Borthan. I wanted to own a piece of Earth, too, some potsherd, some bit of stone, some battered coin, as a tangible link to the world at the heart of man's wanderings. And I longed for some other Earthman to come to Borthan, so that I could ask him ten thousand thousand questions, so that I could beg a slice of Earth for myself, but none came, and I grew up, and my obsession with the first of man's planets faded.

Then Schweiz crossed my way.

Schweiz was a man of commerce. Many Earthmen are. At the time I met him he had been on Borthan a couple of years as representative of an exporting firm based in a solar system not far from our own; he dealt in manufactured goods and sought our furs and spices in return. During his stay in Manneran, he had become entangled in controversy with a local importer over a cargo of stormshield furs from the northwestern coast; the man tried to give Schweiz poor quality at a higher-than-contracted price, Schweiz sued, and the case went to the Port Justiciary. This was about three years ago, and a little more than three years after the retirement of Segvord Helalam.

The facts of the case were clear-cut and there was no doubt about the judgment. One of the lower justices approved Schweiz's plea and ordered the importer to make good on his contract with the swindled Earthman. Ordinarily I would not have become involved in the matter. But when the papers on the case came to High Justice Kalimol for routine review just prior to affirmation of verdict, I glanced at them and saw that the plaintiff was an Earthman.

Temptation speared me. My old fascination with that race – my delusion of fangs and tendrils and extra eyes – took hold of me again. I had to talk with him. What did I hope to get from him? The answers to the questions that had gone unanswered when I was a boy? Some clue to the nature of the forces that had driven mankind to the stars? Or merely amusement, a moment of diversion in an overly placid life?

I asked Schweiz to report to my office.

He came in almost on the run, a frantic, energetic figure in clothes of flamboyant style and tone. Grinning with a manic glee, he slapped my palm in greeting, dug his knuckles into my desktop, pushed himself back a few steps, and began to pace the room.

'The gods preserve you, your grace!' he cried.

I thought his odd demeanor, his coiled-spring bounciness and his wild-eyed intensity, stemmed from fear of me, for he had good reason to worry, called in by a powerful official to discuss a case that he thought he had won. But I found later that Schweiz's mannerisms were expressions of his own seething nature, not of any momentary and specific tension.

He was a man of middle height, very sparely built, not a scrap of fat on his frame. His skin was tawny and his hair was the color of dark honey; it hung down in a straight flow to his shoulders. His eyes were bright and mischievous, his smile quick and sly, and he radiated a boyish vigor, a dynamic enthusiasm, that charmed me just then, though it would eventually make him an exhausting companion for me. Yet he was no boy: his face bore the first lines of age and his hair, abundant though it was, was starting to go thin at the crown.

'Be seated,' I said, for his capering was disturbing me. I wondered how to launch the conversation. How much could I ask him before he claimed Covenant at me and sealed his lips? Would he talk about himself and his world? Had I any right to pry into a foreigner's soul in a way that I would not dare do with a man of Borthan? I would see. Curiosity drove me. I picked up the sheaf of documents on his case, for he was looking at the file unhappily, and held them toward him, saying, 'One places the first matters first. Your verdict has been affirmed. Today High Justice Kalimol gives his seal and within a moonrise you'll have your money.'

'Happy words, your grace.'

'That concludes the legal business.'

'So short a meeting? It seems hardly necessary to have paid this call to exchange only a moment's talk, your grace.'

'One must admit,' I said, 'that you were summoned here to discuss things other than your lawsuit.'

'Eh, your grace?' He looked baffled and alarmed.

'To talk of Earth,' I said. 'To gratify the idle inquisitiveness of a bored bureaucrat. Is that all right? Are you willing to talk a while, now that you've been lured here on the pretense of business? You know, Schweiz, one has always been fascinated by Earth and by Earthmen.' To win some rapport with him, for he still was frowning and mistrustful, I told him the story of the two other Earthmen I had known, and of my childhood belief that they should be alien in form. He relaxed and listened with pleasure, and before I was through he was laughing heartily. 'Fangs!' he cried. 'Tendrils!' He ran his hands over his face. 'Did you really think that, your grace? That Earthmen were such bizarre creatures? By all the gods, your grace, I wish I had some strangeness about my body, that I could give you amusement!'

I flinched each time Schweiz spoke of himself in the first person. His casual obscenities punctured the mood I had attempted to build. Though I tried to pretend nothing was amiss, Schweiz instantly realized his blunder, and leaping to his feet in obvious distress, said, 'A thousand pardons! One tends to forget one's grammar sometimes, when one is not accustomed to—'

'No offense is taken,' I said hastily.

'You must understand, your grace, that old habits of speech die hard, and in using your language one sometimes slips into the mode most natural for himself, even though—'

'Of course, Schweiz. A forgivable lapse.' He was trembling. 'Besides,' I said, winking, 'I'm a grown man. Do you think I'm so easily shocked?' My use of the vulgarities was deliberate, to put him at his ease. The tactic worked; he subsided, calming. But he took no license from the incident to use gutter talk with me again that morning, and in fact was careful to observe the niceties of grammatical etiquette for a long time thereafter, until such things had ceased to matter between us.

I asked him to tell me now about Earth, the mother of us all.

'A small planet,' he said. 'Far away. Choked in its own ancient wastes; the poisons of two thousand years of carelessness and overbreeding stain its skies and its seas and its land. An ugly place.'

'In truth, ugly?'

'There are still some attractive districts. Not many of them, and nothing to boast about. Some trees, here and there. A little grass. A lake. A waterfall. A valley. Mostly the planet is a dunghole. Earthmen often wish they could uncover their early ancestors, and bring them to life again, and then throttle them. For their selfishness. For their lack of concern for the generations to come. They filled the world with themselves and used everything up.'

'Is this why Earthmen built empires in the skies, then, to escape the filth of their home world?'

'Part of it is that, yes,' Schweiz said. 'There were so many billions of people. And those who had the strength to leave all went out and up. But it was more than running away, you know. It was a hunger to see strange things, a hunger to undertake journeys, a hunger to make fresh starts. To create new and better worlds of man. A string of Earths across the sky.'

'And those who did not go?' I asked. 'Earth still has those other billions of people?' I was thinking of Velada Borthan and its sparse forty or fifty millions.

'Oh, no, no. It's almost empty now, a ghost-world, ruined cities, cracking highways. Few live there any longer. Fewer are born there every year.'

'But you were born there?'

'On the continent called Europe, yes. One hasn't seen Earth for almost thirty years, though. Not since one was fourteen.'

'You don't look that old,' I said.

'One reckons time in Earthlength years,' Schweiz explained. 'By your figuring one is only approaching the age of thirty.'

'Also this one,' I said. 'And here also is one who left his homeland before reaching manhood.' I was speaking freely, far more freely than was proper, yet I could not stop myself. I had drawn out Schweiz, and felt an impulse to offer something of my own in return. 'Going out from Salla as a boy to seek his fortune in Glin, then finding better luck in Manneran after a while. A wanderer, Schweiz, like yourself.'

'It is a bond between us, then.'

Could I presume on that bond? I asked him, 'Why did you leave Earth?'

'For the same reasons as everyone else. To go where the air is clean and a man stands some chance to become something. The only ones who spend their whole lives there are those who can't help but stay.'

'And this is the planet that all the galaxy reveres!' I said in wonder. 'The world of so many myths! The planet of boys' dreams! The center of the universe – a pimple, a boil!'

'You put it well.'

'Yet it is revered.'

'Oh, revere it, revere it, certainly!' Schweiz cried. His eyes were aglow. 'The foundation of mankind! The grand originator of the species! Why not revere it, your grace? Revere the bold beginnings that were made there. Revere the high ambitions that sprang from its mud. And revere the terrible mistakes, too. Ancient Earth made mistake after mistake, and choked itself in error, so that you would be spared from having to pass through the same fires and torments.' Schweiz laughed harshly. 'Earth died to redeem you starfolk from sin. How's that for a religious notion? A whole liturgy could be composed around that idea. A priestcraft of Earth the redeemer.' Suddenly he leaned forward and said, 'Are you a religious man, your grace?'

I was taken aback by the thrusting intimacy of his question. But I put up no barriers.

'Certainly,' I said.

'You go to the godhouse, you talk to the drainers, the whole thing?'

I was caught. I could not help but speak.

'Yes,' I said. 'Does that surprise you?'

'Not at all. Everyone on Borthan seems to be genuinely religious. Which amazes one. You know, your grace, one isn't religious in the least, oneself. One tries, one has always tried, one has worked *so hard* to convince oneself that there are superior beings out there who guide destiny, and sometimes one almost makes it, your grace, one almost believes, one breaks through into faith, but then skepticism shuts things down every time. And one ends by saying, no, it isn't possible, it can't be, it defies logic and common sense. Logic and common sense!'

'But how can you live all your days without a closeness to something holy?'

'Most of the time, one manages fairly well. Most of the time.'

'And the rest of the time?'

'That's when one feels the impact of knowing one is entirely alone in the universe. Naked under the stars, and the starlight hitting the exposed skin, burning, a cold fire, and no one to shield one from it, no one to offer a hiding place, no one to pray to, do you see? The sky is ice and the ground is ice and the soul is ice, and who's to warm it? There isn't anyone. You've convinced yourself that no one exists who can give comfort. One wants some system of belief, one wants to submit, to get down and kneel, to be governed by metaphysics, you know? To believe, to have faith! And one can't. And that's when the terror sets in. The dry sobs. The nights of no sleeping.' Schweiz's face was flushed and wild with excitement; I wondered if he could be entirely sane. He reached across the desk, clamped his hand over mine – the gesture stunned me, but I did not pull back – and said hoarsely, 'Do you believe in gods, your grace?'

'Surely.'

'In a literal way? You think there's a god of travelers, and a god of fishermen, and a god of farmers, and one who looks after septarchs, and—'

'There is a force,' I said, 'that gives order and form to the universe. The force manifests itself in various ways, and for the sake of bridging the gap between ourselves and that force, we regard each of its manifestations as a "god," yes, and extend our souls to this manifestation or that one, as our needs demand. Those of us who are without learning accept these gods literally, as beings with faces and personalities. Others realize that they are metaphors for the aspects of the divine force, and not a tribe of potent spirits living overhead. But there is no one in Velada Borthan who denies the existence of the force itself.'

'One feels such fierce envy of that,' said Schweiz. 'To be raised in a culture that has coherence and structure, to have such assurance of ultimate verities, to feel yourself part of a divine scheme – how marvelous that must be! To enter into a system of belief – it would almost be worth putting up with this society's great flaws, to have something like that.'

'Flaws?' Suddenly I found myself on the defensive. 'What flaws?'

Schweiz narrowed his gaze and moistened his lips. Perhaps he was calculating whether I would be hurt or angered by what he meant to say. '*Flaws* was possibly too strong a word,' he replied. 'One might say instead, this society's limits, its – well, its narrowness. One speaks now of the necessity to shield one's self from one's fellow men that you impose. The taboos against reference to self, against frank discourse, against any opening of the soul—'

'Has one not opened his soul to you today in this very room?'

'Ah,' Schweiz said, 'but you've been speaking to an alien, to one who is no part of your culture, to someone you secretly suspect of having tendrils and fangs! Would you be so free with a citizen of Manneran?'

'No one else in Manneran would have asked such questions as you have been asking.'

'Maybe so. One lacks a native's training in self-repression. These questions about your philosophy of religion, then – do they intrude on your privacy of soul, your grace? Are they offensive to you?'

'One has no objections to talking of such things,' I said, without much conviction.

'But it's a taboo conversation, isn't it? We weren't using naughty words, except that once when one slipped, but we were dealing in naughty ideas, establishing a naughty relationship. You let your wall down a little way, eh? For which one is grateful. One's been here so long, years now, and one hasn't ever talked freely with a man of Borthan, not once! Until one sensed today that you were willing to open yourself a bit. This has been an extraordinary experience, your grace.' The manic smile returned. He moved jerkily about the office. 'One had no wish to speak critically of your way of life here,' he said. 'One wished in fact to praise certain aspects of it, while trying to understand others.'

'Which to praise, which to understand?'

'To understand your habit of erecting walls about yourselves. To praise the ease with which you accept divine presence. One envies you for that. As one said, one was raised in no system of belief at all, and is unable to let himself be overtaken by faith. One's head is always full of nasty skeptical questions. One is constitutionally unable to accept what one can't see or feel, and so one must always be *alone*, and one goes around the galaxy seeking

for the gateway to belief, trying this, trying that, and one never finds—'
Schweiz paused. He was flushed and sweaty. 'So you see, your grace, you
have something precious here, this ability to let yourselves become part of a
larger power. One would wish to learn it from you. Of course, it's a matter of
cultural conditioning. Borthan still knows the gods, and Earth has outlived
them. Civilization is young on this planet. It takes thousands of years for the
religious impulse to erode.'

'And,' I said, 'this planet was settled by men who had strong religious beliefs, who specifically came here to preserve them, and who took great pains
to instill them in their descendants.'

'That too. Your Covenant. Yet that was – what, fifteen hundred, two thousand years ago? It could all have crumbled by now, but it hasn't. It's stronger
than ever. Your devoutness, your humility, your denial of self—'

'Those who couldn't accept and transmit the ideals of the first settlers,' I
pointed out, 'were not allowed to remain among them. That had its effect on
the pattern of the culture, if you'll agree that such traits as rebelliousness and
atheism can be bred out of a race. The consenters stayed; the rejecters went.'

'You're speaking of the exiles who went to Sumara Borthan?'

'You know the story, then?'

'Naturally. One picks up the history of whatever planet one happens to
be assigned to. Sumara Borthan, yes. Have you ever been there, your grace?'

'Few of us visit that continent,' I said.

'Ever thought of going?'

'Never.'

'There are those who do go there,' Schweiz said, and gave me a strange
smile. I meant to ask him about that, but at that moment a secretary entered
with a stack of documents, and Schweiz hastily rose. 'One doesn't wish to
consume too much of your grace's valuable time. Perhaps this conversation
could be continued at another hour?'

'One hopes for the pleasure of it,' I told him.

29

When Schweiz was gone I sat a long while with my back to my desk, closing
my eyes and replaying in my mind the things we had just said to one another.
How readily he had slipped past my guard! How quickly we had begun to
speak of inner matters! True, he was an otherworlder, and with him I did
not feel entirely bound by our customs. Yet we had grown dangerously close

so extraordinarily fast. Ten minutes more and I might have been as open as a bondbrother to him, and he to me. I was astounded and dismayed by my easy dropping of propriety, by the way he had drawn me slyly into such intimacy.

Was it wholly his doing? I had sent for him, I had been the first to ask the close questions. I had set the tone. He had sensed from that some instability in me, and he had seized upon it, quickly flipping the conversation about, so that I was the subject and he the interrogator. And I had gone along with it. Reluctantly but yet willingly, I had opened to him. I was drawn to him, and he to me. Schweiz the tempter! Schweiz the exploiter of my weakness, hidden so long, hidden even from myself! How could he have known I was ready to open?

His high-pitched rapid speech still seemed to echo in the room. Asking. Asking. Asking. And then revealing. *Are you a religious man? Do you believe in literal gods? If only I could find faith! How I envy you. But the flaws of your world. The denial of self. Would you be so free with a citizen of Manneran? Speak to me, your grace. Open to me. I have been alone here so long.*

How could he have known, when I myself did not know?

A strange friendship had been born. I asked Schweiz to dine at home with me; we feasted and we talked, and the blue wine of Salla flowed and the golden wine of Manneran, and when we were warmed by our drinking we discussed religion once more, and Schweiz's difficulties with faith, and my convictions that the gods were real. Halum came in and sat with us an hour, and afterward remarked to me on the power of Schweiz to loosen tongues, saying, 'You seemed more drunk than you have ever been, Kinnall. And yet you shared only three bottles of wine, so it must have been something else that made your eyes shine and your words so easy.' I laughed and told her that a recklessness came over me when I was with the Earthman, that I found it hard to abide by custom with him.

At our next meeting, in a tavern by the Justiciary, Schweiz said, 'You love your bondsister, eh?'

'Of course one loves one's bondsister.'

'One means, though, you *love* her.' With a knowing snigger.

I drew back, tense. 'Was one then so thoroughly wined the other night? What did one say to you of her?'

'Nothing,' he replied. 'You said it all to her. With your eyes, with your smile. And no words passed.'

'May we talk of other things?'

'If your grace wishes.'

'This is a tender theme, and painful.'

'Pardon, then, your grace. One only meant to confirm one's guess.'

'Such love as that is forbidden among us.'

'Which is not to say that it doesn't sometimes exist, eh?' Schweiz asked, and clinked his glass against mine.

In that moment I made up my mind never to meet with him again. He looked too deep and spoke too freely of what he saw. But four days afterward, coming upon him on a pier, I invited him to dine a second time. Loimel was displeased by the invitation. Nor would Halum come, pleading another engagement; when I pressed her, she said that Schweiz made her uncomfortable. Noim was in Manneran, though, and joined us at the table. We all drank sparingly, and the conversation was a stilted and impersonal one, until, with no perceptible shifting of tone, we found ourselves telling Schweiz of the time when I had escaped from Salla in fear of my brother's jealousies, and Schweiz was telling us of his departure from Earth; when the Earthman went home that night, Noim said to me, not altogether disapprovingly, 'There are devils in that man, Kinnall.'

30

'This taboo on self-expression,' Schweiz asked me when we were together another time. 'Can you explain it, your grace?'

'You mean the prohibition against saying "I" and "me"?'

'Not that, so much as the whole pattern of thought that would have you deny there are such things as "I" and "me,"' he said: 'The commandment that you must keep your private affairs private at all times, except only with bond-kin and drainers. The custom of wall-building around oneself that affects even your grammar.'

'The Covenant, you mean?'

'The Covenant,' said Schweiz.

'You say you know our history?'

'Much of it.'

'You know that our forefathers were stern folk from a northern climate, accustomed to hardship, mistrustful of luxury and ease, who came to Borthan to avoid what they saw as the contaminating decadence of their native world?'

'Was it so? One thought only that they were refugees from religious persecution.'

'Refugees from sloth and self-indulgence,' I said. 'And, coming here, they established a code of conduct to protect their children's children against corruption.'

'The Covenant.'

'The Covenant, yes. The pledge they made each to each, the pledge that each of us makes to all his fellow men on his Naming Day. When we swear never to force our turmoils on another, when we vow to be strong-willed and hardy of spirit, so that the gods will continue to smile on us. And so on and so on. We are trained to abominate the demon that is self.'

'Demon?'

'So we regard it. A tempting demon, that urges us to make use of others instead of relying on our own strengths.'

'Where there is no love of self, there is neither friendship nor sharing,' said Schweiz.

'Perhaps so.'

'And thus there is no trust.'

'We specify areas of responsibility through contract,' I said. 'There is no need for knowledge of the souls of others, where law rules. And in Velada Borthan no one questions the rule of law.'

'You say you abominate self,' said Schweiz. 'It seems, rather, that you glorify it.'

'How so?'

'By living apart from one another, each in the castle of his skull. Proud. Unbending. Aloof. Uncaring. The reign of self indeed, and no abomination of it!'

'You put things oddly,' I said. 'You invert our customs, and think you speak wisely.'

'Has it always been like this,' Schweiz asked, 'since the beginning of settlement in Velada Borthan?'

'Yes,' I said. 'Except among those malcontents you know of, who fled to the southern continent. The rest of us abide by the Covenant. And our customs harden: thus we not may not talk of ourselves in the first person singular, since this is a raw exposure of self, but in medieval times this could be done. On the other hand, some things soften. Once we were guarded even in giving our names to strangers. We spoke to one another only when absolutely necessary. We show more trust nowadays.'

'But not a great deal.'

'But not a great deal,' I admitted.

'And is there no pain in this for you? Every man sealed against all others? Do you never say to yourselves that there must be a happier way for humans to live?'

'We abide by the Covenant.'

'With ease or with difficulty?'

'With ease,' I said. 'The pain is not so great, when you consider that we have bond-kin, with whom we are exempted from the rule of selflessness.

And the same with our drainers.'

'To others, though, you may not complain, you may not unburden a sorrowful soul, you may not seek advice, you may not expose your desires and needs, you may not speak of dreams and fantasies and romance, you may not talk of anything but chilly, impersonal things.' Schweiz shuddered. 'Pardon, your grace, but one finds this a harsh way to live. One's own search has constantly been for warmth and love and human contact, for sharing, for opening, and this world here seems to elevate the opposite of what one prizes most highly.'

'Have you had much luck,' I asked, 'finding warmth and love and human contact?'

Schweiz shrugged. 'It has not always been easy.'

'For us there is never loneliness, since we have bond-kin. With Halum, with Noim, with such as these to offer comfort, why does one need a world of strangers?'

'And if your bond-kin are not close at hand? If one is wandering, say, far from them in the snows of Glin?'

'One suffers, then. And one's character grows tougher. But that is an exceptional situation. Schweiz, our system may force us into isolation, yet it also guarantees us love.'

'But not the love of husband for wife. Not the love of father for child.'

'Perhaps not.'

'And even the love of bond-kin is limited. For you yourself, eh, have admitted that you feel a longing for your bondsister Halum that cannot be—'

I cut him off, telling him sharply, 'Speak of other things!' Color flared in my cheeks; my skin grew hot.

Schweiz nodded and smiled a chastened smile. 'Pardon, your grace. The conversation became too intense; there was loss of control, but no injury meant.'

'Very well.'

'The reference was too personal. One is abashed.'

'You meant no injury,' I said, guilty over my outburst, knowing he had stung me at a vulnerable place and that I had overreacted to the bite of truth. I poured more wine. We drank in silence for a time.

Then Schweiz said, 'May one make a proposal, your grace? May one invite you to take part in an experiment that may prove interesting and valuable to you?'

'Go on,' I said, frowning, ill at ease.

'You know,' he began, 'that one has long felt uncomfortably conscious of his solitary state in the universe, and that one has sought without success some means of comprehending his relationship to that universe. For you, the method lies in religious faith, but one has failed to reach such faith because of his unfortunate compulsion toward total rationalism. Eh? One cannot break through to that larger sense of *belonging* by words alone, by prayer alone, by ritual alone. This thing is possible for you, and one envies you for it. One finds himself trapped, isolated, sealed up in his skull, condemned to metaphysical solitude: a man apart, a man on his own. One does not find this state of godlessness enjoyable or desirable. You of Borthan can tolerate the sort of emotional isolation you impose on yourselves, since you have the consolations of your religion, you have drainers and whatever mystical mergings-with-the-gods the act of draining gives you; but the one who speaks to you now has no such advantages.'

'All this we have discussed many times,' I said. 'You spoke of a proposal, an experiment.'

'Be patient, your grace. One must explain oneself fully, step by step.'

Schweiz flashed me his most charming smile, and turned on me eyes that were bright with visionary schemes. His hands roamed the air expressively, conjuring up invisible drama, as he said, 'Perhaps your grace is aware that there are certain chemical substances – drugs, yes, call them drugs – that allow one to make an opening into the infinite, or at least to have the illusion that one has made such an opening – to attain a brief and tentative glimpse into the mystic realms of the intangible. Eh? Known for thousands of years, these drugs, used in the days before Earthmen ever went to the stars. Employed in ancient religious rites. Employed by others as a substitute for religion, as a secular means of finding faith, the gateway to the infinite for such as this one, who can get there no other way.'

'Such drugs are forbidden in Velada Borthan,' I said.

'Of course, of course! For you they offer a means of sidestepping the processes of formal religion. Why waste time at a drainer's if you can expand your soul with a pill? Your law is wise on this point. Your Covenant could not survive if you allowed these chemicals to be used here.'

'Your proposal, Schweiz,' I said.

'One first must tell you that he has used these drugs himself, and found them not entirely satisfactory. True, they open the infinite. True, they let one merge with the Godhead. But only for moments: a few hours at best. And at the end of it, one is as alone as before. It is the illusion of the soul's opening, not the opening itself. Whereas this planet produces a drug that can provide the real thing.'

'What?'

'In Sumara Borthan,' said Schweiz, 'dwell those who fled the rule of the Covenant. One is told that they are savages, going naked and living on roots and seeds and fish; the cloak of civilization has dropped away from them and they have slipped back into barbarism. So one learned from a traveler who had visited that continent not long ago. One also learned that in

Sumara Borthan they use a drug made from a certain powdered root, which has the capacity of opening mind to mind, so that each can read the inmost thoughts of the other. It is the very opposite of your Covenant, do you see? They know one another from the soul out, by way of this drug they eat.'

'One has heard stories of the savagery of those folk,' I said.

Schweiz put his face close to mine. 'One confesses himself tempted by the Sumaran drug. One hopes that if he could ever get inside another mind, he could find that community of soul for which he has searched so long. It might be the bridge to the infinite that he seeks, the spiritual transformation. Eh? In quest of revelations he has tried many substances. Why not this?'

'If it exists.'

'It exists, your grace. This traveler who came from Sumara Borthan brought some of it with him to Manneran, and sold some of it to the curious Earthman.' Schweiz drew forth from a pocket a small glossy envelope, and held it toward me. It contained a small quantity of some white powder; it could have been sugar. 'Here it is,' he said.

I stared at it as if he had pulled out a flask of poison.

'Your proposal?' I demanded. 'Your experiment, Schweiz?'

'Let us share the Sumaran drug,' he said.

31

I might have slapped the powder from his hand and ordered his arrest. I might have commanded him to get away from me and never come near again. I might at the very least have cried out that it was impossible I would ever touch any such substance. But I did none of those things. I chose instead to be coolly intellectual, to show casual curiosity, to remain calm and play conversational games with him. Thus I encouraged him to lead me a little deeper into the quicksand.

I said, 'Do you think that one is so eager to contravene the Covenant?'

'One thinks that you are a man of strong will and inquiring mind, who would not miss an opportunity for enlightenment.'

'Illegal enlightenment?'

'All true enlightenment is illegal at first, within its context. Even the religion of the Covenant: were your forefathers not driven out of other worlds for practicing it?'

'One mistrusts such analogy-making. We are not talking of religions

237

now. We talk of a dangerous drug. You ask one to surrender all the training of his lifetime, and open himself to you as he has never done even to bond-kin, even to a drainer.'

'Yes.'

'And you imagine that one might be willing to do such a thing?'

'One imagines that you might well emerge transformed and cleansed, if you could bring yourself to try,' Schweiz said.

'One might also emerge scarred and twisted.'

'Doubtful. Knowledge never injures the soul. It only purges that which encrusts and saps the soul.'

'How glib you are, Schweiz! Look, though: can you believe it would be possible to give one's inner secrets to a stranger, to a foreigner, to an otherworlder?'

'Why not? Better to a stranger than to a friend. Better to an Earthman than a fellow citizen. You'd have nothing to fear: the Earthman would never try to judge you by the standards of Borthan. There'd be no criticisms, no disapprovals of what's under your skull. And the Earthman will leave this planet in a year or two, on a journey of hundreds of light-years, and what then will it matter that your mind once merged with his?'

'Why are you so eager to have this merger happen?'

'For eight moontimes,' he said, 'this drug has been in one's pocket, while one hunts for someone to share it with. It looked as though the search would be in vain. Then one met you, and saw your potential, your strength, your hidden rebelliousness—'

'One is aware of no rebelliousness, Schweiz. One accepts his world completely.'

'May one bring up the delicate matter of your attitude toward your bond-sister? That seems a symptom of a fundamental discontent with the restrictions of your society.'

'Perhaps. Perhaps not.'

'You would know yourself better after sampling the Sumaran drug. You would have fewer perhapses and more certainties.'

'How can you say this, if you haven't had the drug yourself?'

'So it seems to one.'

'It is impossible,' I said.

'An experiment. A secret pact. No one would ever know.'

'Impossible.'

'Is it that you fear to share your soul?'

'One is taught that such sharing is unholy.'

'The teachings can be wrong,' he said. 'Have you never felt the temptation? Have you never tasted such ecstasy in a draining that you wished you might undergo the same experience with someone you loved, your grace?'

Again he caught me in a vulnerable place. 'One has had such feelings oc-casionally,' I admitted. 'Sitting before some ugly drainer, and imagining it was Noim instead, or Halum, and that the draining was a two-way flow—'

'Then you already long for this drug, and don't realize it!'

'No. No.'

'Perhaps,' Schweiz suggested, 'it is the idea of opening to a stranger that dismays you, and not the concept of opening itself. Perhaps you would take this drug with someone other than the Earthman, eh? With your bond-brother? With your bondsister?'

I considered that. Sitting down with Noim, who was to me like a second self, and reaching his mind on levels that had never been available to me before, and he reaching mine. Or with Halum – or with Halum—

Schweiz, you tempter!

He said, after letting me think a while, 'Does the idea please you? Here, then. One will surrender his chance with the drug. Take it, use it, share it with one whom you love.' He pressed the envelope into my hand. It fright-ened me; I let it fall to the table as if it were aflame.

I said, 'But that would deprive you of your hoped-for fulfillment.'

'No matter. One can get more of the drug. One may perhaps find another partner for the experiment. Meanwhile you would have known the ecstasy, your grace. Even an Earthman can be unselfish. Take it, your grace. Take it.'

I gave him a dark look. 'Would it be, Schweiz, that this talk of taking the drug yourself was only pretense? That what you really look for is someone to offer himself as an experimental subject, so you can be sure the drug is safe before you risk it?'

'You misunderstand, your grace.'

'Maybe not. Maybe this is what you've been driving toward.' I saw myself administering the drug to Noim, saw him falling into convulsions before my eyes as I made ready to bring my own dose to my lips. I pushed the en-velope back toward Schweiz. 'No. The offer is refused. One appreciates the generosity, but one will not experiment on his loved ones, Schweiz.'

His face was very red. 'This implication is unwarranted, your grace. The offer to relinquish one's own share of the drug was made in good faith, and at no little cost to one's own plans. But since you reject it, let us return to the original proposition. The two of us will sample the drug, in secrecy, as an experiment in possibilities. Let us find out together what its powers may be and what doors it can open for us. We would have much to gain from this adventure, one is sure.'

'One sees what you would have to gain,' I said. 'But what purpose is there in it for—'

'Yourself?' Schweiz chuckled. Then he rammed me with the barbed hook. 'Your grace, by making the experiment you would learn that the drug is safe, you would discover the proper dosage, you would lose your fear of the mind-opening itself. And then, after obtaining a further supply of the drug, you would be properly prepared to use it for a purpose from which your fears now hold you back. You could take the drug together with the only person whom you truly love. You could use it to open your mind to your bondsister Halum, and to open hers to you.'

32

There is a story they tell to children who are still learning the Covenant, about the days when the gods had not yet ceased to walk the world in human form, and the first men had not yet arrived on Borthan. The gods at that time did not know they were divine, for they had no mortals about them for comparison, and so they were innocent beings, unaware of their powers, who lived in a simple way. They dwelled in Manneran (this is the source of Manneran's claim to superior holiness, the legend that it was once the home of the gods) and ate berries and leaves, and went without clothing except in the mild Mannerangi winter, when they threw shawls of animal hide loosely over their shoulders. And there was nothing godlike about them.

One day two of these ungodlike gods decided they would go off to see something of the world. The idea for making such a journey came first to the god whose secret name is Kinnall, now the god who looks after wayfarers. (Yes, he for whom I was named.) This Kinnall invited the goddess Thirga to join him, she whose responsibility now is the protection of those who are in love. Thirga shared Kinnall's restlessness and off they went.

From Manneran they walked west along the southern coast until they came to the shores of the Gulf of Sumar. Then they turned north, and passed through Stroin Gap just by the place where the Huishtor Mountains come to an end. They entered the Wet Lowlands, which they found less to their liking, and finally they ventured into the Frozen Lowlands, where they thought they would perish of the cold. So they turned south again, and this time they found themselves staring at the inland slopes of the Threishtor Mountains. There seemed no way for them to cross over this mighty range. They followed its eastern foothills south, but could not get out of the Burnt Lowlands, and they suffered great hardships, until at last they stumbled upon Threish Gate, and made their way through that difficult pass into the cool and foggy province of Threish.

On their first day in Threish the two gods discovered a place where a spring flowed out of a hillside. The opening in the hillside was nine-sided, and the rock surrounding the opening was so bright that it dazzled the eye, for it rippled and iridesced, and glowed with many colors constantly pulsing and changing, red and green and violet and ivory and turquoise and many more. And the water that came forth was of the same shimmering quality, having in it every color anyone ever had seen. The stream flowed only a short distance this way, and then was lost in the waters of a much larger brook, in which all the wondrous colors vanished.

Kinnall said, 'We have wandered a long while in the Burnt Lowlands, and our throats are dry from thirst. Shall we drink?' And Thirga said, 'Yes, let us drink,' and knelt by the opening in the hillside. She cupped her hands and filled them with the glittering water, and poured it into her mouth, and Kinnall drank also, and the taste of the water was so sweet that they thrust their faces right against the flow of the spring, gulping down all they could.

As they did this they experienced strange sensations of their bodies and minds. Kinnall looked toward Thirga and realized that he could see the thoughts within her soul, and they were thoughts of love for him. And she looked toward him, and saw his thoughts as well. 'We are different now,' Kinnall said, and he did not even need words to convey his meaning, for Thirga understood him as soon as his thought formed. And she replied, 'No, we are not different, but are merely able to understand the use of the gifts we have always had.'

And it was true. For they had many gifts, and they had never used them before. They could rise in the air and travel like birds; they could change the shape of their bodies; they could walk through the Burnt Lowlands or the Frozen Lowlands and feel no discomfort; they could live without taking in food; they could halt the aging of their flesh and become as young as they pleased; they could speak without saying words. All these things they might have done before coming to the spring, except that they had not known how, and now they were capable of using the skills with which they had been born. They had learned, by drinking the water of the bright spring, how to go about being gods.

Even so, they did not yet know that they were gods.

After some time they remembered the others who lived in Manneran, and flew back to tell them about the spring. The journey took only an instant. All their friends crowded round as Kinnall and Thirga spoke of the miracle of the spring, and demonstrated the powers they had mastered. When they were done, everyone in Manneran resolved to go to the spring, and set out in a long procession, through Stroin Gap and the Wet Lowlands and up the eastern slopes of the Threishtors to Threish Gate. Kinnall and Thirga flew above them, guiding them from day to day. Eventually they reached the place of the spring, and one by one they drank of it and became as gods. Then they scattered, some returning to Manneran, some going to Salla, some going even to Sumara Borthan or the far continents of Umbis, Dabis, and Tibis, since, now that they were as gods, there were no limits on the speed of their travel, and they wished to see those strange places. But Kinnall and Thirga settled down beside the spring in eastern Threish and were content to explore one another's soul.

Many years passed, and then the starship of our forefathers came down in Threish, near the western shore. Men had at last reached Borthan. They built a small town and went about the task of collecting food for themselves. A certain man named Digant, who was among these settlers, ventured deep into the forest in search of meat-animals, and became lost, and roamed and roamed until finally he came to the place where Kinnall and Thirga lived. He had never seen any such as they before, nor they anyone such as he.

'What sort of creatures are you?' he asked.

Kinnall replied, 'Once we were quite ordinary, but now we do quite well, for we never grow old, and we can fly faster than any bird, and our souls are open to each other, and we can take on any shape we please.'

'Why, then, you are gods!' Digant cried.

'Gods? What are gods?'

And Digant explained that he was a man, and had no such powers as theirs, for men must use words to talk, and can neither fly nor change their shape, and grow older with each journey of the world around the sun, until the time of dying comes. Kinnall and Thirga listened with care, comparing themselves to Digant, and when he was done speaking they knew it was true, that he was a man and they were gods.

'Once we were almost like men ourselves,' Thirga admitted. 'We felt hunger and grew old and spoke only by means of words and had to put one foot in front of the other to get from place to place. We lived like men out of ignorance, for we did not know our powers. But then things changed.'

'And what changed them?' Digant asked.

'Why,' said Kinnall in his innocence, 'we drank from that glistening spring, and the water of it opened our eyes to our powers and allowed us to become as gods. That was all.'

Then Digant's soul surged with excitement, for he told himself that he too could drink from the spring, and then he would join this pair in godhood. He would keep the spring a secret afterward, when he returned to the settlers on the coast, and they would worship him as their living god, and treat him with reverence, or he would destroy them. But Digant did not dare ask Kinnall and Thirga to let him drink from the spring, for he feared that they would refuse him, being jealous of their divinity. So he hatched a scheme to get them away from that place.

'Is it true,' he asked them, 'that you can travel so fast that you are able to visit every part of this world in a single day?'

Kinnall assured him that this was true.

'It seems difficult to believe,' said Digant.

'We will give you proof,' Thirga said, and she touched her hand to Kinnall's, and the two gods went aloft. They soared to the highest peak of the Threishtors and gathered snowflowers there; they descended into the Burnt Lowlands and scooped up a handful of the red soil; in the Wet Lowlands they collected herbs; by the Gulf of Sumar they took some liquor from a flesh-tree; on the shores of the Polar Gulf they pried out a sample of the eternal ice; then they leaped over the top of the world to frosty Tibis, and began their journey through the far continents, so that they might bring back to the doubting Digant something from every part of the world.

The moment Kinnall and Thirga had departed on this enterprise, Digant rushed to the spring of miracles. There he hesitated briefly, afraid that the gods might return suddenly and strike him down for his boldness; but they did not appear, and Digant thrust his face into the flow and drank deeply, thinking, Now I too shall be as a god. He filled his gut with the glowing water and swayed and grew dizzy, and fell to the ground. Is this godhood, he wondered? He tried to fly and could not. He tried to change his shape and could not. He failed in all these things because he had been a man to begin with, and not a god, and the spring could not change a man into a god, but could only help a god to realize his full powers.

But the spring gave Digant one gift. It enabled him to reach into the minds of the other men who had settled in Threish. As he lay on the ground, numb with disappointment, he heard a tiny tickling sound in the middle of his mind, and paid close heed to it and realized he was hearing the minds of his friends. And he found a way of amplifying the sound so that he could hear everything clearly: yes, and this was the mind of his wife, and this was the mind of his sister, and this was the mind of his sister's husband, and Digant could look into any of them and any other mind, reading the innermost thoughts. This is godhood, he told himself. And he probed their minds deeply, flushing out all their secrets. Steadily he increased the scope of his power until every mind at once was connected to his. Forth from them he drew the privacies of their souls, until, intoxicated with his new power, swollen with the pride of his godhood, he sent out a message to all those minds from his mind, saying, 'HEAR THE VOICE OF DIGANT. IT IS DIGANT THE GOD THAT YOU SHALL WORSHIP.'

When this terrible voice broke into their minds, many of the settlers in Threish fell down dead with shock, and others lost their sanity, and others ran about in wild terror, crying, 'Digant has invaded our minds! Digant has invaded our minds!' And the waves of fear and pain coming out of them were so intense that Digant himself suffered greatly, falling into a paralysis and stupor, though his dazed mind continued to roar, 'HEAR THE VOICE OF DIGANT. IT IS DIGANT THE GOD THAT YOU SHALL WORSHIP.' Each time that great cry went forth, more settlers died and more lost their reason, and Digant, responding to the mental tumults he had caused, writhed and shook in agony, wholly unable to control the powers of his brain.

Kinnall and Thirga were in Dabis when this occurred, drawing forth from a marsh a triple-headed worm to show to Digant. The bellowings of Digant's mind sped around the world even to Dabis, and, hearing those sounds, Kinnall and Thirga left off what they were doing and hurried back to Threish. They found Digant close to death, his brain all but burned out, and they found the settlers of Threish dead or mad; and they knew at once how this had come to pass. Swiftly they brought an end to Digant's life, so that there would be silence in Threish. Then they went among the victims of the would-be god, and raised all the dead and healed all the injured. And lastly they sealed the opening in the hillside with a seal that could not be broken, for it was plain to them that men must not drink of that spring, but only gods, and all the gods had already taken their draughts of it. The people of Threish fell on their knees before those two, and asked in awe, 'Who are you?' and Kinnall and Thirga replied, 'We are gods, and you are only men.' And that was the beginning of the end of the innocence of the gods. And after that time it was forbidden among men to seek ways of speaking mind to mind, because of the harm that Digant had done, and it was written into the Covenant that one must keep one's soul apart from the souls of others, since only gods can mingle souls without destroying one another, and we are not gods.

33

Of course I found many reasons to postpone taking the Sumaran drug with Schweiz. First, High Justice Kalimol departed on a hunting trip, and I told Schweiz that the doubled pressures of my work in his absence made it impossible for me to undertake the experiment just then. Kalimol returned; Halum fell ill; I used my worry over her as the next excuse. Halum recovered; Noim invited Loimel and myself to spend a holiday at his lodge in southern Salla. We came back from Salla; war broke out between Salla and Glin, creating complex maritime problems for me at the Justiciary. And so the weeks went. Schweiz grew impatient. Did I mean to take the drug at all? I could not give him an answer. I did not truly know. I was afraid. But always there burned in me the temptation he had planted there. To reach out, godlike, and enter Halum's soul—

I went to the Stone Chapel, waited until Jidd could see me, and let myself be drained. But I kept back from Jidd all mention of Schweiz and his drug, fearing to reveal that I toyed with such dangerous amusements. Therefore the draining was a failure, since I had not fully opened my soul to the drainer; and I left the Stone Chapel with a congestion of the spirit, tense and morose. I saw clearly now that I must necessarily yield to Schweiz, that what he offered was an ordeal through which I must pass, for there was no escaping it. He had found me out. Beneath my piety I was a potential traitor to the Covenant. I went to him.

'Today,' I said. 'Now.'

34

We needed seclusion. The Port Justiciary maintains a country lodge in the hills two hours northwest of the city of Manneran, where visiting dignitaries are entertained and treaties of trade negotiated. I knew that this lodge was not currently in use, and I reserved it for myself for a three-day span. At midday I picked Schweiz up in a Justiciary car and drove quickly out of the city. There were three servants on duty at the lodge – a cook, a chambermaid, a gardener. I warned them that extremely delicate discussions would be taking place so that they must on no account cause interruptions or offer distractions. Then Schweiz and I sealed ourselves in the inner living quarters. 'It would be best,' he said, 'to take no food this evening. Also they recommend that the body be absolutely clean.'

The lodge had an excellent steambath. We scrubbed ourselves vigorously, and when we came out we donned loose, comfortable silken robes. Schweiz's eyes had taken on the glassy glitter that came over them in moments of high excitement. I felt frightened and uneasy, and began to think that I would suffer some terrible harm out of this evening. Just then I regarded myself as one who was about to undergo surgery from which his chances of recovery were slight. My mood was sullen resignation: I was willing, I was here, I was eager to make the plunge and have done with it.

'Your last chance,' Schweiz said, grinning broadly. 'You can still back out.'

'No.'

'You understand that there are risks, though? We are equally inexperienced in this drug. There are dangers.'

'Understood,' I said.

'Is it also understood that you enter this voluntarily, and under no coercion?'

I said, 'Why this delay, Schweiz? Bring out your potion.'

'One wishes to assure himself that your grace is fully prepared to meet any consequences.'

In a tone of heavy sarcasm I said, 'Perhaps there should be a contract between us, then, in the proper fashion, relieving you of any liability in case one wishes later to press a claim for damage to the personality—'

'If you wish, your grace. One does not feel it necessary.'

'One wasn't serious,' I said. I was fidgety now. 'Can it be that you're nervous about it too, Schweiz? That you have some doubts?'

'We take a bold step.'

'Let's take it, then, before the moment goes by. Bring out the potion, Schweiz. Bring out the potion.'

'Yes,' he said, and gave me a long look, his eyes to mine, and clapped his hands in childlike glee. And laughed in triumph. I saw how he had manipulated me. Now I was begging him for the drug! Oh, devil, devil!

From his traveling case he fetched the packet of white powder. He told me to get wine, and I ordered two flasks of chilled Mannerangi golden from the kitchen, and he dumped half the contents of the packet into my flask, half into his. The powder dissolved almost instantly: for a moment it left a cloudy gray wake, and then there was no trace of it. We gripped our flasks. I remember looking across the table at Schweiz and giving him a quick smile; he described it to me later as the pale, edgy smirk of a timid virgin about to open her thighs. 'It should all go down at once,' Schweiz said, and he gulped his wine and I gulped mine, and then I sat back, expecting the drug to hit me instantly. I felt a faint giddiness, but that was only the wine doing its work in my empty gut. 'How long does it take to begin?' I asked. Schweiz shrugged. 'It will be some while yet,' he replied. We waited in silence. Testing myself, I tried to force my mind to go forth and encounter his, but I felt nothing. The sounds of the room became magnified: the creak of floorboards, the rasping of insects outside the window, the tiny hum of the bright electric light. 'Can you explain,' I said hoarsely, 'the way this drug is thought to operate?' Schweiz answered, 'One can tell you only what was told to him. Which is, that the potential power to link one mind to another exists in all of us from birth, only we have evolved a chemical substance in the blood that inhibits the power. A very few are born without the inhibitor, and these have the gift of reaching minds, but most of us are forever blocked from achieving this silent communication, except when for some reason the production of the hormone ceases of its own accord and our minds open for a while. When this occurs it is often mistaken for madness. This drug of Sumara Borthan, they say, neutralizes the natural inhibitor in our blood, at least for a short time, and permits us to make contact with one another, as we would normally do if we lacked the counteracting substance in the blood. So one has heard.' To this I answered, 'We all might be supermen, then, but we are crippled by our own glands?' And Schweiz, gesturing grandly, said, 'Maybe it is that there were good biological reasons for evolving this protection against our own powers. Eh? Or maybe not.' He laughed. His face had turned very red. I asked him if he really believed this story of an inhibitory hormone and a counterinhibitory drug, and he said that he had no grounds for making judgment. 'Do you feel anything yet?' I asked. 'Only the wine,' he said. We waited. Perhaps it will do nothing, I thought, and I will be reprieved. We waited. At length Schweiz said, 'It may be beginning now.'

35

I was at first greatly aware of the functioning of my own body: the *thud-thud* of my heart, the pounding of the blood against the walls of arteries, the movements of fluids deep within my ears, the drifting of corpuscular bodies across my field of vision. I became enormously receptive to external stimuli, currents of air brushing my cheek, a fold of my robe touching my thigh, the pressure of the floor against the sole of my foot. I heard an unfamiliar sound as of water tumbling through a distant gorge. I lost touch with my surroundings, for as my perceptions intensified the range of them also narrowed, and I found myself incapable of perceiving the shape of the room, for I saw nothing clearly except in a constricted tunnel at the other end of which was Schweiz; beyond the rim of this tunnel there was only haze. Now I was frightened, and fought to clear my mind, as one may make a conscious effort to free the brain of the muddle caused by too much wine; but the harder I struggled to return to normal perception, the more rapidly did the pace of change accelerate. I entered a state of luminous drunkenness, in which brilliant radiant rods of colored light streamed past my face, and I was certain I must have sipped from Digant's spring. I felt a rushing sensation, like that of air moving swiftly against my ears. I heard a high whining sound that was barely audible at first, but swept up in crescendo until it took on tangibility and appeared to fill the room to overflowing, yet the sound was not painful. The chair beneath me throbbed and pulsated in a steady beat that seemed tuned to some patient pulsation of our planet itself. Then, with no discernible feeling of having crossed a boundary, I realized that my perceptions had for some time been double: now I was aware of a second heartbeat, of a second spurt of blood within vessels, of a second churning of intestines. But it was not mere duplication, for these other rhythms were different, setting up complex symphonic interplays with the rhythms of my own body, creating percussive patterns that were so intricate that the fibers of my mind melted in the attempt to follow them. I began to sway in time with these beats, to clap my hands against my thighs, to snap my fingers; and, looking down my vision-tunnel, I saw Schweiz also swaying and clapping and snapping, and realized whose bodily rhythms it was I had been receiving. We were locked together. I had difficulty now distinguishing his heartbeat from my own, and sometimes, glancing across the table at him, I saw my own reddened, distorted face. I experienced a general liquefying of reality, a breaking down of walls and restraints; I was unable to maintain a sense of Kinnall Darival as an individual; I thought not in terms of *he* and *I*, but of *we*. I had lost not only my identity but the concept of self itself.

At that level I remained a long while, until I started to think that the power of the drug was receding. Colors grew less brilliant, my perception of the room became more conventional, and I could again distinguish Schweiz's body and mind from my own. Instead of feeling relief that the worst was over, though, I felt only disappointment that I had not achieved the kind of mingling of consciousness that Schweiz had promised.

But I was mistaken.

The first wild rush of the drug was over, yes, yet we were only now coming into the true communion. Schweiz and I were apart but nevertheless together. This was the real selfbaring. I saw his soul spread out before me as though on a table, and I could walk up to the table and examine those things that were on it, picking up this utensil, that vase, these ornaments, and studying them as closely as I wished.

Here was the looming face of Schweiz's mother. Here was a swollen pale breast streaked with blue veins and tipped by an enormous rigid nipple. Here were childhood furies. Here were memories of Earth. Through the eyes of Schweiz I saw the mother of worlds, maimed and shackled, disfigured and discolored. Beauty gleamed through the ugliness. This was the place of his birth, this disheveled city; these were highways ten thousand years old; these were the stumps of ancient temples. Here was the node of first love. Here were disappointments and departures. Betrayals, here. Shared confidences, here. Growth and change. Corrosion and despair. Journeys. Failures. Seductions. Confessions. I saw the suns of a hundred worlds.

And I passed through the strata of Schweiz's soul, inspecting the gritty layers of greed and the boulders of trickery, the oily pockets of maliciousness, the decaying loam of opportunism. Here was self incarnate; here was a man who had lived solely for his own sake.

Yet I did not recoil from the darkness of Schweiz.

I saw beyond those things. I saw the yearning, the god-hunger in the man, Schweiz alone on a lunar plain, splayfooted on a black shield of rock under a purple sky, reaching up, grasping, taking hold of nothing. Sly and opportunistic he might be, yes, but also vulnerable, passionate, honest beneath all his capering. I could not judge Schweiz harshly. He was I. I was he. Tides of self engulfed us both. If I were to cast Schweiz down, I must also cast down Kinnall Darival. My soul was flooded with warmth for him.

I felt him, too, probing me. I erected no barriers about my spirit as he came to explore it. And through his own eyes I saw what he was seeing in me. My fear of my father. My awe of my brother. My love for Halum. My flight into Glin. My choosing of Loimel. My petty faults and my petty virtues. Everything, Schweiz. Look. Look. Look. And it all came back refracted through his soul, nor did I find it painful to observe. Love of others begins with love of self, I thought suddenly.

In that instant the Covenant fell and shattered within me.

Gradually Schweiz and I pulled apart, though we remained in contact some time longer, the strength of the bond ebbing steadily. When it broke at last, I felt a shivering resonance, as if a taut string had snapped. We sat in silence. My eyes were closed. I was queasy in the pit of my stomach and conscious, as I had never been conscious before, of the gulf that keeps each of us forever alone. After some long time I looked across the room at Schweiz.

He was watching me, waiting for me. He wore that demonic look of his, the wild grin, the bright-eyed gleam, only now it seemed to me less a look of madness than a reflection of inner joy. He appeared younger now. His face was still flushed.

'I love you,' he said softly.

The unexpected words were bludgeons. I crossed my wrists before my face, palms out, protecting myself.

'What upsets you so much?' he asked. 'My grammar or my meaning?'

'Both.'

'Can it be so terrible to say, *I love you?*'

'One has never – one does not know how to—'

'To react? To respond?' Schweiz laughed. 'I don't mean I love you in any physical way. As if that would be so hideous. But no. I mean what I say, Kinnall. I've been in your mind and I liked what I saw there. I love you.'

'You talk in "I,"' I reminded him.

'Why not? Must I deny self even now? Come on: break free, Kinnall. I know you want to. Do you think what I just said to you is obscene?'

'There is such a strangeness about it.'

'On my world those words have a holy strangeness,' said Schweiz. 'And here they're an abomination. Never to be allowed to say "I love you," eh? A whole planet denying itself that little pleasure. Oh, no, Kinnall, no, no, no!'

'Please,' I said faintly. 'One still has not fully adjusted to the things the drug did. When you shout at one like that—'

But he would not subside.

'You were in my mind too,' he said. 'What did you find there? Was I so loathsome? Get it out, Kinnall. You have no secrets from me now. The truth. The truth!'

'You know, then, that one found you more admirable than one had expected.'

Schweiz chuckled. 'And I the same! Why are we afraid of each other now, Kinnall? I told you: I love you! We made contact. We saw there were areas of trust. Now we have to change, Kinnall. You more than me, because you have farther to go. Come. Come. Put words to your heart. Say it.'

'One can't.'

'Say "I."'

'How difficult that is.'

'Say it. Not as an obscenity. Say it as if you love yourself.'

'Please.'

'Say it.'

'I,' I said.

'Was that so awful? Come, now. Tell me how you feel about me. The truth. From the deepest levels.'

'A feeling of warmth – of affection, of trust—'

'Of love?'

'Of love, yes,' I admitted.

'Then say it.'

'Love.'

'That isn't what I want you to say.'

'What, then?'

'Something that hasn't been said on this planet in two thousand years, Kinnall. Now say it. I—'

'I—'

'Love you.'

'Love you.'

'I love you.'

'I – love – you.'

'It's a beginning,' Schweiz said. Sweat streamed down his face and mine. 'We start by acknowledging that we can love. We start by acknowledging that we have selves *capable* of loving. Then we begin to love. Eh? We begin to love.'

36

Later I said, 'Did you get from the drug what you were looking for, Schweiz?'

'Partially.'

'How so, partially?'

'I was looking for God, Kinnall, and I didn't quite find him, but I got a better idea of where to look. What I did find was how not to be alone any more. How to open my mind fully to someone else. That's the first step on the road I want to travel.'

'One is happy for your sake, Schweiz.'

'Must you still talk to me in that third-person lingo?'

'I can't help myself,' I said. I was terribly tired. I was beginning to feel afraid of Schweiz again. The love I bore for him was still there, but now suspicion was creeping back. Was he exploiting me? Was he milking a dirty little pleasure out of our mutual exposures? He had pushed me into becoming a selfbarer. His insistence on my speaking in 'I' and 'me' to him – was that a token of my liberation, was it something beautiful and pure, as he claimed, or was it only a reveling in filth? I was too new to this. I could not sit placidly while a man said, *I love you.*

'Practice it,' Schweiz said. 'I. I. I. I.'

'Stop. Please.'

'Is it that painful?'

'It's new and strange to me. I need – there, you see? – I need to slide into this more gradually.'

'Take your time, then. Don't let me rush you. But don't ever stop moving forward.'

'One will try. I will try,' I said.

'Good.' After a moment he said, 'Would you try the drug again, ever?'

'With you?'

'I don't think there's any need for that. I mean with someone like your bondsister. If I offered you some, would you use it with her?'

'I don't know.'

'Are you afraid of the drug now?'

I shook my head. 'That isn't easy for me to answer. I need time to come to terms with the whole experience. Time to think about it, Schweiz, before getting involved again.'

'You've tasted the experience. You've seen that there's only good to be had from it.'

'Perhaps. Perhaps.'

'Without doubt!' His fervor was evangelical. His zeal tempted me anew.

Cautiously I said, 'If more were available, I would seriously consider trying it again. With Halum, maybe.'

'Good!'

'Not immediately. But in time. Two, three, four moontimes from now.'

'It would have to be farther from now than that.'

'Why?'

Schweiz said, 'This was my entire stock of the drug that we used this evening. I have no more.'

'But you could get some, if you tried?'

'Oh, yes. Yes, certainly.'

'Where?'

'In Sumara Borthan,' he said.

37

When one is new to the ways of pleasure, it is not surprising to find guilt and remorse following first indulgence. So was it with me. In the morning of our second day at the lodge I awoke after troubled sleep, feeling such shame that I prayed the ground to swallow me. What had I done? Why had I let Schweiz goad me into such foulness? Selfbaring! Selfbaring! Sitting with him all night, saying 'I' and 'me' and 'me' and 'I,' and congratulating myself on my new freedom from convention's strangling hand! The mists of day brought a mood of disbelief. Could I have actually opened myself like that? Yes, I must, for within me now were memories of Schweiz's past, which I had not had access to before. And myself within him, then. I prayed for a way of undoing what I had done. I felt I had lost something of myself by surrendering my apartness. You know, to be a selfbarer is not a pretty thing among us, and those who expose themselves gain only a dirty pleasure from it, a furtive kind of ecstasy. I insisted to myself that I had done nothing of that, but had embarked rather on a spiritual quest; but even as I put the phrase to myself it sounded portentous and hypocritical, a flimsy mask for shabby motives. And I was ashamed, for my sake, for my sons' sake, for the sake of my royal father and his royal forefathers, that I had come to this. I think it was Schweiz's 'I love you' that drove me into such an abyss of regret, more than any other single aspect of the evening, for my old self saw those words as doubly obscene, even while the new self that was struggling to emerge insisted that the Earthman had meant nothing shameful, neither with his 'I' nor with his '*love.*' But I rejected my own argument and let guilt engulf me. What had I become, to trade endearments with another man, an Earthborn merchant, a lunatic? How could I have given my soul to him? Where did I stand, now that I was so wholly vulnerable to him? For a moment I considered killing Schweiz, as a way of recovering my privacy. I went to him where he slept, and saw him with a smile on his face, and I could feel no hatred for him then.

That day I spent mostly alone. I went off into the forest and bathed at a cool pond; then I knelt before a firethorn tree and pretended it was a drainer, and confessed myself to it in shy whispers; afterward I walked through a brambly woods, coming back to the lodge thorned and smudged. Schweiz asked me if I felt unwell. No, I told him, nothing is wrong. I said little that evening, but huddled in a floating-chair. The Earthman, more talkative than ever, a torrent of buoyant words, launched himself into the details of a grand scheme for an expedition to Sumara Borthan to bring back sacks of the drug, enough to transform every soul in Manneran, and I listened without commenting, for everything had become unreal to me, and that project seemed no more strange than anything else.

I hoped the ache of my soul would ease once I was back in Manneran and at my desk in the Justiciary. But no. I came into my house and Halum was there with Loimel, the cousins exchanging clothes with one another, and at the sight of them I nearly turned and fled. They smiled warm woman-smiles at me, secret smiles, the token of the league they had formed between themselves all their lives, and in despair I looked from my wife to my bondsister, from one cousin to the other, receiving their mirrored beauty as a double sword in my belly. Those smiles. Those knowing eyes! They needed no drug to pull the truths from me.

Where have you been, Kinnall?
To a lodge in the forest, to play at selfbaring with the Earthman.
And did you show him your soul?
Oh, yes, and he showed his.
And then?
Then we spoke of love. I love you, he said, and one replied, I love you.
What a wicked child you are, Kinnall!
Yes, Yes. Where can one hide from his shame?

This silent dialogue whirled through my brain in an instant, as I came toward them where they sat beside the courtyard fountain. Formally I embraced Loimel, and formally I embraced my bondsister, but I kept my eyes averted from theirs, so sharp was my guilt. It was the same in the Justiciary office for me. I translated the glances of the underlings into accusing glares. *There is Kinnall Darival, who revealed all our mysteries to Schweiz of Earth. Look at the Sallan selfbarer slink by us! How can he stand his own reek?* I kept to myself and did my work poorly. A document concerning some transaction of Schweiz's crossed my desk, throwing me into dismay. The thought of facing Schweiz ever again appalled me. It would have been no great chore for me to revoke his residence permit in Manneran, using the authority of the High Justice; poor payment for the trust he showed me, but I came close to doing it, and checked myself only out of a deeper shame even than I already bore.

On the third day of my return, when my children too had begun to wonder what was wrong with me, I went to the Stone Chapel to seek healing from the drainer Jidd.

It was a damp day of heavy heat. The soft furry sky seemed to hang in looping folds over Manneran, and everything was coated in glistening beads of bright moisture. That day the sunlight was a strange color, almost white, and the ancient black stone blocks of the holy building gave off blinding reflections as though they were edged with prisms; but once inside the chapel, I found myself in dark, cool, quiet halls. Jidd's cell had pride of place in the chapel's apse, behind the great altar. He awaited me already robed; I had reserved his time hours in advance. The contract was ready. Quickly I signed and gave him his fee. This Jidd was no more lovely than any other of his trade, but just then I was almost pleased by his ugliness, his jagged knobby nose and thin long lips, his hooded eyes, his dangling earlobes. Why mock the man's face? He would have chosen another for himself, if he had been consulted. And I was kindly disposed to him, for I hoped he would heal me. Healers were holy men. *Give me what I need from you, Jidd, and I will bless your ugly face!* He said, 'Under whose auspices will you drain?'

'The god of forgiving.'

He touched a switch. Mere candles were too common for Jidd. The amber light of forgiveness came from some concealed gas-jet and flooded the chamber. Jidd directed my attention toward the mirror, instructing me to behold my face, put my eyes to my eyes. The eyes of a stranger looked back at me. Droplets of sweat clustered in the roots of my beard, where the flesh of my cheeks could be seen. *I love you*, I said silently to the strange face in the mirror. Love of others begins with love of self. The chapel weighed on me; I was in terror of being crushed beneath a block of the ceiling. Jidd was saying the preliminary words. There was nothing of love in them. He commanded me to open my soul to him.

I stammered. My tongue turned upon itself and was knotted. I gagged; I choked; I pulled my head down and pressed it to the cold floor. Jidd touched my shoulder and murmured formulas of comfort until my fit softened. We began the rite a second time. Now I traveled more smoothly through the preliminaries, and when he asked me to speak, I said, as though reciting lines that had been written for me by someone else, 'These days past one went to a secret place with another, and we shared a certain drug of Sumara Borthan that unseals the soul, and we engaged in selfbaring together, and now one feels remorse for his sin and would have forgiveness for it.'

Jidd gasped, and it is no little task to astonish a drainer. That gasp nearly punctured my will to confess; but Jidd artfully recovered control, coaxing me onward with bland priestly phrases, until in a few moments the stiffness left my jaws and I was spilling everything out. My early discussions of the drug with Schweiz. (I left him unnamed. Though I trusted Jidd to maintain the secrecy of the draining, I saw no spiritual gain for myself in revealing to anyone the name of my companion in sin.) My taking of the drug at the lodge. My sensations as the drug took hold. My exploration of Schweiz's soul. His entry into mine. The kindling of deep affection between us as our union of spirit developed. My feeling of alienation from the Covenant while under the drug's influence. That sudden conviction of mine that the denial of self which we practice is a catastrophic cultural error. The intuitive realization that we should deny our solitude instead, and seek to bridge the gulfs between ourselves and others, rather than glorying in isolation. Also I confessed that I had dabbled in the drug for the sake of eventually reaching the soul of Halum; hearing from me this admission of yearning for my bond-sister was old stuff to Jidd by now. And then I spoke of the dislocations I had experienced since coming out of my drug-trance: the guilt, the shame, the doubt. At last I fell silent. There before me, like a pale globe glowing in the dimness, hung the facts of my misdeeds, tangible and exposed, and already I felt cleaner for having revealed them. I was willing now to be brought back into the Covenant. I wanted to be purged of my aberration of selfbaring. I hungered to do penance and resume my upright life. I was eager to be healed, I was begging for absolution and restoration to my community. But I could not feel the presence of the god. Staring into the mirror, I saw only my own face, drawn and sallow, the beard in need of combing. When Jidd began to recite the formulas of absolution, they were merely words to me, nor did my soul lift. I was cut off from all faith. The irony of that distracted me: Schweiz, envying me for my beliefs, seeking through the drug to understand the mystery of submission to the supernatural, had stripped me of my access to the gods. There I knelt, stone knees on stone floor, making hollow phrases, while wishing that Jidd and I could have taken the drug together, so there might have been true communion between us. And I knew that I was lost.

'The peace of the gods be with you now,' said Jidd.

'The peace of the gods is upon one.'

'Seek no more for false succor, and keep your self to yourself, for other paths lead only to shame and corruption.'

'One will seek no other paths.'

'You have bondsister and bondbrother, you have a drainer, you have the mercies of the gods. You need no more.'

'One needs no more.'

'Go in peace, then.'

I went, but not in his kind of peace, for the draining had been a leaden thing, meaningless and trifling. Jidd had not reconciled me to the Covenant: he had simply demonstrated the degree of my separation from it. Unmoved though I had been by the draining, however, I emerged from the Stone Chapel somehow purged of guilt. I no longer repented my selfbaring. Perhaps this was some residual effect of the draining, this inversion of my purpose in going to Jidd, but I did not try deeply to analyze it. I was content to be myself and to be thinking these thoughts. My conversion at that instant was complete. Schweiz had taken my faith from me, but he had given me another in its place.

38

That afternoon a problem came to me concerning a ship from Threish and some false cargo manifests, and I went to a pier to verify the facts. There by chance I encountered Schweiz. Since parting from him a few days before, I had dreaded meeting him again; it would be intolerable, I thought, to look into the eyes of this man who had beheld my entire self. Only by keeping apart from him could I eventually persuade myself that I had not, in fact, done with him what I had done. But then I saw him near me on the pier. He clutched a thick sheaf of invoices in one hand and was shaking the other furiously at some watery-eyed merchant in Glinish dress. To my amazement I felt none of the embarrassment I had anticipated, but only warmth and pleasure at the sight of him. I went to him. He clapped my shoulder; I clapped his. 'You look more cheerful now,' he said.

'Much.'

'Let me finish with this scoundrel and we'll share a flask of golden, eh?'

'By all means,' I said.

An hour later, as we sat together in a dockside tavern, I said, 'How soon can we leave for Sumara Borthan?'

39

The voyage to the southern continent was conducted as though in a dream. Not once did I question the wisdom of undertaking the journey, nor did I pause to ask myself why it was necessary for me to take part in person, rather than let Schweiz make the trip alone, or send some hireling to gather the drug on our behalf. I simply set about the task of arranging for our passage.

No commercial shipping goes regularly between Velada Borthan and Sumara Borthan. Those who would travel to the southern continent must charter a vessel. This I did, through the instrumentality of the High Justiciary, using intermediaries and dummy signatories. The vessel I chose was no Mannerangi craft, for I did not care to be recognized when we sailed, but rather a ship of the western province of Velis that had been tied down in Manneran Harbor for the better part of a year by a lawsuit. It seemed there was some dispute over title to the ship going on in its home port, and the thicket of injunctions and counterinjunctions had succeeded in making it impossible for the vessel to leave Manneran after its last voyage there. The captain and crew were bitter over this enforced idleness and had already filed a protest with the Justiciary; but the High Justice had no jurisdiction over a lawsuit that was being fought entirely in the courts of Velis, and we therefore had had to continue the stay on the vessel's departure until word came from Velis that title was clear. Knowing all this, I issued a decree in the High Justice's name that would permit the unfortunate craft temporarily to accept charters for voyages to points 'between the River Woyn and the eastern shore of the Gulf of Sumar.' That usually was taken to mean any point along the coast of the province of Manneran, but I specified also that the captain might hire himself out for trips to the northern coast of Sumara Borthan. Doubtless that clause left the poor man puzzled, and it must have puzzled him even more when, a few days later, he was approached by my agents and asked to make a voyage to that very place.

Neither Loimel nor Halum nor Noim nor anyone else did I tell of my destination. I said only that the Justiciary required me to go abroad for a short while. At the Justiciary I was even less specific, applying to myself for a leave of absence, granting it at once, and informing the High Justice at the last possible moment that I was not going to be available for the immediate future.

To avoid complications with the collectors of customs, among other things, I picked as our port of departure the town of Hilminor, in south-western Manneran on the Gulf of Sumar. This is a medium-sized place that depends mainly on the fishing trade, but which serves also as a halfway stop for ships traveling between the city of Manneran and the western provinces. I arranged to meet our chartered captain in Hilminor; he then set out for that town by sea, while Schweiz and I made for it in a groundcar.

It was a two-day journey via the coastal highway, through a countryside ever more lush, ever more densely tropical, as we approached the Gulf of Sumar. Schweiz was in high spirits, as was I. We talked to one another in the first person constantly; to him it was nothing, of course, but I felt like a wicked boy sneaking off to whisper 'I' and 'me' in a playmate's ear. He and I speculated on what quantity of the Sumaran drug we would obtain, and what we would do with it. No longer was it just a question of my getting some to use with Halum: we were talking now of proselytizing everyone and bringing about a wholesale liberation of my self-stifling countrymen. That evangelical approach had crept gradually into our plans almost without my realizing it, and had swiftly become dominant.

We came to Hilminor on a day so hot the sky itself seemed to break out in blisters. A shimmering dome of heat covered everything; and the Gulf of Sumar, as it lay before us, was golden-skinned in the fierce sunlight. Hilminor is rimmed by a chain of low hills, which are thickly forested on the seaward side and desert on the landward; the highway curved through them, and we stopped at one point so that I could show Schweiz the flesh-trees that covered the parched inland slopes. A dozen of the trees were clustered in one place. We walked through crackling tinder-dry underbrush to reach them: twice the height of men they were, with twisted limbs and thick pale bark, spongy to the touch like the flesh of very old women. The trees were scarred from repeated tapping of their sap, making them look all the more repugnant. 'Can we taste the fluid?' Schweiz asked. We had no implements for making the tap, but just then a girl of the town came along, perhaps ten years old, half-naked, tanned a deep brown to hide the dirt; she was carrying an auger and a flask, and evidently had been sent out by her family to collect flesh-tree sap. She looked at us sourly. I produced a coin and said, 'One would show his companion the taste of the flesh-tree.' Still a sour look; but she jammed her auger into the nearest tree with surprising force, twisted it, withdrew, and caught the gush of clear thick fluid. Sullenly she handed her flask to Schweiz. He sniffed it, took a cautious lick, finally had a gulp. And whooped in delight. 'Why isn't this stuff sold all over Velada Borthan?' he asked.

'The whole supply comes from one little area along the Gulf,' I told him. 'Most of it's consumed locally, and a lot gets shipped to Threish, where it's almost an addiction. That doesn't leave much left over for the rest of the continent. You can buy it in Manneran, of course, but you have to know where to look.'

'You know what I'd like to do, Kinnall? I'd like to start a flesh-tree plantation, grow them by the thousands and get enough juice bottled so we not only could market it all over Velada Borthan, but could set up an export deal. I—'

'Devil!' the girl cried, and added something incomprehensible in the coast dialect, and snatched the flask from his hand. She ran off wildly, knees high, elbows outthrust, several times looking back to make a finger-jabbing sign of contempt or defiance at us. Schweiz, bewildered, shook his head. 'Is she crazy?' he asked.

'You said "I" three times,' I said. 'Very careless.'

'I've slipped into bad habits, talking with you. But can it really be such a filthy thing to say?'

'Filthier than you'll ever imagine. That girl is probably on her way to tell her brothers about the dirty old man who obscened at her on the hillside. Come on: let's get into town before we're mobbed.'

'Dirty old man,' Schweiz murmured. 'Me!'

I pushed him into the groundcar and we hurried toward the port of Hilminor.

40

Our ship rode at anchor, a small squat craft, twin screws, auxiliary sail, hull painted blue and gold. We presented ourselves to the captain – Khrisch was his name – and he greeted us blandly by the names we had assumed. In late afternoon we put out to sea. At no time during the voyage did Captain Khrisch question us about our purposes, nor did any of his ten crewmen. Surely they were fiercely curious about the motives of anyone who cared to go to Sumara Borthan, but they were so grateful to be out of their escrow even for this short cruise that they were chary of offending their employers by too much prying.

The coast of Velada Borthan dipped from sight behind me and ahead lay only the grand open sweep of the Strait of Sumar. No land at all could be seen, neither aft nor fore. That frightened me. In my brief career as a Glinish seaman I had never been far from the coast, and during stormy moments I had soothed myself with the comforting deceit that I might always swim to shore if we capsized. Here, though, the universe seemed all to be of water. As evening approached, a gray-blue twilight settled over us, stitching sky seamlessly to sea, and it became worse for me: now there was only our little bobbing, throbbing ship adrift and vulnerable in this directionless, dimensionless void, this shimmering anti-world where all places melted into a single nonplace. I had not expected the strait to be so wide. On a map I had seen in the Justiciary only a few days before, the strait had had less breadth than my little finger; I had assumed that the cliffs of Sumara Borthan would be visible to us from the earliest hours of the voyage; yet here we were amid nothingness. I stumbled to my cabin and plunged face first onto my bunk, and lay there shaking, calling upon the god of travelers to protect me. Bit by bit I came to loathe myself for this weakness. I reminded myself that I was a septarch's son and a septarch's brother and another septarch's cousin, that in Manneran I was a man of the highest authority, that I was the head of a house and a slayer of hornfowl. All this did me no good. What value is lineage to a drowning man? What use are broad shoulders and powerful muscles and a skill at swimming, when the land itself has been swallowed up, so that a swimmer would have no destination? I trembled. I think I may have wept. I felt myself dissolving into that gray-blue void. Then a hand lightly caught my shoulder. Schweiz. 'The ship is sound,' he whispered. 'The crossing is a short one. Easy. Easy. No harm will come.'

If it had been anyone else who had found me like that, any other man except perhaps Noim, I might have killed him or myself, to bury the secret of my shame.

I said, 'If this is what it is like to cross the Strait of Sumar, how can one travel between the stars without going mad?'

'One grows accustomed to travel.'

'The fear – the emptiness—'

'Come above.' Gently. 'The night is very beautiful.'

Nor did he lie. Twilight was past and a black bowl pocked with fiery jewels lay over us. Near cities one cannot see the stars so well, because of the lights and the haze. I had looked upon the full glory of the heavens while hunting in the Burnt Lowlands, yes, but then I had not known the names of what I saw. Now, Schweiz and Captain Khrisch stood close alongside me on deck, taking turns calling out the names of stars and constellations, vying with each other to display their knowledge, each one pouring his astronomy into my ear as though I were a terrified child who could be kept from screaming only by a constant flow of distractions. See? See? And see, there? I saw. A host of our neighboring suns, and four or five of the neighboring planets of our system, and even a vagrant comet that night. What they taught me stayed with me. I could step out of my cabin now, I believe, here in the Burnt Lowlands, and call off the stars the way Schweiz and the captain called them off to me aboard ship in the Strait of Sumar. How many more nights do I have, I wonder, on which I will be free to look at the stars?

Morning brought an end to fear. The sun was bright, the sky was lightly fleeced, the broad strait was calm, and it did not matter to me that land was beyond sight. We glided toward Sumara Borthan in an almost imperceptible way; I had to study the surface of the sea with care to remind myself we were in motion. A day, a night, a day, a night, a day, and then the horizon sprouted a green crust, for there was Sumara Borthan. It provided a fixed point for me, except that we were the fixed point, and Sumara Borthan was making for it. The southern continent slid steadily toward us, until at last I saw a rim of bare yellow-green rock stretching from east to west, and atop those naked cliffs rose a thick cap of vegetation, lofty trees knitted together by heavy vines to form a closed canopy, stubbier shrubs clustering in the darkness below, everything cut down the side as if to reveal the jungle's edge to us in cross-section. I felt not fear but wonder at the sight of that jungle. I knew that not one of those trees and plants grew in Velada Borthan; the beasts and serpents and insects of this place were not those of the continent of my birth; what lay before us was alien and perhaps hostile, an unknown world awaiting the first footstep. In a tumble of tangled imaginings I dropped down the well of time, and saw myself as an explorer peeling the mystery from a newly found planet. Those gigantic boulders, those slender, high-crowned trees, those dangling snaky vines, all were products of a raw, elemental mystery straight out of evolution's belly, which now I was about to penetrate. That dark jungle was the gate to something strange and terrible, I thought, yet I was not frightened so much as I was stirred, deeply moved, by the vision of those sleek cliffs and tendriled avenues. This was the world that existed before man came. This was as it was when there were no godhouses, no drainers, no Port Justiciary: only the silent leafy paths, and the surging rivers scouring the valleys, and the unplumbed ponds, and the long heavy leaves glistening with the jungle's exhalations, and the unhunted prehistoric beasts turning in the ooze, and the fluttering winged things that knew no fear, and the grassy plateaus, and the veins of precious metals, a virgin kingdom, and over everything brooding the presence of the gods, of the god, of the god, waiting for the time of worshipers. The lonely gods who did not yet know they were divine. The lonely god.

Of course the reality was nothing so romantic. There was a place where the cliffs dipped to sea level and yielded to a crescent harbor, and here a squalid settlement existed, the shacks of a few dozen Sumarnu who had taken to living here so that they might meet the needs of such ships as occasionally did come from the northern continent. I had thought that all the Sumarnu lived somewhere in the interior, naked tribesmen camping down by the volcanic peak Vashnir, and that Schweiz and I would have to hack our way through the whole apocalyptic immensity of this mysterious land, unguided and uncertain, before we found what passed for civilization and made contact with anyone who might sell us that for which we had come.

Instead, Captain Khrisch brought his little ship smartly to shore by a crumbling wooden pier, and as we stepped forth a small delegation of Sumarnu came to offer us a sullen greeting.

You know my fantasy of fanged and grotesque Earthmen. So, too, I instinctively expected these people of the southern continent to look in some way alien. I knew it was irrational; they were, after all, sprung from the same stock as the citizens of Salla and Manneran and Glin. But had these centuries in the jungle not transformed them? Had their disavowal of the Covenant not laid them open to infiltration by the vapors of the forest, and turned them into unhuman things? No and no. They looked to me like peasants of any province's back country. Oh, they wore unfamiliar ornaments, old jeweled pendants and bracelets of an un-Veladan sort, but there was nothing else about them, neither tone of skin nor shape of face nor color of hair, that set them apart from the men I had always known.

There were eight or nine of them. Two, evidently the leaders, spoke the dialect of Manneran, though with a troublesome accent. The others showed no sign of understanding northern languages, but chattered among themselves in a tongue of clicks and grunts. Schweiz found communication easier than I did, and entered into a long conversation, so difficult for me to follow that I soon ceased to pay attention. I wandered off to inspect the village, and was inspected in turn by goggle-eyed children – the girls here walked about naked even after they were of the age when their breasts had sprouted – and when I returned Schweiz said, 'It's all arranged.'

'What is?'

'Tonight we sleep here. Tomorrow they'll guide us to a village that produces the drug. They don't guarantee we'll be allowed to buy any.'

'Is it only sold at certain places?'

'Evidently. They swear there's none at all available here.'

I said, 'How long a journey will it be?'

'Five days. On foot. Do you like jungles, Kinnall?'

'I don't know the taste of them yet.'

'It's a taste you're going to learn,' said Schweiz.

He turned now to confer with Captain Khrisch, who was planning to go off on some expedition of his own along the Sumaran coast. Schweiz arranged to have our ship back at this harbor waiting for us when we returned from our trip into the jungle. Khrisch's men unloaded our baggage – chiefly trade-goods for barter, mirrors and knives and trinkets, since the Sumarnu had no use for Veladan currency – and got their ship out into the strait before night fell.

Schweiz and I had a shack for ourselves, on a lip of rock overlooking the harbor. Mattresses of leaves, blankets of animal hide, one lopsided window, no sanitary facilities: this is what the thousands of years of man's voyage through the stars have brought us to. We haggled over the price of our lodgings, finally came to an agreement in knives and heat-rods, and at sundown were given our dinner. A surprisingly tasty stew of spicy meats, some angular red fruits, a pot of half-cooked vegetables, a mug of what might have been fermented milk – we ate what was given us, and enjoyed it more than either of us had expected, though we made edgy jokes about the diseases we were likely to catch. I poured out a libation to the god of travelers, more out of habit than conviction. Schweiz said, 'So you still believe, after all?' I replied that I found no reason not to believe in the gods, though my faith in the teachings of men had been greatly weakened.

This close to the equator, darkness came on swiftly, a sudden black curtain rolling down. We sat outside a little while, Schweiz favoring me with some more astronomy, and testing me on what I had already learned. Then we went to bed. Less than an hour later, two figures entered our shack; I was still awake and sat up instantly, imagining thieves or assassins, but as I groped for a weapon a stray moonbeam showed me the profile of one of the intruders, and I saw heavy breasts swinging. Schweiz, out of the dark far corner, said, 'I think they're included in tonight's price.' Another instant and warm naked flesh pressed against me. I smelled a pungent odor, and touched a fat haunch and found it coated in some spicy oil: a Sumarnu cosmetic, I found out afterward. Curiosity warred with caution in me. As I had when a boy taking lodgings in Glain, I feared catching a disease from the loins of a woman of a strange race. But should I not experience the southern kind of loving? From Schweiz's direction I heard the slap of meat on meat, hearty laughter, liquid lip-noises. My own girl wriggled impatiently. Parting the plump thighs, I explored, aroused, entered. The girl squirmed into what I suppose was the proper native position, lying on her side, facing me, one leg flung over me and her heel jammed hard against my buttocks. I had not had a woman since my last night in Manneran; that and my old problem of haste undid me, and I unloaded myself in the usual premature volleys. My girl called out something, probably in derision of my manhood, to her moaning and sighing companion in Schweiz's corner, and got a giggled answer. In rage and chagrin I forced myself to revive and, pumping slowly, grimly, I ploughed her anew, though the stink of her breath nearly paralyzed me, and her sweat, mingling with her oil, formed a nauseous compound. Eventually I pushed her over the brink of pleasure, but it was cheerless work, a tiresome chore. When it was done she nipped my elbow with her teeth: a Sumarnu kiss, I think it was. Her gratitude. Her apology. I had done her good service after all. In the morning I scanned the village maidens, wondering which lass it was had honored me with her caresses. All of them gaptoothed, sagbreasted, fisheyed: let my couchmate have been none of the ones I saw. For days afterward I kept uneasy watch on my organ, expecting it each morning to be broken out in red spots or running sores; but all I caught from her was a distaste for the Sumarnu style of passion.

41

Five days. Six, actually: either Schweiz had misunderstood, or the Sumarnu chieftain was poor at counting. We had one guide and three bearers. I had never walked so much before, from dawn to sunset, the ground yielding and bouncy beneath my feet. The jungle rising, a green wall, on both sides of the narrow path. Astonishing humidity, so that we swam in the air, worse than on the worst day in Manneran. Insects with jeweled eyes and terrifying beaks. Slithering many-legged beasts rushing past us. Strugglings and horrid cries in the underbrush, just beyond sight. The sunlight falling in dappled streaks, barely making it through the canopy high above. Flowers bursting from the trunks of trees: parasites, Schweiz said. One of them a puffy yellow thing that had a human face, goggly eyes, a gaping pollen-smeared mouth. The other even more bizarre, for from the midst of its red and black petals rose a parody of genitalia, a fleshy phallus, two dangling balls. Schweiz, shrieking with amusement, seized the first of these that we found, wrapped his hand around the floral cock, bawdily flirted with it and stroked it. The Sumarnu muttered things; perhaps they were wondering if they had done right to send girls to our shack that night.

We crept up the spine of the continent, emerging from the jungle for a day and a half to climb a good-sized mountain, then more jungle on the other side. Schweiz asked our guide why we had not gone around the mountain instead of over it, and was told that this was the only route, for poison-ants infested all the surrounding lowlands: very cheering. Beyond the mountain lay a chain of lakes and streams and ponds, many of them thick with gray toothy snouts barely breaking the surface. All this seemed unreal to me. A few days' sail to the north lay Velada Borthan, with its banking houses and its groundcars, its customs collectors and its godhouses. That was a tamed continent, but for its uninhabitable interior. Man had made no impact at all, though, on this place where we marched. Its disorderly wildness oppressed me – that and the heavy air, the sounds in the night, the unintelligible conversations of our primitive companions.

On the sixth day we came to the native village. Perhaps three hundred wooden huts were scattered over a broad meadow at a place where two rivers of modest size ran together. I had the impression that there once had been a larger town here, possibly even a city, for on the borders of the settlement I saw grassy mounds and humps, quite plausibly the site of ancient ruins. Or was that only an illusion? Did I need so badly to convince myself that the Sumarnu had regressed since leaving our continent, that I had to see evidences of decline and decay wherever I looked?

The villagers surrounded us: not hostile, only curious. Northerners were uncommon sights. A few of them came close and touched me, a timid pat on the forearm, a shy squeeze of the wrist, invariably accompanied by a quick little smile. These jungle folk seemed not to have the sullen sourness of those who lived in the shacks by the harbor. They were gentler, more open, more childlike. Such little taint of Veladan civilization as had managed to stain the harbor folk had darkened their spirits; not so here, where contact with northerners was less frequent.

An interminable parley began among Schweiz, our guide, and three of the village elders. After the first few moments Schweiz was out of it: the guide, indulging in long cascades of verbal embellishments footnoted by frantic gesticulations, seemed to be explaining the same thing over and over to the villagers, who constantly made the same series of replies to him. Neither Schweiz nor I could understand a syllable of it. At last the guide, looking agitated, turned to Schweiz and poured forth a stream of Sumarnu-accented Mannerangi, which I found almost wholly opaque but which Schweiz, with his tradesman's skill at communicating with strangers, was able to penetrate. Schweiz said finally to me, 'They're willing to sell to us. Provided we can show them that we're worthy of having the drug.'

'How do we do that?'

'By taking some with them, at a love-ritual this evening. Our guide's been trying to talk them out of it, but they won't budge. No communion, no merchandise.'

'Are there risks?' I asked.

Schweiz shook his head. 'It doesn't seem that way to me. But the guide has the idea that we're only looking for profit in the drug, that we don't mean to use it ourselves but intend to go back to Manneran and sell what we get for many mirrors and many heat-rods and many knives. Since he thinks we aren't users, he's trying to protect us from exposure to it. The villagers also think we aren't users, and they're damned if they'll turn a speck of the stuff over to anyone who's merely planning to peddle it. They'll make it available only to true believers.'

'But we *are* true believers,' I said.

'I know. But I can't convince our man of that. He knows enough about northerners to know that they keep their minds closed at all times, and he wants to pamper us in our sickness of soul. But I'll try again.'

Now it was Schweiz and our guide who parleyed, while the village chiefs stood silent. Adopting the gestures and even the accent of the guide, so that both sides of the conversation became unintelligible to me, Schweiz pressed and pressed and pressed, and the guide resisted all that the Earthman was telling him, and a feeling of despair came over me so that I was ready to suggest that we give up and go empty-handed back to Manneran. Then Schweiz somehow broke through. The guide, still suspicious, clearly asked Schweiz whether he really wanted what he said he wanted, and Schweiz emphatically said he did, and the guide, looking skeptical, turned once more to the village chiefs. This time he spoke only briefly with them, and then briefly again with Schweiz. 'It's been settled,' Schweiz told me. 'We'll take the drug with them tonight.' He leaned close and touched my elbow. 'Something for you to remember. When you go under: *be loving*. If you can't love them, all is lost.'

I was offended that he had found it necessary to warn me.

42

Ten of them came for us at sundown and led us into the forest east of the village. Among them were the three chieftains and two other older men, along with two young men and three women. One of the women was a handsome girl, one a plain girl, and one quite old. Our guide did not go with us; I am not sure whether he was not invited to the ceremony or simply did not feel like taking part.

We marched a considerable distance. No longer could we hear the cries of children in the village or the barking of domestic animals. Our halting-place was a secluded clearing, where hundreds of trees had been felled and the dressed logs laid out in five rows as benches, to form a pentagonal amphi-theater. In the middle of the clearing was a clay-lined fire-pit, with a great heap of firewood neatly stacked beside it; as soon as we arrived, the two young men commenced building a towering blaze. On the far side of the woodpile I saw a second clay-lined pit, about twice as wide as a large man's body; it descended diagonally into the ground and gave the appearance of being a passage of no little depth, a tunnel offering access to the depths of the world. By the glow of the firelight I tried to peer into it from where I stood, but I was unable to see anything of interest.

Through gestures the Sumarnu showed us where we should sit: at the base of the pentagon. The plain girl sat beside us. To our left, next to the tunnel entrance, sat the three chiefs. To our right, by the fire-pit, were the two young men. In the far right corner sat the old woman and one of the old men; the other old man and the handsome girl went to the far left corner. Full darkness was upon us by the time we were seated. The Sumarnu now removed what little clothing they wore, and, seeing them obviously beckoning to us to do the same, Schweiz and I stripped, piling our clothes on the benches behind us. At a signal from one of the chiefs the handsome girl rose and went to the fire, poking a bough into it until she had a torch; then, approaching the slanting mouth of the tunnel, she wriggled awkwardly feet-first into it, holding the torch high. Girl and torch disappeared entirely from view. For a little while I could see the flickering light of the firebrand coming from below, but soon it went out, sending up a gust of dark smoke. Shortly the the girl emerged, without the torch. In one hand she carried a thick-rimmed red pot, in the other a long flask of green glass. The two old men – high priests? – left their benches and took these things from her. They began a tuneless chant, and one, reaching into the pot, scooped from it a handful of white powder – the drug! – and dropped it into the flask. The other solemnly shook the flask from side to side in a mixing motion. Meanwhile the old woman – a priestess? – had prostrated herself by the mouth of the tunnel and began to chant in a different intonation, a jagged gasping rhythm, while the two young men flung more wood on the fire. The chanting continued for a good many minutes. Now the girl who had descended into the tunnel – a slim high-breasted wench with long silken red-brown hair – took the flask from the old man and brought it to our side of the fire, where the plain girl, stepping forward, received it reverently with both hands. Solemnly she carried it to the three seated chieftains and held it toward them. The chieftains now joined the chanting for the first time. What I thought of as the Rite of the Presentation of the Flask went on and on; I was fascinated at first, finding delight in the strangeness of the ceremony, but soon I grew bored and had to amuse myself by trying to invent a spiritual content for what was taking place. The tunnel, I decided, symbolized the genital opening of the world-mother, the route to her womb, where the drug – made from a root, from something growing underground – could be obtained. I devised an elaborate metaphorical construct involving a mother-cult, the symbolic meaning of carrying a lighted torch into the world-mother's womb, the use of plain and handsome girls to represent the universality of womanhood, the two young fire-warders as guardians of the chieftains' sexual potency, and a great deal more, all of it nonsense, but – so I thought – an impressive enough scheme to be assembled by a bureaucrat like myself, of no great intellectual powers. My pleasure in my own musings evaporated abruptly when I realized how patronizing I was being. I was treating these Sumarnu like quaint savages, whose chants and rites were of mild aesthetic interest but could not possibly have any serious content. Who was I to take this lofty attitude? I had come to them, had I not, begging the drug of enlightenment that my soul craved; which of us then was the superior being? I assailed myself for my snobbery. *Be loving.* Put aside courtly sophistication. Share their rite if you can, and at the least show no contempt for it, feel no contempt, *have* no contempt. *Be loving.* The chieftains were drinking now, each taking a sip, handing the flask back to the plain-looking girl, who when all three had sipped began to move about the circle, bringing the flask first to the old men, then to the old woman, then to the handsome girl, then to the young fire-tenders, then to Schweiz, then to me. She smiled at me as she gave me the flask. By the fire's leaping light she seemed suddenly beautiful. The flask contained a warm gummy wine; I nearly gagged as I drank. But I drank. The drug entered my gut and journeyed thence to my soul.

43

We all became one, the ten of them and the two of us. First there were the strange sensations of going up, the heightening of perception, the loss of bearings, the visions of celestial light, the hearing of eerie sounds; then came the detecting of other heartbeats and bodily rhythms about me, the doubling, the overlapping of awarenesses; then came the dissolution of self, and we became one, who had been twelve. I was plunged into a sea of souls and I perished. I was swept into the Center of All Things. I had no way of knowing whether I was Kinnall the septarch's son, or Schweiz the man of old Earth, or the fire-tenders, or the chiefs, or the priests, or the girls, or the priestess, for they were inextricably mixed up in me and I in them. And the sea of souls was a sea of love. How could it be anything else than that? We were each other. Love of self bound us each to each, all to all. Love of self is love of others; love of others is love of self. And I loved. I knew more clearly than ever why Schweiz had said to me, *I love you*, as we were coming out of the drug the first time – that odd phrase, so obscene on Borthan, so incongruous in any case when man is speaking to man. I said to the ten Sumarnu, *I love you*, though not in words, for I had no words that they would understand, and even if I had spoken to them in my own tongue and they had understood, they would have resented the foulness of my words, for among my people *I love you* is an obscenity, and no help for it. *I love you.* And I meant it, and they accepted the gift of my love. I who was part of them. I who not long ago had patronized them as amusing primitives worshiping bonfires in the woods. Through them I sensed the sounds of the forest and the heaving of the tides, and, yes, the merciful love of the great world-mother, who lies sighing and quaking beneath our feet, and who has bestowed on us the drug-root for the healing of our sundered selves. I learned what it is to be Sumarnu and live simply at the meeting-place of two small rivers. I discovered how one can lack groundcars and banking houses and still belong to the community of civilized humanity. I found out what half-souled things the people of Velada Borthan have made of themselves in the name of holiness, and how whole it is possible to be, if one follows the way of the Sumarnu. None of this came to me in words or even in a flow of images, but rather in a rush of received knowledge, knowledge that entered and became part of me after a manner I can neither describe nor explain. I hear you saying now that I must be either lying or lazy, to offer you as little specific detail of the experience as I have done. But I reply that one cannot put into words that never *was* in words. One can deal only in approximations, and one's best effort can be nothing more than a distortion, a coarsening of the truth. For I must transform perceptions into words and set them down as my skills permit, and then you must pick my words from the page and convert them into whatever system of perceptions your mind habitually employs, and at each stage of this transmission a level of density leaches away, until you are left only with the shadow of what befell me in the clearing in Sumara Borthan. So how can I explain? We were dissolved in one another. We were dissolved in love. We who had no language in common came to total comprehension of our separate selves. When the drug at length lost its hold on us, part of me remained in them and part of them remained in me. If you would know more than that, if you would have a glimpse of what it is to be released from the prison of your skull, if you would taste love for the first time in your life, I say to you, look for no explanations fashioned out of words, but put the flask to your lips. Put the flask to your lips.

44

We had passed the test. They would give us what we wanted. After the sharing of love came the haggling. We returned to the village, and in the morning our bearers brought out our cases of trade-goods, and the three chieftains brought out three squat clay pots, with the white powder visible within them. And we heaped up a high stack of knives and mirrors and heat-rods, and they carefully poured quantities of powder from two of the pots into the third. Schweiz did most of the bargaining. The guide we had brought from the coast was of little value, for, though he could talk these chieftains' language, he had never talked to their souls. In fact the bargaining inverted itself suddenly, with Schweiz happily piling still more trinkets into the price, and the chiefs responding by adding more powder to our bowl, everyone laughing in a sort of hysterical good nature as the contest of generosity grew more frenzied. In the end we gave the villagers everything we had, keeping only a few items for gifts to our guide and bearers, and the villagers gave us enough of the drug to snare the minds of thousands.

Captain Khrisch was waiting when we reached the harbor. 'One sees you have fared well,' he remarked.

'Is it so obvious?' I asked.

'You were worried men when you went into this place. You are happy men coming out of it. Yes, it is obvious.'

On the first night of our voyage back to Manneran, Schweiz called me into his cabin. He had the pot of white powder out, and he had broken the seal. I watched as he carefully poured the drug into little packets of the kind in which that first dose had come. He worked in silence, scarcely glancing at me, filling some seventy or eighty packets. When he was done, he counted out a dozen of them to one side. Indicating the others, he said, 'Those are for you. Hide them well about your luggage, or you'll need all your power with the Port Justiciary to get them safely past the customs collectors.'

'You've given me five times as much as you've taken,' I protested.

'Your need is greater,' Schweiz told me.

45

I did not understand what he meant by that until we were in Manneran again. We landed at Hilminor, paid Captain Khrisch, went through a minimum of inspection formalities (how trusting the port officials were, not very long ago!), and set out in our groundcar for the capital. Entering the city of Manneran by the Sumar Road, we passed through a crowded district of marketplaces and open-air shops, where I saw thousands of Mannerangi jostling, haggling, bickering. I saw them driving their hard bargains and whipping out contract forms to close the deals. I saw their faces, pinched, guarded, the eyes bleak and unloving. And I thought of the drug I carried and told myself, *If only I could change their frosty souls.* I had a vision of myself going among them, accosting strangers, drawing this one aside and that, whispering gently to each of them, 'I am a prince of Salla and a high official of the Port Justiciary, who has put such empty things aside to bring happiness to mankind, and I would show you how to find joy through self-baring. Trust me: I love you.' No doubt some would flee from me as soon as I began to speak, frightened by the initial obscenity of my 'I am,' and others might hear me out and then spit in my face and call me a madman, and some might cry for the police; but perhaps there would be a few who would listen, and feel tempted, and come off with me to a quiet dockside room where we could share the Sumaran drug. One by one I would open souls, until there were ten in Manneran like me – twenty – a hundred – a secret society of selfbarers, knowing one another by the warmth and love in their eyes, going about the city unafraid to say 'I' or 'me' to their fellow initiates, giving up not merely the grammar of politeness but all the poisonous denials of self-love that that grammar implied. And then I would charter Captain Khrisch again for a voyage to Sumara Borthan, and return laden with packets of white powder, and continue on through Manneran, I and those who now were like me, and we would go up to this one and that, smiling, glowing, to whisper, 'I would show you how to find joy through selfbaring. Trust me: I love you.'

There was no role for Schweiz in this vision. This was not his planet; he had no stake in transforming it. All that interested him was his private spiritual need, his hunger to break through to a sense of the godhood. He had begun that breakthrough already, and could complete it on his own, apart. Schweiz had no need to skulk about the city, seducing strangers. And this was why he had given me the greater share of our Sumaran booty: I was the evangelist, I was the new prophet, I was the messiah of openness, and Schweiz realized that before I did. Until now he had been the leader – drawing me into his confidence, getting me to try the drug, luring me off to Sumara Borthan, making use of my power in the Port Justiciary, keeping me at his side for companionship and reassurance and protection. I had been in his shadow throughout. Now he would cease to eclipse me. Armed with my little packets, I alone would launch the campaign to change a world.

It was a role I welcomed. All my life I had been overshadowed by one man or another, so that for all my strength of body and ability of mind I had come to seem second-rate to myself. Perhaps that is a natural defect of being born a septarch's second son. First there had been my father, whom I could never hope to equal in authority, agility, or might; then Stirron, whose kingship brought only exile for me; then my master in the Glinish logging camp; then Segvord Helalam; then Schweiz. All of them men of determination and prestige, who knew and held their places in our world, while I wandered in frequent bewilderment. Now, in the middle of my years, I could at last emerge. I had a mission. I had purpose. The spinners of the divine design had brought me to this place, had made me who I was, had readied me for my task. In joy I accepted their command.

46

There was a girl I kept for my sport, in a room on the south side of Manneran, in the tangle of old streets back of the Stone Chapel. She claimed to be a bastard of the Duke of Kongoroi, spawned when the duke was on a state visit to Manneran in the days of my father's reign. Perhaps her story was true. Certainly she believed it. I was in the habit of going to her twice or thrice each moontime for an hour of pleasure, whenever I felt too stifled by the routine of my life, whenever I felt boredom's hand at my throat. She was simple but passionate: lusty, available, undemanding. I did not hide my identity from her, but I gave her none of my inner self, and none was expected; we talked very little, and there was no question of love between us. In return for the price of her lodgings, she let me make occasional use of her body, and the transaction was no more complex than that: a touching of skins, a sneeze of the loins. She was the first to whom I gave the drug. I mixed it with golden wine. 'We will drink this,' I said, and when she asked me why, I replied, 'It will bring us closer together.' She asked, in no great curiosity, what it would do to us, and I explained, 'It will open self to self, and make all walls transparent.' She offered no protests – no talk of the Covenant, no whining about privacy, no lectures of the evils of selfbaring. She did as she was told, convinced I would bring no harm to her. We took the dose, and then we lay naked on her couch waiting for the effects to begin. I stroked her cool thighs, kissed the tips of her breasts, playfully nibbled her earlobes, and soon the strangeness started, the buzzing and the rush of air, and we began to detect one another's heartbeats and pulse. 'Oh,' she said. 'Oh, one feels so peculiar!' But it did not frighten her. Our souls drifted together and were fused in the clear white light coming from the Center of All Things. And I discovered what it was like to have only a slit between my thighs, and I learned how it is to wriggle one's shoulders and have heavy breasts slap together, and I felt eggs throbbing and impatient in my ovaries. At the height of our voyage we joined our bodies. I felt my rod slide into my cavern. I felt myself moving against myself. I felt the slow sucking oceanic tide of ecstasy beginning to rise somewhere at my dark hot moist core, and I felt the hot prickling tickle of impending ecstasy dancing along my tool, and

I felt the hard hairy shield of my chest crushing against the tender globes of my breasts, and I felt lips on my lips, tongue on my tongue, soul in my soul. This union of our bodies endured for hours, or so it seemed. And in that time my self was open to her, so that she could see in it all she chose, my boyhood in Salla, my flight to Glin, my marriage, my love for my bondsister, my weaknesses, my self-deceptions, and I looked into her and saw the sweetness of her, the giddiness, the moment of first finding blood on her thighs, the other blood of a later time, the image of Kinnall Darival as she carries it in her mind, the vague and unformed commandments of the Covenant, and all the rest of her soul's furniture. Then we were swept away by the storms of our senses. I felt her orgasm and mine, mine and mine, hers and hers, the double column of frenzy that was one, the spasm and the spurt, the thrust and the thrust, the rise and the fall. We lay sweaty and sticky and exhausted, the drug still thundering through our joined minds. I opened my eyes and saw hers, unfocused, the pupils dilated. She gave me a lopsided smile. 'I – I – I – I – I,' she said. 'I!' The wonder of it seemed to daze her. 'I! I! I!' I planted a kiss between her breasts and felt the brush of my lips myself. 'I love you,' I said.

47

There was a clerk in the Port Justiciary, a certain Ulman, half my age and clearly a man of promise, whom I had come to like. He knew my power and my ancestry and showed no awe of me over that; his respect for me was based entirely on my skills in evaluating and handling the problems of the Justiciary. I kept him late one day and called him into my office when the others were gone. 'There is this drug of Sumara Borthan,' I said, 'that allows one mind freely to enter another.' He smiled and said that he had heard of it, yes, but understood it was difficult to obtain and dangerous to use. 'There is no danger,' I answered. 'And as for the difficulty of obtaining it—' I drew forth one of my little packets. His smile did not fade, though dots of color came into his cheeks. We took the drug together in my office. Hours later, when we left for our homes, I gave him some so that he could take it with his wife.

48

In the Stone Chapel I dared to reach out to a stranger, a short, thickbodied man in princely clothes, possibly a member of the septarch's family. He had the clear serene eyes of a man of good faith and the poise of one who has looked within himself and is not displeased by what he has seen. But when I spoke my words to him, he shoved me away and cursed me with such fury that his anger became contagious; maddened by his words, I nearly struck him in blind frenzy. '*Selfbarer! Selfbarer!*' The shout echoed through the holy building, and people emerged from rooms of meditation to stare. It was the worst shame I had known in years. My exalted mission came into another perspective: I saw it as filthy, and myself as something pitiful, a creeping slinking dog of a man driven by who knew what compulsion to expose his shabby soul to strangers. My anger drained from me and fear flowed in: I slipped into the shadows and out a side door, dreading arrest. For a week I walked about on tiptoe, forever looking back over my shoulder. But nothing pursued me except my panging conscience.

49

The moment of insecurity passed. Again I saw my mission whole, and recognized the merit of what I had pledged myself to do, and felt only sorrow for the man in the Stone Chapel who had spurned my gift. And in a single week I found three strangers who would share the drug with me. I wondered how I could ever have doubted myself. But other seasons of doubt lay ahead.

50

I tried to arrive at a theoretical basis for my use of the drug, to construct a new theology of love and openess. I studied the Covenant and many of its commentaries, attempting to discover why the first settlers of Velada

Borthan had found it necessary to deify mistrust and concealment. What did they fear? What were they hoping to preserve? Dark men in a dark time, with mindsnakes creeping through their skulls. In the end I came to no real understanding of them. They were convinced of their own virtue. They had acted for the best. Thou shalt not thrust the inwardness of thy soul upon thy fellow man. Thou shalt not unduly examine the needs of thine own self. Thou shalt deny thyself the easy pleasures of intimate conversation. Thou shalt stand alone before thy gods. And so we had lived, these hundreds of years, unquestioning, obedient, keeping the Covenant. Maybe nothing keeps the Covenant alive now, for most of us, except simple politeness: we are unwilling to embarrass others by baring ourselves, and so we go locked up, our inner wounds festering, and we speak our language of third-person courtliness. Was it time to create a new Covenant? A bond of love, a testament of sharing? Hidden in my rooms at home, I struggled to write one. What could I say that would be believed? That we had done well enough following the old ways, but at grievous personal cost. That the perilous conditions of the first settling no longer obtained among us, and certain customs, having become handicaps rather than assets, could be discarded. That societies must evolve if they are not to decay. That love is better than hate and trust is better than mistrust. But little of what I wrote convinced me. Why was I attacking the established order of things? Out of profound conviction, or merely out of the hunger for dirty pleasures? I was a man of my own time; I was embedded firmly in the rock of my upbringing even as I toiled to turn that rock to sand. Trapped in the tension between my old beliefs and my still unformed new ones, I swung a thousand times a day from pole to pole, from shame to exaltation. As I labored over the draft of my new Covenant's preamble one evening, my bondsister Halum unexpectedly entered my study. 'What are you writing?' she asked pleasantly. I covered one sheet with another. My face must have reflected my discomfort, for hers showed signs of apology for having intruded. 'Official reports,' I said. 'Foolishness. Dull bureaucratic trivia.' That night I burned all I had written, in a paroxysm of self-contempt.

51

In those weeks I took many voyages of exploration into unknown lands. Friends, strangers, casual acquaintances, a mistress: companions on strange journeys. But through all the early phase of my time of changes I said not a word to Halum about the drug. To share it with her had been my original goal, that had brought the drug to my lips in the first place. Yet I feared to approach her. It was cowardice that kept me back: what if, by coming to know me too well, she ceased to love me?

52

Several times I came close to broaching the subject with her. I held myself back. I did not dare to move toward her. If you wish you may measure my sincerity by my hesitation; how pure, you may ask, was my new creed of openness, if I felt that my bondsister would be above such a communion? But I will not pretend there was any consistency in my thinking then. My liberation from the taboos on selfbaring was a willed thing, not a natural evolution, and I had constantly to battle against the old habits of our custom. Though I talked in 'I' and 'me' with Schweiz and some of the others with whom I had shared the drug, I was never comfortable in doing so. Vestiges of my broken bonds still crept together to shackle me. I looked at Halum and knew that I loved her, and told myself that the only way to fulfill that love was through the joining of her soul and mine, and in my hand was the powder that would join us. And I did not dare. And I did not dare.

53

The twelfth person with whom I shared the Sumaran drug was my bondbrother Noim. He was in Manneran to spend a week as my guest. Winter had come, bringing snow to Glin, hard rains to Salla, and only fog to Manneran, and northerners needed little prodding to come to our warm province. I had not seen Noim since the summer before, when we had hunted together in the Huishtors. In this last year we had drifted apart somewhat; in a sense Schweiz had come to take Noim's place in my life, and I no longer had quite the same need for my bondbrother.

Noim now was a wealthy landowner in Salla, having come into the inheritance of the Condorit family as well as the lands of his wife's kin. In manhood he had become plump, though not fat; his wit and cunning were not hidden deep beneath his new layers of flesh. He had a sleek, well-oiled look, with dark unblemished skin, full, complacent lips, and round sardonic eyes. Little escaped his attention. Upon arriving at my house he surveyed me with great care, as though counting my teeth and the lines about my eyes, and, after the formal bondbrotherly greetings, after the presentation of his gift and the one he had brought from Stirron, after we had signed the contract of host and guest, Noim said unexpectedly, 'Are you in trouble, Kinnall?'

'Why do you ask that?'

'Your face is sharper. You've lost weight. Your mouth – you hold it in a quirky grin that doesn't announce a relaxed man within. Your eyes are red-rimmed and they don't want to look directly into other eyes. Is anything wrong?'

'These have been the happiest months of one's life,' I said, a shade too vehemently, perhaps.

Noim ignored my disclaimer. 'Are you having problems with Loimel?'

'She goes her way, and one goes his own.'

'Difficulties with the business of the Justiciary, then?'

'Please, Noim, won't you believe that—'

'Your face has changes inscribed in it,' he said. 'Do you deny there have been changes in your life?'

I shrugged. 'And if so?'

'Changes for the worse?'

'One does not think so.'

'You're being evasive, Kinnall. Come: what's a bondbrother for, if not to share problems?'

'There are no problems,' I insisted.

'Very well.' And he let the matter drop. But I saw him watching me that evening, and again the next day at morning's meal, studying me, probing me. I could never hide anything from him. We sat over blue wine and talked of the Sallan harvest, talked of Stirron's new program of reforming the tax structure, talked of the renewed tensions between Salla and Glin, the bloody border raids that had lately cost me the life of a sister. And all the while Noim watched me. Halum dined with us, and we talked of our childhood, and Noim watched me. He flirted with Loimel, but his eyes did not wander from me. The depth and intensity of his concern preyed on me. He would be asking questions of others, soon, trying to get from Halum or from Loimel some notion of what might be bothering me, and he might stir up trouble-some curiosities in them that way. I could not let him remain ignorant of the central experience of his bondbrother's life. Late the second night, when everyone else had retired, I took Noim to my study, and opened the secret place where I stored the white powder, and asked him if he knew anything of the Sumaran drug. He claimed not to have heard of it. Briefly I described its effects to him. His expression darkened; he seemed to draw in on himself. 'Do you use this stuff often?' he asked.

'Eleven times thus far.'

'Eleven – *why*, Kinnall?'

'To learn the nature of one's own self, through sharing that self with others.'

Noim laughed explosively: it was almost a snort. 'Selfbaring, Kinnall?'

'One takes up odd hobbies in one's middle years.'

'And with whom have you played this game?'

I said, 'Their names don't matter. No one you would know. People of Manneran, those with some adventure in their souls, those who are willing to take risks.'

'Loimel?'

Now it was my turn to snort. 'Never! She knows nothing of this at all.'

'Halum, then?'

I shook my head. 'One wishes one had the courage to approach Halum. So far one has concealed everything from her. One fears she's too virginal, too easily shocked. It's sad, isn't it, Noim, when one has to hide something as exciting as this, as wonderfully rewarding, from one's bondsister.'

'From one's bondbrother too,' he observed testily.

'You would have been told in time,' I said. 'You would have been offered your chance to experience the communion.'

His eyes flashed. 'Do you think I'd want it?'

His deliberate obscenity earned only a faint smile from me. 'One hopes one's bondbrother will share all of one's experiences. At present the drug opens a gulf between us. One has gone again and again to a place you have never visited. Do you see, Noim?'

Noim saw. He was tempted; he hovered at the edge of the abyss; he chewed his lips and tugged at his earlobes, and everything that passed across his mind was as transparent to me as if we had already shared the Sumaran powder. For my sake he was uneasy, knowing that I had seriously strayed from the Covenant and might soon find myself in grave spiritual and legal trouble. For his own sake he was gnawed by curiosity, aware that selfbaring with one's bondbrother was no great sin and half-eager to know the kind of communion he might have with me under the drug. Also his eyes revealed a glint of jealousy, that I comprehended these things at that moment, though I confirmed them later when Noim's soul was open to me.

We said nothing to one another about these matters for several days. He came with me to my office, and watched in admiration as I dealt with matters of the highest national significance. He saw the clerks bowing in and out of my presence, and also the clerk Ulman, who had had the drug, and whose cool familiarity with me touched off suspicious vibrations in Noim's sensitive antennae. We visited with Schweiz, and emptied many a flask of good wine, and discussed religious topics in a hearty, earnest, drunken way. ('All my life,' said Schweiz, 'has been a quest for plausible reasons to believe in what I know to be irrational.') Noim noticed that Schweiz did not always observe the grammatical niceties. Another night we dined with a group of Mannerangi nobles in a voluptuous house in the hills overlooking the city: small birdlike men, overdressed and fidgety, and huge handsome young wives. Noim was displeased by these effete dukes and barons with their talk of commerce and jewelry, but he grew more irritable when the chatter turned to the rumor that a mind-unsealing drug from the southern continent was now procurable in the capital. To this I made only polite interjections of surprise; Noim glared at me for my hypocrisy, and even refused a dish of tender Mannerangi brandy, so tight-strung were his nerves. The day after, we went to the Stone Chapel together, not for draining but merely to view the relics of the early times, for Noim had developed antiquarian interests. The drainer Jidd happened to wander through the cloister at his devotions and smiled oddly at me: I saw Noim at once calculating whether I had drawn even the priest into my subversions. A sizzling tension was building in Noim during those days, for he clearly longed to return to the subject of our early conversation, yet could not bring himself to it. I made no move toward reopening that theme. It was Noim who made the move, finally, on the eve of his departure for his home in Salla. 'This drug of yours—' he began hoarsely.

He said he felt he could not regard himself as my true bondbrother unless he sampled it. Those words came from him at great cost. His elegant clothes were rumpled by his restlessness, and a fine line of beaded perspiration stood out on his upper lip. We went to a room where no one could intrude, and I prepared the potion. As he took the flask, he briefly flashed at me his familiar grin, impudent and sly and bold, but his hand was shaking so badly he nearly spilled the drink. The drug took effect quickly for both of us. It was a night of thick humidity with a dense greasy mist covering the city and its suburbs, and it seemed to me that fingers of that mist were sliding into our room through the partly opened window: I saw shimmering, pulsating strands of cloud groping at us, dancing between my bondbrother and myself. The early sensations of druggedness disturbed Noim, until I explained that everything was normal, the twinned heartbeats, the cottony head, the high whining sounds in the air. Now we were open. I looked into Noim and saw not only his self but his image of his self, encrusted with shame and self-contempt; there was in Noim a fierce and burning loathing of his imagined flaws, and the flaws were many. He held himself accused of laziness, lack of discipline and ambition, irreligiousness, a casual concern with high obligations, and physical and moral weakness. Why he saw himself in this way

I could not understand, for the true Noim was there beside the image, and the true Noim was a tough-minded man, loyal to those he loved, harsh in judgment of folly, clear-sighted, passionate, energetic. The contrast between Noim's Noim and the world's was startling: it was as though he were capable of correctly evaluating everything but his own worth. I had seen such disparities before on these drug voyages; in fact they were universal in all but Schweiz, who had not been trained from childhood in self-denial; yet they were sharper in Noim than in anyone else.

Also I saw, as I had seen before, my own image refracted through Noim's sensibility: a far nobler Kinnall Darival than I recognized. How he idealized me! I was all he hoped to be, a man of action and valor, a wielder of power, an enemy of everything that was frivolous, a practitioner of the sternest inner discipline and devotion. Yet this image bore traces of a new overlay of tarnish, for was I not also now a Covenant-defiling selfbarer, who had done this and this and that and that with eleven strangers, and who now had lured his own bondbrother into criminal experimentation? And also Noim found in me the true depth of my feelings for Halum, and upon making that discovery, which confirmed old suspicions, he altered his image of me once again, not for the better. Meanwhile I showed Noim how I had always seen him – quick, clever, capable – and showed him too his own Noim and the objective Noim as well, while he gave me a view of the selves of mine he now could see beside that idealized Kinnall. These mutual explorations continued a long time. I thought the exchanges were immensely valuable, since only with Noim could I attain the necessary depth of perspective, the proper parallax of character, and he only with me; we had great advantages over a pair of strangers meeting for the first time by way of the Sumaran drug. When the spell of the potion began to lift, I felt myself exhausted by the intensity of our communion, and yet ennobled, exalted, transformed.

Not so Noim. He looked depleted and chilled. He could barely lift his eyes to mine. His mood was so frigid that I dared not break in on it, but remained still, waiting for him to recover. At length he said, 'Is it all over?'

'Yes.'

'Promise one thing, Kinnall. Will you promise?'

'Say it, Noim.'

'That you never do this thing with Halum! Is it a promise? Will you promise it, Kinnall? Never. Never. Never.'

54

Several days after Noim's departure some guilty impulse drove me to the Stone Chapel. To fill the time until Jidd could see me, I roamed the halls and byways of the dark building, pausing at altars, bowing humbly to half-blind scholars of the Covenant holding debate in a courtyard, brushing away ambitious minor drainers who, recognizing me, solicited my trade. All about me were the things of the gods, and I failed to detect the divine presence. Perhaps Schweiz had found the godhood through the souls of other men, but I, dabbling in selfbaring, somehow had lost that other faith, and it did not matter to me. I knew that in time I would find my way back to grace under this new dispensation of love and trust that I hoped to offer. So I lurked in the godhouse of godhouses, a mere tourist.

I went to Jidd. I had not had a draining since immediately after Schweiz first had given me the Sumaran drug. The little crooknosed man remarked on that as I took the contract from him. The pressures of the Justiciary, I explained, and he shook his head and made a chiding sound. 'You must be full to overflowing,' Jidd said. I did not reply, but settled down before his mirror to peer at the lean, unfamiliar face that dwelled in it. He asked me which god I would have, and I told him the god of the innocent. He gave me a queer look at that. The holy lights came on. With soft words he guided me into the half-trance of confession. What could I say? That I had ignored my pledge, and gone on to use the selfbaring potion with everyone who would take it from me? I sat silent. Jidd prodded me. He did something I had never known a drainer to do before: hearkened back to a previous draining, and asked me to speak again of this drug whose use I had admitted earlier. Had I used it again? I pushed my face close to the mirror, fogging it with my breath. Yes. Yes. One is a miserable sinner and one has been weak once more. Then Jidd asked me how I had obtained this drug, and I said that I had taken it, the first time, in company with one who had purchased it from a man who had been to Sumara Borthan. Yes, Jidd said, and what was the name of this companion? That was a clumsy move: immediately I was on guard. It seemed to me that Jidd's question went far beyond the needs of a draining, and certainly could have no relevance to my own condition of the moment. I refused therefore to give him Schweiz's name, which led the drainer to ask me, a little roughly, if I feared he would breach the secrecy of the ritual.

Did I fear that? On rare occasions I had held things back from drainers out of shame, but never out of fear of betrayal. Naïve I was, and I had full faith in the ethics of the godhouse. Only now, suddenly suspicious, with that suspicion having been planted by Jidd himself, did I mistrust Jidd and all his tribe. Why did he want to know? What information was he after? What could I gain, or he, by my revealing my source of the drug? I replied tautly, 'One seeks forgiveness for oneself alone, and how can telling the name of one's companion bring that? Let him do his own confessing.' But of course there was no chance that Schweiz would go to a drainer; thus I had come down to playing wordgames with Jidd. All value had leaked from this draining, leaving me with an empty husk. 'If you would have peace from the gods,' Jidd said, 'you must speak your soul fully.' How could I do that? Confess the seduction of eleven people into selfbaring? I had no need of Jidd's forgiveness. I had no faith in his good will. Abruptly I stood up, a little dizzy from kneeling in the dark, swaying a bit, almost stumbling. The sound of distant hymn-singing floated past me, and a trace of the scent of the precious incense of a plant of the Wet Lowlands. 'One is not ready for draining today,' I told Jidd. 'One must examine one's soul more closely.' I lurched toward the door. He looked puzzledly at the money I had given him. 'The fee?' he called. I told him he could keep it.

55

The days became mere vacant rooms, separating one journey with the drug from the next. I drifted idle and detached through all my responsibilities, seeing nothing of what was around me, living only for my next communion. The real world dissolved; I lost interest in sex, wine, food, the doings of the Port Justiciary, the friction between neighboring provinces of Velada Borthan, and all other such things, which to me now were only the shadows of shadows. Possibly I was using the drug too frequently. I lost weight and existed in a perpetual haze of blurred white light. I had difficulties in sleeping, and for hours found myself twisting and shifting, a blanket of muggy tropical air clamping me to my mattress, a haggard insomniac with an ache in his eyeballs and grittiness under his lids. I walked tired through my days and blinking through my evenings. Rarely did I speak with Loimel, nor did I touch her, and hardly ever did I touch any other woman. I fell asleep at midday once while lunching with Halum. I scandalized High Justice Kalimol by replying to one of his questions with the phrase 'It seems to me—' Old Segvord Helalam told me I looked ill, and suggested I go hunting with my sons in the Burnt Lowlands. Nevertheless the drug had the power of bringing me alive. I sought out new sharers, and found it ever more easy to make contact with them, for often now they were brought to me by those who had already made the inner voyage. An odd group they were: two dukes, a marquis, a whore, a keeper of the royal archives, a seacaptain in from Glin, a septarch's mistress, a director of the Commercial and Seafarers Bank of Manneran, a poet, a lawyer from Velis here to confer with Captain Khrisch, and many more. The circle of selfbarers was widening. My supply of the drug was nearly consumed, but now there was talk among some of my new friends of outfitting a new expedition to Sumara Borthan. There were fifty of us by this time. Change was becoming infectious; there was an epidemic of it in Manneran.

56

Sometimes, unexpectedly, in the blank dead time between one communion and another, I underwent a strange confusion of the self. A block of borrowed experience that I had stowed in the dark depths of my mind might break loose and float up into the higher levels of consciousness, intruding itself into my own identity. I remained aware of being Kinnall Darival, the septarch's son of Salla, and yet there was suddenly among my memories a segment of the self of Noim, or Schweiz, or one of the Sumarnu, or someone else of those with whom I had shared the drug. For the length of that splicing of selves – a moment, an hour, half a day – I walked about unsure of my past, unable to determine whether some event fresh in my mind had really befallen me, or had come to me through the drug. This was disturbing but not really frightening, except the first two or three times. Eventually I learned to distinguish the quality of these unearned memories from that of my genuine past, through familiarity with the textures of each. The drug had made me many people, I realized. Was it not better to be many than to be something less than one?

57

In early spring a lunatic heat settled over Manneran, coupled with such frequent rains that all the city's vegetation went mad, and would have swallowed every street if not given a daily hacking. It was green, green, green, every-where: green haze in the sky, green rain falling, green sunlight sometimes breaking through, broad glossy green leaves unfurling on every balcony and in every garden plot. A man's own soul can mildew in that. Green, too, were the awnings on the street of the spice-merchants' shops. Loimel had given me a long list of things to purchase, delicacies from Threish and Velis and the Wet Lowlands, and in a docile husbandly way I went to obtain them, since the street of spice was only a short walk from the Justiciary. She was mounting a grand feast to celebrate the Naming Day of our eldest daugh-ter, who was at last going to come into the adult-name we had intended for her: Loimel. All the great ones of Manneran had been invited to look on as my wife acquired a namesake. Among the guests would be several who had covertly sampled the Sumaran drug with me, and I took private pleasure in that; Schweiz, though, had not been invited, since Loimel deemed him coarse, and in any event he had left Manneran on some business trip just as the weather was beginning to go berserk.

I moved through the greenness to the best of the shops. A recent rain had ended and the sky was a flat green plaque resting on the rooftops. To me came delicious fragrances, sweetnesses, pungencies, clouds of tongue-tickling flavors. Abruptly there were black bubbles coursing through my skull and for a moment I was Schweiz haggling on a pier with a skipper who had just brought a cargo of costly produce in from the Gulf of Sumar. I halted to enjoy this tangling of selves. Schweiz faded; through Noim's mind I smelled the scent of newly threshed hay on the Condorit estates, under a delicious late-summer sun; then suddenly and surprisingly I was the bank director with my hand tight on some other man's loins. I cannot convey to you the impact of that last bolt of transferred experience, brief and incan-descent. I had taken the drug with the bank director not very long before, and I had seen nothing in his soul, then, of his taste for his own sex. It was not the kind of thing I would overlook. Either I had manufactured this vision gratuitously, or he had somehow shielded that part of his self from me, keeping his predilections sealed until this instant of breaking through. Was such a partial sealing possible? I had thought one's mind lay fully open. I was not upset by the nature of his lusts, only by my inability to reconcile what I had just experienced with what had come to me from him on the day of our drug-sharing. But I had little time to ponder the problem, for, as I stood gaping outside the spice-shop, a thin hand fell on mine and a guarded voice said, 'I must talk to you secretly, Kinnall.' *I*. The word jolted me from my dreaming.

Androg Mihan, keeper of the archives of Manneran's prime septarch, stood beside me. He was a small man, sharp-featured and gray, the last you would think to seek illegal pleasures; the Duke of Sumar, one of my early conquests, had led him to me. 'Where shall we go?' I asked, and Mihan indicated a disreputable-looking lower-class godhouse across the street. Its drainer lounged outside, trying to stir up business. I could not see how we could talk secretly in a godhouse, but I followed the archivist anyway; we entered the godhouse and Mihan told the drainer to fetch his contract forms. The moment the man was gone, Mihan leaned close to me and said, 'The police are on their way to your house. When you return home this evening you will be arrested and taken to prison on one of the Sumar Gulf's isles.'

'Where do you learn this?'

'The decree was verified this morning and has passed to me for filing.'

'What charge?' I asked.

'Selfbaring,' Mihan said. 'Accusation filed by agents of the Stone Chapel. There is also a secular charge: use and distribution of illegal drugs. They have you, Kinnall.'

'Who is the informer?'

'A certain Jidd, said to be a drainer in the Stone Chapel. Did you let the tale of the drug be drained from you?'

'I did. In my innocence. The sanctity of the godhouse—'

'The sanctity of the dunghouse!' Androg Mihan said vehemently. 'Now you must flee! The full force of the government is mustered against you.'

'Where shall I go?'

'The Duke of Sumar will shelter you tonight,' said Mihan. 'After that – I do not know.'

The drainer now returned, bearing a set of contracts. He gave us a proprietary smile and said, 'Well, gentlemen, which of you is to be first?'

'One has remembered another appointment,' Mihan said.

'One feels suddenly unwell,' I said.

I tossed the startled drainer a fat coin and we left the godhouse. Outside, Mihan pretended not to know me, and we went our separate ways without a word. Not for a moment did I doubt the truth of his warning. I had to take flight; Loimel would have to purchase her own spices. I hailed a car and went at once to the mansion of the Duke of Sumar.

58

This duke is one of the wealthiest in Manneran, with sprawling estates along the Gulf and in the Huishtor foothills, and a splendid home at the capital set amidst a park worthy of an emperor's palace. He is hereditary customs-keeper of Stroin Gap, which is the source of his family's opulence, since for centuries they have skimmed a share of all that is brought forth to market out of the Wet Lowlands. In his person this duke is a man of great ugliness or remarkable beauty, I am not sure which: he has a large flat triangular head, thin lips, a powerful nose, and strange dense tightly curled hair that clings like a carpet to his skull. His hair is entirely white, yet his face is unlined. His eyes are huge and dark and intense. His cheeks are hollow. It is an ascetic face, which to me always seemed alternately saintly and monstrous, and sometimes the both at once. I had been close with him almost since my arrival in Manneran so many years before; he had helped Segvord Helalam into power, and he had stood soulbinder to Loimel at our wedding ceremony. When I took up the use of the Sumaran drug, he divined it as if by telepathy, and in a conversation of marvelous subtlety learned from me that I had the drug, and arranged that he should take it with me. That had been four moonrises earlier, in late winter.

Arriving at his home, I found a tense conference in progress. Present were most of the men of consequence whom I had inveigled into my circle of selfbarers. The Duke of Mannerangu Smor. The Marquis of Woyn. The bank director. The Commissioner of the Treasury and his brother, the Procurator-General of Manneran. The Master of the Border. And five or six others of similar significance. Archivist Mihan arrived shortly after I did.

'We are all here now,' the Duke of Mannerangu Smor said. 'They could sweep us up with a single stroke. Are the grounds well guarded?'

'No one will invade us,' said the Duke of Sumar, a trifle icily, clearly offended by the suggestion that common police might burst into his home. He turned his huge alien eyes on me. 'Kinnall, this will be your last night in Manneran, and no help for it. You are to be the scapegoat.'

'By whose choice?' I asked.

'Not ours,' the duke replied. He explained that something close to a coup d'etat had been attempted in Manneran this day, and might well yet succeed: a revolt of junior bureaucrats against their masters. The beginning, he said, lay in my having admitted my use of the Sumaran drug to the drainer Jidd. (Around the room faces darkened. The unspoken implication was that I had been a fool to trust a drainer, and now must pay the price of my folly. I had not been as sophisticated as these men.) Jidd, it seemed, had leagued himself with a cabal of disaffected minor officials, hungry for their turn at power. Since he was drainer to most of the great men of Manneran, he was in an extraordinarily good position to aid the ambitious, by betraying the secrets of the mighty. Why Jidd had chosen to contravene his oaths in this fashion was not yet known. The Duke of Sumar suspected that in Jidd familiarity had bred contempt, and after listening for years to the melancholy outpourings of his powerful clients, he had grown to loathe them: exasperated by their confessions, he found pleasure in collaborating in their destruction. (This gave me a new view of what a drainer's soul might be like.) Hence Jidd had, for some months now, been slipping useful facts to rapacious subordinates, who had threatened their masters with them, often to considerable effect. By admitting my use of the drug to him, I had made myself vulnerable, and he had sold me to certain folk of the Justiciary who wished to have me out of office.

'But this is absurd!' I cried. 'The only evidence against me is protected by the sanctity of the godhouse! How can Jidd place a complaint against me based on what I've drained to him? I'll have him up on charges for violation of contract!'

'There is other evidence,' the Marquis of Woyn said sadly.

'There is?'

'Using what he heard from your own lips,' the Marquis said, 'Jidd was able to guide your enemies into channels of investigaton. They have found a certain woman who admitted to them that you gave her a strange drink that opened her eyes to you—'

'The beasts.'

'They have also,' the Duke of Sumar said, 'been able to link several of us to you. Not all, but several. This morning some of us were presented, by their own subordinates, with demands to resign their offices or face exposure. We met these threats firmly, and those who made them are now under detention, but there is no telling how many allies they have in high places. It is possible that by next moonrise we will all have been cast down and new men will hold our power. However, I doubt this, since, so far as we can determine, the only solid evidence so far is the confession of the slut, who has implicated only you, Kinnall. The accusations made by Jidd will of course be inadmissible, though they can do damage anyway.'

'We can destroy her credibility,' I said. 'I'll claim I never knew her. I'll—'

'Too late,' said the Procurator-General 'Her deposition is on record. I've had a copy from the Grand Justiciar. It will stand up. You're hopelessly implicated.'

'What will happen?' I asked.

'We will crush the ambitions of the blackmailers,' said the Duke of Sumar, 'and send them into poverty. We will break Jidd's prestige and drive him from the Stone Chapel. We will deny all of the charges of selfbaring that may be brought against us. You, however, must leave Manneran.'

'Why?' I looked at the duke in perplexity. 'I'm not without influence. If you can withstand the charges, why not I?'

'Your guilt is on record,' the Duke of Mannerangu Smor said. 'If you flee, it can be claimed that you alone, and this girl you corrupted, were the only

ones involved, and the rest is merely the fabrication of self-serving underlings trying to overthrow their masters. If you stay and try to fight a hopeless
case, you'll eventually bring us all down, as your interrogation proceeds.'

It was wholly plain to me now.

I was dangerous to them. My strength might be broken in court and their
guilt thus exposed. Thus far I was the only one indicted, and I was the only
one vulnerable to the processes of Mannerangi justice. They were vulnerable solely through me, and if I went, there was no way of getting at them.
The safety of the majority required my departure. Moreover: my naïve faith
in the godhouse, which had led me rashly to confess to Jidd, had led to this
tempest, which otherwise might have been avoided. I had caused all this; I
was the one who must go.

The Duke of Sumar said, 'You will remain with us until the dark hours of
night, and then my private groundcar, escorted by bodyguards as though it
were I who was traveling, will take you to the estate of the Marquis of Woyn.
A riverboat will be waiting there. By dawn you will be across the Woyn and
into your homeland of Salla, and may the gods journey at your side.'

59

Once more a refugee. In a single day all the power I had accumulated in
fifteen years in Manneran was lost. Neither high birth nor high connections
could save me: I might have ties of marriage or love or politics to half the
masters of Manneran, yet they were helpless in helping me. I have made it
seem as if they had forced me into exile to save their own skins, but it was
not like that. My going was necessary, and it brought as much sorrow to
them as to me.

I had nothing with me but the clothes I wore. My wardrobe, my weapons,
my ornaments, my wealth itself, must remain behind in Manneran. As a
boy-prince fleeing from Salla to Glin, I had had the prudence to transfer
funds ahead of myself, but now I was cut off. My assets would be sequestered; my sons would be paupered. There had been no time for preparations.

Here at least my friends were of service. The Procurator-General, who was
nearly of a size with me, had brought several changes of handsome clothing. The Commissioner of the Treasury had obtained for me a fair fortune
in Sallan currency. The Duke of Mannerangu Smor pulled two rings and
a pendant from his own body, so that I should not go unadorned into my
native province. The Marquis of Woyn pressed on me a ceremonial dagger

and his heat-rod, with a hilt worked with precious gems. Mihan promised to speak with Segvord Helalam, and tell him the details of my downfall; Segvord would be sympathetic, Mihan believed, and would protect my sons with all his influence, and keep them untainted by their father's indictment.

Lastly, the Duke of Sumar came to me at the deepest time of the night, when I sat alone sourly eating the dinner I had had no time for earlier, and handed me a small jeweled case of bright gold, of the sort one might carry medicine in. 'Open it carefully,' he said. I did, and found it brimming with white powder. In amazement I asked him where he had obtained this; he had lately sent agents secretly to Sumara Borthan, he replied, who had returned with a small supply of the drug. He claimed to have more, but I believe he gave me all he had.

'In an hour's time you will leave,' said the duke, to smother my gush of gratitude.

I asked to be allowed to make a call first.

'Segvord will explain matters to your wife,' the duke said.

'One did not mean one's wife. One meant one's bondsister.' In speaking of Halum I could not drop easily into the rough grammar we selfbarers affected. 'One has had no chance to make one's farewell to her.'

The duke understood my anguish, for he had been within my soul. But he would not grant me the call. Lines might be tapped; he could not risk having my voice go forth from his home this night. I realized then how delicate a position even he must be in, and I did not force the issue. I could call Halum tomorrow, when I had crossed the Woyn and was safe in Salla.

Shortly it was time for me to depart. My friends had already gone, some hours since; the duke alone led me from the house. His majestic ground-car waited, and a corps of bodyguards on individual powercycles. The duke embraced me. I climbed into the car and settled back against the cushions. The driver opaqued the windows, hiding me from view though not interfering with my own vision. The car rolled silently forward, picked up speed, plunged into the night, with my outriders, six of them, hovering about it like insects. It seemed that hours went by before we came even to the main gate of the duke's estate. Then we were on the highway. I sat like a man carved of ice, scarcely thinking of what had befallen me. Northward lay our route, and we went at such a rate that the sun was not yet up when we reached the margin of the Marquis of Woyn's estate, on the border between Manneran and Salla. The gate opened; we shot through; the road cut across a dense forest, in which, by moonlight, I could see sinister parasitic growths like hairy ropes tangling tree to tree. Suddenly we erupted into a clearing and I beheld the banks of the River Woyn. The car halted. Someone in dark robes helped me out, as though I were a dodderer, and escorted me down the spongy bank to a long narrow pier, barely visible in the thick mist rising off the breast of the river. A boat was tied up, no great craft, hardly more than a dinghy. Yet it traveled at great speed across the broad and turbulent Woyn. Still I felt no inner response to my banishment from Manneran. I was like one who has gone forth in battle and had his right leg sliced off at the thigh by a fire-bolt, and who now lies in a tumbled heap, staring calmly at his stump and sensing no pain. The pain would come, in time.

Dawn was near. I could make out the shape of the Sallan side of the river. We pulled up at a dock that jutted out of a grassy bank, plainly some nobleman's private landing. Now I felt my first alarm. In a moment I would step ashore in Salla. Where would I find myself? How would I reach some settled region? I was no boy, to beg rides from passing trucks. But all this had been settled for me hours before. As the boat bumped the shoulder of the pier, a figure emerged in the dimness and extended a hand: Noim. He drew me forth and clasped me in a tight hug. 'I know what has happened,' he said. 'You will stay with me.' In his emotion he abandoned polite usage with me for the first time since our boyhood.

60

At midday, from Noim's estate in southwestern Salla, I phoned the Duke of Sumar to confirm my safe arrival – it was he, of course, who had arranged for my bondbrother to meet me at the border – and then I put through a call to Halum. Segvord had told her just a few hours earlier of the reasons for my disappearance. 'How strange this news is,' she said. 'You never spoke of the drug. Yet it was so important to you, for you risked everything to use it. How could it have had such a role in your life, and yet be kept a secret from your bondsister?' I answered that I had not dared to let her know of my preoccupation with it, for fear I might be tempted to offer it to her. She said, 'Is opening yourself then to your bondsister so terrible a sin?'

61

Noim treated me with every courtesy, indicating that I could stay with him as long as I wished – weeks, months, even years. Presumably my friends in

Manneran would succeed eventually in freeing some of my assets, and I would buy land in Salla and take up the life of a country baron; or perhaps Segvord and the Duke of Sumar and other men of influence would have my indictment quashed, so that I could return to the southern province. Until then, Noim told me, his home was mine. But I detected a subtle coolness in his dealings with me, as if this hospitality was offered only out of respect for our bonding. Only after some days did the source of his remoteness reach the surface. Sitting late past dinner in his great whitewashed feasting-hall, we were talking of childhood days – our main theme of conversation, far safer than any talk of recent events – when Noim suddenly said, 'Is that drug of yours known to give people nightmares?'

'One has heard of no such cases, Noim.'

'Here's a case, then. One who woke up drenched with chilly sweat night after night, for weeks after we shared the drug in Manneran. One thought one would lose one's mind.'

'What kind of dreams?' I asked.

'Ugly things. Monsters. Teeth. Claws. A sense of not knowing who one is. Pieces of other minds floating through one's own.' He gulped at his wine. 'You take the drug for *pleasure*, Kinnall?'

'For knowledge.'

'Knowledge of what?'

'Knowledge of self, and knowledge of others.'

'One prefers ignorance, then.' He shivered. 'You know, Kinnall, one was never a particularly reverent person. One blasphemed, one stuck his tongue out at drainers, one laughed at the god-tales they told, yes? You've nearly converted one into a man of faith with that stuff. The terror of opening one's mind – of knowing that one has no defenses, that you can slide right into one's soul, and are doing it – it's impossible to take.'

'Impossible for you,' I said. 'Others cherish it.'

'One leans toward the Covenant,' said Noim. 'Privacy is sacred. One's soul is one's own. There's a dirty pleasure in baring it.'

'Not baring. Sharing.'

'Does it sound prettier that way? Very well: there's a dirty pleasure in sharing it, Kinnall. Even though we are bondbrothers. One came away from you last time feeling soiled. Sand and grit in the soul. Is this what you want for everyone? To make us all feel filthy with guilt?'

'There need be no guilt, Noim. One gives, one receives, one comes forth better than one was—'

'Dirtier.'

'Enlarged. Enhanced. More compassionate. Speak to others who have tried it,' I said.

'Of course. As they come streaming out of Manneran, landless refugees, one will question them about the beauty and wonder of selfbaring. Excuse me: self-sharing.'

I saw the torment in his eyes. He wanted still to love me, but the Sumaran drug had shown him things – about himself, perhaps about me – that made him hate the one who had given the drug to him. He was one for whom walls are necessary; I had not realized that. What had I done, to turn my bond-brother into my enemy? Perhaps if we could take the drug a second time, I might make things more clear to him – but no, no hope of that. Noim was frightened by inwardness. I had transformed my blaspheming bondbrother into a man of the Covenant. There was nothing I could say to him now.

After some silence he said, 'One must make a request of you, Kinnall.'

'Anything.'

'One hesitates to place boundaries on a guest. But if you have brought any of this drug with you from Manneran, Kinnall, if you hide it somewhere in your rooms – get rid of it, is that understood? There must be none of it in this house. Get rid of it, Kinnall.'

Never in my life had I lied to my bondbrother. Never.

With the jeweled case the Duke of Sumar had given me blazing against my breastbone, I said solemnly to Noim, 'You have nothing to fear on that account.'

62

Not many days later the news of my disgrace became public in Manneran, and swiftly reached Salla. Noim showed me the accounts. I was described as the chief adviser to the High Justice of the Port, and openly labeled a man of the greatest authority in Manneran, who, moreover, had blood ties to the prime septarchs of Salla and Glin – and yet, despite these attainments and preferments, I had fallen away from the Covenant to take up unlawful self-baring. I had violated not merely propriety and etiquette, but also the laws of Manneran, through my use of a certain proscribed drug from Sumara Borthan that dissolves the god-given barriers between soul and soul. Through abuse of my high office, it was said, I had engineered a secret voyage to the southern continent (poor Captain Khrisch! Had he been arrested too?) and had returned with a large quantity of the drug, which I had devilishly forced on a lowborn woman whom I was keeping; I had also circulated the foul stuff among certain prominent members of the nobility, whose names were being withheld because of their thorough repentance. On the eve of my arrest I had escaped to Salla, and good riddance to me: if I attempted to return to Manneran, I would immediately be apprehended. Meanwhile I would be tried in absentia, and, according to the Grand Justiciar, there could be little doubt of the verdict. By way of restitution to the state for the great injury I had done the fabric of social stability, I would be required to forfeit all my lands and property, except only a portion to be set aside for the maintenance of my innocent wife and children. (Segvord Helalam, then, had at least accomplished that.) To prevent my highborn friends from transferring my assets to me in Salla before the trial, all that I possessed was already sequestered in anticipation of the Grand Justiciar's decree of guilt. Thus spake the law. Let others who would make selfbaring monsters of themselves beware!

63

I made no secret of my whereabouts in Salla, for I had no reason now to fear the jealousy of my royal brother. Stirron as a boy newly on the throne might have been driven to eliminate me as a potential rival, but not the Stirron who had ruled for more than seventeen years. By now he was an institution in Salla, well loved and an integral part of everyone's existence, and I was a stranger, barely remembered by the older folk and unknown to the younger, who spoke with a Mannerangi accent and who had been publicly branded with the shame of selfbaring. Even if I cared to overthrow Stirron, where would I find followers?

In truth I was hungry for the sight of my brother. In times of storm one turns to one's earliest comrades; and with Noim estranged from me and Halum on the far side of the Woyn, I had only Stirron left. I had never resented having had to flee Salla on his account, for I knew that had our ages been reversed I would have caused him to flee the same way. If our relationship had grown frosty since my flight, it was a frost of his making, arising from his guilty conscience. Some years had passed, now, since my last visit to Salla City: perhaps my adversities would open his heart. I wrote Stirron a letter from Noim's place, formally begging sanctuary in Salla. Under Sallan law I had to be taken in, for I was one of Stirron's subjects and was guilty of no crime committed on Sallan soil: yet I thought it best to ask. The charges lodged against me by the Grand Justiciar of Manneran, I admitted, were true, but I offered Stirron a terse and (I think) eloquent justification of my deviation from the Covenant. I closed the letter with expressions of my unwavering love for him, and with a few reminiscences of the happy times we had had before the burdens of the septarchy had descended on him.

I expected Stirron in return to invite me to visit him at the capital, so that he could hear from my own lips an explanation of the strange things I had done in Manneran. A brotherly reunion was surely in order. But no summons to Salla City came. Each time the telephone chimed, I rushed toward it, thinking it might be Stirron calling. He did not call. Several weeks of tension and gloom passed; I hunted, I swam, I read, I tried to write my new Covenant of love. Noim remained aloof from me. His one experience at soul sharing had thrust him into so deep an embarrassment that he hardly dared to meet my eyes, for I was privy to all his innerness, and that had become a wedge between us.

At last came an envelope bearing the septarch's imposing seal. It held a letter signed by Stirron, but I pray it was some steely minister, and not my brother, who composed that pinch-souled message. In fewer lines than I have fingers, the septarch told me that my request for sanctuary in the province of Salla was granted, but only on the condition that I forswear the vices I had learned in the south. If I were caught just once spreading the use of selfbaring drugs in Salla, I would be seized and driven into exile. That was all my brother had to say. Not a syllable of kindness. Not a shred of sympathy. Not an atom of warmth.

64

At the crest of the summer Halum came unexpectedly to visit us. The day of her arrival, I had gone riding far out across Noim's land, following the track of a male stormshield that had burst from its pen. An accursed vanity had led Noim to acquire a clutch of these vicious furbearing mammals, though they are not native to Salla and thrive poorly there: he kept twenty or thirty of them, all claws and teeth and angry yellow eyes, and hoped to breed them into a profitable herd. I chased the escaped male through woods and plain, through morning and midday, hating it more with each hour, for it left a trail of the mutilated carcasses of harmless grazing beasts. These stormshields kill for sheer love of slaughter, taking but a bite or two of flesh and abandoning the rest to scavengers. Finally I cornered it in a shadowy box-canyon. 'Stun it and bring it back whole,' Noim had instructed me, conscious of the animal's value: but when trapped it rushed at me with such ferocity that I gave it the full beam, and gladly slew it. For Noim's sake I took the trouble to strip off the precious hide. Then, weary and depressed, I rode without stopping back to the great house. A strange groundcar was parked outside, and beside it was Halum. 'You know the summers in Manneran,' she explained. 'One planned to go as usual to the island, but then one thought, it would be good to take a holiday in Salla, with Noim and Kinnall.'

She had by then entered her thirtieth year. Our women marry between fourteen and sixteen, are done bearing their children by twenty-two or twenty-four, and at thirty have begun to slide into middle age, but time had left Halum untouched. Not having known the tempests of marriage and the travails of motherhood, not having spent her energies on the grapplings of the conjugal couch or the lacerations of childbed, she had the supple, pliant body of a girl: no fleshy bulges, no sagging folds, no exploded veins, no thickening of the frame. She had changed only in one respect, for in recent years her dark hair had turned silvery. This was but an enhancement, however, since it gleamed with dazzling brilliance, and offered agreeable contrast to the deep tan of her youthful face.

In her luggage was a packet of letters for me from Manneran: messages from the duke, from Segvord, from my sons Noim and Stirron and Kinnall, from my daughters Halum and Loimel, from Mihan the archivist, and several others. Those who wrote did so in tense, self-conscious style. They were the letters one might write to a dead man if one felt guilty at having survived him. Still, it was good to hear these words out of my former life. I regretted not finding a letter from Schweiz; Halum told me she had heard nothing from him since before my indictment, and thought he might well have left our planet. Nor was there any word from my wife. 'Is Loimel too busy to write a line or two?' I asked, and Halum, looking embarrassed, said softly that Loimel never spoke of me these days: 'She seems to have forgotten that she was married.'

Halum also had brought a trove of gifts for me from my friends across the Woyn. They were startling in their opulence: massy clusters of precious metals, elaborate strings of rare gems. 'Tokens of love,' Halum said, but I was not fooled. One could buy great estates with this heap of treasure. Those who loved me would not humiliate me by transferring cash to my account in Salla, but they could give me these splendors in the ordinary way of friendship, leaving me free to dispose of them according to my needs.

'Has it been very sad for you, this uprooting?' Halum asked. 'This sudden going into exile?'

'One is no stranger to exile,' I told her. 'And one still has Noim for bondlove and companionship.'

'Knowing that it would cost you what it did,' she said, 'would you play with the drug a second time, if you could turn time backward by a year?'

'Beyond any doubt.'

'Was it worth the loss of home and family and friends?'

'It would be worth the loss of life itself,' I replied, 'if only one could be assured by that that all of Velada Borthan would come to taste the drug.'

That answer seemed to frighten her: she drew back, she touched the tips of her fingers to her lips, perhaps becoming aware for the first time of the intensity of her bondbrother's madness. In speaking those words I was not uttering mere rhetorical overstatement, and something of my conviction must have reached Halum. She saw that I believed, and, seeing the depth of my commitment, feared for me.

Noim spent many of the days that followed away from his lands, traveling to Salla City on some family business and to the Plain of Nand to inspect property he was thinking of buying. In his absence I was master of the estate, for the servants, whatever they might think of my private life, did not dare to question my authority to my face. Daily I rode out to oversee the workers in Noim's fields, and Halum rode with me. Actually little overseeing was demanded of me, since this was midway in the seasons between planting and harvest, and the crops looked after themselves. We rode for pleasure, mainly, pausing here for a swim, there for a lunch at the edge of the woods. I showed her the stormshield pens, which did not please her, and took her among the gentler animals of the grazing fields, who came up and amiably nuzzled her.

These long rides gave us hours each day to talk. I had not spent so much time with Halum since childhood, and we grew wonderfully close. We were cautious with one another at first, not wishing to get too near the bone with our questions, but soon we spoke as bond-kin should. I asked her why it was she had never married, and she answered me simply, 'One never encountered a suitable man.' Did she regret having gone without husband and children? No, she said, she regretted nothing, for her life had been tranquil and rewarding; yet there was wistfulness in her tone. I could not press her further. On her part she questioned me about the Sumaran drug, trying to learn from me what merits it had that had led me to run such risks. I was amused by the way she phrased her inquiries: trying to sound earnest and sympathetic and objective, yet nonetheless unable to hide her horror at what I had done. It was as though her bondbrother had run amok and butchered twenty people in a marketplace, and she now wished to discover, by means of patient and good-humored questioning, just what had been the philosophical bases that had led him to take up mass murder. I also tried to maintain a temperate and dispassionate manner, so that I would not sear her with my intensity as I had done in that first interchange. I avoided all evangelizing, and, as calmly and soberly as I could, I explained to her the effects of the drug, the benefits I gained from it, and my reasons for rejecting the stony isolation of self that the Covenant imposes on us. Shortly a curious metamorphosis came over both her attitude and mine. She became less the highborn lady striving with well-meant warmth to understand the criminal, and more the student attempting to grasp the mysteries revealed by an initiated master. And I became less the descriptive reporter, and more the prophet of a new dispensation. I spoke in flights of lyricism of the raptures of soulsharing; I told her of the strange wonder of the early sensations, as one begins to open, and of the blazing moment of union with another human consciousness; I depicted the experience as something far more intimate than any meeting of souls one might have with one's bond-kin, or any visit to a drainer. Our conversations became monologues. I lost myself in verbal ecstasies, and came down from them at times to see Halum, silver-haired and eternally young, with her eyes sparkling and her lips parted in total fascination. The outcome was inevitable. One scorching afternoon as we walked slowly through the aisles in a field of grain that rose chest-high on her, she said without warning, 'If the drug is available to you here, may your bondsister share it with you?' I had converted her.

65

That night I dissolved some pinches of the powder in two flasks of wine. Halum looked uncertain as I handed one to her, and her uncertainty rebounded to me, so that I hesitated to go through with our project; but then she gave me a magical smile of tenderness and drained her flask. 'There is no flavor of it,' she said, as I drank. We sat talking in Noim's trophy-hall, decked with hornfowl spears and draped with stormshield furs, and as the drug began to take effect Halum started to shiver; I pulled a thick black hide from the wall and draped it about her shoulders, and through it I held her until the chill was past.

Would this go well? Despite all my propagandizing I was frightened. In every man's life there is something he feels driven to do, something that pricks him at the core of his soul so long as it remains undone, and yet as he approaches the doing of it he will know fear, for perhaps to fulfill the obsession will bring him more pain than pleasure. So with me and Halum and the Sumaran drug. But my fear ebbed as the drug took hold. Halum was smiling. Halum was smiling.

The wall between our souls became a membrane, through which we could slide at will. Halum was the first to cross it. I hung back, paralyzed by prudery, thinking even now that it would be an intrusion on my bondsister's maidenhood for me to enter her mind, and also a violation of the commandment against bodily intimacies between bond-kin. So I dangled in this absurd trap of contradictions, too inhibited to practice my own creed, for some moments after the last barriers had fallen; meanwhile Halum, realizing at last that nothing prevented her, slipped unhesitatingly into my spirit. My instant response was to try to shield myself: I did not want her to discover this or this or that, and particularly to learn of my physical desire for her. But after a moment of this embarrassed flurrying I ceased trying to plaster my soul with figleaves, and went across into Halum, allowing the true communion to begin, the inextricable entanglement of selves.

I found myself – it would be more accurate to say, I lost myself – in corridors with glassy floors and silvered walls, through which there played a cool sparkling light, like the crystalline brightness one sees reflected from the white sandy bottom of a shallow tropical cove. This was Halum's virginal inwardness. In niches along these corridors, neatly displayed, were the shaping factors of her life, memories, images, odors, tastes, visions, fantasies, disappointments, delights. A prevailing purity governed everything. I saw no trace of the sexual ecstasies, nothing of the fleshly passions. I cannot tell you whether Halum, out of modesty, took care to shield the area of her sexuality from my probings, or had thrust it so far from her own consciousness that I could not detect it.

She met me without fear and joined me in joy. I have no doubt of that. When our souls blended, it was a complete union, without reservation, without qualification. I swam through the glittering depths of her, and the grime of my soul dropped from me: she was healing, she was cleansing. Was I staining her even as she was refining and purifying me? I cannot say. I cannot say. We surrounded and engulfed one another, and supported one another, and interpenetrated one another; and here mingling with myself was the self of Halum, who all my life had been my staff and my courage, my ideal and my goal, this cool incorruptible perfect incarnation of beauty; and perhaps as this corruptible self of mine put on incorruption, the first corrosive plague sprouted on her shining incorruptibility. I cannot say. I came to her and she came to me. At one point in our journey through one another I encountered a zone of strangeness, where something seemed coiled and knotted: and I remembered that time in my youth, when I was setting out from Salla City on my flight into Glin, when Halum had embraced me at Noim's house, and I had thought I detected in her embrace a tremor of barely suppressed passion, a flicker of the hunger of the body. For me. For me. And I thought that I had found that zone of passion again, only when I looked more closely at it, it was gone, and I beheld the pure gleaming metallic surface of her soul. Perhaps both the first time and the second it was something I manufactured out of my own churning desires, and projected on her. I cannot say. Our souls were twined; I could not have known where I left off and Halum began.

We emerged from the trance. The night was half gone. We blinked, we shook our foggy heads, we smiled uneasily. There is always that moment, coming out of the drug's soul-intimacy, when one feels abashed, one thinks one has revealed too much, and one wants to retract what one has given. Fortunately that moment is usually brief. I looked at Halum and felt my body afire with holy love, a love that was not at all of the flesh, and I started to say to her, as Schweiz had once said to me, *I love you.* But I choked on the word. The 'I' was trapped in my teeth, like a fish in a weir. *I. I. I. I love you, Halum. I.* If I could only say it. *I.* It would not come. It was there, but could not get past my lips. I took her hands between mine, and she smiled a serene moonlike smile, and it would have been so easy then to hurl the words out, except that something imprisoned them. *I. I.* How could I speak to Halum of love, and couch my love in the syntax of the gutter? I thought then that she would not understand, that my obscenity would shatter everything. Foolishness: our souls had been one, how then could a mere phrasing of words disturb anything? Out with it! *I love you.* Faltering, I said, 'There is – such love in one – for you – such love, Halum—'

She nodded, as if to say, *Don't speak, your clumsy words break the spell.* As if to say, *Yes, there is in one such love for you also, Kinnall.* As if to say, *I love you, Kinnall.* Lightly she got to her feet, and went to the window: cold summer moonlight on the formal garden of the great house, the bushes and trees white and still. I came up behind her and touched her at the shoulders, very gently. She wriggled and made a little purring sound. I thought all was well with her. I was certain all was well with her.

We held no post-mortems on what had taken place between us this evening. That, too, seemed to threaten a puncturing of the mood. We could discuss our trance tomorrow, and all the tomorrows beyond that. I went with her back to her room, not far down the hallway from my own, and kissed her timidly on the cheek, and had a sisterly kiss from her; she smiled again, and closed the door behind her. In my own room I sat awhile awake, reliving everything. The missionary fervor was kindled anew in me. I would become an active messiah again, I vowed, going up and down this land of Salla spreading the creed of love; no more would I hide here at my bondbrother's place, broken and adrift, a hopeless exile in my own nation. Stirron's warning meant nothing to me. How could he drive me from Salla? I would make a hundred converts in a week. A thousand, ten thousand. I would give the drug to Stirron himself, and let the septarch proclaim the new dispensation from his own throne! Halum had inspired me. In the morning I would set out, seeking disciples.

There was a sound in the courtyard. I looked out and saw a groundcar:

Noim had returned from his business trip. He entered the house; I heard him in the hallway, passing my room; then there came the sound of knocking. I peered into the corridor. He stood by Halum's door, talking to her. I could not see her. What was this, that he would go to Halum, who was nothing but a friend to him, and fail to greet his own bondbrother? Unworthy suspicions woke in me – unreal accusations. I forced them away. The conversation ended; Halum's door closed; Noim, without noticing me, continued toward his own bedroom.

Sleep was impossible for me. I wrote a few pages, but they were worthless, and at dawn I went out to stroll in the gray mists. It seemed to me that I heard a distant cry. Some animal seeking its mate, I thought. Some lost beast wandering at daybreak.

66

I was alone at breakfast. That was unusual but not surprising: Noim, coming home in the middle of the night after a long drive, would have wanted to sleep late, and doubtless the drug had left Halum exhausted. My appetite was powerful, and I ate for the three of us, all the while planning my schemes for dissolving the Covenant. As I sipped my tea one of Noim's grooms burst wildly into the dining-hall. His cheeks were blazing and his nostrils were flared, as if he had run a long way and was close to collapse. 'Come,' he cried, gasping. 'The stormshields—' He tugged at my arm, half dragging me from my seat. I rushed out after him. He was already far down the unpaved road that led to the stormshield pens. I followed, wondering if the beasts had escaped in the night, wondering if I must spend the day chasing monsters again. As I neared the pens I saw no signs of a breakout, no clawed tracks, no torn fences. The groom clung to the bars of the biggest pen, which held nine or ten stormshields. I looked in. The animals were clustered, bloody-jawed, bloody-furred, around some ragged meaty haunch. They were snarling and quarreling over the feast scattered across the ground. Had some unfortunate farm beast strayed among these killers by darkness? How could such a thing have happened? And why would the groom see fit to haul me from my breakfast to show it to me? I caught his arm and asked him what was so strange about the sight of stormshields devouring their kill. He turned a terrible face to me and blurted in a strangled voice, 'The lady – the lady—'

67

Noim was brutal with me. 'You lied,' he said. 'You denied you were carrying the drug, but you lied. And you gave it to her last night. Yes? Yes? Yes? Don't hide anything now, Kinnall. You gave it to her!'

'You spoke with her,' I said. I could barely manage words. 'What did she tell you?'

'One stopped by her door, because one thought one heard the sound of sobbing,' Noim answered. 'One inquired if she was well. She came out: her face was strange, it was full of dreams, her eyes were as blank as pieces of polished metal, and yes, yes, she had been weeping. And one asked what was wrong, whether there had been any trouble here. No, she said, all was well. She said you and she had talked all evening. Why was she weeping, then? She shrugged and smiled again and closed the door. But that look in her eyes – it was the drug, Kinnall! Against all your vows, you gave it to her! And now – and now—'

'Please,' I said softly. But he went on shouting, loading me with accusations, and I could not reply.

The grooms had reconstructed everything. They had found the path of Halum's feet in the dew-moist sandy road. They had found the door ajar of the house that gives access to the stormshield pens. They had found marks of forcing on the inner door that leads to the feeding-gate itself. She had gone through; she had carefully opened the feeding-gate, and just as carefully closed it behind her, to loose no killers on the sleeping estate; then she had offered herself to the waiting claws. All this between darkness and dawn, perhaps even while I strolled in a different part. That cry out of the mists – Why? Why? Why? Why?

68

By early afternoon such few possessions as I had were packed. I asked Noim for the loan of a groundcar, and he granted it with a brusque wave of his fingers. There was no question of remaining here any longer. Not only were there echoes of Halum resonating everywhere about, but also I had to go apart, into some place where I could think undisturbed, and examine all that I had done and that I hoped to do. Nor did I wish to be here when the district police carried out their inquest into Halum's death.

Had she been unable to face me again, the morning after having given her soul away? She had gone gladly enough into the sharing of selves. But afterward, in that rush of guilty reappraisal that often follows the first opening, she may have felt another way: old habits of reticence reasserting themselves, a sudden cascading sense of horror at what she had revealed. And the quick irreversible decision, the frozen-faced trek to the stormshield pens, the ill-considered passing of the final gate, the moment of regret-within-regret as the animals pounced and she realized she had carried her atonement too far. Was that it? I could think of no other explanation for that plunge from serenity to despair, except that it was a second thought, a reflex of shock that swept her to doom. And I was without a bondsister, and had lost bondbrother too, for Noim's eyes were merciless when he looked at me. Was this what I had intended, when I dreamed of opening souls?

'Where will you go?' Noim asked. 'They'll jail you in Manneran. Take one step into Glin with your drug and you'll be flayed. Stirron will hound you out of Salla. Where, then, Kinnall? Threish? Velis? Or maybe Umbis, eh? Dabis? No! By the gods, it will be Sumara Borthan, won't it? Yes. Among your savages, and you'll have all the selfbaring you'll need there, yes? Yes?'

Quietly I said, 'You forget the Burnt Lowlands, Noim. A cabin in the desert – a place to think, a place of peace – there is so much one must try to understand, now—'

'The Burnt Lowlands? Yes, that's good, Kinnall. The Burnt Lowlands in high summer. A fiery purge for your soul. Go there, yes. Go.'

69

Alone, I drove northward along the flank of the Huishtors, and then westward, on the road that leads to Kongoroi and Salla's Gate. More than once I thought of swerving the car and sending it tumbling over the highway's rim, and making an end. More than once, as the first light of day touched my eyelids in some back-country hostelry, I thought of Halum and had to struggle to leave my bed, for it seemed so much easier to go on sleeping. Day and night and day and night and day, and a few days more, and I was deep into West Salla, ready to go up the mountains and through the gate. While resting one night in a town midway into the uplands I discovered that an order was out in Salla for my arrest. Kinnall Darival, the septarch's son, a man of thirty years, of this height and having these features, brother to the Lord Stirron, was wanted for monstrous crimes: selfbaring, and the use of a dangerous drug, which against the explicit orders of the septarch he was offering to the unwary. By means of this drug the fugitive Darival had driven his own bondsister insane and in her madness she had perished in a horrible way. Therefore all citizens of Salla were enjoined to apprehend the evildoer, for whom a heavy reward would be paid.

If Stirron knew why Halum had died, then Noim had told him everything. I was lost. When I reached Salla's Gate, I would find officers of the West Sallan constabulary waiting for me, for my destination was known. Yet in that case why had the announcement not informed the populace that I was heading for the Burnt Lowlands? Possibly Noim had held back some of what he knew, so that I could make an escape.

I had no choice but to go forward. It would take me days to reach the coast, and I would find all of Salla's ports alerted for me when I got there; even if I slipped on board a vessel, where would I go? Glin? Manneran? Similarly it was hopeless thinking of getting somehow across the Huish or the Woyn, into the neighboring provinces: I was already proscribed in Manneran, and surely I would find a chilly greeting in Glin. The Burnt Lowlands it would have to be, then. I would stay there some while, and then perhaps try to make my way out via one of the Threishtor passes, to start a new life on the western coast. Perhaps.

I brought provisions in the town, at a place that serves the needs of hunters entering the Lowlands: dried food, some weapons, and condensed water, enough to last me by careful expansion for several moontimes. As I made my purchases I thought the townsfolk were eyeing me strangely. Did they recognize me as the depraved prince whom the septarch sought? No one moved to seize me. Possibly they knew there was a cordon across Salla's Gate, and would take no risks with such a brute, when there were police in plenty to capture me on top of Kongoroi. Whatever the reason, I got out of the town unbothered, and set out now on the final stretch of the highway. In the past I had come this way only in winter, when snow lay deep; even now there were patches of dirty whiteness in shadowy corners, and as the road rose, the snow thickened, until near Kongoroi's double summit everything lay mantled in it. Timing my ascent carefully, I managed things so that I came to the great pass well after sundown, hoping that darkness would protect me in case of a roadblock. But the gate was unguarded. My car's lights were off as I drove the last distance – I half expected to go over the edge – and I made the familiar left turn, which brought me into Salla's Gate, and I saw no one there. Stirron had not had time to close the western border, or else he did not think I would be so mad as to flee that way. I went forward, and through the pass, and slowly down the switchbacks on the western face of Kongoroi, and when dawn overtook me I was into the Burnt Lowlands, choking in the heat, but safe.

70

Near the place where the hornfowl nest I found this cabin, about where I remembered it to be. It was without plumbing, nor were the walls even whole, yet it would do. It would do. The awful heat of the place would be my purge. I set up housekeeping inside, laying out my things, unpacking the journal-paper I had bought in the town for this record of my life and deeds, setting the jeweled case containing the last of the drug in a corner, piling my clothing above it, sweeping away the red sand. On my first full day of residence I busied myself camouflaging my groundcar, so that it would not betray my presence when searchers came: I drove it into a shallow ravine, so that its top barely broke the level of the ground, and collected woody ground-plants to make a covering for it, throwing sand atop the interwoven stems of the plants. Only sharp eyes would see the car when I was done. I made careful note of the place, lest I fail to find it myself when I was ready to leave.

For some days I simply walked the desert, thinking. I went to the place where the hornfowl struck my father down, and had no fear of the sharp-beaked circling birds: let them have me too. I considered the events of my time of changes, asking myself, *Is this what you wanted, Is this what you hoped to bring about, Does this satisfy you?* I relived each of my many soul sharings, from that with Schweiz to that with Halum, asking, *Was this good? Were there mistakes that could have been avoided? Did you gain, or did you lose, by what you did?* And I concluded that I had gained more than I had lost, although my losses had been terrible ones. My only regrets were for poor tactics, not for faulty principles. If I had stayed with Halum until her uncertainties had fled, she might not have given way to the shame that destroyed her. If I had been more open with Noim – if I had stayed in Manneran to confront my enemies – if – if – if – and yet, I had no regrets for having done my changing, but just that I had bungled my revolution of the soul. For I was convinced of the wrongness of the Covenant and of our way of life. Your way of life. That Halum had seen fit to kill herself after two hours of experiencing human love was the most scathing possible indictment of the Covenant.

And finally – not too many days ago – I began to write what you have been reading. My fluency surprised me; perhaps I verged even on glibness, though it was hard for me at first to use the grammar I imposed on myself. *I am Kinnall Darival and I mean to tell you all about myself.* So I began my memoir. Have I been true to that intent? Have I concealed anything? Day upon day my pen has scratched paper, and I have put myself down whole for you, with no cosmetic alterations of the record. In this sweatbox of a cabin have I laid myself bare. Meanwhile I have had no contact with the outside world, except for occasional hints, possibly irrational, that Stirron's agents are combing the Burnt Lowlands for me. I believe that guards are posted at the gates leading into Salla, Glin, and Manneran; and probably at the western passes as well; and also in Stroin Gap, in case I try to make my way to the Gulf of Sumar through the Wet Lowlands. My luck has held well, but soon they must find me. Shall I wait for them? Or shall I move on, trusting to fortune, hoping to find an unguarded exit? I have this thick manuscript. I value it now more than my life itself. If you could read it, if you could see how I have stumbled and staggered toward knowledge of self, if you could receive from it the vibrations of my mind – I have put everything down, I think, in this autobiography, in this record of self, in this document unique in the history of Velada Borthan. If I am captured here, my book will be captured with me, and Stirron will have it burned.

I must move on, then. But—

A sound? Engines?

A groundcar coming swiftly toward my cabin over the flat red land. I am found. It is done. At least I was able to write this much.

71

Five days have passed since the last entry, and I am still here. The groundcar was Noim's. He came not to arrest me but to rescue me. Cautiously, as if expecting me to open fire on him, he crept about my cabin, calling, 'Kinnall? Kinnall?' I went outside. He tried to smile, but he was too tense to manage it. He said, 'One thought you would be somewhere near this place. The place of the hornfowl – it still haunts you, eh?'

'What do you want?'

'Stirron's patrols are searching for you, Kinnall. Your path was traced as far as Salla's Gate. They know you're in the Burnt Lowlands. If Stirron knew you as well as your bondbrother does, he'd come straight here with his troops. Instead they're searching to the south, on the theory that you mean to go into the Wet Lowlands to the Gulf of Sumar, and get a ship to Sumara

Borthan. But they're bound to start hunting for you in this region once they discover you haven't been down there.'

'And then?'

'You'll be arrested. Tried. Convicted. Jailed or executed. Stirron thinks you're the most dangerous man on Velada Borthan.'

'I am,' I said.

Noim gestured toward the car. 'Get in. We'll slip through the blockade. Into West Salla, somehow, and down to the Woyn. The Duke of Sumar will meet you and put you aboard some vessel heading out. You can be in Sumara Borthan by next moonrise.'

'Why are you helping me, Noim? Why should you bother? I saw the hate in your eyes when I left you.'

'Hate? Hate? No, Kinnall, no hate, only sorrow. One is still your—' He paused. With an effort, he said, '*I'm* still your bondbrother. I'm pledged to your welfare. How can I let Stirron hunt you like a beast? Come. Come. I'll get you safely out of here.'

'No.'

'No?'

'We're certain to be caught. Stirron will have you, too, for aiding a fugitive. He'll seize your lands. He'll break your rank. Don't make a useless sacrifice for me, Noim.'

'I came all the way into the Burnt Lowlands to fetch you. If you think I'll go back without—'

'Let's not quarrel over it,' I said. 'Even if I escape, what is there for me? To spend the rest of my life hiding in the jungles of Sumara Borthan, among people whose language I can't speak and whose ways are alien to me? No. No. I'm tired of exile. Let Stirron take me.'

Persuading Noim to leave me here was no little task. We stood in the midday fire for eternal minutes, arguing vehemently. He was determined to effect this heroic rescue, despite the almost certain probability that we would both be captured. This he was doing out of a sense of duty, not out of love, for I could see that he still held Halum's death to my account. I would not have his disgrace scored against me as well, and told him so: he had done nobly to make this journey, but I could not go with him. Finally he began to yield, but only when I swore I would at least make some effort to save myself. I promised that I would set out for the western mountains, instead of sitting here where Stirron would surely find me. If I reached Velis or Threish safely, I said, I would notify Noim in some way, so that he would cease to fear my fate. And then I said, 'There is one thing you can do for me.' I brought my manuscript out of the cabin – a great heap of paper, red scribbling on grayish rough sheets. In this, I said, he would find the whole story: my entire self encapsulated, and all the events that had brought me to the Burnt Lowlands.

I asked him to read it, and to pass no judgment on me until he had. 'You will find things in here that will horrify and disgust you,' I warned him. 'But I think you'll also find much that will open your eyes and your soul. Read it, Noim. Read it with care. Think about my words.' And I asked one last vow of him, by our oath of bonding: that he keep my book safely preserved, even if the temptation came over him to burn it. 'These pages hold my soul,' I told him. 'Destroy the paper and you destroy me. If you loathe what you read, hide the book away, but do no harm to it. What shocks you now may not shock you a few years from now. And someday you may want to show my book to others, so that you can explain what manner of man your bond-brother was, and why he did what he did.' *And so that you may change them as I hope my book will change you*, I said silently. Noim vowed this vow. He took my sheaf of pages and stored them in the hold of his groundcar. We embraced; he asked me again if I would not ride away with him; again I refused; I made him say once more that he would read my book and preserve it; once more he swore he would; then he entered the groundcar and drove slowly toward the east. I entered the cabin. The place where I had kept my manuscript was empty, and I felt a sudden hollowness, I suppose much like that of a woman who has carried a child for the full seven moontimes and now finds her belly flat again. I had poured all of myself into those pages. Now I was nothing, and the book was all. Would Noim read it? I thought so. And would he preserve it? Very likely he would, though he might hide it in the darkest corner of his house. And would he someday show it to others? This I do not know. But if you have read what I have written, it is through the kindness of Noim Condorit; and if he has let it be read, then I have prevailed over his soul after all, as I hope to prevail over yours.

72

I had said to Noim that I would remain in the cabin no longer, but would set out for the west in an attempt to save myself. Yet I found myself unwilling to leave. The sweltering shack had become my home. I stayed a day, and another day, and a third, doing nothing, wandering the blazing solitude of the Burnt Lowlands, watching the hornfowl circle. On the fifth day, as you perhaps are able to see, I fell into the habit of autobiography again, and sat down at the place where I had lately spent so many hours sitting, and wrote a few new pages to describe my visit from Noim. Then I let three days more go by, telling myself that on the fourth I would dig my groundcar out of the red sand and head westward. But on the morning of that fourth day Stirron and his men found my hiding place, and now it is the evening of that day, and I have an hour or two more to write, by the grace of the Lord Stirron. And when I have done with this, I will write no more.

73

They came in six well-armed groundcars, and surrounded my cabin, and called on me through loudspeakers to surrender. I had no hope of resisting them, nor any desire to try. Calmly – for what use was fear? – I showed myself, hands upraised, at the cabin door. They got out of their cars, and I was amazed to find Stirron himself among them, drawn out of his palace into the Lowlands for an out-of-season hunting party with his brother as quarry. He wore all his finery of office. Slowly he walked toward me. I had not seen him in some years, and I was appalled by the signs of age on him: shoulders rounded, head thrust forward, hair thinning, face deeply lined, eyes yellowed and dim. The profits of half a lifetime of supreme power. We regarded one another in silence, like two strangers seeking a point of contact. I tried to find in him that boy, my playmate, my elder brother, whom I had loved and lost so long ago, and I saw only a grim old man with trembling lips. A septarch is trained to mask his inner feelings, yet Stirron was able to hold nothing secret from me, nor could he keep one consistent expression: I saw his face, one look tumbling across the other, tokens of imperial rage, bewilderment, sorrow, contempt, and something that I took to be a sort of suppressed love. At length I spoke first, inviting him into my cabin for a conference. He hesitated, perhaps thinking I had assassination in mind, but after a moment he accepted in right kingly manner, waving to his bodyguard to wait outside. When we were alone within, there was another silent spell, which this time he broke, saying, 'One has never felt such pain, Kinnall. One scarcely believes what one has heard about you. That you should stain our father's memory—'

'Is it such a stain, Lord Septarch?'

'To foul the Covenant? To corrupt the innocent – your bondsister among the victims? What have you been doing, Kinnall? *What have you been doing?*'

A terrible fatigue came over me, and I closed my eyes, for I scarcely knew where to begin explaining. After a moment I found strength. I reached toward him, smiling, taking his hand, and said, 'I love you, Stirron.'

'How sick you are!'

'To talk of love? But we came out of the same womb! Am I not to love you?'

'Is this how you talk now, only in filth?'

'I talk as my heart commands me.'

'You are not only sick but sickening,' said Stirron. He turned away and spat on the sandy floor. He seemed a remote medieval figure to me, trapped behind his dour kingly face, imprisoned in his jewels of office and his robes of state, speaking in gruff, distant tones. How could I reach him?

I said, 'Stirron, take the Sumaran drug with me. I have a little left. I'll mix it for us, and we'll drink it together, and in an hour or two our souls will be one, and you'll understand. I swear, you'll understand. Will you do it? Kill me afterward, if you still want to, but take the drug first.' I began to bustle about, making ready the potion. Stirron caught my wrist and halted me. He shook his head with the slow, heavy gesture of one who feels an infinite sadness. 'No,' he said. 'Impossible.'

'Why?'

'You will not fuddle the mind of the prime septarch.'

'I'm interested in *reaching* the mind of my brother Stirron!'

'As your brother, one wishes only that you may be healed. As prime septarch, one must avoid harm, for one belongs to one's people.'

'The drug is harmless, Stirron,'

'Was it harmless for Halum Helalam?'

'Are you a frightened virgin?' I asked. 'I've given the drug to scores of people. Halum is the only one who reacted badly – Noim too, I suppose, but he got over it. And—'

'The two people in the world closest to you,' said Stirron, 'and the drug harmed them both. Now you offer it to your brother?'

It was hopeless. I asked him again, several times, to risk an experiment with the drug, but of course he would not touch it. And if he had, would it have availed me anything? I would have found only iron in his soul.

I said, 'What will happen to me now?'

'A fair trial, followed by an honest sentence.'

'Which will be what? Execution? Imprisonment for life? Exile?'

Stirron shrugged. 'It is for the court to decide. Do you take one for a tyrant?'

'Stirron, why does the drug frighten you so? Do you know what it does? Can I make you see that it brings only love and understanding? There's no need for us to live as strangers to each other, with blankets around our souls. We can speak ourselves out. We can reach forth. We can say "I," Stirron, and not have to apologize for having selves. *I. I. I.* We can tell each other what gives us pain, and help each other to escape that pain.' His face darkened; I think he was sure I was mad. I went past him, to the place where I had put down the drug, and quickly mixed it, and offered a flask to him. He shook his head. I drank, impulsively gulping it, and offered the flask again to him. 'Go on,' I said. 'Drink. Drink! It won't begin for a while. Take it now, so we'll be open at the same time. Please, Stirron!'

'I could kill you myself,' he said, 'without waiting for the court to act.'

'Yes! Say it, Stirron! I! Myself! Say it again!'

'Miserable selfbarer. My father's son! If I talk to you in "I," Kinnall, it's because you deserve no better than filth from me.'

'It doesn't need to be filth. Drink, and understand.'

'Never.'

'Why do you oppose it, Stirron? What frightens you?'

'The Covenant is sacred,' he said. 'To question the Covenant is to question the whole social order. Turn this drug of yours loose in the land and all reason collapses, all stability is lost. Do you think our forefathers were villains? Do you think they were fools? Kinnall, they understood how to create a lasting society. Where are the cities of Sumara Borthan? Why do they still live in jungle huts, while we have built what we have built? You'd put us on their road, Kinnall. You'd break down the distinctions between right and wrong, so that in a short while law itself would be washed away, and every man's hand would be lifted against his fellow, and where would be your love and universal understanding then? No, Kinnall. Keep your drug. One still prefers the Covenant.'

'Stirron—'

'Enough. The heat is intolerable. You are arrested; now let us go.'

74

Because the drug was in me, Stirron agreed to let me have a few hours alone, before we began the journey back to Salla, so that I would not have to travel while my soul was vulnerable to external sensations. A small mercy from the lord septarch: he posted two men as guards outside my cabin, and went off with the others to hunt hornfowl until the coming of dusk.

Never had I taken the drug without a sharer. So the strangenesses came upon me and I was alone with them, to hear the throbbings and the whinings and the rushings, and then, as the walls fell away from my soul, there was no one for me to enter, and no one to enter me. Yet I could detect the souls of my guards – hard, closed, metallic – and I felt that with some effort

I could reach even into them. But I did not, for as I sat by myself I was launched on a miraculous voyage, my self expanding and soaring until I encompassed this our entire planet, and all the souls of mankind were merged into mine. And a wondrous vision came upon me. I saw my bondbrother Noim making copies of my memoir, and distributing them to those he could trust, and other copies were made from those, to circulate through the provinces of Velada Borthan. And out of the southern land now came shiploads of the white powder, sought not merely by an elite, not only by the Duke of Sumar and the Marquis of Woyn, but by thousands of ordinary citizens, by people hungry for love, by those who found the Covenant turning to ashes, those who wished to reach one another's souls. And though the guardians of the old order did what they could to halt the movement, it could not be stopped, for the former Covenant had run its course, and now it was clear that love and gladness could no longer be suppressed. Until at last a network of communication existed, shining filaments of sensory perception linking one to one to one to all. Until at last even the septarchs and the justiciars were swept up in the tide of liberation, and all the world joined in joyous communion, each of us open to all, and the time of changes was complete; the new Covenant was established. I saw all this from my shabby cabin in the Burnt Lowlands. I saw the bright glow encompassing the world, shimmering, flickering, gaining power, deepening in hue. I saw walls crumbling. I saw the brilliant red blaze of universal love. I saw new faces, changed and exultant. Hands touching hands. Selves touching selves. This vision blazed in my soul for half a day, filling me with joy such as I had never experienced at any time, and my soaring spirit wandered in realms of dream. And only as the drug began to ebb from me did I realize that it was nothing but a fantasy.

Perhaps it will not always be a fantasy. Perhaps Noim will find readers for what I have written, and perhaps others will be persuaded to follow my path, until there are enough like me, and the changes become irreversible and universal. It has happened before. I will disappear, I the forerunner, I the anticipator, I the martyred prophet. But what I have written will live, and through me you will be changed. It may yet be that this is no idle dream.

This final page has been set down as twilight descends. The sun hastens toward the Huishtors. Soon, as Stirron's prisoner, I will follow it. I will take this little manuscript with me, hidden somewhere about me, and if I have good fortune I will find some way of giving it to Noim, so that it can be joined to the pages he has already had from me. I cannot say if I will succeed, nor do I know what will become of me and of my book. And you who read this are unknown to me. But I can say this: If the two parts have become one, and you read me complete, you may be sure that I have begun to prevail. Out of that joining can come only changes for Velada Borthan, changes for all of you. If you have read this far, you must be with me in soul. So I say to you, my unknown reader, that I love you and reach my hand toward you, I who was Kinnall Darival, I who have opened the way, I who promised to tell you all about myself, and who now can say that the promise has been fulfilled. Go and seek. Go and touch. Go and love. Go and be open. Go and be healed.

LORD VALENTINE'S CASTLE

For David Hartwell
Page Cuddy
John Bush
– they pushed very gently

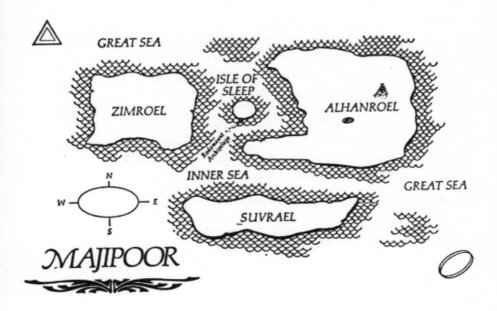

GREAT SEA

ZIMROEL

ISLE OF
SLEEP

ALHANROEL

GREAT SEA

INNER SEA

Rodamaunt Archipelago

N

W   E

S

SUVRAEL

MAJIPOOR

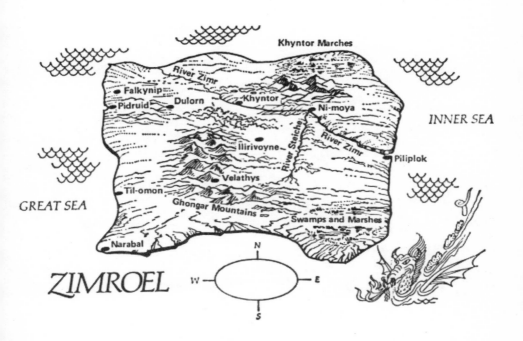

Khyntor Marches

River Zimr

Falkynip

Pidruid   Dulorn   Khyntor

Ni-moya

INNER SEA

Ilirivoyne   River Steiche   River Zimr

Piliplok

Velathys

Til-omon

Ghongar Mountains

Swamps and Marshes

GREAT SEA

Narabal

N

W   E

S

ZIMROEL

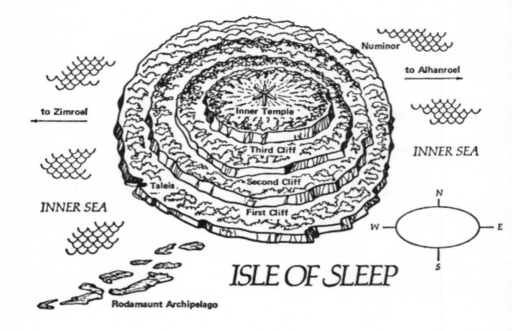

Numinor

to Alhanroel →

← to Zimroel

Inner Temple

Third Cliff

Second Cliff

Taleis

First Cliff

INNER SEA

INNER SEA

ISLE OF SLEEP

Rodamaunt Archipelago

N
W — E
S

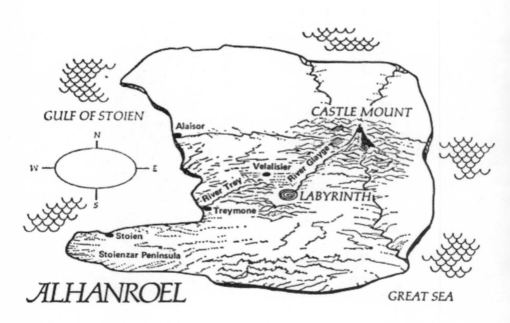

GULF OF STOIEN

CASTLE MOUNT

Alaisor

N
1V — E
S

Velalisier

River Glayge

River Trey

LABYRINTH

Treymone

Stoien

Stoienzar Peninsula

ALHANROEL

GREAT SEA

CASTLE

SLAYGE VALLEY AND
CASTLE MOUNT

Amblemorn

Makroprosopos

Velalisier

Pendiwane

River Glayge

Lake Roghoiz

LABYRINTH

N

W

E

S

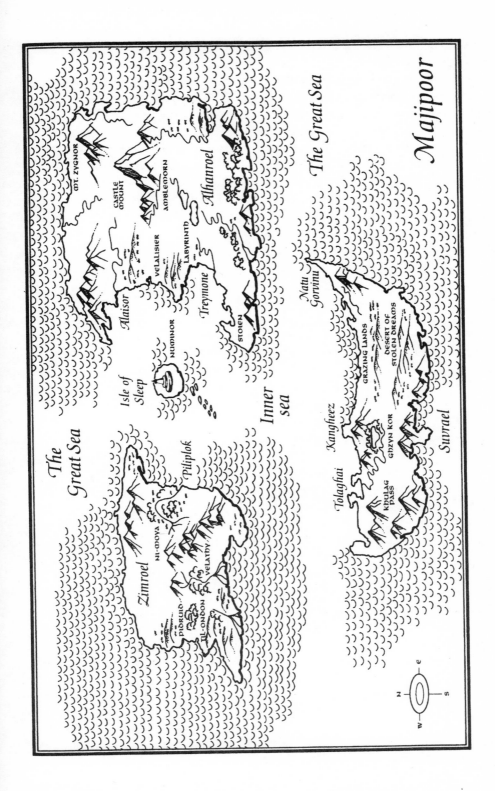

PART I

The Book of
the King of Dreams

1

And then, after walking all day through a golden haze of humid warmth that gathered about him like fine wet fleece, Valentine came to a great ridge of outcropping white stone overlooking the city of Pidruid. It was the provincial capital, sprawling and splendid, the biggest city he had come upon since – since? – the biggest in a long while of wandering, at any rate.

There he halted, finding a seat at the edge of the soft, crumbling white ridge, digging his booted feet into the flaking ragged stone, and he sat there staring down at Pidruid, blinking as though newly out of sleep. On this summer day twilight was still some hours away, and the sun hung high to the southwest beyond Pidruid, out over the Great Sea. I will rest here for a while, Valentine thought, and then I will go down into Pidruid and find lodging for the night.

As he rested he heard pebbles tumbling past him from a higher point on the ridge. Unhurriedly he looked back the way he had come. A young herdsman had appeared, a boy with straw-colored hair and a freckled face, leading a train of fifteen or twenty mounts down the hill road. They were fat sleek purple-skinned beasts, obviously well looked after. The boy's own mount looked older and less plump, a wise and toughened creature.

'Hoy!' he called down to Valentine. 'Where are you bound?'

'Pidruid. And you?'

'The same. Bringing these mounts to market. Thirsty work it is, too. Do you have wine?'

'Some,' Valentine said. He tapped the flask at his hip, where a fiercer man might wear a weapon. 'Good red mid-country wine. I'll be sorry to see the last of it.'

'Give me a drink and I'll let you ride into town with me.'

'Done,' said Valentine.

He got to his feet as the boy dismounted and scrambled down the ridge toward him. Valentine offered him the flask. The boy was no more than fourteen or fifteen, he guessed, and small for his age, though deep through the chest and brawny. He came hardly elbow-high to Valentine, who was tall but not unusually so, a sturdy man just above middle height, with wide flat shoulders and big capable hands.

The boy swirled the wine in the flask, inhaled in a knowing way, nodded his approval, took a deep gulp, sighed. 'I've been eating dust all the way from

Falkynkip! And this sticky heat – it chokes you! Another dry hour and I'd have been a dead one.' He returned the wine to Valentine. 'You live in town?'

Valentine frowned. 'No.'

'Here for the festival, then?'

'Festival?'

'You don't know?'

Valentine shook his head. He felt the pressure of the boy's bright, mocking eyes, and was confused. 'I've been traveling. I haven't followed the news. Is this festival time in Pidruid?'

'This week it is,' said the boy. 'Beginning on Starday. The grand parade, the circus, the royal celebration. Look down there. Don't you see *him* entering the city even now?'

He pointed. Valentine sighted along the boy's outstretched arm and squinted, peering at Pidruid's southern corner, but all he saw was a jumble of green-tiled rooftops and a tangle of ancient streets following no rational plan. Again he shook his head. 'There,' the boy said impatiently. 'Down by the harbor. See? The ships? The five tremendous ones, with *his* banner flying from the rigging? And there's the procession, coming through Dragon Gate, just beginning to march Black Highway. I think that's his chariot, coming up now by the Arch of Dreams. Don't you see? Is there something wrong with your eyes?'

'I don't know the city,' said Valentine mildly. 'But yes, I see the harbor, the five ships.'

'Good. Now follow along inland a little way – the big stone gate? And the wide highway running through it? And that ceremonial arch, just this side of—'

'I see it now, yes.'

'And his banner over the chariot?'

'Whose banner? If I sound dim, forgive me, but—'

'Whose? Whose? Lord Valentine's banner! Lord Valentine's chariot! Lord Valentine's bodyguard marching through the streets of Pidruid! Don't you know the Coronal has arrived?'

'I didn't.'

'And the festival! Why do you think there's a festival at this time of summer, if not to welcome the Coronal?'

Valentine smiled. 'I've been traveling and I haven't followed the news. Would you like more wine?'

'There's not much left,' the boy said.

'Go on. Finish it. I'll buy more in Pidruid.'

He handed over the flask and turned toward the city again, letting his gaze travel down the slope and across the woodsy suburbs to the dense and teeming city, and outward toward the waterfront, and to the great ships, the banners, the marching warriors, the chariot of the Coronal. This must be a great moment in the history of Pidruid, for the Coronal ruled from far-off Castle Mount, all the way on the other side of the world, so distant that he and it were almost legendary, distances being what they were on this world of Majipoor. Coronals of Majipoor did not come often to the western continent. But Valentine was oddly unmoved by the knowledge of the presence of his glittering namesake down below there. I am here and the Coronal is here, he thought, and he will sleep tonight in some splendid palace of the masters of Pidruid, and I will sleep in some pile of hay, and then there will be a grand festival, and what is that to me? He felt almost apologetic, being so placid in the face of the boy's excitement. It was a discourtesy.

He said, 'Forgive me. I know so little of what's been happening in the world these past months. Why is the Coronal here?'

'He makes the grand processional,' said the boy. 'To every part of the realm, to mark his coming to power. This is the new one, you know. Lord Valentine, only two years on his throne. The brother to Lord Voriax who died. You knew that, that Lord Voriax was dead, that Lord Valentine was our Coronal?'

'I had heard,' said Valentine vaguely.

'Well, that's he, down there in Pidruid. Touring the realm for the first time since he got the Castle. He's been down south all month, in the jungle provinces, and yesterday he sailed up the coast to Pidruid, and tonight he enters the city, and in a few days there'll be the festival, and food and drink for everyone, games, dancing, delights, a great market too, where I'll sell these animals for a fortune. Afterward he travels overland through the whole continent of Zimroel, from capital to capital, a journey of so many thousands of miles it makes my head ache to think of it, and from the eastern shore he'll sail back to Alhanroel and Castle Mount, and none of us in Zimroel will see him again for twenty years or more. A fine thing it must be to be Coronal!' The boy laughed. 'That was good wine. My name's Shanamir. What's yours?'

'Valentine.'

'Valentine? *Valentine?* An auspicious name!'

'A common one, I'm afraid.'

'Put *Lord* in front of it and you'd be the Coronal!'

'It's not as easy as that. Besides, why would I want to be Coronal?'

'The power,' said Shanamir, wide-eyed. 'The fine clothes, the food, the wine, the jewels, the palaces, the women—'

'The responsibility,' Valentine said somberly. 'The burden. Do you think a Coronal does nothing but drink golden wine and march in grand processions? Do you think he's put there just to enjoy himself?'

The boy considered. 'Perhaps not.'

'He rules over billions upon billions of people, across territories so huge we can't comprehend them. Everything falls on his shoulders. To carry out the decrees of the Pontifex, to sustain order, to support justice in every land – it tires me to think of it, boy. He keeps the world from collapsing into chaos. I don't envy him. Let him have the job.'

Shanamir said, after a moment, 'You're not as stupid as I first thought, Valentine.'

'Did you think I was stupid, then?'

'Well, simple. Easy of mind. Here you are a grown man, and you seem to know so little of certain things, and I half your age and I have to explain. But perhaps I misjudge you. Shall we go down into Pidruid?'

2

Valentine had his pick of the mounts the boy was taking to the market; but they all seemed alike to him, and after making a pretense of choosing he picked one at random, vaulting lightly into the creature's natural saddle. It was good to ride, after so long on foot. The mount was comfortable, as well it might be, for they had been bred for comfort for thousands of years, these artificial animals, these witchcraft-creatures out of the old days, strong and tireless and patient, able to convert any sort of trash into food. The skill of making them was long forgotten, but now they bred of themselves, like natural animals, and it would be a slow business getting about on Majipoor without them.

The road to Pidruid led along the high ridge for more than a mile, then began sudden sharp switchbacks down into the coastal plain. Valentine let the boy do most of the talking as they made the descent. Shanamir came, he said, from a district two and a half days' journey inland, to the northeast; there he and his brothers and his father raised mounts for sale at Pidruid market, and turned a good living at it; he was thirteen years old, and had a high opinion of himself; he had never been outside the province of which Pidruid was the capital, but someday he meant to go abroad, to travel every-where on Majipoor, to make the pilgrimage to the Isle of Sleep and kneel before the Lady, to cross the Inner Sea to Alhanroel and achieve the ascent of Castle Mount, even to go down south, maybe, beyond the steaming trop-ics, into the burnt and barren domain of the King of Dreams, for what was the use of being alive and healthy on a world as full of wonders as Majipoor if you did not journey hither and thither about on it?

'And you, Valentine?' he asked suddenly. 'Who are you, where from, whither bound?'

Valentine was caught by surprise, lulled by the boy's prattle and the steady gentle rhythm of the mount as it padded down the broad twisting road, and the burst of jabbing questions left him unprepared. He said only, 'I come from the eastern provinces, I have no plans beyond Pidruid. I'll stay here until I have reason to leave.'

'Why have you come?'

'Why not?'

'Ah,' said Shanamir. 'All right. I know purposeful evasion when I hear it. You're the younger son of a duke in Ni-moya or Piliplok, and you sent someone a mischievous dream and were caught at it, and your father gave you a pouch of money and told you to vanish to the far side of the continent. Right?'

'Precisely,' Valentine said, with a wink.

'And you're loaded with royals and crowns and you're going to set yourself up like a prince in Pidruid and drink and dance until your last coin is gone, and then you'll hire aboard a seagoing vessel and ship out for Alhanroel, and you'll take me with you as your squire. Isn't that so?'

'You have it exactly, my friend. Except for the money. I neglected to provide for that part of your fantasy.'

'But you have *some* money,' said Shanamir, not so playfully now. 'You aren't a beggar, are you? They're very hard on beggars in Pidruid. They don't allow any sort of vagrancy down there.'

'I have a few coins,' Valentine said. 'Enough to carry me through festival time and a bit beyond. And then I'll see.'

'If you do go to sea, take me with you, Valentine.'

'If I do, I will,' he promised.

They were halfway down the slope now. The city of Pidruid lay in a great basin along the coast, rimmed by low gray hills on the inland side and along much of the shore, save only where a break in the outer range allowed the ocean to spill through, forming a blue-green bay that was Pidruid's magnificent harbor. As he approached sea level here in late afternoon Valentine felt the offshore breezes blowing toward him, cool, fragrant, breaking the heat. Already white shoals of fog were rolling toward the shore out of the west, and there was a salty tang to the air, thick as it was now with water that had embraced the fishes and sea-dragons only hours before. Valentine was awed by the size of the city that lay before him. He could not remember ever having seen a larger one; but there was so much, after all, that he could not remember.

This was the edge of the continent. All of Zimroel lay at his back, and for all he knew he had walked it from end to end, from one of the eastern ports indeed, Ni-moya or Piliplok, except that he knew himself to be a young man, not very young but young enough, and he doubted that it was possible to have made such a journey on foot in one lifetime, and he had no recollection of having been on any sort of mount until this afternoon. On the other hand, he seemed to know how to ride, he had lifted himself knowledgeably into the beast's broad saddle, and that argued that he must have ridden at least part of the way before. It did not matter. He was here now, and he felt no restlessness; since Pidruid was where he had somehow arrived, Pidruid was where he would stay, until there was reason to go elsewhere. He lacked Shanamir's hunger for travel. The world was so big it did not bear thinking about, three great continents, two enormous seas, a place that one could comprehend fully only in dreams, and even then not bring much of the truth of it away into the waking world. They said this Lord Valentine the Coronal lived in a castle eight thousand years old, with five rooms for every year of its existence, and that the castle sat upon a mountain so tall it pierced the sky, a colossal peak thirty miles high, on whose slopes were fifty cities as big as Pidruid. Such a thing as that did not bear much thought either. The world was too big, too old, too populous for one man's mind. I will live in this city of Pidruid, Valentine thought, and I will find a way to pay for my food and lodging, and I will be happy.

'Naturally you don't have a bed reserved in an inn,' Shanamir said.

'Of course not.'

'It stands to reason you wouldn't. And naturally everything in town is full, this being festival time and the Coronal already here. So where will you sleep, Valentine?'

'Anywhere. Under a tree. On a mound of rags. In the public park. That looks like a park there, over to the right, that stretch of green with the tall trees.'

'You remember what I told you about vagrants in Pidruid? They'll find you and lock you deep for a month, and when they let you out they'll have you sweeping dung until you can buy your way out of your fine, which at the pay of a dung-sweeper will take you the rest of your life.'

'At least dung-sweeping's steady work,' Valentine said.

Shanamir didn't laugh. 'There's an inn the mount-sellers stay at. I'm known there, or rather my father is. We'll get you in somehow. But what would you have done without me?'

'Become a dung-sweeper, I suppose.'

'You sound as though you really wouldn't mind.' The boy touched his mount's ear, halting it, and looked closely at him. 'Doesn't *anything* matter to you, Valentine? I don't understand you. Are you a fool, or simply the most carefree man on Majipoor?'

'I wish I knew,' said Valentine.

At the foot of the hill the ridge road joined with a grand highway that came running down out of the north and curved westward toward Pidruid. The new road, wide and straight along the valley floor, was rimmed with low white markers stamped with the double crest of Pontifex and Coronal, the labyrinth and the starburst, and was paved in smooth blue-gray stuff of light resiliency, a springy, flawless roadbed that probably was of great antiquity, as were so many of the best things of this world. The mounts plodded tirelessly. Synthetic things that they were, they scarcely understood fatigue, and would clop from Pidruid to Piliplok without resting and without complaining. From time to time Shanamir glanced back, checking for strays, since the beasts were not tied; but they remained blandly in their places, one after another, blunt snout of one close behind coarse ropy tail of another, along the flank of the highway.

Now the sun was faintly tinged with late-day bronze, and the city lay close before them. A stunning sight presented itself in this part of the road: on both shoulders of it had been planted noble trees, twenty times the height of a man, with slim tapering trunks of dark bluish bark and mighty crowns of glistening greenish-black leaves sharp as daggers. Out of those crowns burst astounding clusters of bloom, red tipped with yellow, that blazed like beacons as far as Valentine could see.

'What are those trees?' he asked.

'Fireshower palms,' Shanamir said. 'Pidruid is famous for them. They grow only near the coast and flower just one week a year. In the winter they drop sour berries, that make a strong liquor. You'll drink it tomorrow.'

'The Coronal has picked a good moment to come here, then.'

'Not by chance, I imagine.'

On and on the twin column of brilliant trees stretched, and they followed along, until open fields yielded to the first country villas, and then suburban tracts thick with more modest homes, and then a dusty zone of small factories, and finally the ancient wall of Pidruid itself, half as high as a fireshower tree, pierced by a pointed arch set with archaic-looking battlements. 'Falkynkip Gate,' Shanamir announced. 'The eastern entrance to Pidruid. Now we enter the capital. Eleven million souls here, Valentine, and all the races of Majipoor to be found, not just humans, no, everything here, all mixed together, Skandars and Hjorts and Liimen and all the rest. Even, so they say, a little group of Shapeshifters.'

'Shapeshifters?'

'The old race. The first natives.'

'We call them something else,' Valentine said vaguely. '*Metamorphs*, is it?'

'The same. Yes. I've heard they're called that in the east. You have a strange accent, do you know that?'

'No stranger than yours, friend.'

Shanamir laughed. 'To me your accent's strange. And I have no accent at all. I speak normal speech. You shape your words with fancy sounds. "*We call them Metamorphs,*"' he said, mimicking. 'That's how you sound to me. Is that Ni-moyan talk?'

Valentine replied only with a shrug.

Shanamir said, 'They frighten me, Shapeshifters. Metamorphs. This would be a happier planet without them. Sneaking around, imitating others, working mischief. I wish they would keep to their own territory.'

'Mostly they do, is that not so?'

'Mostly. But they say a few live in each city. Plotting who knows what kind of trouble for the rest of us.' Shanamir leaned across toward Valentine, caught his arm, peered solemnly into his face. 'One might meet one anywhere. Sitting on a ridge looking out toward Pidruid on a hot afternoon, for example.'

'So you think I'm a Metamorph in masquerade?'

The boy cackled. 'Prove that you aren't!'

Valentine groped for some way to demonstrate his authenticity, found none, and made a terrifying face instead, stretching his cheeks as though they were rubber, twisting his lips in opposite directions, rolling his eyeballs high. 'My true visage,' he said. 'You have discovered me.' And they laughed, and passed on through Falkynkip Gate into the city of Pidruid.

Within the gate everything seemed much older, the houses built in a curious angular style, humpbacked walls swelling outward and upward to tiled roofs, and the tiles themselves often chipped and broken, and interspersed with heavy clumps of low fleshy-leaved roof-weeds that had gained footholds in cracks and earthy pockets. A heavy layer of fog hovered over the city, and it was dark and cool beneath it, with lights glowing in almost every window. The main highway split, and split again, until now Shanamir was leading his animals down a much narrower street, though still a fairly straight one, with secondary streets coiling off from it in every direction. The streets were thick with folk. Such crowds made Valentine obscurely uncomfortable; he could not recall having had so many others so close about him at once, almost at his elbow, smack up against his mount, pushing, darting about, a jostling mob of porters, merchants, mariners, vendors, people from the hill country like Shanamir bringing animals or produce to the market, tourists in fine robes of glowing brocades, and little boys and girls underfoot everywhere. Festival time in Pidruid! Gaudy banners of scarlet cloth were strung across the street from the upper stories of buildings, two and three on every block, emblazoned with the starburst crest, hailing in bright green lettering Lord Valentine the Coronal, bidding him be welcome to this his westernmost metropolis.

'Is it far to your inn?' Valentine asked.

'Halfway across town. Are you hungry?'

'A little. More than a little.'

Shanamir signaled to his beasts and they marched obediently into a cobbled cul-de-sac between two arcades, where he left them. Then, dismounting, he pointed out a tiny grimy booth across the street. Skewered sausages hung grilling over a charcoal flame. The counterman was a Liiman, squat and hammer-headed, with pocked gray-black skin and three eyes that glowed like coals in a crater. The boy pantomimed, and the Liiman passed two skewers of sausages to them, and poured tumblers of pale amber beer. Valentine produced a coin and laid it on the counter. It was a fine thick coin, bright and gleaming, with a milled edge, and the Liiman looked at it as though Valentine had offered him a scorpion. Hastily Shanamir scooped up the piece and put down one of his own, a squarish coppery coin with a triangular hole punched in the center. The other he returned to Valentine. They retreated to the cul-de-sac with their dinner.

'What did I do wrong?' Valentine asked.

'With that coin you could buy the Liiman and all his sausages, and a month of beer! Where did you get it?'

'Why, from my purse.'

'Are there more like that in there?'

'It could be,' said Valentine. He studied the coin, which bore on one face the image of an old man, gaunt and withered, and on the other the visage of a young and vigorous one. The denomination was fifty royals. 'Will this be too valuable to use anywhere?' he asked. 'What will it buy, in truth?'

'Five of my mounts,' Shanamir said. 'A year's lodgings in princely style. Transportation to Alhanroel and back. Any of those. Perhaps even more. To most of us it would be many months' wages. You have no idea of the value of things?'

Valentine looked abashed. 'It would seem that way.'

'These sausages cost ten weights. A hundred weights make a crown, ten crowns make a royal, and this is fifty of those. Now do you follow? I'll change it for you at the market. Meanwhile keep it to yourself. This is an honest city and a safe one, more or less, but with a purse full of those you tempt fate. Why didn't you tell me you were carrying a fortune?' Shanamir gestured broadly. 'Because you didn't know, I suppose. There's such a strange innocence about you, Valentine. You make me feel like a man, and I'm only a boy. You seem so much like a child. Do you know anything? Do you even know how old you are? Finish your beer and let's move along.'

Valentine nodded. One hundred weights to a crown, he thought, ten crowns to a royal, and he wondered what he would have said had Shanamir pressed him on the matter of his age. Twenty-eight? Thirty-two? He had no idea. What if he were asked in earnest? Thirty-two, he decided. That had a good sound to it. Yes, I am thirty-two years old, and ten crowns make a royal, and the shining piece that shows the old man and the young one is worth fifty of those.

3

The road to Shanamir's inn led squarely through the heart of Pidruid, across districts that even at this late hour were crowded and hectic. Valentine asked if that was on account of the visit of the Coronal, but Shanamir said no, the city was like this all the time, for it was the major port of the western coast of Zimroel. From here went vessels to every major port of Majipoor: up and down this busy coast, but also across the Inner Sea on the enormous journey to Alhanroel, a voyage requiring the better part of a year, and there was even some commerce with the sparsely populated southern continent, Suvrael, the sun-blasted lair of the King of Dreams. When Valentine thought of the totality of Majipoor he felt oppressed by the weight of the world, the sheer mass of it, and yet he knew that was foolish, for was not Majipoor a light and airy place, a giant bubble of a planet, huge but without much substance, so that one felt forever buoyant, forever afloat? Why this leaden sense of pressure across his back, why these moments of unfounded dismay? He led himself quickly back to an easier mood. Soon he would sleep, and the morning would be a day of new marvels.

'We cross the Golden Plaza,' said Shanamir, 'and on the far side of it we take Water Road, that leads to the piers, and our inn is ten minutes out that way. You'll find the plaza amazing.'

Indeed it was, such of it as Valentine was able to see: a vast rectangular space, wide enough to drill two armies in, bordered on all four sides by immense square-topped buildings on whose broad flat faces were inlaid dazzling designs in gold leaf, so that by the evening's torchlight the great towers blazed with reflected light and were more brilliant than the fireshower trees. But there was no crossing the plaza tonight. A hundred paces from its eastern entrance it was roped off with thick braided cord of red plush, behind which stood troops in the uniform of the Coronal's bodyguard, smug, impassive, arms folded across their green-and-gold jerkins. Shamamir leaped from his mount and trotted forward, and spoke quickly with a vendor. When he returned he said angrily, 'They have it entirely blocked. May the King of Dreams send them prickly sleep tonight!'

'What's happening?'

'The Coronal has taken lodging in the mayor's palace – that's the tallest building, with the jagged golden swirls on its walls, on the far side over there – and nobody can get near it tonight. We can't even go around the plaza's inner rim, because there's such a mob piled up there, waiting for a glimpse of Lord Valentine. So it's a detour for us, an hour or more, the long way around. Well, sleep isn't that important, I suppose. Look, there he is!'

Shanamir indicated a balcony high on the facade of the mayor's palace. Figures had emerged on it. At this distance they were no larger than mice, but mice of dignity and grandeur, clad in sumptuous robes; Valentine could see at least that much. There were five of them, and the central personage was surely the Coronal. Shanamir was straining and standing on tiptoe for a better view. Valentine could make out very little: a dark-haired man, possibly bearded, in a heavy white steetmoy-fur robe over a doublet in green or light blue. The Coronal stood at the front of the balcony, spreading his arms toward the crowd, who made the starburst symbol with their outstretched fingers and shouted his name again and again: 'Valentine! Valentine! Lord Valentine!'

And Shanamir, at Valentine's side, cried out too: 'Valentine! Lord Valentine!'

Valentine felt a fierce shudder of revulsion. 'Listen to them!' he muttered. 'Yelling as if he's the Divine Itself, come down for dinner in Pidruid. He's only a man, isn't he? When his bowels are full he empties them, yes?'

Shanamir blinked in shock. 'He's the Coronal!'

'He means nothing to me, even as I mean less than nothing to him.'

'He governs. He administers justice. He holds back chaos. You said those things yourself. Aren't such things worthy of your respect?'

'Respect, yes. But not my worship.'

'To worship the king is nothing new. My father has told me of olden times. They had kings as far back as Old Earth itself, and I'll bet they were worshiped, Valentine, in scenes far more wild than what you see here tonight.'

'And some were drowned by their own slaves, and some were poisoned by their chief ministers, and some were smothered by their wives, and some were overthrown by the people they pretended to serve, and every last one was buried and forgotten,' Valentine felt himself growing surprisingly warm with anger. He spat in disgust. 'And many lands on Old Earth got along without kings altogether. Why do we need them on Majipoor? These expensive Coronals, and the weird old Pontifex hiding in his Labyrinth, and the sender of bad dreams out of Suvrael – No, Shanamir, I may be too simple to understand it, but it makes no sense to me. This frenzy! These screams of delight! No one screams delight, I'll wager, when the Mayor of Pidruid rides through the streets.'

'We need kings,' Shanamir insisted. 'This world is too big to be ruled by mayors alone. We need great and potent symbols, monarchs who are almost like gods, to hold things together. Look. Look.' The boy pointed toward the balcony. 'Up there, that little figure in the white robe: the Coronal of Majipoor. You feel nothing go shivering down your back when I say that?'

'Nothing.'

'You get no thrill, knowing that there are twenty billion people on this world and only one is Coronal, and that tonight you behold him with your own eyes, something which you will never do again? You feel no awe?'

'None.'

'You're a strange one, Valentine. I've never met anyone like you at all. How could anyone be untouched by the sight of the Coronal?'

'I am,' said Valentine, shrugging, a little puzzled by it himself. 'Come, let's get out of here. This mob tires me. Let's find the inn.'

It was a long journey around the plaza, for all streets ran into it but few ran parallel to it, and Valentine and Shanamir had to move in ever-widening circles while trying to proceed westward, with the train of mounts clopping placidly wherever Shanamir led. But at last they emerged from a district of hotels and fine shops into one of warehouses and lofts, and approached the edge of the waterfront, and came finally to a weatherbeaten inn of warped black timbers and frayed thatching, with stables to the rear. Shanamir housed his beasts and went through a courtyard to the innkeeper's quarters, leaving Valentine alone in the shadows. He waited a long while. It seemed to him that even here he could hear the blurred and muffled cries: '*Valentine ... Valentine ... Lord Valentine!*' But it meant nothing to him that multitudes were crying his name, for it was the name of another.

Shanamir returned in time, sprinting lightly and silently across the yard.

'It's arranged. Give me some money.'

'The fifty?'

'Smaller. Much smaller. A half-crown or so.'

Valentine groped for coins, sorted through them by dim lamplight, handed several well-worn pieces to Shanamir. 'For the lodging?' he asked.

'To bribe the doorkeeper,' Shanamir replied. 'Places to sleep are hard to come by tonight. Crowding in one more means less room for everybody, and if someone counts heads and complains, it's the doorkeeper must back us up. Follow me and say nothing.'

They went in. The place smelled of salt air and mildew. Just within, a fat grayish-faced Hjort sat like an enormous toad at a desk, arranging playing-cards in patterns. The rough-skinned creature barely looked up. Shanamir laid the coins before him and the Hjort signaled with an almost imperceptible flicker of its head. Onward, to a long narrow windowless room, lit by three widely spaced glowfloats that yielded a hazy reddish light. A row of mattresses spanned the length of the room, one close by the next on the floor, and nearly all of them were occupied. 'Here,' Shanamir said, nudging one with the tip of his boot. He stripped off his outer clothes and lay down, leaving room for Valentine. 'Dream well,' the boy said.

'Dream well,' said Valentine, and kicked off his boots and shed his top-garments, and dropped down beside him. Distant shouts echoed in his ears, or perhaps in his mind. It astonished him how weary he was. There might be dreams tonight, yes, and he would watch carefully for them so that he could sift them for meaning, but first there would be deep sleep, the sleep of the utterly exhausted. And in the morning? A new day. Anything might befall. Anything.

4

There was a dream, of course, somewhere toward the depth of the night. Valentine placed himself at a distance from it and watched it unfold, as he had been taught from childhood. Dreams held great significance; they were messages from the Powers that ruled the world, by which one was to guide one's life; they were ignored only at one's peril, for they were manifestations of the deepest truth. Valentine saw himself crossing a vast purple plain under a baleful purple sky and a swollen amber sun. He was alone and his face was drawn, his eyes were tense and strained. As he marched, ugly fissures opened in the ground, gaping cracks that were bright orange within, and things popped forth like children's toys popping from a box, laughing shrilly at him and swiftly retreating into the fissures as they closed.

That was all. Not a full dream, then, for it had no story, no pattern of conflicts and resolution. It was only an image, a bizarre scene, a slice from some larger canvas not yet revealed to him. He could not even tell whether it was a sending from the Lady, the blessed Lady of the Isle of Sleep, or from the malevolent King of Dreams. He lay half awake, pondering it awhile, and decided at last to give it no deeper consideration. He felt oddly adrift, cut free from his own inner self: it was as though he had not even existed the day before yesterday. And even the wisdom of dreams was concealed from him now.

He slept again, a sleep unbroken except when a light patter of rain fell briefly but noisily, and he was unaware of further dreams. Early light woke him: warm golden-green light pouring in through the far end of the long narrow hall. The door stood open. Shanamir was nowhere about. Valentine was alone, except for a couple of snorers deeper into the room.

Valentine rose, stretched, flexed his arms and legs, dressed. He washed at a basin against the wall, and stepped out into the courtyard, feeling alert, energetic, ready for whatever this day might bring. The morning air was thick with moisture, but warm and bright, and last night's fog had altogether burned off; out of a clear sky came the throbbing heat of the summer sun. In the courtyard grew three great vines, one along each wall, with gnarled woody trunks broader than a man's waist, and shovel-shaped glossy leaves of a deep bronze hue, the new growth bright red. The vine was abloom with showy yellow blossoms like little trumpets, but also it bore ripened fruit, heavy blue-white berries glistening with beads of wetness. Valentine plucked one boldly and ate it: sweet, tart as well, with the headiness of very young wine. He had another, then reached for a third and thought better of it.

Circling the courtyard, he peered into the stables and saw Shanamir's mounts munching quietly on bits of straw, but no Shanamir. Off on business, perhaps. Onward now around a bend, and the odor of grilled fish came to him and made him tingle with sudden hunger. He pushed open a rickety door and found himself in a kitchen where a small weary-looking man was cooking breakfast for half a dozen lodgers of several races. The cook looked at Valentine without interest.

'Am I too late to eat?' Valentine asked softly.

'Take a seat. Fish and beer, thirty weights.'

He found a half-crown piece and laid it on the stove. The cook pushed a few coppers back at him and threw another fillet onto his griddle. Valentine took a seat against the wall. Several of the diners got up to depart, and one, a slender, lithe young woman with close-clipped black hair, paused near him. 'The beer's in that pitcher,' she said. 'You help yourself around here.'

'Thank you,' said Valentine, but she was already out the door.

He poured a mugful – it was heavy, tangy stuff, thick against his tongue. In a minute he had his fish, crisply cooked and sweet. He ate it swiftly. 'Another?' he said to the cook, who eyed him sourly but complied.

As he ate, Valentine became aware that a lodger at the next table – a Hjort, thick-bodied and puffy-faced, with pebble-textured ashen skin and big bulging eyes – was peering intently at him. The strange surveillance made Valentine uncomfortable. After a time he glanced directly back at the Hjort, who blinked and looked quickly away.

Some moments later the Hjort turned to Valentine again and said, 'Just got here, did you?'

'Last night.'

'Staying long?'

'Through the festival, at least,' Valentine said.

Definitely there was something about the Hjort that he instinctively disliked. Perhaps it was merely his looks, for Valentine found Hjorts un-attractive, coarse and bloated creatures. But that was unkind, he knew. Hjorts bore no responsibility for the way they looked, and they probably found humans equally disagreeable, pale scrawny things with disgustingly smooth skins.

Or possibly it was the intrusion on his privacy that bothered him, the staring, the questions. Or maybe just the way the Hjort was decorated with fleshy daubs of orange pigment. Whatever it was, it made him feel queasy and bothered.

But he felt mild guilt for such prejudices and he had no wish to be un-sociable. By way of atoning he offered a lukewarm smile and said, 'My name is Valentine. I'm from Ni-moya.'

'Long way to come,' said the Hjort, chewing noisily.

'You live near here?'

'Little way south of Pidruid. Name's Vinorkis. Dealer in haigus hides.' The Hjort sliced fussily at his food. After a moment he returned his attention to Valentine, letting his great fishy eyes rest fixedly on him. 'You traveling with that boy?'

'Not really. I met him on my way into Pidruid.'

The Hjort nodded. 'Going back to Ni-moya after the festival?'

The flow of questions was becoming an annoyance. But Valentine still hesitated to be impolite even in the face of this impoliteness. 'I'm not sure yet,' he said.

'Thinking of staying here, then?'

Valentine shrugged. 'I really have no plans at all.'

'Mmm,' the Hjort said. 'fine way to live.'

It was impossible to tell, from the Hjort's flat nasal inflection, whether that was meant as praise or sarcastic condemnation. But Valentine hardly cared. He had sufficiently met his social responsibilities, he decided, and fell silent. The Hjort likewise seemed to have no more to say. He finished his breakfast, pushed back his chair with a screech, and in his ungainly Hjor-tish way lurched toward the door, saying, 'Off to the marketplace now. See you around.'

Eventually Valentine wandered out into the courtyard, where now an odd game was in progress. Eight figures stood near the far wall, throwing dag-gers back and forth to one another. Six of them were Skandars, big rough shaggy beings with four arms and coarse gray pelts, and the other two were human. Valentine recognized those two as having been breakfasting when he entered the kitchen – the sleek slim dark-haired woman and a lean, hard-eyed man with eerie white skin and long white hair. The daggers flew with astonishing speed, glittering as they flashed in the morning sun, and there was grim concentration on everyone's face. No one dropped a blade, no one ever seemed to catch one by the sharp side, and Valentine could not even count the number of daggers passing back and forth; everyone appeared constantly to be throwing and catching, all hands full and more weapons traveling through the air. Jugglers, he thought, practicing their trade, getting ready to perform at the festival. The Skandars, four-armed and powerfully built, performed prodigies of coordination, but the man and the woman held their own in the patterns, juggling as deftly as the others. Valentine stood at a safe distance, watching in fascination as the daggers flew.

Then one of the Skandars grunted a 'Hup!' and the pattern changed: the six aliens began to direct their weapons only at one another, doubling and redoubling the intensity with which they passed, and the two humans moved a short way apart. The girl grinned at Valentine. 'Hoy, come join us!'

'What?'

'Play the game with us!' Her eyes sparkled mischievously.

'A very dangerous game, I'd say.'

'All the best games are dangerous. Here!' Without warning, she flipped a dagger toward him. 'What's your name, fellow?'

'Valentine,' he said in a sort of gasp, and desperately nipped the dagger by its haft as it went shooting past his ear.

'Nicely caught,' said the white-haired man. 'Try this!'

He tossed a blade too. Valentine laughed and caught it, a little less awkwardly, and stood there with one in each hand. The aliens, wholly ignoring the byplay, continued methodically to send cascades of weapons flashing back and forth.

'Return the throw,' the girl called.

Valentine frowned. He tossed it too carefully, absurdly fearful of skewering her, and the dagger described a limp arc and landed at her feet.

'You can do better,' she said scornfully.

'Sorry,' he said.

He threw the other one with more vigor. She plucked it calmly, and took another from the white-haired man, and sent first one, then the other, toward Valentine. There was no time to think. Snap and snap and he caught them both. Sweat broke out on his forehead, but he was getting into the rhythm of it.

'Here,' he called. He gave one to her and took another from the white-haired one, and sent a third through the air, and found one coming at him and then another, and he wished that these were play daggers, blunt of blade, but he knew that they were not and he stopped fretting about it. The thing to do was to make oneself into a kind of automaton, keeping the body centered and aware, looking always toward the incoming dagger and letting the outgoing one fly of its own accord. He moved steadily, catching, throwing, catching, throwing, always one blade coming toward him and one departing. Valentine realized that a true juggler would be using both hands at once, but he was no juggler and it was all he could manage to co-ordinate catching and throwing. Yet he was doing well. He wondered how soon it would be before the inevitable blunder came and he was cut. The jugglers laughed as the tempo increased. He laughed with them, easily, and went on catching and throwing for a good two or three minutes before he felt his reflexes blurring from the strain. This was the moment to stop. He caught and deliberately dropped each of the blades in turn, until all three lay at his feet, and he bent over, chuckling, slapping his thighs, breathing hard.

The two human jugglers applauded. The Skandars had not ceased their formidable whirling of blades, but now one cried another 'Hup,' and the sextet of aliens reeled in their daggers and moved off without a further word, disappearing in the direction of the sleeping-quarters.

The young woman danced over to Valentine.

'I'm Carabella,' she said. She was no taller than Shanamir, and could not have been more than a few years out of girlhood. There was an irrepressible vitality bubbling within her small, muscular frame. She wore a light green doublet of close weave and a triple strand of polished quanna-shells at her throat, and her eyes were as dark as her hair. Her smile was warm and invit-ing. 'Where have you juggled before, fellow?' she asked.

'Never,' said Valentine. He dabbed at his sweaty forehead. 'A tricky sport. I don't know why I wasn't cut.'

'*Never?*' cried the white-haired one. 'Never juggled before? That was a show of natural skill and nothing else?'

'I suppose it has to be called that,' Valentine said with a shrug.

'Can we believe that?' the white-haired man asked.

'I think so,' Carabella said. 'He was good, Sleet, but he had no form. Did you see how his hands moved after the daggers, out to here, across to here, a little nervous, a little eager, never waiting for the hafts to come to the proper place? And his throws, how hurried, how wild? No one who has been trained in the art could easily have pretended to such clumsiness, and why should he? This Valentine's eye is good, Sleet, but he tells the truth. He's never thrown.'

'His eye is more than good,' Sleet muttered. 'He has a quickness I envy greatly. He has a gift.'

'Where are you from?' Carabella asked.

'The east,' said Valentine obliquely.

'I thought so. Your speech is somewhat odd. You come from Velathys? Khyntor, maybe?'

'From that direction, yes.'

Valentine's lack of specificity was not lost on Carabella, nor on Sleet; they exchanged quick glances. Valentine wondered if they could be father and daughter. Probably not. Sleet, Valentine saw, was not nearly as old as he had seemed at first. Of middle years, yes, but hardly old; the bleached look of his skin and of his hair exaggerated his age. He was a compact, taut man with thin lips and a short, pointed white beard. A scar, pale now but once no doubt quite vivid, ran across one cheek from ear to chin.

Carabella said, 'We are from the south, I from Til-omon, Sleet from Narabal.'

'Here to perform at the Coronal's festival?'

'Indeed. Newly hired by the troupe of Zalzan Kavol the Skandar, to help them fulfill the Coronal's recent decree concerning employment of humans. And you? What has brought you to Pidruid?'

'The festival,' said Valentine.

'To do business?'

'Merely to see the games and parades.'

Sleet laughed knowingly. 'No need to be coy with us, friend. Hardly a disgrace to be selling mounts in the market. We saw you come in with the boy last night.'

'No,' Valentine said. 'I met the young herdsman only yesterday, as I was approaching the city. The animals are his. I merely accompanied him to the inn, because I was a stranger here. I have no trade of my own.'

One of the Skandars reappeared in a doorway. He was of giant size, half again as tall as Valentine, a formidable hulking creature, heavy-jawed and fierce, with narrow yellow eyes. His four arms hung well below his knees and terminated in hands like great baskets. 'Come inside!' he called brusquely.

Sleet saluted and trotted off. Carabella lingered a moment, grinning at Valentine.

'You are very peculiar,' she said. 'You speak no lies, yet nothing you say sounds right. I think you yourself have little knowledge of your own soul. But I like you. You give off a glow, do you know that, Valentine? A glow of innocence, of simplicity, of warmth, or – of something else. I don't know.' Almost shyly she touched two fingers to the side of his arm. 'I do like you. Perhaps we'll juggle again.'

And she was gone, scampering off after Sleet.

5

He was alone, and there was no sign of Shanamir, and although he found himself wishing mightily he could spend the day with the jugglers, with

Carabella, there was no way he could do that. And the morning was still young. He was without plan, and that troubled him, but not excessively. There was all of Pidruid for him to explore.

Out he went, down winding streets heavy with foliage. Lush vines and trees with thick weeping limbs sprouted everywhere, thriving in the moist warm salt air. From far away came band music, a gay if somewhat strident wheezing and pumping melody, maybe a rehearsal for the grand parade. A small river of foaming water rushed along the gutter, and the wildlings of Pidruid frolicked in it, mintuns and mangy dogs and little prickly-nosed droles. Busy, busy, busy, a teeming city where everyone and everything, even the stray animals, had something important to do and were doing it in a hurry. All but Valentine, who strolled aimlessly, following no particular route. He paused now to peer into some dark shop festooned with bolts and swatches of fabric, now into some musty repository of spices, now into some choice and elegant garden of rich-hued blossoms sandwiched between two tall narrow buildings. Occasionally people glanced at him as though marveling that he could allow himself the luxury of sauntering.

In one street he stopped to watch children playing a game, a sort of pantomime, one little boy with a strip of golden cloth tied as a circlet around his forehead making menacing gestures in the center of a ring, and the others dancing around him, pretending to be terrified, singing:

> *The old King of Dreams*
> *Sits on his throne.*
> *He's never asleep.*
> *He's never alone.*
> *The old King of Dreams*
> *Comes in the night.*
> *If you've been bad*
> *He'll give you a fright.*
> *The old King of Dreams*
> *Has a heart made of stone.*
> *He's never asleep*
> *He's never alone.*

But when the children realized that Valentine was watching, they turned and made grotesque gestures at him, grimacing, crooking their arms, pointing. He laughed and moved on.

By mid-morning he was at the waterfront. Long elbow-angled piers thrust far out into the harbor, and every one seemed a place of mad activity. Longshoremen of four or five races were unloading cargo vessels that bore the arms of twenty ports on all three continents; they used floaters to bring the bales of goods down to dockside and convey them to the warehouses, but there was plenty of shouting and angry maneuvering as the immensely heavy bundles were jockeyed this way and that. As Valentine watched from the shadow of the wharf, he felt a rough thump between his shoulders, and whirled to find a puffy-faced choleric Hjort pointing and waving arms. 'Over there,' the Hjort said. 'We need six more to work the Suvrael ship!'

'But I'm not—'

'Quick! Hurry!'

Very well. Valentine was not disposed to argue; he moved out onto the pier and joined a group of longshoremen who were bellowing and roaring as they guided a cargo of livestock downward. Valentine bellowed and roared with them, until the animals, squealing long-faced yearling blaves, were on their way toward the stockyard or slaughterhouse. Then he quietly slipped away and moved down the quay until he came to an idle pier.

He stood there peacefully for some minutes, staring out across the harbor toward the sea, the bronze-green whitecapped sea, squinting as though if he tried hard enough he could see around the bend of the globe to Alhanroel and its Castle Mount, rising heaven-high. But of course there was no seeing Alhanroel from here, across tens of thousands of miles of ocean, across a sea so broad that certain entire planets might conveniently be fitted between the shores of one continent and the other. Valentine looked down, between his feet, and let his imagination plummet into Majipoor's depths, wondering what lay straight through the planet from here. The western half of Alhanroel, he suspected. Geography was vague and puzzling to him. He seemed to have forgotten so much of his schoolboy knowledge, and had to struggle to remember anything. Possibly right now he was diametrically across the world from the lair of the Pontifex, the terrifying Labyrinth of the old and reclusive high monarch. Or perhaps, more likely, the Isle of Sleep lay downward from here, the blessed Isle where the sweet Lady dwelled, in leafy glades where her priests and priestesses endlessly chanted, sending benevolent messages to the sleepers of the world. Valentine found it hard to believe that such places existed, that there were such personages in the world, such Powers, a Pontifex, a Lady of the Isle, a King of Dreams, even a Coronal, though he had beheld the Coronal with his own eyes only last night. Those potentates seemed unreal. What seemed real was the dockside at Pidruid, the inn where he had slept, the grilled fish, the jugglers, the boy Shanamir and his animals. All else was mere fantasy and mirage.

The day was warm now and growing quite humid, although a pleasant breeze blew toward shore. Valentine was hungry again. At a stand at the edge of the quay he bought, for a couple of coppers, a meal of strips of raw blue-fleshed fish marinated in a hot spicy sauce and served on slivers of wood. He washed it back with a beaker of fireshower wine, startling golden stuff that tasted hotter even than the sauce. Then he thought of returning to the inn. But he realized that he knew neither the name of the inn nor the name of its street, only that it lay a short distance inland from the waterfront district. Small loss if he never found it, for he had no possessions except those he carried on him; but the only people he knew in all of Pidruid were Shanamir and the jugglers, and he did not want to part from them so soon.

Valentine started back and promptly lost himself in a maze of indistinguishable alleyways and streetlets that ran back and forth across Water Road. Three times he found inns that seemed the right one, but each, when he approached it closely, proved to be some other. An hour passed, or more, and it grew to be early afternoon. Valentine understood that it would be impossible for him to find the inn, and there was a pang of sadness at that, for he thought of Carabella and the touch of her fingers to the side of his arm, and the quickness of her hands as she caught the knives, and the brightness of her dark eyes. But what is lost, he thought, is lost, and no use weeping over it. He would find himself a new inn and new friends before dark.

And then he turned a corner and discovered what must surely be Pidruid market.

It was a vast enclosed space nearly as huge as the Golden Plaza, but there were no towering palaces and hotels with golden façades here, only an endless sprawl of tile-roofed sheds and open stockyards and cramped booths. Here was every fragrance and stink in the world, and half the produce of the universe for sale. Valentine plunged in, delighted, fascinated. Sides of meat hung from great hooks in one shed. Barrels of spice, spilling their contents, occupied another. In one stockyard were giddy spinner-birds, standing taller than Skandars on their preposterous bright legs, pecking and kicking at one another while dealers in eggs and wool bargained over them. In another were tanks of shining serpents, coiling and twisting like streaks of angry flame; nearby was a place where small seadragons, gutted and pithed, lay stacked for sale in foul-smelling heaps. Here was a place of public scribes, doing letters for the unlettered, and here a moneychanger deftly haggling for currencies of a dozen worlds, and here a row of sausage-stands, fifty of them and identical, with identical-looking Liimen side by side tending their smoky fires and twirling their laden skewers.

And fortunetellers, and sorcerers, and jugglers, though not the jugglers Valentine knew, and in a clear space squatted a storyteller, relating for coppers some involuted and all but incomprehensible adventure of Lord Stiamot, the famed Coronal of eight thousand years ago, whose deeds now were the stuff of myth. Valentine listened for five minutes but could make no sense of the tale, which held fifteen or twenty off-duty porters in rapture. He went on, past a booth where a golden-eyed Vroon with a silver flute played slinky tunes to charm some three-headed creature in a wicker basket, past a grinning boy of about ten who challenged him to a game involving shells and beads, past an aisle of vendors who were selling banners that bore the Coronal's starburst, past a fakir who hovered suspended over a vat of some nasty-looking hot oil, past an avenue of dream-speakers and a passageway thronged with drug-dealers, past the place of the interpreters and the place of the jewel-sellers, and at last, after turning a corner where all manner of cheap garments were for sale, he arrived at the stockyard where mounts were sold.

The sturdy purple beasts were lined up flank to flank by the hundreds, maybe even the thousands, standing impassively and peering without interest at what appeared to be an auction taking place before their noses. Valentine found the auction as difficult to follow as the storyteller's tale of Lord Stiamot: buyers and sellers faced each other in two long rows, and made hacking gestures across their wrists at one another, supplementing those movements with grimaces, the banging together of fists, and the sudden outward thrust of elbows. Nothing was said, and yet much evidently was communicated, because scribes stationed along the row constantly scribbled deeds of sale that were validated by thumb-chops in green ink, and frantic clerks affixed tags stamped with the labyrinth seal of the Pontifex to the haunches of one beast after another. Moving along the line of the auction, Valentine at last came upon Shanamir, hacking and elbowing and banging fists with consummate ferocity. In minutes it was all over; and the boy came bounding out of the line with a whoop of joy. He caught Valentine by the arm and whirled him gleefully about.

'All sold! All sold! And at a premium price!' He held out a wad of chits that a scribe had given him. 'Come with me to the treasury, and then it's nothing left but play for us! How late did you sleep?'

'Late, I suppose. The inn was almost empty.'

'I didn't have the heart to wake you. You were snoring like a blave. What have you been doing?'

'Exploring the waterfront, mainly. I stumbled into the marketplace while trying to get back to the inn. It was by luck I came upon you.'

'Ten minutes more and you'd have missed me forever,' said Shanamir. 'Here. This place.' He tugged at Valentine's wrist and pulled him into a long, brightly lit arcade where clerks behind wickers were changing chits into coins. 'Give me the fifty,' Shanamir murmured. 'I can have it broken for you here.'

Valentine produced the thick gleaming coin and stood aside while the boy joined a line. Minutes later Shanamir returned. 'These are yours,' he said, dumping into Valentine's outstretched purse a shower of money, some five-royal pieces and a jingle of crowns. 'And these are mine,' the boy said, grinning wickedly and holding up three big fifty-royal pieces of the kind he had just changed for Valentine. He popped them into a moneyband under his jerkin. 'A profitable trip, it was. At festival time everyone's in a fever to spend his money fast. Come, now. Back to the inn, and let's celebrate with a flask of fireshower wine, eh? The treat's mine!'

The inn, it turned out, was no more than fifteen minutes from the market, on a street that suddenly looked familiar as they entered it. Valentine suspected that he had come within a block or two of it in his fruitless quest. No matter: he was here, and with Shanamir. The boy, relieved at being rid of his animals and excited over the price he had had for them, chattered on and on about what he would do in Pidruid before he returned to his countryside home – the dancing, the games, the drinking, the shows.

As they sat in the tavern of the inn at work on Shanamir's wine, Sleet and Carabella appeared. 'May we join you?' Sleet asked.

Valentine said to Shanamir, 'These are jugglers, members of a Skandar troupe here to play in the parade. I met them this morning.' He made introductions. They took seats and Shanamir offered them drinks.

'Have you been to market?' said Sleet.

'Been and done,' Shanamir said. 'A good price.'

'And now?' Carabella asked.

'The festival for a few days,' said the boy. 'And home to Falkynkip, I suppose.' He looked a little crestfallen at the thought.

'And you?' Carabella said, glancing at Valentine. 'Do you have plans?'

'To see the festival.'

'And then?'

'Whatever seems right.'

They were finished with the wine. Sleet gestured sharply and a second flask appeared. It was poured around generously. Valentine felt his tongue tingling with the heat of the liquor, and his head becoming a little light.

Carabella said, 'Would you think to be a juggler, and join our troupe, then?'

It startled Valentine. 'I have no skill!'

'You have skill aplenty,' said Sleet. 'What you lack is training. That we could supply, Carabella and I. You would learn the trade quickly. I take an oath on it.'

'And I would travel with you, and live the life of a wandering player, and go from town to town, is that it?'

'Exactly.'

Valentine looked across at Shanamir. The boy's eyes were shining at the prospect. Valentine could almost feel the pressure of his excitement, his envy.

'But what is all this about?' Valentine demanded. 'Why invite a stranger, a novice, an ignoramus like me, to become one of your number?'

Carabella signaled to Sleet, who quickly left the table. She said, 'Zalzan Kavol will explain. It is a necessity, not a caprice. We are shorthanded, Valentine, and we have need of you.' She added, 'Besides, have you anything other to do? You seem adrift in this city. We offer you companionship as well as a livelihood.'

A moment and Sleet returned with the giant Skandar. Zalzan Kavol was an awesome figure, massive, towering. He lowered himself with difficulty into a seat at their table: it creaked alarmingly beneath his bulk. Skandars came from some windswept, icy world far away, and though they had been settled on Majipoor for thousands of years, working in rough trades needing great strength or unusual quickness of eye, they had a way of eternally looking angry and uncomfortable in Majipoor's warm climate. Perhaps it was only a matter of their natural facial features, Valentine thought, but he found Zalzan Kavol and others of his kind an offputtingly bleak tribe.

The Skandar poured himself a stiff drink with his two inner arms and spread the outer pair wide across the table as though he were taking possession of it. In a harsh rumbling voice he said, 'I watched you do the knives with Sleet and Carabella this morning. You can serve the purpose.'

'Which is?'

'I need a third human juggler, and in a hurry. You know what the new Coronal has lately decreed concerning public entertainers?'

Valentine smiled and shrugged.

Zalzan Kavol said, 'It is foolishness and stupidity, but the Coronal is young and I suppose must let fly some wild shafts. It has been decreed that in all troupes of performers made up of more than three individuals, one third of the troupe must be Majipoori citizens of human birth, this to be effective as of this month.'

'A decree like that,' said Carabella, 'can accomplish nothing but to set race against race, on a world where many races have lived in peace for thousands of years.'

Zalzan Kavol scowled. 'Nevertheless the decree exists. Some jackal in the Castle must have told this Lord Valentine that the other races are growing too numerous, that the humans of Majipoor are going hungry when we work. Foolishness, and dangerous. Ordinarily no one would pay attention to such a decree, but this is the festival of the Coronal, and if we are to be licensed to perform we must obey the rules, however idiotic. My brothers and I have earned our keep as jugglers for years, and done no harm to any human by it, but now we must comply. So I have found Sleet and Carabella in Pidruid, and we are working them into our routines. Today is Twoday. Four days hence we perform in the Coronal's parade, and I must have a third human. Will you apprentice yourself to us, Valentine?'

'How could I learn juggling in four days?'

'You will be merely an apprentice,' said the Skandar. 'We will find something of a juggling nature for you to do in the grand parade that will disgrace neither yourself nor us. The law does not, as I see it, require all members of the troupe to have equal responsibilities or skills. But three of us must be human.'

'And after the festival?'

'Come with us from town to town.'

'You know nothing about me, and you invite me to share your lives?'

'I know nothing about you and I *want* to know nothing about you. I need a juggler of your race. I'll pay your room and board wherever we go, and ten crowns a week besides. Yes?'

Carabella's eyes had an odd glint, as though she were telling him, *You can ask twice that wage and get it, Valentine.* But the money was unimportant. He would have enough to eat and a place to sleep, and he would be with Carabella and Sleet, who were two of the three human beings he knew in this city, and, he realized with some confusion, in all the world. For there was a vacancy in him where a past should be: he had hazy notions of parents, and cousins and sisters, and a childhood somewhere in eastern Zimroel, and schooling and travels, but none of it seemed real to him, nothing had density and texture and substance. And there was a vacancy in him where a future should be, too. These jugglers promised to fill it. But yet—

'One condition,' Valentine said.

Zalzan Kavol looked displeased. 'Which is?'

Valentine nodded toward Shanamir. 'I think this boy is tired of raising mounts in Falkynkip, and may want to travel more widely. I ask that you offer him a place in your troupe as well—'

'*Valentine!*' the boy cried.

'—as groom, or valet, or even a juggler if he has the art,' Valentine went on, 'and that if he is willing to go with us, you accept him along with me. Will you do that?'

Zalzan Kavol was silent a moment, as if in calculation, and there was a barely audible growling sound from somewhere deep within his shaggy form. At length he said, 'Have you any interest in joining us, boy?'

'Have I? *Have* I?'

'I feared as much,' said the Skandar morosely. 'Then it is done. We hire the both of you at thirteen crowns the week with room and board. Done?'

'Done,' said Valentine.

'Done!' cried Shanamir.

Zalzan Kavol knocked back the last of the fireshower wine. 'Sleet, Carabella, take this stranger to the courtyard and begin making a juggler out of him. You come with me, boy. I want you to have a look at our mounts.'

6

They went outside. Carabella darted off to the sleeping-quarters to fetch equipment. Watching her run, Valentine took pleasure in her graceful movements, imagining the play of supple muscles beneath her garments. Sleet plucked blue-white berries from one of the courtyard vines and popped them into his mouth.

'What are they?' Valentine asked.

Sleet tossed him one. 'Thokkas. In Narabal, where I was born, a thokka vine will sprout in the morning and be as high as a house by afternoon. Of course the soil bursts with life in Narabal, and the rain falls every dawn. Another?'

'Please.'

With a deft quick wrist-flip Sleet chucked a berry over. It was the smallest of gestures, but effective. Sleet was an economical man, bird-light, without an ounce of excess flesh, his gestures precise, his voice dry and controlled. 'Chew the seeds,' he advised Valentine. 'They promote virility.' He managed a thin laugh.

Carabella returned, bearing a great many colored rubber balls that she juggled briskly as she crossed the yard. When she reached Valentine and Sleet she flipped one of the balls to Valentine and three to Sleet, without breaking stride. Three she retained.

'Not knives?' Valentine asked.

'Knives are showy things. Today we deal in fundamentals,' Sleet said. 'We deal in the philosophy of the art. Knives would be a distraction.'

'Philosophy?'

'Do you think juggling's a mere trick?' the little man asked, sounding wounded. 'An amusement for the gapers? A means of picking up a crown or two at a provincial carnival? It is all those things, yes, but first it is a way of life, friend, a creed, a species of worship.'

'And a kind of poetry,' said Carabella.

Sleet nodded. 'Yes, that too. And a mathematics. It teaches calmness, control, balance, a sense of the placement of things and the underlying structure of motion. There is silent music to it. Above all there is discipline. Do I sound pretentious?'

'He means to sound pretentious,' Carabella said. There was mischief in her eyes. 'But everything he says is true. Are you ready to begin?'

Valentine nodded.

Sleet said, 'Make yourself calm. Cleanse your mind of all needless thought and calculation. Travel to the center of your being and hold yourself there.'

Valentine planted his feet flat on the ground, took three deep breaths, relaxed his shoulders so that he could not feel his dangling arms, and waited.

'I think,' said Carabella, 'that this man lives most of the time at the center of his being. Or else that he is without a center and so can never be far from it.'

'Are you ready?' Sleet asked.

'Ready.'

'We will teach you basics, one small thing at a time. Juggling is a series of small discrete motions done in quick sequence, that give the appearance of constant flow and simultaneity. Simultaneity is an illusion, friend, when you are juggling and even when you are not. All events happen one at a time.' Sleet smiled coldly. He seemed to be speaking from ten thousand miles away. 'Close your eyes, Valentine. Orientation in space and time is essential. Think of where you are and where you stand in relation to the world.'

Valentine pictured Majipoor, mighty ball hanging in space, half of it or more than half engulfed by the Great Sea. He saw himself standing rooted at Zimroel's edge with the sea behind him and a continent unrolling before him, and the Inner Sea punctuated by the Isle of Sleep, and Alhanroel beyond, rising on its nether side to the great swollen bulge of Castle Mount, and the sun overhead, yellow with a bronze-green tint, sending blistering rays down on dusty Suvrael and into the tropics, and warming everything else, and the moons somewhere on the far side of things, and the stars farther out, and the other worlds, the worlds from which the Skandars came and the Hjorts and the Liimen and all the rest, even the world from which his own folk had emigrated, Old Earth, fourteen thousand years ago, a small blue world absurdly tiny when compared to Majipoor, far away, half forgotten in some other corner of the universe, and he journeyed back down across the stars to this world, this continent, this city, this inn, this courtyard, this small plot of moist yielding soil in which his boots were rooted, and told Sleet he was ready.

Sleet and Carabella stood with arms hanging straight, elbows at their sides, and brought their forearms up to a level position, cupped hands outstretched, one ball in the right hand. Valentine imitated them. Sleet said, 'Pretend that a tray of precious gems rests on your hands. If you move your shoulders or elbows, or raise or lower your hands, the gems will spill. Eh? The secret of juggling is to move your body as little as possible. Things move; you control them; you remain still.' The ball that Sleet held traveled suddenly from his right hand to the left, though there had not been a flicker of motion in his body. Carabella's ball did the same. Valentine, imitating, threw the ball from hand to hand, conscious of effort and movement.

Carabella said, 'You use too much wrist and much too much elbow. Let the cup of your hand open suddenly. Let the fingers stretch apart. You are releasing a trapped bird – so! The hand opens, the bird flies upward.'

'No wrist at all?' Valentine asked.

'Little, and conceal what you use. The thrust comes from the palm of your hand. So.'

Valentine tried it. The shortest of upward movements of the forearm, the quickest of snaps with the wrist; propulsion from the center of his hand and from the center of his being. The ball flew to his cupped left hand.

'Yes,' said Sleet. 'Again.'

Again. Again. Again. For fifteen minutes the three of them popped balls from one hand to the other. They made him send the ball in a neat un-varying arc in front of his face, holding it in a plane with his hands, and they would not permit him to reach upward or outward for a catch; hands waited, ball traveled. After a time he was doing it automatically. Shanamir emerged from the stables and stared, bemused, at the singleminded tossing; then he wandered away. Valentine did not halt. This hardly seemed juggling, this rigid one-ball toss, but it was the event of the moment and he gave him-self up to it entirely.

He realized eventually that Sleet and Carabella had stopped throwing, that he alone was proceeding, like a machine. 'Here,' said Sleet, and flipped him a thokka-berry fresh from the vine. Valentine caught it between ball-tosses and held it as if thinking he might be asked to juggle with it, but no, Sleet pantomimed that he was to eat it. His reward, his incentive.

Carabella now put a second ball in his left hand and a third next to the original one in his right. 'Your hands are big,' she said. 'This will be easy for you. Watch me, then do as I do.'

She popped a ball back and forth between her hands, catching it by making a four-pointed basket out of three fingers and the ball she held in the center of each hand. Valentine imitated her. Catching the ball was harder with a full hand than with an empty one, but not greatly so, and soon he was flawless.

'Now,' said Sleet, 'comes the beginning of art. We make an exchange – so.'

One ball traveled in a face-high arc from Sleet's right hand to his left. As it journeyed, he made room for it in his left by popping the ball he held there upward and across, under the incoming ball, into his right. The maneuver seemed simple enough, a quick reciprocal toss, but when Valentine tried it the balls collided and went bounding away. Carabella, smiling, retrieved them. He tried again with the same result, and she showed him how to throw the first ball so it would come down on the far side of his left hand, while the other traveled inside its trajectory when he launched it rightward. He needed several tries to master it, and even after he did he sometimes failed to make the catch, his eyes going in too many directions at once. Meanwhile

Sleet, machinelike, completed exchange after exchange. Carabella drilled Valentine in the double throw for what seemed like hours, and perhaps was. He grew bored, at first, once he was perfect at it, and then he passed through boredom into a state of utter harmony, knowing that he could throw the balls like this for a month without wearying or dropping one.

And suddenly he perceived that Sleet was juggling all three at once.

'Go on,' Carabella urged. 'It only *looks* impossible.'

He made the shift with an ease that surprised him, and evidently sur- prised Sleet and Carabella too, because she clapped her hands and he, with- out breaking rhythm, released a grunt of approval. Intuitively Valentine threw the third ball as the second was moving from his left hand to the right; he made the catch and returned the toss, and then he was going, a throw, a throw, a throw and a catch, a throw and a catch, a throw, always a ball on a rising arc and one descending into the waiting hand and one wait- ing to be thrown, and he kept it up for three, four, five interchanges before he realized the difficulty of what he was doing and broke his timing, sending all three balls spraying across the courtyard as they collided.

'You have a gift,' Sleet murmured. 'A definite gift.'

Valentine was embarrassed by the collision, but the fact that he had dropped the balls did not appear to matter nearly as much as that he had been able to juggle them all on the first try. He rounded them up and began again, Sleet facing him and continuing the sequence of tosses that he had never interrupted. Mimicking Sleet's stance and timing, Valentine began to throw, dropped two balls on the first try, reddened and muttered apologies, started again, and this time did not stop. Five, six, seven inter- changes, ten, and then he lost count, for they no longer seemed like inter- changes but all part of one seamless process, infinite and never-ending. Somehow his consciousness was split, one part making precise and accurate catches and tosses, the other monitoring the floating and descending balls, making rapid calculation of speed, angle, and rate of descent. The scan- ning part of his mind relayed data instantly and constantly to the part of his mind that governed the throwing and catching. Time seemed divided into an infinity of brief strokes and yet, paradoxically, he had no sense of sequence: the three balls seemed fixed in their places, one perpetually in mid-air, one in each of his hands, and the fact that at each moment a different ball held one of those positions was inconsequential. Each was all. Time was timeless. He did not move, he did not throw, he did not catch: he only observed the flow, and the flow was frozen outside time and space. Now Valentine saw the mystery of the art. He had entered into infinity. By split- ting his consciousness he had unified it. He had traveled to the inner nature of movement, and had learned that movement was illusion and sequence an error of perception. His hands functioned in the present, his eyes scanned the future, and nevertheless there was only this moment of now.

And as his soul journeyed toward the heights of exultation, Valentine perceived, with the barest flicker of his otherwise transcendent consciousness, that he was no longer standing rooted to the place, but somehow had begun to move forward, drawn magically by the orbiting balls, which were drifting subtly away from him. They were receding across the courtyard with each series of throws – and he experienced them now as a series once again, rather than as an infinite seamless continuum – and he was having to move faster and faster to keep pace with them, until he was virtually running, staggering, lurching around the yard, Sleet and Carabella scrambling to avoid him, and finally the balls were out of his reach altogether, beyond even his last desperate lunge. They bounced off in three directions.

Valentine dropped to his knees, gasping. He heard the laughter of his instructors and began to laugh with them.

'What happened?' he asked finally. 'I was going so well – and then – and then—'

'Small errors accumulate,' Carabella told him. 'You get carried away by the wonder of it all, and you throw a ball slightly out of the true plane and you reach forward to catch it, and the reaching causes you to make the next throw out of plane as well, and the next, and so on until everything drifts away from you, and you give chase, and in the end pursuit is impossible. It happens to everyone at the beginning. Think nothing of it.'

'Pick up the balls,' said Sleet. 'In four days you juggle before the Coronal.'

7

He drilled for hours, going no further than the three-ball cascade but repeating it until he had penetrated the infinite a dozen times, moving from boredom to ecstasy to boredom so often that boredom itself became ecstasy. His clothing was soaked with sweat, clinging to him like warm wet towels. Even when one of Pidruid's brief light rainshowers began he continued to throw the balls. The rain ended and gave way to a weird twilight glow, the early evening sun masked by light fog. Still Valentine juggled. A crazy intensity overcame him. He was dimly aware of figures moving about the courtyard, Sleet, Carabella, the various Skandars, Shanamir, strangers, coming and going, but he paid no attention. He had been an empty vessel into which this art, this mystery, had been poured, and he dared not stop, for fear he would lose it and be drained and hollow once again.

Then someone came close and he was suddenly empty-handed, and he understood that Sleet had intercepted the balls, one by one, as they arced past his nose. For a moment Valentine's hands went on moving anyway in persistent rhythms. His eyes would not focus on anything but the plane through which he had been throwing the balls.

'Drink this,' Carabella said gently, and put a glass to his lips. Fireshower wine: he drank it like water. She gave him another. 'You have a miraculous gift,' she told him. 'Not only coordination but concentration. You frightened us a little, Valentine, when you would not stop.'

'By Starday you will be the best of us,' said Sleet. 'The Coronal himself will single you out for applause. Eh, Zalzan Kavol? What do you say?'

'I say he is soaking wet and needs clean clothes,' the Skandar rumbled. He handed Sleet some coins. 'Go to the bazaar, buy something that fits him before the booths close. Carabella, take him out back to the cleanser. We eat in half an hour.'

'Come with me,' Carabella said.

She led Valentine, who still was dazed, through the courtyard to the sleeping-quarters, and behind them. A crude open-air cleanser had been rigged against the side of the building. 'The animal!' she said angrily. 'He could have given you a word of praise. But praise isn't his way, I suppose. He was impressed, all right.'

'Zalzan Kavol?'

'Impressed – yes, astonished. But how could he praise a human? You have only two arms! Well, praise isn't his way. Here. Get out of those.'

Quickly she stripped, and he did the same, dropping his soggy garments to the ground. By bright moonlight he saw her nakedness and was delighted. Her body was slim and lithe, almost boyish but for the small round breasts and the sudden flaring of the hips below her narrow waist. Her muscles lay close beneath the skin and were well developed. A flower had been tattooed in green and red on the crest of one flat buttock.

She led him under the cleanser and they stood close together as the vibrations rid them of sweat and grime. Then, still naked, they returned to the sleeping-quarters, where Carabella produced a fresh pair of trousers in soft gray fabric for herself, and a clean jerkin. By then Sleet had come back from the bazaar with new clothes for Valentine; a dark-green doublet with scarlet trim, tight red trousers, and a light cloak of blue that verged on black. It was a costume far more elegant than the one he had shed. Wearing it, he felt like one raised to some high rank, and moved with conscious hauteur as he accompanied Sleet and Carabella to the kitchen.

Dinner was stew – an anonymous meat at its base, and Valentine did not dare ask – washed down with copious drafts of fireshower wine. The six Skandars sat at one end of the table, the four humans at the other, and there was little conversation. At meal's end Zalzan Kavol and his brothers rose without a word and strode out.

'Have we offended them?' Valentine asked.

'It is their normal politeness,' said Carabella.

The Hjort who had spoken to him at breakfast, Vinorkis, now crossed the room and hovered by Valentine's shoulder, staring down in that fishy-eyed way of his: evidently it was a habit. Valentine smiled awkwardly.

Vinorkis said, 'Saw you juggling in the yard this afternoon. You're pretty good.'

'Thank you.'

'Hobby of yours?'

'Actually, I've never done it before. But the Skandars seem to have hired me for their troupe.'

The Hjort looked impressed. 'Really? And will you go on tour with them?'

'So it appears.'

'Whereabouts?'

'I have no idea,' said Valentine. 'Perhaps it hasn't even been decided yet. Wherever they want to go will be good enough for me.'

'Ah, the free-floating life,' Vinorkis said. 'I've meant to try it myself. Perhaps your Skandars would hire me, too.'

'Can you juggle?'

'I can keep accounts. I juggle figures.' Vinorkis laughed vehemently and gave Valentine a hearty slap on the back. 'I juggle figures! Do you like that? Well, good night to you!'

'Who was that?' Carabella asked, when the Hjort was gone.

'I met him at breakfast this morning. A local merchant, I think.'

She made a face. 'I don't think I like him. But it's so easy not to like Hjorts. Ugly things!' She rose gracefully and stretched. 'Shall we go?'

He slept soundly again that night. To dream of juggling might have been expected, after the afternoon's events, but instead he found himself once more on the purple plain – a disturbing sign, for the Majipoori know from childhood that dreams of recurring aspect have extra significance, probably dark. The Lady rarely sends recurring dreams, but the King is given to the practice. Again the dream was a fragment. Mocking faces hovered in the sky. Whirlpools of purple sand churning alongside the path, as if creatures with busy claws and clacking palps were moving beneath. Spikes sprouted from the ground. The trees had eyes. Everything held menace, ugliness, foreboding. But the dream was without characters and without events. It communicated only sinister foreboding.

The world of dreams yielded to the world of daybreak. This time he was the first to waken, when the earliest strands of light entered the hall. Next to him Shanamir slumbered blissfully. Sleet lay coiled like a serpent far down the hall, and near him was Carabella, relaxed, smiling in her dreams. The Skandars evidently slept elsewhere; the only aliens in the room were a couple of lumpish Hjorts and a trio of Vroons tangled in a weave of limbs that defied comprehension. From Carabella's trunk Valentine took three of the juggling balls, and went outside into the misty dawn to sharpen his burgeoning skills.

Sleet, emerging an hour later, found him at it and clapped his hands. 'You have the passion, friend. You juggle like one possessed. But don't tire yourself so soon. We have more complicated things to teach you today.'

The morning's lesson had to do with variations on the basic position. Now that Valentine had mastered the trick of throwing three balls so that one was always in the air – and he had mastered it, no question of that, attaining in one afternoon a control of technique that Carabella said had taken her many days of practice – they had him moving about, walking, trotting, turning corners, even skipping, all the while keeping the cascade going. He juggled the three balls up a flight of stairs and down again. He juggled in a squatting position. He juggled standing on one leg like the solemn gihorna-birds of the Zimr Marsh. He juggled while kneeling. By now he was absolutely secure in the harmony of eye and hand, and what the rest of his body might be doing had no effect on that.

In the afternoon Sleet moved him to new intricacies: throwing the ball from behind his back in mid-volley, throwing it up under one leg, juggling with crossed wrists. Carabella taught him how to bounce a ball against a wall and work the return smoothly into the flow, and how to send a ball from one hand to the other by letting it hit the back of his hand, instead of catching and throwing. These things he grasped swiftly. Carabella and Sleet had stopped complimenting him on the quickness of his mastery – it was patronizing to shower him constantly with praise – but he did not fail to observe the little glances of astonishment that often passed between them, and that pleased him.

The Skandars juggled in another part of the courtyard, rehearsing the act they would do in the parade, a miraculous thing involving knives and sickles and blazing torches. Occasionally Valentine glanced over, marveling at what the four-armed ones were achieving. But mainly he concentrated on his own training.

So went Seaday. On Fourday they began teaching him how to juggle with clubs instead of balls. This was a challenge, for although the principles were mainly the same, clubs were bigger and clumsier, and it was necessary for Valentine to throw them higher in order to have time to make the catches. He began with one club, tossing it from hand to hand. This is how you hold it, said Carabella, this is how you throw, this is how you catch, and he did as she said, bending a thumb now and then but soon learning the skills. 'Now,' she said, 'put two balls in your left hand and the club in your right,' and he threw, confused for a moment by the differences in mass and spin, but not for long, and after that it was two clubs in his right hand and a ball in his left, and late Fourday afternoon he worked with three clubs, wrists aching and eyes tight with strain, working all the same, unwilling and almost unable to stop.

That evening he asked, 'When will I learn how to throw the clubs with another juggler?'

Carabella smiled. 'Later. After the parade, as we travel eastward through the villages.'

'I could do it now,' he said.

'Not in time for the parade. You've performed wonders, but there are limits to what you can master in three days. If we had to juggle with a novice, we'd be forced to come down to your level, and the Coronal won't take much joy in that.'

He admitted the justice of what she said. Still, he longed for the time when he would take part in the interplay of the jugglers, and pass clubs or knives or torches with them as a member of a single many-souled entity in perfect coordination.

There was rain Fourday night, unusually heavy rain for subtropical Pidruid in summer, when quick showers were the rule, and Fiveday morning the courtyard was spongy-wet and tricky of footing. But the sky was clear and the sun was bright and hot.

Shanamir, who had been roaming the town during the days of Valentine's training, reported that preparations for the great parade were well advanced. 'Ribbons and streamers and flags everywhere,' he said, standing at a wary distance as Valentine began a morning warmup with the three clubs. 'And the starburst banner – they've lined the route with it, from Falkynkip Gate to Dragon Gate, and out Dragon and all along the waterfront, is what I hear, miles and miles of decoration, even cloth of gold, and green paint in the roadway. They say the cost runs to thousands of royals.'

'Who pays?' Valentine asked.

'Why, the people of Pidruid,' said Shanamir in surprise. 'Who else? Those of Ni-moya? Those of Velathys?'

'Let the Coronal himself pay for his festival, I'd say.'

'And whose money would that be, except the taxes of the whole world! Why should cities in Alhanroel pay for festivals in Zimroel? Besides, it's an honor to host the Coronal! Pidruid pays gladly. Tell me: how do you manage to throw a club and catch one at the same time with the same hand, Valentine?'

'Throw comes first, my friend. By only a little. Watch very carefully.'

'I *am* watching. I still can't figure it out.'

'When we have time, after the parade's done with, I'll show you how it works.'

'Where are we going after here?'

'I don't know. Eastward, Carabella told me. We'll go wherever there's a fair or a carnival or a festival that will hire jugglers.'

'Will I become a juggler too, Valentine?'

'If you want to. I thought you wanted to go to sea.'

'I just want to travel,' said Shanamir. 'It doesn't have to be by sea. So long as I don't have to go back to Falkynkip. Eighteen hours a day in the stables, currying mounts – oh, no, not for me, not any more! Do you know, the night I left home I dreamed I had learned how to fly. It was a dream from the Lady, Valentine, I knew it at once, and the flying meant I would go where I hoped to go. When you told Zalzan Kavol he had to take me along if he wanted you, I trembled. I thought I was going to – going to – I felt all—' He caught himself. 'Valentine, I want to be a juggler as good as you are.'

'I'm not very good. I'm only a beginner.' But, growing bold, Valentine threw the clubs in lower, faster arcs, showing off.

'I can't believe you just learned how on Twoday.'

'Sleet and Carabella are good instructors.'

'I never saw anyone learn anything so fast, though,' Shanamir said. 'You must have an extraordinary mind. I'll bet you were someone important before you became a wanderer, yes. You seem so cheerful, so – simple, and yet – and yet—'

'Hidden depths,' Valentine said amiably, trying to throw a club from behind his back and hurling it with an agonizing crack against his left elbow. All three clubs splattered to the wet ground, and he winced and rubbed the bruise. 'A master juggler,' he said. 'You see? Ordinarily it takes weeks of training to learn to hit your elbow like that!'

'You did it to change the subject,' Shanamir said, sounding more than half serious.

8

Starday morning, parade day, the Coronal's day, the first day of the grand festival of Pidruid, and Valentine lay curled in sleep, dreaming a quiet dream of lush green hills and limpid pools flecked with blue and yellow pond-anemones, when fingers poking in his ribs awakened him. He sat up, blinking and mumbling. Darkness: long before dawn. Carabella crouching over him: he sensed the catlike grace of her, heard her light laughter, picked up the creamy fragrance of her skin.

'Why so early?' he asked.

'To get a good place when the Coronal goes by. Hurry! Everyone's up already.'

He scrambled to his feet. His wrists were a little sore from juggling with the clubs, and he held out his arms, letting his hands loll and flop. Carabella grinned and took them in hers and looked up at him.

'You'll juggle magnificently today,' she said softly.

'I hope so.'

'There's no doubt of it, Valentine. Whatever you set out to do, you'll do supremely well. That's the sort of person you are.'

'You know what sort of person I am?'

'Of course I do. Better than you know, I suspect. Valentine, can you tell the difference between sleeping and waking?'

He frowned. 'I don't follow you.'

'There are times when I think it's all the same to you, that you're living a dream or dreaming a life. Actually I didn't think that. Sleet did. You fascinate him, and Sleet doesn't fascinate easily. He's been everywhere, he's seen much, he's seen through everything, and yet he talks constantly of you, he tries to comprehend you, to see into your mind.'

'I didn't realize I was so interesting. I find myself boring.'

'Others don't.' Her eyes were sparkling. 'Come, now. Dress, eat, off to the parade. In the morning we watch the Coronal go by, in the afternoon we perform, and at night – at night—'

'Yes? At night?'

'At night we hold festival!' she cried, and sprang away from him and out the door.

In the morning mist the troupe of jugglers headed for the place that Zalzan Kavol had secured for them along the grand processional highway. The Coronal's route began in the Golden Plaza, where he was lodged; from there he would move eastward along a curving boulevard that led out one of the city's secondary gates, and around to the great road on which Valentine and Shanamir had entered Pidruid, the one bordered by twin columns of fireshower palms in bloom, and thence via Falkynkip Gate back into the city, and across it down Water Road through the Arch of Dreams and out Dragon Gate to the waterfront, to the edge of the bay, where a reviewing stand had been erected in Pidruid's chief stadium. So the parade was double in nature: first a progress of the Coronal past the people, and then the people past the Coronal. It was an event that would last all through the day and into the night beyond, and probably toward Sunday's dawn.

Because the jugglers were part of the royal entertainment, it was necessary for them to take up a position somewhere near the waterfront end of things; otherwise they would never be able to cross the congested city in time to reach the stadium for their own performance. Zalzan Kavol had obtained a choice location for them close by the Arch of Dreams, but it meant that they would spend the better part of the day waiting for the parade to come to them. No help for it. On foot they cut diagonally through the back streets, emerging at last at the lower end of Water Road. As Shanamir had reported, the city was lavishly decorated, cluttered with ornament, banners and bunting dangling from every building, every lightglobe. The roadbed itself had been freshly painted in the Coronal's colors, gleaming bright green bordered by golden stripes.

At this early hour the route was already lined with viewers, and no open spaces, but a space in the crowd swiftly was made when the Skandar jugglers appeared and Zalzan Kavol produced his sheaf of tickets. People on Majipoor normally tended to courtesy and graceful accommodation. Besides, there were few who cared to argue points of precedence with six surly Skandars.

And then the waiting. The morning was warm and swiftly growing hot, and there was nothing for Valentine to do but stand and wait, staring at the empty highway, at the ornate black polished stonework of the Arch of Dreams, Carabella jammed up against his left side, Shanamir pushed close on the right. Time ticked infinitely slowly that morning. The wells of conversation quickly ran dry. One moment of diversion came when Valentine picked a startling phrase out of the murmur of conversation from the rows behind him:

'—can't see what all this cheering's about. I don't trust him one bit.'

Valentine listened more carefully. A pair of spectators – Ghayrogs, by the slippery sound of their voices – were talking about the new Coronal, and not in any complimentary way.

'—issuing too many decrees, if you ask me. Regulating this, regulating that, getting his fingers in here and there. No need for it!'

'He wants to show that he's on the job,' the other said mildly.

'No need! No need! Things went along well enough under Lord Voriax, and Lord Malibor before him, without all these fussy rules. Smacks of insecurity, if you ask me.'

'Quiet! Today of all days, this is no way to talk.'

'If you ask me, the boy's not sure he's really Coronal yet, so he makes sure we all take notice of him. If you ask me.'

'I didn't ask you.' In worried tones.

'And another thing. These imperial proctors all over the place, suddenly. What's he doing? Setting up his own world-wide police? Spying for the Coronal, are they? What for? What's he up to?'

'If he's up to anything, you'll be the first one pulled in. Will you be quiet?'

'I mean no harm,' the first Ghayrog said. 'Look, I carry the starburst banner like everyone else! Am I loyal, or am I loyal? But I don't like the way things are going. It's a citizen's right to worry about the state of the realm, isn't it? If matters are not to our liking, we should speak up. That's our tradition, isn't it? If we allow small abuses now, who knows what sort of things he'll be doing five years on!'

Interesting, Valentine thought. For all this frantic cheering and waving, the new Coronal was not universally loved and admired. How many of these others, he wondered, are merely pumping up their enthusiasm out of fear or self-interest?

The Ghayrogs fell silent. Valentine scanned for other conversations, but heard nothing of interest. Again time crawled. He turned his attention to the Arch, and studied it until he had memorized its features, the carved images of ancient Powers of Majipoor, heroes of the murky past, generals in the early Metamorph Wars, Coronals who antedated even legendary Lord Stiamot, Pontifexes of antiquity, Ladies offering benign blessings. The Arch, said Shanamir, was the oldest surviving thing in Pidruid and the holiest, nine thousand years old, carved from blocks of black Velathyntu marble that were immune to the ravages of the weather. To pass beneath it was to ensure the protection of the Lady and a month of useful dreams.

Rumors of the Coronal's progress across Pidruid enlivened the morning. The Coronal, it was said, had left the Golden Plaza; had entered by way of Falkynkip Gate; had paused to bestow double handfuls of five-crown pieces in the sectors of the city inhabited primarily by Vroons and Hjorts; had stopped to comfort a wailing infant; had halted to pray at the shrine of his late brother Lord Voriax; had found the heat too great and was resting for some hours at midday; had done this, had done that, had done something else. The Coronal, the Coronal, the Coronal! All attention was on the Coronal this day. Valentine pondered what sort of life it must be, constantly making grand circuits of this sort, showing oneself in city after city on eternal parade, smiling, waving, throwing coins, taking part in unending gaudy spectacle, demonstrating in one's physical person the embodiment of the power of the government, accepting all this homage, this noisy public excitement, and somehow still managing to hold the reins of the government. Or were there reins to hold? The system was so ancient it probably ran of its own accord. A Pontifex, old and by tradition reclusive, hidden in a mysterious Labyrinth somewhere in central Alhanroel, making the decrees by which the world was ruled, and his heir and adopted son the Coronal reigning as executive officer and prime minister from atop Castle Mount, except when he was engaged in ceremonial progresses such as this – and was either of them needed except as a symbol of majesty? This was a peaceful, sunny, playful world, so Valentine thought, though no doubt it had a dark side hidden somewhere, or else why would a King of Dreams have arisen to challenge the authority of the blessed Lady? These rulers, this constitutional pomp, this expense and tumult – no, Valentine thought, it had no meaning, it was a survival out of some distant era when perhaps it all had had necessity. What had meaning now? To live each day, to breathe sweet air, to eat and drink, to sleep soundly. The rest was foolishness.

'The Coronal comes!' someone cried.

So the cry had arisen, ten times in the past hour, and no Coronal had come. But now, just about noon, it seemed that in fact he was drawing near.

The sound of cheering preceded him: a distant roar, like the crashing of the sea, that spread as a propagating wave along the line of march. As it grew louder, heralds on sprightly mounts appeared in the roadway, moving almost at a gallop, managing occasional trumpet-blasts through lips that must be sore and weary after all this time. And then, mounted on a floater that carried them briskly along, several hundred of the Coronal's personal bodyguard in the green-and-gold starburst uniform, a carefully selected group, both men and women, humans and others, the cream of Majipoor, standing at attention aboard their vehicle, looking, Valentine thought, very dignified and a trifle silly.

And now the Coronal's own chariot was in sight.

It, too, was floater-mounted, hovering several feet above the pavement and moving quickly forward in a ghostly way. Lavishly bedecked with glittering fabric and thick white quarterings sewn from what might well have been the fur of rare beasts, it had an appropriate look of majesty and costliness. On it rode half a dozen of the high officials of the city of Pidruid and the surrounding province, all of them clad in robes of state, mayors and dukes and such, and among them, mounted on a raised platform of some silken scarlet wood, extending his arms benevolently to the onlookers on either side of the road, was Lord Valentine the Coronal, second most luminous of the Powers of Majipoor, and – since his adoptive imperial father the Pontifex was aloof and never to be seen by ordinary mortals – perhaps the truest embodiment of authority that could be beheld in this world.

'Valentine!' the cry arose. 'Valentine! Lord Valentine!'

Valentine studied his royal namesake as intently as earlier he had examined the inscriptions on the ancient black Arch of Dreams. This Coronal was an imposing figure, a man of more than middle height, powerful-looking, with strong shoulders and long sturdy arms. His skin was of a rich olive hue, his hair was black and cut to fall just below his ears, his dark beard was a short stiff fringe at his chin.

As the tumult of cheers descended on him, Lord Valentine turned graciously to one side and another, acknowledging, inclining his body slightly, offering his outstretched hands to the air. The floater drifted swiftly past the place where Valentine and the jugglers stood, and in that interval of proximity the Coronal turned toward them, so that for an electric moment Valentine and Lord Valentine had their eyes locked on one another. It seemed that a contact passed between them, a spark leaped the gap. The Coronal's smile was brilliant, his bright dark eyes held a dazzling gleam, his robes of state themselves seemed to have life and power and purpose, and Valentine stood transfixed, caught by the sorcery of imperial might. For an instant he comprehended Shanamir's awe, the awe of all these people at the presence among them of their prince. Lord Valentine was only a man, true, he needed to void his bladder and fill his gut, he slept at night and rose yawning in the morning like ordinary mortals, he had dirtied his diapers when a babe and would drool and doze when he was old, and yet, and yet, he moved in sacred circles, he dwelled on Castle Mount, he was the living son of the Lady of the Isle of Sleep and had been taken as son by the Pontifex Tyeveras, as had his brother, dead Voriax, before him, he had lived most of his life close to the founts of power, he had had given into his charge the government of all this colossal world and its teeming multitudes, and, thought Valentine, such an existence changes one, it sets one apart, it gives one an aura and a strangeness. And as the chariot of the Coronal floated by, Valentine perceived that aura and was humbled by it.

Then the chariot was past and the moment was gone, and there was Lord Valentine retreating in the distance, still smiling, still extending his arms, still nodding graciously, still flashing his brilliant gaze at this citizen and that, but Valentine no longer felt himself in the presence of grace and might. Instead he felt vaguely soiled and cheated, and did not know why.

'Come quickly,' Zalzan Kavol grunted. 'We must get ourselves to the stadium now.'

That much was simple. Everyone in Pidruid except the bedridden and the imprisoned stood stationed along the line of parade. The auxiliary streets were empty. In fifteen minutes the jugglers were at the waterfront, in ten more they approached the huge bayside stadium. Here a crowd had already begun to form. Thousands jammed the wharfs just beyond the stadium to have a second glimpse of the Coronal as he arrived.

The Skandars formed themselves into a wedge and cut brutally through this mob, Valentine and Sleet and Carabella and Shanamir following in their wake. Performers were instructed to report to the staging area at the stadium's rear, a great open space fronting the water, and a kind of madness already prevailed there, with hundreds of costumed artists jostling for position. Here were giant gladiators of Kwill who made even the Skandars look frail, and teams of acrobats clambering impatiently over each other's shoulders, and an entire nude corps de ballet, and three orchestras of strange outworldly instruments, tuning up in bizarre discord, and animal-trainers tugging strings that controlled floater-borne beasts of improbable size and ferocity, and freaks of every description – a man who weighed a thousand pounds, a woman eleven feet high and slender as a black bamboo rod, a Vroon with two heads, Liimen who were triplets and joined by a rope of ghastly blue-gray flesh from waist to waist to waist, someone whose face was like a hatchet and whose lower body was like a wheel – and so much more that Valentine was dizzied by the sights and sounds and smells of this congregation of the bewildering.

Frantic clerks wearing municipal sashes were trying to arrange these performers into an orderly procession. Some sort of order of march actually existed; Zalzan Kavol barked an identification at a clerk and received in return a number that marked his troupe's place in line. But then it was their task to find their neighbors in the line, and that was not so easy, for everyone in the staging area was in constant motion and finding numbers was like trying to attach name-tags to waves in the sea.

Eventually the jugglers found their place, well back in the crowd, jammed in between a group of acrobats and one of the orchestras. After that there was no moving about, and once more they stood in place for hours. The performers were offered refreshments as they waited: servitors moved among them bearing bits of skewered meat and globelets of green or gold wine, for which no fee was asked. But the air was warm and heavy, and the reek of so many close-packed bodies of so many races and metabolisms made Valentine feel faint. In an hour, he thought, I will be juggling before the Coronal. How odd that sounds! He was aware of Carabella close beside him, jaunty, buoyant, always smiling, unfailingly energetic. 'May the Divine spare us from having to do this ever again,' she whispered.

At last there was some sense of movement far away near the gate to the stadium, as if some stopcock had been pulled and eddy-currents were drawing the first performers out of the staging area. Valentine stood on tiptoe but had no clear idea of what was happening. The better part of an hour went by before any sort of motion was apparent at their end of the assemblage. Then the line began to go steadily forward.

From within the stadium came sounds: music, screeching beasts, laughter, applause. The orchestra that preceded Zalzan Kavol's troupe now was ready to enter – twenty players, of three non-human races, bearing fanciful instruments unknown to Valentine, swirls of shining brass pipe and strange lopsided drums and small five-bodied fifes and the like, everything oddly delicate, but the sound they made was not delicate at all when they struck up and began their march. The last of the musicians disappeared through the great double gates of the stadium and an officious major-domo strutted forward to bar the access of the jugglers.

'Zalzan Kavol and his troupe,' the major-domo announced.

'We are here,' said Zalzan Kavol.

'You will wait for the signal. Then you enter and follow those musicians in procession from left to right around the stadium. Do not begin to perform until you pass the large green flag that bears the Coronal's emblem. When you reach the pavilion of the Coronal, pause and make obeisance, and hold your place for sixty seconds, performing your act, before moving onward. When you reach the far gate, depart from the arena at once. You will be paid your fee as you leave. Is everything clear?'

'Quite,' said Zalzan Kavol.

The Skandar turned to his troupe. He had until this moment been nothing other than brusque and rough, but suddenly he displayed another side, for he reached three of his arms toward his brothers, and clasped hands with them, and something that seemed almost like a loving smile appeared on his harsh face. Then the Skandar embraced Sleet, and then Carabella, and then he drew Valentine toward him and said, as gently as a Skandar could, 'You have learned quickly and you show signs of mastery. You were only a convenience for us, but I am pleased now that you are among us.'

'Thank you,' said Valentine solemnly.

'Jugglers!' the major-domo barked.

Zalzan Kavol said, 'It's not every day that we juggle for a Power of Majipoor. Let this be our finest performance.'

He gestured and the troupe moved through the mighty double gates.

Sleet and Carabella led the way, juggling five knives that they exchanged with one another in staccato patterns constantly varying: then, after a space, Valentine walked alone, juggling his three clubs with a taut intensity likely to conceal the simplicity of his routine; and, behind him, the six Skandar brothers, making utmost use of their twenty-four arms to fill the air with a preposterous miscellany of flying objects. Shanamir, as a kind of esquire, concluded the march, making no performance, merely serving as a human punctuation mark.

Carabella was exuberant, irrepressible: she did high-springs, clicking her heels, clapping her hands, and yet never missing a beat, while beside her Sleet, whiplash-quick, compact, dynamic, made himself a veritable well of energy as he snatched knives from the air and returned them to his partner. Even somber economical Sleet allowed himself a quick implausible somersault while the soft air of Majipoor under the light pull of gravity held the knives aloft for the necessary fraction of a second.

Around the stadium they marched, taking their rhythm from the strident squeaks and tootles and thumps of the orchestra before them. The vast throng, jaded already with novelty after novelty, hardly reacted, but no matter: the jugglers' allegiance was to their art, not to the sweaty faces barely visible in the distant seats.

Valentine had devised yesterday, and privately practiced, a fancy flourish for his routine. The others knew nothing of it, for there were risks in such things for a novice, and a royal performance was perhaps not the right place for a risk – although, he thought, more truthfully a royal performance was the most proper place for extending oneself to the fullest.

So he grasped two of his clubs in his right hand and hurled them high, and as he did so he heard the grunting '*Hoy!*' of surprise from Zalzan Kavol, but there was no time to think on that, for the two clubs were descending and Valentine sent the one in his left hand up between them in a soaring double flip. Deftly he caught one falling club in each hand, sent the one in his right hand aloft, caught the double-flipped one as it dropped, and went serenely and with great relief into his familiar cascade of clubs, looking neither to the right nor to the left as he trailed Carabella and Sleet around the perimeter of the gigantic stadium.

Orchestras, acrobats, dancers, animal-trainers, jugglers, before him and aft, thousands of blank faces in the seats, ribbon-bedecked arcades of grandees – Valentine saw none of it except in the most subliminal way. Throw, throw, throw and catch, throw and catch, throw and catch, on and on, until in the corner of his eye he saw the brilliant green-and-gold draperies flanking the royal pavilion. He turned to face the Coronal. This was a difficult moment, for now he had to divide his attention: keeping the clubs flying, he sought for Lord Valentine himself, and found him, halfway up the sloping pavilion. Valentine prayed for another jolt of interchanged energy, another quick flash of contact with the Coronal's searing eyes. He threw automatically, precisely, each club rising its allotted distance and arcing over to land between his thumb and fingers, and as he did so he searched the Coronal's face, but no, no jolt of energy this time, for the prince was distracted, he did not see the juggler at all, he stared in boredom across the whole width of the stadium, toward some other act, perhaps some fang-and-claw animal number, perhaps the bare-rumped ballet-dancers, perhaps at nothing at all. Valentine persevered, counting out the full sixty seconds of his homage, and toward the end of his minute it seemed to him the Coronal did indeed glance his way a fraction of an instant, but no more than that.

Then Valentine moved on. Carabella and Sleet were already approaching the exit. Valentine turned in a half circle where he stood, and grinned high-heartedly at the Skandars, who marched forward under a dancing canopy of axes and fiery torches and sickles and hammers and pieces of fruit, adding object after object to the multitude of things they whirled aloft. Valentine juggled at them a moment before continuing his solitary orbit of the stadium.

And onward, and outward through the far gate. And caught his clubs and held them as he passed into the outer worlds. Again, as he left the presence of the Coronal, he felt a letdown, a weariness, an emptiness, as though Lord Valentine did not truly radiate energy but merely drained it from others, giving the illusion of a bright out-flashing aura, and when moved beyond him one experienced only a sense of loss. Besides, the performance was over; Valentine's moment of glory had come and gone, and no one apparently had noticed.

Except Zalzan Kavol, who looked dour and irritable. 'Who taught you that two-club throw?' he demanded, the moment he came through the gate.

'No one,' said Valentine. 'I invented it myself.'

'And if you had dropped your clubs out there?'

'Did I drop them?'

'That was no place for fancy tricks,' the Skandar muttered. Then he softened a bit. 'But I do admit you carried yourself well.' From a second majordomo he received a purse of coins, and dumped them into his two outer hands, counting quickly through them. Most he pocketed, but he tossed one to each of his brothers, and one apiece to Sleet and Carabella, and then, after some thought, smaller coins to Valentine and Shanamir.

Valentine saw that he and Shanamir had each received half a crown, and the others a crown apiece. Not important: money was of no real account so long as a few crowns jingled in his pouch. The bonus, however small, was unexpected. He would squander it gleefully tonight on strong wine and spicy fish.

The long afternoon was nearly over. Fog rising off the sea was bringing an early darkness to Pidruid. In the stadium, the sounds of circus still resounded. The poor Coronal, Valentine thought, would be sitting there far into the night.

Carabella tugged at his wrist.

'Come now,' she whispered urgently. 'Our work is done! Now we make festival!'

9

She sprinted off into the crowd, and Valentine, after a moment's confusion, followed her. His three clubs, fastened by a cord to his waist, clumped awkwardly into his thighs as he ran. He thought he had lost her, but no, she was in sight now, taking high bouncy strides, turning and grinning saucily back at him, waving him on. Valentine caught up with her on the great flat steps that led down to the bay. Barges had been towed into the near harbor, with pyres of slender logs piled on them in intricate patterns, and already, though it was hardly night yet, a few of them had been torched and were burning with a cool green glow, sending up scarcely any smoke.

The entire city had been converted, during the day, into a playground. Carnival booths had sprung up like toadstools after summer rain; revelers in strange costumes swaggered along the quays; there was music on all sides, laughter, a feverish excitement. As the darkness deepened, new fires blazed, and the bay became a sea of colored light; and out of the east erupted some kind of pyrotechnic display, a skyrocket of piercing brilliance that soared to a point high overhead and burst, sending dazzling streamers downward to the tips of Pidruid's highest buildings.

A frenzy was on Carabella, and a frenzy crept into Valentine too. Hand in hand they raced recklessly through the city, from booth to booth, scattering coins like pebbles as they played. Many of the booths were games of skill, knocking down dolls with balls or upsetting some carefully balanced construct. Carabella, with her juggler's eye and juggler's hand, won nearly everything she tried, and Valentine, though less skilled, took his share of prizes too. At some booths the winnings were mugs of wine or morsels of meat; at others they were silly stuffed animals or banners bearing the Coronal's emblem, and these things they abandoned. But they ate the meat, they gulped the wine, and they grew flushed and wild as the night moved on.

'Here!' Carabella cried, and they joined a dance of Vroons and Ghayrogs and drunken Hjorts, a capering circle-dance that seemed to have no rules. For long minutes they pranced with the aliens. When a leathery-faced Hjort embraced Carabella she hugged it back, clasping it so tightly that her small strong fingers sank deeply into its puffy hide, and when a female Ghayrog, all snaky locks and myriad swaying breasts, pressed herself against Valentine he accepted her kiss and returned it with more enthusiasm than he would have expected himself to muster.

And then it was onward again, into a open-walled theater where angular puppets were enacting a drama in jerky stylized movements, and on into an arena where, at a cost of a few weights, they watched sea-dragons swim in menacing circles round and round in a glistening tank, and onward from there to a garden of animate plants from Alhanroel's southern shore, ropy tentacular things and tall trembling rubbery columns with surprising eyes near their summits. 'Feeding time in half an hour,' the keeper called, but Carabella would not stay, and with Valentine in tow she plunged off through the gathering darkness.

Fireworks exploded again, now infinitely more effective against the backdrop of night. There was a triple starburst that gave way to the image of Lord Valentine filling half the sky, and then a dazzle of green and red and blue that took the form of the Labyrinth and yielded to the gloomy visage of old Pontifex Tyeveras, and after a moment, when the colors had cleared, a new explosion threw a sheet of fire across the heavens, out of which coalesced the beloved features of the great royal mother, the Lady of the Isle of Sleep, smiling down on Pidruid with all of love. The sight of her so deeply moved Valentine that he would have fallen to his knees and wept, a mysterious and startling response. But there was no room in the crowd for any of that. He stood trembling an instant. The Lady faded into the darkness. Valentine slipped his hand against Carabella's and held it tightly.

'I need more wine,' he whispered.

'Wait. There's one more to come.'

Indeed. Another skyrocket, another burst of color, this one jagged and uncouth to the eye, yellows and reds, and out of it another face, heavy-jawed and somber-eyed, that of the fourth of the Powers of Majipoor, that darkest and most ambiguous figure of the hierarchy, the King of Dreams, Simonan Barjazid. A hush fell over the crowd, for the King of Dreams was no one's friend, though all acknowledged his power, lest he bring bad fortune and dread punishment.

Now they went for wine. Valentine's hand shook and he downed two mugs quickly, while Carabella looked at him in some concern. Her fingers played with the strong bones of his wrist, but she asked no questions. Her own wine she left barely touched.

The next door that opened before them in the festival was that of a wax museum, in the shape of a miniature Labyrinth, so that when they stumbled inside there was no turning back, and they gave the waxen keeper their three-weight pieces and went forward. Out of the darkness emerged heroes of the realm done in cunning simulation, moving, even speaking in archaic dialects. This tall warrior announced himself to be Lord Stiamot, conqueror of the Metamorphs, and this was the fabled Lady Thiin, his mother, the warrior-Lady who in person led the defense of the Isle of Sleep when it was besieged by aborigines. To them came one claiming to be Dvorn, the first Pontifex, a figure almost as remote in time from the era of Stiamot as Stiamot was from the present, and near him was Dinitak Barjazid, the first King of Dreams, a personage far less ancient. Deeper into the maze went Carabella and Valentine, encountering a host of dead Powers, a cleverly chosen assortment of Pontifexes and Ladies and Coronals, the great rulers Confalume and Prestimion and Dekkeret, and the Pontifex Arioc of curious fame, and last of all, presiding over the exit, the image of a ruddy-faced man in tight black garments, perhaps forty years of age, black-haired and dark-eyed and smiling, and he needed to offer no introductions, for this was Voriax, the late Coronal, brother to Lord Valentine, cut down in the prime of his reign two years past, dead in some absurd hunting accident after holding power only eight years. The image bowed and reached forth its hands, and exclaimed, 'Weep for me, brothers and sisters, for I was supreme and perished before my time, and my fall was all the greater since I fell from so lofty a height. I was Lord Voriax, and think long on my fate.'

Carabella shuddered. 'A gloomy place, and a gloomy finish to it. Away from here!'

Once more she led him breathlessly through the festival grounds, through gaming-halls and arcades and brilliantly lit pavilions, past dining-tables and pleasure-houses, never halting, floating birdlike from place to place, until finally they turned a corner and were in darkness, beyond the zone of revelry altogether. From behind them came the raucous sounds of fading merriment and the dwindling glow of garish light; as they moved forward they encountered the fragrance of heavy blossoms, the silence of trees. They were in a garden, a park.

'Come,' Carabella murmured, taking him by the hand.

They entered a moonlit glade where the trees had been pleached overhead to form a tightly woven bower. Valentine's arm slipped easily around her taut, narrow waist. The soft warmth of the day lay trapped under these close-tangled trees, and from the moist soil rose the creamy sweet aroma of huge fleshy flowers, bigger across than a Skandar's head. The festival and all its chaotic excitement seemed ten thousand miles away.

'This is where we'll stay,' Carabella announced.

With exaggerated chivalry he spread his cloak, and she drew him to the ground and slid easily and swiftly into his arms. They lay secluded between two high dense bushes of gray-green sticklike branches. A stream ran not far from them and only the most slender gleams of brightness entered overhead.

Fastened to Carabella's hip was a tiny pocket-harp of intricate workmanship. She drew it forth now, strummed a brief melodious prelude, and began to sing in a cool, pure voice:

> My love is fair as is the spring,
> As gentle as the night,
> My love is sweet as stolen fruit,
> My love is clear and bright
> Not all the richness of the land,
> Nor all the gems of sea,
> Nor all the wealth of Castle Mount
> Is worth my love to me.

'How lovely that is,' Valentine murmured. 'And your voice – your voice is so beautiful—'

'Do you sing?' she asked.

'Why – yes, I suppose so.'

She handed him the harp. 'Sing for me now. One of your favorites.'

He turned the little instrument over in his hand, puzzled, and said after a moment, 'I don't know any songs.'

'No songs? No songs? Come, you must know a few!'

'All gone from my mind, so it seems.'

Carabella smiled and took back her harp. 'I'll teach you a few, then,' she said. 'But not now, I think.'

'No. Not now.'

He touched his lips to hers. She purred and chuckled, and her embrace grew tighter. As his eyes became accustomed to the darkness he could see her more clearly, small pointed face, bright sly eyes, glossy tumbling black hair. Her nostrils flared with expectation. He drew back momentarily from what was to occur, obscurely fearing that some sort of contract was about to be sealed, but then he put those fears behind him. It was festival night, and he wanted her, and she him, Valentine's hands slipped down her back, came forward, felt the cage of her ribs lying just below the skin. He remembered her as she had looked standing naked under the cleanser: muscle and bone, bone and muscle, not much meat on her except at thighs and buttocks. A compact bundle of energy. In a moment she was naked again, and so was he. He saw that she was trembling, but not from chill, not on this balmy humid night in this secret bower. A strange, almost frightening intensity seemed to grip her. He stroked her arms, her face, her muscular shoulders, the small hard-tipped spheres of her breasts. His hand found the sleek skin along the inside of her thighs, and she let out her breath sharply and pulled him to her.

Their bodies moved in easy rhythms, as though they had been lovers for months and were well practiced with one another. Her slender powerful legs clasped his waist and they rolled over and over, until they came almost to the edge of the stream and could feel its chilly spray on their sweaty skins. They paused there, laughing, and rolled back the other way. This time they came to rest against one of the gray-green bushes, Carabella pulling him downward, taking the thrust of his weight without difficulty.

'Now!' she cried, and he heard her hiss and moan, and then her fingers dug deep into his flesh and a furious spasm racked her body, and in that same instant he gave himself up fully to the forces that were sweeping through him.

Afterward he lay gasping and half dazed in her embrace, listening to the booming of his own heart.

'We'll sleep here,' she whispered. 'No one will trouble us on this night.' She stroked his forehead, pushing his soft yellow hair back from his eyes, smoothing it into place. Lightly she kissed the tip of his nose. She was casual, playful, kittenish: that dark erotic intensity was gone from her, burned away in the fires of passion. But he felt shaken, stunned, confused. For him there had been sudden sharp ecstasy, yes. But in that moment of ecstasy he had found himself peering through gates of dazzling light into a mysterious realm without color or form or substance, and he had teetered precariously on the brink of that unknown before tumbling back into the world of this reality.

He could not speak. Nothing he might say seemed appropriate. He had not expected such disorientation to come out of the act of love. Carabella evidently sensed the disquiet in him, for she said nothing, only held him, rocked him gently, drew his head against her breast, sang softly to him.

In the warmth of the night he drifted gradually into sleep.

When the dream-images came, they were harsh and terrifying.

He was carried back yet again to that bleak, familiar purple plain. The same mocking faces leered at him from the purple sky, but this time he was not alone. Looming up against him was a figure of dark visage and heavy, oppressive physical presence whom Valentine understood to be his brother, although in the fierce crackling glow of the amber sun he could not clearly see the other man's features. And the dream enacted itself against a background of somber music, the low keening note of mind-music that denoted the peril-dream, the threat-dream, the death-dream.

The two men were locked in a bitter duel, and only one would come forth from the duel alive.

'Brother!' Valentine cried in shock and horror. 'No!' He stirred and twisted and came swimming up to the surface of sleep, and hovered there for an instant. But his training lay too deep for that. One did not flee dreams, one did not reject them no matter how appalling. One entered fully into them and accepted their guidance; one came to grips with the unthinkable in dreams, and to avoid it then meant the inevitability of confronting it, and being defeated by it, in waking life.

Deliberately Valentine drove himself downward again, through the borderland between wakefulness and sleep, and felt stealing about him once more the malign presence of his enemy, his brother.

They were armed with swords, but the contest was unequal, for Valentine's weapon was a flimsy rapier, the brother's a massive saber. Through skill and agility Valentine tried desperately to slip his sword past his brother's guard. Impossible. With slow weighty strokes the other parried steadily, sweeping Valentine's frail blade aside and driving him inexorably backward over the rough gullied terrain.

Vultures circled overhead. Out of the sky came a hissing death-song. There would be blood spilling soon, and a life returning to the Source.

Step by step Valentine yielded, knowing that a ravine lay just behind him and further retreat soon would be forestalled. His arm was aching, his eyes pounded with fatigue, there was the gritty taste of sand in his mouth, his last strength ebbing. Backward – backward—

'Brother!' he cried in anguish. 'In the name of the Divine—'

His plea drew harsh laughter and a sharp obscenity. The saber descended in a mighty swing. Valentine thrust out his blade and was shaken by a terrible body-numbing shiver as metal rang against metal and his light sword was snapped to a stump. In the same moment he tripped over a dry sand-scoured snag of wood and tumbled heavily to the ground, landing in a tangle of thorny creeping stems. The huge man with the saber reared above him, blotting out the sun, filling the sky. The death-song took on a murderous screeching intensity of timbre; the vultures fluttered and swooped.

The sleeping Valentine moaned and trembled. He turned again, huddled close against Carabella, took warmth from her as the dread cold of the death-dream enveloped him. It would be so easy to awaken now, to escape the horror and violence of these images, to swim to safety on the shores of consciousness. But no. With fierce discipline he thrust himself again into the nightmare. The giant figure laughed. The saber rose high. The world lurched and crumbled beneath his fallen body. He commended his soul to the Lady and waited for the blow to descend.

And the blow of the saber was awkward and lame, and with a foolish thud his brother's sword buried itself deep in the sand, and the texture and thrust of the dream was altered, for no longer did Valentine hear the wailing hiss of death-songs, and now he found everything reversed, found currents of new and unexpected energy pouring into him. He leaped to his feet. His brother tugged at the saber, cursed, struggled to pull it from the ground, and Valentine snapped it with a contemptuous kick.

He seized the other man barehanded.

Now it was Valentine who commanded the duel, and his cowering brother who retreated before a shower of blows, sagging now to his knees as Valentine battered him, growling like a wounded bear, shaking his bloody head from side to side, taking the beating and offering no defense, murmuring only, 'Brother … brother …' as Valentine pounded him to the sand.

He lay still and Valentine stood victor over him.

Let it be dawn, Valentine prayed, and released himself from sleep.

It was still dark. He blinked and clasped his arms to his sides and shivered. Violent frenzied images, fragmented but potent, swam in his troubled mind.

Carabella studied him thoughtfully.

'Are you all right?' she asked.

'I dreamed.'

'You cried out three times. I thought you would wake. A strong dream?'

'Yes.'

'And now?'

'I'm puzzled. Troubled.'

'Tell me your dream.'

It was an intimate request. And yet were they not lovers? Had they not gone down into the world of sleep together, partners in the night's quest?

'I dreamed that I fought with my brother,' he said hoarsely. 'That we dueled with swords in a hot barren desert, that he came close to killing me, that at the last moment I rose from the ground and found new strength and – and – and I beat him to death with my fists.'

Her eyes glittered like an animal's in the darkness: she watched him like some wary beady-eyed drole.

'Do you always have such ferocious dreams?' she asked after a time.

'I don't think so. But—'

'Yes?'

'Not only the violence. Carabella, I have no brother!'

She laughed. 'Do you expect dreams to correspond exactly to reality? Valentine, Valentine, where were you taught? Dreams have a truth deeper than the reality we know. The brother of your dream could be anyone or no one: Zalzan Kavol, Sleet, your father, Lord Valentine, the Pontifex Tyeveras, Shanamir, even me. You know that unless they be specific sendings, dreams transform all things.'

'I know, yes. But what does it mean, Carabella? To duel with a brother – to be killed, almost, by him – to slay him instead—'

'You want me to speak your dreams for you?' she said, surprised.

'It speaks nothing to me except fear and mystery.'

'You were badly frightened, yes. You were soaked with sweat and you cried out again and again. But painful dreams are the most revealing ones, Valentine. Speak it for yourself.'

'My brother – I have no brother—'

'I told you, it doesn't matter.'

'Did I make war against myself, then? I don't understand. I have no enemies, Carabella.'

'Your father,' she suggested.

He considered that. His father? He searched for a face that he could give to the shadowy man with the saber, but he found only more darkness.

'I don't remember him,' Valentine said.

'Did he die when you were a boy?'

'I think so.' Valentine shook his head, which was beginning to throb. 'I don't remember. I see a big man – his beard is dark, his eyes are dark—'

'What was his name? When did he die?'

Valentine shook his head again.

Carabella leaned close. She took his hands in hers and said softly, 'Valentine, where were you born?'

'In the east.'

'Yes, you've said that. Where? What city, what province?'

'Ni-moya?' he said vaguely.

'Are you asking me or telling me?'

'Ni-moya,' he repeated. 'A big house, a garden, near the bend of the river. Yes. I see myself there. Swimming in the river. Hunting in the duke's forest. Am I dreaming that?'

'Are you?'

'It feels like – something I've read. Like a story I've been told.'

'Your mother's name?'

He began to reply, but when he opened his mouth no name came.

'She died young too?'

'Galiara,' Valentine said without conviction. 'That was it. Galiara.'

'A lovely name. Tell me what she looked like.'

'She – she had—' He faltered. 'Golden hair, like mine. Sweet smooth skin. Her eyes – her voice sounded like – it's so hard, Carabella!'

'You're shaking.'

'Yes.'

'Come. Here.' Once again she drew him close. She was much smaller than he, and yet she seemed very much stronger now, and he took comfort from her closeness. Gently she said, 'You don't remember anything, do you, Valentine?'

'No. Not really.'

'Not where you were born or where you came from or what your parents looked like or even where you were last Starday, isn't that so? Your dreams can't guide you because you have nothing to speak against them.' Her hands roamed his head; her fingers probed delicately but firmly into his scalp.

'What are you doing?' he asked.

'Looking to see if you've been hurt. A blow on the head can take the memory away, you know.'

'Is there anything there?'

'No. No, nothing. No marks. No bumps. But that doesn't mean anything. It could have happened a month or two ago. I'll look again when the sun has risen.'

'I like the feel of your hands touching me, Carabella,'

'I like touching you,' she said.

He lay quietly against her. The words that had passed between them just now troubled him intensely. Other people, he realized, had rich memories of their childhood and adolescence, and knew the names of their parents and were sure of the place where they had been born, and he had nothing but his overlay of hazy notions, this mist of thin untrustworthy memories covering a well of blankness, yes, and he had known that the blankness was there but had chosen not to peer into it. Now Carabella had forced that upon him. Why, he wondered, was he unlike others? Why were his memories without substance? Had he taken some blow on the head, as she suggested? Or was it just that his mind was dim, that he lacked the capacity to retain the imprints of experience, that he had wandered for years across the face of Majipoor, erasing each yesterday as each new day dawned?

Neither of them slept again that night. Toward morning, quite suddenly, they began to make love again, in silence, in a kind of driven purposeful way quite different from the earlier playful union; and then they rose, still saying nothing, and bathed in the chilly little brook, and dressed and made their way through town to the inn. There were still some bleary-eyed revelers staggering in the streets as the bright eye of the sun rose high over Pidruid.

10

At Carabella's prompting Valentine took Sleet into his confidence, and told him of his dream and of the conversation that followed it. The little white-haired juggler listened thoughtfully, never interrupting, looking increasingly solemn.

He said when Valentine had done, 'You should seek guidance from a dream-speaker. This is too strong a sending to be ignored.'

'Do you think it is a sending, then?'

'Possibly it is,' said Sleet.

'From the King?'

Sleet spread his hands and contemplated his fingertips. 'It could be. You will have to wait and pay close heed. The King never sends simple messages.'

'It could be from the Lady just as well,' Carabella offered. 'The violence of it shouldn't deceive us. The Lady sends violent dreams when the need exists.'

'And some dreams,' said Sleet with a smile, 'come neither from the Lady nor from the King, but up out of the depths of our own foggy minds. Who can tell unaided? Valentine, see a dream-speaker.'

'Would a dream-speaker help me find my memories, then?'

'A dream-speaker or a sorcerer, yes. If dreams are no guidance to your past, nothing will be.'

'Besides,' said Carabella, 'a dream so strong should not go unexamined.

There is your responsibility to be considered. If a dream commands an action, and you choose not to pursue that action—' She shrugged. 'Your soul will answer for it, and swiftly. Find a speaker, Valentine.'

'I had hoped,' Valentine said to Sleet, 'that you would have some wisdom in these things.'

'I am a juggler. Find a speaker.'

'Can you recommend one in Pidruid?'

'We will be leaving Pidruid shortly. Wait until we are a few days' journey from the city. You will have richer dreams to give the speaker by then.'

'I wonder if this is a sending,' said Valentine. 'And from the King? What business would the King of Dreams have with a wanderer like me? I hardly think it possible. With twenty billion souls on Majipoor, how could the King find time to deal with any but the most important?'

'In Suvrael,' said Sleet, 'at the palace of the King of Dreams, are great machines that scan this entire world, and send messages into the minds of millions of people every night. Who knows how those millions are chosen? One thing they tell us when we are children, and I know it has truth: at least once before we leave this world, we will feel the touch of the King of Dreams against our spirit, each and all of us. I know that I have.'

'You?'

'More than once.' Sleet touched his lank, coarse white hair. 'Do you think I was born white-haired? One night I lay in a hammock in the jungles outside Narabal, no juggler then, and the King came to me as I slept and placed commands upon my soul, and when I awakened my hair was like this. I was twenty-three years old.'

'Commands?' Valentine blurted. 'What commands?'

'Commands that turn a man's hair from black to white between darkness and dawn,' Sleet said. Obviously he wished to say no more. He got to his feet and glanced at the morning sky as though checking the elevation of the sun. 'I think we've had enough talk for now, friend. There still are crowns to earn at the festival. Would you learn a few new tricks before Zalzan Kavol sends us out to work?'

Valentine nodded. Sleet fetched balls and clubs; they went out into the courtyard.

'Watch,' said Sleet, and he stood close behind Carabella. She held two balls in her right hand, he one in his left, and they put their other arms around one another. 'This is half-juggling,' Sleet said. 'A simple thing even for beginners, but it looks extremely challenging.' Carabella threw; Sleet threw and caught; at once they were in the rhythm of interchange, easily passing the balls back and forth, one entity with four legs and two minds and two juggling arms. Indeed it did look taxing, Valentine thought. Sleet called out, 'Feed the clubs to us now!'

As Valentine delivered each club with a quick sharp toss to Carabella's right hand, she worked it into the sequence, one, two, three, until balls and clubs flew from her to Sleet, from Sleet to her, in a dizzying cascade. Valentine knew from his own private trials how difficult it was to deal with that many objects. Five balls would be in his compass in another few weeks, he hoped; four clubs might be feasible soon too; but to handle three of each at the same time, and coordinate this half-juggling as well, was a feat that amazed him with admiration. And some jealousy too, he realized oddly, for here was Sleet with his body tight up against Carabella's, forming a single organism with her, and only a few hours ago she had lain with him by the side of that brook in the Pidruid park.

'Try it,' Sleet said.

He stepped aside and Carabella put herself in front of Valentine, arm and arm. They worked with three balls only. At first Valentine had problems judging the height and force of his throws, and sometimes sent the ball popping beyond Carabella's reach, but in ten minutes he had the knack of it and in fifteen they were working together as smoothly as if they had been doing the act for years. Sleet encouraged him with lively applause.

One of the Skandars appeared, not Zalzan Kavol but his brother Erfon, who even as Skandars went was dour and chill. 'Are you ready?' he asked gruffly.

The troupe performed that afternoon in the private park of one of the powerful merchants of Pidruid, who was giving an entertainment for a provincial duke, Carabella and Valentine performed their new half-juggling routine, the Skandars did something flamboyant with dishes and crystal goblets and cooking-pans, and, as a climax, Sleet was led forth to juggle blindfolded.

'Is this possible?' Valentine asked, awed.

'Watch!' said Carabella.

Valentine watched, but few others did, for this was Sunday after the great Starday frenzy, and the lordlings who had ordered this performance were a weary, jaded bunch, half asleep, bored with the skills of the musicians and acrobats and jugglers they had hired. Sleet stepped forward carrying three clubs and planted himself in a firm, confident way, standing a moment with his head cocked as though listening to the wind that blows between the worlds, and then, catching his breath sharply, he began to throw.

Zalzan Kavol boomed, 'Twenty years of practice, lords and ladies of Pidruid! The keenest sense of hearing is necessary for this! He detects the rustle of the clubs against the atmosphere as they fly from hand to hand!'

Valentine wondered how even the keenest sense of hearing could detect anything against the hum of conversation and the clink of dishes and the loud ostentatious pronouncements of Zalzan Kavol, but Sleet made no errors. That the juggling was difficult even for him was obvious: normally he was smooth as a machine, tireless as a loom, but now his hands were moving in sudden sharp skips and lunges, grasping hastily at a club that was spinning up almost out of reach, snatching with desperate quickness at one that had fallen nearly too far. Still, it was miraculous juggling. It was as if Sleet had some chart in his mind of the location of each of the moving clubs, and put his hand where he expected a club to fall, and found it there, or close enough. He did ten, fifteen, twenty exchanges of the clubs, and then gathered all three to his chest, flipped the blindfold aside, took a deep bow. There was a pattering of applause. Sleet stood rigid. Carabella came to him and embraced him, Valentine clapped him lustily on the shoulder, and the troupe left the stage.

In the dressing room Sleet was quivering from strain and beads of sweat glistened on his forehead. He gulped fireshower wine without restraint, as though it were nothing. 'Did they pay attention?' he asked Carabella. 'Did they even notice?'

'Some did,' she said gently.

Sleet spat. 'Pigs! Blaves! They have not enough skill to walk from one side of a room to the other, and they sit their chattering when – when an artist – when—'

Valentine had never seen Sleet show temper before. This blind juggling, he decided, was not good for the nerves. He seized the livid Sleet by both shoulders and leaned close. 'What matters,' he said earnestly, 'is the display of skill, not the manners of the audience. You were perfect.'

'Not quite,' Sleet said sullenly. 'The timing—'

'Perfect,' Valentine insisted, 'You were in complete command. You were majestic. How could you care what drunken merchants might say or do? Is it for their souls or yours that you mastered the art?'

Sleet managed a weak grin. 'The blind juggling cuts deep into the soul.'

'I would not see you in such pain, my friend.'

'It passes. I feel a little better now.'

'Your pain was self-inflicted,' Valentine said. 'It was unwise to allow yourself such outrage. I say again: you were perfect, and nothing else is important.' He turned to Shanamir. 'Go to the kitchen and see if we might have some meat and bread. Sleet has worked too hard. He needs new fuel, and fireshower wine isn't enough.'

Sleet looked merely tired now, instead of tense and furious. He reached forth a hand. 'Your soul is warm and kind, Valentine. Your spirit is a gentle and sunny one.'

'Your pain pained me.'

'I'll guard my wrath better,' Sleet said. 'And you're right, Valentine: we juggle for ourselves. *They* are incidental. I should not have forgotten that.'

Twice more in Pidruid Valentine saw the blind juggling done; twice more he saw Sleet stalk from the stage, rigid and drained. The attention of the onlookers, Valentine realized, had nothing to do with Sleet's fatigue. It was a demonic hard thing to do, was all, and the price the small man paid for his skill was a high one. When Sleet suffered, Valentine did what he could to beam comfort and strength to him. There was great pleasure for Valentine in serving the other man in that way.

Twice more, too, Valentine had dark dreams. One night the apparition of the Pontifex came to him and summoned him into the Labyrinth, and inward he went, down its many passageways and incomprehensible avenues, and the image of gaunt old Tyeveras floated like a will-o'-the-wisp before him, leading him onward to the core, until at last he attained some inner realm of the great maze and suddenly the Pontifex vanished, and Valentine stood alone in a void of cold green light, all footing gone, falling endlessly toward the center of Majipoor. And another night it was the Coronal, riding in his chariot across Pidruid, who beckoned him and invited him to a game of counters, and they threw the dice and moved the markers, and what they played with was a packet of bleached knucklebones, and when Valentine asked whose bones they were, Lord Valentine laughed and tugged at his stiff black fringe of a beard and fastened his dazzling harsh eyes on him and said, 'Look at your hands,' and Valentine looked, and his hands were without fingers, mere pink globes at his wrists.

These dreams Valentine shared once more with Carabella and with Sleet. But they offered him no dream-speaking, only repeated their advice that he go to some priestess of the slumber-world once they had left Pidruid.

Departure now was imminent. The festival was breaking up; the Coronal's ships no longer stood in the harbor; the roads were crowded with the outflow, as the people of the province made their way homeward from the capital. Zalzan Kavol instructed his troupe to finish whatever business remained to be done in Pidruid that morning, for on Seaday afternoon they would take to the highway.

The announcement left Shanamir strangely quiet, and dejected. Valentine noticed the boy's moodiness. 'I thought you'd be eager to move along. Finding the city too exciting to leave?'

Shanamir shook his head. 'I could go anytime.'

'Then what is it?'

'Last night a dream came to me of my father and brothers.'

Valentine smiled. 'Homesickness already, and you haven't even left the province?'

'Not homesickness,' Shanamir said bleakly. 'They were tied and lying in the road, and I was driving a team of mounts, and they cried out to me for help, and I drove right on, over their helpless bodies. One doesn't have to go to a dream-speaker for understanding of a dream like that.'

'So is it guilt at abandoning your duties at home?'

'Guilt? Yes. The *money*!' Shanamir said. There was an edge on his voice, as though he were a man trying to explain something to a dull child. He tapped his waist. 'The money, Valentine. I carry in here some hundred sixty royals from the sale of my animals, have you forgotten? A fortune! Enough to pay my family's way all this year and part of next! They depend on my coming back safely to Falkynkip with it.'

'And you were planning not to give it to them?'

'I am hired by Zalzan Kavol. What if his route lies another way? If I bring the money home, I might never find you all again as you wander over Zimroel. If I go off with the jugglers I steal my father's money, that he's expecting, that he needs. You see?'

'Simply enough solved,' Valentine said. 'Falkynkip is how far from here?'

'Two days fast, three days ordinary.'

'Quite close. Zalzan Kavol's route, I'm sure, has not yet been fixed. I'll speak to him right now. One town's as good as the next to him. I'll cajole him into taking the Falkynkip road out of here. When we're close to your father's ranch, you'll slip away by night, give the money quietly to one of your brothers, slip back to us before dawn. And then no guilt will attach, and you'll be free to proceed on your way.'

Shanamir's eyes widened. 'You think you can win a favor from that Skandar? How?'

'I can try.'

'He'll strike you to the ground in anger if you ask for anything. He wants no interference with his plans, any more than you'd allow a flock of blaves to vote on how you should run your affairs.'

'Let me talk to him,' said Valentine, 'and we'll see. I have reason to think Zalzan Kavol's not as rough within as he'd like us to believe. Where is he?'

'Seeing after his wagon, readying it for the journey. Do you know where that is?'

'Toward the waterfront,' Valentine said. 'Yes. I know.'

The jugglers traveled between cities in a fine wagon that was parked in a lot several blocks from the inn, for it was too broad of beam to bring down these narrow streets. It was an imposing and costly vehicle, noble and majestic, made with the finest workmanship by artisans of one of the inland provinces. The wagon's main frame was of long pale spars of light, springy wingwood, cunningly laminated into wide arching strips with a colorless fragrant glue and bound with resilient withes found in the southern marshes. Over this elegant armature sheets of tanned stickskin had been stretched and stitched into place with thick yellow fibers drawn from the stick-creatures' own gristly bodies.

Approaching it now, Valentine found Erfon Kavol and another of the Skandars, Gibor Haern, diligently oiling the wagon's traces, while from within came deep booming shouts of rage, so loud and violent that the wagon seemed to sway from side to side.

'Where is your brother?' Valentine asked.

Gibor Haern nodded sourly toward the wagon. 'This would not be a wise moment to intrude.'

'I have business with him.'

'*He* has business,' said Erfon Kavol, 'with the thieving little sorcerer we pay to guide us through the provinces, and who would resign our service in Pidruid just as we are making ready to leave. Go in, if you will, but you will regret it.'

The angry cries from the wagon grew more vociferous. Suddenly the door of the wagon burst open and a tiny figure sprang forth, a wizened old Vroon no bigger than a toy, a doll, a little feather-light creature, with ropy tentacular limbs and skin of a faded greenish tint and huge golden eyes now bright with fear. A smear of something that might be pale yellow blood covered the Vroon's angular cheek close beside its beak of a mouth.

Zalzan Kavol appeared an instant later, a terrifying figure in the doorway, his fur puffed with wrath, his vast basketlike hands impotently churning the air. To his brothers he cried, 'Catch him! Don't let him get away!'

Erfon Kavol and Gibor Haern rose ponderously and formed a shaggy wall blocking the Vroon's escape. The little being, trapped, panicky, halted and whirled and threw himself against Valentine's knees.

'Lord,' the Vroon murmured, clinging hard, 'protect me! He is insane and would kill me in his anger!'

Zalzan Kavol said, 'Hold him there, Valentine.'

The Skandar came forward. Valentine pushed the cowering Vroon out of sight behind him and faced Zalzan Kavol squarely. 'Control your temper, if you will. Murder this Vroon and we'll all be stuck in Pidruid forever.'

'I mean no murder,' Zalzan Kavol rumbled. 'I have no appetite for years of loathsome sendings.'

The Vroon said tremulously, 'He *means* no murder, only to throw me against a wall with all his strength.'

Valentine said, 'What is the quarrel? Perhaps I can mediate.'

Zalzan Kavol scowled. 'This dispute does not concern you. Get out of the way, Valentine.'

'Better that I don't, until your fury has subsided.'

Zalzan Kavol's eyes blazed. He advanced until he was no more than a few feet from Valentine, until Valentine could smell the anger-sharpened scent of the rough-thatched Skandar. Zalzan Kavol still seethed. It may be, Valentine thought, that he will throw both of us against the wall. Erfon

Kavol and Gibor Haern stared from the side: possibly they had never seen their brother defied before. There was silence a long moment. Zalzan Kavol's hands twitched convulsively, but he remained where he was.

At length he said, 'This Vroon is the wizard Autifon Deliamber, whom I hire to show me the inland roads and to guard me against the deceits of the Shapeshifters. All this week he has enjoyed a holiday at my expense in Pidruid; now it is time to leave and he tells me to find another guide, that he has lost interest in traveling from village to village. Is this your sense of how contracts are kept, wizard?'

The Vroon answered, 'I am old and weary and my sorceries grow stale, and sometimes I think I start to forget the road. But if you still wish it, I'll accompany you as before, Zalzan Kavol.'

The Skandar looked astounded.

'*What?*'

'I've changed my mind,' said Autifon Deliamber blandly, letting go his fearful clutch of Valentine's legs and stepping out into view. The Vroon coiled and opened his many rubbery boneless arms as if a dread tension were being discharged from them, and peered boldly up at the enormous Skandar. 'I will keep to my contract,' he declared.

Bewilderedly Zalzan Kavol said, 'For an hour and a half you've been swearing you'll remain here in Pidruid, ignoring all my entreaties and even ignoring my threats, driving me into such rage that I was ready to smash you to pulp, to my own grievous harm as well as yours, for dead sorcerers give poor service and the King of Dreams would rack me fearfully for such a thing, and still you were stubborn, still you denied the contract and told me to make shift elsewhere for a guide. And now at a moment's notice you retract all that?'

'I do.'

'Will you have the grace to tell me why?'

'No reason,' said the Vroon, 'except perhaps that this young man pleases me, that I admire his courage and his kindness and the warmth of his soul, and because he goes with you I will go with you again, for his sake and no other reason. Does that gratify your curiosity, Zalzan Kavol?'

The Skandar growled and sputtered in exasperation and gestured fiercely with his outer pair of hands, as though trying to pull them free of a tangle of birdnet vines. For an instant it seemed he might burst out in some new uprising of uncontrollable anger, that he was controlling himself only by supreme effort.

He said at last, 'Out of my sight, wizard, before I hurl you against a wall anyway. And may the Divine guard your life if you aren't here to depart with us this afternoon.'

'At the second hour after midday,' Autifon Deliamber said courteously.

'I will be punctual, Zalzan Kavol.' To Valentine he added, 'I thank you for protecting me. I am indebted to you, and will make repayment sooner than you think.'

The Vroon slipped quickly away.

Zalzan Kavol said after a moment, 'It was a foolishness of you to come between us, Valentine. There could have been violence.'

'I know.'

'And if I had injured you both?'

'I felt you would have held your anger. I was right, yes?'

Zalzan Kavol offered his sunless Skandar equivalent of a smile. 'I held my anger, true, but only because I was so amazed at your insolence that my own surprise halted me. Another moment – or had Deliamber continued to thwart me—'

'But he agreed to honor the contract,' Valentine pointed out.

'He did, indeed. And I suppose I too am indebted to you, then. Hiring a new guide might have delayed us for days. I thank you, Valentine,' said Zalzan Kavol with clumsy grace.

'Is there truly a debt between us?'

The Skandar suddenly was taut with suspicion. 'How do you mean?'

'I need a small favor of you. If I have done you service, may I now ask my return?'

'Go on.' Zalzan Kavol's voice was frosty.

Valentine took a deep breath. 'The boy Shanamir is from Falkynkip. Before he takes to the road with us, he has an urgent errand to perform there. A matter of family honor.'

'Let him go to Falkynkip, then, and rejoin us wherever we may be.'

'He fears he won't be able to find us if he parts from us.'

'What are you asking, Valentine?'

'That you arrange our route so that we pass within a few hours' journey of the boy's home.'

Zalzan Kavol stared balefully at Valentine. Bleakly he said, 'I am told by my guide that my contract is worthless, and then I am halted from action by an apprentice juggler, and then I am asked to plan my journey for the sake of a groom's family honor. This is becoming a taxing day, Valentine.'

'If you have no urgent engagements elsewhere,' said Valentine hopefully, 'Falkynkip is only two or three days' journey to the northeast. And the boy—'

'Enough!' cried Zalzan Kavol. 'The Falkynkip road it is, And then no more favors. Leave me now. Erfon! Haern! Is the wagon ready for the road?'

11

The wagon of Zalzan Kavol's troupe was as splendid within as without. The floor was of dark shining planks of nightflower wood, buffed to a bright finish and pegged together with consummate artifice. To the rear, in the passenger compartment, graceful strings of dried seeds and tassels dangled from the vaulted ceiling, and the walls were covered with swirl-patterned fur hangings, intricate carved inlays, banners of gossamer-sheer fabrics. There was room for five or six people of Skandar bulk to ride back there, though not in any spacious way. Mid-cabin was a place for the storage of belongings, trunks and parcels and juggling gear, all the paraphernalia of the troupe, and up front, on a raised platform open to the sky, was a driver's seat wide enough for two Skandars or three humans.

Huge and princely though the wagon was, a vehicle fit for a duke or even a Coronal, it was altogether airy and light, light enough to float on a vertical column of warm air generated by magnetic rotors whirling in its belly. So long as Majipoor spun on its axis, so would the rotors, and when the rotors were spinning the wagon would drift a foot or so above the ground, and could readily be drawn along by a harnessed team of mounts.

In late morning they finished loading their goods aboard, and went to the inn for lunch. Valentine was startled to see the Hjort with the orange-daubed whiskers, Vinorkis, appear at this point and take a seat beside Zalzan Kavol. The Skandar hammered on the table for attention and bellowed, 'Meet our new road manager! This is Vinorkis, who will assist me in making bookings, look after our properties, and handle all manner of chores that now fall to me!'

'Oh, no,' Carabella muttered under her breath. 'He's hired a Hjort? That weird one who's been staring at us all week?'

Vinorkis smiled a ghastly Hjort smile, showing triple bands of rubbery chewing-cartilage, and peered about in a goggle-eyed way.

Valentine said, 'So you were serious about joining us! I thought that was a joke, about your juggling figures.'

'It is well known that Hjorts never make jokes,' said Vinorkis gravely, and broke into vociferous laughter.

'But what becomes of your trade in haigus hides?'

'Sold my stock entirely at market,' the Hjort replied. 'And I thought of you, not knowing where you'd be tomorrow, and not caring. I admired that. I envied that. I asked myself, Are you going to peddle haigus hides all your days, Vinorkis, or will you try something new? A traveling life, perhaps? So

I offered my services to Zalzan Kavol when I happened to overhear he was in need of an assistant. And here I am!'

'Here you are,' said Carabella sourly. 'Welcome!'

After a hearty meal they began their departure. Shanamir led Zalzan Kavol's quartet of mounts from the stable, talking softly and soothingly to the animals as the Skandars tied them into the traces. Zalzan Kavol took the reins; his brother Heitrag sat beside him, with Autifon Deliamber squeezed in alongside. Shanamir, on his own mount, rode alongside. Valentine clambered into the snug, luxurious passenger compartment along with Carabella, Vinorkis, Sleet, and the other four Skandars. There was much rearranging of arms and legs to fit everyone in comfortably.

'Hoy!' Zalzan Kavol cried sharply, and it was off and out, through Falkynkip Gate and eastward down the grand highway on which Valentine had entered Pidruid just a week ago Moonday.

Summer's warmth lay heavily on the coastal plain, and the air was thick and moist. Already the spectacular blossoms of the fireshower palms were beginning to fade and decay, and the road was littered with fallen petals, like a crimson snowfall. The wagon had several windows – thin, tough sheets of stick-skin, the best quality, carefully matched, perfectly transparent – and in an odd solemn silence Valentine watched Pidruid dwindle and disappear, that great city of eleven million souls where he had juggled before the Coronal and tasted strange wines and spicy foods and spent a festival night in the arms of the dark-haired Carabella.

And now the road lay open before him, and who knew what travels awaited, what adventures would befall?

He was without plan, and open to all plans. He itched to juggle again, to master new skills, to cease being an apprentice and to join with Sleet and Carabella in the most intricate of maneuvers, and perhaps even to juggle with the Skandars themselves. Sleet had warned him about that: that only a master could risk juggling with them, for their double sets of arms gave them an advantage no human could hope to match. But Valentine had seen Sleet and Carabella throwing with the Skandars, and maybe in time he would do so as well. A high ambition! he thought. What more could he ask than to become a master worthy of juggling with Zalzan Kavol and his brothers!

Carabella said, 'You look so happy all of a sudden, Valentine.'

'Do I?'

'Like the sun. Radiant. Light streams from you.'

'Yellow hair,' he said amiably, 'It gives that illusion.'

'No. No. A sudden smile—'

He pressed his hand against hers. 'I was thinking of the road ahead. A free and hearty life. Wandering zigzag across Zimroel, and stopping to perform, and learning new routines. I want to become the best human juggler on Majipoor!'

'You stand a good chance,' Sleet said. 'Your natural skills are enormous. You need only the training.'

'For that I count on you and Carabella.'

Carabella said quietly, 'And while you were thinking of juggling, Valentine, I was thinking about you.'

'And I about you,' he whispered, abashed. 'But I was ashamed to say it aloud.'

The wagon now had reached the switchbacked ridge road that led upward to the great inland plateau. It climbed slowly. In places the angles of the road were so sharp that the wagon could barely execute the turns, but Zalzan Kavol was as cunning a driver as he was a juggler, and brought the vehicle safely around each tight corner. Soon they were at the top of the ridge. Distant Pidruid now looked like a map of itself, flattened and foreshortened, hugging the coast. The air up here was drier but hardly cooler, and in late afternoon the sun unleashed ghastly blasts, a mummifying heat from which there could be no escape before sundown.

That night they halted in a dusty plateau village along the Falkynkip road. A disturbing dream came to Valentine again as he lay on a scratchy mattress stuffed with straw: once more he moved among the Powers of Majipoor. In a vast echoing stone-floored hall the Pontifex sat enthroned at one end and the Coronal at the other, and set in the ceiling was a terrifying eye of light, like a small sun, that cast a merciless white glare. Valentine bore some message from the Lady of the Isle, but he was unsure whether to deliver it to Pontifex or Coronal, and whichever Power he approached receded to infinity as Valentine neared. All night long he trudged back and forth over that cold slippery floor, reaching hands in supplication toward one Power or the other, and always they floated away.

He dreamed again of Pontifex and Coronal the next night, in a town on the outskirts of Falkynkip. This was a hazy dream, and Valentine remembered nothing of it except impressions of fearsome royal personages, enormous pompous assemblies, and failures of communication. He awoke with a feeling of deep and aching discontent. Plainly he was receiving dreams of high consequence, but he was helpless to interpret them. 'The Powers obsess you and will not let you rest,' Carabella said in the morning. 'You seem tied to them by unbreakable cords. It isn't natural to dream so frequently of such mighty figures. I think surely these are sendings.'

Valentine nodded. 'In the heat of the day I imagine I feel the hands of the King of Dreams pressing coldly on my temples. And when I close my eyes his fingers enter my soul.'

Alarm flashed in Carabella's eyes. 'Can you be sure they are his sendings?'

'Not sure, no. But I think—'

'Perhaps the Lady—'

'The Lady sends kinder, softer dreams, so I believe,' said Valentine. 'These are sendings of the King, I much fear. But what does he want of me? What crime have I done?'

She frowned. 'In Falkynkip, Valentine, take yourself to a speaker, as you promised.'

'I'll look for one, yes.'

Autifon Deliamber, joining the conversation unexpectedly, said, 'May I make a recommendation?'

Valentine had not seen the wizened little Vroon approach. He looked down, surprised.

'Pardon,' the sorcerer said offhandedly. 'I happened to overhear. You are troubled by sendings, you think?'

'They could be nothing else.'

'Can you be certain?'

'I'm certain of nothing. Not even of my name, or yours, or the day of the week.'

'Sendings are rarely ambiguous. When the King speaks, or the Lady, we know without doubt,' Deliamber said.

Valentine shook his head. 'My mind is clouded these days. I hold nothing sure. But these dreams vex me, and I need answers, though I hardly know how to frame my questions.'

The Vroon reached up to take Valentine's hand with one of his delicate, intricately branched tentacles. 'Trust me. Your mind may be clouded, but mine is not, and I see you clearly. My name is Deliamber, and yours is Valentine, and this is Fiveday of the ninth week of summer, and in Falkynkip is the dream-speaker Tisana, who is my friend and ally, and who will help you find your proper path. Go to her and say that I give her greetings and love. Time has come for you to begin to recover from the harm that has befallen you, Valentine.'

'Harm? Harm? What harm is that?'

'Go to Tisana,' Deliamber said firmly.

Valentine sought Zalzan Kavol, who was speaking with some person of the village. Eventually the Skandar was done, and turned to Valentine, who said, 'I ask leave to spend Starday night apart from the troupe, in Falkynkip.'

'Also a matter of family honor?' asked Zalzan Kavol sardonically.

'A matter of private business. May I?'

The Skandar shrugged an elaborate four-shouldered shrug. 'There is something strange about you, something troublesome to me. But do as you wish. We perform in Falkynkip anyway, tomorrow, at the market fair. Sleep where you like, but be ready to leave early Sunday morning, eh?'

12

Falkynkip was nothing in the way of being a city to compare with huge sprawling Pidruid, but all the same was far from insignificant, a county seat that served as metropolis for a ranching district of great size. Perhaps three quarters of a million people lived in and about Falkynkip, and five times as many in the outlying countryside. But its pace was different from Pidruid's, Valentine observed. Possibly its location on this dry, hot plateau rather than along the mild and humid coast had something to do with that: but people moved deliberately here, with stolid, unhurried manners.

The boy Shanamir made himself scarce on Starday. He had indeed slipped off secretly the night before to his father's farm some hours north of the city, where – so he told Valentine the next morning – he had left the money he had earned in Pidruid and a note declaring that he was going off to seek adventure and wisdom, and had managed to get away again without being noticed. But he did not expect his father to take lightly the loss of so skilled and useful a hand, and fearing that municipal proctors would be out in search of him, Shanamir proposed to spend the rest of his stay in Falkynkip hidden in the wagon. Valentine explained this to Zalzan Kavol, who agreed, with his usual acrid grace.

That afternoon at the fair the jugglers came marching boldly out, Carabella and Sleet leading the way, he banging a drum, she tapping a tambourine and singing a lilting jingle:

> Spare a royal, spare a crown,
> Gentlefolk, come sit ye down.
> Astonishment and levity—
> Come and see our jugglery!
> Spare an inch and spare a mile,
> Gentlefolk, we'll make you smile.
> Cup and saucer, ball and chair,
> Dancing lightly in the air!
> Spare a moment, spare a day,
> And we'll spin your cares away,
> A moment's time, a coin well spent,
> Will bring you joy and wonderment.

But levity and wonderment were far from Valentine's spirit that day, and he juggled poorly. He was tense and uneasy from too many nights of troubled sleep, and also was inflamed with ambitions that went beyond his present skills, which led him to overreach himself. Twice he dropped clubs, but Sleet had shown him ways of pretending that that was part of the routine, and the crowd seemed forgiving. Forgiving himself was a harder matter. He crept off sullenly to a wine-stand while the Skandars took the center of the stage.

From a distance he watched them working, the six huge shaggy beings weaving their twenty-four arms in precise and flawless patterns. Each juggled seven knives while constantly throwing and receiving others, and the effect was spectacular, the tension extreme, as the silent interchange of sharp weapons went on and on. The placid burghers of Falkynkip were spellbound.

Watching the Skandars, Valentine regretted all the more his own faulty performance. Since Pidruid he had yearned to go before an audience again – his hands had twitched for the feel of clubs and balls – and he had finally had his moment and had been clumsy. No matter. There would be other marketplaces, other fairs. All across Zimroel the troupe would wander, year after year, and he would shine, he would dazzle audiences, they would cry out for Valentine the juggler, they would demand encore after encore, until Zalzan Kavol himself looked black with jealousy. A king of jugglers, yes, a monarch, a Coronal of performers! Why not? He had the gift. Valentine smiled. His dour mood was lifting. Was it the wine, or his natural good spirits reasserting themselves? He had been at the art only a week, after all, and look what he had achieved already! Who could say what wonders of eye and hand he would perform when he had had a year or two of practice?

Autifon Deliamber was at his side. 'Tisana is to be found in the Street of Watermongers,' the diminutive sorcerer said. 'She expects you shortly.'

'Have you spoken to her of me, then?'

'No,' said Deliamber.

'But she expects me. Hah! Is it by sorcery?'

'Something of that,' the Vroon said, giving a Vroonish wriggle of the limbs that amounted to a shrug. 'Go to her soon.'

Valentine nodded. He looked across: the Skandars were done, and Sleet and Carabella were demonstrating one-arm juggling. How elegantly they moved together, he thought. How calm, how confident they were, how crisp of motion. And how beautiful she is. Valentine and Carabella had not been lovers since the night of the festival, though sometimes they had slept side by side; it was a week now, and he had felt aloof and apart from her, though nothing but warmth and support had come from her to him. These dreams were the problem, draining and distracting him. To Tisana, then, for a speaking, and then, perhaps tomorrow, to embrace Carabella again—

'The Street of Watermongers,' he said to Deliamber. 'Very well. Will there be a sign marking her dwelling?'

'Ask,' Deliamber said.

As Valentine set out, the Hjort Vinorkis stepped from behind the wagon and said, 'Off for a night on the town, are you?'

'An errand,' Valentine said.

'Want some company?' the Hjort laughed his coarse, noisy laugh. 'We could hit a few taverns together, hoy? I wouldn't mind getting away from all this jugglery for a few hours.'

Uneasily Valentine said, 'It's the sort of thing one must do by oneself.'

Vinorkis studied him a moment. 'Not too friendly, are you?'

'Please. It's exactly as I said: I must do this alone. I'm not going tavern-crawling tonight, believe me.'

The Hjort shrugged. 'All right. Be like that, see if I care. I just wanted to help you have fun – show you the town, take you to a couple of my favorite places—'

'Another time,' said Valentine quickly.

He strode off toward Falkynkip.

The Street of Watermongers was easy enough to find – this was an orderly town, no medieval maze like Pidruid, and there were neat and comprehensible city maps posted at every major intersection – but finding the home of the dream-speaker Tisana was a slower business, for the street was long and those he asked for directions merely pointed over their shoulders toward the north. He followed along steadfastly and by early evening reached a small gray rough-shingled house in a residential quarter far from the marketplace. It bore on its weatherworn front door two symbols of the Powers, the crossed lightning-bolts that stood for the King of Dreams, and the triangle-within-triangle that was the emblem of the Lady of the Isle of Sleep.

Tisana was a sturdy woman of more than middle years, heavy-bodied and of unusual height, with a broad strong face and cool searching eyes. Her hair, thick and unbound, black streaked with swaths of white, hung far down her shoulders. Her arms, emerging bare from the gray cotton smock that she wore, were solid and powerful, although swinging dewlaps of flesh hung from them. She seemed a person of great strength and wisdom.

She greeted Valentine by name and bade him be comfortable in her house.

'I bring you, as you must already know, the greetings and love of Autifon Deliamber,' he said.

The dream-speaker nodded gravely. 'He has sent advance word, yes. That rascal! But his love is worth receiving, for all his tricks. Convey the same from me to him.' She moved around the small dark room, closing draperies, lighting three thick red candles, igniting some incense. There was little furniture, only a high-piled woven rug in tones of gray and black, a venerable wooden table on which the candles stood, and a tall clothes-cabinet in antique style. She said, as she made her preparations, 'I've known Deliamber nearly forty years, would you believe it? It was in the early days of the reign of Tyeveras that we met, at a festival in Piliplok, when the new Coronal came to town, Lord Malibor that drowned on the sea-dragon hunt. The little Vroon was tricky even then. We stood there cheering Lord Malibor in the streets, and Deliamber said, "He'll die before the Pontifex, you know," the way someone might predict rain when the south wind blows. It was a terrible thing to say, and I told him so. Deliamber didn't care. A strange business, when the Coronal dies first, when the Pontifex lives on and on. How old d'ye think Tyeveras is by now? A hundred? A hundred twenty?'

'I have no idea,' said Valentine.

'Old, very old. He was Coronal a long while before he entered the Labyrinth. And he's been in there for three Coronal-reigns, can you imagine? I wonder if he'll outlive Lord Valentine too.' Her eyes came to rest on Valentine's. 'I suppose Deliamber knows that too. Will you have wine with me now?'

'Yes,' Valentine said, uncomfortable with her blunt, outgoing manner and with the sense she gave him of knowing far more about him than he knew himself.

Tisana produced a carven stone decanter and poured two generous drinks, not the spicy fireshower wine of Pidruid but some darker, thicker vintage, sweet with undertastes of peppermint and ginger and other, more mysterious, things. He took a quick sip, and then another, and after the second she said casually, 'It contains the drug, you know.'

'Drug?'

'For the speaking.'

'Oh. Of course. Yes.' His ignorance embarrassed him. Valentine frowned and stared into his goblet. The wine was dark red, almost purple, and its surface gave back his own distorted reflection by candlelight. What was the procedure? he wondered. Was he supposed now to tell his recent dreams to her? Wait and see, wait and see. He drained the drink in quick uneasy gulps and immediately the old woman refilled, topping off her own glass, which she had barely touched.

She said, 'A long time since your last speaking?'

'Very long, I'm afraid.'

'Evidently. This is the moment when you give me my fee, you know. You'll find the price somewhat higher than you remember.'

Valentine reached for his purse. 'It's been so long—'

'—that you don't remember. I ask ten crowns now. There are new taxes, and other bothers. In Lord Voriax's time it was five, and when I first took up speaking, in the reign of Lord Malibor, I got two or two and a half. Is ten a burden for you?'

It was a week's pay for him from Zalzan Kavol, above his room and board;

but he had arrived in Pidruid with plenty of money in his purse, he knew not how or why, close on sixty royals, and much of that remained. He gave the dream-speaker a royal and she dropped the coin negligently into a green porcelain bowl on the table. He yawned. She was watching him closely. He drank again; she did also, and refilled; his mind was growing cloudy. Though it was still early at night, he would soon be sleepy.

'Come now to the dream-rug,' she said, blowing out two of the three candles.

She pulled off her smock and was naked before him.

That was unexpected. Did dream-speaking involve some sort of sexual contact? With this old woman? Not that she seemed so old now: her body looked a good twenty years younger than her face, not a girl's body by any means, but still firm-fleshed, plump but unwrinkled, with heavy breasts and strong smooth thighs. Perhaps these speakers were some sort of holy prostitutes, Valentine thought. She beckoned to him to undress, and he cast his clothes aside. They lay down together on the thick woolen rug in the half-darkness, and she drew him into her arms, but there was nothing at all erotic about the embrace – more maternal, if anything, an all-enfolding engulfment. He relaxed. His head was against her soft warm bosom and it was hard for him to stay awake. The scent of her was strong in his nostrils, a sharp pleasant aroma like that of the gnarled and ageless needle-trees that grew on the high peaks of the north just below the snow-line, an odor that was crisp and pungent and clean. She said softly. 'In the kingdom of dreams the only language spoken is that of truth. Be without fear as we embark together.'

Valentine closed his eyes.

High peaks, yes, just below the snow-line. A brisk wind blew across the crags, but he was not at all cold, though his feet were bare against the dry stony soil. A trail lay before him, a steeply sloping path in which broad gray flagstones had been laid to form a gigantic staircase leading into a mist-wrapped valley, and without hesitation Valentine started the descent. He understood that these images were not yet those of his dream, only of the prelude, that he had only begun his night's journey and was still merely on the threshold of sleep. But as he went downward he passed others, making the ascent, figures familiar to him from recent nights, the Pontifex Tyeveras with parchment skin and withered face, laboring up the steps in feeble quavering manner, and Lord Valentine the Coronal clambering with bold assertive strides, and dead Lord Voriax floating serenely just above the steps, and the great warrior-Coronal Lord Stiamot out of eight thousand years past, brandishing some mighty staff around the tip of which furious storms swirled, and was this not the Pontifex Arioc who had resigned the Labyrinth six thousand years before to proclaim himself a woman, and become Lady of the Isle of Sleep instead? And this the great ruler Lord Confalume, and the equally great Lord Prestimion who had succeeded him, under whose two long reigns Majipoor had attained its peak of wealth and power? And then came Zalzan Kavol with the wizard Deliamber on his back, and Carabella, naked and nut-brown, sprinting with unfailing vigor, and Vinorkis, goggling and gaping, and Sleet, juggling balls of fire as he cimbed, and Shanamir, and a Liiman selling sizzling sausages, and the gentle sweet-eyed Lady of the Isle, and the old Pontifex again, and the Coronal, and a platoon of musicians, and twenty Hjorts bearing the King of Dreams, terrible old Simonan Barjazid, in a golden litter. The mists were thicker down here, the air more dank, and Valentine found his breath coming in short painful bursts, as though instead of descending from the heights he had been climbing all the time, working his way by awful struggle above the line of needle-trees, into the bare granite shields of the high mountains, barefoot on burning strands of snow, swaddled in gray blankets of cloud that concealed all of Majipoor from him.

There was noble austere music in the heavens now, awesome choirs of brass playing solemn and somber melodies suitable for the robing-ceremony of a Coronal. And, indeed, they were robing him, a dozen crouching servants placing on him the cloak of office and the starburst crown, but he shook his head lightly and brushed them away, and with his own hands he removed the crown and handed it to his brother of the menacing saber, and shrugged off his fine robes and distributed them in strips to the poor, who used them to make bindings for their feet, and word went out to all the provinces of Majipoor that he had resigned his high office and given up all power, and once more he found himself on the flagstone steps, descending the mountain trail, seeking that valley of mists that lay in the unattainable beyond.

'But why do you go downward?' asked Carabella, blocking his path, and he had no answer to that, so that when little Deliamber pointed upward he shrugged meekly and began a new ascent, through fields of brilliant red and blue flowers, through a place of golden grass and lofty green cedars. He perceived that this was no ordinary peak he had been climbing and descending and climbing anew, but rather Castle Mount itself, that jutted thirty miles into the heavens, and his goal was that bewildering all-encompassing ever-expanding structure at its summit, the place where the Coronal dwelled, the castle that was called Lord Valentine's Castle but that had, not long before, been Lord Voriax's Castle and before that Lord Malibor's Castle, and other names before that, names of all those mighty princes who had ruled from Castle Mount, each putting his imprint on the growing castle and giving his name to it while he lived there, all the way back to Lord Stiamot the conqueror of the Metamorphs, he who was the first to dwell on Castle Mount and built the modest keep out of which all the rest had sprouted. I will regain the Castle, Valentine told himself, and I will take up residence.

But what was this? Workmen by the thousands, dismantling the enormous edifice! The work of demolition was well under way, and all the outer wings were taken apart, the place of buttresses and arches that Lord Voriax had built, and the grand trophy-room of Lord Malibor, and the great library that Tyeveras had added in his days as Coronal, and much else, all those rooms now mere piles of bricks laid in neat mounds on the slopes of the Mount, and they were working inward toward more ancient wings, to the garden-house of Lord Confalume and the armory of Lord Dekkeret and the archive-vault of Lord Prestimion, removing those places brick by brick like locusts sweeping over the fields at harvest-time. 'Wait!' Valentine cried. 'No need to do this! I am back, I will take up my robes and crown once again!' But the work of destruction continued, and it was as if the castle were made of sand and the tides were sweeping in, and a gentle voice said, 'Too late, too late, much too late,' and the watchtower of Lord Arioc was gone and the parapets of Lord Thimin were gone and the observatory of Lord Kinniken was gone with all its star-watching apparatus, and Castle Mount itself was shuddering and swaying as the removal of the castle disrupted its equilibrium, and workmen now were running frantically with bricks in their hands, seeking flat places on which to stack them, and a dread eternal night had come and baleful stars swelled and writhed in the sky, and the machineries that held back the chill of space atop Castle Mount were failing, so that the warm mild air was flowing moonward, and there was sobbing in the depths of the planet and Valentine stood amid the scenes of disruption and gathering chaos, holding forth outstretched fingers to the darkness.

The next thing he knew, morning light was in his eyes, and he blinked and sat up, confused, wondering what inn this was and what he had been doing the night before, for he lay naked on a thick woolly rug in a warm strange room, and there was an old woman moving about, brewing tea, perhaps—

Yes. The dream-speaker Tisana, and this was Falkynkip, in the Street of Watermongers—

His nakedness discomforted him. He rose and dressed quickly.

Tisana said, 'Drink this. I'll put some breakfast up, now that you're finally awake.'

He looked dubiously at the mug she handed him.

'Tea,' she said. 'Nothing but tea. The time for dreaming is long past.'

Valentine sipped at it while she bustled around the small kitchen. There was a numbness in his spirit, as though he had caroused himself into insensibility and now had a reckoning to pay; and he knew there had been strange dreams, a whole night of them, but yet he felt none of the malaise of the soul that he had known upon awakening these past few mornings, only that numbness, a curious centered calmness, almost an emptiness. Was that the purpose of visiting a dream-speaker? He understood so little. He was like a child loose in this vast and complex world.

They ate in silence. Tisana seemed to be studying Valentine intently across the table. Last night she had chattered much before the drug had taken its effect, but now she seemed subdued, reflective, almost withdrawn, as if she needed to be apart from him while preparing to speak his dream.

At length she cleared the dishes and said, 'How do you feel?'

'Quiet within.'

'Good. Good. That's important. To go away from a dream-speaker in turmoil is a waste of money. I had no doubts, though. Your spirit is strong.'

'Is it?'

'Stronger than you know. Reverses that would crush an ordinary person leave you untouched. You shrug off disaster and whistle in the face of danger.'

'You speak very generally,' Valentine said.

'I am an oracle, and oracles are never terribly specific,' she replied lightly.

'Are my dreams sendings? Will you tell me that, at least?'

She was thoughtful a moment. 'I am uncertain.'

'But you shared them! Aren't you able to know at once if a dream comes from the Lady or the King?'

'Peace, peace, this is not so simple,' she said, waving a palm at him. 'Your dreams are not sendings of the Lady, this I know.'

'Then if they are sendings, they are of the King.'

'Here is the uncertainty. They have an aura of the King about them in some way, yes, but not the aura of sendings. I know you find that hard to fathom: so do I. I do believe the King of Dreams watches your doings and is concerned with you, but it doesn't seem to me that he's been entering your sleep. It confounds me.'

'Has anything like this been known to you before?'

The dream-speaker shook her head. 'Not at all.'

'Is this my speaking, then? Only more mysteries and unanswered questions?'

'You haven't had the speaking yet,' Tisana answered.

'Forgive my impatience.'

'No forgiveness is needed. Come, give me your hands, and I'll make a speaking for you.' She reached for him across the table, and grasped and held him, and after a long while said, 'You have fallen from a high place, and now you must begin to climb back to it.'

He grinned. 'A high place?'

'The highest.'

'The highest place on Majipoor,' he said lightly, 'is the summit of Castle Mount. Is *that* where you would have me climb?'

'There, yes.'

'A very steep ascent you lay upon me. I could spend my entire life reaching and climbing that place.'

'Nevertheless, Lord Valentine, that ascent awaits you, and it is not I who lays it on you.'

He gasped at her use of the royal title to him, and then burst out laughing at the grossness of it, the tastelessness of her joke. 'Lord Valentine! Lord Valentine? No, you do me far too much honor, Madame Tisana. Not *Lord* Valentine. Only Valentine, Valentine the juggler, is all, the newest of the troupe of Zalzan Kavol the Skandar.'

Her gaze rested steadily on him. Quietly she said, 'I beg your pardon. I meant no offense.'

'How could it offend me? But put no royal titles on me, please. A juggler's life is royal enough for me, even if my dreams may sometimes be high-flown ones.'

Her eyes did not waver. 'Will you have more tea?' she asked.

'I promised the Skandar I'd be ready for departure early in the morning, and so I must leave soon. What else does the speaking hold for me?'

'The speaking is over,' said Tisana.

Valentine had not expected that. He was awaiting interpretations, analysis, exegesis, counsel. And all he had had from her—

'I have fallen and I must climb back on high. That's all you tell me for a royal?'

'Fees for everything grow larger nowadays,' she said without rancor. 'Do you feel cheated?'

'Not at all. This has been valuable for me, in its fashion.'

'Politely said, but false. Nevertheless you have received value here. Time will make that clear to you.' She got to her feet, and Valentine rose with her. There was about her an aura of confidence and strength. 'I wish you a good journey,' she said, 'and a safe ascent.'

13

Autifon Deliamber was the first to greet him when he returned from the dream-speaking. In the quiet of dawn the little Vroon was practicing a sort of juggling near the wagon, with shards of some glittering ice-bright crystal-line substance: but this was wizard-juggling, for Deliamber only pretended to throw and catch, and appeared actually to be moving the shards by power of mind alone. He stood beneath the brilliant cascade and the shimmering slivers coursed through the air in a circle above him like a wreath of bright light, remaining aloft although Deliamber never touched them.

As Valentine approached, the Vroon gave a twitch of his tentacle-tips and the glassy shards fell instantly inward to form a close-packed bundle that Deliamber snatched deftly from the air. He held them forth to Valentine. 'Pieces of a temple building from the Ghayrog city of Dulorn, that lies a few days' journey east of here. A place of magical beauty, it is. Have you been there?'

The enigmas of the dream-speaking night still lay heavy on Valentine, and he had no taste for Deliamber's flamboyant spirit this early in the morning. Shrugging, he said, 'I don't remember.'

'You'd remember, if you had. A city of light, a city of frozen poetry!' The Vroon's beak clacked: a Vroonish sort of smile. 'Or perhaps you wouldn't remember. I suppose not: so much is lost to you. But you'll be there again soon enough.'

'Again? I never was there.'

'If you were there once, you'll be there again when we get there. If not, not. However it may be for you, Dulorn is our next stop, so says our beloved Skandar.' Deliamber's mischievous eyes probed Valentine's. 'I see you learned a great deal at Tisana's.'

'Let me be, Deliamber.'

'She's a marvel, isn't she?'

Valentine attempted to go past. 'I learned nothing there,' he said tightly. 'I wasted an evening.'

'Oh, no, no, no! Time is never wasted. Give me your hand, Valentine.' The Vroon's dry, rubbery tentacle slipped around Valentine's reluctant fingers. Solemnly Deliamber said, 'Know this, and know it well: *time is never wasted*. Wherever we go, whatever we do, everything is an aspect of education. Even when we don't immediately grasp the lesson.'

'Tisana told me approximately the same thing as I was leaving,' Valentine murmured sullenly. 'I think you two are in conspiracy. But what did I learn? I dreamed again of Coronals and Pontifexes. I climbed up and down mountain trails. The dream-speaker made a silly, tiresome joke on my name. I rid myself of a royal better spent on wine and feasting. No, I achieved nothing.' He attempted to withdraw his hand from Deliamber's grip, but the Vroon held him with unexpected strength. Valentine felt an odd sensation, as of a chord of somber music rolling through his mind, and somewhere beneath the surface of his consciousness an image glimmered and flashed, like some sea-dragon stirring and sounding in the depths, but he was unable to perceive it clearly: the core of the meaning eluded him. Just as well. He feared to know what was stirring down there. An obscure and incomprehensible anguish flooded his soul. For an instant it seemed to him that the dragon in the depths of his being was rising, was swimming upward through the murk of his clouded memory toward the levels of awareness. That frightened him. Knowledge, terrifying and menacing knowledge, was hidden within him, and now was threatening to break loose. He resisted. He fought. He saw little Deliamber staring at him with terrible intensity, as if trying to lend him the strength he needed to accept that dark knowledge, but Valentine would not have it. He pulled his hand free with sudden violent force and went lurching and stumbling toward the Skandar wagon. His heart was pounding fiercely, his temples throbbed, he felt weak and dizzy. After a few uncertain steps he turned and said angrily, 'What did you do to me?'

'I merely touched my hand to yours.'

'And gave me great pain!'

'I may have given you access to your own pain,' said Deliamber quietly. 'Nothing more than that. The pain is carried within you. You have been unable to feel it. But it's struggling to awaken within you, Valentine. There's no preventing it.'

'I mean to prevent it.'

'You have no choice but to heed the voices from within. The struggle has already begun.'

Valentine shook his aching head. 'I want no pain and no struggles. I've been a happy man, this last week.'

'Are you happy when you dream?'

'These dreams will pass from me soon. They must be sendings intended for someone else.'

'Do you believe that, Valentine?'

Valentine was silent. After a moment he said, 'I want only to be allowed to be what I want to be.'

'And that is?'

'A wandering juggler. A free man. Why do you torment me this way, Deliamber?'

'I would gladly have you be a juggler,' the Vroon said gently. 'I mean you no sorrow. But what one wants often has little connection with what may be marked out for one on the great scroll.'

'I will be a master juggler,' said Valentine, 'and nothing more than that, and nothing less.'

'I wish you well,' Deliamber said courteously, and walked away.

Slowly Valentine let his breath escape. His entire body was tense and stiff, and he squatted and put his head down, stretching out first his arms and then his legs, trying to rid himself of these strange knots that had begun to invade him. Gradually he relaxed a little, but some residue of uneasiness remained, and the tension would not leave him. These tortured dreams, these squirming dragons in his soul, these portents and omens—

Carabella emerged from the wagon and stood above him as he stretched and twisted. 'Let me help,' she said, crouching down beside him. She pushed him forward until he lay sprawled flat, and her powerful fingers dug into the taut muscles of his neck and back. Under her ministrations he grew somewhat less tense, yet his mood remained dark and troubled.

'The speaking didn't help you?' she asked softly.

'No.'

'Can you talk about it?'

'I'd rather not,' he said.

'Whatever you prefer.' But she waited expectantly, her eyes alert, shining with warmth and compassion.

He said, 'I barely understood the things the woman was telling me. And what I understood I can't accept. But I don't want to talk about it.'

'Whenever you do, Valentine, I'm here. Whenever you feel the need to tell someone—'

'Not right now, Perhaps never.' He sensed her reaching toward him, eager to heal the pain in his soul as she had grappled with the tensions in his body. He could feel the love flooding from her to him. Valentine hesitated. He did battle within himself. Haltingly he said, 'The things the speaker told me—'

'Yes.'

No. To talk of these things was to give them reality, and they had no reality, they were absurdities, they were fantasies, they were foolish vapors.

'—were nonsense,' Valentine said. 'What she said isn't worth discussing.'

Carabella's eyes reproached him. He looked away from her.

'Can you accept that?' he asked roughly. 'She was a crazy old woman and she told me a lot of nonsense, and I don't want to discuss it, not with you, not with anyone. It was *my* speaking. I don't have to share it. I—' He saw the shock on her face. In another moment he would be babbling. He said in an entirely different tone of voice, 'Get the juggling balls, Carabella.'

'Now?'

'Right now.'

'But—'

'I want you to teach me the exchange between jugglers, the passing of the balls. Please.'

'We're due to leave in half an hour!'

'Please,' he said urgently.

She nodded and sprinted up the steps of the wagon, returning a moment later with the balls. They moved apart, to an open place where they would have room, and Carabella flipped three of the balls to him. She was frowning.

'What's wrong?' he asked.

'Learning new techniques when the mind is troubled is never a good idea.'

'It might calm me,' he said. 'Let's try.'

'As you wish.' She began to juggle the three balls she held, by way of warming up. Valentine imitated her, but his hands were cold, his fingers unresponsive, and he had trouble doing this simplest of all routines, dropping the balls several times. Carabella said nothing. She continued to juggle while he launched one abortive cascade after another. His temper grew edgy. She would not tell him again that this was the wrong moment for attempting such things, but her silence, her look, even her stance, all said it more forcefully than words. Valentine desperately sought to strike a rhythm. *You have fallen from a high place*, he heard the dream-speaker saying, *and now you must begin to climb back to it.* He bit his lip. How could he concentrate, with such things intruding? Hand and eye, he thought, hand and eye, forget all else. Hand and eye. *Nevertheless, Lord Valentine, that ascent awaits you, and it is not I who lays it on you.* No. No. No. No. His hands shook. His fingers were rods of ice. He made a false move and the balls went scattering.

'Please, Valentine,' Carabella said mildly.

'Get the clubs.'

'It'll be even worse with them. Do you want to break a finger?'

'The clubs,' he said.

Shrugging, she gathered up the balls and went into the wagon. Sleet emerged, yawned, nodded a casual greeting to Valentine. The morning was beginning. One of the Skandars appeared and crawled under the wagon to adjust something. Carabella came out bearing six clubs. Behind her was Shanamir, who gave Valentine a quick salute and went to feed the mounts. Valentine took the clubs. Conscious of Sleet's cool eyes on him, he put himself into the juggling position, threw one club high, and botched the catch. No one spoke. Valentine tried again. He managed to get the three clubs into sequence, but for no more than thirty seconds; then they spilled, one landing unpleasantly on his toe. Valentine caught sight of Autifon Deliamber watching the scene from a distance. He picked up the clubs again, Carabella, facing him, patiently juggled her three, studiously ignoring him. Valentine threw the clubs, got them started, dropped one, started again, dropped two, started yet again, made a faulty grab and bent his left thumb badly out of place.

He tried to pretend that nothing had gone wrong. Once more he picked up the clubs, but this time Sleet came over and took Valentine lightly by both wrists.

'Not now,' he said. 'Give me the clubs.'

'I want to practice.'

'Juggling isn't therapy. You're upset about something, and it's ruining your timing. If you keep this up you can do damage to your rhythms that will take you weeks to undo.'

Valentine tried to pull free, but Sleet held him with surprising strength.

Carabella, impassive, went on juggling a few feet away. After an instant Valentine yielded. With a shrug he surrendered the clubs to Sleet, who scooped them up and took them back into the wagon. A moment later Zalzan Kavol stepped outside, elaborately scratched his pelt fore and aft with several of his hands as though searching in it for fleas, and boomed, 'Everybody in! Let's move it along!'

14

The road to the Ghayrog city of Dulorn took them eastward through lush, placid farming country, green and fertile under the eye of the summer sun. Like much of Majipoor this was densely populated terrain, but intelligent planning had created wide agricultural zones bordered by busy strip-cities, and so the day went, through an hour's worth of farms, an hour's worth of town, an hour of farms, an hour of town. Here in the Dulorn Rift, the broad sloping lowland east of Falkynkip, the climate was particularly suited for farming, for the Rift was open at its nothern end to the polar rainstorms that constantly drenched Majipoor's temperate arctic, and the subtropical heat was made moderate by gentle, predictable precipitation. The growing season lasted year round: this was the time for harvesting the sweet yellow stajja tubers, from which a bread was made, and for planting such fruits as niyk and glein.

The beauty of the landscape lightened Valentine's bleak outlook. By easy stages he ceased to think about things that did not bear thinking about, and allowed himself to enjoy the unending procession of wonders that was the planet of Majipoor. The black slender trunks of niyk-trees planted in rigid and complex geometrical patterns danced against the horizon; teams of Hjort and human farmers in rural costumes moved like invading armies across the stajja-fields, plucking the heavy tubers; now the wagon glided quietly through a district of lakes and streams, and now through one where curious blocks of white granite jutted tooth-fashion from the smooth grassy plains.

At midday they entered a place of particularly strange beauty, one of the many public forest preserves. At the gateway a sign glowing with green luminosity proclaimed:

BLADDERTREE PRESERVE

Located here is an outstanding virgin tract of Dulorn Bladdertree. These trees manufacture lighter-than-air gases which keep their upper branches buoyant. As they approach maturity their trunks and root systems atrophy, and they become epiphytic in nature, dependent almost entirely on the atmosphere for nourishment. Occasionally in extreme old age a tree will sever its contact with the ground entirely and drift off to found a new colony far away. Bladdertrees are found both in Zimroel and in Alhanroel but have become rare in recent times. This grove set aside for the people of Majipoor by official decree, 12th Pont. Confalume Cor. Lord Prestimion.

The jugglers followed the forest trail silently on foot for some minutes without seeing anything unusual. Then Carabella, who led the way, passed through a thicket of dense blue-black bushes and cried out suddenly in surprise.

Valentine ran to her side. She was standing in wonder in the midst of marvels.

Bladdertrees were everywhere, in all stages of their growth. The young ones, no higher than Deliamber or Carabella, were curious ungainly-looking shrublets with thick, swollen branches of a peculiar silvery hue that emerged at awkward angles from squat fleshy trunks. But in trees fifteen or twenty feet tall, the trunks had begun to attentuate and the limbs to inflate, so that now the bulging boughs appeared topheavy and precarious, and in even older trees the trunks had shriveled to become nothing more than rough, scaly guy-ropes by which the trees' buoyant crowns were fastened to the ground. High overhead they floated and bobbed in the gentlest breeze, leafless, turgid, the branches puffed up like balloons. The silvery color of the young branches became, in maturity, a brilliant translucent gleam, so that the trees seemed like glass models of themselves, shining brightly in the shafts of sunlight through which they danced and weaved. Even Zalzan Kavol seemed moved by the strangeness and beauty of the trees. The Skandar approached one of the tallest, its gleaming swollen crown floating far overhead, and carefully, almost reverently, encircled its taut narrow stem with his fingers. Valentine thought Zalzan Kavol might be minded to snap the stem and send the bladdertree floating away like a glittering kite, but no, the Skandar seemed merely to be marking the slenderness of the stem, and after a moment he stepped back, muttering to himself.

For a long while they wandered among the bladdertrees, studying the little ones, observing the stages of growth, the gradual narrowing of the trunks and bloating of the limbs. The trees were leafless and no flowers were apparent: it was difficult to believe that they were vegetable creations at all, so vitreous did they seem. It was a place of magic. The darkness of his earlier mood now seemed a mystery to Valentine. On a planet where such beauty abounded, how could one have any need for brooding or fretting?

'Here,' Carabella called. 'Catch!'

She had gauged the change in his spirits and had gone to the wagon for the juggling balls. Now she threw three of them to him and he went easily into the basic cascade, and she the same, in a clearing surrounded by glistening bladdertrees.

Carabella stood facing him, just a few feet away. They juggled independently for three or four minutes, until a symmetry of phase encompassed them and they were throwing in identical rhythms. Now they juggled together, mirroring one another, Valentine feeling a deeper calmness settling over him with each cycle of throws: he was balanced, centered, tuned. The bladdertrees, stirring lightly in the wind, showered him with dazzles of refracted light. The world was silent and serene.

'When I tell you,' Carabella said quietly, 'throw the ball from your right hand to my left, at precisely the height you'd throw it if you were giving it to yourself. One ... two ... three ... four ... five ... *pass*!' And on *pass* he threw to her on a firm straight arc, and she to him. He managed, just barely, to catch the incoming ball and work it into the rhythm, continuing his own cascade, and counting off until it was time to pass again. Back – forth – back – forth – *pass*—

It was hard at first, the hardest juggling he had ever done, but yet he could do it, he was doing it without blundering, and after the first few passes he was doing it without awkwardness, smoothly exchanging throws with Carabella as though he had practiced this routine with her for months. He knew that this was extraordinary, that no one was supposed to master intricate patterns like this on the first try: but as before, he moved swiftly toward the core of the experience, placed himself in a region where nothing existed but hand and eye and the moving balls, and failure became not merely impossible but inconceivable.

'Hoy!' Sleet cried. 'Over here now!'

He too was juggling. Momentarily Valentine was baffled by this multiplication of the task, but he forced himself to remain in automatic mode, to throw when it seemed appropriate, to catch what came to him, and constantly to keep the balls that remained to him moving between his hands. So when Sleet and Carabella began to exchange balls he was able to stay in the pattern, and catch from Sleet instead of Carabella. 'One – two – one – two—' Sleet called, taking up a position between Valentine and Carabella and making himself the leader of the group, feeding the balls first to one, then to the other, in a rhythm that remained rock-steady for a long while and then accelerated comically to a pace far beyond Valentine's abilities. Suddenly there were dozens of balls in the air, or so it seemed, and Valentine grasped wildly at all of them and lost them all and collapsed, laughing, onto the warm springy turf.

'So there are some limits to your skills, eh?' Sleet said gaily. 'Good! Good! I was beginning to wonder whether you were mortal!'

Valentine chuckled. 'Mortal enough, I fear.'

'Lunch!' Deliamber called.

He presided over a pot of stew hanging from a tripod above a glowglobe. The Skandars, who had been doing some practice of their own in another part of the grove, appeared as if conjured from the soil and helped themselves with ungracious eagerness. Vinorkis too was quick to fill his plate. Valentine and Carabella were the last to be served, but he hardly cared. He was sweating the good sweat of exertion well exerted, and his blood was pounding and his skin was tingling, and his long night of unsettling dreams seemed far behind him, something he had left in Falkynkip.

All that afternoon the wagon sped eastward. This was definitely Ghayrog country now, inhabited almost exclusively by that glossy-skinned reptilian-looking race. When nightfall came the troupe was still half a day's journey from the provincial seat of Dulorn, where Zalzan Kavol had arranged some sort of theatrical booking. Deliamber announced that a country inn lay not far ahead, and they went on until they came to it.

'Share my bed,' Carabella said to Valentine.

In the corridor going to their chamber they passed Deliamber, who paused a moment, touching their hands with tentacle-tips and murmuring, 'Dream well.'

'Dream well,' Carabella repeated automatically.

But Valentine did not offer the customary response with her, for the touch of the Vroon sorcerer's flesh to his hand set the dragon stirring within his soul again, and he was disquieted and grave, as he had been before the miracle of the bladdertree grove. It was as though Deliamber had appointed himself the enemy of Valentine's tranquility, arousing in him inarticulate fears and apprehensions against which he had no defense. 'Come,' Valentine muttered hoarsely to Carabella.

'In a hurry, are you?' She laughed a light tinkling laugh, but it died away quickly when she saw his expression. 'Valentine, what is it? What's the matter?'

'Nothing.'

'Nothing?'

'May I be allowed moods, as other human beings sometimes have?'

'When your face changes like that, it's like a shadow passing over the sun. And so suddenly—'

'Something about Deliamber,' Valentine said, 'disturbs and alarms me. When he touched me—'

'Deliamber's harmless. Mischievous, like all wizards, especially Vroonish ones, especially small ones. There's dark mischief in very small people. But you have nothing to fear from Deliamber.'

'Truly so?' He closed the door, and she was in his arms.

'Truly,' she said. 'You have nothing to fear from anyone, Valentine. Everyone who sees you loves you. There's no one who would injure you in this world.'

'How good to believe that,' he said, as she drew him down on the bed.

They embraced, and his lips touched hers gently, and then with more force, and soon their bodies were entwined. He had not made love with her for over a week, and he had looked forward to it with intense longing and delight. But the incident in the hallway had robbed him of desire, had left him numb and isolated, and that mystified and depressed him. Carabella must have sensed the coolness in him, but evidently she chose to ignore it, for her lithe energetic body sought his with fervor and passion. He forced himself to respond, and then after a minute he was no longer forcing, was nearly as enthusiastic as she, but still he stood outside his own sensations, a mere spectator as they made love. It was over quickly, and the light was out, although moonlight entering their window cast a harsh chilly glow over their faces.

'Dream well,' Carabella murmured.

'Dream well,' he replied.

She was asleep almost at once. He held her, keeping her warm slim body close against him, feeling no sleepiness himself. After a time he rolled away and drew himself into his favorite sleep position, on his back, arms folded across his chest, but no sleep came, only fitful dreamless dozing. He diverted himself by counting blaves, by imagining himself juggling in patterns of surpassing intricacy with Sleet and Carabella, by trying to relax his entire body one muscle at a time. Nothing worked. Wide awake, he propped himself on one arm and lay looking down at Carabella, lovely in the moonlight.

She was dreaming. A muscle flickered in her cheek; her eyes moved beneath their lids; her breasts rose and fell in jagged rhythms; she put her knuckles to her lips, murmured something in a thick unintelligible voice, drew her knees tightly to her chest. Her lean bare form looked so beautiful that Valentine wanted to reach out to her, to stroke her cool thighs, to touch his lips lightly to her small rigid nipples, but no, it was uncouth to interrupt a dreamer, it was an unforgivable breach of civility. So he was content to watch her, and to love her from afar, and to savor the reawakened desire that he felt.

Carabella cried out in terror.

Her eyes opened, but she saw nothing – the sign of a sending. A shudder went rippling the length of her body. She trembled and turned to him, still asleep, still dreaming, and he held her while she whimpered and moaned, giving her dream-service, dream-comfort, protecting her against the darkness of the spirit by the strength of his arms, and at last the fury of her dream ran its course and she relaxed, limp, sweat-soaked, against his chest.

She lay still for some moments, until Valentine thought she had fallen peacefully asleep. No. She was awake, but motionless, as if contemplating her dream, confronting it, trying to carry it upward into the realm of wakefulness. Suddenly she sat upright and gasped and covered her mouth with her hands. Her eyes were wild and glassy.

'My lord!' she whispered. She backed away from him, scuttling across the bed in a strange crablike crawl, holding one arm folded above her breasts and the other as a kind of shield across her face. Her lips were quivering. Valentine reached for her, but she pulled away in horror and threw herself to the rough wooden floor, where she crouched in an eerie huddle, folded inward on herself as if trying to conceal her nakedness.

'Carabella?' he said, bewildered.

She looked up at him. 'Lord – lord – please – let me be, lord—'

And bowed again, and made the starburst with her fingers, the two-handed gesture of obeisance that one makes only when one comes before the Coronal.

15

Wondering whether it might be he and not she that had been dreaming, and the dream still going on, Valentine rose, found a robe for Carabella to wear, put on one of his own garments. Still she crouched apart from him, stunned and shattered. When he tried to comfort her she pulled away, huddling still deeper into herself.

'What is it?' he asked. 'What happened, Carabella?'

'I dreamed – I dreamed that you were—' She faltered. 'So real, so terrible—'

'Tell me. I'll speak your dream for you, if I can.'

'It needs no speaking. It speaks for itself.' She made the starburst sign at him again. In a cold, low, inflectionless voice she said, 'I dreamed that you were the true Coronal Lord Valentine, that you had been robbed of your power and all your memory, and set into another's body, and turned loose near Pidruid to roam and live an idle life while someone else ruled in your stead.'

Valentine felt himself at the edge of a great abyss, and the ground crumbling beneath his feet.

'Was this a sending?' he asked.

'It was a sending. I know not from whom, Lady or King, but it was no dream of mine, it was something that was placed in my mind from outside. I saw you, lord—'

'Stop calling me that.'

'—atop Castle Mount, and your face was the face of the other Lord Valentine, the dark-haired one we juggled for, and then you came down from the Mount to travel on the grand processional in all the lands, and while you were in the south, in my own city of Til-omon it was, they gave you a drug and seized you in your sleep and changed you into this body and cast you out, no one was the wiser that you had been magicked out of your royal powers. And I have touched you, lord, and shared your bed, and been familiar with you in a thousand ways, and how will I be forgiven, lord?'

'Carabella?'

She cowered and trembled.

'Look up, Carabella. Look at me.'

She shook her head. He knelt before her, and touched his hand to her chin. She shuddered as though he had marked her with acid. Her muscles were rigid. He touched her again.

'Raise your head,' he said gently. 'Look at me.'

She looked up, slowly, timidly, the way one might look into the face of the sun, fearing the brightness.

He said, 'I am Valentine the juggler and nothing more.'

'No, lord.'

'The Coronal is a dark-haired man, and my hair is golden.'

'I beg you, lord, let me be. You frighten me.'

'A wandering juggler frightens you?'

'It is not who you are that frightens me. The person you are is a friend I have come to love. It is *who you have been*, lord. You have stood beside the Pontifex and tasted the royal wine. You have walked in the highest rooms of Castle Mount. You have known the fullest power of the world. It was a true dream, lord, it was as clear and real as anything I have ever seen, a sending beyond doubt, not to be questioned. And you are rightful Coronal, and I have touched your body and you have touched mine, and it is sacrilege a thousand times over for an ordinary woman like me to approach a Coronal so closely. And I will die for it.'

Valentine smiled. 'If I was ever Coronal, love, it was in another body, and there's nothing holy about the one you embraced tonight. But I was never Coronal.'

Her gaze rested squarely on him. Her tone was less quavering as she said, 'You remember nothing of your life before Pidruid. You were unable to tell me your father's name, and you told me of your childhood in Ni-moya and didn't believe it yourself, and you guessed at a name for your mother. Is this not true?'

Valentine nodded.

'And Shanamir has told me you had much money in your purse, but had no idea what any of it was worth, and tried to pay a sausageman with a fifty-royal piece. True?'

He nodded again.

'As though you had lived all your life at court, perhaps, and never handled money? You know so little, Valentine! You have to be taught – like a child.'

'Something has happened to my memory, yes. But does that make me Coronal?'

'The way you juggle, so naturally, as though all skills are yours if you want them – the way you move, the way you hold yourself, the radiance that comes from you, the sense you give everyone that you were born to hold power—'

'Do I give that?'

'We have talked of little else, since you came among us. That you must be a fallen prince, some exiled duke perhaps. But then my dream – it leaves no doubt, lord—'

Her face was white with strain. For a moment she had overcome her awe, but only for a moment, and now she trembled again. And the awe was contagious, it seemed, for Valentine himself began to feel fear, a coldness of the skin. Was there truth in any of this? Was he an anointed Coronal that had touched hands with Tyeveras in the heart of the Labyrinth and at the summit of Castle Mount?

He heard the voice of the dream-speaker Tisana. *You have fallen from a high place, and now you must begin to climb back to it,* she had said. Impossible. Unthinkable. *Nevertheless, Lord Valentine, that ascent awaits you, and it is not I who lays it on you.* Unreal. Impossible. And yet his dreams, that brother who would have slain him, and whom he had slain instead, and those Coronals and Pontifexes moving through the chambers of his soul, and all the rest. Could it be? Impossible. Impossible.

He said, 'You mustn't fear me, Carabella.'

She shivered. He reached for her and she shied away, crying, 'No! Don't touch me! My lord—'

Tenderly he said, 'Even if I was once Coronal – and how strange and foolish that sounds to me – even if, Carabella, I am Coronal no longer, I am not in any anointed body, and what has taken place between us is no sacrilege. I am Valentine the juggler now, whoever I may have been in a former life.'

'You don't understand, lord.'

'I understand that a Coronal is a man like any other, only he bears more responsibilities than others, but there is nothing magical about him and nothing to fear except his power, and I have none of that. If ever I had.'

'No,' she said. 'A Coronal is touched by the highest grace, and it never goes from him.'

'Anyone can be Coronal, given the right training and the right cast of mind. One isn't bred for it. Coronals have come from every district of Majipoor, every level of society.'

'Lord, you don't understand. To have been Coronal is to be touched by grace. You have ruled, you have walked on Castle Mount, you have been adopted into the line of Lord Stiamot and Lord Dekkeret and Lord Prestimion, you are brother to Lord Voriax, you are *the son of the Lady of the Isle.* And I am to think of you as an ordinary man? I am to have no fear of you?'

He stared at her in shock.

He remembered what had gone through his own mind when he stood in the streets and beheld Lord Valentine the Coronal in the procession, and had felt himself in the presence of grace and might, and had realized that to be Coronal was to become a being set apart, a personage of aura and strangeness, one who holds power over twenty billion, who carries in himself the energies of thousands of years of famed princes, who is destined to go on to the Labyrinth one day and wear the authority of the Pontifex. Incomprehensible as all this was to him, it was sinking in, and he was dumbfounded and overwhelmed by it. But it was absurd. To fear himself? To sink down in awe at his own imaginary majesty? He was Valentine the juggler, and nothing more!

Carabella was sobbing. In another moment she would be hysterical. The Vroon, surely, would have some sleeping potion that would give her ease.

'Wait,' Valentine said. 'I'll be back in a moment. I'll ask Deliamber for something to calm you.'

He darted from the room, down the hall, wondering which room was the sorcerer's. All doors were closed. He debated knocking at random, hoping not to blunder in on Zalzan Kavol, when a dry voice said out of the darkness from a point somewhere below his elbow, 'Do you have trouble sleeping?'

'Deliamber?'

'Here. Close by you.'

Valentine peered, narrowing his eyes, and made out the Vroon sitting cross-tentacled in the hallway in some kind of posture of meditation. Deliamber rose.

'I thought you might come in search of me soon,' he said.

'Carabella has had a sending. She needs a drug to quiet her spirit. Do you have anything useful?'

'No drugs, no. A touch, though – it can be done. Come.' The little Vroon glided along the corridor and into the room that Valentine shared with Carabella. She had not moved, still huddled pitifully beside the bed with her robe wrapped carelessly about her. Deliamber went to her at once; his ropy tendrils delicately enfolded her shoulders, and she loosened her tautly held muscles, and slumped as though rendered boneless. The sound of her heavy breathing was loud in the room. After a moment she looked up, calmer now, but still with a dazed, frozen look in her eyes.

She gestured toward Valentine and said, 'I dreamed that he was – that he had been—' She hesitated.

'I know,' said Deliamber.

'It is not true,' Valentine said thickly. 'I am only a juggler.'

Mildly Deliamber said, 'You are only a juggler *now*.'

'You believe this nonsense too?'

'It was obvious from the first. When you stepped between the Skandar and me. This is the act of a king, I told myself, and I read your soul—'

'What?'

'A professional trick. I read your soul, and saw what had been done to you—'

'But such a thing is impossible!' Valentine protested. 'To take a man's mind from his body, and put it in another's, and put another's mind in his—'

'Impossible? No,' Deliamber said. 'I think not. There have been tales coming out of Suvrael that studies into this art are being done at the court of the King of Dreams. For several years now the rumors of strange experiments have trickled forth.'

Valentine stared sullenly at his fingertips. 'It could not be done.'

'So I thought, too, when first I heard it. But then I considered. There are many wizardries nearly as great whose secrets I myself know, and I am only a minor wizard. The seeds of such an art have long existed. Maybe some Suvraelu sorcerer has found a way to germinate those seeds at last. Valentine, if I were you I would not reject the possibility.'

'A change of bodies?' Valentine said, bewildered. 'This is not my true body? Whose would it be, then?'

'Who knows? Some unlucky man struck down by accident, drowned perhaps, or choked on a piece of meat, or the victim of some evil toadstool unwisely eaten. Dead, anyway, in some manner that left his body reasonably whole; and taken with the hour of death to some secret place, there to have the Coronal's soul transplanted into the empty shell, and then another man, giving up his own body forever, quickly taking possession of the Coronal's vacated skull, possibly retaining much of the Coronal's own memory and mind in union with his own, so that he can carry on the masquerade of ruling as though he were the true monarch—'

'I accept none of this as remotely real,' said Valentine stubbornly.

'Nevertheless,' Deliamber said, 'when I looked into your soul I saw everything even as I describe it to you now. And felt more than a little fear – in my trade one doesn't often meet Coronals, or stumble on such evidence of gross treason – and I took a moment to compose myself, and asked myself if I would not be wiser to forget what I had seen, and for a time I seriously considered it. But then I knew that I could not, that I would be whipped with monstrous dreams until the end of my days if I ignored what I knew. I told myself that there is much in the world that is in need of repair, and I would, Divine willing, be part of the fixing. And now the fixing has begun.'

Valentine said, 'There is nothing to it.'

'For the sake of argument, say that there is,' Deliamber urged. 'Pretend that they came upon you in Til-omon and cast you from your body and put a usurper upon the throne. Suppose that is the case. What would you do then?'

'Nothing at all.'

'No?'

'Nothing,' said Valentine forcefully. 'Let him be Coronal who *wants* to be Coronal. I think power is a sickness and governing is a folly for madmen. If I once dwelled on Castle Mount, so be it, but I am not there now, and nothing in my being impels me to go back there. I'm a juggler and a good one getting better, and a happy man. Is the Coronal happy? Is the Pontifex? If I have been cast out of power, I regard it as good fortune. I would not now resume the burden.'

'It is what you were destined to carry.'

'Destined? Destined?' Valentine laughed. 'Just as fair to say that I was destined to be Coronal a little while, and then to be displaced by someone more fitting. One must be crazy to be a ruler, Deliamber, and I'm sane. The government is a burden and a chore. I would not accept it.'

'You will,' Deliamber said. 'You've been tampered with and you are not yourself. But once a Coronal, forever a Coronal. You will be healed and come into your own again, Lord Valentine.'

'Don't use that title!'

'It will be yours again,' said Deliamber.

Valentine angrily shook the suggestion away. He looked toward Carabella: she was asleep on the floor, head against the bed. Carefully he lifted her and put her under the coverlet. To Deliamber he said, 'It grows late, and there's been much foolishness tonight. My head hurts from all this heavy talk. Do to me what you did to her, wizard, and grant me sleep, and say no more to me of responsibilities that have never been mine and are never going to be mine. We must perform tomorrow, and I want to be rested for it.'

'Very well. Get into bed.'

Valentine settled in beside Carabella. The Vroon touched him lightly, then with more force, and Valentine felt his mind growing cloudy. Sleep came upon him easily, like a thick white mist sweeping up out of the ocean at twilight. Good. Good. Willingly he relinquished consciousness.

And in the night he dreamed, and there was about the dream a bright fierce glow that had the unmistakable aspect of a sending, for it was a dream vivid beyond imagining.

He saw himself crossing the harsh and terrible purple plain that he had visited so often in recent slumber. This time he knew without question where the plain was: no realm of fantasy, but the distant continent of Suvrael, that lay beneath the unshielded glare of the naked sun, and these fissures in the ground were scars of summer, where what little moisture the soil contained had been sucked forth. Ugly twisted plants with swollen grayish leaves lay limp against the ground, and things with thorns and weird angular joints grew tall. Valentine walked swiftly, in the heat and the merciless biting wind and the skin-cracking dryness. He was late, overdue at the palace of the King of Dreams, where he had been hired to perform.

The palace now loomed before him, sinister, black-shadowed, all spidery turrets and jagged porticoes, a building as spiky and forbidding as the plants of the desert. More a jail than a palace it seemed, at least in its outer aspect, but inside everything was different, cool and luxurious, with fountains in the courtyards, and soft plush draperies, and a scent of flowers in the air. Servants bowed and beckoned to him, leading him to inner chambers, stripping away his sand-crusted clothes, bathing him, drying him in feathery towels, giving him fresh clothes, elegant jeweled robes, offering him chilled sherberts, icy wine of a silvery hue, morsels of unknown delicate meats, and at last bringing him to the great high-vaulted throne-room where the King of Dreams sat in state.

At a vast distance Valentine saw him enthroned: Simonan Barjazid, the malign and unpredictable Power who from this wind-swept desert territory sent his messages of terrible import all through Majipoor. He was a heavy-bodied man, his face beardless, fleshy-jowled, eyes deep-set and ringed with dark circles, and around his close-cropped stubbly head he wore the golden diadem of his power, the thought-amplifying apparatus that a Barjazid had devised a thousand years ago. To Simonan's left sat his son Cristoph, fleshy like his father, and at his right hand was his son Minax, the heir, a man of lean and forbidding aspect, dark-skinned and sharp-faced, as if honed by the desert winds.

The King of Dreams, with a casual wave of his hand, ordered Valentine to begin.

It was knives he juggled, ten, fifteen of them, thin shining stilettos that would pierce right through his arm if they dropped wrongly, but he handled them with ease, juggling as only Sleet might do, or perhaps Zalzan Kavol, a virtuoso display of skill. Valentine stood still, making only the tiniest flicking motions of his hands and wrists, and the knives soared aloft and flashed with keen brilliance, coursing high through the air and falling perfectly back to his waiting fingers, and as they rose and fell, rose and fell, the arc that they described took on an alteration of form, no longer a mere cascade but becoming the starburst emblem of the Coronal, blades pointing outward as they flew through the air, and abruptly, as Valentine approached the climax of his performance, the knives froze in mid-air, and hovered there just above his questing fingers, and would not descend to them.

And from behind the throne came a scowling fierce-eyed man who was Dominin Barjazid, the third of the sons of the King of Dreams, and he strode toward Valentine and with an easy contemptuous gesture swept the starburst of knives from the air, thrusting them into the sash of his robe.

The King of Dreams smiled mockingly. 'You are an excellent juggler, Lord Valentine. At last you find a proper occupation.'

'I am Coronal of Majipoor,' Valentine replied.

'Were. Were. Were. You are a wanderer now, and fit to be nothing more.'

'Lazy,' said Minax Barjazid.

'Cowardly,' said Cristoph Barjazid. 'Idle.'

'A shirker of duty,' Dominin Barjazid declared.

'Your rank is forfeit,' said the King of Dreams. 'Your office is vacated. Go. Go and juggle, Valentine the juggler. Go, idler. Go, wanderer.'

'I am Coronal of Majipoor,' Valentine repeated firmly.

'No longer,' said the King of Dreams. He touched his hands to the diadem at his forehead and Valentine rocked and shook as if the ground had opened at his feet, and he stumbled and fell, and when he looked up again he saw that Dominin Barjazid now was clad in the green doublet and ermine robe of a Coronal, and had altered in appearance so that his face was the face of Lord Valentine and his body was the body of Lord Valentine, and out of the juggling knives that he had taken from Valentine he had fashioned the starburst crown of a Coronal, which his father Simonan Barjazid now placed upon his brow.

'See?' the King of Dreams cried. 'Power passes to the worthy! Go, juggler! Go!'

And Valentine fled into the purple desert, and saw the angry swirls of a sandstorm racing toward him out of the south, and tried to escape, but the storm came at him from all directions. He roared, 'I am Lord Valentine the Coronal!' but his voice was lost in the wind and he felt sand in his teeth. He shouted, 'This is treason, to usurp the power!' and his shout was blown away. He looked toward the palace of the King of Dreams, but it was no longer to be seen, and a great and shattering sense of eternal loss overwhelmed him.

He woke.

Carabella lay peacefully beside him. The first pale light of dawn was entering the room. Although it had been a monstrous dream, a sending of the most portentous sort, he felt utterly calm. For days now he had tried to deny the truth, but there was no rejecting it now, however bizarre, however fantastic it seemed. In another body he had once been Coronal of Majipoor, and body and identity had been stolen somehow from him. Could it be? A dream of such urgency could scarcely be dismissed or ignored. He sorted through the deepest places of his mind, trying to uncover memories of power, ceremonies on the Mount, glimpses of royal pomp, the taste of responsibility. Nothing. Nothing whatever. He was a juggler, and nothing more than a juggler, and he could remember no shred of his life before Pidruid: it was as if he had been born on that hillside, moments before Shanamir the herdsman had encountered him, born there with money in his purse and a flask of good red wine at his hip and a scattering of false memories in his mind.

And if it was true? If he was Coronal?

Why, then, he must go forth, for the sake of the commonwealth of Majipoor, to overthrow the tyrant and reclaim his rightful position. There would be that obligation upon him. But the notion was absurd. It created a dryness in his throat and a pounding in his chest, close to panic. To overthrow that dark-haired man of power, who had ridden in pomp through Pidruid? How could that possibly be done? How even come near a Coronal, let alone push him from his perch? That it had been done once – maybe – was no argument that it could be done again, and by a wandering juggler, an easy-natured young man who felt no compelling urge to tackle the impossible. Besides, Valentine saw in himself so little aptitude for governing. If he had in fact been Coronal, he must have had years of training on Castle Mount, a lengthy apprenticeship in the ways and uses of power; but not a trace of that was left to him now. How could he pretend to be a monarch, with none of a monarch's skills in his head?

And yet – and yet—

He glanced down at Carabella. She was awake; her eyes were open; she was watching him in silence. The awe was still upon her, but no longer the terror.

She said, 'What will you do, lord?'

'Call me Valentine, now and ever.'

'If you so command me.'

'I do so command you,' he said.

'And tell me – Valentine: what will you do?'

'Travel with the Skandars,' he replied. 'Continue to juggle. Master the art more thoroughly. Keep close watch on my dreams. Bide my time, seek to comprehend. What else can I do, Carabella?' He put his hand lightly to hers, and momentarily she shrank from his touch, and then did not, but pressed her other hand above his. He smiled. 'What else can I do, Carabella?'

PART II

The Book of
the Metamorphs

1

The Ghayrog city of Dulorn was an architectural marvel, a city of frosty brilliance that extended for two hundred miles up and down the heart of the great Dulorn Rift. Though it covered so huge an area, the city's predominant thrust was vertical: great shining towers, fanciful of design but severely restrained in material, that rose like tapered fangs from the soft gypsum-rich ground. The only approved building material in Dulorn was the native stone of the region, a light, airy calcite of high refractive index, that glittered like fine crystal, or perhaps like diamond. Out of this the Dulornese had fashioned their sharp-tipped high-rise structures and embellished them with parapets and balconies, with enormous flamboyant flying buttresses, with soaring cantilevered ribs, with stalactites and stalagmites of sparkling facets, with lacy bridges far above the streets, with colonnades and domes and pendentives and pagodas. The juggling troupe of Zalzan Kavol, approaching the city from the west, came upon it almost exactly at noon, when the sun stood straight overhead and streaks of white flame seemed to dance along the flanks of the titanic towers. Valentine caught his breath in wonder. Such a vast place! Such a wondrous show of light and form!

Fourteen million people dwelled in Dulorn, making it one of the larger cities of Majipoor, although by no means the largest. On the continent of Alhanroel, so Valentine had heard, a city of this size would be nothing remarkable, and even here on the more pastoral continent of Zimroel there were many that matched or surpassed it. But surely no place could equal its beauty, he thought. Dulorn was cold and fiery, both at once. Its gleaming spires insistently claimed one's attention, like chill, irresistible music, like the piercing tones of some mighty organ rolling out across the darkness of space.

'No country inns for us here!' Carabella cried happily. 'We'll have a hotel, with fine sheets and soft cushions!'

'Will Zalzan Kavol be so generous?' Valentine asked.

'Generous?' Carabella laughed. 'He has no choice. Dulorn offers only luxurious accommodations. If we sleep here, we sleep in the street or we sleep like dukes: there's nothing between.'

'Like dukes,' Valentine said. 'To sleep like dukes. Why not?'

He had sworn her, that morning before leaving the inn, to say nothing to anyone about last night's events, not to Sleet, not to any of the Skandars, not even, should she feel the need to seek one, to a dream-speaker. He had demanded the oath of silence from her in the name of the Lady, the Pontifex, and the Coronal. Furthermore he had compelled her to continue to behave toward him as though he had always been, and for the rest of his life would remain, merely Valentine the wandering juggler. In extracting the oath from her Valentine had spoken with force and dignity worthy of a Coronal, so that poor Carabella, kneeling and trembling, was as frightened of him all over again as if he were wearing the starburst crown. He felt more than a little fraudulent about that, for he was far from convinced that the strange dreams of the previous night were to be taken at face value. But still, those dreams could not lightly be dismissed, and so precautions must be taken, secrecy, guile. They came strangely to him, such maneuvers. He swore Autifon Deliamber also to the oath, wondering as he did so how much he could trust a Vroon and a sorcerer, but there seemed to be sincerity in Deliamber's voice as he vowed to keep his confidence.

Deliamber said, 'And who else knows of these matters?'

'Only Carabella. And I have her bound by the same pledge.'

'You've said nothing to the Hjort?'

'Vinorkis? Not a word. Why do you ask?'

The Vroon replied, 'He watches you too carefully. He asks too many questions. I have little liking for him.'

Valentine shrugged. 'It's not hard to dislike Hjorts. But what do you fear?'

'He guards his mind too well. His aura is a dark one. Keep your distance from him, Valentine, or he'll bring you trouble.'

The jugglers entered the city and made their way down broad dazzling avenues to their hotel, guided by Deliamber, who seemed to have a map of every corner of Majipoor engraved in his mind. The wagon halted in front of a tower of splendid height and awesome fantasy of architecture, a place of minarets and arched vaults and shining octagonal windows. Descending from the wagon, Valentine stood blinking and gaping in awe.

'You look as though you've been clubbed on the head,' Zalzan Kavol said gruffly. 'Never seen Dulorn before?'

Valentine made an evasive gesture. His porous memory said nothing to him of Dulorn: but who, once having seen this city, could forget it?

Some comment seemed called for. He said simply, 'Is there anything more glorious on all of Majipoor?'

'Yes,' the gigantic Skandar replied. 'A tureen of hot soup. A mug of strong wine. A sizzling roast over an open fire. You can't eat beautiful architecture. Castle Mount itself isn't worth a stale turd to a starving man.' Zalzan Kavol snorted in high self-approbation and, hefting his luggage, strode into the hotel.

Valentine called bemusedly after him, 'But I was speaking only of the beauty of cities!'

Thelkar, usually the most taciturn of the Skandars, said, 'Zalzan Kavol admires Dulorn more than you would believe. But he'd never admit it.'

'He admits admiration only for Piliplok, where we were born,' Gibor Haern put in. 'He feels it's disloyal to say a good word for anyplace else.'

'Shh!' cried Erfon Kavol. 'He comes!'

Their senior brother had reappeared at the hotel door. 'Well?' Zalzan Kavol boomed. 'Why are you standing about? Rehearsal in thirty minutes!' His yellow eyes blazed like those of some beast of the woods. He growled, clenched his four fists menacingly, and vanished again.

An odd master, Valentine thought. Somewhere far beneath that shaggy hide, he suspected, lay a person of civility and even – who could tell? – of kindness. But Zalzan Kavol worked hard at his bearishness.

The jugglers were booked to perform at the Perpetual Circus of Dulorn, a municipal festivity that was in progress during every hour of the day and on every day of the year. The Ghayrogs, who dominated this city and its surrounding province, slept not nightly but seasonally, for two or three months at a time mainly in winter, and when they were awake were insatiable in their demand for entertainment. According to Deliamber they paid well and there were never enough itinerant performers in this part of Majipoor to satisfy their needs.

When the troupe gathered for the afternoon practice session, Zalzan Kavol announced that tonight's engagement was due to take place between the fourth and sixth hours after midnight.

Valentine was unhappy about that. This night in particular he was eager for the guidance that dreams might bring, after last night's weighty revelations. But what chance could there be for useful dreams if he spent the most fertile hours of the night on stage?

'We can sleep earlier,' Carabella observed. 'Dreams come at any hour. Or do you have an appointment for a sending?'

It was a sly teasing remark, for one who had trembled in awe of him not so much earlier. He smiled to show he had taken no offense – he could see self-doubt lurking just beneath her mockery of him – and said, 'I might not sleep at all, knowing that I must rise so early.'

'Have Deliamber touch you as he did last night,' she suggested.

'I prefer to find my own path into sleep,' he said

Which he did, after a stiff afternoon of practice and a satisfying dinner of wind-dried beef and cold blue wine at the hotel. He had taken a room by himself here, and before he entered the bed – cool smooth sheets, as Carabella had said, fit for a duke – he commended his spirit to the Lady of the Isle and prayed for a sending from her, which was permissible and frequently done, though not often effective. It was the Lady now whose aid he most dearly needed. If he was in truth a fallen Coronal, then she was his fleshly mother as well as his spiritual one, and might confirm him in his identity and direct him along his quest.

As he moved into sleep, he tried to visualize the Lady and her Isle, to reach out across the thousands of miles to her and create a bridge, some spark of consciousness over that immense gap, by which she could make contact with him. He was hampered by the empty places in his memory. Presumably any adult Majipooran knew the features of the Lady and the geography of the Isle as well as he did the face of his own mother and the outskirts of his city, but Valentine's crippled mind gave him mainly blanks, which had to be filled by imagination and chance. How had she looked that night in the fireworks over Pidruid? A round smiling face, long thick hair. Very well. And the rest? Suppose the hair is black and glossy, black like that of her sons Lord Valentine and dead Lord Voriax. The eyes are brown, warm, alert. The lips full, the cheeks lightly dimpled, a fine network of wrinkles at the corners of the eyes. A stately, robust woman, yes, and she strolls through a garden of lush floriferous bushes, yellow tanigales and camellias and eldirons and purple thwales, everything rich with tropical life; she pauses to pluck a blossom and fasten it in her hair, and moves on, along white marble flagstones that wind sinuously between the shrubs, until she emerges on a broad stone patio set into the side of the hill on which she dwells, looking down on the terraces upon terraces descending in wide sweeping curves toward the sea. And she looks westward to far-off Zimroel, she closes her eyes, she thinks of her lost wandering outcast son in the city of the Ghayrogs, she gathers her force and broadcasts sweet messages of hope and courage to Valentine exiled in Dulorn—

Valentine slipped into deep sleep.

And indeed the Lady came to him as he dreamed. He encountered her not on the hillside below her garden, but in some empty city in a wasteland, a ruined place of weatherbeaten sandstone pillars and shattered altars. They approached one another from opposite sides of a tumbledown forum under ghostly moonlight. But her face was veiled and she kept it averted from him: he recognized her by the heavy coils of her dark hair and by the fragrance of the creamy-petaled eldiron flower beside her ear, and knew that he was in the presence of the Lady of the Isle, but he wanted her smile to warm his soul in this bleak place, he wanted the comfort of her gentle eyes, and he saw only the veil, the shoulders, the side of her head. 'Mother?' he asked uncertainly. 'Mother, it's Valentine! Don't you know me? Look at me, mother!'

Wraithlike she drifted past him, and disappeared between two broken columns inscribed with scenes of the deeds of the great Coronals, and was gone.

'Mother?' he called.

The dream was over. Valentine struggled to make her return, but could not. He awakened and lay peering into the darkness, seeing that veiled figure once more and searching for meaning. She hadn't recognized him. Was he so effectively transformed that not even his own mother could perceive who lay hidden in this body? Or had he never been her son, so that there was no reason for her to know him? He lacked answers. If the soul of dark-haired Lord Valentine was embedded in the body of fair-haired Valentine, the Lady of the Isle in his dream had given no sign of it, and he was as far from understanding as he had been when he closed his eyes.

What follies I pursue, he thought. What implausible speculations, what madnesses!

He eased himself back into sleep.

And almost at once, so it seemed, a hand touched his shoulder and someone rocked him until he came reluctantly into wakefulness. Carabella.

'Two hours after midnight,' she told him. 'Zalzan Kavol wants us down by the wagon in half an hour. Did you dream?'

'Inconclusively. And you?'

'I remained awake,' she answered. 'It seemed safest. Some nights one prefers not to dream.' She said timidly, as he began to dress, 'Will I share your room again, Valentine?'

'Would you like to?'

'I have given oath to act with you as I acted before – before I knew – Oh, Valentine, I was so frightened! But yes. Yes, let's be companions again, and even lovers. Tomorrow night!'

'What if I am Coronal?'

'Please. Don't ask such questions.'

'What if I am?'

'You've ordered me to call you Valentine and to regard you as Valentine. This I'll do, if you'll let me.'

'Do you believe I'm Coronal?'

'Yes,' she whispered.

'It no longer frightens you?'

'A little. Just a little. You still seem human to me.'

'Good.'

'I've had a day to get used to things. And I'm under an oath. I must think of you as Valentine. I swore by the Powers to that.' She grinned impishly. 'I swore an oath to the Coronal that I would pretend you are not Coronal, and so I must be true to my pledge, and treat you casually, and call you Valentine, and show no fear of you, and behave as though nothing has changed. And so I can share your bed tomorrow night?'

'Yes.'

'I love you, Valentine.'

He pulled her lightly to him. 'I thank you for overcoming your fear. I love you, Carabella.'

'Zalzan Kavol will be angry if we're late,' she said.

2

The Perpetual Circus was housed in a structure altogether opposite from those most typical of Dulorn: a giant flat unadorned drum of a building, perfectly circular and no more than ninety feet high, that stood by itself on a huge tract of open land on the eastern perimeter of the city. Within, a great central space provided an awesome setting for the stage, and around it ran the seating ring, tier upon tier in concentric circles rising to the roof.

The place could hold thousands, perhaps hundreds of thousands. Valentine was startled to see how nearly full it was, here at what was for him the middle of the night. Looking outward into the audience was difficult, for the stage-lights were in his eyes, but he was able to perceive enormous numbers of people sitting or sprawling in their seats. Nearly all were Ghayrogs, though he caught sight of the occasional Hjort or Vroon or human making a late night of it. There were no places on Majipoor entirely populated by one race – ancient decrees of the government, going back to the earliest days of heavy non-human settlement, forbade such concentrations except on the Metamorph reservation – but the Ghayrogs were a particularly clannish lot, and tended to cluster together in and around Dulorn up to the legal maximum. Though warm-blooded and mammalian, they had certain reptilian traits that made them unlovable to most other races: quick-flicking forked red tongues, grayish scaly skin of a thick, polished consistency, cold green unblinking eyes. Their hair had a medusoid quality, black succulent strands that coiled and writhed unsettlingly, and their odor, both sweet and acrid at once, was not charming to non-Ghayrog nostrils.

Valentine's mood was subdued as he moved out with the troupe onto the stage. The hour was all wrong: his body-cycles were at low ebb, and though he had had enough sleep, he had no enthusiasm for being awake just now. Once again he carried the burden of a difficult dream. That rejection by the Lady, that inability to make contact with her, what did it signify? When he was only Valentine the juggler, significance was insignificant to him: each day had a path of its own, and he had no worries about larger patterns, only to increase the skill of hand and eye from one day to the next. But now that these ambiguous and disturbing revelations had been visited upon him he was forced to consider dreary long-range matters of purpose and destiny and the route on which he was bound. He had no liking for that. Already he tasted a keen nostalgic sorrow for the good old times of the week before last, when he had wandered busy Pidruid in happy aimlessness.

The demands of his art quickly lifted him out of this brooding. There was no time, under the glare of the spotlights, to think of anything except the work of performing.

The stage was colossal, and many things were happening on it at once. Vroon magicians were doing a routine involving floating colored lights and bursts of green and red smoke; an animal-trainer just beyond had a dozen fat serpents standing on their tails; a dazzling group of dancers with grotesquely attenuated bodies sprayed in many-faceted silver glowstuff did austere leaps and carries; several small orchestras in widely separated regions played the tinny and tootling woodwind music beloved of the Ghayrogs; there was a one-finger acrobat, a high-wire woman, a levitator, a trio of glassblowers engaged in fashioning a cage for themselves, an eel-eater, and a platoon of berserk clowns, along with much more beyond Valentine's range of vision. The audience, slouching and lounging out there in the half-darkness, had an easy time watching all this, for, Valentine realized, the giant stage was in gentle motion, turning slowly on hidden bearings, and in the course of an hour or two would make a complete circuit, presenting each group of performers in turn to every part of the auditorium. 'It all floats on a pool of quicksilver,' Sleet whispered. 'You could buy three provinces with the value of the metal.'

With so much competition for the eyes of the onlookers, the jugglers had brought forth some of their finest effects, which meant that the novice Valentine was largely excluded, left to toss clubs to himself and occasionally to feed knives or torches to the others. Carabella was dancing atop a silver globe two feet in diameter that rolled in irregular circles as she moved: she juggled five spheres that glowed with brilliant green light. Sleet had mounted stilts, and rose even taller than the Skandars, a tiny figure far above everyone, coolly flipping from hand to hand three huge red-and-black-speckled eggs of the moleekahen, that he had bought at market that evening. If he dropped an egg from so great a height, the splash would be conspicuous and the humiliation enormous, but never since Valentine had known him had Sleet dropped anything, and he dropped no eggs tonight. As for the six Skandars, they had arranged themselves in a rigid star-pattern, standing with their backs to one another, and were juggling flaming torches. At carefully coordinated moments each would hurl a torch backward over his outer shoulder to his brother at the opposite side of the star. The interchanges were made with wondrous precision, the trajectories of the flying torches were flawlessly timed to create splendid crisscrossing patterns of light, and not a hair on any Skandar's hide was scorched as they casually snatched from the air the firebrands that came hurtling past them from their unseen partners.

Round and round the stage they went, performing in stints of half an hour at a stretch, with five minutes to relax in the central well just below the stage, where hundreds of other off-duty artists gathered. Valentine longed to be doing something more challenging than his own little elementary juggle, but Zalzan Kavol had forbidden it: he was not yet ready, the Skandar said, though he was doing excellently well for a novice.

Morning came before the troupe was allowed to leave the stage. Payment here was by the hour, and hiring was governed by silent response-meters beneath the seats of the audience, monitored by cold-eyed Ghayrogs in a booth in the well. Some performers lasted only a few minutes before universal boredom or disdain banished them, but Zalzan Kavol and his company, who had been guaranteed two hours of work, remained on stage for four. They would have been kept for a fifth if Zalzan Kavol had not been dissuaded by his brothers, who gathered around him for a brief and intense argument.

'His greed,' Carabella said quietly, 'will lead him to embarrass himself yet. How long does he think people can throw those torches around before someone slips up? Even Skandars get tired eventually.'

'Not Zalzan Kavol, from the looks of it,' Valentine said.

'*He* may be a juggling machine, yes, but his brothers are mortal. Rovorn's timing is starting to get ragged. I'm glad they had the courage to make a stand.' She smiled. 'And I was getting pretty tired too.'

So successfully were the jugglers received in Dulorn that they were hired for four additional days. Zalzan Kavol was elated – the Ghayrogs gave their entertainers high wages – and declared a five-crown bonus for everyone.

All well and good, Valentine thought. But he had no wish to settle in indefinitely among the Ghayrogs. After the second day, restlessness began to make him chafe.

'You wish to be moving on,' Deliamber said – a statement, not a question.

Valentine nodded. 'I begin to glimpse the shape of the road ahead of me.'

'To the Isle?'

'Why do you bother speaking with people,' Valentine said lightly, 'if you see everything within their minds?'

'I did no mind-peeking this time. Your next move is obvious enough.'

'Go to the Lady, yes. Who else can truly tell me who I am?'

'You still have doubts,' Deliamber said.

'I have no evidence other than dreams.'

'Which speak powerful truths.'

'Yes,' Valentine said, 'but dreams can be parables, dreams can be metaphors, dreams can be fantasies. It's folly to speak them literally without confirmation. And the Lady can give confirmation, or so I hope. How far is it to the Isle, wizard?'

Deliamber briefly closed his large golden eyes.

'Thousands of miles,' he said. 'We are now perhaps a fifth of the way across Zimroel. You must make your way eastward through Khyntor or Velathys, and around the territory of the Metamorphs, and then perhaps by riverboat via Ni-moya to Piliplok, where the pilgrim-ships leave for the Isle.'

'How long will that take?'

'To reach Piliplok? At our present pace, about fifty years. Wandering with these jugglers, stopping here and there for a week at a time—'

'What if I left the troupe and went on my own?'

'Six months, possibly. The river journey is swift. The overland section takes much longer. If we had airships as they do on other worlds it would be a matter of a day or two to Piliplok, but of course we do without many devices on Majipoor that other people enjoy.'

'Six months?' Valentine frowned. 'And the cost, if I hired a vehicle and a guide?'

'Perhaps twenty royals. You'll juggle a long time to earn that much.'

'When I get to Piliplok,' Valentine said, 'what then?'

'You book passage to the Isle. The voyage is a matter of weeks. When you reach the Isle you take lodging on the lowest terrace and begin the ascent.'

'The ascent?'

'A course of prayer, purification, and initiation. You move upward from terrace to terrace until you reach the Terrace of Adoration, which is the threshold to Inner Temple. You know nothing of any of this?'

'My mind, Deliamber, has been meddled with.'

'Of course.'

'At Inner Temple, then?'

'You are now an initiate. You serve the Lady as an acolyte, and if you seek an audience with her, you undergo special rites and await the summoning dream.'

Uneasily Valentine said, 'How long does this entire process take, the terraces, the initiation, the service as acolyte, the summoning dream?'

'It varies. Five years, sometimes. Ten. Forever, conceivably. The Lady has no time for each and every pilgrim.'

'And there's no more direct way of gaining audience?'

Deliamber uttered the thick coughing sound that was his laugh. 'What? Knock on the temple door, cry out that you are her changeling son, demand entry?'

'Why not?'

'Because,' the Vroon said, 'the outer terraces of the Isle are designed as filters to keep such things from happening. There are no easy channels of communication to the Lady, and deliberately so. It would take you years.'

'I'd find a way,' Valentine stared levelly at the little wizard. 'I could reach her mind, if I were on the Isle. I could cry out to her, I could persuade her to summon me. Perhaps.'

'Perhaps.'

'With your assistance it could be done.'

'I feared that was coming,' said Deliamber dryly.

'You have some skill at making sendings. We could reach, if not the Lady herself, then those close to her. Step by step, drawing ourselves closer to her, cutting short the interminable process on the terraces—'

'It could be done, possibly,' Deliamber said. 'Do you believe I'm minded to make the pilgrimage with you, though?'

Valentine regarded the Vroon in silence for a long time.

'I'm certain of it,' he said finally. 'You play at reluctance, but you've engineered my every motive to impel me toward the Isle. With you at my side. Am I right? Eh, Deliamber? You're more eager to have me get there than I am myself.'

'Ah,' the sorcerer said. 'It comes out now!'

'Am I right?'

'If you resolve to go to the Isle, Valentine, I will be at your side. But are you resolved?'

'Sometimes.'

'Intermittent resolutions lack potency,' said Deliamber.

'Thousands of miles. Years of waiting. Toil and intrigue. Why do I want to do this, Deliamber?'

'Because you are Coronal, and must be again.'

'The first may be true, though I have mighty doubts of it. The second is open to question.'

Deliamber's look was crafty. 'You prefer to live under the rule of a usurper?'

'What's the Coronal and his rule to me? He's half a world away on Castle Mount and I'm a wandering juggler.' Valentine extended his fingers and stared at them as though he had never seen his hands before. 'I could spare myself much effort if I remained with Zalzan Kavol and let the other, whoever he may be, keep the throne. Suppose he's a wise and just usurper? Where's the benefit for Majipoor, if I do all this work merely to put myself back in his place? Oh, Deliamber, Deliamber, do I sound like a king at all, when I say these things? Where's my lust for power? How can I ever have been a ruler, when I so obviously don't care about what's happened?'

'We've spoken of this before. You have been tampered with, my lord. Your spirit as well as your face has been changed.'

'Even so. My royal nature, if ever I had one, is altogether gone from me. That lust for power—'

'Twice you've used the phrase,' Deliamber said. 'Lust has nothing to do with it. A true king doesn't lust for power: responsibility lusts for him. And takes him, and possesses him. This Coronal is new, he has done little yet but make the grand processional, and already the people grumble at his early decrees. And you ask if he will be wise and just? How can any usurper be just? He is a criminal, Valentine, and he rules already with a criminal's guilty fears eating at his dreams, and as time goes on those fears will poison him and he will be a tyrant. Can you doubt that? He will remove anyone who threatens him – will kill, even, if need be. The poison that courses in his veins will enter the life of the planet itself, will affect every citizen. And you, sitting here looking at your fingers, do you see no responsibility? How can you talk of *sparing yourself much effort*? As if it hardly matters who is the king. It matters very much who is the king, my lord, and you were chosen and trained for it, and not by lottery. Or do you believe anyone can become Coronal?'

'I do. By random stroke of fate.'

Deliamber laughed harshly. 'Possibly that was true nine thousand years ago. There is a dynasty, my Lord.'

'An adoptive dynasty?'

'Precisely. Since the time of Lord Arioc, and maybe even earlier, Coronals have been chosen from among a small group of families, no more than a hundred clans, all of them dwellers on Castle Mount and close participants in the government. The next Coronal is already in training, though only he and a few advisers know who he is, and two or three replacements for him must also have been chosen. But now the line is broken, now an intruder has pushed his way in. Nothing but evil can come of that.'

'What if the usurper is simply the heir-in-waiting, who grew tired of waiting?'

'No,' said Deliamber. 'Inconceivable. No one deemed qualified to be Coronal would overthrow a lawfully consecrated prince. Besides, why the mummery of pretending to be Lord Valentine, if he is another?'

'I grant you that.'

'Grant me also this: that the person atop Castle Mount now has neither right nor qualification for being there, and must be cast down, and you are the only one who can do it.'

Valentine sighed. 'You ask a great deal.'

'History asks a great deal,' said Deliamber. 'History has demanded, on a thousand worlds across many thousands of years, that intelligent beings choose between order and anarchy, between creation and destruction, between reason and unreason. And the forces of order and creation and reason have been focused always in a single leader, a king, if you will, or a president, a chairman, a grand minister, a generalissimo, use whatever word you wish,

427

a monarch by some name or other. Here it is the Coronal, or more accurately the Coronal ruling as the voice of the Pontifex who was once Coronal, and it matters, my lord, it matters very much, who is to be Coronal and who is not to be Coronal.'

'Yes,' Valentine said. 'Perhaps.'

'You'll go on wavering from *yes* to *perhaps* a long while,' said Deliamber. 'But *yes* will govern, in the end. And you will make the pilgrimage to the Isle, and with the Lady's blessing you will march on Castle Mount and take your rightful place.'

'The things you say fill me with terror. If ever I had the ability to rule, if ever I was given the training for it, these things have been burned from my mind.'

'The terror will fade. Your mind will be made whole in the passing of time.'

'And time passes, and here we sit in Dulorn, to amuse the Ghayrogs.'

Deliamber said, 'Not much longer. We'll find our way eastward, my lord. Have faith in that.'

There was something contagious about Deliamber's assurance. Valentine's hesitations and uncertainties were gone – for the moment. But when Deliamber had departed, Valentine gave way to uncomfortable contemplation of certain hard realities. Could he simply hire a couple of mounts and set off for Piliplok with Deliamber tomorrow? What about Carabella, who had suddenly become very important to him? Abandon her here in Dulorn? And Shanamir? The boy was attached to Valentine, not to the Skandars: he neither could nor would be left. There was the cost, then, of a journey for four across nearly all of vast Zimroel, food, lodging, transportation, then the pilgrim-ship to the Isle, and what then of expenses on the Isle while he schemed to gain access to the Lady? Autifon Deliamber had guessed it might cost twenty royals for him to travel alone to Piliplok. The cost, for the four of them, or for the five if Sleet were added, though Valentine had no idea if Sleet would care to come, might run a hundred royals or more, a hundred fifty perhaps to the lowest terrace of the Isle. He sorted through his purse. Of the money he had had upon him when he found himself outside Pidruid, he had more than sixty royals left, plus a royal or two that he had earned with the troupe. Not enough, not nearly enough. Carabella, he knew, was almost without money; Shanamir had dutifully returned to his family the hundred sixty royals from the sale of his mounts; and Deliamber, if he had any wealth, would not in old age be hauling himself through the countryside under contract to a crowd of ruffian Skandars.

So, then? Nothing to do but wait, and plan, and hope that Zalzan Kavol intended a generally eastward route. And save his crowns and bide his time, until the moment was ripe for going to the Lady.

3

A few days after their departure from Dulorn, purses bulging with the generous Ghayrog pay, Valentine drew Zalzan Kavol aside to ask him about the direction of travel. It was a gentle late-summer day, and here, where they were camped for lunch along the eastern slope of the Rift, a purple mist enfolded everything, a low thick clammy cloud that took its delicate lavender color from pigments in the air, for there were deposits of skuvva-sand just north of here and the winds were constantly stirring the stuff aloft.

Zalzan Kavol looked uncomfortable and irritable in this weather. His gray fur, purpled now by droplets of mist, was clumped in comic bunches, and he rubbed at it, trying to restore it to its proper nap. Probably not the best moment for such a conference, Valentine realized, but it was too late: the issue had been broached.

Zalzan Kavol said hollowly, 'Which of us is the leader of this troupe, Valentine?'

'You are, beyond question.'

'Then why do you try to govern me?'

'I?'

'In Pidruid,' the Skandar said, 'you asked me to go next to Falkynkip, for the convenience of your herdsman squire's family honor, and I remind you that you forced me to hire the herdsman boy in the first place, though he is no juggler and never will be. In these things I yielded, I know not why. There was also the matter of your interfering in my quarrel with the Vroon—'

'My interference had benefit,' Valentine pointed out, 'as you yourself admitted at the time.'

'True. But interference of itself is unfamiliar to me. Do you understand that I am absolute master of this troupe?'

Valentine shrugged lightly. 'No one disputes that.'

'But do you understand it? My brothers do. They are aware that a body can have only one head – unless it's a Su-Suheris body, and we're not talking of those – and here I am the head, it is from my mind that plans and instructions flow, and mine alone.' Zalzan Kavol flashed an austere smile. 'Is this tyranny? No. This is simple efficiency. Jugglers can never be democrats, Valentine. One mind designs the patterns, one alone, or there is chaos. Now what do you want with me?'

'Only to know the shape of our route.'

With barely suppressed anger Zalzan Kavol said, 'Why? You are in our employ. You go where we go. Your curiosity is misplaced.'

'It doesn't seem that way to me. Some routes are more useful to me than others.'

'Useful? To you? You have plans? You told me you had no plans!'

'I do now.'

'What do you plan, then?'

Valentine took a deep breath. 'Ultimately to make the pilgrimage to the Isle, and become a devotee of the Lady. Since the pilgrim-ships sail from Piliplok, and all of Zimroel lies between us and Piliplok, it would be valuable to me to know whether you plan to go in some other direction, let's say down to Velathys, or maybe back to Til-omon or Narabal, instead of—'

'You are discharged from my service,' Zalzan Kavol said icily.

Valentine was astounded. '*What?*'

'Terminated. My brother Erfon will give you ten crowns as your settlement. I want you on your way within an hour.'

Valentine felt his cheeks growing hot. 'This is totally unexpected! I merely asked—'

'You merely asked. And in Pidruid you merely asked, and in Falkynkip you merely asked, and next week in Mazadone you would merely ask. You annoy my tranquillity, Valentine, and this cancels out your promise as a juggler. Besides, you are disloyal.'

'Disloyal? To what? To whom?'

'You hire on with us, but secretly mean to use us as the vehicle to get you to Piliplok. Your commitment to us is insincere. I call that treachery.'

'When I hired on with you, I had nothing else in mind but to travel with your troupe wherever you went. But things have changed, and now I see reason to make the pilgrimage.'

'Why did you allow things to change? Where's your sense of duty to your employers and teachers?'

'Did I hire on with you for life?' Valentine demanded. 'Is it treachery to discover that one has a goal more important than tomorrow's performance?'

'That diversion of energy,' said Zalzan Kavol, 'is what leads me to be rid of you. I want you thinking about juggling every hour of the day, and not about the departure date of pilgrim-ships from Shkunibor Pier.'

'There would be no diversion of energy. When I juggle, I juggle. And I'd resign from the troupe when we approached Piliplok. But until then—'

'Enough,' Zalzan Kavol said. 'Pack. Go. Take yourself swiftly to Piliplok and sail to the Isle, and may you fare well. I have no further need of you.'

The Skandar seemed altogether serious. Scowling in the purple mist, slapping at the soggy patches in his pelt. Zalzan Kavol swung heavily around and began to walk away. Valentine trembled in tension and dismay. The thought of leaving now, of traveling alone to Piliplok, left him aghast; and beyond that he felt part of this troupe, more so than he had ever been aware, a member of a close-knit team, and would not willingly be sundered. At least not now, not yet, while he could remain with Carabella and Sleet and even the Skandars, whom he respected without liking, and continue to increase his skills of eye and hand while moving eastward toward whatever strange destiny Deliamber seemed to have in mind for him.

'Wait!' Valentine called. 'What about the law?'

Zalzan Kavol glared over his shoulder. 'Which law?'

'The one requiring you to keep three human jugglers in your employ,' said Valentine.

'I will hire the herdsman boy in your place,' Zalzan Kavol retorted, 'and teach him whatever skills he can learn.' And he stalked off.

Valentine stood stunned. His conversation with Zalzan Kavol had taken place in a grove of small golden-leafed plants that evidently were psychosensitive: for, he noticed now, the plants had folded their intricate compound leaflets in the course of the quarrel, and looked shriveled and blackened for ten feet on all sides of him. He touched one. It was crisp and lifeless, as though it had been torched. He felt abashed at being a party to such destruction.

'What happened?' Shanamir asked, appearing suddenly and staring in wonder at the withered foliage. 'I heard yelling. The Skandar—'

'Has fired me,' said Valentine vacantly, 'because I asked him which way we were going next, because I admitted to him that I intended eventually to journey on pilgrimage to the Isle and wondered if his route would suit my purpose.'

Shanamir gaped. 'You are to make the pilgrimage? I never knew!'

'A recent decision.'

'Why, then,' the boy cried, 'we'll make it together, won't we? Come, we'll pack our things, we'll steal a couple of mounts from these Skandars, we'll leave at once!'

'Do you mean that?'

'Of course!'

'It's thousands of miles to Piliplok. You and I, and no one to guide us, and—'

'Why not?' Shanamir asked. 'Look, we ride to Khyntor, and there we take a riverboat to Ni-moya, and on from there down the Zimr to the coast, and at Piliplok we buy passage on the pilgrim-ship, and – what's wrong, Valentine?'

'I belong with these people. I'm learning an art from them. I – I—' Valentine broke off in confusion. Was he a juggler-in-training, or a Coronal-in-exile? Was it his purpose to plod along with shaggy Skandars, yes, with Carabella and Sleet also, or was it incumbent on him to move by the fastest means toward the Isle, and then with the Lady's help toward Castle Mount? He was confounded by these uncertainties.

'The cost?' Shanamir said. 'Is that what worries you? You had fifty royals and more in Pidruid. You must have some of that left. I have a few crowns myself. If we need more, you can work as a juggler on the riverboat, and I could curry mounts, I suppose, or—'

'Where are you planning to go?' said Carabella, coming abruptly upon them out of the forest. 'And what has happened to these sensitivos here? Is there trouble?'

Briefly Valentine told her of his talk with Zalzan Kavol.

She listened in silence, with her hand to her lips; and, when he was done, she darted off abruptly, without a word, in the direction Zalzan Kavol had taken.

'Carabella?' Valentine called. But already she was out of sight.

'Let's go,' said Shanamir. 'We can be out of here in half an hour, and by nightfall we'll be miles away. Look, you pack our things. I'll take two of the mounts and lead them around through the woods, down the slope toward the little lake we passed when we came in, and you meet me down there by the grove of cabbage trees.' Shanamir waved his hands impatiently. 'Hurry! I've got to get the mounts while the Skandars aren't around, and they might come back at any minute!'

Shanamir vanished into the forest. Valentine stood frozen. To leave now, so suddenly, with so little time to prepare himself for this upheaval? And what of Carabella? Not even a goodbye? Deliamber? Sleet? He started toward the wagon to gather his few possessions, halted, plucked indecisively at the dead leaves of the poor sensitivo plants, as though by pruning the withered stalks he could instantly induce new growth. Gradually he compelled himself to see the brighter side. This was a disguised blessing. If he stayed with the jugglers, it would delay by months or even years the confrontation with reality that obviously lay in store for him. And Carabella, if any truth lay in the shape of things that began to emerge, could be no part of that reality, anyway. So, then, it behooved him to shrug away his shock and distress, and to take to the highway, bound for Piliplok and the pilgrim-ships. Come, he told himself, get moving, collect your things. Shanamir's waiting by the cabbage trees with the mounts. But he could not move.

And then Carabella came bounding toward him, face aglow.

'It's all fixed,' she said. 'I got Deliamber to work on him. You know, a little trick here and there, a bit of a touch with the tip of a tentacle – the usual wizardry. He's changed his mind. Or we've changed it for him.'

Valentine was startled by the intensity of his feeling of relief. 'I can stay?'

'If you'll go to him and ask forgiveness.'

'Forgiveness for what?'

Carabella grinned. 'That doesn't matter. He took offense, the Divine only knows why! His fur was wet. His nose was cold. Who knows? He's a Skandar, Valentine, he has his own weird sense of what's right and wrong, he's not required to think the way humans do. You got him angry and he discharged you. Ask him politely to take you back, and he will. Go on, now. Go.'

'But – but—'

'But what? Are *you* going to stand on pride now? Do you want to be re-hired or don't you?'

'Of course I do.'

'Then go,' Carabella said. She seized him by the arm and gave a little tug, to budge him as he stood there faltering and fumbling, and as she did so, it must have occurred to her whose arm it was she was tugging, for she sucked in her breath and let go of him and moved away, hovering as if on the verge of kneeling and making the starburst symbol. 'Please?' she said softly. 'Please go to him, Valentine? Before he changes his mind again? If you leave the troupe, I'll have to leave it too, and I don't want to. Go. Please.'

'Yes,' said Valentine. She led him over the spongy mist-moistened ground to the wagon. Zalzan Kavol sat sulkily on the steps, huddling in a cloak in the damp, close warmth of the purple mist. Valentine approached him and said straightforwardly, 'It was not my intent to anger you. I ask your pardon.'

Zalzan Kavol made a low growling sound, almost below the threshold of audibility.

'You are a nuisance,' the Skandar said. 'Why am I willing to forgive you? From now on you will not speak to me unless I have spoken to you first. Understood?'

'Understood, yes.'

'You will make no attempt to influence the route we travel.'

'Understood,' said Valentine.

'If you irritate me again, you will be terminated without severance pay and you will have ten minutes to get out of my sight, no matter where we are, even if we are camped in the midst of a Metamorph reservation and nightfall is coming, do you understand?'

'I understand,' Valentine said.

He waited, wondering if he would be asked to bow, to kiss the Skandar's hairy fingers, to grovel in obeisance. Carabella, standing to one side, seemed to be holding her breath, as though expecting some explosion to come from the spectacle of a Power of Majipoor begging forgiveness from an itinerant Skandar juggler.

Zalzan Kavol regarded Valentine disdainfully, as he might have regarded a cold fish of uncertain vintage presented to him in a congealed sauce for dinner. Acidulously he said, 'I am not required to provide my employees with information of no concern to them. But I will tell you, anyway, that Piliplok is my native city, and I return there from time to time, and it is my purpose to arrive there eventually. How soon it will be depends on what engagements I can arrange between here and there: but be informed that our route lies generally eastward, although there may be some departures from that path, for we have a livelihood to earn. I hope this pleases you. When we reach Piliplok, you may resign from the troupe if you still have it in mind to undergo the pilgrimage, but if you induce any members of the troupe other than the herdsman boy to accompany you on that voyage, I will ask an injunction against it in the Coronal's Court, and prosecute you to the fullest. Understood?'

'Understood,' said Valentine, though he wondered whether he would deal honorably with the Skandar on this point.

'Lastly,' said Zalzan Kavol, 'I ask you to remember that you are paid a good many crowns a week, plus expenses and bonuses, to perform in this troupe. If I detect you filling your mind with thoughts of the pilgrimage, or of the Lady and her servants, or of anything else but how to throw things into the air and catch them in a theatrically suitable manner, I'll revoke your employment. In these last few days you've already seemed unacceptably moody, Valentine. Change your ways. I need three humans for this troupe, but not necessarily the ones I have now. Understood?'

'Understood,' Valentine said.

'Go, then.'

Carabella said, as they walked away, 'Was that terribly unpleasant for you?'

'It must have been terribly pleasant for Zalzan Kavol.'

'He's just a hairy animal!'

'No,' said Valentine gravely. 'He's a sentient being equal to ourselves in civil rank, and never speak of him as anything else. He only *looks* like an animal.' Valentine laughed, and after a moment Carabella laughed with him, a trifle edgily. He said, 'In dealing with people who are enormously touchy on matters of honor and pride, I think it's wisest to be accommodating to their needs, especially if they're eight feet tall and provide you with your wages. At this point I need Zalzan Kavol far more than he needs me.'

'And the pilgrimage?' she asked. 'Are you really planning to undergo it? When did you decide that?'

'In Dulorn. After conversation with Deliamber. There are questions about myself I must answer, and if anyone can help me with those answers, it's the Lady of the Isle. So I'll go to her, or try to. But all that's far in the future, and I've sworn to Zalzan Kavol not to think of such things.' He took her hand in his. 'I thank you, Carabella, for repairing matters between Zalzan Kavol and me. I wasn't at all ready to be discharged from the troupe. Or to lose you so soon after I had found you.'

'Why do you think you would have lost me,' she asked, 'if the Skandar had insisted on letting you go?'

He smiled. 'I thank you for that, too. And now I should go down to the cabbage-tree grove, and tell Shanamir to return the mounts that he's stolen for us.'

4

In the next few days the landscape began to grow surpassingly strange, and Valentine had more cause for gladness that he and Shanamir had not tried to proceed by themselves.

The district between Dulorn and the next major city, Mazadone, was relatively thinly populated. Much of it, according to Deliamber, was a royal forest preserve. That bothered Zalzan Kavol, for jugglers would not find employment in forest preserves, nor, for that matter, in low-lying swampy farmland occupied mainly by rice paddies and lusavender-seed plantations; but there was no choice but to follow the main forest highway, since nothing more promising lay to the north or south. On they went, in generally humid and drizzly weather, through a region of villages and farms and occasional thick stands of the fat-trunked comical cabbage trees, short and squat, with massive white fruits sprouting directly from their bark. But as Mazadone Forest Preserve drew closer, the cabbage trees gave way to dense thickets of singing ferns, yellow-fronded and glassy of texture, that emitted piercing discordant sounds whenever they were approached, shrill high-pitched bings and twangs and bleeps, nasty screeches and scrapes. That would not have been so bad – the unmelodious song of the ferns had a certain raucous charm, Valentine thought – but the fern thickets were inhabited by bothersome small creatures far more disagreeable than the plants, little toothy winged rodents known as dhiims, that came flapping up out of hiding every time the proximity of the wagon touched off the fern-song. The dhiims were about the length and breadth of a small finger, and were covered by fine golden fur; they arose in such numbers that they clouded the air, and swarmed about indignantly, sometimes nipping with their tiny but effective incisors. The thickly furred Skandars up front in the driver's seat largely ignored them, merely swatting at them when they clustered too close, but the usually stolid mounts were bothered, and balked in the traces several times. Shanamir, sent out to placate the animals, suffered half a dozen painful bites; and as he scurried back into the wagon a good many dhiims entered with him. Sleet took a frightening nip on his cheek near his left eye, and Valentine, beset by dozens of infuriated creatures at once, was bitten on both arms. Carabella methodically destroyed the dhiims with a stiletto used in the juggling act, skewering them with single-minded determination and great skill, but it was an ugly half hour before the last of them was dead.

Beyond the territory of the dhiims and the singing ferns, the travelers entered into a region of curious appearance, a broad open area of meadows out of which rose hundreds of black granite needles just a few feet wide and perhaps eighty feet high, natural obelisks left behind by some unfathomable geological event. To Valentine it was a region of delicate beauty; to Zalzan Kavol it was merely one more place to pass quickly through, en route to the next festival where jugglers might be hired; but to Autifon Deliamber it seemed something else, a place giving sign of possible menace. The Vroon leaned forward, staring keenly for a long moment through the wagon's windows at the obelisks. 'Wait,' he called finally to Zalzan Kavol.

'What is it?'

'I want to check something. Let me out.'

Zalzan Kavol grunted impatiently and tugged on the reins. Deliamber scrambled from the wagon, moving in his supple ropy-limbed Vroonish glide toward the odd rock formations, disappearing among them, coming occasionally into view as he zigzagged from one thin pinnacle to the next.

When he returned, Deliamber looked glum and apprehensive.

'See there,' he said, pointing. 'Do you make out vines far up, stretched from that rock to that, and from that to that, and on over to there? And some small animals crawling about on the vines?'

Valentine could just barely discern a network of slender glossy red lines high on the pinnacles, forty or fifty feet or more above the ground. And yes, half a dozen apelike beasts moving from obelisk to obelisk like acrobats, swinging freely by hands and feet.

'It looks like birdnet vine,' said Zalzan Kavol in a puzzled tone.

'It is,' Deliamber said.

'But why do they not stick to it?' What are those animals, anyway?'

'Forest-brethren,' the Vroon answered. 'Do you know of them?'

'Tell me.'

'They are troublesome. A wild tribe, native to central Zimroel, not usually found this far west. The Metamorphs are known to hunt them for food or perhaps for sport, I'm not sure which. They have intelligence, though of a low order, something greater than dogs or droles, less than civilized folk. Their gods are dwikka-trees; they have some sort of tribal structure; they know how to use poisoned darts, and cause problems for wayfarers. Their sweat contains an enzyme that makes them immune to the stickiness of birdnet vine, which they employ for many purposes.'

'If they annoy us,' Zalzan Kavol declared, 'we will destroy them. Onward!'

Once past the region of the obelisks they saw no further traces of forest-brethren that day. But on the next, Deliamber once again spied ribbons of birdnet vine in the treetops, and a day after that the travelers, now deep in the forest preserve, came upon a grove of trees of truly colossal mass, which, the Vroonish wizard said, were dwikkas, sacred to the forest-brethren. 'This explains their presence so far from Metamorph territory,' said Deliamber. 'These must be a migrating band, come west to pay homage in this forest.'

The dwikkas were awesome. There were five of them, set far apart in otherwise empty fields. Their trunks, covered with bright-red bark that grew in distinct plates with deep fissures between, were greater in diameter than the long axis of Zalzan Kavol's wagon; and though they were not particularly tall, no higher than a hundred feet or so, their mighty limbs, each as thick as the trunk of an ordinary tree, spread out to such a distance that whole legions might take shelter under the dwikka's gigantic canopy. On stalks as thick as a Skandar's thigh sprouted the leaves, great leathery black things the size of a house, that drooped heavily, casting an impenetrable shade. And from each branch hung suspended two or three elephantine yellowish fruits, bumpy irregular globes a good twelve or fifteen feet in width. One of them had recently fallen, it appeared, from the nearest tree – perhaps on a rainy day when the ground was soft, for its weight had dug a shallow crater in which it lay, split apart, revealing large glistening many-angled black seeds in the mass of scarlet pulp.

Valentine could understand why these trees were gods to the forest-brethren. They were vegetable monarchs, imperious, commanding. He was quite willing to sink to his knees before them himself.

Deliamber said, 'The fruit is tasty. Intoxicating, in fact, to the human metabolism and to some others.'

'To Skandars?' asked Zalzan Kavol.

'To Skandars, yes.'

Zalzan Kavol laughed. 'We'll try it. Erfon! Thelkar! Gather pieces of the fruit for us!'

Nervously Deliamber said, 'The talismans of the forest-brethren are embedded in the ground before each tree. They've been here recently, and might return, and if they find us desecrating the grove they will attack, and their darts can kill.'

'Sleet, Carabella, stand guard to the left. Valentine, Shanamir, Vinorkis, over there. Cry out if you see even one of the little apes.' Zalzan Kavol gestured at his brothers. 'Collect the fruit for us,' he ordered. 'Haern, you and I will defend the situation from here. Wizard, remain with us.' Zalzan Kavol took two energy-throwers from a rack and gave one to his brother Haern.

Deliamber clucked and muttered in disapproval. 'They move like ghosts, they come out of nowhere—'

'Enough,' said Zalzan Kavol.

Valentine took up a lookout position fifty yards ahead of the wagon, and peered warily beyond the last of the dwikka-trees into the dark, mysterious forest. He expected to have a fatal dart come winging toward him at any moment. It was an uncomfortable feeling. Erfon Kavol and Thelkar, carrying a big wicker basket between them, made their way toward the fallen fruit, pausing every few steps to look in all directions. When they reached it, they began cautiously to edge around to the far side of it.

'What if a bunch of forest-brethren are sitting behind that thing right now,' Shanamir asked, 'having a little feast? Suppose Thelkar stumbles over them and—'

A tremendous and terrifying whoop and a roar, such as might come from an outraged bull bidlak interrupted in its mating, erupted from the vicinity of the dwikka-fruit. Erfon Kavol, looking panic-stricken, came galloping back into view and rushed toward the wagon, followed a moment later by an equally daunted Thelkar.

'Beasts!' cried a ferocious voice. 'Pigs and fathers of pigs! Rape a woman enjoying her lunch, will you? I'll teach you to rape! I'll fix you, so you'll never rape again! Stand your ground, hairy animals! Stand, I say, stand!'

Out from behind the dwikka-fruit came the largest human woman Valentine had ever seen, a creature so vast she was a proper companion to these trees, and seemed perfectly in scale with them. She stood close to seven feet tall, perhaps more, and her gigantic body was a mountain of flesh rising on legs as sturdy as pillars. A close-fitting shirt and gray leather trousers were her garments, and the shirt was open nearly to the waist, revealing huge jouncing globes of breasts the size of a man's head. Her hair was a mop of wild orange curls; her blazing eyes were pale piercing blue. She carried a vibration-sword of imposing length, which she swung about her with such force that Valentine, a hundred feet away, could feel the breeze it stirred. Her cheeks and breasts were smeared with the scarlet juice of the dwikka-fruit's meat.

In weighty strides she thundered toward the wagon, crying rape and demanding vengeance.

'What is this?' Zalzan Kavol asked, looking as bemused as Valentine had ever seen him. He glared at his brothers. 'What did you do to her?'

'We never touched her,' said Efron Kavol. 'We were looking for forest-brethren back there, and Thelkar came upon her unexpectedly, and stumbled, and caught her arm to steady himself—'

'You said you never touched her,' Zalzan Kavol snapped.

'Not *that* way. It was only an accident, a stumble.'

'Do something,' Zalzan Kavol said hastily to Deliamber, for the giant woman was almost upon them now.

The Vroon, looking pale and cheerless, stepped in front of the wagon and lifted many tentacles toward the apparition that towered, almost Skandar-high, above him.

'Peace,' Deliamber said mildly to the onrushing giantess. 'We mean you no harm.' As he spoke he gestured with manic purposefulness, casting some sort of pacifying spell that manifested itself as a faint bluish glow in the air before him. The huge woman appeared to respond to it, for she slowed her advance and managed to come to a halt a few feet from the wagon.

There she stood, sullenly whipping the vibration-sword back and forth at her side. After a moment she pulled her shirt together in front, fastening it inadequately. Glowering at the Skandars, she indicated Erfon and Thelkar and said in a deep booming voice, 'What were those two planning to do to me?'

Deliamber replied, 'They had simply gone to collect pieces of the dwikka-fruit. See the basket they were carrying?'

'We had no idea you were there,' Thelkar murmured. 'We walked around behind the fruit to check for hidden forest-brethren, is all.'

'And fell upon me like the oaf you are, and would have violated me if I hadn't been armed, eh?'

'I lost my footing,' Thelkar insisted. 'There was no intention of molesting you. I was on guard for forest-brethren, and when instead I encountered someone of your size—'

'What? More insults?'

Thelkar took a deep breath. 'That is to say – it was unexpected when I – when you—'

Erfon Kavol said, 'We had no thought—'

Valentine, who had been observing all of this in gathering amusement, now came over and said, 'If they were minded for rape, would they have attempted it in front of so large an audience? We are of your kind here. We wouldn't have tolerated it.' He indicated Carabella. 'That woman is as fierce in her way as you are in yours, my lady. Be assured that if these Skandars had tried to do you any injury, she alone would have prevented it. It was a simple misunderstanding, nothing more. Put down your weapon and feel no peril among us.'

The giantess looked somewhat soothed by the courtliness and charm of Valentine's speech. Slowly she lowered the vibration-sword, allowing it to go inert, and fastened it at her hip.

'Who are you?' she asked querulously. 'What is all this procession traveling here?'

'My name is Valentine, and we are traveling jugglers, and this Skandar is Zalzan Kavol, the master of our troupe.'

'And I am Lisamon Hultin,' the giantess responded, 'who hires as bodyguard and warrior, though there's been little of that lately.'

'And we are wasting time,' said Zalzan Kavol, 'and should be on our way, if we are properly forgiven for having intruded on your repose.'

Lisamon Hultin nodded brusquely. 'Yes, be on your way. But are you aware this is dangerous territory?'

'Forest-brethren?' Valentine asked.

'All over the place. The woods are thick with them, just ahead.'

'And yet you feel no fear of them?' Deliamber remarked.

'I speak their language,' Lisamon Hultin said. 'I have negotiated a private treaty with them. Do you think I'd dare be munching on dwikka-fruit otherwise? I may be fat but not between the ears, little sorcerer.' She stared at Zalzan Kavol. 'Where are you bound?'

'Mazadone,' replied the Skandar.

'Mazadone? Is there work for you in Mazadone?'

'We hope to learn that,' Zalzan Kavol said.

'There's nothing for you there. I come from Mazadone just now. The duke is lately dead and three weeks of mourning have been decreed in the entire province. Or do you jugglers perform at funerals?'

Zalzan Kavol's face darkened. 'No work in Mazadone? No work in the whole province? We have expenses to meet! We have already gone unpaid since Dulorn! What will we do?'

Lisamon Hultin spat out a chunk of dwikka-fruit pulp. 'That's no sorrow of mine. Anyway, you can't get to Mazadone.'

'What?'

'Forest-brethren. They've blocked the road a few miles ahead. Asking tribute of wayfarers, I think, something absurd like that. They won't let you through. Lucky if they don't fill you with their darts.'

'They'll let us through!' Zalzan Kavol exclaimed.

The warrior-woman shrugged. 'Not without me, they won't.'

'You?'

'I told you, I speak their language. I can buy you a way through, with a little haggling. Are you interested? Five royals ought to do it.'

'What use do forest-brethren have for money?' the Skandar asked.

'Oh, not for them,' she said airily. 'Five for me. I'll offer other things to them. Deal?'

'Absurd. Five royals is a fortune!'

'I don't bargain,' she said evenly. 'There is honor in my profession. Good luck on the road ahead.' She favored Thelkar and Erfon Kavol with a frigid stare. 'If you wish, you may have some of the dwikka-fruit before you go. But better not be munching on it when you meet the brethren!'

She turned with massive dignity and walked to the great fruit beneath the tree. Drawing her sword, she hacked off three large chunks and shoved them disdainfully toward the two Skandars, who somewhat uneasily nudged them into the wicker basket.

Zalzan Kavol said, 'Into the wagon, all of you! We have a long way to Mazadone!'

'You won't travel far today,' said Lisamon Hultin, and released a gale of derisive laughter. 'You'll be back here soon enough – if you survive!'

5

The poisoned darts of the forest-brethren preoccupied Valentine for the next few miles. Sudden horrible death held no appeal for him, and the woods were thick and mysterious, with vegetation of a primordial sort, fern-trees with silvery spore-sheaths and glassy-textured horsetails a dozen feet high and thickets of bunch-fungus, pale and pocked with brown craters. In a place of such strangeness anything might happen, and probably would.

But the juice of the dwikka-fruit eased tensions mightily. Vinorkis sliced up one huge chunk and passed cubes of it around: it was piercingly sweet of flavor and granular in texture, dissolving quickly against the tongue, and whatever alkaloids it contained went swiftly through the blood to the brain, faster than the strongest wine. Valentine felt warm and cheerful. He slouched back in the passenger cabin, one arm around Carabella, the other around Shanamir. Up front, Zalzan Kavol evidently was more relaxed as well, for he stepped up the pace of the wagon, pushing it to a rollicking speed not much in keeping with his dour, cautious practices. The usually self-contained Sleet, slicing up more dwikka-fruit, began to sing a rowdy song:

> Lord Barhold came to Belka Strand
> With crown and chain and pail.
> He meant to force old Gornup's hand
> And make him eat his—

The wagon pulled suddenly to a halt, so suddenly that Sleet lurched forward and came close to falling into Valentine's lap, and a slab of soft wet dwikka-fruit smacked into Valentine's face. Laughing and blinking, he wiped himself clean. When he could see again, he found that everyone was gathered at the front of the wagon, peering out between the Skandars on the driver's seat.

'What is it?' he asked.

'Birdnet vine,' said Vinorkis, sounding quite sober. 'Blocking the road. The giantess told the truth.'

Indeed. The sticky, tough red vine had been laced from fern-tree to fern-tree at a dozen angles, forming a sturdy and resilient chain both broad and thick. The forest flanking the road was altogether impenetrable here; the birdnet vine sealed the highway. There was no way the wagon could proceed.

'How hard is it to cut?' Valentine asked.

Zalzan Kavol said, 'We could do it in five minutes with energy-throwers. But look there.'

'Forest-brethren,' Carabella said softly.

They were everywhere, swarming in the woods, hanging from every tree although getting no closer to the wagon than a hundred yards or so. They seemed less like apes at close range, more like savages of an intelligent species. They were small, naked beings with smooth blue-grey skin and thin limbs. Their hairless heads were narrow and long, with sloping flat foreheads, and their elongated necks were flimsy and fragile. Their chests were shallow, their frames meatless and bony. All of them, both men and woman, wore dart-blowers of reeds strapped to their hips. They pointed at the wagon, chattered to one another, made little hissing whistling sounds.

'What do we do?' Zalzan Kavol asked Deliamber.

'Hire the warrior-woman, I would think.'

'Never!'

'In that case,' said the Vroon, 'let us prepare to camp in the wagon until the end of our days, or else go back toward Dulorn and find some other road to travel.'

'We could parley with them,' the Skandar said. 'Go out there, wizard. Speak to them in dream-language, monkey-language, Vroon-language, any words that will work. Tell them we have urgent business in Mazadone, that we must perform at the funeral of the duke, and they will be severely punished if they delay us.'

Deliamber said calmly to Zalzan Kavol, '*You* tell them.'

'I?'

'Whichever of us steps out of the wagon first is apt to be skewered by their darts. I prefer to yield the honor. Perhaps they will be intimidated by your great size and hail you as their king. Or perhaps not.'

Zalzan Kavol's eyes blazed. 'You refuse?'

'A dead sorcerer,' Deliamber said, 'will not guide you very far on this planet. I know something of these creatures. They are unpredictable and very dangerous. Pick another messenger, Zalzan Kavol. Our contract doesn't require me to risk my life for you.'

Zalzan Kavol made his growling sound of displeasure, but he let the issue drop.

Stymied, they sat tight for long minutes. The forest-brethren began to descend from the trees, remaining at a considerable distance from the wagon. Some of them danced and cavorted now in the roadway, setting up a ragged, tuneless chanting, formless and atonal, like the droning of huge insects.

Erfon Kavol said, 'A blast from the energy-thrower would scatter them. It wouldn't take long for us to incinerate the bird-net vine. And then—'

'And then they'd follow us through the forest pumping darts at us whenever we showed our faces,' said Zalzan Kavol. 'No. There may be thousands of them all around us. They see us: we can't see them. We can't hope to win by using force against them.' Moodily the big Skandar wolfed down the last of the dwikka-fruit. Again he sat in silence for a few moments, scowling, occasionally shaking fists at the tiny folk blocking the path. At length he said in a bitter rumble, 'Mazadone is still some day's journey away, and that woman said there was no work to be had there anyway, so we'll have to go on to Borgax or maybe even Thagobar, eh, Deliamber? Weeks more before we earn another crown. And here we sit, trapped in the forest by little apes with poisoned darts. Valentine?'

Startled, Valentine said, 'Yes?'

'I want you to slip out of the wagon the back way and return to that warrior-woman. Offer her three royals to get us out of this.'

'Are you serious?' Valentine asked.

Carabella, with a little gasp, said, 'No! I'll go instead!'

'What's this?' said Zalzan Kavol in irritation.

'Valentine is – he is – he gets lost easily, he becomes distracted, he – he might not be able to find—'

'Foolishness,' the Skandar said, waving his hands impatiently. 'The road is straight. Valentine is strong and quick. And this is dangerous work. You have skills too valuable to risk, Carabella. Valentine will have to go.'

'Don't do it,' Shanamir whispered.

Valentine hesitated. He had not much liking for the idea of leaving the relative safety of the wagon to travel on foot alone in a forest infested with deadly creatures. But someone had to do it, and not one of the slow, ponderous Skandars, nor the splay-footed Hjort. To Zalzan Kavol he was the most expendable member of the troupe; perhaps he was. Perhaps he was expendable even to himself.

He said, 'The warrior-woman told us her price was five royals.'

'Offer her three.'

'And if she refuses? She said it was against her honor to bargain.'

'Three,' Zalzan Kavol said. 'Five royals is an immense fortune. Three is an absurd enough price to pay.'

'You want me to run miles through a dangerous forest to offer someone an inadequate price for a job that absolutely must be done?'

'Are you refusing?'

'Pointing out folly,' said Valentine. 'If I'm to risk my life, there must be the hope of achievement. Give me five royals for her.'

'Bring her back here,' the Skandar said, 'and I'll negotiate with her.'

'Bring her back yourself,' said Valentine.

Zalzan Kavol considered that. Carabella, tense and pale, sat shaking her head. Sleet warned Valentine with his eyes to hold his position. Shanamir, red-faced, trembling, seemed about ready to burst forth with anger. Valentine wondered if this time he had pushed the Skandar's always volatile temper too far.

Zalzan Kavol's fur stirred as though spasms of rage were contorting his powerful muscles. He seemed to be holding himself in check by furious effort. Doubtless Valentine's latest show of independence had enraged him almost to the boiling point; but there was a glint of calculation in the Skandar's eyes, as though he were weighing the impact of Valentine's open defiance against the need he had for Valentine to do this service. Perhaps he was even asking himself whether his thrift might be foolishness here.

After a long tense pause Zalzan Kavol let out his breath in an explosive hiss and, scowling, reached for his purse. Sourly he counted out the five gleaming one-royal pieces.

'Here,' he grunted. 'And hurry.'

'I'll go as fast as I can.'

'If running is too great a burden.' said Zalzan Kavol, 'go out the front way, and ask the forest-brethren if you may have leave to unhitch one of our mounts, and ride back to her in comfort. But do it quickly, whichever you choose.'

'I'll run,' Valentine replied, and began to unfasten the wagon's rear window.

His shoulder blades itched in anticipation of the thwock of a dart between them the moment he emerged. But no thwocks came, and soon he was running lightly and easily down the road. The forest that had looked so sinister from the wagon looked much less so now, the vegetation unfamiliar but hardly ominous, not even the pockmarked bunch-fungus, and the fern trees seemed nothing but elegant as their spore-sheaths glistened in the afternoon sun. His long legs moved in steady rhythm, and his heart pumped uncomplainingly. The running was relaxing, almost hypnotic, as soothing to him as juggling.

He ran a long while, paying no heed to time and distance, until it seemed he surely must have gone far enough. But how could he have run unknowingly past anything so conspicuous as five dwikka-trees? Had he carelessly taken some fork in the road and lost the path? It seemed unlikely. So he simply ran on, and on and on, until eventually the monstrous trees, with the great fallen fruit beneath the closest of them, came into view.

The giantess seemed nowhere around. He called out her name, he peered behind the dwikka-fruit, he made a circuit of the entire grove. No one. In dismay he contemplated running onward, back halfway to Dulorn, maybe, to find her. Now that he had stopped, he felt the effects of his jog: muscles were protesting in his calves and thighs, and his heart was thumping in an unpleasant way. He had no appetite for more running just now.

But then he caught sight of a mount tethered a few hundred yards back of the dwikka-tree grove – an oversize beast, broad-backed and thick-legged, suitable for carrying Lisamon Hultin's bulk. He went to it, and looked beyond, and saw a roughly hacked trail leading toward running water.

The ground sloped off sharply, and gave way to a jagged cliff. Valentine peered over the edge. A stream emerged from the forest here and tumbled down the face of the cliff to land in a rock basin perhaps forty feet below; and alongside that pool, sunning herself after a bath, was Lisamon Hultin. She lay face down, her vibration-sword close beside her. Valentine looked with awe at her wide muscular shoulders, her powerful arms, the massive columns of her legs, the vast dimpled globes of her buttocks.

He called to her.

She rolled over at once, sat up, looked about her.

'Up here,' he said. She glanced in his direction, and discreetly he turned his head away, but she only laughed at his modesty. Rising, she reached for her clothing in a casual, unhurried way.

'You,' she said. 'The gentle-spoken one. Valentine. You can come down here. I'm not afraid of you.'

'I know you dislike being disturbed at your repose,' Valentine said mildly, picking his way down the steep rocky path. By the time he had reached the bottom she had her trousers on and was struggling to pull her shirt over her mighty breasts. He said, 'We came to the roadblock.'

'Of course.'

'We need to get on to Mazadone. The Skandar has sent me to hire you.' Valentine produced Zalzan Kavol's five royals. 'Will you help us?'

She eyed the shining coins in his hand.

'The price is seven and a half.'

Valentine pursed his lips. 'You told us five, before.'

'That was before.'

'The Skandar has given me only five royals to pay you.'

She shrugged and began to unfasten her shirt. 'In that case, I'll continue to sunbathe. You may stay or not, as you wish, but keep your distance.'

Quietly Valentine said, 'When the Skandar tried to beat down your price, you refused to bargain, telling him that there is honor in your profession. My notion of honor would require me to abide by a price once I quoted it.'

She put her hands to her hips and laughed, a laugh so vociferous he thought it would blow him away. He felt like a plaything beside her: she outweighed him by more than a hundred pounds, and stood at least a head taller. She said, 'How brave you are, or how stupid! I could destroy you with a slap of my hand, and you stand here lecturing me about faults of honor!'

'I think you wouldn't harm me.'

She studied him with new interest. 'Perhaps not. But you take risks, fellow. I offend easily and I do more damage than I intend, sometimes, when I lose my temper.'

'Be that as it may. We have to get to Mazadone, and only you can call off the forest-brethren. The Skandar will pay five royals and no more.' Valentine knelt and put the five brilliant coins in a row on the rock by the pool. 'However, I have a little money of my own. If it'll settle the issue, I'll add that to the fee.' He fished in his purse until he found a royal piece, found another, laid a half-royal beside it, and looked up hopefully.

'Five will be enough,' Lisamon Hultin said.

She scooped up Zalzan Kavol's coins, left Valentine's, and went scrambling up the path.

'Where's your mount?' she asked, untethering her own.

'I came on foot.'

'On foot? On *foot*? You ran all that way?' She peered at him. 'What a loyal employee you are! Does he pay you well, to give such service and take such risks?'

'Not particularly.'

'No, I suppose not. Well, climb on behind me. This beast would never even notice a little extra weight.'

She clambered onto the mount, which, though large for its kind, seemed dwarfed and frail once she was on it. Valentine, after some hesitation, got on behind her and clamped his hands around her waist. For all her bulk there was nothing fat about her: solid muscle girdled her hips.

The mount cantered out of the dwikka-tree grove and down the road. The wagon, when they came to it, was still shut up tight, and forest-brethren still danced and chattered in and around the trees behind the blockade.

They dismounted. Lisamon Hultin walked without sign of fear to the front of the wagon and called something to the forest-brethren in a high, shrill voice. There was a reply of similar pitch from the trees. Again she called; again she was answered; then a long, feverish colloquy ensued, with many brief expostulations and interjections.

She turned to Valentine. 'They will open the gate for you,' she said. 'For a fee.'

'How much?'

'Not money. Services.'

'What services can we render for forest-brethren?'

She said, 'I told them you are jugglers, and I explained what it is that jugglers do. They'll let you proceed if you'll perform for them. Otherwise they intend to kill you and make toys of your bones, but not today, for today is a holy day among the forest-brethren and they kill no one on holy days. My advice to you is to perform for them, but do as you wish.' She added, 'The poison that they use does not act particularly quickly.'

6

Zalzan Kavol was indignant – perform for monkeys? perform without fee? – but Deliamber pointed out that the forest-brethren were somewhat higher on the evolutionary scale than monkeys, and Sleet observed that they had not had their practice today and the workout would do them some good, and Erfon Kavol clinched the matter by arguing that it would not really be a free performance, since it was being traded for passage through this part of the forest, which these creatures effectively controlled. And in any case they had no choice in the matter: so out they came, with clubs and balls and sickles, but not the torches, for Deliamber suggested that the torches might frighten the forest-brethren and cause them to do unpredictable things. In the clearest space they could find they began to juggle.

The forest-brethren watched raptly. Hundreds upon hundreds of them trooped from the forest and squatted alongside the road, staring, nibbling their fingers and their slender prehensile tails, making soft chittering comments to one another. The Skandars interchanged sickles and knives and clubs and hatchets, Valentine whirled clubs aloft, Sleet and Carabella performed with elegance and distinction, and an hour went by, and another, and the sun began to slink off in the direction of Pidruid, and still the forest-brethren watched, and still the jugglers juggled, and nothing was done about unwinding the birdnet vine from the trees.

'Do we play for them all night?' Zalzan Kavol demanded.

'Hush,' said Deliamber. 'Give no offense. Our lives are in their hands.'

They used the opportunity to rehearse new routines. The Skandars polished an interception number, stealing throws from one another in a way that was comical in beings so huge and fierce. Valentine worked with Sleet and Carabella on the interchange of clubs. Then Sleet and Valentine threw clubs rapidly at one another while first Carabella and then Shanamir turned handsprings daringly between them. And so it went, on into a third hour. 'These forest-brethren have had five royals' worth of entertainment from us already,' Zalzan Kavol grumbled. 'When does this end?'

'You juggle very capably,' said Lisamon Hultin. 'They enjoy your show immensely. I enjoy it myself.'

'How pleasant for you,' Zalzan Kavol said sourly.

Twilight was approaching. Apparently the coming of darkness signaled some shift in mood for the forest-brethren, for without warning they lost interest in the performance. Five of them, of presence and authority, came forward and set about ripping down the barricade of birdnet vine. Their small sharp-fingered hands dealt easily with the stuff, that would have tangled anyone else hopelessly in snarls of sticky fiber. In a few minutes the way was clear, and the forest-brethren, chattering, faded into the darkness of the woods.

'Have you wine?' Lisamon Hultin asked, as the jugglers gathered their gear and prepared to move along. 'All this watching has given me a powerful thirst.'

Zalzan Kavol began to say something miserly about supplies running low, but too late: Carabella, with a sharp glare at her employer, produced a flask. The warrior-woman tipped it back, draining it in one long lusty gulp. She wiped her lips with the sleeve of her shirt and belched.

'Not bad,' she said. 'Dulornese?'

Carabella nodded.

'Those Ghayrogs know how to drink, snakes that they are! You won't find anything like it in Mazadone.'

Zalzan Kavol said, 'Three weeks of mourning, you say?'

'No less. All public amusements forbidden. Yellow mourning-stripes on every door.'

'Of what did the duke die?' Sleet asked.

The giantess shrugged. 'Some say it was a sending from the King, that frightened him to death, and others that he choked on a gobbet of half-cooked meat, and still others that he indulged in an excess with three of his concubines. Does it matter? He's dead, that's not to be disputed, and the rest is trifles.'

'And no work to be had,' said Zalzan Kavol gloomily.

'No, nothing as far as Thagobar and beyond.'

'Weeks without earnings,' the Skandar muttered.

Lisamon Hultin said, 'It must be unfortunate for you. But I know where you could find good wages just beyond Thagobar.'

'Yes,' Zalzan Kavol said. 'In Khyntor, I suppose.'

'Khyntor? No, times are lean there, I hear. A poor harvest of clennet-puffs this summer, and the merchants have tightened credit, and I think there's little money to be spent on entertainments. No, I speak of Ilirivoyne.'

'*What?*' Sleet cried, as though he had been struck by a dart.

Valentine sorted through his knowledge, came up with nothing, and whispered to Carabella, 'Where's that?'

'Southeast of Khyntor.'

'But southeast of Khyntor is the Metamorph territory.'

'Exactly.'

Zalzan Kavol's heavy features took on an animated cast for the first time since encountering the roadblock. He swung round and said, 'What work is there for us in Ilirivoyne?'

'The Shapeshifters hold festival there next month,' Lisamon Hultin replied. 'There'll be harvest-dancing and contests of many kinds and merrymaking. I've heard that sometimes troupes from the imperial provinces enter the reservation and earn huge sums at festival-time. The Shapeshifters regard imperial money lightly and are quick to dispose of it.'

'Indeed,' Zalzan Kavol said. The chilly light of greed played across his face. 'I had heard the same thing, long ago. But it never occurred to me to test its truth.'

'You'll test it without me!' Sleet cried suddenly.

The Skandar glanced at him. 'Eh?'

Sleet showed intense strain, as though he had been doing his blind-juggling routine all afternoon. His lips were taut and bloodless, his eyes were fixed and unnaturally bright. 'If you go to Ilirivoyne,' he said tensely, 'I will not accompany you.'

'I remind you of our contract,' said Zalzan Kavol.

'Nevertheless. Nothing in it obliges me to follow you into Metamorph territory. Imperial law is not valid there, and our contract lapses the moment we enter the reservation. I have no love for the Shapeshifters and refuse to risk my life and soul in their province.'

'We'll talk about this later, Sleet.'

'My response will be the same later.'

Zalzan Kavol looked about the circle. 'Enough of this. We've lost hours here. I thank you for your help,' he said without warmth to Lisamon Hultin.

'I wish you a profitable journey,' she said, and rode off into the forest.

Because they had consumed so much time at the roadblock, Zalzan Kavol chose to keep the wagon moving through the night, contrary to his usual practice. Valentine, exhausted by a lengthy run and hours of juggling, and feeling some lingering haziness from the dwikka-fruit he had eaten, fell asleep sitting up in the back of the wagon and knew nothing more until morning. The last he heard was a forceful discussion of the notion of venturing into Metamorph territory: Deliamber suggesting that the perils of

Ilirivoyne had been exaggerated by rumor, Carabella noting that Zalzan Kavol would be justified in prosecuting Sleet, and expensively, if he broke his contract, and Sleet insisting with almost hysterical conviction that he dreaded the Metamorphs and would not go within a thousand miles of them. Shanamir and Vinorkis, too, expressed fear of the Shapeshifters, who they said were sullen, tricky, and dangerous

Valentine woke to find his head nestled cozily in Carabella's lap. Bright sunlight streamed into the wagon. They were camped in some broad and pleasant park, a place of sweeping blue-gray lawns and narrow sharp-angled trees of great height. Low rounded hills surrounded everything.

'Where are we?' he asked.

'Outskirts of Mazadone. The Skandar drove like a madman all night long.' Carabella laughed prettily. 'And you slept like one who has been dead a long time.'

Outside, Zalzan Kavol and Sleet were engaged in heated argument a few yards from the wagon. The small white-haired man seemed half again his normal size with rage. He paced back and forth, pounded fist into palm, shouted, scuffed at the ground, once seemed at the verge of launching a physical attack on the Skandar, who seemed, for Zalzan Kavol, remarkably calm and forbearing. He stood with all his arms folded, looming high over Sleet and making only an occasional quiet cold reply to his outbursts.

Carabella turned to Deliamber. 'This has continued long enough. Wizard, can you intervene, before Sleet says something really rash?'

The Vroon looked melancholy. 'Sleet has a terror of the Metamorphs that goes beyond all reason. Perhaps it's connected with that sending of the King that he had, long ago in Narabal, that turned his hair white in a single evening. Or perhaps not. In any case, it may be wisest for him to withdraw from the troupe, whatever the consequences.'

'But we need him!'

'And if he thinks terrible things will befall him in Ilirivoyne? Can we ask him to subject himself to such fears?'

'Perhaps I can calm him,' Valentine said.

He rose to go outside, but at that instant Sleet, face dark and set, stormed into the wagon. Without a word the compact little juggler began to stuff his few possessions into a pack; then he swept out, his fury unabated, and striding past the motionless Zalzan Kavol, began to march at a startling clip toward the low hills to the north.

Helplessly they watched him. No one made a move to pursue until Sleet was nearly out of sight. Then Carabella said, 'I'll go after him. I can get him to change his mind.'

She ran off toward the hills.

Zalzan Kavol called to her as she went past him, but she ignored him. The

Skandar, shaking his head, summoned the others from the wagon.

'Where is she going?' he asked.

'To try to bring Sleet back,' said Valentine.

'Hopeless. Sleet has chosen to leave the troupe. I'll see to it that he regrets his defection. Valentine, greater responsibilities now will fall upon you, and I'll add five crowns a week to your salary. Is this acceptable?'

Valentine nodded. He thought of Sleet's quiet, steady presence in the troupe, and felt a pang of loss.

The Skandar continued, 'Deliamber, I have, as you might suspect, decided to seek work for us among the Metamorphs. Are you familiar with the routes to Ilirivoyne?'

'I have never been there,' the Vroon answered. 'But I know where it is.'

'And which is the quickest way?'

'To Khyntor from here, I think, and then eastward by riverboat some four hundred miles, and at Verf there's a road due south into the reservation. Not a smooth road, but wide enough for the wagon, so I believe. I will study it.'

'And how long will it take for us to reach Ilirivoyne, then?'

'Perhaps a month, if there are no delays.'

'Just in time for the Metamorph festival,' said Zalzan Kavol. 'Perfect! What delays do you anticipate?'

Deliamber said, 'The usual. Natural disasters, breakdown of the wagon, local disturbances, criminal interferences. Things are not as orderly in mid-continent as they are on the coasts. There are risks involved in traveling in those parts.'

'You bet there are!' boomed a familiar voice. 'Protection is what you need!'

The formidable presence of Lisamon Hultin suddenly was among them.

She looked rested and relaxed, not at all as though she had ridden all night, nor was her mount particularly spent. In a puzzled voice Zalzan Kavol said, 'How did you get here so quickly?'

'Forest trails. I'm big, but not so big as your wagon, and I can take back ways. Going to Ilirivoyne, are you?'

'Yes,' said the Skandar.

'Good. I knew you would. And I've come after you to offer my services. I'm out of work, you're going into dangerous parts – it's a logical partnership. I'll escort you safely to Ilirivoyne, that I guarantee!'

'Your wages are too high for us.'

She grinned. 'You think I always get five royals for a little job like that? I charged so much because you made me angry, tromping in on me while I was trying to have a private feed. I'll get you to Ilirivoyne for another five, no matter how long it takes.'

'Three,' said Zalzan Kavol sternly.

'You never learn, do you?' The giantess spat almost at the Skandar's feet.

'I don't haggle. Get yourselves to Ilirivoyne without me, and good fortune attend you. Though I doubt it will.' She winked at Valentine. 'Where are the other two?'

'Sleet refused to go to Ilirivoyne. He went roaring out of here ten minutes ago.'

'I don't blame him. And the woman?'

'She went after him, to talk him into returning. Up there.' Valentine pointed to the path winding up into the hills.

'*There?*'

'Between that hill and that.'

'Into the mouthplant grove?' There was disbelief in Lisamon Hultin's voice.

'What is that?' Valentine asked.

Deliamber, at the same moment, said, 'Mouthplants? Here?'

'The park is dedicated to them,' the giantess declared. 'But there are warning signs at the foot of the hills. They went up that trail? On foot? The Divine protect them!'

Exasperated, Zalzan Kavol said, 'They can eat him twice, for all I care. But I need her!'

'As do I,' said Valentine. To the warrior-woman he said, 'Possibly if we rode up there now, we could find them before they enter the mouthplant grove.'

'Your master feels he can't afford my services.'

'Five royals?' Zalzan Kavol said. 'From here to Ilirivoyne?'

'Six,' she said coolly.

'Six, then. But get them back! Get her, at least!'

'Yes,' said Lisamon Hultin in disgust. 'You people have no sense, but I have no work, so we deserve each other, perhaps. Take one of those mounts,' she said to Valentine, 'and follow me.'

'You want him to go?' Zalzan Kavol wailed. 'I'll have no humans at all in my troupe!'

'I'll bring him back,' the giantess said. 'And, with luck, the other two also.' She clambered onto her mount. 'Come,' she said.

7

The path into the hills was gently sloping, and the blue-gray grass looked soft as velvet. It was hard to believe that anything menacing dwelled in this lovely park. But as they reached the place where the path began to rise at a sharper angle, Lisamon Hultin grunted and indicated a bare wooden stake set in the ground. Beside it, half hidden by grass, was a fallen sign. Valentine saw only the words

DANGER
NO FOOT TRAFFIC
BEYOND THIS

in large red letters. Sleet, in his rage, had not noticed; Carabella, perhaps in her urgent haste, had failed to see the sign also, or else had ignored it.

Quickly now the path climbed, and just as quickly it leveled off on the far side of the hills, in a place that was no longer grassy but densely wooded. Lisamon Hultin, riding just ahead of Valentine, slowed her mount to a walk as they entered a moist and mysterious copse where trees with slender, strong-ribbed trunks grew at wide intervals, shooting up like bean-stalks to create a thickly interlaced canopy far overhead.

'See, there, the first mouthplants,' the giantess said. 'Filthy things! If I had the keeping of this planet, I'd put the torch to all of them, but our Coronals tend to be nature-lovers, so it seems, and preserve them in royal parks. Pray that your friends have had the wisdom to stay clear of them!'

On the bare forest floor, in the open spaces between the trees, grew stemless plants of colossal size. Their leaves, four or five inches broad and eight or nine feet in length, sharp-toothed along their sides and metallic of texture, were arranged in loose rosettes. At the center of each gaped a deep cup a foot in diameter, half filled with a noxious-looking greenish fluid, out of which a complex array of stubby organs projected. It seemed to Valentine that there were things like knife-blades in there, and paired grinders that could come together nastily, and still other things that might have been delicate flowers partly submerged.

'These are flesh-eating plants,' Lisamon Hultin said. 'The forest floor is underlain by their hunting tendrils, which sense the presence of small animals, capture them, and carry them to the mouth. Observe.'

She guided her mount toward the closest of the mouthplants. When the animal was still at least twenty feet from it, something like a live whip suddenly began to writhe in the decaying forest duff. It broke free of the ground to coil itself with a terrifying snapping sound around the animal's pastern just above the hoof. The mount, placid as usual, sniffed in puzzlement as the tendril began to exert pressure, trying to pull it toward the gaping mouth in the plant's central cup.

The warrior-woman, drawing her vibration-sword, leaned down and sliced quickly through the tendril. It snapped back as the tension was released, almost to the cup itself, and at the same time a dozen other tendrils rose from the ground, flailing the air furiously on all sides of the plant.

She said, 'The mouthplant lacks the strength to tug anything so big as a mount into its maw. But the mount wouldn't be able to break free. In time it would weaken and die, and then it might be pulled in. One of these plants would live for a year on that much meat.'

Valentine shuddered. Carabella, lost in a forest of such things? Her lovely voice stilled forever by some ghastly plant? Her quick hands, her sparkling eyes – no. No. The thought chilled him.

'How can we find them?' he asked. 'It might already be too late.'

'How are they called?' the giantess asked. 'Shout their names. They must be near.'

'*Carabella!*' Valentine roared with desperate urgency. '*Sleet! Carabella!*'

A moment later he heard a faint answering shout; but Lisamon Hultin had heard it first, and was already going forward. Valentine saw Sleet ahead, down on one knee on the forest floor, and that knee dug in deep to keep him from being dragged into a mouthplant by the tendril that encircled his other ankle. Crouching behind him was Carabella, her arms thrust through his and hooked tight around his chest in a desperate attempt to hold him back. All about them excited tendrils belonging to neighboring plants snapped and coiled in frustration. Sleet held a knife, with which he sawed uselessly at the powerful cable that held him; and there was a trail of skid-marks in the duff, showing that he had already been drawn four or five feet toward the waiting mouth. Inch by inch he was losing the struggle for his life.

'Help us!' Carabella called.

With a stroke of her sword Lisamon Hultin severed the tendril grasping Sleet. He recoiled sharply as he was freed, toppling backward and coming within an eyeblink of being seized around the throat by the tendril of another plant; but with an acrobat's easy grace he rolled over, avoiding the groping filament, and sprang to his feet. The warrior-woman caught him about the chest and lifted him quickly to a place behind her on her mount. Valentine now approached Carabella, who stood shaken and trembling in a safe place between two sets of the thrashing tendrils, and did the same for her.

She clung to him so tightly that his ribs ached. He twisted himself around and embraced her, stroking her gently, nuzzling her ear with his lips. His relief was overwhelming and startling: he had not realized how much she had come to mean to him, nor how little he had cared about anything just now except that she was all right. Gradually her terror subsided, but he could feel her still quivering at the horror of the scene. 'Another minute,' she whispered. 'Sleet was starting to lose his foothold – I could feel him slipping toward that plant—' Carabella winced. 'Where did she come from?'

'She took some shortcut through the forest. Zalzan Kavol has hired her to protect us on the way to Ilirivoyne.'

'She's already earned her fee,' Carabella said.

'Follow me,' Lisamon Hultin ordered.

She chose a careful route out of the mouthplant grove, but for all her care her mount was seized twice by the leg, and Valentine's once. Each time, the giantess cut the tendril away, and in moments they were out into the clearing and riding back down the path toward the wagon. A cheer went up from the Skandars as they reappeared.

Zalzan Kavol regarded Sleet coldly. 'You chose an unwise route for your departure,' he observed.

'Not nearly so unwise as the one you've picked,' said Sleet. 'I beg you excuse me. I will go on toward Mazadone by foot, and seek some sort of employment there.'

'Wait,' Valentine said.

Sleet looked at him inquiringly.

'Let's talk. Come walk with me.' Valentine laid his arm over the smaller man's shoulders and drew him aside, off into a grassy glade, before Zalzan Kavol could provoke some new wrath in him.

Sleet was tense, wary, guarded. 'What is it, Valentine?'

'I was instrumental in getting Zalzan Kavol to hire the giantess. But for that, you'd be tidbits for the mouthplant now.'

'For that I thank you.'

'I want more than thanks from you,' said Valentine. 'It could be said that you're indebted to me for your life, in a way.'

'That may be.'

'Then I ask by way of repayment that you withdraw your resignation.'

Sleet's eyes flashed. 'You don't know what you ask!'

'The Metamorphs are strange and unsympathetic creatures, yes. But Deliamber says they're not as menacing as often reported. Stay with the troupe, Sleet.'

'You think I'm being whimsical in quitting?'

'Not at all. But irrational, perhaps.'

Sleet shook his head. 'I had a sending from the King, once, in which a Metamorph imposed on me a terrible fate. One listens to such sendings. I have no desire to go near the place where those beings dwell.'

'Sendings don't always bear the literal truth.'

'Agreed. But often they do. Valentine, the King told me I would have a wife that I loved more dearly than my art itself, a wife who juggled with me the way Carabella does, but far more closely, so much in tune with my rhythms that it was as if we were one person.' Sweat broke out on Sleet's scarred face, and he faltered, and almost did not go on, but after a moment he said, 'I dreamed, Valentine, that the Shapeshifters came one day and stole that wife of mine, and substituted for her one of their own people, disguised so cunningly that I couldn't tell the difference. And that night, I dreamed, we performed before the Coronal, before Lord Malibor that ruled then and drowned soon after, and our juggling was perfection, it was a harmony unequaled in all of my life, and the Coronal feasted us with fine meats and wines, and gave us a bedchamber draped with silks, and I took her in my arms and began to make love, and as I entered her she changed before me and was a Metamorph in my bed, a thing of horror, Valentine, with rubbery gray skin and gristle instead of teeth, and eyes like dirty puddles, who kissed me and pressed close against me. I have not sought the body of a woman,' Sleet said, 'since that night, out of dread that some such thing might befall me in the embrace. Nor have I told this story to anyone. Nor can I bear the prospect of going to Ilirivoyne and finding myself surrounded by creatures with Shapeshifter faces and Shapeshifter bodies.'

Compassion flooded Valentine's spirit. In silence he held the smaller man for a moment, as if with the strength of his arms alone he could eradicate the memory of the horrific nightmare that had maimed his soul. When he released him Valentine said slowly, 'Such a dream is truly terrible. But we are taught to use our dreams, not to let ourselves be crushed by them.'

'This one is beyond my using, friend. Except to warn me to stay clear of Metamorphs.'

'You take it too straightforwardly. What if something more oblique was intended? Did you have the dream spoken, Sleet?'

'It seemed unnecessary.'

'It was you who urged me to see a speaker, when I dreamed strangely in Pidruid! I remember your very words. The King never sends simple messages, you said.'

Sleet offered an ironic smile. 'We are always better doctors for others than for ourselves, Valentine. In any event, it's too late to have a fifteen-year-old dream spoken, and I am its prisoner now.'

'Free yourself!'

'How?'

'When a child has a dream that he is falling, and awakens in fright, what does his parent say? That falling dreams are not to be taken seriously, because one doesn't really get hurt in dreams? Or that the child should be thankful for a falling dream, because such a dream is a good dream, that it speaks of power and strength, that the child was not falling but flying, to a place where he would have learned something, if he had not allowed anxiety and fear to shake him loose of the dream-world?'

'That the child should be thankful for the dream,' said Sleet.

'Indeed. And so too with all other "bad" dreams: we must not be frightened, they tell us, but be grateful for the wisdom of dreams, and act on it.'

'So children are told, yes. Even so, adults don't always handle such dreams better than children. I recall some cries and whimpers coming from you in your sleep of late, Valentine.'

'I try to learn from my dreams, however dark they may be.'

'What do you want from me, Valentine?'

'That you come with us to Ilirivoyne.'

'Why is that so important to you?'

Valentine said, 'You belong to this troupe. We are a whole with you and broken without you.'

'The Skandars are masterly jugglers. It hardly matters what the human performers contribute. Carabella and I are with the troupe for the same reason as you, to comply with a stupid law. You'll earn your pay whether I'm with you or not.'

'I learn the art from you, though.'

'You can learn from Carabella. She's as skilled as I am, and is your lover besides, who knows you better than I ever could. And the Divine spare you,' said Sleet in a suddenly terrifying voice, 'from losing her to the Shapeshifters in Ilirivoyne!'

'It isn't something I fear,' said Valentine. He extended his hands toward Sleet. 'I would have you remain with us.'

'*Why?*'

'I value you.'

'And I value you, Valentine. But it would give me great pain to go where Zalzan Kavol would have us go. Why is it so urgent for you to insist on my enduring that pain?'

'You might be healed of that pain,' said Valentine, 'if you go to Ilirivoyne and find that the Metamorphs are only harmless primitives.'

'I can live with my pain,' Sleet replied. 'The price of that healing seems too high.'

'We can live with the most horrible wounds. But why not attempt to cure them?'

'There is some other thing not being spoken here, Valentine.'

Valentine paused and let his breath out slowly. 'Yes,' he said.

'What is it, then?'

With some hesitation Valentine said, 'Sleet, have I figured in your dreams at all, since we met in Pidruid?'

'You have, yes.'

'In what way?'

'How does this matter?'

'Have you dreamed,' said Valentine, 'that I might be somewhat unusual in Majipoor, someone of more distinction and power than I myself comprehend?'

'Your bearing and poise told me that at our first meeting. And the phenomenal skill with which you learned our art. And the content of your own dreams that you've shared with me.'

'And who am I, in those dreams, Sleet?'

'A person of might and grace, fallen through deceit from his high position. A duke, maybe. A prince of the realm.'

'Or higher?'

Sleet licked his lips. 'Higher, yes. Perhaps. What do you want with me, Valentine?'

'To accompany me to Ilirivoyne and beyond.'

'Do you tell me that there's truth in what I've dreamed?'

'This I'm yet to learn,' said Valentine. 'But I think there's truth in it, yes. I feel more and more strongly that there must be truth in it. Sendings tell me there's truth in it.'

'My lord—' Sleet whispered.

'Perhaps.'

Sleet looked at him in amazement and began to fall to his knees. Valentine caught him hastily and held him upright. 'None of that,' he said. 'The others can see. I want nobody to have an inkling of this. Besides, there remain great areas of doubt. I would not have you kneeling to me, Sleet, or making starbursts with your fingers, or any of that, while I am still uncertain of the truth.'

'My lord—'

'I remain Valentine the juggler.'

'I am frightened now, my lord. I came within a minute of a foul death today, and this frightens me more, to stand here quietly talking with you about these things.'

'Call me Valentine.'

'How can I?' Sleet asked.

'You called me Valentine five minutes ago.'

'That was before.'

'Nothing has changed, Sleet.'

Sleet shook the idea away. 'Everything has changed, my lord.'

Valentine sighed heavily. He felt like an imposter, like a fraud, manipulating Sleet in this way, and yet there seemed purpose to it, and genuine need. 'If everything has changed, then will you follow me as I command? Even to Ilirivoyne?'

'If I must,' said Sleet, dazed.

'No harm of the kind you fear will come to you among the Metamorphs.

You'll emerge from their country healed of the pain that has racked you. You do believe that, don't you, Sleet?'

'It frightens me to go there.'

'I need you by me in what lies ahead,' said Valentine. 'And through no choice of mine, Ilirivoyne has become part of my journey. I ask you to follow me there.'

Sleet bowed his head. 'If I must, my lord.'

'And I ask you, by the same compulsion, to call me Valentine and show me no more respect in front of the others than you would have shown me yesterday.'

'As you wish,' Sleet said.

'*Valentine.*'

'Valentine,' said Sleet reluctantly. 'As you wish – Valentine.'

'Come, then.'

He led Sleet back to the group. Zalzan Kavol was, as usual, pacing impatiently; the others were preparing the wagon for departure. To the Skandar Valentine said, 'I've talked Sleet into withdrawing his resignation. He'll accompany us to Ilirivoyne.'

Zalzan Kavol looked altogether dumbfounded. 'How did you manage to do that?'

'Yes,' said Vinorkis. 'What did you say to him, anyway?'

With a cheerful smile Valentine said, 'It would be tedious to explain, I think.'

8

The pace of the journey now accelerated. All day long the wagon purred along the highway, and sometimes well into the evening. Lisamon Hultin rode alongside, though her mount, sturdy as it was, needed more rest than those that drew the wagon, and occasionally she fell behind, catching up as opportunity allowed: carrying her heroic bulk was no easy task for any animal.

On they went through a tamed province of city after city, broken only by modest belts of greenery that barely obeyed the letter of the density laws. This province of Mazadone was a place where commercial pursuits kept many millions employed, for Mazadone was the gateway to all the territories of northwestern Zimroel for goods coming from the east, and the chief transshipment point for overland conveyance of merchandise of Pidruid and

Til-omon heading eastward. They passed quickly in and out of a host of interchangeable and forgettable cities, Cynthion and Apoortel and Doirectine, Mazadone city itself, Borgax and Thagobar beyond it, all of them subdued and quiescent during the mourning period for the late duke, and strips of yellow dangling everywhere as sign of sorrow. It seemed to Valentine a heavy thing to shut down an entire province for the death of a duke. What would these people do, he wondered, over the death of a Pontifex? How had they responded to the premature passing of the Coronal Lord Voriax two years ago? But perhaps they took the going of their local duke more seriously, he thought, for he was a visible figure, real and present among them, whereas to people of Zimroel, thousands of miles separated from Castle Mount or Labyrinth, the Powers of Majipoor must seem largely abstract figures, mythical, legendary, immaterial. On a planet so large as this no central authority could govern with real efficiency, only symbolic control; Valentine suspected that much of the stability of Majipoor depended on a social contract whereby the local governors – the provincial dukes and the municipal mayors – agreed to enforce and support the edicts of the imperial government, provided that they might do as they pleased within their own territories.

How, he asked himself, can such a contract be upheld when the Coronal is not the anointed and dedicated prince, but some usurper, lacking in the grace of the Divine through which such fragile social constructs are sustained?

He found himself thinking more and more upon such matters during the long, quiet, monotonous hours of the eastward journey. Such thoughts surprised him with their seriousness, for he had grown accustomed to the lightness and simplicity of his mind since the early days of Pidruid, and he could feel a progressive enrichment and growing complexity of mental powers now. It was as if whatever spell had been laid upon him was wearing thin, and his true intellect was beginning to emerge.

If, that is, any such magic had actually befallen him as his gradually forming hypothesis required.

He was still uncertain. But his doubts were weakening from day to day.

In dreams now he often saw himself in positions of authority. One night it was he, not Zalzan Kavol, who led the band of jugglers; on another he presided in princely robes over some high council of the Metamorphs, whom he saw as eerie foglike wraiths that would not hold the same shape more than a minute at a time; a night later he had a vision of himself in the marketplace at Thagobar, dispensing justice to the cloth-sellers and vendors of bangles in their noisy little disputes.

'You see?' Carabella said. 'All these dreams speak of power and majesty.'

'Power? Majesty? Sitting on a barrel in a market and expounding on equity to dealers in cotton and linen?'

'In dreams many things are translated. These visions are metaphors of high might.'

Valentine smiled. But he had to admit the plausibility of the interpretation.

One night as they were nearing the city of Khyntor there came to him a most explicit vision of his supposed former life. He was in a room paneled with the finest and rarest of woods, glistening strips of semotan and bannikop and rich dark swamp mahogany, and he sat before a sharp-angled desk of burnished palisander, signing documents. The starburst crest was at his right hand; obsequious secretaries hovered about; and the enormous curving window before him revealed an open gulf of air, as though it looked out upon the titanic slope of Castle Mount. Was this a fantasy? Or was it some fugitive fragment of the buried past that had broken free and come floating up in his sleep to approach the surface of his conscious mind? He described the office and the desk to Carabella and to Deliamber, hoping they could tell him how the office of the Coronal looked in reality, but they had no more idea of that than they did of what the Pontifex had for breakfast. The Vroon asked him how he had perceived himself when sitting at that palisander desk; was he golden-haired, like the Valentine who rode in the jugglers' wagon, or dark, like the Coronal who had made grand processional through Pidruid and the western provinces?

'Dark,' said Valentine immediately. Then he frowned. 'Or is that so? I was sitting at the desk, not looking at the man who was there because I *was* the man. And yet – and yet—'

Carabella said, 'In the world of dreams we often see ourselves with our own eyes.'

'I could have been both fair and dark. Now one, now the other – the point escaped me. Now one, now the other, eh?'

'Yes,' Deliamber said.

They were almost into Khyntor now, after too many days of steady, wearying overland travel. This, the major city of north-central Zimroel, lay in rugged, irregular terrain, broken by lakes and highlands and dark, virtually impassable forests. The route chosen by Deliamber took the wagon through the city's southwestern suburbs, known as Hot Khyntor because of the geothermal marvels there – great hissing geysers, and a broad steaming pink lake that bubbled and gurgled ominously, and a mile or two of gray rubbery-looking fumaroles from which, every few minutes, came clouds of greenish gases accompanied by comic belching sounds and deeper, stranger subterranean groans. Here the sky was heavy with big-bellied clouds the color of dull pearls, and although the last of summer still held the land, there was a cool autumnal quality to the thin, sharp wind that blew from the north.

The River Zimr, largest in Zimroel, divided Hot Khyntor from the city proper. When the travelers came upon it, the wagon emerging suddenly from an ancient district of narrow streets to enter a broad esplanade leading to Khyntor Bridge, Valentine gasped with amazement.

'What is it?' Carabella asked.

'The river – I never expected it to be as big as this!'

'Are rivers unfamiliar to you?'

'There are none of any consequence between Pidruid and here,' he pointed out. 'I remember nothing clearly before Pidruid.'

'Compared with the Zimr,' said Sleet, 'there are no rivers of any consequence anywhere. Let him be amazed.'

To the right and left, so far as Valentine could see, the dark waters of the Zimr stretched to the horizon. The river was so broad here that it looked more like a bay. He could barely make out the square-topped towers of Khyntor on the far shore. Eight or ten mighty bridges spanned the waters here, so vast that Valentine wondered how it had been possible to build them at all. The one that lay directly ahead, Khyntor Bridge, was four highways wide, a structure of looping arches that rose and descended and rose and descended in great leaps from bank to bank; a short way downstream was a bridge of entirely different design, a heavy brick roadbed resting on astounding lofty piers, and just upstream was another that seemed made of glass, and gleamed with a dazzling brightness. Deliamber said, 'That is Coronal Bridge, and to our right the Bridge of the Pontifex, and farther downstream is the one known as the Bridge of Dreams. All of them are ancient and famous.'

'But why try to bridge the river at a place where it's so wide?' Valentine asked in bewilderment.

Deliamber said, 'This is one of the narrowest points.'

The Zimr's course, declared the Vroon, was some seven thousand miles, rising northwest of Dulorn at the mouth of the Rift and flowing in a southeasterly direction across all of upper Zimroel toward the coastal city of Piliplok on the Inner Sea. This happy river, navigable for its entire length, was a swift and phenomenally broad stream that flowed in grand sweeping curves like some amiable serpent. Its shores were occupied by hundreds of wealthy cities, major inland ports, of which Khyntor was the most westerly. On the far side of Khyntor, running off to the northeast and only dimly visible in the cloudy sky, were the jagged peaks of the Khyntor Marches, nine great mountains on whose chilly flanks lived tribes of rough, high-spirited hunters. These people could be found in Khyntor much of the year, exchanging hides and meat for manufactured goods.

That night in Khyntor, Valentine dreamed he was entering the Labyrinth to confer with the Pontifex.

This was no vague and misty dream, but one with sharp, painful clarity.

He stood under harsh winter sunlight on a barren plain, and saw before him a roofless temple with flat white walls, which Deliamber told him was the gateway to the Labyrinth. The Vroon and Lisamon Hultin were with him, and Carabella too, walking in a protective phalanx, but when Valentine stepped out onto the bare slate platform between those white walls he was alone. A being of sinister and forbidding aspect confronted him. This creature was of alien shape, but belonged to none of the non-human forms long settled on Majipoor – neither Liiman nor Ghayrog nor Vroon nor Skandar nor Hjort nor Su-Suheris, but something mysterious and disturbing, a muscular thick-armed creature with cratered red skin and a blunt dome of a head out of which blazed yellow eyes bright with almost intolerable rage. This being demanded Valentine's business with the Pontifex in a low, resonant voice.

'Khyntor Bridge is in need of repair,' Valentine replied. 'It is the ancient duty of the Pontifex to deal with such matters.'

The yellow-eyed creature laughed. 'Do you think the Pontifex will care?'

'It is my responsibility to summon his aid.'

'Go, then.' The guardian of the portal beckoned with sardonic politeness and stepped aside. As Valentine went past, the being uttered a chilling snarl, and slammed shut a gateway behind Valentine. Retreat was impossible. Before him lay a narrow winding corridor, sourcelessly lit by some cruel white light that numbed the eyes. For hours Valentine descended on a spiral path. Then the walls of the corridor widened, and he found himself in another roofless temple of white stone, or perhaps the same one as before, for the pockmarked red-skinned being again blocked his way, growling with that unfathomable anger.

'Behold the Pontifex,' the creature said.

And Valentine looked beyond it into a darkened chamber and saw the imperial sovereign of Majipoor seated upon a throne, clad in robes of black and scarlet, and wearing the royal tiara. And the Pontifex of Majipoor was a monster with many arms and many legs, and the face of a man but the wings of a dragon, and he sat shrieking and roaring upon the throne like a madman. A terrible whistling sound came from his lips, and the smell of the Pontifex was a frightful stink, and the black leathery wings flailed the air with fierce intensity, buffeting Valentine with cold gales. 'Your majesty,' Valentine said, and bowed, and said, again, 'Your majesty.'

'Your lordship,' replied the Pontifex. And laughed, and reached for Valentine and tugged him forward, and then Valentine was on the throne and the Pontifex, laughing insanely, was fleeing up the brightly lit corridors, running and flapping wings and raving and shrieking, until he was lost from sight.

Valentine woke, wet with perspiration, in Carabella's arms. She showed a look of concern bordering on fear, as if the terrors of his dream had been only too obvious to her, and she held him a moment, saying nothing, until he had had a chance to comprehend the fact that he was awake. Tenderly she stroked his cheeks. 'You cried out three times,' she told him.

'There are occasions,' he said after gulping a little wine from a flask beside the bed, 'when it seems more wearying to sleep than to remain awake. My dreams are hard work, Carabella.'

'There's much in your soul that seeks to express itself, my lord.'

'It expresses itself in a very strenuous way,' Valentine said, and nestled down against her breasts. 'If dreams are the source of wisdom, I pray to grow no wiser before dawn.'

9

In Khyntor, Zalzan Kavol booked passage for the troupe aboard a riverboat bound toward Ni-moya and Piliplok. They would be journeying only a short way down the river, though, to the minor city of Verf, gateway to the Metamorph territory.

Valentine regretted having to leave the riverboat at Verf, when he could easily, for another ten or fifteen royals, sail all the way to Piliplok and take ship for the Isle of Sleep. That, after all, and not the Shapeshifter reservation, was his most urgent immediate destination: the Isle of the Lady, where perhaps he might find confirmation of the visions that tormented him. But that was not to be, just yet.

Destiny, Valentine thought, could not be rushed. Thus far things had moved with deliberate speed but toward some definite, if not always understandable, goal. He was no longer the cheerful and simple idler of Pidruid, and, although he had no sure knowledge of what it was he was becoming, he had a definite sense of inner transition, of boundaries passed and not to be recrossed. He saw himself as an actor in some vast and bewildering drama the climactic scenes of which were still far away in space and time.

The riverboat was a grotesque and fanciful structure, but not without a beauty of sorts. Oceangoing ships such as had been in port at Pidruid were designed for grace and sturdiness, since they would face journeys of thousands of miles between harbors; but the riverboat, a short-haul vessel, was squat and broad-beamed, more of a floating platform than a ship, and as if to compensate for the inelegance of its design its builders had festooned it with ornament – a great soaring bridge topped with triple figureheads painted in brilliant reds and yellows, an enormous central courtyard almost like a village plaza, with statuary and pavilions and game-parlors, and, at the stern, an upswept superstructure of many levels in which passengers were housed. Belowdecks were cargo holds, steerage quarters, dining halls, and cabins for the crew, as well as the engine room, from which two gigantic smokestacks sprouted that came curving up the sides of the hull and rose skyward like the horns of a demon. The entire frame of the ship was of wood, metal being too scarce on Majipoor for such large-scale enterprises and stone being generally deemed undesirable for maritime use; and the carpenters had exerted their imaginations over nearly every square foot of the surface, decorating it with scrollwork, bizarre dadoes, outjutting joists, and similar flourishes of a hundred kinds.

The riverboat seemed a vast and teeming microcosm. As they waited for sailing, Valentine and Deliamber and Carabella strolled the deck, thronged with citizens of many districts and of all the races of Majipoor. Valentine saw frontiersmen from the mountains beyond Khyntor, Ghayrogs in the finery affected in Dulorn, people of the humid southlands in cool white linens, travelers in sumptuous robes of crimson and green which Carabella said were typical of western Alhanroel, and many others. The ubiquitous Liimen sold their ubiquitous grilled sausages; officious Hjorts strutted about in uniforms of the riverboat line, giving information and instructions to those who asked and to many who did not; a Su-Suheris family in diaphanous green robes, conspicuous because of their unlikely doubleheaded bodies and aloof, imperious mien, drifted like emissaries from the world of dreams through the crowds, who gave way in automatic deference. And there was one small group of Metamorphs on deck that afternoon.

Deliamber saw them first. The little Vroon made a clucking sound and touched Valentine's hand. 'See them? Let's hope Sleet doesn't.'

'Which ones?' Valentine asked.

'By the railing. Standing alone, looking uneasy. They wear their natural form.'

Valentine stared. There were five of them, perhaps a male and a female adult and three younger ones. They were slender, angular, long-legged beings, the older ones taller than he, with a frail, insubstantial look to them. Their skins were sallow, almost green in hue. Their faces approached the human pattern in construction, except that their cheekbones were sharp as blades, their lips were almost nonexistent and their noses were reduced to mere bumps, and their eyes, set on angles that sloped inward toward the center, were tapered and without pupils. Valentine was unable to decide whether these Metamorphs bore themselves with arrogance or with timidity: certainly they must regard themselves as in hostile territory aboard this riverboat, these natives of the ancient race, these descendants of those who had possessed Majipoor before the coming of the first Earthborn settlers fourteen thousand years ago. He could not take his eyes from them.

'How is the changing of shape accomplished?' he asked.

'Their bones are not joined like those of most races,' answered Deliamber. 'Under muscular pressure they will move and take up new patterns. Also they have mimicry cells in their skins, that allow them to alter color and texture, and there are other adaptations. An adult can transform itself almost instantaneously.'

'And what purpose does this serve?'

'Who can say? Most likely the Metamorphs ask what purpose there was in creating races in this universe that are unable to shift shape. It must have some value to them.'

'Very little,' said Carabella acidly, 'if they could have such powers and still have their world snatched away from them.'

'Shifting shape is not enough of a defense,' Deliamber replied, 'when people travel from one star to another to steal your home.'

The Metamorphs fascinated Valentine. To him they represented artifacts of Majipoor's long history, archaeological relics, survivors from the era when there were no humans here, nor Skandars nor Vroons nor Ghayrogs, only these fragile green people spread out across a colossal planet. Before the settlers came – the intruders, ultimately the conquerors. How long ago it had been! He wished they would perform a transformation as he watched, perhaps turn into Skandars or Liimen before his eyes. But they remained unwavering in their identities.

Shanamir, looking agitated, appeared suddenly out of the crowd. He seized Valentine's arm and blurted, 'Do you know what's on board with us? I heard the cargo-handlers talking. There's a whole family of Shape—'

'Not so loud,' Valentine said. 'Look yonder.'

The boy looked and shivered. 'Scary things, they are.'

'Where's Sleet?'

'On the bridge, with Zalzan Kavol. They're trying to get a permit to perform tonight. If he sees them—'

'He'll have to confront Metamorphs sooner or later,' Valentine murmured. To Deliamber he said, 'Is it uncommon for them to be seen outside their reservation?'

'They are found everywhere, but never in great numbers, and rarely in their own form. There might be eleven of them living in Pidruid, say, and six in Falkynkip, nine in Dulorn—'

'Disguised?'

'Yes, as Ghayrogs or Hjorts or humans, whatever seems best in a certain place.'

The Metamorphs began to leave the deck. They moved with great dignity, but, unlike the little Su-Suheris group, there was nothing imperious about them; they seemed rather to give an impression of wishing they were invisible.

Valentine said, 'Do they live in their territory by choice or compulsion?'

'Some of each, I think. When Lord Stiamot completed the conquest, he forced them to leave Alhanroel entirely. But Zimroel was barely settled then, just the coastal outposts, and they were allowed most of the interior. They chose only the territory between the Zimr and the southern mountains, though, where access could easily be controlled, and withdrew into that. By now there's a tradition that the Metamorphs dwell only in that territory, except for the unofficial few living out in the cities. But I have no idea whether that tradition has force of law. Certainly they pay little attention to the decrees that emerge from the Labyrinth or Castle Mount.'

'If imperial law matters so little to them, are we not taking great risks in going to Ilirivoyne?'

Deliamber laughed. 'The days when Metamorphs attacked outsiders for the sheer love of vengeance are long over, so I am assured. They are a shy and sullen people, but they will do us no harm, and we'll probably leave their country intact and well laden with the money that Zalzan Kavol loves so much. Look, here he comes now.'

The Skandar, with Sleet beside him, approached, looking self-satisfied.

'We have arranged for the right to perform,' he announced. 'Fifty crowns for an hour's work, right after dinner! We'll give them our simplest tricks, though. Why exert ourselves before we get to Ilirivoyne?'

'No,' Valentine said. 'We should do our best.' He looked hard at Sleet. 'There's a party of Metamorphs aboard this boat. Perhaps they'll carry the word of our excellence ahead of us to Ilirivoyne.'

'Wisely argued,' said Zalzan Kavol.

Sleet was taut and fearful. His nostrils flickered, his lips compressed, he made holy signs with his left hand at his side. Valentine turned to him and said in a low voice, 'Now the process of healing begins. Juggle for them tonight as you would for the court of the Pontifex.'

Hoarsely Sleet said, 'They are my enemies!'

'Not these. They are not the ones of your dream. Those have done you all the damage that lay in their power, and it was long ago.'

'It sickens me to be on the same boat.'

'There's no leaving it now,' Valentine said. 'There are only five of them. A small dose – good practice for meeting what awaits us in Ilirivoyne.'

'Ilirivoyne—'

'There is no avoiding Ilirivoyne,' said Valentine. 'Your pledge to me, Sleet—'

Sleet regarded Valentine in silence a moment.

'Yes, my lord,' he whispered.

'Come, then. Juggle with me: we both need practice. And remember to call me Valentine!'

They found a quiet place belowdecks and worked out with the clubs; there was an odd reversal in their roles at first, for Valentine juggled flawlessly, while Sleet was as clumsy as a tyro, dropping the clubs constantly and in several instances bruising his fingers. But in a few minutes his disciplines asserted themselves. He filled the air with clubs, interchanging them with Valentine in patterns of such complexity that it left Valentine laughing and gasping, and finally he had to beg a halt and ask Sleet to return to more manageable cascades.

That night at the deckside performance – the first since the impromptu event staged for the amusement of the forest-brethren – Zalzan Kavol ordered a program that they had never done before an audience. The jugglers divided into three groups of three – Sleet, Carabella, and Valentine; Zalzan Kavol, Thelkar, and Gibor Haern; Heitrag Kavol, Rovorn, and Erfon Kavol – and engaged in simultaneous triple exchanges in the same rhythm, one group of Skandars juggling knives, the other flaming torches, and the humans silver clubs. It was one of the most severe tests of his skills that Valentine had yet experienced. The symmetry of the routine depended on perfection. One dropped implement by any of the nine would ruin the total effect. He was the weakest link; on him the entire impact of the performance depended, therefore.

But he dropped no clubs, and the applause, when the jugglers had ended their act in a flurry of high throws and jaunty catches, was overwhelming. As he took his bows Valentine noticed the family of Metamorphs seated only a few rows away. He glanced at Sleet, who bowed and bowed again, ever more deeply.

As they skipped from the stage Sleet said, 'I saw them when we started, and then I forgot about them. I forgot about them, Valentine!' He laughed. 'They were nothing at all like the creature I remember from my dream.'

10

The troupe slept that night in a dank, crowded hold in the bowels of the riverboat. Valentine found himself jammed between Shanamir and Lisamon Hultin on the thinly cushioned floor, and the proximity of the warrior-woman seemed to guarantee that he would have no sleep, for her snoring was a fierce insistent buzz, and more distracting even than the snore was the fear that as her vast body rolled and thrashed about beside him he would be crushed beneath it. Several times indeed she fetched up against him and he was hard put to extricate himself. But soon she lay more quietly, and he felt sleep stealing over him.

A dream came in which he was Coronal, Lord Valentine of the olive skin and black beard, and sat once more in Castle Mount wielding the seals of power, and then somehow he was in a southern city, a moist steaming tropical place of giant vines and gaudy red blossoms, a city that he knew to be Til-omon at the far side of Zimroel, and he attended there a grand feast in his honor. There was another high guest at the table, a somber-eyed man with coarse skin, who was Dominin Barjazid, second son of the King of Dreams, and Dominin Barjazid poured wine in honor of the Coronal, and offered toasts, crying out long life and predicting a glorious reign, a reign to rank with those of Lord Stiamot and Lord Prestimion and Lord Confalume. And Lord Valentine drank, and drank again, and grew flushed and merry, and offered toasts of his own, to his guest and to the mayor of Til-omon and to the duke of the province, and to Simonan Barjazid the King of Dreams, and to the Pontifex Tyeveras, and to the Lady of the Isle, his own beloved mother, and the goblet was filled and filled once again, amber wine and red wine and the blue wine of the south, until finally he could drink no more, and went to his bedchamber and dropped instantly into sleep. As he slept figures moved about him, the men of Dominin Barjazid's entourage, lifting him and carrying him wrapped in silken sheets, taking him somewhere, and he could give no resistance, for it seemed to him that his arms and legs would not obey him, as if this were a dream, this scene within a dream. And Valentine beheld himself on a table in a secret room, and now his hair was yellow and his skin was fair, and it was Dominin Barjazid who wore the face of the Coronal.

'Take him to some city in the far north,' said the false Lord Valentine, 'and turn him loose, and let him make his own way upon the world.'

The dream would have continued, but Valentine found himself smothering in his sleep, and came up into consciousness to discover Lisamon Hultin sprawled against him with one of her beefy arms over his face. With some effort he freed himself, but then there was no returning to sleep.

In the morning he said nothing to anyone of his dream: it was becoming time, he suspected, to keep the information of the night to himself, for they were starting to border on affairs of state. This was the second time he had dreamed of having been supplanted as Coronal by Dominin Barjazid, and Carabella, weeks ago, had dreamed that enemies unknown had drugged him and stolen his identity. All these dreams might yet prove to be nothing but fantasy or parable, but Valentine inclined now to doubt that. There was too strong a consistency to them, too frequent a repetition of underlying structures.

And if a Barjazid now wore the starburst crown? What then, what then?

The Valentine of Pidruid would have shrugged and said, no matter, one overlord is the same as another; but the Valentine now sailing from Khyntor to Verf took a more thoughtful view of things. There was a balance of power in this world, a balance carefully designed over a span of thousands of years, a system that had been evolving since Lord Stiamot's time, or perhaps earlier, out of whatever forgotten polities had ruled Majipoor in the first centuries of the settlement. And in that system an inaccessible Pontifex ruled through the vehicle of a vigorous and dynamic Coronal of his own choosing, with the official known as the King of Dreams functioning to execute the commands of the government and chastise lawbreakers by virtue of his entry into the minds of sleepers, and the Lady of the Isle, mother of the Coronal, contributing a tempering of love and wisdom. There was strength to the system, or else it could not have endured so many thousands of years; under it, Majipoor was a happy and prosperous world, subject, true, to the frailties of flesh and the vagaries of nature, but mainly free of conflict and suffering. What now, Valentine wondered, if a Barjazid of the King's blood were to put aside a lawfully constituted Coronal and interpose himself in that divinely ordained balance? What harm to the commonwealth, what disruption of public tranquillity?

And what might be said of a fallen Coronal who chooses to accept his altered destiny and leaves the usurper unchallenged? Was that not an abdication, and had there ever been an abdication of a Coronal in Majipoor's history? Would he not there by become a co-conspirator in Dominin Barjazid's overthrow of order?

The last of his hesitations were going from him. It had seemed a comical thing, or a bizarre one, to Valentine the juggler when the first hints had come to him that he might be truly Lord Valentine the Coronal. That had been an absurdity, a lunacy, a farce. No longer. The texture of his dreams carried the weight of plausibility. A monstrous thing had happened, indeed. The full import of it was only now coming clear to him. And it was his task, that he must accept without further question, to set things right.

But how? Challenge an incumbent Coronal? Rise up in juggler's costume to claim Castle Mount?

He spent the morning quietly, giving no hint of his thoughts. Mostly he remained at the rail, staring at the far-off shore. The river's immensity was beyond his understanding: at some points here it was so wide that no land could be seen, and in other places what Valentine took to be the shore turned out to be islands, themselves of great size, with miles of water between their farther sides and the riverbank. The flow of the river was strong, and the huge riverboat was being swept rapidly along eastward.

The day was bright, and the river rippled and glinted in the sparkling sunlight. In the afternoon a light rain began to fall, out of clouds so compact that the sunlight remained bright around them. The rain increased in intensity and the jugglers were forced to cancel their second performance, to Zalzan Kavol's great annoyance. They huddled under cover.

That night Valentine took care to sleep beside Carabella, and left the snores of Lisamon Hultin for the Skandars to cope with. He waited almost eagerly for revealing new dreams. But what came to him was useless, the ordinary formless hodgepodge of fantasy and chaos, of nameless streets and unfamiliar faces, of bright lights and garish colors, of absurd disputes, disjointed conversations, and unfocused images, and in the morning the riverboat arrived at the port of Verf on the river's southern bank.

11

'The province of the Metamorphs,' said Autifon Deliamber, 'is named Piurifayne, after the name by which the Metamorphs call themselves in their own language, which is Piurivar. It is bounded on the north by the outlying suburb of Verf, on the west by the Velathys Scarp, on the south by the substantial range of mountains known as the Gonghars, and on the east by by the River Steiche, an important tributary of the Zimr. I have beheld each of those boundary zones with my own eyes, though I have never entered Piurifayne itself. To enter is difficult, for the Velathys Scarp is a sheer wall a mile high and three hundred miles long; the Gonghars are stormswept and disagreeable; and the Steiche is a wild unruly river full of rapids and turbulence. The only rational way in is through Verf and down through Piurifayne Gate.'

The jugglers now were only a few miles north of that entrance, having left the drab mercantile city of Verf as quickly as possible. The rain, light but insistent, had continued all morning. The countryside here was unexciting, a place of light sandy soil and dense stands of dwarf trees with pale green bark and narrow, twittering leaves. There was little conversation in the wagon. Sleet seemed lost in meditation, Carabella juggled three red balls obsessively in the mid-cabin space, the Skandars who were not driving engaged in some intricate game played with slivers of ivory and packets of black drole-whiskers, Shanamir dozed, Vinorkis made entries in a journal he carried, Deliamber entertained himself with minor incantations, the lighting of tiny necromantic candles, and other wizardly amusements, and Lisamon Hultin, who had hitched her mount to the team drawing the wagon so that she could come in from the rain, snored like a beached sea-dragon, awakening now and then to gulp a globelet of the cheap gray wine she had bought in Verf.

Valentine sat in a corner, up against a window, thinking of Castle Mount. What could it be like, a mountain thirty miles high? A single stone shaft rising like a colossal tower into the dark night of space? If Velathys Scarp, a mile high, was as Deliamber said an impassable wall, what sort of barrier was a thing thirty times as tall? What shadow did Castle Mount cast when the sun was in the east? A dark stripe running the length of the Alhanroel? And how were the cities on its lofty slope provided with warmth, and air to breathe? Some machines of the ancients, Valentine had heard, that manu-factured heat and light, and dispensed sweet air, miraculous machines of that forgotten technological era of thousands of years ago, when the old arts brought from Earth still were widely practiced here; but he could no more comprehend how such machines might work than he understood what forces operated the engines of memory in his own mind to tell him that this dark-haired woman was Carabella, this white-haired man Sleet. He thought too of Castle Mount's highest reaches, and that building of forty thousand rooms at its summit, Lord Valentine's Castle now, Lord Voriax's not so long ago, Lord Malibor's when he was a boy in that childhood he no longer re-membered. Lord Valentine's Castle! Was there really such a place, or was the Castle and its Mount only a fable, a vision, a fantasy such as comes in dreams? Lord Valentine's Castle! He imagined it clinging to the mountain-top like a coat of paint, a bright splash of color just a few molecules thick, or so it would seem against the titanic scale of that impossible mountain, a splash that coursed irregularly down the flank of the summit in a ten-tacular way, hundreds of rooms extending on this face, hundreds more on that, a cluster of great chambers extending themselves pseudopod-fashion here, a nest of courtyards and galleries over there. And in its innermost place the Coronal in all grandeur, dark-bearded Lord Valentine, except that the Coronal would not be there now, he would still be making his grand processional through the realm, in Ni-moya by now or some other eastern city. And I, thought Valentine, I once lived on that Mount? Dwelled in that Castle? What did I do, when I was Coronal – what decrees, what appoint-ments, what duties? The whole thing was inconceivable, and yet, he felt the conviction growing in him, there was fullness and density and substance to the phantom bits of memory that drifted through his mind. He knew now that he had been born not in Ni-moya by the river's bend, as the false recol-lections planted in his mind had it, but rather in one of the Fifty Cities high up on the Mount, almost at the verge of the Castle itself, and that he had been reared among the royal caste, among that cadre from which princes were chosen, that his childhood and boyhood had been one of privilege and comfort. He still had no memory of his father, who must have been some high prince of the realm, nor could be recall anything of his mother except that her hair was dark and her skin was swarthy, as his once had been, and – a memory rushed into his awareness out of nowhere – and that she had embraced him a long while one day, weeping a little, before she told him that Voriax had been chosen as Coronal in the place of the drowned Lord Malibor, and she would go thenceforth to live as Lady on the Isle of Sleep. Was there truth to that, or had he imagined it just now? He would have been – Valentine paused, calculating – twenty-two years old, very likely, when Voriax came to power. Would his mother have embraced him at all? Would she have wept, on becoming Lady? Or rather rejoice, that she and her eldest son were chosen Powers of Majipoor? To weep and to rejoice at once, maybe. Valentine shook his head. These mighty scenes, these moments of potent history: would he ever regain access to them, or was he always to labor under the handicap placed upon him by those who had stolen his past?

There was a tremendous explosion in the distance, a long low ground-shaking boom that brought everyone in the wagon to attention. It continued for several minutes and gradually subsided to a quiet throb, then to silence.

'What was that?' Sleet cried, groping in the rack for an energy-thrower.

'Peace, peace,' Deliamber said. 'It is the sound of Piurifayne Fountain. We are approaching the boundary.'

'Piurifayne Fountain?' Valentine asked.

'Wait and see,' Deliamber told him.

The wagon came to a halt a few minutes later. Zalzan Kavol turned round from the driver's seat and yelled, 'Where's that Vroon? Wizard, there's a roadblock up ahead!'

'We are at Piurifayne Gate,' said Deliamber.

A barricade made of stout glossy yellow logs lashed with a bright emerald twine spanned the narrow roadway, and to the left of it was a guardhouse occupied by two Hjorts in customs-official uniform of gray and green. They ordered everyone out of the wagon and into the rain, though they themselves were under a protective canopy.

'Where bound?' asked the fatter Hjort.

'Ilirivoyne, to play at the Shapeshifter festival. We are jugglers,' said Zalzan Kavol.

'Permit to enter Piurifayne Province?' the other Hjort demanded.

'No such permits are required,' Deliamber said.

'You speak too confidently, Vroon. By decree of Lord Valentine the Coronal more than a month past, no citizens of Majipoor enter the Metamorph territory except on legitimate business.'

'Ours is legitimate business,' growled Zalzan Kavol.

'Then you would have a permit.'

'But we knew nothing of the need for one!' the Skandar protested.

The Hjorts looked indifferent to that. They seemed ready to turn their attention to other matters.

Zalzan Kavol glanced toward Vinorkis as though expecting him to have some sort of influence with his compatriots. But the Hjort merely shrugged. Zalzan Kavol glared at Deliamber next and said, 'It falls within your responsibilities, wizard, to advise me of such matters.'

The Vroon shrugged. 'Not even wizards can learn of changes in the law that happen while they travel in forest preserves and other remote places.'

'But what do we do now? Turn back to Verf?'

The idea seemed to bring a glow of delight to Sleet's eyes. Reprieved from this Metamorph adventure after all! But Zalzan Kavol was fuming. Lisamon Hultin's hand strayed to the hilt of her vibration-sword. Valentine stiffened at that.

He said quietly to Zalzan Kavol, 'Hjorts are not always incorruptible.'

'A good thought,' the Skandar murmured.

Zalzan Kavol drew forth his money-pouch. Instantly the attention of the Hjorts sharpened. This was indeed the right tactic, Valentine decided.

'Perhaps I have found the necessary document,' said Zalzan Kavol. Ostentatiously removing two one-crown pieces from the pouch, he caught a Hjort's rough-skinned puffy hand in one of his, and with the others pressed a coin into each palm, smiling his most self-satisfied smile. The Hjorts exchanged glances, and they were not glances of bliss. Contemptuously they allowed the coins to fall to the muddy ground.

'A crown?' Carabella muttered in disbelief. 'He expected to buy them with a *crown*?'

'Bribing an officer of the imperial government is a serious offense,' the fatter Hjort declared ominously. 'You are under arrest and remanded for trial to Verf. Remain in your vehicle until appropriate escort can be found for you.'

Zalzan Kavol looked outraged. He whirled, began to say something to Valentine, choked it off, gestured angrily at Deliamber, made a growling noise, and spoke in a low voice and in the Skandar language to the three nearest of his brothers. Lisamon Hultin again began to finger the sword-hilt. Valentine felt despair. There would be two dead Hjorts here in another moment, and the jugglers would all be criminal fugitives at the edge of Piurifayne. That was not likely to speed his journey to the Lady of the Isle.

'Do something quickly,' Valentine said under his breath to Autifon Deliamber.

But the Vroonish sorcerer was already in motion. Stepping forward, he snatched up the money and offered it again to the Hjorts, saying, 'Your pardon, but you must have dropped these small coins.' He dropped them into the Hjorts' hands, and at the same time allowed the tips of his tentacles to coil lightly about their wrists for an instant.

When he released them, the thinner Hjort said, 'Your visa is good for three weeks only, and you must leave Piurifayne by way of this gate. Other exit points are illegal for you.'

'Not to mention very dangerous,' added the other. He gestured and unseen figures pulled the barricade sideways fifteen feet along a buried track, so that there was room for the wagon to proceed.

As they entered the wagon Zalzan Kavol said furiously to Valentine. 'In the future, give me no illegal advice! And you, Deliamber: make yourself aware of the regulations that apply to us. This could have caused us great delay, and much loss of income.'

'Perhaps if you had tried bribing with royals instead of crowns,' Carabella said beyond the Skandar's range of hearing, 'we would have had a simpler time of it.'

'No matter, no matter,' Deliamber said. 'We were admitted, were we not? It was only a small sorcery, and cheaper than a heavy bribe.'

'These new laws,' Sleet began. 'So many decrees!'

'A new Coronal,' said Lisamon Hultin. 'He wants to show his power. They always do. They decree this, they decree that, and the old Pontifex goes along with everything. This one decreed me right out of a job, do you know that?'

'How so?' Valentine asked.

'I was bodyguard to a merchant in Mazadone, much afraid of jealous rivals. This Lord Valentine placed a new tax on personal bodyguards for anyone below noble rank, amounting to my whole year's salary; and my employer, damn his ears, let me go on a week's notice! Two years, and it was goodbye, Lisamon, thank you very much, take a bottle of my best brandy as your going-away gift.' She belched resonantly. 'One day I was a defender of his miserable life, the next I was a superfluous luxury, and all thanks to Lord Valentine! Oh, poor Voriax! D'ye think his brother had him murdered?'

'Guard your tongue!' Sleet snapped, 'Such things aren't done on Majipoor.'

But she persisted. 'A hunting accident, was it? And the last one, old Malibor, drowned while out fishing? Why are our Coronals suddenly dying so strangely? It never happened before like this, did it? They went on to become Pontifex, they did, and hid themselves away in the Labyrinth and lived next to forever, and now we have Malibor feeding the sea-dragons and Voriax taking a careless bolt in the forest.' She belched again. 'I wonder. Up there on Castle Mount, maybe they're getting too hungry for the taste of power.'

'Enough,' Sleet said, looking uncomfortable with such talk.

'Once a new Coronal's picked, all the rest of the princes are finished, you know, no hope of advancement. Unless, unless, unless, unless the Coronal should die, and back they go into the hopper to be picked again. When Voriax died and this Valentine came to rule, I said—'

'Stop it!' Sleet cried.

He rose to his full height, which was hardly chest-high to the warrior-woman, and his eyes blazed as if he planned to chop her off at the thighs to equalize matters between them. She remained at her ease, but her hand again was wandering toward her sword. Smoothly Valentine interposed himself.

'She means no offense to the Coronal,' he said gently. 'She is fond of wine, and it loosens her tongue.' And to Lisamon Hultin he said, 'Forgive him, will you? My friend is under strain in this part of the world, as you know.'

A second enormous explosion, five times as loud and fifty times as frightening as the one that had occurred half an hour earlier, interrupted the discussion. The mounts reared and squealed; the wagon lurched; Zalzan Kavol shouted ferocious curses from the driver's seat.

'Piurifayne Fountain,' Deliamber announced. 'One of the great sights of Majipoor, well worth getting wet to see.'

Valentine and Carabella rushed from the wagon, the others close behind. They had come to an open place in the road, where the forest of little green-boled trees fell away to create a kind of natural amphitheater, completely without vegetation, running perhaps half a mile back from the highway. At its farther end a geyser was in eruption, but a geyser that was to the ones Valentine had seen at Hot Khyntor as a sea-dragon is to a minnow. This was a column of frothing water that seemed taller than the tallest tower in Dulorn, a white shaft rising five hundred feet, six hundred, possibly even more, roaring out of the ground with incalculable force. At its upper end, where its unity broke and gave way to streamers and spouts and ropes of water that darted off in many directions, a mysterious light appeared to glow, kindling a whole spectrum of hues at the fringes of the column, pinks and pearls and crimsons and pale lavenders and opals. A warm spray filled the air.

The eruption went on and on – an incredible volume of water driven by incredible might into the sky. Valentine felt his entire body massaged by the subterranean forces that were at work. He stared in awe and wonder, and it was almost with shock that he realized that the event was ending, the column now was shrinking, no more than four hundred feet, three hundred, now just a pathetic strand of white sinking toward the ground, now only forty feet, thirty, and then gone, gone, vacant air where that stunning shaft had been, droplets of warm moisture as its only revenant.

'Every thirty minutes,' Autifon Deliamber informed them. 'As long as the Metamorphs have lived on Majipoor, so it is said, that geyser has never been a minute late. It is a sacred place to them. See? There are pilgrims now.'

Sleet caught his breath and began making holy signs. Valentine put a steadying hand to his shoulder. Indeed Metamorphs, Shapeshifters, Piurivars, a dozen or more of them, gathered at a kind of wayside shrine not far ahead. They were looking at the travelers, and, Valentine thought, not in a particularly friendly way. Several of the aborigines in the front of the group stepped briefly behind others, and when they reappeared they looked strangely blurred and indistinct, but that was not all, for they had undergone transformations. One had sprouted great cannonballs of breasts, in caricature of Lisamon Hultin, and another had grown four shaggy Skandararms, and another was mimicking Sleet's white hair. They made a curious thin sound which might have been the Metamorph version of laughter, and then the entire group slipped away into the forest.

Valentine did not release his grip on Sleet's shoulder until he felt some of the tension ebb from the little juggler's rigid body. Lightly he said, 'A good trick that is! If we could do that – perhaps grow some extra arms in the middle of our act – what do you say, Sleet, would you like that?'

'I would like to be in Narabal,' Sleet said, 'or Piliplok, or someplace else very far from here.'

'And I in Falkynkip, feeding slops to my mounts,' said Shanamir, who looked pale and shaken.

'They mean us no harm,' Valentine said. 'This will be an interesting experience, one that we will never forget.'

He smiled broadly. But there were no smiles about him, not even on Carabella, Carabella the inextinguishably buoyant. Zalzan Kavol himself looked oddly discomforted, as if perhaps he might now be having second thoughts about the wisdom of pursuing his love of royals into the Metamorph province. Valentine could not, by sheer force of optimistic energy alone, give his companions much cheer. He looked toward Deliamber.

'How far is it to Ilirivoyne?' he asked.

'It lies somewhere ahead,' the Vroon replied. 'How far, I have no idea. We will come to it when we come to it.'

It was not an encouraging reply.

12

This was primordial country, timeless, unspoiled, an outpost of time's early dawn of civilized and housebroken Majipoor. The Shapeshifters lived in rain-forest land, where daily downpours cleansed the air and let vegetation run riot. Out of the north came the frequent storms, down into that natural funnel formed by Velathys Scarp and the Gonghars; and as the moist air rose in the ascent of the Gonghar foothills, gentle rains were released, that soaked the light spongy soil. Trees grew tall and slender-trunked, sprouting high and forming thick canopies far overhead; networks of creepers and lianas tied the treetops together; cascades of dark leaves, tapering, drip-tipped, glistened as if polished by the rain. Where there were breaks in the forest, Valentine could see distant green-cloaked mist-wrapped mountains, heavy-shouldered, forbidding, great mysterious bulks crouching on the land. Of wildlife there was little, at least not much that let itself be seen: an occasional red-and-yellow serpent slithering along a bough, an infrequent green-and-scarlet bird or toothy web-winged brown aerolizard fluttering overhead, and once a frightened bilantoon that scampered delicately in front of the wagon and vanished into the woods with a flurry of its sharp little hooves and a panicky wigwagging of its upturned tufted tail. Probably forest-brethren lurked here, since several groves of dwikka-trees came into view. And no doubt the streams were thick with fish and reptiles, the forest floor teemed with burrowing insects and rodents of fantastic hue and shape, and for all Valentine knew, each of the innumerable dark little lakes held its own monstrous submerged amorfibot, that arose by night to prowl, all neck and teeth and beady eyes, for whatever prey came within reach of its massive body. But none of these things made themselves apparent as the wagon sped southward over the rough, narrow wilderness road.

Nor were the Piurivars themselves much in evidence – now and then a well-worn trail leading into the jungle, or a few flimsy wickerwork huts visible just off the road, or a party of half a dozen pilgrims heading on foot up toward the shrine at the fountain. They were, said Deliamber, a folk that lived by hunting and fishing, and collecting wild fruits and nuts, and a certain amount of agriculture. Possibly their civilization had once been more advanced, for ruins had been discovered, especially on Alhanroel, of large stone cities thousands of years old, that might have dated from early Piurivar times before the starships arrived – although, Deliamber said, there were some historians who maintained that the ruins were those of ancient human settlements, founded and destroyed in the turbulent pre-Pontifical period twelve to thirteen thousand years ago. At any rate the Metamorphs, if they had ever had a more complex way of life, now preferred to be forest-dwellers. Whether that was retrogression or progress Valentine could not say.

By mid-afternoon the sound of Piurifayne Fountain could no longer be heard behind them, and the forest was more open, more thickly settled. The road was unmarked, and, unexpectedly, it forked in a place where no clues were to be had to anything beyond. Zalzan Kavol looked for guidance to Deliamber, who looked to Lisamon Hultin.

'Damn my gut if I could say,' the giantess boomed. 'Pick one at random. We've got a fifty-fifty chance of getting to Ilirivoyne on it.'

But Deliamber had a better idea, and knelt down in the mud to cast an inquiry-spell. He took from his pack a couple of cubes of a wizardy incense. Shielding them from the rain with his cloak, he ignited them to create a pale brown smoke. This he inhaled, while waving his tentacles in intricate curlicues.

The warrior-woman snorted and said, 'It's only a fraud. He'll wiggle his arms for a while and then he'll make a guess. Fifty-fifty for Ilirivoyne.'

'The left fork,' Deliamber announced eventually.

It was good sorcery or else lucky guessing, for shortly signs of Metamorph occupation increased. There were no more isolated scatterings of lonely huts, but now little clumps of wickerwork dwellings, eight or ten or more close together every hundred yards, and then even closer. There was much foot traffic too, mainly aboriginal children carrying light burdens in slings dangling from their heads. Many stopped as the wagon went by, and stared and pointed and made little chittering sounds between their teeth.

Definitely they were approaching a large settlement. The road was crowded with children and older Metamorphs, and dwellings were numerous. The children were an unsettling crew. They seemed to be practicing their immature skills at transformation as they walked along, and took many forms, most of them bizarre: one had sprouted legs like stilts, another had tentacular Vroonish arms that dangled almost to the ground, a third had swollen its body to a globular mass supported by tiny props. 'Are we the circus entertainers,' Sleet asked, 'or are they? These people sicken me!'

'Peace,' Valentine said softly.

In a grim voice Carabella said, 'I think some of the entertainments here are dark ones. Look.'

Just ahead were a dozen large wicker cages by the side of the road. Teams of bearers, having apparently just put them down, were resting beside them. Through the bars of the cages small long-fingered hands were thrust, and some prehensile tails coiling in anguish. As the wagon drew alongside, Valentine saw that the cages were full of forest-brethren, jammed three and four together, on their way to Ilirivoyne for – what? To be slaughtered for food? To be tormented at the festival? Valentine shivered.

'Wait!' Shanamir blurted, as they rode past the final cage. 'What's that in there?'

The last cage was bigger than the others, and what it held was no forest-brother, but rather some other sort of captive, a being of obvious intelligence, tall and strange, with dark blue skin, fierce and desolate purple eyes of extraordinary intensity and luminosity, and a wide, thin-lipped slash of a mouth. Its clothing – a fine green fabric – was ripped and tattered, and splotched with dark stains, possibly blood. It gripped the bars of its cage with terrible force, shaking and tugging at them, and cried out hoarsely at the jugglers for help in an odd, totally unfamiliar accent. The wagon went on.

Chilled, Valentine said to Deliamber, 'That is no being of Majipoor!'

'No,' Deliamber said. 'None that I've seen before.'

'I saw one once,' Lisamon Hultin put in. 'An offworlder, native to some star close by here, though I forget the name of it.'

'But what would offworlders be doing here?' Carabella asked. 'There's little traffic between the stars these days, and few ships come to Majipoor.'

'Still, some do,' Deliamber said. 'We're not yet totally cut off from the starlanes, though certainly we're considered a backwater in the commerce of the worlds. And—'

'Are you all mad?' Sleet burst out in exasperation. 'Sitting here like scholars, discussing the commerce between the worlds, and in that cage is a civilized being crying for help, who probably will be stewed and eaten at the Metamorph festival? And we pay no attention to its cries, but ride blithely onward into their city?' He made a tormented sound of anger and went rushing forward to the Skandars on the driver's seat. Valentine, fearing trouble, went after him. Sleet tugged at Zalzan Kavol's cloak. 'Did you see it?' he demanded. 'Did you hear? The offworlder in the cage?'

Without turning, Zalzan Kavol said, 'So?'

'You'll ignore its cries?'

'This is no affair of ours,' the Skandar replied evenly. 'Shall we liberate the prisoners of an independent people? They must have some reason for arresting that being.'

'Reason? Yes, to cook him for dinner! And we'll be in the next pot. I ask you to go back and release—'

'Impossible.'

'At least let's ask of it why it's caged! Zalzan Kavol, we may be riding blithely to our deaths! Are you in such a hurry to reach Ilirivoyne that you'll ride right past someone who may know something about conditions here, and who is in such a plight?'

'What Sleet says has wisdom in it,' Valentine remarked.

'Very well!' Zalzan Kavol snorted. He pulled the wagon to a halt. 'Go and investigate, Valentine. But be quick about it.'

'I'll go with him,' Sleet said.

'Stay here. If he feels he needs a bodyguard, let him take the giantess.'

That seemed sensible. Valentine beckoned to Lisamon Hultin, and they got down from the wagon and strode back toward the place of the cages.

Instantly the forest-brethren set up a frantic screeching and a banging on their bars. The Metamorph bearers – armed, Valentine noticed now, with effective-looking short dirks of polished horn or wood – unhurriedly formed themselves into a phalanx in the road, keeping Valentine and Lisamon Hultin from a closer approach to the large cage. One Metamorph, plainly the leader, stepped forward and waited with menacing calmness for inquiries.

Valentine said quietly to the giantess, 'Will he speak our language?'

'Probably. Try it.'

'We are a troupe of roving jugglers,' Valentine said in a loud, clear voice, 'come to perform at the festival we hear you hold at Ilirivoyne. Are we near Ilirivoyne now?'

The Metamorph, half a head taller than Valentine, though much flimsier of build, seemed amused.

'You are in Ilirivoyne,' was the cool, remote reply.

Valentine moistened his lips. These Metamorphs gave off a thin, sharp odor, acrid but not disagreeable. Their strangely sloped eyes were frighteningly expressionless. He said, 'To whom would we go to make arrangements for performing in Ilirivoyne?'

'The Danipiur interviews all strangers who come to Ilirivoyne. You will find her at the House of Offices.'

The Metamorph's frosty self-contained manner was disconcerting. After a moment Valentine said, 'One thing more. We see that in that large cage you keep a being of an unfamiliar sort. May I ask, for what purpose?'

'Punishment.'

'A criminal?'

'So it is said,' The Metamorph replied distantly. 'Why does this concern you?'

'We are strangers in your land. If strangers are placed in cages here, we might prefer to find employment somewhere else.'

There was a flicker of some emotion – amusement? contempt? – around the Metamorph's mouth and nostrils. 'Why should you fear such a thing? Are you criminals?'

'Hardly.'

'Then you will not be caged. Pay your respects to the Danipiur and address further questions to her. I have important tasks to complete.'

Valentine looked toward Lisamon Hultin, who shrugged. The Metamorph walked away. There was nothing more to do but return to the wagon.

The bearers were lifting the cages and fastening them to poles laid across their backs. From the large cage came a roar of anger and despair.

13

Ilirivoyne was neither a city nor a village, but something intermediate, a forlorn concentration of many low, impermanent-looking structures of withes and light woods, arranged along irregular unpaved streets that seemed to stretch for considerable distances into the forest. The place had a makeshift look, as though Ilirivoyne might have been located elsewhere a few years ago and might be in an altogether other district a few years hence. That it was festival-time in Ilirivoyne was signaled, apparently, by fetish-sticks of some sort planted in front of almost every house, thick shaven stakes to which bright ribbons and bits of fur had been attached; also on many streets scaffolding had been erected, as for performances, or, thought Valentine uneasily, for tribal rites of some darker kind.

Finding the House of Offices and the Danipiur was simple. The main street opened into a broad plaza bordered on three sides by small domed buildings with ornately woven roofs, and on the fourth by a larger structure, the first three-story building they had seen in Ilirivoyne, with an elaborate garden of globular thick-stemmed gray-and-white shrubs in front of it. Zalzan Kavol drew the wagon into a clearing just outside the plaza.

'Come with me,' the Skandar said to Deliamber. 'We'll see what we can arrange.'

They were inside the House of Offices a long while. When they emerged, a female Metamorph of great presence and authority was with them, doubtless the Danipiur, and the three stood together by the garden in elaborate conversation. The Danipiur pointed; Zalzan Kavol alternately nodded and shook his head; Autifon Deliamber, dwarfed between the two tall beings, made frequent graceful gestures of diplomatic conciliation. Finally Zalzan Kavol and the Vroon returned to the wagon. The Skandar's mood seemed brighter.

'We've come just in time,' he announced. 'The festival has already begun. Tomorrow night is one of the major holidays.'

'Will they pay us?' Sleet asked.

'So it would seem,' said Zalzan Kavol. 'But they will supply us with no food, and no lodging either, for Ilirivoyne is without hostelries. And there are certain specified zones of the city that we may not enter. I have had friendlier welcomes in other places. But also less friendly ones now and then, I suppose.'

Crowds of solemn, silent Metamorph children trailed after them as they moved the wagon from the plaza to an area just back of it where they could park. In late afternoon they held a practice session, and though Lisamon Hultin did her formidable best to clear the young Metamorphs from the scene and keep them away, it was impossible to prevent them from slipping back, emerging between trees and out of bushes to stare at the jugglers. Valentine found it unnerving to work in front of them, and he was plainly not the only one, for Sleet was tense and uncharacteristically awkward, and even Zalzan Kavol, the master of masters, dropped a club for the first time in Valentine's memory. The silence of the children was disturbing – they stood like blank-eyed statues, a remote audience that drained energy and gave none in return – but even more troublesome was their trick of metamorphosis, their way of slipping from one shape to another as casually as a human child might suck its thumb. Mimicry was their apparent purpose, for the forms they took were crude, half-recognizable versions of the jugglers, such as the older Metamorphs had attempted earlier at Piurifayne Fountain. The children held the forms only briefly – their skills seemed feeble – but in the pauses between routines Valentine saw them now sprouting golden hair for him, white for Sleet, black for Carabella, or making themselves bearish and many-armed like the Skandars, or trying to imitate faces, individual features, expressions, everything done in a distorted and unflattering way.

The travelers slept crammed aboard the wagon that night, one packed close upon the other, and all night, so it seemed, a steady rain fell, Valentine only occasionally was able to sleep; he dropped into light dozes, but mainly he lay awake listening to Lisamon Hultin's lusty snoring or the even more grotesque sounds coming from the Skandars. Somewhere in the night he must have had some real sleep, for a dream came to him, hazy and incoherent, in which he saw the Metamorphs leading a procession of prisoners, forest-brethren and the blue-skinned alien, up the road toward Piurifayne Fountain, which erupted and rose above the world like a colossal white mountain. And again toward morning he slept soundly for a time, until Sleet woke him by shaking his shoulder a little before dawn.

Valentine sat up, rubbing his eyes. 'What is it?'

'Come outside. I have to talk.'

'It's still dark!'

'Even so. Come!'

Valentine yawned, stretched, got creakily to his feet. He and Sleet picked their way carefully over the slumbering forms of Carabella and Shanamir, went warily around one of the Skandars, and down the steps of the wagon. The rain had stopped, but the morning was dark and chilly, and a nasty fog rose from the ground.

'I have had a sending,' Sleet said, 'From the Lady, I think.'

'Of what sort?'

'About the blue-skinned one, in the cage, that they said was a criminal going to be punished. In my dream he came to me and said he was no criminal at all, but only a traveler who had made the error of entering Shapeshifter territory, and had been captured because it's their custom to sacrifice a stranger in Piurifayne Fountain at festival-time. And I saw how it is done, the victim bound hand and foot and left in the basin of the Fountain, and when the explosion comes he is hurled far into the sky.'

Valentine felt a chill that did not come from the morning mist. 'I dreamed something similar,' he said.

'In my dream I heard more,' Sleet went on. 'That we are in danger too, not perhaps from sacrifice but in danger all the same. And if we rescue the alien, he will help us to safety, but if we leave him to die, we will not leave Piurivar country alive. You know I fear these Shapeshifters, Valentine, but this dream is something new. It came to me with the clarity of a sending. It ought not to be dismissed as more fears of foolish Sleet.'

'What do you want to do?'

'Rescue the alien.'

Valentine said uneasily, 'And if he really was a criminal? By what right do we meddle in Piurivar justice?'

'By right of sending,' said Sleet. 'Are those forest-brethren criminals too? I saw them also go into the Fountain. We are among savages, Valentine.'

'Not savages, no. But strange folk, whose way is not like the ways of Majipoor.'

'I'm determined to set the blue-skinned one free. If not with your help, then by myself.'

'Now?'

'What better time?' Sleet asked. 'It's still dark. Quiet. I'll open the cage; he'll slip off into the jungle.'

'You think the cage is unguarded? No, Sleet. Wait. This makes no sense. You'll jeopardize us all if you act now. Let me try to find out more about this prisoner and why he's caged, and what's intended for him. If they do mean to sacrifice him, they'd do it at some high point of the festival. There's time.'

'The sending is on me now,' Sleet said.

'I dreamed a dream something like yours.'

'But not a sending.'

'Not a sending, no. Still, enough to let me think your dream holds truth. I'll help you, Sleet. But not now. This isn't the moment for it.'

Sleet looked restless. Clearly in his mind he was already on the way to the place of the cages, and Valentine's opposition was thwarting him.

'Sleet?'

'Yes?'

'Hear me. This is not the moment. There is time.'

Valentine looked steadily at the juggler. Sleet returned his gaze with equal steadfastness for a moment; then, abruptly, his resolve broke and he lowered his eyes.

'Yes, my lord,' he said quietly.

During the day Valentine tried to gain information about the prisoner, but with little success. The cages, eleven holding forest-brethren and the twelfth holding the alien, now had been installed in the plaza opposite the House of Offices, stacked in four tiers with the alien's cage alone on high, far above the ground. Piurivars armed with dirks guarded them.

Valentine approached, but he was only halfway across the plaza when he was stopped. A Metamorph told him, 'This is forbidden for you to enter.'

The forest-brethren began frantically to rattle their bars. The blue-skinned one called out, thickly accented words that Valentine could barely understand. Was the alien saying, 'Flee, fool, before they kill you too!' or was that only Valentine's heightened imagination at work? The guards held a tight cordon around the place. Valentine turned away. He attempted to ask some children nearby if they could explain the cages to him; but they looked at him in obstinate silence, giving him cool blank-eyed stares and murmuring to one another and making little partial metamorphoses that mimicked his fair hair, and then they scattered and ran as though he were some sort of demon.

All morning long Metamorphs entered Ilirivoyne, swarming in from the outlying forest settlements. They brought with them decorations of many sorts, wreaths and buntings and draperies and mirror-bedecked posts and tall poles carved with mysterious runes; everyone seemed to know what to do, and everyone was intensely busy. No rain fell after sunrise. Was it by witchcraft, Valentine wondered, that the Piurivars provided a rare dry day for their high holiday, or only coincidence?

By mid-afternoon the festivities were under way. Small bands of musicians played heavy, pulsating, jangling music of eccentric rhythm, and throngs of Metamorphs danced a slow and stately pattern of interweavings, moving almost like sleepwalkers. On certain streets races were run, and judges stationed at points along the course engaged in intricate arguments as the racers went past them. Booths apparently constructed during the night dispensed soups, stews, beverages, and grilled meats.

Valentine felt like an intruder in this place. He wanted to apologize to the Metamorphs for having come among them at their holiest time. Yet no one but the children seemed to be paying the slightest attention to them, and the children evidently regarded them as curiosities brought here for their amusement. Young shy Metamorphs lurked everywhere, flashing jumbled imitations of Deliamber and Sleet and Zalzan Kavol and the rest, but never allowing anyone to get close to them.

Zalzan Kavol had called a rehearsal for late afternoon, back of the wagon.

Valentine was one of the first to arrive, glad of an excuse to remove himself from the crowded streets. He found only Sleet and two of the Skandars.

It seemed to him that Zalzan Kavol was eyeing him in an odd way. There was something new and disturbing about the quality of the Skandar's attentiveness. After a few minutes Valentine was so troubled by it that he said, 'Is something wrong?'

'What would be wrong?'

'You seem out of countenance.'

'I? I? Nothing's the matter. A dream, is all. I was thinking on a dream I had last night.'

'You dreamed of the blue-skinned prisoner?'

Zalzan Kavol looked baffled. 'Why do you think that?'

'I did, and Sleet.'

'My dream had nothing at all to do with the blue-skinned one,' the Skandar replied. 'Nor do I wish to discuss it. It was foolishness, mere foolishness.' And Zalzan Kavol, moving away, picked up a double brace of knives and began to juggle them in an edgy, absent-minded way.

Valentine shrugged. It had not even occurred to him that Skandars had dreams, let alone that they might have troublesome ones. But of course: they were citizens of Majipoor, they shared in all the attributes of people here, and so they must live full and rich dream-lives like everyone else, with sendings from King and Lady, and stray intrusions from the minds of lesser beings, and upwellings of self from their own deeper reaches, even as humans did, or, Valentine supposed, Hjorts and Vroons and Liimen. Still, it was curious. Zalzan Kavol was so guarded of emotion, so unwilling to let anything of himself be seen by others save greed and impatience and irritation, that Valentine found it strange that he would admit something so personal as that he was pondering a dream.

He wondered if Metamorphs had meaningful dreams, and sendings, and all of that.

The rehearsal went well. Afterward the jugglers made a light and not very satisfying dinner of fruits and berries that Lisamon Hultin had gathered in the forest, and washed it down with the last of the wine they had brought from Khyntor. Bonfires now were blazing in many streets of Ilirivoyne, and the discordant music of the various bands set up weird clashing near-harmonies. Valentine had assumed the performance would take place in the plaza, but no, Metamorphs in what perhaps were priestly costumes came at darkness to escort them to some entirely other part of town, a much larger oval clearing that already was ringed by hundreds or even thousands of expectant onlookers. Zalzan Kavol and his brothers went over the ground carefully, checking for pitfalls and irregularities that might disrupt their movements. Sleet usually took part in that, but, Valentine noticed abruptly,

Sleet had vanished somewhere between the rehearsal place and this clearing. Had his patience run out, had he gone off to do something rash? Valentine was just about to set out in search when Sleet appeared, breathing lightly as though he had just been jogging.

'I went to the plaza,' he said in a low voice. 'The cages are still piled up. But most of the guards must be off at the dancing. I was able to exchange a few words with the prisoner before I was chased.'

'And?'

'He said he's to be sacrificed at midnight in the Fountain, exactly as in my sending. And tomorrow night the same will happen to us.'

'What?'

'I swear it by the Lady,' said Sleet. His eyes were like augers. 'It was under pledge to you, my lord, that I came into this place. You assured me no harm would befall me.'

'Your fears seemed irrational.'

'And now?'

'I begin to revise my opinion,' Valentine said. 'But we'll get out of Ilirivoyne in good health. I pledge you that. I'll speak with Zalzan Kavol after the performance, and after I've had a chance to confer with Deliamber.'

'It would please me more to get on the road sooner.'

'The Metamorphs are feasting and drinking this evening. They'll be less likely to notice our departure later,' said Valentine, 'and less apt to pursue us, if pursuit is their aim. Besides, do you think Zalzan Kavol would agree to cancel a performance merely on the rumor of danger? We'll do our act, and then we'll begin to extricate ourselves. What do you say?'

'I am yours, my lord,' Sleet replied.

14

It was a splendid performance, and no one was in better form than Sleet, who did his blind-juggling routine and carried it off flawlessly. The Skandars flung torches at one another with giddy abandon, Carabella cavorted on the rolling globe, Valentine juggled while dancing, skipping, kneeling, and running. The Metamorphs sat in concentric circles around them, saying little, never applauding, peering in at them out of the foggy darkness with unfathomable intensity of concentration.

Working to such an audience was hard. It was worse than working in rehearsal, for no one expects an audience then, but now there were thousands

of spectators and they were giving nothing to the performers; they were
statue-still, as the children had been, an austere audience that offered neither
approval nor disapproval but only something that had to be interpreted as
indifference. In the face of that, the jugglers presented ever more taxing and
marvelous numbers, but for more than an hour they could get no response.

And then, astoundingly, the Metamorphs began a juggling act of their
own, an eerie dreamlike counterfeit of what the troupe had been doing.

By two and threes they came forward from the darkness, taking up
positions in the center of the ring only a few yards from the jugglers. As
they did so they swiftly shifted forms, so that six of them now wore the look
of bulky shaggy Skandars, and one was small and lithe and much like Carabella, and one had Sleet's compact form, and one, yellow-haired and tall,
wore the image of Valentine. There was nothing playful about this donning
of the jugglers' bodies: to Valentine it seemed ominous, mocking, distinctly
threatening, and when he looked to the side at the non-performing members of the troupe he saw Autifon Deliamber making worried gestures with
his tentacles, Vinorkis scowling, and Lisamon Hultin rocking evenly back
and forth on the balls of her feet as if readying herself for combat.

Zalzan Kavol looked disconcerted also by this development.

'Continue,' he said in a ragged tone. 'We are here to perform for them.'

'I think,' said Valentine, 'we are here to amuse them, but not necessarily
as performers.'

'Nevertheless, we are performers, and we will perform.'

He gave a signal and launched, with his brothers, into a dazzling interchange of multitudinous sharp and dangerous objects. Sleet, after a moment's hesitation, scooped up a handful of clubs and began to throw them
in cascades, as did Carabella. Valentine's hands were chilled; he felt no willingness in them to juggle.

The nine Metamorphs alongside them were beginning to juggle now too.

It was only counterfeit juggling, dream-juggling, with no true art or skill
to it. It was mockery and nothing more. They held in their hands rough-
skinned black-fruits, and bits of wood, and other ordinary things, and threw
them from hand to hand in a child's parody of juggling, now and again
failing to make even those simple catches and bending quickly to retrieve
what they had dropped. Their performance aroused the audience as nothing
that the true jugglers had done had managed to do. The Metamorphs now
were humming – was this their form of applause? – and rocking rhythmically, and clapping hands to knees, and, Valentine saw, some of them were
transforming themselves almost at random, taking on odd alternate forms,
human or Hjort or Su-Suheris as the whim struck, or modeling themselves
after the Skandars or Carabella or Deliamber. At one point he saw six or
seven Valentines in the rows nearest him.

Performing was all but impossible in such a circus of distractions, but the jugglers clung grimly to their routines for some minutes more, doing poorly now, dropping clubs, missing beats, breaking up long-familiar combinations. The humming of the Metamorphs grew in intensity.

'Oh, look, look!' Carabella cried suddenly.

She gestured toward the nine mock jugglers, and pointed at the one who represented Valentine.

Valentine gasped.

What the Metamorph was doing defied all comprehension, and struck him rigid with terror and astonishment. For it had begun to oscillate between two forms. One was the Valentine-image, the tall, wide-shouldered, big-handed, golden-haired young man.

And the other was the image of Lord Valentine the Coronal.

The metamorphosis was almost instantaneous, like the flashing of a light. One moment Valentine saw his twin before him, and the next instant there was, in his place, the black-bearded fierce-eyed Coronal, a figure of might and presence, and then he was gone and the simple juggler was back. The humming of the crowd became louder: they approved of the show. Valentine ... Lord Valentine ... Valentine ... Lord Valentine ...

As he watched, Valentine felt a trail of icy chill go down his back, felt his scalp prickle, his knees quiver. There was no mistaking the import of this bizarre pantomime. If ever he had hoped for confirmation of all that had swept through him these weeks since Pidruid, he was getting it now. But here? In this forest town, among these aboriginal folk?

He looked into his own mimicked face.

He looked into the face of the Coronal.

The other eight jugglers leaped and pranced in a nightmarish dance, their legs rising high and stamping down, the false Skandar-arms waving and thumping against their sides, the false Sleet-hair and Carabella-hair wild in the night wind, and the Valentine-figure remained still, alternating one face and the other, and then it was over; nine Metamorphs stood in the center of the circle, holding out their hands to the audience, and the rest of the Piurivars were on their feet and dancing in the same wild way.

The performance was ended. Still dancing, the Metamorphs streamed out into the night, toward the booths and games of their festival.

Valentine, stunned, turned slowly and saw the frozen, astonished faces of his companions. Zalzan Kavol's jaw sagged, his arms dangled limply. His brothers clustered close behind him, their eyes wide in awe and shock. Sleet looked frighteningly pale; Carabella the opposite, her cheeks flushed, almost feverish. Valentine held out a hand toward them. Zalzan Kavol came stumbling forward, dazed, all but tripping over his own feet. The giant Skandar paused a few feet from Valentine. He blinked, he ran his tongue over his lips, he seemed to be working hard to make his voice function at all.

Finally he said, in a tiny, preposterous voice: 'My lord ...?'

First Zalzan Kavol and then his five brothers dropped hesitantly and awkwardly to their knees. With trembling hands Zalzan Kavol made the starburst symbol; his brothers did the same. Sleet, Carabella, Vinorkis, Deliamber, all knelt as well. The boy Shanamir, looking frightened and baffled, stared open-mouthed at Valentine. He seemed paralyzed with wonder and surprise. Slowly he bent to the ground also.

Lisamon Hultin cried out, 'Have you all gone crazy?'

'Down and pay homage!' Sleet ordered her hoarsely. 'You saw it, woman! He is the Coronal! Down and pay homage!'

'The Coronal?' she repeated in confusion.

Valentine stretched his arms out over them all in a gesture that was as much one of comfort as blessing. They were frightened of him and of what had just befallen; so too was he, but his fear was passing quickly, and in its place came strength, conviction, sureness. The sky itself seemed to cry at him: You are Lord Valentine who was Coronal on Castle Mount, and you shall have the Castle again one day, if you fight for it. Through him now flowed the power of his former imperial office. Even here, in this rainswept remote hinterland, in this ramshackle aboriginal town, here with the sweat of juggling still on his body, here in these coarse common clothes, Valentine felt himself to be what he once had been, and although he did not understand what metamorphosis had been worked on him to make him what he now was, he no longer questioned the reality of the messages that had come in dreams. And he felt no guilt, no shame, no deceitfulness, at receiving this homage from his stupefied companions.

'Up,' he said gently. 'All of you. On your feet. We must get out of this place. Shanamir, round up the mounts. Zalzan Kavol, get the wagon ready.' To Sleet he said, 'Everyone should be armed. Energy-throwers for those who know how to use them, juggling knives for the rest. See to it.'

Zalzan Kavol said heavily, 'My lord, there is in all this the flavor of a dream. To think that all these weeks I traveled with – to think I spoke roughly to – that I quarreled with—'

'Later,' Valentine said. 'We have no time for discussing these things now.'

He turned to Lisamon Hultin, who seemed busy in some conversation with herself, moving her lips, gesturing, explaining things to herself, debating these bewildering events. In a quiet, forceful voice Valentine said, 'You were hired only to bring us as far as Ilirivoyne. I need you to give us your strength as we escape. Will you stay with us to Ni-moya and beyond?'

'They made the starburst at you,' she said puzzledly. 'They all kneeled. And the Metamorphs – they—'

'I was once Lord Valentine of Castle Mount. Accept it. Believe it. The realm has fallen into dangerous hands. Remain at my side, Lisamon, as I journey east to set things right.'

She put her huge meaty hand over her mouth and looked at him in amazement.

Then she began to sag into an homage, but he shook his head, caught her by the elbow, would not let her kneel. 'Come,' he said. 'That doesn't matter now. Out of here!'

They gathered up their juggling gear and sprinted through the darkness toward the wagon, far across town. Shanamir and Carabella had already taken off, and were running well ahead. The Skandars moved in a single ponderous phalanx, shaking the ground beneath them; Valentine had never seen them move so quickly before. He ran just behind them, alongside Sleet. Vinorkis, splay-footed and slow, struggled to keep pace with them. To the rear was Lisamon Hultin. She had scooped up Deliamber and was carrying the little wizard perched in the crook of her left arm; in her right she bore her unsheathed vibration-sword.

As they neared the wagon Sleet said to Valentine, 'Shall we free the prisoner?'

'Yes.'

He beckoned to Lisamon Hultin. She put Deliamber down and followed him.

With Sleet in the lead, they ran toward the plaza. To Valentine's relief it was all but empty, no more than a handful of Piurivar guards on duty. The twelve cages still were stacked in tiers at the far end, four on the bottom, then rows of four and three, and the one containing the blue-skinned alien perched on top. Before the guards could react Lisamon Hultin was among them, seizing them two at a time and hurling them far across the plaza.

'Take no lives,' Valentine warned.

Sleet, monkey-swift, was scrambling up the stack of cages. He reached the top and began to cut through the thick withes that held the cage door shut. With brisk sawing motions of the knife he slashed while Valentine held the withes taut. In a moment the last of the fibers was severed and Valentine hoisted the door. The alien clambered out, stretching his cramped limbs and looking questioningly at his rescuers.

'Come with us,' Valentine said. 'Our wagon is over there, beyond the plaza. Do you understand?'

'I understand,' said the alien. His voice was deep, harsh, resonant, with a sharp clipped edge to each syllable. Without another word he swung himself down past the cages of the forest-brethren to the ground, where Lisamon Hultin had finished dealing with the Metamorph guards and was piling them tidily in a heap.

Impulsively Valentine sliced through the lashings on the cage of forest-brethren nearest to him. The busy little hands of the creatures reached through the bars and pulled the latch, and out they came. Valentine went on to the next cage. Sleet had already descended.

'One moment,' Valentine called. 'The job's not quite done.'

Sleet drew his knife and set to work. In moments all the cages were open, and the forest-brethren, dozens of them, were disappearing into the night.

As they ran to the wagon Sleet said, 'Why did you do that?'

'Why not?' Valentine asked. 'They want to live too.'

Shanamir and the Skandars had the wagon ready to go, the mounts hitched, the rotors turning. Lisamon Hultin was the last one in; she slammed the door behind her and yelled to Zalzan Kavol, who took off immediately.

And just in time, for half a dozen Metamorphs appeared and began running frantically after them, shouting and gesticulating. Zalzan Kavol stepped up the wagon's speed. Gradually the pursuers fell behind and were lost to sight as the wagon entered the utter darkness of the jungle.

Sleet peered worriedly back. 'Do you think they're still following us?'

'They can't keep up with us,' said Lisamon Hultin. 'And they travel only by foot. We're safely out of there.'

'Are you sure?' Sleet asked. 'What if they have some side route to take in catching up with us?'

'Worry about that when we must,' said Carabella. 'We're moving quickly.' She shuddered. 'And let it be a long while before we see Ilirivoyne again!'

They fell silent. The wagon glided swiftly onward.

Valentine sat slightly apart from the others. It was inevitable, yet it distressed him, for he was still more Valentine than Lord Valentine, and it was strange and disagreeable to set himself up above his friends. But there was no helping it. Carabella and Sleet, learning privately of his identity, had come to terms with it privately in their own ways; Deliamber, who had known the truth before Valentine himself, had never been overly awed by it; but the others, whatever suspicions they may have had that Valentine was something more than a happy-go-lucky wanderer, were dumfounded by the open acknowledgment of his rank that had come out of the grotesque Metamorph performance. They stared; they were speechless; they sat in stiff, unnatural postures, as if afraid to slouch in the presence of a Coronal. But how should one behave in the presence of a Power of Majipoor? They could not sit here constantly making starbursts at him. The gesture seemed absurd to Valentine anyway, a comical outpoking of the fingers and nothing more: his growing sense of his own importance did not seem to include much spirit of self-importance yet.

The alien introduced himself as Khun of Kianimot, a world of a star relatively close by Majipoor. He seemed a dark and brooding sort, with a crystalline anger and despair at his core, something integral to his being, that expressed itself, Valentine thought, in the set of his lips and the tone of his voice and particularly in the intense gaze of his strange, haunted purple eyes. Of course it was possible, Valentine conceded, that he was projecting his own human notions of expression onto this alien being, and that perhaps Khun was, as Kianimot folk went, a person of total jollity and amiability. But he doubted that.

Khun had come to Majipoor two years before, on business that he chose not to explain. It was, he said bitterly, the greatest mistake of his life, for among the merry Majipoorans he had been parted from all his money, he had unwisely embarked on a journey to Zimroel unaware that there was no starport on that continent from which he could depart for his home world, and he had even more foolishly ventured into Piurivar territory, thinking he could recoup his losses in some sort of trade with the Metamorphs. But they had seized him instead and thrust him in the cage, and held him prisoner for weeks, meaning to give him to the Fountain on the high night of their festival.

'Which would perhaps have been best,' he said. 'One quick blast of water and all this wandering would be at an end. Majipoor makes me weary. If I am destined to die on this world of yours, I think I would prefer it to be soon.'

'Pardon us for rescuing you,' Carabella said sharply.

'No. No. I mean no ingratitude. But only—' Khun paused. 'This place has been grief for me. So too was Kianimot. Is there any place in the universe where life does not mean suffering?'

'Has it been that bad?' asked Carabella. 'We find it tolerable here. Even the worst is tolerable enough, considering the alternative.' She laughed. 'Are you always this gloomy?'

The alien shrugged. 'If you are happy, I admire and envy you. I find existence painful and life meaningless. But these are dark thoughts for one who has just been rescued. I thank you for your aid. Who are you, and what rashness brought you to Piurifayne, and where do you go now?'

'We are jugglers,' said Valentine, with a sharp glance at the others. 'We came to this province because we thought there was work for us here. And if we succeed in getting away from this place, we'll head for Ni-moya, and down the river to Piliplok.'

'And from there?'

Valentine gestured vaguely. 'Some of us will make the pilgrimage to the Isle. Do you know what that is? And the others – I can't say where they'll go.'

'I must reach Alhanroel,' Khun said. 'My only hope lies in going home, which is impossible from this continent. In Piliplok perhaps I can arrange passage across the sea. May I travel with you?'

'Of course.'

'I have no money.'

'We see that,' said Valentine. 'It makes no difference.'

The wagon moved on swiftly through the night. No one slept, except in occasional quick naps. A light rain was falling now. In the darkness of the forest, dangers might lie on any side, but there was a paradoxical comfort in not being able to see anything, and the wagon sped on unmolested.

After an hour or so Valentine looked up and saw Vinorkis standing before him, gaping like a gaffed fish and quivering with what must be unbearable tension.

'My lord?' he said in a tiny voice.

Valentine nodded to the Hjort. 'You're trembling, Vinorkis.'

'My lord – how do I say this? – I have a terrible confession to make—'

Sleet opened his eyes and glared bleakly. Valentine signaled him to be calm.

Vinorkis said, 'My lord—' and faltered. He began again. 'My lord, in Pidruid a man came to me and said, "There is a tall fair-haired stranger at a certain inn and we believe he has committed monstrous crimes." And this man offered me a bag of crowns if I would keep close by the fair-haired stranger, and go wherever he went, and give news of his doings to the imperial proctors every few days.'

'A spy?' Sleet blurted. His hand flew to the dagger at his hip.

'Who was this man who hired you?' Valentine asked quietly.

The Hjort shook his head. 'Someone in the service of the Coronal, by the way he dressed. I never knew his name.'

'And you gave these reports?' Valentine said.

'Yes, my lord,' Vinorkis murmured, staring at his feet. 'In every city. After a time I hardly believed that you could be the criminal they said you were, for you seemed kind and gentle and sweet of soul, but I had taken their money, and there was more money for me every time I reported—'

'Let me kill him now,' Sleet muttered harshly.

'There'll be no killing,' Valentine said. 'Neither now nor later.'

'He's dangerous, my lord!'

'Not any longer.'

'I never trusted him,' Sleet said. 'Nor did Carabella, nor Deliamber. It wasn't just that he was Hjort. There was always something shifty about him, sly, insinuating. All those questions, all that sucking around for information—'

Vinorkis said, 'I ask pardon. I had no idea whom I was betraying, my lord.'

'You believe that?' Sleet cried.

'Yes,' Valentine said. 'Why not? He had no more idea who I was than – than I did. He was told to trail a fair-haired man and give information to the government. Is that so evil a thing? He was serving his Coronal, or so he thought. His loyalty must not be repaid by your dagger, Sleet.'

'My lord, sometimes you are too innocent,' Sleet said.

'Perhaps true. But not this time. We have much to gain by forgiving this man, and nothing at all by slaying him.' To the Hjort Valentine said, 'You have my pardon, Vinorkis. I ask only that you be as loyal to the true Coronal as you've been to the false.'

'You have my pledge, my lord.'

'Good. Get yourself some sleep, now, and put away your fear.'

Vinorkis made the starburst and backed away, settling down in mid-cabin beside two of the Skandars.

Sleet said, 'That was unwise, my lord. What if he continues to spy on us?'

'In these jungles? Messages to whom?'

'And when we leave the jungles?'

'I think he can be trusted,' said Valentine. 'I know, this confession may have been only a double ruse, to lull us into casting aside our suspicions. I'm not as naïve as you think, Sleet. I charge you to keep private watch over him when we reach civilization again – just in case. But I think you'll find his repentance is genuine. And I have uses for him that will make him valuable to me.'

'Uses, my lord?'

'A spy can lead us to other spies. And there'll be other spies, Sleet. We may want Vinorkis to maintain his contacts with the imperial agents, eh?'

Sleet winked. 'I see your meaning, my lord!'

Valentine smiled, and they fell silent.

Yes, he told himself, Vinorkis's horror and remorse were genuine. And provided much that Valentine needed to know; for if the Coronal had been willing to pay good sums to have an insignificant wanderer followed from Pidruid to Ilirivoyne, how insignificant could that wanderer actually be? Valentine felt a weird prickling along his skin. More than anything else, Vinorkis's confession was a confirmation of all that Valentine had discovered about himself. Surely, if the technique that had been used to cast him from his body was new and relatively untried, the conspirators would be uncertain about how permanent the mind-wiping would be, and would hardly dare to allow the outcast Coronal to roam about the land free and unobserved. A spy, then, and probably others close by; and the threat of quick preventive action if word got back to the usurper that Valentine was beginning to recover his memory. He wondered how carefully the imperial forces were tracking him, and at what point they would choose to intercept him on his journey toward Alhanroel.

Onward the wagon moved in the blackness of night. Deliamber and Lisamon Hultin conferred endlessly with Zalzan Kavol about the route;

the other main Metamorph settlement, Avendroyne, lay somewhere to the southeast of Ilirivoyne, in a gap between two great mountains, and it seemed likely that the road they were on would take them there. To ride blithely into another Metamorph town hardly seemed wise, of course. Word must have gone on ahead of the freeing of the prisoner and the escape of the wagon. Still, there was even greater peril in trying to go back toward Piurifayne Fountain.

Valentine, not at all sleepy, re-enacted the Metamorph pantomime a hundred times in his mind. It had the quality of a dream, yes, but no dream was so immediate: he had been close enough to touch his Metamorph counterpart; he had seen, beyond all doubt, those shifts of features from fair to dark, dark to fair. The Metamorphs knew the truth, more clearly than he himself. Could they read souls, as Deliamber sometimes did? What had they felt, knowing they had a fallen Coronal in their midst? No awe, certainly: Coronals were nothing to them, mere symbols of their own defeat thousands of years ago. It must have seemed terribly funny to them to have a successor to Lord Stiamot tossing clubs at their festival, amusing them with silly tricks and dances, far from the splendors of Castle Mount, a Coronal in their own muddy wooden village. How strange, he thought. How much like a dream.

15

Toward dawn huge rounded mountains became visible, with a broad notch between them, Avendroyne could not be far. Zalzan Kavol, with a deference he had never shown before, came aft to consult Valentine on strategy. Lie low in the woods all day, and wait until nightfall to try to get past Avendroyne? Or attempt a bold daylight passage?

Leadership was unfamiliar to Valentine. He pondered a moment, trying to look far-seeing and thoughtful.

At length he said, 'If we go forward by day, we are too conspicuous. On the other hand, if we waste all day hiding here, we give them more time to prepare plans against us.'

'Tonight,' Sleet pointed out, 'is the high festival again in Ilirivoyne, and probably here also. We might slip by them while they're merrymaking, but in daylight we have no chance.'

'I agree,' said Lisamon Hultin.

Valentine looked around. 'Carabella?'

'If we wait, we give the Ilirivoyne people time to overtake us. I say go onward.'

'Deliamber?'

The Vroon delicately touched tentacle-tips together. 'Onward. Bypass Avendroyne, double back toward Verf. There'll be a second road to the Fountain from Avendroyne, surely.'

'Yes,' Valentine said. He looked to Zalzan Kavol. 'My thoughts run with Deliamber and Carabella. What of yours?'

Zalzan Kavol scowled. 'Mine say, let the wizard make this wagon fly, and take us tonight to Ni-moya. Otherwise, continue on without waiting.'

'So be it,' said Valentine, as if he had made the decision single-handedly. 'And when we approach Avendroyne, we'll send scouts out to find a road that bypasses the town.'

On they went, moving more cautiously as daybreak arrived. The rain was intermittent, but when it came now it was no gentle spatter, more an almost tropical downpour, a heavy cannonade of drops that rattled with malign force against the wagon's roof. To Valentine the rain was welcome: perhaps it would keep the Metamorphs indoors as they went through.

There were signs of outskirts now, scattered wicker huts. The road forked and forked again, Deliamber offering a guess at each point of division, until finally they knew they must be close to Avendroyne. Lisamon Hultin and Sleet rode out as scouts, and returned in an hour with good news: one of the two roads just ahead ran right into the heart of Avendroyne, where festival preparations were under way, and the other curved toward the northeast, bypassing the city entirely and going through what looked like a farming district on the farther slopes of the mountains.

They took the northeast road. Uneventfully they passed the Avendroyne region.

Now, in late afternoon, they journeyed down the mountain pass and into a broad thickly forested plain, rainswept and dark, that marked the eastern perimeter of Metamorph territory. Zalzan Kavol drove the wagon furiously onward, pausing only when Shanamir insisted that the mounts absolutely had to rest and forage; virtually tireless they might be, and of synthetic origin, but living things were what they were, and now and then they needed to halt. The Skandar yielded reluctantly; he seemed possessed by desperate need to put Piurifayne far behind him.

Toward twilight, as they went in heavy rain through rough, irregular country, trouble came suddenly upon them.

Valentine was riding in mid-cabin, with Deliamber and Carabella; most of the others were sleeping, and Heitrag Kavol and Gibor Haern were driving. There came a crashing, crackling, smashing sound from ahead, and a moment later the wagon jolted to a stop.

'Tree down in the storm!' Heitrag Kavol called. 'Road blocked in front of us!'

Zalzan Kavol muttered curses and tugged Lisamon Hultin awake. Valentine saw nothing but green ahead, the entire crown of some forest giant blocking the road. It might take hours or even days to clear that. The Skandars, hoisting energy-throwers to their shoulders, went out to investigate. Valentine followed. Darkness was falling rapidly. The wind was gusty, and shafts of rain swept almost horizontally into their faces.

'Let's get to work,' Zalzan Kavol growled, shaking his head in annoyance. 'Thelkar! You start cutting from down there! Rovorn! The big side branches! Erfon—'

'It might be swifter,' Valentine suggested, 'to back up and look for another fork in the road.'

The idea startled Zalzan Kavol, as if the Skandar would never in a century have conceived such a notion. He mulled it for a moment. 'Yes,' he said finally. 'That does make some sense. If we—'

And a second tree, larger even than the first, toppled to the ground a hundred yards behind them. The wagon was trapped.

Valentine was the first to comprehend what must be happening. 'Into the wagon, everyone! It's an ambush!' He rushed toward the open door.

Too late. Out of the darkening forest came a stream of Metamorphs, fifteen or twenty of them, perhaps even more, bursting silently into their midst. Zalzan Kavol let out a terrible cry of rage and opened fire with his energy-thrower; the blaze of light cast a strange lavender glow over the roadside and two Metamorphs fell, charred hideously. But in the same instant Heitrag Kavol uttered a strangled gurgle and dropped, a weapon shaft through his neck, and Thelkar fell, clutching at another in his chest.

Suddenly the rear end of the wagon was ablaze. Those within came scrambling out, Lisamon Hultin leading the way with her vibration-sword high. Valentine found himself attacked by a Metamorph wearing his own face; he kicked the creature away, pivoted, slashed a second one with the knife that was his only weapon. That was strange, to inflict a wound. In weird fascination, he watched the bronze-hued fluid begin to flow.

The Valentine Metamorph came at him again. Claws went for his eyes. Valentine dodged, twisted, stabbed. The blade sank deep and the Metamorph reeled back, clutching at its chest. Valentine trembled in shock, but only for an instant. He turned to confront the next.

This was a new experience for him, this fighting and killing, and it made his soul ache. But to be gentle now was to invite a quick death. He thrust and cut, thrust and cut. From behind him he heard Carabella call, 'How are you doing?'

'Holding – my – own—' he grunted.

Zalzan Kavol, seeing his magnificent wagon on fire, howled and caught a Metamorph by the waist and hurled it into the pyre; two more rushed at him, but another Skandar seized them and snapped them like sticks with each pair of hands. In the frantic melee Valentine caught sight of Carabella wrestling with a Metamorph, forcing it to the ground with the powerful forearm muscles years of juggling had developed; and there was Sleet, ferociously vindictive, pounding another with his boots in savage joy. But the wagon was burning. The wagon was burning. The woods were full of Metamorphs, night was swiftly coming on, the rain was a torrent, and the wagon was burning.

As the heat of the fire increased, the centre of the battle shifted from the roadside to the forest, and matters became even more confused, for in the darkness it was hard to tell friend from foe. The Metamorph trick of shape-shifting added another complication, although in the frenzy of the fight they were unable to hold their transformations for long, and what seemed to be Sleet, or Shanamir, or Zalzan Kavol, reverted quickly to its native form.

Valentine fought savagely. He was slippery with his own sweat and the blood of Metamorphs, and his heart hammered mightily with the furious exertion. Panting, gasping, never still an instant, he waded through the tangle of enemies with a zeal that astonished him, never pausing for an instant's rest. Thrust and cut, thrust and cut—

The Metamorphs were armed with only the simplest of weapons, and, though there seemed to be dozens of them, their numbers soon were dwindling rapidly. Lisamon Hultin was doing awful destruction with her vibration-sword, swinging it two-handed and lopping off the boughs of trees as well as the limbs of Metamorphs. The surviving Skandars, spraying energy-bolts wildly around the scene, had ignited half a dozen trees and had littered the ground with fallen Metamorphs. Sleet was maiming and slaughtering as if he could in one wild minute avenge himself for all the pain he fancied the Metamorphs had brought upon him. Khun and Vinorkis too were fighting with passionate energy.

As suddenly as the ambush had begun, it was over.

By the light of the fires Valentine could see dead Metamorphs everywhere. Two dead Skandars lay among them. Lisamon Hultin bore a bloody but shallow wound on one thigh; Sleet had lost half his jerkin and had taken several minor cuts; Shanamir had clawmarks across his cheek. Valentine too felt some trifling scratches and nicks, and his arms had a leaden ache of fatigue. But he had not been seriously harmed. Deliamber, though – where was Deliamber? The Vroon wizard was nowhere to be seen. In anguish Valentine turned to Carabella and said, 'Did the Vroon stay in the wagon?'

'I thought we all came out when it burst afire.'

Valentine frowned. In the silence of the forest the only sounds were the terrible hissing and crackling of fire and the quiet mocking patter of the rain. 'Deliamber?' Valentine called. 'Deliamber, where are you?'

'Here,' answered a high-pitched voice from above. Valentine looked up and saw the sorcerer clinging to a sturdy bough, fifteen feet off the ground. 'Warfare is not one of my skills,' Deliamber explained blandly, swinging outward and letting himself drop into Lisamon Hultin's arms.

Carabella said, 'What do we do now?'

Valentine realized that she was asking him. He was in command. Zalzan Kavol, kneeling by his brothers' bodies, seemed stunned by their deaths and by the loss of his precious wagon.

He said, 'We have no choice but to cut through the forest. If we try to take the main road we'll meet more Metamorphs. Shanamir, what of the mounts?'

'Dead,' the boy sobbed. 'Every one. The Metamorphs—'

'On foot, then. A long wet journey it will be, too. Deliamber, how far do you think we are from the River Steiche?'

'A few days' journey, I suspect. But we have no sure notion of the direction.'

'Follow the slope of the land,' Sleet said. 'Rivers won't lie uphill from here. If we keep going east we're bound to hit it.'

'Unless a mountain stands in our way,' Deliamber remarked.

'We'll find the river,' Valentine said firmly. 'The Steiche flows into the Zimr at Ni-moya, is that right?'

'Yes,' said Deliamber, 'but its flow is turbulent.'

'We'll have to chance it. A raft, I suppose, will be the quickest to build. Come. If we stay here much longer we'll be set upon again.'

They could salvage nothing from the wagon, neither clothing nor food nor belongings nor their juggling gear – all lost, every scrap, everything but what had been on them when they came forth to meet the ambushers. To Valentine that was no great loss; but to some of the others, particularly the Skandars, it was overwhelming. The wagon had been their home a long while.

It was difficult to get Zalzan Kavol to move from the spot. He seemed frozen, unable to abandon the bodies of his brothers and the ruin of his wagon. Gently Valentine urged him to his feet. Some of the Metamorphs, he said, might well have escaped in the skirmish; they could soon return with reinforcements; it was perilous to remain here. Quickly they dug shallow graves in the soft forest floor and laid Thelkar and Heitrag Kavol to rest. Then, in steady rain and gathering darkness, they set out in what they hoped was an easterly direction.

For over an hour they walked, until it became too dark to see; then they camped miserably in a little soggy huddle, clinging to one another until dawn. At first light they rose, cold and stiff, and picked their way onward through the tangled forest. The rain, at least, had stopped. The forest here was less of a jungle, and gave them little challenge, except for an occasional swift stream that had to be forded with care. At one of those, Carabella lost her footing and was fished out by Lisamon Hultin; at another it was Shanamir who was swept downstream, and Khun who plucked him to safety. They walked until midday, and rested an hour or two, making a scrappy meal of raw roots and berries. Then they went on until darkness.

And passed two more days in the same fashion.

And on the third came to a grove of dwikka-trees, eight fat squat giants in the forest, with monstrous swollen fruits hanging from them.

'Food!' Zalzan Kavol bellowed.

'Food sacred to the forest-brethren,' Lisamon Hultin said. 'Be careful!'

The famished Skandar, nevertheless, was on the verge of cutting down one of the enormous fruits with his energy-thrower when Valentine said sharply, 'No! I forbid it!'

Zalzan Kavol stared incredulously. For an instant his old habits of command asserted themselves, and he glared at Valentine as if about to strike him. But he kept his temper in check.

'Look,' Valentine said.

Forest-brethren were emerging from behind every tree. They were armed with their dart-blowers; and seeing the slender apelike creatures encircling them, Valentine in his weariness felt almost willing to be slain. But only for a moment. He recovered his spirits and said to Lisamon Hultin, 'Ask them if we may have food and guides to the Steiche. If they ask a price, we can juggle for them with stones, or pieces of fruit, I suppose.'

The warrior-woman, twice as tall as the forest-brethren, went into their midst and talked with them a long time. She was smiling when she returned.

'They are aware,' she said, 'that we are the ones who freed their brothers in Ilirivoyne!'

'Then we are saved!' cried Shanamir.

'News travels swiftly in this forest,' Valentine said.

Lisamon Hultin went on, 'We are their guests. They will feed us. They will guide us.'

That night the wanderers ate richly on dwikka-fruit and other forest delicacies, and there was actually laughter among them for the first time since the ambush. Afterward the forest-brethren performed a sort of dance for them, a monkeyish prancing thing, and Sleet and Carabella and Valentine responded with impromptu juggling using objects collected in the forest. Afterward Valentine slept a deep, satisfying sleep. In his dreams he had the gift of flight, and saw himself soaring to the summit of Castle Mount.

And in the morning a party of chattering forest-brethren led them to the

River Steiche, three hours' journey from the dwikka-tree grove, and bade them farewell with little twittering cries.

The river was a sobering sight. It was broad, though nothing remotely like the mighty Zimr, and it sped northward with startling haste, flowing so energetically that it had carved out a deep bed bordered in many places by high rocky walls. Here and there ugly stone snags rose above the water, and downstream Valentine could see white eddies of rapids.

The building of rafts took a day and a half. They cut down the young slim trees that grew by the riverbank, trimmed and trued them with knives and sharp stones, lashed them together with vines. The results were hardly elegant, but the rafts, though crude, did look reasonably riverworthy. There were three altogether – one for the four Skandars, one for Khun, Vinorkis, Lisamon Hultin, and Sleet, and one occupied by Valentine, Carabella, Shanamir, and Deliamber.

'We will probably become separated as we go downriver,' Sleet said. 'We should choose a meeting-place in Ni-moya.'

Deliamber said, 'The Steiche and the Zimr flow together at a place called Nissimorn. There is a broad, sandy beach there. Let us meet at Nissimorn Beach.'

'At Nissimorn Beach, yes,' Valentine said.

He cut loose the cord that bound his raft to the shore, and was carried off into the river.

The first day's journey was uneventful. There were rapids, but not difficult ones, and they poled safely past them. Carabella showed skill at handling the raft, and deftly steered them around the occasional rocky patches.

After a time the rafts became separated, Valentine's taking some subcurrent and moving rapidly ahead of the other two. In the morning he waited, hoping the others would catch up. But there was no sign of them and eventually he decided to depart.

On, on, on, for the most part swept easily along, with occasional moments of anxiety in the white-water stretches. By afternoon of the second day the course was becoming rougher. The land seemed to dip here, sloping downward as the Zimr drew near, and the river, following the line of descent, plunged and bucked. Valentine began to worry about waterfalls ahead. They had no charts, no notion of dangers: they took everything as it came. He could only trust to luck that this swift water would deliver them safely to Ni-moya.

And then? By boat to Piliplok, and by pilgrim-ship to the Isle of Sleep, and somehow procure an interview with the Lady his mother, and then? And then? How did one claim the Coronal's throne, when one's face was not the face of Lord Valentine the rightful ruler? By what claim, by what authority? It seemed to Valentine an impossible quest. He might be better remaining here in the forest, ruling over his little band. They, readily enough, accepted him for what he thought himself to be; but in that world of billions of strangers, in that vast empire of giant cities that lay beyond the edge of the horizon, how, how, how would he ever manage to convince the unbelievers that he, Valentine the juggler, was—

No. These thoughts were foolish. He had never, not since he had appeared, shorn of memory and past, on the verge overlooking Pidruid, felt the need to rule over others; and if he had come to command this little group, it was more by natural gift and by Zalzan Kavol's default than out of any overt desire on his part. And yet he was in command, however tentatively and delicately. So it would be as he traveled onward through Majipoor. He would take one step at a time, and do that which seemed right and proper, and perhaps the Lady would guide him, and if the Divine so willed it he would one day stand again on Castle Mount, and if that was not part of the great plan, why, that would be acceptable also. There was nothing to fear. The future would unroll serenely in its own true course, as it had done since Pidruid. And—

'*Valentine!*' Carabella shouted.

The river seemed to sprout giant stony teeth. There were boulders everywhere, and monstrous white whirlpools, and, just ahead, an ominous tumbling descent, a place where the Steiche leaped out into space and went roaring down a series of steps to a valley far below. Valentine gripped his pole, but no pole could help him now. It lodged between two snags and was ripped from his grasp; a moment later there was a ghastly grinding sound as the flimsy raft, battered by submerged rocks, swung around at right angles to its course and split apart. He was hurled into the chilly stream and swept forward like a cork. For a moment he grasped Carabella by the wrist; but then the current pulled her free, and as he clutched desperately for her he was engulfed by the swift water and driven under.

Gasping and choking, Valentine struggled to get his head above the water. When he did, he was already far downstream. The wreckage of the raft was nowhere in sight.

'Carabella?' he yelled. 'Shanamir? Deliamber? Hoy! Hoy!'

He roared until his voice was ragged, but the booming of the rapids so thoroughly covered his cries that he could scarcely hear them himself. A terrible sense of pain and loss numbed his spirit. All gone, then? His friends, his beloved Carabella, the wily little Vroon, the clever, cocky boy Shanamir, all swept to death in an instant? No. No. Unthinkable. That was an agony far worse than this business, still unreal to him, of being a Coronal thrust from the Castle. What did that mean? These were beings of flesh and blood, dear to him; that was only a title and power. He would not stop calling their names as the river threw him about. '*Carabella!*' he shouted. '*Shanamir!*'

Valentine clawed at rocks, trying to halt his willy-nilly descent, but he was in the heart of the rapids now, buffeted and battered by the current and by the stones of the riverbed. Dazed and exhausted, half paralyzed by grief, Valentine gave up struggling and let himself be carried along, down the giant staircase of the river, a tiny plaything spinning and bouncing along. He drew his knees to his chest and wrapped his arms over his head, attempting to minimize the surface he presented to the rocks. The power of the river was awesome. So here is how it ends, he thought, the grand adventure of Valentine of Majipoor, once Coronal, later wandering juggler, now about to be broken to bits by the impersonal and uncaring forces of nature. He commended himself to the Lady whom he thought to be his mother, and gulped air, and went heels over head, head over heels, down and down and down, and struck something with frightening force and thought this must be the end, only it was not the end, and struck something again that gave him an agonizing blow in the ribs, knocking the air from him, and he must have lost consciousness for a time, for he felt no further pain.

And then he found himself lying on a pebble-strewn strand, in a quiet sidestream of the river. It seemed to him that he had been shaken in a giant dice-box for hours, and cast up at random, discarded and useless. His body ached in a thousand places. His lungs felt soggy when he breathed. He was shivering and his skin was covered with goosebumps. And he was alone, under a vast cloudless sky, at the edge of some unknown wilderness, with civilization some unknown distance ahead and his friends perhaps dashed to death on the boulders.

But he was alive. That much was sure. Alone, battered, helpless, grief-stricken, lost ... but alive. The adventure, then, was not ended. Slowly, with infinite effort, Valentine hauled himself out of the surf and tottered to the riverbank, and let himself carefully down on a wide flat rock, and with numb fingers undid his clothing and stretched out to dry himself under the warm friendly sun. He looked toward the river, hoping to see Carabella come swimming along, or Shanamir with the wizard perched on his shoulder. No one. But that doesn't mean they're dead, he told himself. They may have been cast up on farther shores. I'll rest here for a time, Valentine resolved, and then I'll go searching for the others, and then, with them or without, I'll set out onward, toward Ni-moya, toward Piliplok, toward the Isle of the Lady, onward, onward, onward toward Castle Mount or whatever else lies ahead for me. Onward. Onward. Onward.

PART III

The Book of
the Isle of Sleep

1

For what felt like months or perhaps years Valentine lay sprawled naked on his warm flat rock on the pebbly beach where the unruly River Steiche had deposited him. The roar of the river was a constant drone in his ears, oddly soothing. The sunlight enfolded him in a hazy golden nimbus, and he told himself that its touch would heal his bruises and abrasions and contusions, if only he lay still long enough. Vaguely he knew he ought to rise and see about shelter, and begin to search for his companions, but he barely could find the strength to turn from one side to the other.

This was no way, he knew, for a Coronal of Majipoor to conduct himself. Such self-indulgence might be acceptable for merchants or tavernkeepers or even jugglers, but a higher discipline rested upon one who had pretensions to govern. Therefore get to your feet, he told himself, and clothe your body, and start walking northward along the riverbank until you reach those who can help you regain your lofty place. Yes. Up, Valentine! But he remained where he was. He had expended every scrap of energy in him, Coronal or not, during the helter-skelter plunge down the rapids. Lying here like this, he had a powerful sense of the immensity of Majipoor, its many thousands of miles of circumference stretching out beneath his limbs, a planet large enough comfortably to house twenty billion people without crowding, a planet of enormous cities and wondrous parks and forest preserves and sacred districts and agricultural territories, and it seemed to him that if he took the trouble to rise it would be necessary for him to cover all that colossal domain on foot, step by step by step. It seemed simpler to stay where he was.

Something tickled the small of his back, something rubbery and insistent. He ignored it.

'Valentine?'

He ignored that too, for a moment.

The tickling occurred again. But by then it had filtered through his fatigue-dulled brain that someone had spoken his name, and therefore that one of his companions must have survived after all. Joy flooded his soul. With what little energy he could muster, Valentine raised his head and saw the small many-limbed figure of Autifon Deliamber standing beside him. The Vroonish wizard was about to prod him a third time.

'You're alive!' Valentine cried.

'Evidently I am. And so are you, more or less.'

'And Carabella? Shanamir?'

'I have not seen them.'

'As I feared,' Valentine murmured dully. He closed his eyes and lowered his head, and in leaden despair lay once more like jetsam.

'Come,' Deliamber said. 'There is a vast journey ahead of us.'

'I know. That's why I don't want to get up.'

'Are you hurt?'

'I don't think so. But I want to rest, Deliamber. I want to rest a hundred years.'

The sorcerer's tentacles probed and poked Valentine in a dozen places. 'No serious damage,' the Vroon murmured. 'Much of you is still healthy.'

'Much of me isn't,' said Valentine indistinctly. 'What about you?'

'Vroons are good swimmers, even old ones like me. I am unhurt. We should go on, Valentine.'

'Later.'

'Is this how a Coronal of Majip—'

'No,' Valentine said. 'But a Coronal of Majipoor would not have had to shoot the Steiche rapids on a slapped-together log raft. A Coronal would not have been wandering in this wilderness for days and days, sleeping in the rain and eating nothing but nuts and berries. A Coronal—'

'A Coronal would not allow his lieutenants to see him in a condition of indolence and spiritlessness,' Deliamber said sharply. 'And one of them is approaching right now.'

Valentine blinked and sat up. Lisamon Hultin was striding along the beach toward them. She looked a trifle disarranged, her clothing in shreds, her gigantic fleshy body purpled with bruises here and there, but her pace was jaunty and her voice, when she called out to them, was as booming as ever.

'Hoy! Are you intact?'

'I think so,' Valentine answered. 'Have you seen any others?'

'Carabella and the boy, half a mile or so back that way.'

He felt his spirits soar. 'Are they all right?'

'She is, at any rate.'

'And Shanamir?'

'Doesn't want to wake up. She sent me out to look for the sorcerer. Found him sooner than I thought. Phaugh, what a river! That raft came apart so fast it was almost funny!'

Valentine reached for his clothing, found it still wet, and, with a shrug, dropped it to the rocks. 'We must get to Shanamir at once. Have you news of Khun and Sleet and Vinorkis?'

'Didn't see them. I went into the river and when I came up I was alone.'

'And the Skandars?'

'No sign of them at all.' To Deliamber she said, 'Where do you think we are, wizard?'

'Far from anywhere,' the Vroon replied. 'Safely out of the Metamorph lands, at any rate. Come, take me to the boy.'

Lisamon Hultin scooped Deliamber to her shoulder and strode back along the beach, while Valentine limped along behind them, carrying his damp clothing over his arm. After a time they came upon Carabella and Shanamir camped in an inlet of bright white sand surrounded by thick river-reeds with scarlet stems. Carabella, battered and weary-looking, wore only a brief leather skirt. But she seemed in reasonably good shape. Shanamir lay unconscious, breathing slowly, his skin an odd dark hue.

'Oh, Valentine!' Carabella cried, springing up and running to him. 'I saw you swept away – and then – and then – Oh, I thought I'd never see you again!'

He held her close against him. 'And I thought the same. I thought you were lost to me forever, love.'

'Were you hurt?'

'Not permanently,' he said. 'And you?'

'I was tossed and tossed and tossed until I couldn't remember my own name. But then I found a calm place and I swam to shore, and Shanamir was already there. But he wouldn't wake up. And Lisamon came out of the underbrush and said she'd try to find Deliamber, and – Will he be all right, wizard?'

'In a moment,' said Deliamber, arranging his tentacle-tips over the boy's chest and forehead, as if making some transfer of energy. Shanamir grunted and stirred. His eyes opened tentatively, closed, opened again. In a thick voice he began to say something, but Deliamber told him to be silent, to lie still, to let the strength flow back into him.

There was no question of attempting to move on that afternoon. Valentine and Carabella constructed a crude shelter out of reeds; Lisamon Hultin assembled a meager dinner of raw fruit and young pininna-sprouts; and they sat in silence beside the river, watching a spectacular sunset, bands of violet and gold streaking the great dome of the sky, reflections in luminous tones of orange and purple in the water, undertones of pale green, satiny red, silken crimson, and then the first puffs of gray and black, the swift descent of night.

In the morning they all felt able to proceed, though stiff from a night in the open. Shanamir showed no ill effects. Deliamber's care and the natural resilience of youth had restored his vitality.

Patching together their clothing as best they could, they set out to the north, following the beach until it gave out, then continuing through the forest of gawky androdragma-trees and flowering alabandina that flanked the river. The air was soft and mild here, and the sun, descending in dappled splotches through the treetops, gave a welcome warmth to the weary stragglers.

In the third hour of the march Valentine caught the scent of fire just ahead, and what smelled very much like the aroma of grilled fish. He jogged forward, salivating, prepared to buy, beg, if necessary steal, some of that fish, for it had been more days than he cared to count since he had last tasted cooked food. Down a rough talus slope he skidded, into the sunlight on white pebbles, so bright he could barely see. In the glare he made out three figures crouched over a fire by the river's edge, and when he shaded his eyes he discovered that one was a compact human with pale skin and a startling shock of white hair, and another was a long-legged blue-skinned being of alien birth, and the third a Hjort.

'Sleet!' Valentine cried. 'Khun! Vinorkis!'

He ran toward them, slipping and sliding over the rocks.

They watched his wild approach calmly, and when he was close by them Sleet, in casual manner, handed him a stake on which was spitted a fillet of some pink-fleshed river fish.

'Have some lunch,' Sleet said amiably.

Valentine gaped. 'How did you get so far ahead of us? What did you build this fire with? How did you catch the fish? What have you—'

'Your fish will get cold,' Khun said. 'Eat first, questions after.'

Valentine took a hasty bite – he had never tasted anything so delicious, a tender moist meat splendidly seared, surely as elegant a morsel as had ever been served in the feasts on Castle Mount – and, turning, called to his companions to come down the slope. But they were already on their way, Shanamir whooping and cavorting as he ran, Carabella gracefully darting over the rocks, Lisamon Hultin, bearing Deliamber, pounding thunderously toward him.

'There's fish for all!' Sleet proclaimed.

They had caught at least a dozen, which circled sadly in a shallow rock-rimmed pool near the fire. Efficiently Khun plucked them forth and split and gutted them. Sleet held them briefly over the flame and passed them to the others, who ate ravenously.

Sleet explained that when their raft had broken up they had found themselves clinging to a fragment some three logs wide, and had managed to hang on all the way through the rapids and far downstream. They vaguely remembered having seen the beach where Valentine was cast ashore, but had not noticed him on it as they passed by, and they had drifted another few miles before they had recovered enough from their rapids-running to want to let go of their logs and swim to the bank. Khun had caught the fish barehanded: he had, said Sleet, the quickest hands he had ever seen, and would probably make a magnificent juggler. Khun grinned – the first time Valentine had seen anything but a grim expression on his face.

'And the fire?' Carabella asked. 'You started it by snapping your fingers, I suppose?'

'We attempted it,' Sleet answered smoothly. 'But it proved to be strenuous work. So we walked over to the village of fisher-folk just beyond the bend and asked to borrow a light.'

'Fisherfolk?' Valentine said, startled.

'An outpost of Liimen,' said Sleet, 'who evidently don't know that it's their racial destiny to sell sausages in the western cities. They gave us shelter last night, and have agreed to ferry us up to Ni-moya this afternoon, so that we can wait for our friends at Nissimorn Beach,' He smiled. 'I suppose we'll need to hire a second boat now.'

Deliamber said, 'Are we that close to Ni-moya?'

'Two hours by boat, so I'm told, to the place where the rivers flow together.'

Suddenly the world seemed less huge to Valentine, and the chores that awaited him less overwhelming. To have eaten a real meal once again, and to know that a friendly settlement lay nearby, and that he would soon be leaving the wilderness behind, was tremendously cheering. Only one thing troubled him now: the fate of Zalzan Kavol and his three surviving brothers.

The Liiman village was indeed close at hand – perhaps five hundred souls, short flat-headed dark-skinned people whose triple sets of bright fiery eyes regarded the wanderers with little curiosity. They lived in modest thatched huts close beside the river, and raised an assortment of crops in small gardens to supplement the catch that their fleet of crude fishing-boats brought in. Their dialect was a difficult one, but Sleet seemed able to communicate with them and managed to arrange not only another boat but also the purchase, for a couple of crowns, of fresh clothing for Carabella and Lisamon Hultin.

In early afternoon they set out, with four taciturn Liimen as their crew, on the journey to Ni-moya.

The river ran as swift as ever here, but there were few rapids of any consequence, and the two boats sped nicely along through countryside increasingly populous and tame. The steep riverbanks of the uplands gave way, down here, to broad alluvial plains of heavy black silt, and shortly an almost continuous strip of farming villages appeared.

Now the river widened and grew calm, becoming a broad, even waterway with a deep blue glint. The land here was flat and open, and though the settlements on both sides were doubtless goodly cities with populations of many thousands, they seemed mere hamlets, so dwarfed were they by the gigantic surroundings. Ahead lay a dark, immense headwater that seemed to span the entire horizon as though it were the open sea.

'River Zimr,' announced the Liiman at the helm of Valentine's boat. 'Steiche ends here. Nissimorn Beach on left.'

Valentine beheld a huge crescent strand, bordered by a dense grove of palm trees of a peculiarly lopsided shape, purplish fronds jutting up like ruffled feathers. As they drew near, Valentine was startled to see a raft of crudely trimmed logs on the beach, and, sitting beside it, four giant shaggy four-armed figures. The Skandars were waiting for them.

2

Zalzan Kavol saw nothing extraordinary about his voyage. His raft had come to the rapids; he and his brothers had poled their way through, getting jounced about a little, but not seriously; they had continued on downstream to Nissimorn Beach, where they had camped in growing impatience, wondering what was delaying the rest of the party. It had not occurred to the Skandar that the other rafts might have been wrecked in the passage, nor had he seen any of the castaways along the river-bank en route. 'Did you have trouble?' he asked in what seemed to be genuine innocence.

'Of a minor sort,' Valentine replied dryly. 'But we seem to be reunited, and it will be good to sleep in proper lodgings again tonight.'

They resumed the journey, and presently they passed into the great confluence of the Steiche and the Zimr, a water so wide that it was impossible for Valentine to conceive it as the mere meeting-place of two rivers. At the town of Nissimorn on the southwestern shore they parted from the Liimen and boarded the ferry that would take them on across to Ni-moya, largest of the cities of the continent of Zimroel.

Thirty million citizens dwelled here. At Ni-moya the River Zimr made a great bend, changing its course sharply from easterly to southeasterly. There a prodigious megalopolis had taken form. It spread for hundreds of miles along both banks of the river and up several tributaries that flowed in from the north. Valentine and his companions saw first the southern suburbs, residential districts that gave way, in the extreme south, to the agricultural territory stretching down into the Steiche Valley. The main urban zone lay on the north bank, and could only dimly be seen at first, tier upon tier of flat-topped white towers descending toward the river. Ferries by the dozens plied the water here, linking the myriad riverside towns. The crossing took several hours, and twilight was beginning before Ni-moya proper was clearly in view.

The city looked magical. Its lights, just coming on, sparkled invitingly against the backdrop of heavily forested green hills and impeccable white buildings. Giant fingers of piers thrust into the river, and an astounding bustle of vessels great and small lined the waterfront. Pidruid, which had seemed so mighty to Valentine in his early days of wandering, was a minor city indeed compared with this.

Only the Skandars, Khun, and Deliamber had seen Ni-moya before. Deliamber spoke of the city's marvels: its Gossamer Galleria, a mercantile arcade a mile long, raised above the ground on nearly invisible cables; its Park of Fabulous Beasts, where the rarest of Majipoor's fauna, those creatures brought closest to extinction by the spread of civilization, roved in surroundings approximating their natural habitats; its Crystal Boulevard, a glittering street of revolving reflectors that awed the eye; its Grand Bazaar, fifteen square miles of mazelike passageways housing uncountable thousands of tiny shops under continuous roofs of dazzling yellow sparklecloth; its Museum of Worlds, its Chamber of Sorcery, its Ducal Palace, built on a heroic scale said to be surpassed only by Lord Valentine's Castle, and many other things that sounded, to Valentine, more like the stuff of myth and fantasy than anything one might encounter in a real city. But they would see none of these things. The thousand-instrument municipal orchestra, the floating restaurants, the artificial birds with jeweled eyes, and all the rest would have to wait until, if ever the day came, he returned to Ni-moya in a Coronal's robes.

As the ferry neared the slip Valentine called everyone together and said, 'Now we must determine our individual courses. I mean to take passage here for Piliplok, and make my way from there to the Isle. I've prized your companionship this far, and I would have it even longer, but I can offer you nothing except endless journeying and the possibility of an early death. My hope of success is slight and the obstacles are formidable. Will any of you continue with me?'

'To the other side of the world!' Shanamir cried.

'And I,' said Sleet, and Vinorkis the same.

'Would you have doubted me?' Carabella asked.

Valentine smiled. He looked to Deliamber, who said, 'The sanctity of the realm is at stake. How could I not follow the rightful Coronal wherever he asks?'

'This mystifies me,' Lisamon Hultin said. 'I understand none of this business of a Coronal roaming out of his proper body. But I have no other employment, Valentine. I am with you.'

'I thank you all,' Valentine said. 'I will thank you again, and more grandly, in the feasting-hall on Castle Mount.'

Zalzan Kavol said, 'And have you no use for Skandars, my lord?'

Valentine had not expected that. 'Will you come?'

'Our wagon is lost. Our brotherhood is broken by death. We are without our juggling gear. I feel no calling to be a pilgrim, but I will follow you to the Isle and beyond, and so also will my brothers, if you want us.'

'I want you, Zalzan Kavol. Is there such a post as juggler to the royal court? You will have it, I promise!'

'Thank you, my lord,' said the Skandar gravely.

'There is one more volunteer,' said Khun.

'You too?' Valentine said in surprise.

The dour alien replied, 'It matters little to me who is king of this planet where I am stranded. But it matters much to me to behave honorably. I would be dead now in Piurifayne but for you. I owe you my life and I will give you such aid as I can.'

Valentine shook his head. 'We did for you only what any civilized being would do for any other. No debt exists.'

'I see it otherwise. Besides,' said Khun, 'my life until now has been trivial and shallow. I left my native Kianimot for no good reason to come here, and I lived foolishly here and nearly paid with my life, and why go on as I have been going? I will join your cause and make it mine, and perhaps I will come to believe in it, or feel that I do, and if I die to make you king, it will only even the debt between us. With a death well accomplished I can repay the universe for a life poorly spent. Can you use me?'

'With all my heart I welcome you,' Valentine said.

The ferry released a grand blast of its horn and glided smoothly into its slip.

They stayed the night at the cheapest waterfront hotel they could find, a clean but stark place of whitewashed stone walls and communal tubs, and treated themselves to a modestly lavish dinner at an inn nearby. Valentine called for a pooling of funds and appointed Shanamir and Zalzan Kavol joint treasurers, since they seemed to have the finest appreciation of the value and uses of money. Valentine himself had much remaining of the funds he had had in Pidruid, and Zalzan Kavol produced from a hidden pouch a surprising stack of ten-royal pieces. Together they had enough to get them all to the Isle of Sleep.

In the morning they bought passage aboard a riverboat similar to the one that had carried them from Khyntor to Verf, and began their voyage to Piliplok, the great port at the mouth of the Zimr.

For all they had traveled across the face of Zimroel, some thousands of miles still separated them from the east coast. But on the broad breast of the Zimr vessels moved swiftly and serenely. Of course, the riverboat stopped again and again at the innumerable towns and cities of the river,

Larnimisculus and Belka and Clarischanz, Flegit, Hiskuret, Centriun, Obliorn Vale, Salvamot, Gourkaine, Semirod and Cerinor and Haunfort Major, Impemond, Orgeliuse, Dambemuir, and many more, an unending flow of nearly indistinguishable places, each with its piers, its waterfront promenades, its planting of palms and alabandinas, its gaily painted warehouses and sprawling bazaars, its ticket-clutching passengers eager to come on board and impatient for departure once they had ascended the ramp. Sleet whittled juggling clubs out of some scraps of wood he begged from the crew, and Carabella found balls somewhere to juggle, and at meals the Skandars quietly palmed dishware and slipped it out of sight, so that the troupe gradually accumulated implements to work with, and from the third day on they earned some extra crowns by performing on the plaza-deck. Zalzan Kavol gradually regained some of his old gruff self-assurance now that he was performing again, although he still was oddly subdued, his soul moving on tiptoe through situations that once would have called forth angry storms.

This was the native territory of the four Skandars, who had been born in Piliplok and began their careers on circuit through the inland towns of the huge province, ranging as far upriver as Stenwamp and Port Saikforge, a thousand miles from the coast. This familiar countryside brightened them, these rolling tawny hills and bustling little cities of wooden buildings, and Zalzan Kavol spoke lengthily of his early career here, his successes and failures – very few of those – and of a dispute with an impresario that led him to seek fortune at the other end of Zimroel. Valentine suspected that there was some violence involved, perhaps some embroilment with the law, but he asked no questions.

One night after much wine the Skandars even broke into song, for the first time in Valentine's time with them – a Skandar song, mournful and lugubrious, sung in a minor key as the singers shuffled about and about in a slump shouldered circling march:

> *Dark my heart*
> *Dark my fears*
> *Dim my eyes*
> *All full of tears*
> *Death and woe,*
> *Death and woe,*
> *Follow us*
> *Where'er we go.*
> *Far the lands*
> *I used to roam.*
> *Far the hills*
> *And streams of home.*

Death and woe,
Death and woe,
Follow us
Where'er we go.
Seas of dragons,
Lands of pain,
I shall not see
My home again.
Death and woe,
Death and woe,
Follow us
Where'er we go.

The song was so unrelievedly gloomy, and the enormous Skandars looked so absurd as they lurched about chanting it, that it was all that Valentine and Carabella could do to hold back laughter at first. But by the second chorus Valentine actually found himself moved by it, for there seemed real emotion in the song: the Skandars *had* met death and woe, and though they were close to home now, they had spent much of their lives far from Piliplok; and perhaps, Valentine thought, it was a harsh and painful thing to be a Skandar on Majipoor, a shaggy-pelted creature moving ponderously in the warm air among smaller and sleeker beings.

The summer now was over, and in eastern Zimroel it was the dry season, when warm winds blew from the south, vegetation went dormant until the spring rains, and, so said Zalzan Kavol, tempers became short and crimes of passion common. Valentine found this region less interesting than the jungles of the mid-continent or the subtropic floribundance of the far west, though he decided after a few days of close observation that it did have a certain austere beauty of its own, restrained and severe, quite unlike the riotous lushness of the west. All the same, he was pleased and relieved when, after day upon day on this changeless and seemingly unending river, Zalzan Kavol announced that the outskirts of Piliplok were in view.

3

Piliplok was about as old and about as large as its counterpart port on the farther shore of the continent, Pidruid; but the resemblance went no deeper. For Pidruid had been built without a plan, a random tangle of streets and avenues and boulevards winding around one another according to whim, whereas Piliplok had been laid out, untold thousands of years ago, with rigid, almost maniacal, precision.

It occupied a promontory of great magnitude on the southern shore of the mouth of the Zimr. The river here was of inconceivable width, sixty or seventy miles across at the point where it flowed into the Inner Sea, and carrying a burden of silt and debris accumulated in all its swift seven-thousand-mile flow out of the far northwest, it stained the blue-green waters of the ocean with a dark tinge that, it was said, could be seen hundreds of miles out. The north headland at the rivermouth was a chalk cliff a mile high and many miles wide, which even from Piliplok was visible on a clear day, a shining white wall dazzling in the morning light. There was nothing over there that could in any way be used as a harbor, and so it had never been settled, but was set aside as a holy preserve. Devotees of the Lady lived there in a withdrawal from the world so total that no one had intruded on them in a hundred years. But Piliplok was another matter: eleven million people occupying a city that radiated in stern spokes from its magnificent natural harbor. A series of curving bands crossed the axis of these spokes, the inner ones mercantile, then zones of industry and recreation, and in the outer reaches the residential neighborhoods, fairly sharply delimited by levels of wealth and to a lesser degree by race. There was a heavy concentration of Skandars in Piliplok – it seemed to Valentine that every third person on the waterfront belonged to Zalzan Kavol's people – and it was a little intimidating to see so many giant hairy four-armers swaggering about. Here, too, lived many of the aloof and aristocratic two-headed Su-Suheris folk, dealers in luxury commodities, fine fabrics and jewelry and the rarest handicrafts of every province. The air here was crisp and dry, and, feeling the unyielding southerly wind hot against his cheeks, Valentine began to understand what Zalzan Kavol had meant about the short tempers kindled by that wind.

'Does it ever stop blowing?' he asked.

'On the first day of spring,' said Zalzan Kavol.

Valentine hoped to be elsewhere by then. But a problem immediately appeared. With Zalzan Kavol and Deliamber he went to Shkunibor Pier at the eastern end of Piliplok harbor to arrange transport to the Isle. For months now Valentine had imagined himself in this city and at that pier, and it had taken on an almost legendary glamor in his mind, a place of vast perspectives and sweeping architecture; and so it disappointed him more than a little to get there and find that the chief place of embarkation for the pilgrim-ships was a ramshackle, dilapidated structure, peeling green paint on its sides, tattered banners flapping in the wind.

Worse was in store. The pier seemed deserted. After some prowling Zalzan Kavol found a departure schedule posted in a dark corner of the ticket house.

Pilgrim-ships sailed for the Isle the first of every month – except in autumn, when sailings were spaced more widely because of prevailing unfavorable winds. The last ship of the season had departed a week ago Starday. The next left in three months.

'Three months!' Valentine cried, 'What will we do in Piliplok for three months? Juggle in the streets? Beg? Steal? Read the schedule again, Zalzan Kavol!'

'It will say the same,' the Skandar declared. He grimaced. 'I am fond of Piliplok beyond any place, but I have no love for it at wind-time. What foul luck!'

'Do no ships at all sail in this season?' Valentine asked.

'Only the dragon-ships,' said Zalzan Kavol.

'And what are they?'

'Fishing vessels, that prey on the sea-dragons, which come together in herds to mate at this time of year, and are easily taken. Plenty of dragon-ships set forth now. But what use are they to us?'

'How far out to sea do they go?' Valentine asked.

'As far as they must to make their catch. Sometimes as far as the Rodamaunt Archipelago, if the dragons are swarming easterly.'

'Where is that?'

Deliamber said, 'It is a long chain of islands far out in the Inner Sea, perhaps midway from here to the Isle of Sleep.'

'Inhabited?'

'Quite heavily.'

'Good. Surely there's commerce between islands, then. What if we hire one of these dragon-ships to take us on as passengers, and carry us as far as the Archipelago, and there we commission some local captain to transport us to the Isle?'

'Possibly,' Deliamber said.

'There's no rule requiring all pilgrims to arrive by pilgrim-ship?'

'None that I know of,' said the Vroon.

'The dragon-ships will not care to bother with passengers,' Zalzan Kavol objected. 'They never carry any such trade.'

'Would a few royals arouse their interest in doing so?'

The Skandar looked doubtful. 'I have no idea. Their trade's a lucrative one as it is. They might consider passengers a nuisance, or even bad luck. Nor would they necessarily agree to haul us out to the Archipelago, if it happens to lie beyond this year's hunting track. Nor can we be sure, even if we do reach the Archipelago, that anyone there would be willing to carry us farther.'

'On the other hand,' Valentine said, 'it might all be quite easy to arrange. We have money, and I'd rather use it persuading sea-captains to give us passage than spend it on lodgings and food for the next three months in Piliplok. Where can we find the dragon-hunters?'

An entire section of the waterfront spanning three or four miles was set apart for their use, pier after pier after pier, and there were dozens of the huge wooden vessels in harbor, being outfitted for the new hunting season just beginning. The dragon-ships were of one design, and an ominous and morbid one it was, Valentine thought, for they were great bloated things with flaring outbellying hulls and enormous fanciful three-pronged masts, and terrifying toothy figureheads at their prows and long spiky tails at their sterns. Most were decorated along their flanks with bold scarlet-and-yellow eye-patterns or rapacious-looking rows of white teeth; and high abovedecks were bristling cupolas for the harpooners and mammoth winches for the nets, and bloodstained platforms where the butchering took place. To Valentine it was incongruous to make use of such a killer-vessel in reaching the peaceful and holy Isle of Sleep. But he had no other way.

And even this way soon began to seem doubtful. From ship to ship they went, from wharf to wharf, from drydock to drydock, and the dragon-captains listened without interest to their proposal and made swift refusals. Zalzan Kavol did most of the speaking, for the captains were mainly Skandars and might give sympathetic ear to one of their own kind. But no persuasion would sway them.

'You would be a distraction to the crew,' said the first captain. 'Forever stumbling over gear, getting seasick, making special requests for service—'

'We are not chartered to carry passengers,' said the second. 'The rules are strict.'

'The Archipelago lies south of our preferred waters,' the third declared.

'I have long believed,' said the fourth, 'that a dragon-ship that goes to sea with strangers to the guild on board is a ship that will never return to Piliplok. I choose not to test that superstition this year.'

'Pilgrims are no concern of mine,' the fifth told them. 'Let the Lady waft you to the Isle, if she will. You won't get there aboard my ship.'

The sixth also refused, adding that no captain was likely to aid them. The seventh said the same. The eighth, having heard that a party of drylanders was wandering the docks looking for passage, refused even to speak with them.

The ninth captain, a grizzled old Skandar with gaps in her teeth and faded fur, was more friendly than the others, though just as unwilling to make room for them on her vessel. She did, at least, have a suggestion. 'On Prestimion Pier,' she said, 'you will find Captain Gorzval of the *Brangalyn*. Gorzval has made several unlucky voyages and is known to be short of funds; I heard him in a tavern just the other night trying to arrange a loan to pay for repairs to his hull. It may be that some extra revenue from passengers would be useful to him now.'

'And where is Prestimion Pier?' Zalzan Kavol asked.

'The farthest in this line, beyond Dekkeret and Kinnikeh, just west of the salvage-yard.'

A berth close by the salvage-yard seemed appropriate for the *Brangalyn*, Valentine thought bleakly an hour later, upon having his first view of Captain Gorzval's vessel. It looked about ready to be broken up for scrap. It was a smaller and older ship than the others he had seen, and at some point in its long history it must have suffered a staved hull, for in its rebuilding it had become malproportioned, with mismatched timbers and an oddly sloping look to starboard. The painted eyes and teeth along the waterline had lost their luster; the figurehead was awry; the tailspikes had been snapped off eight or ten feet from their mountings, perhaps a petulant swipe by an angry dragon; the masts had lost some of their yards also. Crewmen with a sluggish and dispirited look to them were at work, but not in any very effective way, caulking and coiling ropes and mending sail.

Captain Gorzval himself seemed as weary and worn as his vessel. He was a Skandar not quite as tall as Lisamon Hultin – virtually a dwarf among his race – with a cast in one eye and a stump where his outer left arm should be. His fur was matted and coarse; his shoulders were slumped; his entire look was one of fatigue and defeat. But he brightened immediately at Zalzan Kavol's query about taking passengers to the Rodamaunt Archipelago.

'How many?'

'Twelve. Four Skandars, a Hjort, a Vroon, five humans, and one – other.'

'All pilgrims, you say?'

'All pilgrims.'

Gorzval made the sign of the Lady in a perfunctory way and said, 'You know it's irregular for passengers to travel on a dragonship. But I owe the Lady recompense for past favors received. I'm willing to make an exception. Cash in advance?'

'Of course,' said Zalzan Kavol.

Valentine quickly released his breath. This was a miserable dilapidated ship, and Gorzval probably a third-rate navigator dogged by bad fortune or even downright incompetence; nevertheless, he was willing to take them, and no one else would even entertain the idea.

Gorzval named his price and waited, with obvious tension, to be haggled with. What he asked was less than half what they had unsuccessfully offered the other captains. Zalzan Kavol, bargaining out of habit and pride, no doubt, attempted to cut three royals from that. Gorzval, plainly dismayed, offered a reduction of a royal and a half; Zalzan Kavol appeared ready to shave another few crowns, but Valentine, pitying the hapless captain, cut in quickly to say, 'Done. When do we sail?'

'In three days,' Gorzval said.

It turned out to be four, actually – Gorzval spoke vaguely of some need for additional refitting, by which he meant, Valentine discovered, patching of some fairly serious leaks. He had not been able to afford it until his passengers had hired on. According to the gossip in the dockside taverns, Lisamon Hultin reported, Gorzval had been trying to mortgage part of his catch to raise the money for carpenters, but found no takers. He had, she said, a doubtful reputation: his judgment was inferior, his luck poor, his crew ill-paid and shiftless. Once he had missed the sea-dragon swarm entirely and returned empty to Piliplok; on another voyage he had lost his arm to a lively little dragon not quite as dead as he thought; and on this last one the *Brangalyn* had been struck amidships by an irritated beast and nearly sent to the bottom. 'We might do better,' Lisamon Hultin suggested, 'by trying to swim to the Isle.'

'Possibly we'll bring our captain better luck than he's had,' said Valentine.

Sleet laughed. 'If optimism alone could carry one to the throne, my lord, you'd be on Castle Mount by Winterday.'

Valentine laughed with him. But after the disaster in Piurifayne he hoped he was not leading these folk into new catastrophe aboard this ill-favored vessel. They were following him, after all, on faith alone, on the evidence of dreams and wizardry and an enigmatic Metamorph prank: it would be shame and pain for him if, in his haste to reach the Isle, he caused them more grief. Yet Valentine felt powerful sympathy for the bedraggled stump-armed Gorzval. An unlucky mariner he might be – but a fitting helmsman, perhaps, for a Coronal so frowned upon by fortune that he had managed to lose throne and memory and identity all in a single night!

On the eve of the *Brangalyn*'s departure Vinorkis drew Valentine aside and said in a troubled tone, 'My lord, we are being watched.'

'How do you know?'

The Hjort smiled and preened his orange mustachios. 'When one has done a little spying, one recognizes the traits in others. I've noticed a grayish Skandar lounging around the docks these past few days, asking questions of Gorzval's people. One of the ship's carpenters told me he was curious about the passengers Gorzval had taken on, and about our destination.'

Valentine scowled. 'I hoped we had shaken them off our track in the jungles!'

'They must have discovered us again in Ni-moya, my lord.'

'Then we must lose them again in the Archipelago,' said Valentine. 'And be wary until then of other spies along our way. I thank you, Vinorkis.'

'No thanks are needed, my lord. It is my duty.'

A strong wind blew from the south in the morning when the ship set forth. Vinorkis kept close look for the inquisitive Skandar at the pier during the embarkation, but he was nowhere in view; his work was done, Valentine supposed, and some other informant farther on would continue the surveillance on the usurper's behalf.

The route lay to the east and south; these dragon-ships were accustomed to tack against that constant hostile wind all the way to the hunting-grounds. It was a wearying business, but there was no avoiding it, for the sea-dragons were within the reach of hunters only at this season. The *Brangalyn* had supplementary engine power, but not any great deal of it, fuels of all kinds being so scarce on Majipoor. With a certain majestic clumsiness the *Brangalyn* picked up the side wind and moved out of Piliplok harbor into the open sea.

This was the smaller sea of Majipoor, the Inner Sea, which separated eastern Zimroel from western Alhanroel. It was no trifle – some five thousand miles from shore to shore – yet it was a mere puddle compared with the Great Sea that occupied most of the other hemisphere, an ocean beyond the possibility of navigation, untold thousands of miles of open water. The Inner Sea was more human in scale, and was broken midway between the continents by the Isle of Sleep – itself big enough so that on another world, of less extraordinary size, it would be considered a continent – and by several major island chains.

The sea-dragons spent their lives in unending migration between the two oceans. Round and round the globe they went, taking years or even decades, so far as anyone knew, to make the circumnavigation. Perhaps a dozen great herds of them inhabited the ocean, traveling constantly from west to east. Every summer one of those herds would complete its journey across the Great Sea, passing south of Narabal and up the southern coast of Zimroel toward Piliplok. It was forbidden to hunt them then, for the herd abounded at that time with pregnant cows. By autumn the young were born, the herd now having reached the windswept water between Piliplok and the Isle of Sleep, and the annual hunt began. Out from Piliplok came the dragon-ships in great numbers. The herds were thinned of both young and old, and the survivors made their way back into the tropics, passing south of the Isle of Sleep, rounding the hump of Alhanroel's lengthy Stoienzar Peninsula, and heading on eastward below Alhanroel to the Great Sea, where they would swim unmolested until their time brought them round to Piliplok again.

Of all the beasts of Majipoor, the sea-dragons were by far the largest. Newborn, they were tiny, no more than five or six feet in length, but through all their lives they continued to grow, and their lifespans were long, although no one knew just how long. Gorzval, who let his passengers share his table and proved to be a talkative man now that his anxieties were behind him, was fond of telling tales of the immensity of certain sea-dragons. One that had been taken in the reign of Lord Malibor was a hundred and ninety feet in length, and another, of Confalume's time, two hundred and forty, and in the era when Prestimion was Pontifex and Lord Dekkeret the Coronal they had caught one thirty feet longer than that. But the champion, said Gorzval, was one that had boldly appeared almost in the mouth of Piliplok harbor in the reign of Thimin and Lord Kinniken, and had reliably been measured at three hundred and fifteen feet. That monster, known as Lord Kinniken's dragon, had escaped unharmed because the entire fleet of dragon-ships was then far out to sea. Allegedly it had been sighted again several times by hunters in succeeding centuries, most recently in the year Lord Voriax became Coronal, but no one had ever laid a harpoon on it, and among hunters it had a baleful reputation. 'It must be five hundred feet long by now,' said Gorzval, 'and I pray that some other captain is given the honor of encountering it when it returns to our waters.'

Valentine had seen small sea-dragons, pithed, gutted, salted, and dried, sold in marketplaces all over Zimroel, and on occasion he had tasted their meat, which was dark, tangy, and tough. Dragons less than ten feet long were the ones prepared in this way. The meat of larger ones, up to fifty feet or so, was butchered and sold fresh along the eastern coast of Zimroel, but difficulties of transportation kept it from finding markets far from the sea. Beyond that length the dragons were too old to be edible, but their flesh was rendered into oil that had many purposes, petroleum and other fossil hydrocarbons being scarce on Majipoor, The bones of sea-dragons of all sizes had their uses in architecture, for they were nearly as strong as steel and far more readily obtained, and there was medicinal value in the unborn dragon-eggs, found in quantities of many hundreds of pounds in the abdomens of mature females. Dragon-skin, dragon-wings, dragon this and dragon that, everything was put to some benefit and nothing wasted. 'This, for example, is dragon-milk,' said Gorzval, offering his guests a flask of a pale bluish liquid. 'In Ni-moya or Khyntor they'd pay ten crowns for a flask like this. Here, taste it.'

Lisamon Hultin took a hesitant sip and spat it on the floor. 'Dragon-milk or dragon-piss?' she demanded.

The captain smiled frostily. 'In Dulorn,' he said, 'what you spat out would cost you at least a crown, and you'd count yourself lucky to find some.' He pushed the flask toward Sleet, who shook his head, and then to Valentine. After a moment's pause Valentine put it to his lips.

'Bitter,' he said, 'and a musty taste, but not entirely terrible. What's the secret of its appeal?'

The Skandar patted his thighs. 'Aphrodisiac!' he boomed. 'Stirs the juices! Heats the blood! Prolongs the life!' He pointed jovially at Zalzan Kavol, who, unasked, had taken a robust swig of the stuff. 'See? The Skandar knows! The man of Piliplok doesn't need to be begged to drink it!'

Carabella said, 'Dragon-*milk*? These are mammals?'

'Mammals, yes. The eggs are hatched within, so, and the young born alive, ten or twenty in a litter, rows of nipples all up and down the belly. You think it's odd, milk from dragons?'

'I think of dragons as reptiles,' said Carabella, 'and reptiles give no milk.'

'Think of dragons as dragons, better. You want to taste?'

'Thank you, no,' she replied. 'My juices need no stirring.'

The meals in the captain's cabin were the best part of the voyage, Valentine decided. Gorzval was good-natured and outgoing, as Skandars went, and he set a decent table, with wine and meats and fish of various sorts, including a good deal of dragon-flesh. But the ship itself was creaky and cramped, poorly designed and even more poorly maintained, and the crew, a dozen Skandars and an assortment of Hjorts and humans, was uncommunicative and often downright hostile. Obviously these dragon-hunters were a proud and insular lot, even the crew of a bedraggled vessel like the *Brangalyn*, and resented the presence of outsiders among them as they practiced their mysteries. Only Gorzval seemed at all hospitable; but he clearly felt grateful to them, for their fare was all that had allowed him to get his ship seaworthy.

They were far from land now, in a featureless realm where pale blue ocean met pale blue sky to obliterate all sense of place and direction. The course was south-southeasterly, and the farther they got from Piliplok the warmer grew the wind, hot now and dry as ever. 'We call the wind our sending,' said Gorzval, 'because it comes straight from Suvrael. The little gift of the King of Dreams, it is, as delightful as all his others.' The sea was empty: no islands, no drifting logs, no sign of anything, not even dragons. The dragons had gone far past the coast this year, as they sometimes did, and were basking in the tropical waters close by the fringes of the Archipelago. Occasionally a gihorna-bird passed far overhead, making its autumn migration from the islands to the Zimr Marsh, which was not near the Zimr at all but on the coast five hundred miles south of Piliplok; these long-legged creatures must have made tempting targets, but no one took aim at them. Another tradition of the sea, it seemed.

The first dragons manifested themselves the second week out from Piliplok. Gorzval predicted their arrival a day in advance, having dreamed that they were near. 'Every captain dreams dragons,' he explained. 'Our minds are attuned to them: we feel their souls approaching us. There's a captain, a woman with some teeth out, Guidrag's her name, who can dream them a week away, sometimes more. Heads right to them and they're always there. Me, I'm not that good, can't do better than a day's distance. But nobody's as good as Guidrag, anyway. I do my best. We'll have dragons off the bow in another ten, twelve hours, that's a guarantee.'

Valentine had little confidence in the Skandar captain's guarantees. But in mid-morning the lookout high in the mast sang out, 'Hoy! Dragons ho!'

A great many of them, forty, fifty, maybe more, swarmed just off the *Brangalyn*'s bow. They were big-bellied ungraceful beasts, broad in cross-section like the *Brangalyn* itself, with long thick necks, heavy triangular heads, short tails terminating in flat flaring flukes, and prominent ridges of bony projections running the length of their high-vaulted backs. Their wings were the strangest feature of all – fins, really, for it was inconceivable that these huge creatures should ever take to the air, but they looked far more like wings than fins, batwings, dark and leathery, sprouting from massive stumpy bases below the sea-dragons' neck and sweeping down half the length of their bodies. Most of the dragons kept their wings folded like cloaks, but some had them fully outspread, fanning them out along the axes provided by long fragile-looking finger-bones, and with them they covered the water about them for astonishing spreads, unfurling them like black tarpaulins.

Most of the dragons were young, twenty to fifty feet in length, but there were many newborn ones, six-footers or thereabouts, swimming and splashing freely or else gripping the nipples of their mothers, who tended to be of mid-size range. But among the school drifted a few monsters, half submerged and somnolent, their spine-ridges rising high above the water like the central hills of some floating island. They were unimaginably bulky. It was hard to judge their full magnitude, for their hindquarters tended to droop out of sight, but two or three of them looked at least as large as the ship. As Gorzval passed him on the deck Valentine said, 'We don't have Lord Kinniken's dragon out there, do we?'

The Skandar captain chuckled indulgently. 'Nay, the Kinniken's three times the size of those, at least. Three? More than three! Those are hardly hundred-fifty-footers. I've seen dozens bigger. So will you, friend, before long.'

Valentine tried to imagine dragons three times the size of the biggest out there. His mind rebelled. It was like trying to visualize the full scope of Castle Mount: one simply could not do it

The ship moved in for the kill. It was a smoothly coordinated operation. Boats were lowered, with a lance-wielding Skandar strapped upright in the bow of each. Among the nursing dragons the boats quietly moved, the lancer spearing one here, one there, apportioning the kill among the mothers so that none was aroused by total loss of her young. These young dragons were lashed by their tails to the boats; and as the boats returned to the ship, nets were lowered to hoist the catch. Only when some dozen young dragons had been taken did the hunters go for bigger game. The boats were retracted and the harpooner, a giant Skandar with a naked dull-blue swath across his chest where the fur had long ago been ripped away, took his place in the cupola. Unhurriedly he selected his weapon and nocked it into its catapult while Gorzval maneuvered the ship to give him a good shot at the chosen victim. The harpooner took aim; the dragons grazed on, heedless; Valentine discovered that he was holding his breath and intently squeezing Carabella's hand. Then the gleaming somber shaft of the harpoon was released.

It buried itself to its haft in the blubbery shoulder of a dragon some ninety feet long and instantly the sea came alive.

The wounded dragon lashed the surface with its tail and unfurled its wings, which beat against the water in a titanic fury, as though the animal meant to burst into the air and soar off, dragging the dangling *Brangalyn* behind it. At that first frantic outburst of pain the mother-dragons opened their wings as well, gathering their nurslings into a protective shield, and with powerful strokes of their tails began to move away, while the largest of the herd, the utter monsters, simply sank from view, letting themselves glide into the depths with scarcely a ripple of energy. This left a dozen or so adolescent dragons, who knew that something disturbing was happening but were not sure how to react; they swam in wide circles around their wounded comrade, holding their wings tentatively half-spread and slapping lightly at the water with them. Meanwhile the harpooner, still choosing his weapons in absolute tranquillity, put a second and a third into his prey, close by the first.

'Boats!' cried Gorzval. 'Nets!'

Now began a strange proceeding. Once more the boats were lowered, and the hunters rowed forth. Toward the ring of excited dragons they headed, and hurled into the water grenades of some sort that exploded with dull booming sounds, spreading a thick coating of bright yellow dye. The explosions and, it seemed, the dye sent the remaining dragons into a frenzy of terror. With wild thrashings of wings and tails they swam swiftly out of sight. Only the victim remained, very much alive but held fast. It too was swimming, in an northerly direction, but it towed the entire mass of the *Brangalyn* along behind it, and it was visibly weakened moment by moment by the effort. The boatmen, with their dye-grenades, attempted to force the dragon closer to the ship; at the same time the netmen lowered a colossal webwork of fabric which by some interior mechanism opened and spread out over the water, and closed again when the dragon had entangled itself in its meshes.

'Winches!' Gorzval roared, and the net rose from the water.

The dragon dangled in mid-air. Its enormous weight caused the huge ship to list alarmingly. Far above, the harpooner rose in his cupola for the coup de grace. He gripped the catapult with all four hands and let fly. A ferocious grunt came from him as he released the weapon and an instant later came an answering sound, hollow, agonized, from the dragon. The harpoon penetrated the dragon's skull at a point just behind the great saucerlike green eyes. The mighty wings raked the air in one last terrible convulsion.

The rest was mere butchery. The winches did their work, the dragon was hoisted to the slaughter-block, the stripping of the carcass began. Valentine watched awhile, until the gory spectacle palled: the flensing of the blubber, the securing of the valuable internal organs, the severing of the wings, and all the rest. When he had had enough he went below, and when he returned a few hours later the skeleton of the dragon rose like a museum exhibit over the deck, a great white arch topped by that bizarre spiny ridge, and the hunters were at work disassembling even that.

'You look grim,' Carabella said to him.

'I lack appreciation of this art,' he answered.

It seemed to Valentine that Gorzval could entirely have filled the hold of his vessel, large as it was, with the proceeds of this one school of dragons. But he had chosen a handful of young and only one adult, not by any means the largest, and had deliberately driven the others away. Zalzan Kavol explained that there were quotas, decreed by Coronals in centuries past, to prevent overfishing: herds were to be thinned, not exterminated, and a ship that returned too soon from its voyage would be called to account and subjected to severe penalties. Besides, it was essential to get the dragons quickly on board, before predators arrived, and to process the flesh swiftly; a crew that hunted too greedily would be unable to handle its own catch in an effective and profitable way.

The season's first kill seemed to make Gorzval's crew more mellow. They nodded occasionally at the passengers, even smiled now and then, and went about their own tasks in a relaxed and almost cheerful way. Their sullen silence melted; they laughed, joked, sang on deck:

> *Lord Malibor was fine and bold*
> *And loved the heaving sea,*
> *Lord Malibor came off the Mount,*
> *A hunter for to be.*
> *Lord Malibor prepared his ship,*
> *A gallant sight was she,*
> *With sails of beaten gold,*
> *And masts of ivory.*

Valentine and Carabella heard the singers – it was the squad barreling the blubber – and went aft to listen more closely. Carabella, quickly picking up the simple robust melody, quietly began to finger it on her pocket-harp, adding little fanciful cadenzas between the verses.

> *Lord Malibor stood at the helm*
> *And faced the heaving wave,*

And sailed in quest of the dragon free,
The dragon fierce and brave.
Lord Malibor a challenge called,
His voice did boom and ring.
'I wish to meet, I wish to fight,'
Quoth he, 'the dragon-king.'
'I hear, my lord,' the dragon cried,
And came across the sea.
Twelve miles long and three miles wide
And two miles deep was he.

'Look,' Carabella said. 'There's Zalzan Kavol.'

Valentine glanced across the way. Yes, there was the Skandar, listening at the far side near the rail, all his arms folded, a deepening scowl on his face. He did not seem to be enjoying the song. What was the matter with him?

Lord Malibor stood on the deck
And fought both hard and well.
Thick was the blood that flowed that day
And great the blows that fell.
But dragon-kings are cold and sly,
And rarely are they beaten.
Lord Malibor, for all his strength,
Eventually was eaten.
All sailors bold, who dragons hunt,
Of this grim tale take heed!
Despite all luck and skill, you may
End up as dragon-feed.

Valentine laughed and clapped his hands. That brought an immediate fierce glare from Zalzan Kavol, who strode toward them looking huffy with indignation.

'My lord!' he cried. 'Will you tolerate such irreverent—'

'Not so loud on the *my lord*,' Valentine said crisply. 'Irreverent, you say? What are you talking about?'

'No respect for a terrible tragedy! No respect for a fallen Coronal! No respect for—'

'Zalzan Kavol!' Valentine said slyly. 'Are you such a lover of respectability, then?'

'I know what is right and what is wrong, my lord. To mock the death of Lord Malibor is—'

'Be more easy, my friend,' Valentine said gently, putting his hand on one of the Skandar's gigantic forearms. 'Where Lord Malibor has gone, he is far beyond matters of respect or disrespect. And I thought the song was a delight. If *I* take no offense, Zalzan Kavol, why should you?'

But Zalzan Kavol continued to grumble and bluster. 'If I may say it, my lord, you may not yet be returned to a full sense of the rightness of things. If I were you, I would go to those sailors now and order them never to sing such a thing again in your presence.'

'In my presence?' Valentine said, with a broad grin. 'Why should they care dragon-spittle for my presence? Who am I but a passenger, barely tolerated at all? If I said any such thing, I'd be over the rail in a minute, and dragon-feed myself the next. Eh? Think about it, Zalzan Kavol! And calm yourself, fellow. It's only a silly sailor-song.'

'Nevertheless,' the Skandar muttered, walking stiffly away.

Carabella giggled. 'He takes himself so seriously.'

Valentine began to hum, then to sing:

> *All sailors bold, who dragons hunt,*
> *Of this—*
> *Of this sad tale?—*
> *Of this said tale take heed!*

'Yes, that's it,' he said. 'Love, will you do me a service? When those men are through with their work, draw one of them aside – the red-bearded one, I think, with the deep bass voice – and have him teach you the words. And then teach them to me. And I can sing it to Zalzan Kavol to make him smile, eh? How does it go? Let's see—'

> *'I hear, my lord,' the dragon cried,*
> *And came across the sea.*
> *Twelve miles long and three miles wide*
> *And two miles deep was he—*

A week or thereabouts passed before they sighted dragons again, and in that time not only Carabella and Valentine learned the ditty, but Lisamon Hultin as well, who took pleasure in bellowing it across the decks in her raucous baritone. But Zalzan Kavol continued to growl and snort whenever he heard it.

The second school of dragons was much larger than the first, and Gorzval allowed the taking of some two dozen small ones, one mid-sized, and one titan at least a hundred and thirty feet long. That kept all hands busy for the next few days. The deck ran purple with dragons' blood, and bones and wings were stacked all over the ship as the crew labored to get everything down to storable size. At the captain's table delicacies were offered, from the most mysterious inner parts of the creature, and Gorzval, ever more expansive, brought forth casks of fine wines, quite unsuspected from someone who had been at the edge of bankruptcy. 'Piliplok golden,' he said, pouring with a lavish hand. 'I have saved this wine for some special occasion, and doubtless this is it. You have brought us excellent luck.'

'Your fellow captains will not be joyed to hear that,' Valentine said. 'We might easily have sailed with them, if they had only known how charmed we were.'

'Their loss, our gain. To your pilgrimage, my friends!' cried the Skandar captain.

They were moving now through ever more balmy waters. The hot wind out of Suvrael relented here at the edge of the tropics, and a kinder, moister breeze came to them out of the southwest, from the distant Stoienzar Peninsula of Alhanroel. The water was a deep green hue, sea-birds were numerous, algae grew so thick in places that navigation was sometimes impeded, and brightly colored fish could be seen darting just below the surface – the prey of the dragons, who were flesh-eaters and swam open-mouthed through swarms of lesser sea-creatures. The Rodamaunt Archipelago now lay not far away, Gorzval proposed to complete his haul here: the *Brangalyn* had room for another few large dragons, two more of mid-size, and perhaps forty of the small, and then he would drop his passengers and head for Piliplok to market his catch.

'Dragons ho!' came the lookout's cry.

This was the greatest school yet, hundreds of them, spiny humps rising above the water everywhere. For two days the *Brangalyn* moved among them, slaughtering at will. On the horizon other ships could be seen, but they were far off, for strict rules governed impinging on hunting territory.

Gorzval seemed to glow with the success of his voyage. He himself took frequent turns in the boat-crews, which Valentine gathered was unusual, and once he even made his way to the cupola to wield a harpoon. The ship now was settling low to the waterline with the weight of dragon-flesh.

On the third day dragons were still close about them, undismayed by the carnage and unwilling to scatter. 'One more big one,' Gorzval vowed, 'and then we make for the islands.'

He selected an eighty-footer for the final target.

Valentine had grown bored, and more than bored, with the butchery, and as the harpooner sent his third shaft into the prey he turned away, and walked to the far side of the deck. There he found Sleet, and they stood by the rail, peering off to the east.

'Do you think we can see the Archipelago from here?' Valentine asked.

'I long for solid land again, and an end to the stink of dragon-blood in my nostrils.'

'My eyes are keen, my lord, but the islands are two days' sailing from here, and I think even my vision has limits. But—' Sleet gasped. 'My lord—'

'What is it?'

'An island comes swimming toward us, my lord!'

Valentine stared, but with difficulty at first: it was morning and a brilliant fiery glare lit the surface of the sea. But Sleet took Valentine's hand and pointed with it, and then Valentine saw. A ridged dragon-spine broke the water, a spine that went on and on and on, and below it a vast and implausible bulk was dimly visible.

'Lord Kinniken's dragon!' Valentine said in a choked voice. 'And it comes straight at us!'

4

Kinniken's it might be, or more likely some other not nearly so great, but it was great enough, larger than the *Brangalyn*, and it was bearing down on them steadily and unhesitatingly – either an avenging angel or else an unthinking force, there was no knowing that, but its mass was unarguable.

'Where is Gorzval?' Sleet blurted. 'Weapons – guns—?'

Valentine laughed. 'As easily stop a rock-slide with a harpoon, Sleet. Are you a good swimmer?'

Most of the hunters were preoccupied with their catch. But some had looked the other way now, and there was frantic activity on deck. The harpooner had whirled round and stood outlined against the sky, weapons in every hand. Others had mounted the adjoining cupolas. Valentine, searching for Carabella and Deliamber and the others, caught sight of Gorzval rushing madly toward the helm; the Skandar's face was livid and his eyes were bugging, and he looked like one who stood in the presence of the ministers of death.

'Lower the boats!' someone screamed. Winches turned. Figures ran about wildly. One, a Hjort black-cheeked with fear, shook a fist at Valentine and caught him roughly by the arm, muttering, 'You brought this on us! You should never have been allowed on board, any of you!'

Lisamon Hultin appeared from somewhere and swept the Hjort aside like so much chaff. Then she flung her powerful arms around Valentine as if to protect him from any harm that might come.

'The Hjort was right, you know,' said Valentine calmly. 'We *are* an ill-omened bunch. First Zalzan Kavol loses his wagon, and now poor Gorzval loses—'

There was a ghastly impact as the onrushing dragon crashed broadside into the *Brangalyn*.

The ship heeled over as though it had been pushed by a giant's hand, then rolled dizzyingly back the other way. An awful shudder shook its timbers. A secondary impact came – the wings hitting the hull, the thrashing flukes? – and then another, and the *Brangalyn* bobbed like a cork. 'We're stove in!' a desperate voice cried. Things rolled free on the deck, a giant rendering cauldron breaking its moorings and tumbling over three hapless crewmen, a case of boning-axes ripping loose and skidding over the side. As the ship continued to sway and lurch, Valentine caught a glimpse of the great dragon on the far side, where the recent catch still hung, unbalancing everything; and the monster swung around and headed in for another attack. There could be no doubt now of the purposefulness of its onslaught.

The dragon struck, shoulder-side on; the *Brangalyn* rocked wildly; Valentine grunted as Lisamon Hultin's grip became an almost crushing embrace. He had no idea where any of the others might be, nor whether they would survive. Clearly the ship was doomed. Already it was listing badly as water poured into the hold. The tail of the dragon rose nearly to deck-level and struck again. Everything dissolved into chaos. Valentine felt himself flying; he soared gracefully, he dipped and bobbed, he plunged with elegance and skill toward the water.

He landed in something much like a whirlpool and was drawn down into the terrible turbulent spin.

As he went under Valentine could not help but hear the ballad of Lord Malibor ringing in his mind. In truth that Coronal had taken a fancy to dragon-hunting some ten years back, and had gone out in what was said to be the finest dragon-ship in Piliplok, and the ship had been lost with all hands. No one knew what had happened, but – so it came out of Valentine's spotty recollections – the government had spoken of a sudden storm. More likely, he thought, it had been this killer-beast, this avenger of dragonkind.

Twelve miles long and three miles wide
And two miles deep was he—

And now a second Coronal, successor but one to Malibor, would meet the same fate. Valentine was oddly unmoved by that. He had thought himself dying in the rapids of the Steiche, and had survived that; here, with a hundred miles of sea between him and any sort of safety, and a rampaging monster lashing about close at hand, he was even more surely doomed, but there was no use bemoaning it. The Divine had clearly withdrawn its favor from him. What grieved him was that others whom he loved would die with him, merely because they had been loyal, because they had pledged themselves to follow him on his journey to the Isle, because they had tied themselves to a luckless Coronal and a luckless dragon-captain and now must share their evil destinies.

He was sucked deep into the heart of the ocean and ceased to ponder the tides of luck. He struggled for breath, coughed, choked, spat out water and swallowed more. His head pounded mercilessly. *Carabella*, he thought, and darkness engulfed him.

Valentine had never, since awakening out of his broken past to find himself near Pidruid, given much thought to a philosophy of death. Life held challenges enough for him. He recalled vaguely what he had been taught in boyhood, that all souls return to the Divine Source at their last moment when the release of life-energy comes, and travel over the Bridge of Farewells, the bridge that is the prime responsibility of the Pontifex. But whether there might be truth in that, whether there was a world beyond, and if so of what sort, Valentine had never paused to consider. Now, though, he returned to consciousness in a place so strange that it surpassed the imaginings of even the most fertile of thinkers.

Was this the afterlife? It was a giant chamber, a great silent room with thick moist pink walls and a roof that was in places high and domed, supported by mighty pillars, and in other places drooped until it nearly touched the floor. In that roof were mounted huge glowing hemispheres that emitted a faint blue light, as if by phosphorescence. The air in here was rank and steamy, and had a sharp, bitter flavor, unpleasant and stifling. Valentine lay on his side against a wet slippery surface, rough to the touch, deeply corrugated, quivering with constant deep palpitations and tremors. He put the flat of his hand to it and felt a kind of convulsion deep within. The texture of the ground was like nothing he had known before, and those tiny but perceptible motions within it made him wonder if what he had entered was not the world after death but merely some grotesque hallucination.

Valentine got unsteadily to his feet. His clothing was soaked, he had lost one boot somewhere, his lips burned with the taste of salt, his lungs seemed full of water, and he felt shaky and dazed; furthermore it was hard to keep upright on this unendingly trembling surface. Looking about, he saw by the dim pale luminosity a kind of vegetation, pliant whip-shaped growths, thick and fleshy and leafless, sprouting from the ground. They too writhed with inner animation. Making his way between two lofty pillars and through an area where ceiling and floor almost met, he caught sight of what seemed to be a pond of some greenish fluid. Beyond that he was unable to see in the dimness.

He walked toward the pond and perceived something exceedingly odd in it: hundreds of brightly colored fish, of the kind that he had seen flitting about in the water before the day's hunt had begun. They were not swimming now. They were dead and decaying, flesh stripping away from bones, and below them in the pool was a carpet of similar bones, many feet thick.

Suddenly there was a sound as of the roaring of the wind behind him. Valentine turned. The walls of the chamber were in motion, pulling back, the drooping places in the ceiling retracting to create a vast open space; and a torrent of water came rushing toward him, as high as his hips. He barely had time to reach one of the ceiling-pillars and fling his arms tight about it; then the inrushing of water sluiced about him with tremendous force. He held on. It seemed that half the Inner Sea was pouring past him, and for a moment he thought he would lose his grip, but then the flow subsided and the water drained away through slits that materialized abruptly in the floor – leaving in its wake scores of stranded fish. The floor convulsed; the fleshy whips swept the desperate flopping fish across the floor to the greenish pool; and once they entered it they quickly ceased to move.

Suddenly Valentine understood.

I am not dead, he knew, nor is this any place of afterlife. I am within the belly of the dragon.

He began to laugh.

Valentine threw back his head and let giant guffaws pour from him. What other response was fitting? To cry? To curse? The vast beast had gobbled him whole at a gulp, had sucked in the Coronal of Majipoor as heedlessly as it might a minnow. But he was too big to be propelled into that digestive pond down there, so here he was, camped on the floor of the dragon's maw, in this cathedral of an alimentary canal. What now? Hold court for the fishes? Dispense justice among them as they came sweeping in? Settle down here and spend the rest of his days dining on raw fish stolen from the monster's catch?

It was high comedy, Valentine thought.

But dark tragedy as well, for Sleet and Carabella and young Shanamir and all the others, drawn down to death in the wreck of the *Brangalyn*, victims of their own sympathies and of his awesomely bad luck. For them he felt only anguish. Carabella's lilting voice silenced forever, and Sleet's miraculous skills of hand and eye forever lost, and the rough-souled Skandars no longer to fill the air with whirling multitudes of knives and sickles and torches, and Shanamir cut off before he had fairly begun his life—

Valentine could not bear thinking about them.

For himself, though, there was only cosmic amusement at this absurd plight. To take his mind from grief and pain and loss he laughed again, and stretched his arms wide to the distant walls of the strange room. 'Lord Valentine's Castle, this is!' he cried. 'The throne-room! I invite you all to dine with me in the grand feasting-hall!'

Out of the murky distance a booming voice called, 'By my gut, I accept that invitation!'

Valentine was astounded beyond all measure.

'Lisamon?'

'No, it's the Pontifex Tyeveras and his cross-eyed uncle! Is that you, Valentine?'

'Yes! Where are you?'

'In the gizzard of this stinking dragon! Where are you?'

'Not far from you! But I can't see you!'

'Sing,' she called. 'Stay where you are and sing, and keep singing! I'll try to reach you!'

Valentine began, in the loudest voice he could muster:

> *Lord Malibor was fine and bold*
> *And loved the heaving sea—*

Again the roaring sound came; again the great creature's gullet opened to admit a cascade of sea-water, and a horde of fish; again Valentine clung to a pillar as the influx hit him.

'Oh – by the Divine's toes,' Lisamon cried. 'Hang on, Valentine, hang on!'

He hung on until the force was spent, and slumped against the pillar, soaked, panting. Somewhere in the distance the giantess called to him, and he called back. Her voice grew nearer. She urged him to keep singing, and he did:

> *Lord Malibor stood at the helm*
> *And faced the heaving wave.*
> *And sailed in quest of the dragon free—*

He heard her occasionally bawling a snatch of the ballad herself, with amiably bawdy embellishments, as she approached through the intricacies of the dragon's interior, and then he looked up and saw by the faint luminous light her enormous form looming above him. He smiled at her. She smiled, and laughed, and he laughed with her, and they clasped one another in a wet, slippery embrace.

But the sight of one who had survived put him in mind again of those who surely had not, and plunged him once more into grief and shame. He turned away, biting at his lip.

'My lord?' she said puzzledly.

'Only we two remain, Lisamon.'

'Yes, and praises be for that!'

'But the others – they'd live now, if they hadn't been so stupid as to go chasing across the world with me—'

She caught him by the arm. 'My lord, will mourning them bring them back to life, if dead they be?'

'I know all that. But—'

'We are safe. If we have lost our friends, my lord, that's cause for sorrow indeed, but not for guilt. They followed you of their own free choice, eh, my lord? And if their time has come, well, it is because their time has come, and how could that have been otherwise? Will you give up this grief, my lord, and rejoice that we are safe?'

He shrugged. 'Safe, yes. And yes, grief brings no one back to life. But how safe are we? How long can we survive in here, Lisamon?'

'Long enough for me to cut us free.' She pulled her vibration-sword out of its sheath.

Amazed, he said, 'You think you can hack a path to the outside?'

'Why not? I've cut through worse.'

'At the first touch of that thing to the dragon's flesh it'll dive to the bottom of the sea. We're safer in here than trying to swim up from five miles underneath.'

'It was said of you that you are an optimist at the darkest time,' the warrior-woman declared. 'Where's that optimism now? The dragon lives at the surface. It might thrash a bit, but it won't dive. And if we do emerge five miles down? At least it's a quick death. Can you breathe this foul muck for-ever? Can you wander for long inside a single giant fish?'

Gingerly Lisamon Hultin touched the tip of the vibration-sword to the side wall. The thick moist flesh quivered a bit but did not recoil. 'You see? It's got no nerves in here,' she said, driving the weapon a little deeper and turning it to excavate a cavity. There were tremors and twitches. She kept digging. 'Do you think anyone else was swallowed with us?' she asked.

'Yours was the only voice I've heard.'

'And I only yours. Phaugh, what a monster! I tried to hold you as we went overboard, but when we were struck the last time I lost my grip on you. We came to the same place, anyway.' She had by now opened a hole a foot deep and two feet wide in the side of the dragon's stomach. It seemed hardly to feel the surgery at all. We are like maggots gnawing within it, Valentine thought. Lisamon Hultin said, 'While I cut, you see if you can find anyone else. But don't stray too far, hear?'

'I'll be careful.'

He chose a route along the stomach wall, groping in the half-darkness, pausing twice to hang on through inrushes of water, and calling out con-stantly in the hope that someone might reply. No replies came. Her exca-vation was enormous now; he saw her deep within the dragon's flesh, still hacking away. Gobbets of severed meat were piled on all sides and thick pur-plish blood stained her entire body. She was singing cheerfully as she cut.

Lord Malibor stood on the deck
And fought both hard and well.
Thick was the blood that flowed that day
And great the blows that fell.

'How far do you think it is to the outside?' he asked.

'Half a mile or so'

'Really?'

She laughed. 'I suppose ten or fifteen feet. Here, clear the opening behind me. This meat's piling up faster than I can sweep it away.'

Feeling like a butcher, and not enjoying the sensation much, Valentine seized the chunks of severed flesh and hauled them back out of the cavity, tossing them as far as he could. He shivered in horror as he saw the fleshy whips of the stomach floor seize the meat and sweep it blithely on toward the digestive pond. Any protein was welcome here, so it seemed.

Deeper, deeper they traveled into the dragon's abdominal wall. Valentine tried to calculate the probable width of it, taking the length of the creature at no less than three hundred feet; but the arithmetic became a muddle. They were working in close quarters and in a foul, hot atmosphere. The blood, the raw meat, the sweat, the narrowness of the cavity – it was hard to imagine a more repellent place.

Valentine looked back. 'The hole's closing behind us!'

'Beast that lives forever must have tricks of healing,' the giantess muttered. She thrust and gouged and hacked. Uneasily Valentine watched new flesh sprouting as if by magic, the wound healing with phenomenal speed. What if they became encapsulated in this opening? Smothered by joining flesh? Lisamon Hultin pretended to be unworried, but he saw her working harder, faster, grunting and moaning, standing with colossal legs planted far apart and shoulders braced. The gash was sealed to their rear, pink new meat covering the hole, and now it was closing at the sides. Lisamon Hultin slashed and cut with furious intensity, and Valentine continued his humbler task of clearing the debris, but she was plainly wearying now, her giant strength visibly diminished, and the hole seemed to be closing almost as fast as she could cut.

'Don't know if I – can keep – it up—' she muttered.

'Give me the sword, then!'

She laughed. 'Watch out! You can't do it!' In wild rage she returned to the struggle, bellowing curses at the dragon's flesh as it sprouted around her. It was impossible now to tell where they were; they were burrowing through a realm without landmarks. Her grunts grew sharper and shorter.

'Maybe we should try to go back to the stomach area,' he suggested. 'Before we're trapped so—'

'No!' she roared. 'I think we're getting there! Not so meaty here – tougher, more like muscle – maybe the sheath just under the hide—'

Suddenly sea-water poured in on them.

'We're through!' Lisamon Hultin cried. She turned, seizing Valentine as though he were a doll, and pushed him forward, headfirst into the opening in the monster's flank. Her arms were locked in a fierce grip around his hips. She gave one tremendous thrust and he barely had time to fill his lungs with air before he was projected out through the slippery walls into the cool green embrace of the ocean. Lisamon Hultin emerged just after him, still gripping him tightly, now by his ankle and then by his wrist, and they rocketed upward, upward, rising like corks.

For what seemed like hours they flew toward the surface. Valentine's forehead ached. His ribs soon would burst. His chest was on fire. We are climbing from the very bottom of the sea, he thought bleakly, and we will drown before we reach the air, or our blood will boil the way it does in divers who go too deep in search of the eyestones off Til-omon, or we will be squeezed flat by the pressure, or—

He erupted into clear sweet air, popping nearly the full length of his body out of the water and falling back with a splash. Limply he floated, a straw on the waters, weak, trembling, struggling for breath. Lisamon Hultin floated alongside. The warm beautiful sun blazed wonderfully, straight overhead.

He was alive, and he was unharmed, and he was free of the dragon.

And he bobbed somewhere on the breast of the Inner Sea, a hundred miles from anywhere.

5

When the first moments of exhaustion had passed, he raised his head and peered about. The dragon was still visible, hump and ridge above the surface, only a few hundred yards away. But it seemed placid and appeared to be swimming slowly in the opposite direction. Of the *Brangalyn* there was no trace – only scattered timbers over a broad span of ocean. Nor were other survivors in view.

They swam to the nearest timber, a good-sized strip of the hull, and flung themselves across it. For a long while neither of them spoke. At length Valentine said, 'And now do we swim to the Archipelago? Or should we simply go straight on to the Isle of Sleep?'

'Swimming is hard work, my lord. We could ride on the dragon's back.'

'But how guide him?'

'Tug on the wings,' she suggested.

'I have my doubts of that.'

They were silent again.

Valentine said, 'At least in the belly of the dragon we had a fresh catch of fish delivered every few minutes.'

'And the inn was large,' Lisamon Hultin added. 'But poorly ventilated. I think I prefer it here.'

'But how long can we drift like this?'

She looked at him strangely. 'Do you doubt that we'll be rescued, my lord?'

'It seems reasonably in doubt, yes.'

'It was prophesied to me in a dream from the Lady,' said the giantess, 'that my death would come in a dry place when I was very old. I am still young and this place is the least dry on all of Majipoor, except perhaps the middle of the Great Sea. Therefore there is nothing to fear. I will not perish here, and neither will you.'

'A comforting revelation,' Valentine said, 'But what will we do?'

'Can you accomplish sendings, my lord?'

'I was Coronal, not King of Dreams.'

'But any mind can reach any other, with true intent! Do you think only the King and Lady have such skills? The little wizard Deliamber talked into minds at night, I know that, and Gorzval said he spoke with dragons in his sleep, and you—'

'I am barely myself, Lisamon. Such of my mind as is left to me will send no sendings.'

'Try. Reach out across the waters. To the Lady, your mother, my lord, or to her people on the Isle, or to the folk of the Archipelago. You have the power. I am only a stupid swinger of swords, but you, lord, have a mind that was deemed worthy of the Castle, and now, in the hour of our need—' The giantess seemed transfigured with passion. 'Do it, Lord Valentine! Call for help, and help will come!'

Valentine was skeptical. He knew little of the network of dream-communication that seemed to bind this planet together, it did appear that mind often called to mind, and of course there were the Powers of the Isle and of Suvrael supposedly sending directed messages forth by some means of mechanical amplification, but yet, drifting here on a slab of wood in the ocean, body and clothes filthied with the flesh and blood of the giant beast that lately had swallowed him, spirit so drained by unending adversity that even his legendary sunny faith in luck and miracles was put to rout – how could he hope to summon aid across such a gulf?

He closed his eyes. He sought to concentrate the energies of his mind in a single point deep within his skull. He imagined a glowing spark of light there, a hidden radiance that he could tap and beam forth. But it was useless. He found himself wondering what toothy creature might soon be nibbling at his dangling feet. He distracted himself with fears that any messages he might send would reach only as far as the hazy mind of the dragon nearby, that had destroyed the *Brangalyn* and almost all its people, and now might wish to turn back and finish the job. Still, he tried. For all his doubts, he owed it to Lisamon Hultin to make the attempt. He held himself still, barely breathing, seeking intently to do whatever it might be that could transmit such a message.

On and off during the afternoon and early evening he attempted it. Darkness came on quickly, and the water grew strangely luminescent, flickering with a ghostly greenish light. They did not dare sleep at the same time, for fear they might slip from the timber and be lost; so they took turns, and when it was Valentine's turn he fought hard for wakefulness, thinking more than once that he was losing consciousness. Creatures swam near them in the night, making tracks of cold fire through the luminous wavelets.

From time to time Valentine tried the sending-forth of messages again. But he saw no avail in it.

We are lost, he thought.

Toward morning he gave himself up to sleep, and had perplexing dreams of dancing eels atop the water. Vaguely, while sleeping, he strived to reach far-off minds with his mind, and then he slipped into a slumber too deep for that.

And woke to the touch of Lisamon Hultin's hand on his shoulder.

'My lord?'

He opened his eyes and looked at her in bewilderment.

'My lord, you may stop making sendings now. We are saved!'

'What?'

'A boat, my lord! See? From the east?'

Wearily he raised his head and followed her gesture. A boat, yes, a small one, coming toward them. Oars flashing in the sunlight. Hallucination, he thought. Delusion. Mirage.

But the boat grew larger against the horizon, and then it was there, and hands were groping for him, hauling him up, and he was sprawled feebly against someone and someone else was putting a flask to his lips, a cool drink, wine, water, he had no way of telling, and they were peeling off his soggy befouled garments and wrapping him in something clean and dry. Strangers, two men and a woman, with great manes of tawny hair and clothing of an unfamiliar sort. He heard Lisamon Hultin talking with them, but the words were blurred and indistinct, and he made no attempt to discern their meaning. Had he conjured up these rescuers with his mental broadcast, then? Angels, were they? Spirits? Valentine settled back, hardly caring, totally spent. He thought hazily of drawing Lisamon Hultin aside and telling her to make no mention of his true identity, but he lacked even the energy for that, and hoped she would have sense enough not to compound absurdity with absurdity by saying any such thing. 'He is Coronal of Majipoor in disguise, yes, and the dragon swallowed us both but we were able to cut ourselves free, and—' Yes. Certainly that would have the ring of unanswerable truth to these people. Valentine smiled faintly and drifted into a dreamless sleep.

When he woke he was in a pleasant sunlit room, facing out on a broad golden beach, and Carabella was looking down at him with an expression of grave concern.

'My lord?' she said softly. 'Do you hear me?'

'Is this a dream?'

'This is the island of Mardigile in the Archipelago,' she told him. 'You were picked up yesterday, drifting in the ocean, along with the giantess. These islanders are fisherfolk, who have been scouting the sea for survivors since the ship went down.'

'Who else lives?' Valentine asked quickly.

'Deliamber and Zalzan Kavol are here with me. The Mardigile folk say that Khun, Shanamir, Vinorkis, and some Skandars – I don't know if they're ours – were picked up by boats from a neighboring island. Some of the dragon-hunters escaped in their own boats and have reached the islands too.'

'And Sleet? What of Sleet?'

Carabella showed, for a flashing moment, a look of fear. 'I have no news of Sleet,' she said. 'But the rescue is continuing. He may be safe on one of these islands. There are dozens hereabouts. The Divine has preserved us so far: we will not be cast aside now.' She laughed lightly. 'Lisamon Hultin has told a wonderful story of how you both were swallowed by the great dragon, and hacked your way out with the vibration-sword. The islanders love it. They think it's the most splendid fable since the tale of Lord Stiamot and the—'

'It happened,' Valentine said.

'My lord?'

'The dragon. Swallowing us. She tells the truth.'

Carabella giggled. 'When I first learned in dreams of your real self, I believed that. But when you tell me—'

'Within the dragon,' Valentine said earnestly, 'there were great pillars holding up the vault of the stomach, and an opening at one end through which sea-water came rushing every few minutes, and with it came fish that were pushed by little whips toward a greenish pond where they were digested, and where the giantess and I would have been digested too, if we were less lucky. Did she tell you that? And do you think we spent our time out there inventing a fable to amuse you all?'

Eyes wide, Carabella said, 'She told the same story, yes. But we thought—'

'It's true, Carabella.'

'Then it is a miracle of the Divine, and you will be famous in all time to come!'

'I'm already going to be famous,' said Valentine acidly, 'as the Coronal who lost his throne, and took up juggling for lack of a royal occupation. That will win me a place in the ballads alongside the Pontifex Arioc, who made himself Lady of the Isle. The dragon, now, that only embellishes the legend I'm creating around myself.' His expression changed suddenly. 'You've told me none of these people who I am, I hope?'

'Not a word, my lord.'

'Good. Keep it that way. They have enough difficult things to believe about us, as it is.'

An islander, slim and tanned and with the great sweep of fair hair that seemed the universal style here, brought Valentine a tray of food: some clear soup, a tender piece of baked fish, triangular wedges of a fruit with dark indigo flesh dotted with tiny scarlet seeds. Valentine found himself ravenously hungry.

Afterward he strolled with Carabella on the beach outside his cottage. 'Once again I thought you were lost to me forever,' he said softly. 'I thought I would never hear your voice again.'

'Do I matter that much to you, my lord?'

'More than I could ever tell you.'

She smiled sadly. 'Such pretty words, eh, Valentine? For so I call you, *Valentine*, but you are *Lord* Valentine, and how many fancy women do you have, Lord Valentine, waiting for you on Castle Mount?'

He had now and then been thinking the same thing himself. Had he a lover there? Many of them? An intended bride, even? So much of his past was still shrouded. And if he reached the Castle, and if a woman who had waited for him came forth to him—

'No,' he said. 'You are mine, Carabella, and I am yours, and whatever may have been in the past – if ever anything was – lies in the past now. I have a different face these days. I have a different soul.'

She looked skeptical, but did not challenge what he had said, and he lightly kissed her frown away.

'Sing to me,' he said. 'The song you sang under the bush in Pidruid, the festival-night. *Not all the wealth of Castle Mount*, it went, *Is worth my love to me*. Eh?'

'I know another much like it,' she said, and took up the pocket-harp from her hip:

My love has donned a pilgrim's robe
Afar across the sea
My love has gone to the Isle of Sleep
Across the dreaming sea.
Sweet my love, and fair as dawn
Afar across the sea
Lost my love to an island tall
Across the dreaming sea.
Lady kind of the distant Isle
Afar across the sea
Fill my dreams with my lover's smile
Across the dreaming sea.

'A different sort of song, that one.' Valentine said. 'A sadder one. Sing me that other, love.'

'Another time.'

'Please. This is a time of joy, of reuniting, Carabella. Please.'

She smiled and sighed and took up the harp again.

My love is fair as is the spring,
As gentle as the night,
My love is sweet as stolen fruit—

Yes, he thought. Yes, that one was better. He let his hand rest tenderly on the nape of her neck, and stroked it as they walked along the beach. It was astonishingly beautiful here, warm and peaceful. Birds of fifty hues perched in the tortuous-limbed little trees of the shore, and a crystalline sea, surf-less, transparent, lapped at the fine sand. The air was soft and mild, fragrant with the perfumes of unknown blossoms. From far away came the sound of laughter and of a gay, bright, tinkling music. How tempting it was, Valentine thought, to abandon all fantasies of Castle Mount and settle forever on Mardigile, and go out at dawn on a fishing-boat for the catch, and spend the rest of each day frolicking in the hot sunshine.

But there would be no such abdications for him. In the afternoon Zalzan Kavol and Autifon Deliamber, both healthy and well rested after their ordeals at sea, came to call on him, and soon they were talking of ways and means to continue the journey.

Zalzan Kavol, parsimonious as always, had had the money-pouch on him when the *Brangalyn* went down, and so at least half their treasury had survived, even if Shanamir had lost the rest. The Skandar laid out the glittering coins. 'With this,' he said, 'we can hire these fisherfolk to convey us to the Isle. I have spoken with our hosts. This Archipelago is nine hundred miles in length, and numbers three thousand islands, more than eight hundred of them inhabited. No one here wishes to journey all the way to the Isle, but for a few royals we can hire a large trimaran that will carry us to Rodamaunt Graun, near the mid-point of the chain, and there we can probably find transport the rest of the way.'

'When can we leave?' Valentine asked.

'As soon,' said Deliamber, 'as we are reunited once more. I am told that several of our people are on their way across from the nearby isle of Burbont at this moment.'

'Which ones?'

'Khun, Vinorkis, and Shanamir,' Zalzan Kavol answered, 'and my brothers Erfon and Rovorn. With them is Captain Gorzval. Gibor Haern is lost at sea – I saw him perish, struck by a timber and sent under – and of Sleet there is no news.'

Valentine touched the Skandar's shaggy forearm. 'I grieve for your latest loss.'

Zalzan Kavol's feelings seemed well under control. 'Let us rather rejoice that some of us still live, my lord,' he said quietly.

In early afternoon a boat from Burbont brought the other survivors. There were embraces all round; and then Valentine turned to Gorzval, who stood apart, looking numb and bewildered, rubbing at the stump of his severed arm. The dragon-captain seemed in shock. Valentine would have put his arms around the hapless man, but the instant he approached, Gorzval sank to his knees in the sand and touched his forehead to the ground and stayed there, trembling, arms outspread in the starburst gesture. 'My lord—' he whispered harshly. 'My lord—'

Valentine, displeased, looked around. 'Who has been talking?'

Silence a moment. Then Shanamir, a bit frightened, said, 'I, my lord. I meant no harm. The Skandar seemed so injured by the loss of his ship – I thought to console him by telling him who his passenger had been, that he had become part of the history of Majipoor by giving you voyage. This was before we knew that you had survived the wreck.' The boy's lip quivered. 'My lord, I meant no harm by it!'

Valentine nodded, 'And no harm was done. I forgive you. Gorzval?'

The cowering dragon-captain remained huddled at Valentine's feet.

'Look up, Gorzval. I can't talk to you this way.'

'My lord?'

'Get to your feet.'

'My lord—'

'Please, Gorzval. Get up!'

The Skandar, amazed, peered at Valentine and said, '*Please*, you say? *Please?*'

Valentine laughed. 'I've forgotten the habits of power, I suppose. All right: Up! I command it!'

Shakily Gorzval rose. He was a miserable sight, this little three-armed Skandar, his fur matted, sandy, his eyes bloodshot, his expression downcast.

Valentine said, 'I brought foul luck upon you, and you had no need of more of that. Accept my apologies; and if fortune begins to smile more kindly on me, I will repair the harm you have suffered, someday. I promise you that. What will you do now? Gather your crew and return to Piliplok?'

Gorzval shook his head pathetically. 'I could never go there again. I have no ship, I have no reputation, I have no money. I have lost everything and it can never be regained. My people were released of their indentures when the *Brangalyn* sank. I am alone now. I am ruined.'

'Come with us to the Isle of the Lady, then, Gorzval.'

'My lord?'

'You can't stay here. I think these islanders prefer not to take in settlers, and this is no climate for a Skandar, anyway. Nor can a dragon-hunter become a fisherman, I think, without knowing pain every time he casts his nets. Come with us. If we get no farther than the Isle, you may find peace there in the service of the Lady; and if we continue on our quest, there will be honor for you as we make the ascent of Castle Mount. What do you say, Gorzval?'

'It frightens me to be near you, my lord.'

'Am I so terrifying? Do I have a dragon's mouth? Do you see these people green-faced with fear?' Valentine clapped the Skandar on his shoulder. To Zalzan Kavol he said, 'No one can replace the brothers you have lost. But at least I give you another companion of your own kind. And now let's make arrangements for departure, eh? The Isle is still many days' journey away.'

Within an hour Zalzan Kavol had secured an island craft to carry them eastward in the morning. That evening the hospitable islanders provided them with a splendid feast, cool green wines and sleek sweet fruits and fine fresh sea-dragon flesh. That last made Valentine queasy, and he would have pushed it away, but he saw Lisamon Hultin shoveling it in as though it were the last meal she would eat. As an exercise in self-discipline he decided to force a morsel into his own throat, and found the flavor so irresistible that he renounced on the spot any discomfort that sea-dragons might arouse in his mind. As they ate, sunset came, at an early hour here in the tropics, and an extraordinary one it was, streaking the sky with rich throbbing tones of amber and violet and magenta and gold. Surely these were blessed islands, Valentine thought, extraordinarily joyous places even on a world where most places were happy ones and most lives fulfilled. The population seemed generally homogeneous, handsome long-legged folk of human blood with thick unshorn golden hair and smooth honey-colored skin, though there was a scattering of Vroons and even Ghayrogs among them, and Deliamber said that other islands in the chain had people of different stocks. According to Deliamber, who had been mingling freely since his rescue, the islands were largely out of touch with the mainland continents, and went their way in a world of their own, ignorant of matters of high destiny in the greater world. When Valentine asked one of his hosts if Lord Valentine the Coronal had happened to pass this way on his recent journey to Zimroel, the woman gave him a blank look and said ingenuously, 'Is the Coronal not Lord Voriax?'

'Dead two years or more, I hear,' one of the other islanders declared, and it seemed to come as news to most of the people at the table.

Valentine shared his cottage with Carabella that night. They stood together a long while on the veranda, eyes fixed on the brilliant white track of moonlight gleaming out across the sea toward distant Piliplok. He thought of the sea-dragons grazing in that sea, and of the monster in whose belly he had made that dreamlike sojourn, and, with pain, of his two lost comrades, Gibor Haern and Sleet, one of whom was deep in the sea now, the other perhaps. So great a journey, he thought, remembering Pidruid, Dulorn, Mazadone, Ilirivoyne, Ni-moya, remembering the flight through the forest, the turbulence of the Steiche, the coldness of the Piliplok dragon-captains, the look of the dragon as it bore down on poor Gorzval's doomed vessel. So great a journey, so many thousands of miles, and so many miles yet to cover before he could begin to answer the questions that flooded his soul.

Carabella nestled close beside him, silent. Her attitude toward him was constantly evolving, and now had become a mixture of awe and love, of deference and irreverence, for she accepted and respected him as true Coronal, and yet remembered his innocence, his ignorance, his naïveté, qualities which had not yet left him even now. And clearly she feared she would lose him when he had again come into his own. Simply on the level of dealing daily with the world, she was far more competent than he, far more experienced, and that colored her view of him, making her see him as terrifying and childlike both at once. He understood that and took no issue with it, for, although fragments of his earlier self and princely education returned to him almost daily, and he grew daily more accustomed to the postures of command, most of his former identity still was inaccessible to him and he was, in large part, still Valentine the easy-going wanderer, Valentine the innocent, Valentine the juggler. That darker figure, the Lord Valentine he once had been, that he might someday be again, was a hidden substratum in his spirit, rarely operative but never to be ignored. He thought Carabella was making the best of a difficult position.

She said at last, 'What are you thinking of, Valentine?'

'Sleet. I miss that tough little man.'

'He'll turn up. We'll find him four islands from here.'

'I hope so.' Valentine cupped his arm about her shoulders. 'I think also of all that has happened, and all that will happen. I move as though through a world of dreams, Carabella.'

'Who can tell, really, what is the dream and what is not? We move as the Divine instructs us, and we ask no questions, because there are no answers. Do you know what I mean? There are questions and there are answers, of course. I can tell you what day this is, and what we had for dinner, and how this island is called, if you ask me, but there are no *questions*, there are no *answers*.'

'So I believe also,' Valentine said.

6

Zalzan Kavol had hired one of the grandest fishing-boats on the island, a marvelous turquoise trimaran named *Pride of Mardigile*. It was a splendid fifty-footer rising nobly on its three sleek hulls, and its sails, spotless and dazzling in the morning sunlight, bore bright vermilion edging that gave the craft a festive, jubilant air. Their captain was a man past middle years, one of the most prosperous fishermen of the island, Grigitor by name, tall and sturdy, with hair down to his waist and skin so vigorous it looked to have been oiled; he was one of those who had rescued Deliamber and Zalzan Kavol, when the first alarms of a sinking ship had reached the island. He had a crew of five, his sons and daughters, all strapping and handsome after his image.

The route of the voyage lay first toward Burbont, less than half an hour's sail away, and then into an open channel of shallow greenish water that linked the two outermost islands to the rest. The sea-bottom here was of clean white sand, and sunlight penetrated easily to it, setting off patterns of sparkling coruscations that revealed the undersea dwellers, the rip-toads and the twitch-crabs and the big-leg lobsters, and the gaudy-hued multitudes of fish, and the sinister, lurking sand-eels. Once even a small sea-dragon flitted by, far too close to land for its own good and obviously confused; one of Grigitor's daughters urged that they go after it, but he shook the notion off, saying that their responsibility was to get their passengers swiftly to Rodamaunt Graun.

All morning they sailed, passing three more islands – Richelure, Grialon, Voniaire, said their captain – and at noon they dropped anchor for lunch. Two of Grigitor's children went over the side to hunt, moving like magnificent animals, naked in the brilliant water, quickly spearing crustaceans and fish with rarely a missed thrust. Grigitor himself prepared the meal, cubes of raw white fish marinated in a spicy sauce and washed down with cheering pungent green wine. Deliamber withdrew after eating only a little, and perched himself on the tip of one of the outer hulls, staring intently to the north. After a while Valentine noticed, and would have gone to him, but Carabella caught him by the wrist.

'He is in a trance,' she said. 'Let him be.'

They delayed their departure after lunch by some minutes, until the little Vroon descended from his place and rejoined them. The wizard looked pleased.

'I have cast my mind forth,' he announced, 'and I bring you good news. Sleet lives!'

'Good news indeed!' Valentine cried. 'Where is he?'

'An island in that group,' said Deliamber, gesturing vaguely with a cluster of tentacles. 'He is with several of Gorzval's people who escaped by boat from the disaster.'

Grigitor said, 'Tell me which island, and we'll make for it.'

'It has the shape of a circle, with an opening at one side, and a body of water at its center. The people are dark-skinned and wear their hair in long ringlets, with jewels in their earlobes.'

'Kangrisorn,' said one of Grigitor's daughters instantly.

Her father nodded. 'Kangrisorn it is,' he said. 'Pull up anchor!'

Kangrisorn lay an hour to the windward, somewhat off the route Grigitor had charted. It was one of half a dozen small sandy atolls, mere rings of upraised reef surrounding little lagoons, and it must have been uncommon for people of Mardigile to visit it. For long before the trimaran had entered the harbor children of Kangrisorn were flocking out in boats to view the strangers. They were as dark as the Mardigilese were golden, and just as beautiful in their solemn way, with shining white teeth and hair so black it seemed almost blue. With much laughter and waving of arms they guided the trimaran through the entrance to the lagoon, and there, squatting at the edge of the water, was Sleet indeed, looking sunburned and a bit ragged but mainly intact. He was juggling five or six globes of bleached white coral for an audience that consisted of a few dozen islanders and five members of Gorzval's crew, four humans and a Hjort.

Gorzval seemed apprehensive at encountering his erstwhile employees. He had begun to recover his spirits during the morning's voyage, but now he grew tense and withdrawn as the trimaran entered the lagoon. Carabella was the first off, splashing through the shallow water to embrace Sleet; Valentine followed close behind. Gorzval lurked to the rear, eyes lowered.

'How did you find us?' Sleet asked.

Valentine indicated Deliamber. 'Sorcery. How else? Are you well?'

'I thought I'd die of seasickness getting here, but I've had a day or two to recover.' With a shudder he said, 'And you? I saw you sucked under, and believed all was over.'

'So it seemed,' said Valentine. 'A strange story, which I'll tell you another time. We are all together again, eh, Sleet? All but Gibor Haern,' he added mournfully, 'who perished in the wreck. But we've taken on Gorzval as one of our companions. Come forward, Gorzval! Aren't you pleased to see your men again?'

Gorzval muttered something indistinct and looked between Valentine and the others, meeting no one's eyes. Valentine comprehended the situation and turned to the crew people, meaning to ask them to hold no ill will toward the former captain for a disaster far beyond mortal control. He was taken aback to discover the five of them groveling at his feet.

Sleet said, abashed, 'I thought you were dead, my lord. I couldn't resist telling them my tale.'

'I see,' said Valentine, 'that the news is apt to spread more rapidly than I wish, no matter how solemnly I swear you all to silence. Well, it's pardonable, Sleet.' To the others he said, 'Up. Up. This crawling in the sand does none of us any good.'

They rose. Their contempt for Gorzval was impossible for them to hide; but it was overshadowed by the astonishment they felt at being in the presence of the Coronal. Of the five, Valentine quickly learned, two – the Hjort and one of the humans – chose to remain on Kangrisorn in the hope of finding, eventually, some way to return to Piliplok and resume their trade. The other three begged to accompany him on his pilgrimage.

The new members of the rapidly expanding band were two women – Pandelon and Cordeine, a carpenter and a sailmender – and a man, Thesme, one of the winchwinders. Valentine bade them be welcome, and accepted pledges of allegiance from them, a ceremony that stirred vague discomfort in him. Yet he was growing accustomed to taking on these trappings of rank.

Grigitor and his children had paid no attention to the kneelings and hand-kissings among the passengers. Just as well: until he had conferred with the Lady, Valentine wished not to spread news across the world of his return to self-awareness. He was still uncertain of his strategy and unsure of his powers. Besides, if he advertised his existence he might draw the attention of the present Coronal, who was not likely to stay his hand if he discovered that a pretender was journeying toward Castle Mount.

The trimaran resumed its voyage. From isle to golden isle it went, staying well within the coastal channels and only occasionally venturing into deeper, bluer waters. Past Lormanar and Climidole they sailed, and Secundail, Blayhar Strand, Garhuven, and Wiswis Keep; past Quile and Fruil;

past Dawn-break, Nissemhold, and Thiaquil; past Roazen and Piplinat; and past the great crescent sand-spit known as Damozal. They stopped at the island of Sungyve for fresh water, at Musorn for fruit and leafy vegetables, at Cadibyre for casks of the young pink wine of that island. And after many days of traveling through these small sun-blessed places they pulled into the spacious harbor of Rodamaunt Graun.

This was a large lush island of mountainous origin, surrounded by black volcanic beaches and equipped along its southern shore with a splendid natural breakwater. Rodamaunt Graun was dominant in the Archipelago, by far the largest in the chain, with a population, so Grigitor asserted, of five and a half million. Twin cities spread out like wings from both sides of the harbor, but the flanks of the island's looming central peak were also well populated, with dwellings of rattan and skupik-wood rising in neat ranks almost to mid-point. About the last line of houses the slopes were thickly covered with jungle, and at the highest level rose a plume of thin white smoke, for Rodamaunt Graun was an active volcano. The last eruption, said Grigitor, had occurred less than fifty years before. But that was hard to believe, when one looked at the impeccable houses and the unbroken forest growth above them.

Here the *Pride of Mardigile* would turn back for home, but Grigitor arranged for the voyagers to shift to a trimaran even more noble, the *Rodamaunt Queen*, which would carry them to the Isle of Sleep. Her skipper was one Namurinta, a woman of regal poise and bearing, with long straight hair as white as Sleet's and a youthful, unlined face. Her manner was fastidious and quizzical: she studied her assortment of passengers closely, as if trying to determine what pull had drawn such a mixture into an off-season pilgrimage, but she said only 'If you are refused at the Isle, I will return you to Rodamaunt Graun, but there will be extra costs for your upkeep in that event.'

'Does the Isle often refuse pilgrims?' Valentine asked.

'Not when they come at the proper time. But the pilgrim-ships, as I suppose you know, don't sail in autumn. There may not be facilities ready for receiving you.'

'We've come this far with only minor difficulties,' said Valentine jauntily. He heard Carabella snicker and Sleet make stagy coughing sounds. 'I feel confident,' he went on, 'that we'll meet no obstacles greater than those we've already encountered.'

'I admire your determination,' Namurinta said, and signaled to her crew to prepare for departure.

The Archipelago in its eastern half hooked somewhat to the north, and the islands here were generally unlike Mardigile and its neighbors, being mainly the tops of a submerged mountain chain, not flat coral-based platforms. Studying Namurinta's charts, Valentine concluded that this part of the Archipelago had once been a long tail of a peninsula jutting out of the southwest corner of the Isle of Sleep, but had been swallowed by some rising of the Inner Sea in ancient times. Only the tallest peaks had remained above water; and between the easternmost island of the Archipelago and the coast of the Isle there now lay some hundreds of miles of open sea – a formidable journey for a trimaran, even so well equipped a trimaran as Namurinta's.

But the voyage was uneventful. They stopped at four ports – Hellirache, Sempifiore, Dimmid, and Guadeloom – for water and victuals, sailed on serenely past Rodamaunt Ounze, the last island of the Archipelago, and entered Ungehoyer Channel, which separated the Archipelago from the Isle of Sleep. This was a broad but shallow seaway, richly endowed with marine life and heavily fished by the island folk, all but the easternmost hundred miles, which formed part of the holy perimeter of the Isle. In these waters were monsters of a harmless kind, great balloon-shaped creatures known as volevants that anchored themselves to deep rocks and lived by filtering plankton through their gills; these creatures excreted a constant stream of nutrient matter, which sustained the enormous population of life-forms about them. Valentine saw dozens of volevants in the next few days: swollen globular sacks of a deep carmine hue, fifty to eighty feet across at their upper ends, plainly visible just a few feet below the calm surface. They bore dark semicircular markings on their skins, which Valentine imagined were eyes and noses and lips, so that he saw faces peering gravely up from the water, and it seemed to him that the volevants were beings of the deepest melancholy, philosophers of weight and wisdom reflecting eternally on the ebb and flow of the tides. 'They sadden me,' he told Carabella. 'Forever hovering there, tied by their tails to hidden boulders, swaying slowly as the currents move them. How thoughtful they are!'

'Thoughtful! Primitive gasbags, no cleverer than a sponge!'

'But look carefully at them, Carabella. They want to fly, to soar – they look up at the sky, at the whole world of the air, and long to encounter it, but all they can do is hang below the waves, and sway, and fill themselves with invisible organisms. Just in front of their face lies another world, and it would be death to them to enter it. Are you untouched by that?'

'Silly,' Carabella said.

On the second day in the channel the *Rodamaunt Queen* came upon five fishing-boats that had uprooted a volevant, brought it to the surface, and slit it into gores; they clustered about the huge outspread skin of it, cutting it into smaller sections and stacking them like hides on their decks. Valentine was appalled. When I am Coronal again, he thought, I will prohibit the killing of these creatures, and then he looked at the thought in amazement, asking himself if it was his intention to promulgate laws on the basis of sympathies alone, without study of the facts. He asked Namurinta what use was made of volevant-skin.

'Medicinal,' she replied. 'For the comfort of the very old, when their blood flows sluggishly. One of them provides enough of the drug for all the islands for a year or more: what you see is a rare event.'

When I am Coronal again, Valentine resolved, I will reserve judgment until I am in full possession of the truth, if such a thing is ever possible.

Nevertheless, the imagined solemn profundity of the volevants haunted him with strange emotions, and he was relieved to pass beyond their zone, and into the cool blue waters that bordered the Isle of Sleep.

7

The Isle now lay clearly in view to the east, growing perceptibly larger every hour. Valentine had seen it only in dreams and fantasies, and those based on nothing but his own imaginings and whatever residue of remembered reality still encrusted his mind; and he was not at all prepared for the actuality of the place.

It was immense. That should not have been surprising on a planet itself gigantic, and where so many things were on a scale with the planetary dimensions. But Valentine had misled himself into thinking an island necessarily was something of convenient and accessible scope. He had expected something perhaps two or three times as big as Rodamaunt Graun, which was foolishness: the Isle of Sleep, he saw now, spanned the entire horizon and looked as large from this distance as had the coast of Zimroel when they were a day or two out of Piliplok. An island it was, but by that token so too were Zimroel and Alhanroel and Suvrael; and the only reason the Isle was not called a continent, as were they, was that they were colossal, and the Isle merely very big.

And the Isle was dazzling. Like the promontory across the mouth of the river from Piliplok, it was ramparted by cliffs of pure white chalk that blazed brilliantly in the afternoon sunlight. They formed a wall hundreds of feet high and perhaps hundreds of miles in length across the western face of the Isle. Atop that wall spread a dark-green crown of forest, and, so it seemed, there was a second wall of chalk inland at a higher elevation, topped also by forest, and then a third yet farther from the sea, so that the Isle from this side gave an appearance of tier upon tier of brightness, rising to some unknown and perhaps inaccessible central fastness. He had heard of the terraces of the Isle, which he gathered were artificial constructs of great age, symbolic markers of the ascent toward initiation. But the island itself seemed a place of terraces, natural ones, that enhanced its mystery. Small wonder that this place had become the abode of the sacred on Majipoor.

Namurinta said, pointing, 'That notch in the cliff is Taleis, where the pilgrim-ships land. It's one of the Isle's two harbors; the other's Numinor, over around Alhanroel side. But you must know all this, being pilgrims.'

'We have had little time to study,' said Valentine. 'This pilgrimage came on us suddenly.'

'Will you pass the rest of your lives here in the service of the Lady?' she asked.

'In the service of the Lady, yes,' Valentine said. 'But I think not here. The Isle is only a way-station for some of us, on a much greater journey.'

Namurinta looked puzzled at that, but she asked no further questions.

The wind blew briskly from the southwest here, and carried the *Rodam-aunt Queen* easily and swiftly toward Taleis. Soon the great chalk wall altogether filled the view, and the opening in it was revealed as no mere notch, but a harbor of heroic size, a huge gouge in the whiteness. With sails full, the trimaran entered. Valentine, in the bow, hair streaming in the breeze, was awestruck by the scope of the place, for within the sharp-angled V that was Taleis the cliffs descended almost vertically toward the water from a height of a mile or more, and at their base was a flat strip of land bordered by a broad white beach. At one side were wharfs and piers and docks, everything dwarfed by the scale of this gigantic amphitheater. It was hard to imagine how one could get from this port at the foot of the cliffs to the interior of the island: the place was a natural fortress.

And it was silent. There were no vessels in the harbor and an eerie echoing quietness prevailed, against which the sound of the wind or the screeching of an occasional gull took on magnified significance.

'Is there anyone here?' Sleet asked. 'Who will greet us?'

Carabella closed her eyes. 'To have to go around to the Numinor side now – worse, to return to the Archipelago—'

'No,' Deliamber said. 'We will be met. Fear nothing.'

The trimaran glided toward the shore and came to rest at a vacant pier. The grandeur of the surroundings was overwhelming here, deep in the V of the harbor, with the cliffs rising so high they seemed to be on the verge of toppling. A crewman made the boat fast and they stepped forth.

Deliamber's confidence seemed misplaced. There was no one here. Everything remained still, a silence so mighty that Valentine wanted to put his hands to his ears to shut it out. They waited. They exchanged uncertain glances.

'Let's explore,' he said finally. 'Lisamon, Khun, Zalzan Kavol – examine the buildings to our left. Sleet, Deliamber, Vinorkis, Shanamir – down that way. You, Pandelon, Thesme, Rovorn – to that curve of the beach, and look beyond it. Gorzval, Erfon—'

Valentine, with Carabella and the sailmender Cordeine, went straight ahead, to the foot of the titanic chalk cliffs. Some sort of pathway began there, and angled upward at an impossible slope, close to vertical, toward the upper reaches of the cliff, where it vanished between two white spires. Climbing that path would require the agility of a forest-brother and the gall of a tandy-prancer, Valentine decided. Yet no other place of exit from the beach was apparent. He peered into the small wooden shack at the base of the path and found nothing but a few floater-sleds, presumably used in riding the path. He hauled one out, set it on the thrusting-pad at ground level, and mounted it; but he saw no way of activating it.

Baffled, he returned to the pier. Most of the others had come back already. 'The place is deserted,' said Sleet.

Valentine looked toward Namurinta. 'How long would it take you to carry us around to the Alhanroel side?'

'To Numinor? Weeks. But I would not go there.'

'We have money,' said Zalzan Kavol.

She looked indifferent. 'My trade is fishing. The time of harvest for the thorn-fish is at hand. If I take you to Numinor, I will miss it, and half the gissoon season as well. You could not recompense me for that.'

The Skandar produced a five-royal piece, as though by its glitter alone he could change the captain's mind. But she shook it away.

'For half of what you paid me to bring you from Rodamaunt Graun to here, I'll return you to Rodamaunt Graun, but that's the best I can do for you. In a few months the pilgrim-ships will be sailing again and this harbor will come to life, and then, if you wish, I'll bring you here again for the same half fee. However you decide, I am at your service. But I will sail from this place before it grows dark, and not for Numinor.'

Valentine considered the situation. This was a greater nuisance than being swallowed by the sea-dragon; for he had quickly enough been set free from that, but this unexpected obstacle threatened to delay him well into winter, or even beyond, and all this while Dominin Barjazid ruled at Castle Mount, new laws went forth, history was altered, the usurper consolidated his position. But what, then? He glanced at Deliamber, but the wizard, though he looked bland and untroubled, offered no suggestions. They could not climb this wall. They could not fly it. They could not leap in mighty bounds to the unreachable, infinitely desirable forest groves that cloaked its shoulders. Back to Rodamaunt Graun, then?

'Will you wait with us here a day?' Valentine asked. 'For an additional fee, that is? Possibly in the morning we'll find someone who—'

'I am far from Rodamaunt Graun,' Namurinta replied. 'I yearn to see its shores again. Waiting here another hour, even, would gain you nothing and me even less. The season is wrong; the people of the Lady expect no one to arrive at Taleis, and will not be here.'

Shanamir tugged lightly at Valentine's sleeve. 'You are Coronal of Majipoor,' the boy whispered. '*Command* her to wait! Reveal yourself and force her to her knees!'

Smiling, Valentine said softly, 'I think the trick might not work. I've left my crown elsewhere.'

'Then have Deliamber witch her into yielding!'

That was a possibility. But Valentine disliked it: Namurinta had taken them on in good faith, and by rights was free to leave, and probably was correct that waiting here another day or two or three was pointless. Compelling her to yield by Deliamber's powers was distasteful to him. On the other hand—

'Lord Valentine!' a woman's voice called, far away. 'Here! Come!'

He looked toward the far end of the harbor. It was Pandelon, Gorzval's carpenter, who had gone with Thesme and Rovorn to inspect what lay around the curve. She was waving, beckoning. He sprinted down toward her, the others following after a moment.

When he reached her she led him through the shallow water around a jutting fold of rock that concealed a much smaller beach. There he saw a single-story structure of pink sandstone that bore the triangle-within-triangle emblem of the Lady and was perhaps some sort of shrine. In front of it was a garden of flowering shrubs arranged in symmetrical patterns of red, blue, orange, and yellow blossoms. Two gardeners, a man and a woman, were tending it. They looked up without interest as Valentine approached. Awkwardly he made the sign of the Lady at them, and they returned it more adeptly.

He said, 'We are pilgrims, and need to be told the way to the terraces.'

'You come out of season,' the woman said. Her face was wide and pale, with a sprinkling of pale freckles on it. There was nothing friendly in her voice.

'Because of our eagerness to enter into the Lady's service.'

The woman shrugged and returned to her weeding. The man, a thick-muscled, short-statured person with thinning gray hair, said, 'You should have gone to Numinor at this time of year.'

'We came from Zimroel.'

That produced a minor flicker of attention. 'Through the dragon-winds? You must have had a difficult crossing.'

'There were some troublesome moments,' Valentine said, 'but they lie behind us now. We feel only joy at having reached this Isle at last.'

'The Lady will comfort you,' said the man indifferently, and he began to work with pruning-shears.

After a moment of silence that grew swiftly dismaying, Valentine said, 'And the way to the terraces?'

The freckled woman said, 'You won't be able to operate it.'

'But will you help us?'

Silence again.

Valentine said, 'It would be only a moment, and then we'd disturb you no more. Show us the way.'

'We have our duties here,' said the balding man.

Valentine moistened his lips. This was leading nowhere; and for all he knew, Namurinta had left the other beach five minutes ago and was on her way back to Rodamaunt Graun, marooning them. He looked to Deliamber. Some wizardry compulsion might be in order. Deliamber ignored the hint. Valentine moved toward him and murmured, 'Touch your tentacles to them and inspire them to cooperate.'

'I think my sorceries are of little value on this holy Isle,' said Deliamber. 'Try wizardries of your own.'

'I have none!'

'Try,' said the Vroon.

Valentine confronted the gardeners once again. I am Coronal of Majipoor, he told himself, and I am the son of the Lady whom these two worship and serve. It was impossible to say any of that to the gardeners, but he could transmit it, perhaps, through sheer force of soul. He stood tall and moved toward the center of his being, as he would have done if he were preparing to juggle before the most critical of audiences, and he smiled a smile so warm it might have opened buds on the branches of the flowering shrubs, and after a moment the gardeners, looking up from their work, saw it and showed an unmistakable response, a reaction of surprise, bewilderment, and – submission. He bathed them in glowing love. 'We have come thousands of miles,' he said gently, 'to give ourselves up to the peace of the Lady, and we beg you, in the name of the Divine that we both serve, to assist us on our pathway; for our need is great and we are weary of wandering.'

They blinked, as if the sun had emerged from behind a gray cloud.

'We have our tasks,' said the woman lamely.

'We are not supposed to ascend until the garden is cared for,' the man said, almost in a mumble.

'The garden thrives,' said Valentine, 'and will thrive without your aid for a few hours today. Help us, before the darkness comes. We ask only that you point us on our way, and I tell you that the Lady will reward you for it.'

The gardeners looked troubled. They glanced at one another, and then toward the sky, as though to see how late it was. Frowning, they rose and brushed the sandy soil from their knees, and, like sleepwalkers, moved to the water's edge, and out into the light surf, and around the point to the greater beach, and down toward the foot of the cliff where that vertical path began its skyward climb.

Namurinta was still there, but she was nearly ready for departure. Valentine went to her.

'For your aid we thank you deeply,' he said.

'You are staying?'

'We have found a way to the terraces.'

She smiled in unfeigned pleasure. 'I was not eager to abandon you, but Rodamaunt Graun was calling me. I wish you well as you make your pilgrimage.'

'And I wish you a safe voyage home.'

He turned away.

'One thing,' the captain said.

'Yes?'

'When the woman called to you from down there,' she said, 'she hailed you as *Lord* Valentine. What was the meaning of that?'

'A joke,' said Valentine. 'Only a joke.'

'Lord Valentine is how the new Coronal is named, so I have been told, the one that rules since a year or two past.'

'Yes,' Valentine said. 'But he is a dark-haired man. It was only a joke, a play on names, for I am Valentine too. A safe journey, Namurinta.'

'A fruitful pilgrimage, Valentine.'

He walked toward the cliff. The gardeners had taken several of the floater-sleds from the shack, and had placed them in riding sequence on the thrusting-pad. Silently they gestured the travelers aboard. Valentine mounted the first sled, with Carabella, Deliamber, Shanamir, and Khun. The female gardener went into the shack, where, it seemed, the controls of the floaters must be located, for an instant afterward the sled drifted free of the pad and began the dizzying, terrifying ascent of the towering white cliff.

8

'You have come,' said the acolyte Talinot Esulde, 'to the Terrace of Assessment. Here you will be weighed in the balance. When it is time to move onward, your path takes you to the Terrace of Inception, and then to the

Terrace of Mirrors, where you will confront yourself. If what you see is satisfactory to you and your guides, you move inward to Second Cliff, where another group of terraces awaits you. And so you proceed until the Terrace of Adoration. There, if the favor of the Lady is upon you, you will receive your summons to Inner Temple. But I would not expect that to happen quickly. I would not expect that to happen at all. Those who *expect* to attain the Lady are the least likely to reach her.'

Valentine's mood darkened at that, for not only did he expect to attain the Lady, it was absolutely vital that he do so; and yet he understood what the acolyte was saying. In this holy place one made no demands on the fabric of existence. One surrendered; one gave up demands and needs and desires; one yielded, if one hoped to find peace. This was no place for a Coronal. The essence of a Coronal's being was the wielding of power, wisely if he was capable of wisdom, but in any event steadfastly; the essence of a pilgrim was surrender. In that contradiction he might easily be lost. Yet he had no choice but to go to the Lady.

He had, at least, reached the outer fringes of the Lady's domain. At the top of the cliff they had been greeted by unsurprised acolytes, plainly aware that out-of-season pilgrims were floating toward them. And now, looking pious and faintly absurd in the soft pale robes of pilgrims, they were gathered in a low long building of smooth pink stone near the crest of the cliff. Flags of the same pink stone formed a massive semicircular promenade that stretched for what appeared to be a great distance along the edge of the forest that topped the cliff: this was the Terrace of Assessment. Beyond it lay more forest; the other terraces were farther beyond; and deeper in, not visible from where they were now, rose the second chalk cliff atop the plateau that the outer one formed. A third cliff yet, Valentine knew, rose above the second somewhere hundreds of miles inland, and this was the holiest precinct, where Inner Temple was, where the Lady dwelled. For all that he had traveled so far, it seemed impossible that he would ever complete those last few hundreds of miles.

Night was falling swiftly. He could look back through the circular window behind him and see the darkening sky and the broad dark bosom of the sea, lit only by the purpling light of the vanishing sun as it fled toward Piliplok. There was a speck out there, a scratch on the smooth surface of the water, that he thought and hoped was the trimaran *Rodamaunt Queen*, heading homeward, and out there too were the volevants dreaming their endless dream, and the sea-dragons making their way toward a greater sea, and beyond all that was Zimroel, its teeming cities, its forest preserves and parklands, its festivals, its billions of souls. There was much for him to look back on; but now he must look forward. He stared intently at Talinot Esulde, their first guide in this place, a tall slender person with milk-white skin and a shaven skull, who might be of either sex. Male was Valentine's guess – the height and something about the breadth of shoulders argued that, though not absolutely – but the delicacy of Talinot Esulde's facial bones, notably the fragile curve of the light ridges above the strange blue eyes, argued otherwise.

Talinot Esulde was explaining things: the daily routine of prayer and work and meditation, the system of dream-speaking, the arrangement of living-quarters, the dietary restrictions, which excluded all wines and certain spices, and much else. Valentine tried to master it all, but there were so many regulations and requirements and obligations and customs that they tangled in his mind, and he ceased making the effort after a time, hoping that daily practice would instill the rules in him.

As darkness came Talinot Esulde led them from the indoctrination hall, past the sparkling spring-fed rock pool where they had been bathed before being given their robes and where they would bathe twice each day until they left this terrace, and to the dining-hall, farther from the cliff's rim. Here they were served a simple meal of soup and fish, flavorless and unappealing even though they were furiously hungry. Their servitors were novices like themselves, in robes of light green. The hall, a large one, was only partly full – the hour for dining was almost past, Talinot Esulde pointed out. Valentine looked at his fellow pilgrims. They were of all sorts, perhaps half of human stock, but also a great many Vroons and Ghayrogs, a sprinkling of Skandars, some Liimen, some Hjorts though not very many, and, far across the way, a little insular Su-Suheris group. The net of the Lady caught all the races of Majipoor, it would seem. All but one. 'Do Metamorphs ever seek the Lady?' Valentine asked.

Talinot Esulde smiled seraphically. 'If a Piurivar came to us, we would accept it. But they take no part in our rites. They live to themselves as though they were alone on all of Majipoor.'

'Perhaps some have come here disguised in other forms,' Sleet suggested.

'We would know that,' said Talinot Esulde calmly.

After dinner they were taken to their rooms – individual chambers, hardly bigger than closets, in a hivelike lodge. A couch, a sink, a place for clothes, and nothing more. Lisamon Hultin glowered at hers. 'No wine,' she said, 'and I give up my sword, and now I sleep in this box? I think I'm going to be a failure as a pilgrim, Valentine.'

'Peace, and make the effort. We'll travel through the Isle as swiftly as we can.'

He entered his room, which was between the warrior-woman's and Carabella's. Immediately the lightglobe dimmed, and when he settled in on his couch he found himself disappearing instantly into sleep, though the hour was still early. As consciousness left him a new light glowed softly in his mind, and he beheld the Lady, the unmistakable, unquestionable Lady of the Isle.

Valentine had seen her in dreams many times before since Pidruid, the gentle eyes, the dark hair, the flower at her ear, the olive-hued skin, but now the image was sharper, the vision more detailed, and he noticed the small lines in the corners of her eyes and the tiny green jewels set in her earlobes and the thin silver band that encircled her brow. In his dream he held his hands to her and said, 'Mother, here I am. Call me to you, mother.'

She smiled at him, but she made no answer.

They were in a garden, with alabandinas in bloom all about them. She nipped at the plants with a small golden implement, clipping away flower-buds so the remaining ones would yield larger blossoms. He stood beside her, waiting for her to turn to him, but the work of nipping went on and on, and finally she said, still not looking his way, 'One must give constant attention to one's task if it is to be done properly.'

'Mother, I am Valentine your son!'

'See, each branch has five buds? Let them be and they all will open, but I take two away here, one here, one here, and the blooms are glorious.' And as she spoke the buds unfurled, and the alabandinas filled the air with a fragrance so keen it stunned him, while the great yellow petals stretched forth like platters, revealing the black stamens and pistils within. She touched them lightly, sending a scattering of purple pollen into the air. And said, 'You are who you are, and always will be.' The dream changed, then, with nothing of the Lady remaining in it, but only a bower of thorny bushes waving rigid arms at him, and moleeka-birds of colossal size strutting about, and other images, confused and ever-altering and telling him nothing that had coherent pattern.

When he woke he was expected to report at once to his dream-speaker, not Talinot Esulde but another acolyte of the guide level, this a person named Stauminaup, shaven also and also of ambiguous sex, but more likely than not a woman. These acolytes were of a medium level of initiation, Valentine had learned yesterday. They returned from Second Cliff to serve the needs of novices here.

Dream-speaking on the Isle was nothing like that which he had experienced in Falkynkip with Tisana. There were no drugs, there was no lying-together of bodies. He merely came into the presence of the speaker and described his dream. Stauminaup listened impassively. Valentine suspected that the speaker had had access to his dream as he was experiencing it, and merely wanted to contrast Valentine's account of it with her own perceptions, to see what gulfs and contradictions might lie between. Therefore he presented the dream exactly as he recalled it, saying, as he had in sleep, 'Mother, I am Valentine your son!' and studying Stauminaup for a reaction to that. But he might as well have been studying the chalk face of the cliff.

When he was done the speaker said, 'And what color were the alabandina blooms?'

'Why, yellow, with black centers!'

'A lovely flower. In Zimroel the alabandinas are scarlet, and yellow at the center. Do you like the colors of yours better?'

'I have no preference,' said Valentine.

Stauminaup smiled. 'The alabandinas of Alhanroel are yellow, with black centers. You may go now.'

The speakings were much the same every day: a cryptic comment, or one that was perhaps not so cryptic, but lay open to varying interpretations, only no interpretations ever were offered. Stauminaup was like a repository for his dreams, absorbing them without providing counsel. Valentine became accustomed to that.

He became accustomed, too, to the daily routines of labor. He worked in the garden two hours each morning, doing minor trimming and weeding and much turning of soil, and in the afternoons he was a mason, taking instruction in the art of pointing the flagstones of the terrace. There were long sessions of meditation in which he was given no guidance whatever, only sent off to his room to stare at the walls. He saw hardly anything of his companions of the journey, except when they bathed together, at mid-morning and again just before dinner, in the sparkling pool; and they had little to say. It was easy to get into the rhythm of this place and cast aside all urgencies. The tropic air, the perfume of millions of blossoms, the gentle tone of everything that went on here, lulled and soothed like a warm bath.

But Alhanroel lay thousands of miles to the east, and he was moving not an inch toward his goal so long as he remained at the Terrace of Assessment. Already a week had gone by. During his meditation sessions Valentine entertained fantasies of collecting his people and slipping away by night, passing illicitly through terrace after terrace, scaling Second Cliff and Third, presenting himself ultimately to the Lady at the threshold of her temple; but he suspected they would not get far, in a place where dreams were open books.

So he fretted. He knew that fretting would win him no advancement here, and he taught himself instead to relax, to give himself up utterly to his tasks, to clear his mind of all needs and compulsions and attachments, and thus to open the way toward the dream of summoning by which the Lady would beckon him inward. That had no effect either. He plucked weeds, he cultivated the warm rich soil, he carried buckets of mortar and grout to the farthest reaches of the terrace, he sat crosslegged in his meditation hours with his mind entirely empty, and night after night he went to bed praying that the Lady would appear and tell him, 'It is time for you to come to me,' but nothing happened.

'How long will this continue?' he asked Deliamber at the pool one day. 'It's the fifth week! Or maybe the sixth – I'm losing count. Do I stay here a year? Two? five?'

'Some of the pilgrims among us have done just that,' said the Vroon. 'I spoke with one, a Hjort who served in patrols under Lord Voriax. She has spent four years here and seems quite resigned to staying at the outermost terrace forever.'

'She has no need to go elsewhere. This is a pleasant enough inn, Deliamber. But I—'

'—have urgent appointments to the east,' Deliamber said. 'And therefore you are condemned to remain here. There's a paradox in your dilemma, Valentine. You strive to renounce purpose; but your renunciation itself has a purpose. Do you see? Your speaker surely does.'

'Of course I see. But what do I do? How do I pretend not to care whether I stay here forever?'

'Pretense is impossible. The moment you genuinely don't care, you'll move onward. Not until then.'

Valentine shook his head. 'That's like telling me that my salvation depends on never thinking of gihorna-birds. The harder I'd try not to think of them, the more flocks of gihornas would fly through my mind. What am I to do, Deliamber?'

But Deliamber had no other suggestions. The next day, Valentine learned that Shanamir and Vinorkis had received advancement to the Terrace of Inception.

Two more days passed before Valentine saw Deliamber again. The wizard remarked that Valentine did not look well; and Valentine replied, with an impatience he could not control, 'How do you expect me to look? Do you know how many weeds I've pulled, how much masonry I've pointed, while in Alhanroel a Barjazid sits on Castle Mount and—'

'Peace,' Deliamber said softly. 'This is not like you.'

'Peace? Peace? How long can I be peaceful?'

'Perhaps your patience is being tested. In which case, my lord, you are failing the test.'

Valentine considered that. After a moment he said, 'I admit your logic. But perhaps it's my ingenuity that's being tested. Deliamber, put a summoning-dream into my head tonight.'

'My sorceries, you know, seem of little value on this island.'

'Do it. Try it. Concoct a message from the Lady and plant it in my mind, and then we'll see.'

Deliamber, shrugging, touched his tentacles to Valentine's hands for the moment of thought-transference. Valentine felt the faint distant tingle of contact.

'Your sorceries still work,' he said.

And that night there came to him a dream in which he drifted like a volevant in the bathing-pool, attached to the rocks by some membrane that had sprouted from his feet, and as he sought to free himself the face of the Lady appeared, smiling, in the night sky, and whispered to him, 'Come, Valentine, come to me, come,' and the membrane dissolved, and he floated upward and soared on the breeze, borne by the wind toward Inner Temple.

Valentine relayed the dream to Stauminaup in his dream-speaking session. She listened as though he were telling her of a dream of plucking weeds in the garden. The next night Valentine pretended he had had the same dream, and again she made no comment. He offered the dream on the next, and asked for a speaking of it.

Stauminaup said, 'The speaking of your dream is that no bird flies with another's wings.'

His cheeks reddened. He went slinking away from her chamber.

Five days later, he was told by Talinot Esulde that he had been granted admission to the Terrace of Inception.

'But *why*?' he asked Deliamber.

The Vroon replied. '*Why?* is a useless question in matters of spiritual progress. Obviously something has altered in you.'

'But I've had no legitimate summoning dream!'

'Perhaps you have,' said the sorcerer.

One of the acolytes took him, by foot, through the forest paths to the next terrace. The road was a maze, zigzagging bewilderingly, several times requiring them to turn in what seemed like precisely the wrong direction. Valentine was altogether lost by the time they emerged, some hours later, into a cleared area of immense size. Pyramids of dark-blue stone ten feet high rose there at regular intervals from the pink flagstone of the terrace.

Life was much the same here – menial tasks, meditation, daily dream-speaking, stark ascetic quarters, drab food. But there was also the beginning of holy instruction, an hour each afternoon in which the principles of the grace of the Lady were explained by means of elliptical parables and circuitous dialogues.

Valentine listened restlessly to all that at first. It seemed vague and abstract to him, and it was hard to concentrate on such cloudy matters when what possessed him was a direct political passion – to reach Castle Mount and settle the questioning of the governing of Majipoor. But by the third day it struck him that what the acolyte was saying about the role of the Lady was entirely political. She was a tempering force, Valentine realized, a mortar of love and faith binding together the centers of power on this world. However she worked her magic of dream-sending – and it was impossible to believe the popular myth, that she was in touch with the minds of millions of people every night – it was clear that her calm spirit soothed and eased the planet. The apparatus of the King of Dreams, Valentine knew, sent direct and specific dreams that lashed the guilty and admonished the uncertain, and the sendings of the King could be fierce. But as the warmth of the ocean moderates the climate of the land, so did the Lady make gentle the harsh forces of control on Majipoor, and the theology that had arisen around the person of the Lady as Divine Mother Incarnate was, Valentine now understood, only a metaphor for the division of power that the early rulers of Majipoor had devised.

So he listened with keener interest. He put aside his eagerness to move to loftier terraces for a time, in order to learn more here.

Valentine was entirely alone at this terrace. That was new. Shanamir and Vinorkis were nowhere to be seen – had they been sent on already to the Terrace of Mirrors? – and the rest, so far as he knew, remained behind. Most of all he missed Carabella's sparkling energies and Deliamber's sardonic wisdom, but the others too had become part of his soul in the long difficult journey across Zimroel, and not to have them about him here was discomforting. His days as a juggler seemed long gone and never to be recaptured. Occasionally now he would, in leisure moments, take fruits from the trees and toss them in the old familiar patterns, to the amusement of passing novices and acolytes. One in particular, a thick-shouldered black-bearded man named Farssal, made a point of watching closely whenever Valentine juggled.

'Where did you learn those arts?' Farssal asked.

'In Pidruid,' Valentine said. 'I was with a juggling troupe.'

'It must have been a fine life.'

'It was,' said Valentine, remembering the excitement of standing before the dark-visaged Lord Valentine in the arena at Pidruid, and of stepping out onto the vast stage of Dulorn's Perpetual Circus, and all the rest, unforgettable scenes of his past.

Farssal said, 'Can those skills be taught, or is it an inborn knack?'

'Anyone can learn, anyone with a quick eye and the willingness to concentrate. I learned myself in just a week or two, last year in Pidruid.'

'No! Surely you've juggled all your life!'

'Not before last year.'

'What led you to take it up, then?'

Valentine smiled. 'I needed a livelihood, and there were traveling jugglers in Pidruid for the Coronal's festival, who had need of an extra pair of hands. They taught me quickly, as I could teach you.'

'You could, do you think?'

'Here,' Valentine said, and tossed the black-bearded man one of the fruits he was juggling, a firm green bishawar. 'Throw that back and forth between your hands awhile, to loosen your fingers. You must master a few basic positions, and certain habits of perception, which will take practice, and then—'

'What did you do before you were a juggler?' asked Farssal as he tossed the fruit.

'I wandered about,' said Valentine. 'Here: hold your hands in this fashion—'

He drilled Farssal half an hour, trying to train him as Carabella and Sleet had done for him at the inn in Pidruid. It was a welcome diversion in this placid and monotonous life. Farssal had quick hands and good eyes, and learned rapidly, though not nearly so rapidly as Valentine had. Within a few days he had developed most of the elementary skills and could juggle after a fashion, though not gracefully. He was an outgoing and talkative man, who kept up a steady flow of conversation as he flipped the bishawars from hand to hand. Born in Ni-moya, he said; for many years a merchant in Piliplok; recently overtaken by a spiritual crisis that had thrust him into confusion and then sent him on the Isle pilgrimage. He talked of his marriage, his unreliable sons, his winning and losing huge fortunes at the gaming-tables; and he wanted to know all about Valentine as well, his family, his ambitions, the motives that had brought him to the Lady. Valentine dealt with these queries as plausibly as he could, and turned aside the most awkward ones with quickly contrived dissertations on the art of juggling.

At the end of the second week – toil, study, meditation, periods of free time spent juggling with Farssal, a stable and static round – Valentine felt restlessness coming over him again, the yearning to be moving onward.

He had no idea how many terraces there were – nine? ninety? – but if he spent this much time at each, he might be years in reaching the Lady. Some means of abbreviating the process of ascent was needed.

Counterfeit summoning-dreams did not seem to work. He trotted forth his drifting-in-the-pool dream for Silimein, his dream-speaker here, but she was no more impressed by it than Stauminaup had been. He tried, during his meditation periods and when he was falling asleep at night, to reach forth to the mind of the Lady and implore her to summon him. This produced nothing useful either.

He asked those who sat near him in the dining-hall how long they had been at the Terrace of Inception. 'Two years,' said one. 'Eight months,' said another. They looked untroubled.

'And you?' he asked Farssal.

Farssal said he had arrived only a few days before Valentine. But he felt no impatience about moving on. 'There's no hurry, is there? We serve the Lady wherever we may be, don't you think? So one terrace is as good as another.'

Valentine nodded. He hardly dared disagree.

Late in the third week he thought he caught sight of Vinorkis far across the field of stajja where he was working. But he was not sure – was that a flash of orange on that Hjort's whiskers? – and the distance was too great for shouting. The next day, though, as Valentine stood casually juggling with Farssal near the bathing-pool, he saw Vinorkis, unquestionably Vinorkis, watching from the other side of the plaza. Valentine excused himself and jogged over. After so many weeks sundered from his old companions here, even the Hjort was a welcome sight.

'Then it *was* you in the stajja-fields,' Valentine said.

Vinorkis nodded. 'These past few days I've had several glimpses of you, my lord. But the terrace is so huge – I've never been able to come close. When did you arrive?'

'About a week after you. Are there others of us here?'

'Not so far as I know,' the Hjort replied. 'Shanamir was, but he's moved on. I see you've lost none of your juggling skill, my lord. Who's your partner?'

'A man of Piliplok. Quick with his hands.'

'And with his tongue as well?'

Valentine frowned. 'What do you mean?'

'Have you said much to this man of your past, my lord, or of your future?'

'Of course not.' Valentine stared. 'No, Vinorkis! Surely no spies of the Coronal right here on the Lady's own Isle!'

'Why not? Is it so hard to infiltrate this place?'

'But why do you suspect—'

'Last night, after I glimpsed you in the fields, I came here to make inquiry about you. One of those I spoke to was your new friend, my lord. Asked him if he knew you and he started questioning *me*. Was I your friend, had I known you in Pidruid, why had we come to the Isle, and so on and so on. My lord, I am uneasy when strangers ask questions. Especially in this place, where one is taught to remain apart from others.'

'You may be too suspicious, Vinorkis.'

'Maybe so. But guard yourself anyway, my lord.'

'That I will,' said Valentine. 'He'll learn nothing from me but what he's already had. Which is merely some juggling.'

'He may already know too much about you,' said the Hjort gloomily. 'But let us watch him, even as he watches you.'

The notion that he might be under surveillance even here dismayed him. Was there no sanctuary? Valentine wished he had Sleet beside him, or Deliamber. A spy now might well become an assassin later, as Valentine drew closer to the Lady and became that much more of a peril to the usurper.

But Valentine seemed to be drawing no closer to the Lady. Another week went by in the same fashion as before. Then, just as he was coming to believe he would spend the rest of his days at the Terrace of Inception, and when he was reaching a point where it mattered little to him if he did, he was called from the fields and told to make ready to go on to the Terrace of Mirrors.

9

This third terrace was a place of dazzling beauty, with a glitter that reminded Valentine of Dulorn. It nestled against the base of Second Cliff, a forbidding vertical wall of white chalk that seemed an absolute barrier to further inward progress, and when the sun was in the west the face of the cliff was such a wonder of reflected brilliance that it stunned the eye and wrung gasps of awe from the soul.

Then, too, there were the mirrors – great rough-hewn slabs of polished black stone set edgewise in the ground everywhere about this terrace, so that wherever one looked one encountered one's own image, glowing against a shining inner light. Valentine at first studied himself critically, searching for the changes that his journey had brought upon him, some dimming of the warm radiance that had flowed from him since the Pidruid days, or perhaps marks of weariness or stress. But he saw none of that, only the familiar golden-haired smiling man, and he waved to himself and winked amiably and saluted, and then, after a week or so, ceased to notice his reflection at all. If he had been ordered to ignore the mirrors he would probably have lived in guilty tension, flicking his gaze involuntarily toward them and wrenching it away; but no one here told him what purpose the mirrors served or what attitude he should take toward them, and in time he simply forgot them. This, he realized much later, was the key to forward movement on the Isle: evolution of the spirit from within, a growing ability to discern and discard the irrelevant.

He was entirely alone here. No Shanamir, no Vinorkis, and no Farssal. Valentine kept close watch for the black-bearded man: if indeed he was some sort of spy, he would doubtless find a way to follow Valentine from terrace to terrace. But Farssal did not arrive.

Valentine stayed at the Terrace of Mirrors eleven days and went onward, in the company of five other novices, via a floater-sled to the rim of Second Cliff and the Terrace of Consecration.

From here there was a magnificent view back over the first three terraces, far below, to the distant sea. Valentine could barely see the Terrace of Assessment – only a thin line of pink against the dark green of the forest – but the great Terrace of Inception spread out awesomely at the mid-point of the lower plateau, and the Terrace of Mirrors, just below, blazed like a million bright pyres in noonday light.

It was becoming unimportant to him, now, how swift his pace might be. Time was losing its meaning. He had slipped entirely into the rhythm of the place. He worked in the fields; he attended lengthy sessions of spiritual instruction; he spent much of his time in the darkened stone-roofed building that was the shrine of the Lady, asking, in a way that was not really asking at all, that illumination be granted him. Occasionally he remembered that he had intended to go quickly to the heart of the Isle and to the woman who dwelled there. But there seemed little urgency to any of that now. He had become a true pilgrim.

Beyond the Terrace of Consecration lay the Terrace of Flowers, and beyond that the Terrace of Devotion, and then the Terrace of Surrender. All these were of Second Cliff, as was the Terrace of Ascent, which was the final stage before one went up onto the plateau where the Lady lived. Each of the terraces, Valentine came to understand, completely encircled the island, so that there might be a million votaries in each at any time, or even more, and each pilgrim saw only a tiny segment of the whole as he pursued his course toward the center. How much effort had gone into constructing all this! How many lives had been given over entirely to the Lady's service! And each pilgrim moved within a sphere of silence: no friendships were begun here, no confidences were exchanged, no lovers embraced. Farssal had been a mysterious exception to that custom. It was as though this place existed outside of time and apart from the ordinary rituals of life.

In this middle zone of the Isle there was less emphasis on teaching, more on toil. When he reached Third Cliff, he knew, he would join those who actually carried out the Lady's work in the world at large; for it was not the Lady herself, he now understood, who emanated most sendings to the world, but rather the millions of advanced acolytes of Third Cliff, whose minds and spirits became amplifiers for the Lady's benevolence. Not that everyone reached Third Cliff: many of the older acolytes, he gathered, had spent decades on Second Cliff, performing administrative tasks, with neither the hope nor the desire of moving toward the more taxing responsibilities of the inner zone.

In his third week at the Terrace of Devotion, Valentine was granted what he knew to be an unmistakable summoning-dream.

He saw himself crossing that parched purple plain that had darkened his sleep in Pidruid. The sun was low at the horizon and the sky was harsh and bleak, and ahead of him lay two broad mountain ranges that rose like giant swollen fists. In the jagged boulder-strewn valley between them the last ruddy glimmer of sunlight was visible, a peculiar oily light, ominous, more a stain than a radiance. A cool dry wind blew out of that strangely illuminated valley, and on it came sighing, singing sounds, soft melancholy melodies riding the breeze. Valentine walked for hours but made no progress: the mountains grew no nearer, the desert sands extended themselves infinitely as he trekked, that last shard of light did not depart. His strength was ebbing. Menacing mirages danced before him. He saw Simonan Barjazid, the King of Dreams, and his three sons. He saw the ghastly senile Pontifex roaring on his subterranean throne. He saw monstrous amorfibots crawling sluggishly in the dunes, and the snouts of massive dhumkars rising like augers out of the sands, probing the air for prey. Things hissed and twanged and whispered; insects swarmed in nasty little clouds; a rain of dry sand began to fall, lightly, clogging his eyes and nostrils. He was weary and ready at any moment to yield and halt, to lie down in the sand and let the shifting dunes cover him, but one thing drew him on, for in the valley a glowing figure moved to and fro, a smiling woman, the Lady his mother, and so long as she could be seen there he would not cease pressing forward. He felt the warmth of her presence, the pull of her love. 'Come,' she murmured. 'Come to me, Valentine!' Her arms reached toward him across that terrible desert of monstrosities. His shoulders sagged. His knees weakened. He could not continue, though he knew he must. 'Lady,' he whispered, 'I am at my end, I must rest, I must sleep!' At that the glow between the mountains grew warmer and brighter. 'Valentine,' she called. 'Valentine, my son!' He could scarcely keep his eyes open. It was so tempting to lie down in the warm sand. 'You are my son,' came the voice of the Lady across that impossible distance, 'and I have need of you,' and as she said these words he found new strength, and walked more rapidly, and then began to run lightly over the hard, crusted desert floor, his heart lifting, his stride widening. Now the distances quickly dwindled, and Valentine could see her clearly, awaiting him on a terrace of violet-hued stone, smiling, reaching to him with outstretched arms, calling his name in a voice that rang like the bells of Ni-moya.

He awoke with the sound of her voice still ringing in his mind.

It was dawn. Wondrous energy flooded his spirit. He rose and went down to the great amethystine basin that was the bathing-pool at the Terrace of Devotion, and plunged boldly into the chilly spring-water. Afterward he trotted to the chamber of Menesipta, his dream-speaker here, a compact, fine-honed person with flashing dark eyes and a taut, spare face, and poured forth the dream to her in one long rush of words.

Menesipta sat silently.

The coolness of her response dampened Valentine's exuberance. He remembered going to Stauminaup at the Terrace of Assessment with the fraudulent summoning-dream of the volevant, and how swiftly Stauminaup had dismissed that dream. But this was no fraud. He had no Deliamber here to do witcheries on his mind.

Valentine said at length, 'May I ask an evaluation?'

'The dream has familiar overtones,' Menesipta replied calmly.

'Is that your whole speaking of it?'

She seemed amused. 'What more would you have me say?'

Valentine clenched his fists in frustration. 'If someone came to me for a speaking of such a dream, I would call it a dream of summoning.'

'Very well.'

'Do you agree? Would *you* call it a dream of summoning?'

'If it would please you.'

'Pleasing me isn't the point,' said Valentine, irritated. 'Either the dream was a dream of summoning or it wasn't. What is your view of it?'

Smiling obliquely, the dream-speaker said, 'I call your dream a dream of summoning.'

'And now?'

'Now? Now you have your morning duties to observe.'

'A dream of summoning, as I understand it,' said Valentine tightly, 'is required in order to attain the presence of the Lady.'

'Indeed.'

'Should I not advance now to Inner Temple?'

Menesipta shook her head. 'No one goes from Second Cliff to Inner Temple. Only when you reach the Terrace of Adoration does a summoning-dream suffice of itself to call you inward. Your dream is interesting and important, but it changes nothing. Go to your duties, Valentine.'

Anger throbbed in him as he left her chamber. He knew he was being foolish, that a mere dream could not be enough to sweep him past the remaining hurdles that separated him from the Lady, and yet he had expected so much from it – he had hoped Menesipta would clap her hands and cry out in joy and ship him at once to Inner Temple, and none of that had happened, and the letdown was painful and infuriating.

More pain ensued. As he came from the fields two hours later an acolyte intercepted him and said bluntly, 'You are ordered immediately to the harbor at Taleis, where new pilgrims await your guidance.'

Valentine was stunned. The last thing he wanted now was to be sent back to the starting point.

He was to set out at once, on foot and alone, making his way outward from terrace to terrace and getting himself to the Terrace of Assessment in the shortest possible time. They provided him at the terrace commissary with enough food to see him as far as the Terrace of Flowers. They gave him also a direction-finding device, an amulet to be fastened to his arm, that would scan for buried road-markers and emit a soft high pinging sound.

At midday he left the Terrace of Devotion. But the path he chose was the one inward toward the Terrace of Surrender, not the one that would take him back toward the coast.

The decision came suddenly and with unarguable force. He simply *could not* allow himself to be turned away from the Lady. Slipping off on an unauthorized trek, on this highly disciplined island, held serious risks, but he had no choice.

Valentine circled past the rim of the terrace and found the grassy path that cut diagonally across the recreation field to the main road. There he was supposed to turn left toward the outer terraces. But – feeling extraordinarily conspicuous – he turned right instead and set out briskly toward the interior. Soon he was beyond the settled part of the terrace and the road had narrowed from wide paved highway to earthen track, with forest pressing close on all sides.

Within half an hour he was at a fork in the road. When he started at random down the left-hand branch, the quiet pinging tone of the direction-finding amulet vanished, returning when he had made his way back to the other fork. A useful device, he thought.

He walked steadily until nightfall. Then he camped in a pleasant grove beside a gentle stream, and allowed himself a sparing meal of cheese and sliced meat. He slept fitfully, stretched out on the cool moist ground between two slender trees.

The first pink glimmer of dawn woke him. He stirred, stretched, opened his eyes. A quick splash in the stream, yes, and then a bit of breakfast, and then—

Valentine heard sounds in the forest behind him – twigs snapping, something moving through the bushes. Quietly he slipped behind a thick-trunked tree by the edge of the stream and peered warily around it. And saw a powerfully built black-bearded man emerge from the underbrush, pause by his campsite, look cautiously about.

Farssal.

In a pilgrim's robe. But with a dagger strapped to his left forearm.

Some twenty-five feet separated the two men. Valentine frowned, considering his options, calculated tactics. Where had Farssal found a dagger on this peaceful island? Why was he tracking Valentine through the forest, if not to slay him?

Violence was alien to Valentine. But to take Farssal by surprise seemed the only course that made sense. He rocked back and forth a moment on the balls of his feet, centered his mind as though he were about to juggle, and sprang from his hiding place.

Farssal whirled and managed to get the dagger from its scabbard just as Valentine crashed into him. With a sudden desperate hacking motion Valentine slammed the side of his hand into the underside of Farssal's arm, numbing it, and the dagger dropped to the ground; but an instant later Farssal's meaty aims wrapped Valentine in a crushing grip.

They stood locked, face to face. Farssal was a head shorter than Valentine, but deeper of chest, broader of shoulder, a bull-bodied man. He strained to throw Valentine to the ground; Valentine struggled to break free; neither was able to sway the other, though veins bulged on their foreheads and their faces went red and swollen with strain.

'This is madness,' Valentine murmured. 'Let go, back off. I mean you no harm.'

Farssal only tightened his grip.

'Who sent you?' Valentine asked. 'What do you want with me?'

Silence. The mighty arms, Skandar-strong, continued inexorably pressing inward. Valentine fought for breath. Pain dazed him. He tried to force his elbows outward and snap the hold. No. Farssal's face was ugly and distorted with effort, his eyes fierce, his lips tightly set. And slowly but measurably he was pushing Valentine to the ground.

Resisting that terrible grip was impossible. Valentine abruptly ceased trying, and let himself go limp as a bundle of rags. Farssal, surprised, twisted him to one side; Valentine allowed his knees to buckle, and offered no resistance as Farssal hurled him down. But he landed lightly, on his back with his legs coiled above him, and as Farssal lunged furiously for him Valentine brought his feet up with all his force into the other man's gut. Farssal gasped and grunted and staggered back, stunned. Valentine, springing to his feet, seized Farssal with arms made greatly muscular by months of juggling, and pushed him down roughly to the ground, and held him pinned there, knees against Farssal's outspread arms, hands gripping his shoulders.

How strange this is, Valentine thought, to be fighting hand-to-hand with another being, as though we were unruly children! It had the quality of a dream.

Farssal glared at him in rage, slammed his feet angrily against the ground, tried in vain to push Valentine off.

'Talk to me now,' Valentine said. 'Tell me what this means. Did you come here to kill me?'

'I will say nothing.'

'You who talked so much when we were juggling?'

'That was before.'

'What am I to do with you?' Valentine asked. 'If I let you up, you'll be at me again. But if I hold you here, I hold myself as well!'

'You can't hold me long this way.'

Once more Farssal heaved. His strength was enormous. But Valentine's grip on him was firm. Farssal's face was scarlet; thick cords stood out on his throat; his eyes blazed with fury and frustration. For a long moment he lay still. Then he appeared to gather all his strength, going tense and thrusting upward. Valentine could not withstand that awesome push. There was a wild moment when neither man was in control of the situation, Valentine half flung aside, Farssal writhing and flexing as he tried to roll over. Valentine grabbed Farssal's thick shoulders and attempted to force him back to the ground. Farssal shook him away and his fingers clawed for Valentine's eyes. Valentine ducked below the clutching fingers. Then, without pausing to think about it, he seized Farssal by his coarse black beard and pulled him to one side, slamming his head into a rock that jutted from the moist soil close beside him.

Farssal made a heavy grunting sound and lay still.

Springing to his feet, Valentine seized the fallen dagger and stood above the other. He was trembling, not out of fear but from the release of tension, like a bowstring after the arrow has been let go. His ribs ached from that awful hug, and the muscles of his arms and shoulders were twitching and throbbing in fifty different rhythms.

'Farssal?' he said, nudging him with one foot.

No response. Dead? No. The great barrel of a chest was slowly rising and falling, and Valentine heard the sound of hoarse, ragged breathing.

Valentine hefted the knife. What now? Sleet might say, finish the fallen man off before he came to. Impossible. One did not kill, except in self-defense. One certainly did not kill an unconscious man, would be assassin though he might be. To kill another intelligent being meant a lifetime of punishing dreams, the vengeance of the murdered. But he could scarcely just walk away, leaving Farssal to recover and come after him. Some bird-net-vine would be a useful thing to have just now. Valentine did see another sort of vine, a sturdy-looking liana with green-and-yellow stems as thick as his fingers, scrambling far up the side of the tree; and with some fierce tugging he pulled down five huge strands of it. These he wound tightly around Farssal, who stirred and moaned but did not regain consciousness. In ten minutes Valentine had him securely trussed, bound like a mummy from chest to ankles. He tested the vines and they held tight at his pull.

Valentine gathered his few possessions and hurried away.

The savage encounter in the forest had shaken him badly. Not only the fighting, though that was barbaric enough, and would disturb him a long while; but also the idea that his enemy no longer was content merely to spy on him, but was sending murderers to him. And if that is so, he thought, can I doubt any longer the truth of the visions that tell me I am Lord Valentine?

Valentine barely comprehended the concept of deliberate murder. One absolutely did not take the lives of others. In the world he knew, that was basic. Not even the usurper, overthrowing him, had dared to kill him, for fear of the dark dreams that would come; but evidently now he was willing to accept that dread risk. Unless, Valentine thought, Farssal had resolved on the assassination attempt by himself, as a ghastly way of winning the favor of his employers, when he discovered Valentine slipping away toward the inner zone of the Isle.

A somber business. Valentine shuddered. More than once, as he strode along the forest trails, he looked tensely behind him, half expecting to see the black-bearded man pursuing him again.

But no pursuers came. By mid-afternoon Valentine saw the Terrace of Surrender in the distance, and the flat white face of Third Cliff far beyond it.

No one was likely to notice an unauthorized pilgrim quietly moving about among all these millions. He entered the Terrace of Surrender with what he hoped was an innocent expression, as if he had every right to be there. It was an opulent, spacious place, with a row of lofty buildings of dark blue stone at its eastern end and a grove of bassa-trees in fruit closer at hand. Valentine added half a dozen of the tender, succulent bassa-fruits to his pack and continued to the terrace baths, where he rid himself of the grime of his first day's trek. Growing even bolder, he found the dining-hall and helped himself to soup and stewed meat. And as casually as he had come, he slipped out the far end of the terrace just as night was descending.

Again he slept in an improvised forest bed, dozing and waking often to thoughts of Farssal, and when there was light enough he rose and went onward. The stupefying white wall of Third Cliff loomed high above the forest before him.

All day he walked, and all the next, and still he seemed no closer to the cliff. Traveling on foot through these woods, he was covering, he guessed, no more than fifteen or eighteen miles a day; might it be fifty or eighty to Third Cliff? And then, how far from there to Inner Temple? This journey might take weeks. He walked on. His stride grew ever more springy; this forest life was agreeing with him.

On the fourth day Valentine reached the Terrace of Ascent. He paused briefly to refresh himself, slept in a quiet grove, and in the morning went onward until he arrived at the base of Third Cliff.

He knew nothing of the mechanism that transported the floater-sleds up the cliff walls. From here he could see the small settlement at the floater station, a few cottages, some acolytes working in a field, sleds stacked by the foot of the cliff. He considered waiting until darkness and then trying to run the sleds, but decided against it: climbing that giddy height unaided, using equipment he did not understand, seemed too risky. Forcing the acolytes to aid him was even less to his liking.

One option remained. He tidied his travel-stained robes, donned an air of supreme authority, and advanced at a dignified pace toward the floater station.

The acolytes – there were three of them – regarded him coolly.

He said, 'Are the floaters ready for operation?'

'Have you business on Third Cliff?'

'I do.' Valentine turned on them his most dazzling smile, letting them see, also, an underlying aspect of confidence, strength, total self-assurance. He said crisply, 'I am Valentine of Alhanroel, under special summons to the Lady. They wait for me above to escort me to Inner Temple.'

'Why were we not told of this?'

Valentine shrugged. 'How would I know? Someone's error, obviously. Shall I wait here until the papers arrive for you? Shall the Lady wait for me? Come, get your floaters floating!'

'Valentine of Alhanroel – special summons to the Lady—' The acolytes frowned, shook their heads, peered uncomfortably at one another. 'This is all very irregular. Who did you say is to be your escort up there?'

Valentine took a deep breath. 'The High Speaker Tisana of Falkynkip herself has been sent to fetch me!' he announced resonantly. 'She, too, will be kept waiting while you fidget and fumble! Will you answer to her for this delay? You know what sort of temper the High Speaker has!'

'True, true,' the acolytes agreed nervously, nodding to one another as though such a person actually existed and her wrath were something greatly to be dreaded.

Valentine saw that he had won. With brisk impatient gestures he mobilized them to their tasks, and in a moment he was aboard a sled and floating serenely toward the highest and most sacred of the three cliffs of the Isle of Sleep.

10

The air atop Third Cliff was clear and pure and cool, for this level of the Isle lay thousands of feet above sea level, and up here in the eyrie of the Lady the environment was quite different from that of the two lower steps. The trees were tall and slim, with needlelike leaves and open, symmetrical boughs, and the shrubs and plants about them had a subtropical hardiness to them, thick glossy leaves and sturdy rubbery stems. Looking back, Valentine could not see the ocean from here, only the forested sprawl of Second Cliff and a hint of First Cliff far beyond.

A pathway of elegantly joined stone blocks led from the rim of Third Cliff toward the forest. Unhesitatingly Valentine set out upon it. He had no idea of the topography of this level, only that there were many terraces, and the last of them was the Terrace of Adoration, where one awaited the call to the Lady. He did not expect to get all the way to the threshold of Inner Temple unintercepted: but he would go as far as he could, and when they seized him as a trespasser he would give them his name and ask that it be conveyed to the Lady, and the rest would be subject to her mercy, her grace.

He was halted before he reached the outermost of Third Cliff's terraces.

Five acolytes in the robes of the inner hierarchy, gold with red trim, emerged from the forest and arrayed themselves coolly across his path. There were three men, two women, all of considerable age, and they showed no fear of him at all.

One of the women, white-haired, with thin lips and dark, intense eyes, said, 'I am Lorivade of the Terrace of Shadows and I ask you in the Lady's name how you come to be here.'

'I am Valentine of Alhanroel,' he replied evenly, 'and I am of the Lady's own flesh and would have you take me to her.'

The brazen statement produced no smiles among the hierarchs.

Lorivade said, 'You claim kinship with the Lady?'

'I am her son.'

'Her son's name is Valentine, and he is Coronal on Castle Mount. What madness is this?'

'Bring to the Lady the news that her son Valentine has come to her across the Inner Sea and all of Zimroel, and that he is a fair-haired man, and I ask no more than that.'

One of the men at Lorivade's side said, 'You wear the robes of Second Cliff. It is forbidden for you to have made this ascent.'

With a sigh Valentine said, 'I understand that. My ascent was unauthorized, illegal, and presumptuous. But I claim the highest reasons of state. If my message is delayed in reaching the Lady, you will answer for it.'

'We are not accustomed to threats here,' Lorivade declared.

'I make no threat. I speak only of inevitable consequences.'

A woman to the right of Lorivade said, 'He's a lunatic. We'll have to confine him and treat him.'

'And censure the crew below,' said another man.

'And discover which terrace he's from, and how he was allowed to wander away from it,' said a third.

'I ask only that you send my message to the Lady,' Valentine said quietly.

They surrounded him and, moving in formation, walked him briskly along the forest path to a place where three floaters were parked and a number of younger acolytes waited. Evidently they had been prepared for serious trouble. Lorivade gestured to one of the acolytes and issued brief orders; then the five hierarchs boarded one of the floaters and were borne away.

Acolytes moved toward Valentine. None too gently they caught him and propelled him toward a floater. He smiled and indicated he would make no resistance, but they held him firmly and pushed him roughly into a seat. The floater rose to full hover and, at a signal, the mounts tethered to it began to trot toward the nearby terrace.

It was a place of wide, low buildings and great stone plazas, this Terrace of Shadows, and the shadows that gave it its name were black as the darkest ink, mysterious all-engulfing pools of night that stretched in strangely significant patterns over the abstract stone statuary. But Valentine's tour of the terrace was brief. His captors halted outside a squat stark building without windows; a cunningly fashioned door slid open on silent hinges at the lightest of touches; he was ushered inside.

The door closed and left no trace in the wall.

He was a prisoner.

The room was square, low-ceilinged, and bleak. A single dim glow-float cast a mellow greenish light. There was a cleanser, a sink, a commode, a mattress. Beyond that, nothing.

Would they send his message to the Lady?

Or would they leave him here to grow dusty, while they investigated the irregularities of his advent on Third Cliff, rummaging for weeks in the island bureaucracy?

An hour passed, two, three. Let them send an interrogator, he prayed, an inquisitor, anyone, only not this silence, this boredom, this solitude. He counted paces. The room was not precisely square: one pair of walls was a pace and a half longer than the other pair. He searched for the outlines of the doorway, and could not find them. The fit was seamless, a marvel of design that gave him little cheer. He invented dialogues and silently embellished them: Valentine and Deliamber, Valentine and the Lady, Valentine and Carabella, Valentine and Lord Valentine. But it was an amusement that soon palled.

He heard a faint whining sound and whirled to see a slot open in the wall and a tray come sliding into his cell. They had given him baked fish, a cluster of ivory-colored grapes, a beaker of cool red juice. 'For this repast I thank you kindly,' he said out loud. His fingers probed the wall, seeking the places where the tray had entered: no trace.

He ate. He invented more dialogues, conversing in his mind with Sleet, with the old dream-speaker Tisana, with Zalzan Kavol, with Captain Gorzval. He asked them about their childhoods, their hopes and dreams, their political opinions, their tastes in food and drink and clothing. Again the game wore thin after a while, and he stretched out to sleep.

Sleep was thin too, a shallow doze, broken half a dozen times by white dreary spells of wakefulness. His dreams were patchy ones; through them drifted the Lady, Farssal, the King of Dreams, the Metamorph chieftain, and the hierarch Lorivade, but they offered only muddled and murky words. When he woke, finally, a tray of breakfast had appeared in the room.

A long day passed.

He had never known a day so interminable. There was nothing at all to do, nothing, nothing whatever, an endless stretch of gray nothingness. He would have juggled his dishes, but they were light and flimsy things and it would have been like juggling feathers. He tried to juggle his boots, but he had only two of those and juggling things in twos was a fool's sport. He juggled memories instead, reliving all that had befallen him since Pidruid, but the prospect of an infinity of hours doing that dismayed him. He meditated until there was a dull buzz of fatigue between his ears. He crouched in the center of the room, trying to anticipate the moment when the next meal would arrive, but the tension he generated out of that yielded only feeble entertainment.

On the second night Valentine made an attempt to communicate with the Lady. He prepared himself for sleep, but as his mind began to release itself from consciousness he endeavored to slip into an intermediate place between waking and sleeping, a trance-state of sorts. It was a ticklish business, for if he concentrated too intently he would tip himself back into full wakefulness, and if he relaxed too thoroughly he would fall asleep; he balanced there a long time, at the floating-point, wishing he had taken the opportunity in some quiet part of his Zimroel journey to have Deliamber train him in these matters.

At last he sent forth his spirit.

—Mother?

He imagined his soul coursing high over the Terrace of Shadows and drifting inward, past terrace after terrace, to the core of Third Cliff, to Inner Temple, to the chamber where the Lady of the Isle rested.

—Mother, it's Valentine. It's your son Valentine. I have so much to tell you, mother, and so much to ask! But you have to help me reach you.

Valentine lay still. He was wholly calm. A pure white radiance seemed to glow in his mind.

—Mother, I'm on Third Cliff, in a prison cell in the Terrace of Shadows. I've come so far, mother. But now I'm stopped. Send for me, mother!

—Mother—

—Lady—

—Mother—

He slept.

The radiance still glowed. He perceived the first tingling music of the dream-state, the overture, the initial sensations of contact. Visions came. No longer was he imprisoned. He lay beneath the cool white stars on a great circular platform of finely polished stone, as though an altar, and to him came a white-robed woman with lustrous dark hair, who knelt beside him and touched him lightly, saying in a tender voice, 'You are my son Valentine, and I do acknowledge you before all Majipoor to be my son, and I summon you now to my side.'

That was all. When he woke he could recall nothing of the dream but that.

There was no breakfast tray for him that morning. Was it truly morning, then, or had he awakened in the middle of the night? Hours passed. No tray. Had they forgotten him? Did they plan to starve him to death? He felt a twinge of terror: was that an improvement over boredom? He thought he preferred boredom to terror, but not by much. He called out, but he knew it was useless. This place was sealed like a tomb. Like a tomb. Glumly Valentine looked at the accumulation of old trays, stacked against the far walls. He remembered the wonders and joys of food, the sausages of the Liimen, the fish that Khun and Sleet had grilled on the banks of the Steiche, the flavor of dwikka-fruit, the potent tang of fireshower wine in Pidruid. His hunger was growing intense. And he was frightened. Not bored at all now, but frightened. They had held a meeting, perhaps, and condemned him to death for overwhelming folly.

Minutes. Hours. Half a day gone now.

Folly to think he could touch the Lady's mind in sleep. Folly to think he could float effortlessly into Inner Temple and win her aid. Folly to think he could regain Castle Mount, or that he had ever had it at all. He had propelled himself halfway around the world on no force other than folly, and now, he thought bitterly, he would have the reward of his presumption and his foolishness.

Then at last he heard the familiar faint whine. But it was not the food-slot opening: it was the door.

Two white-haired hierarchs entered the cell. They favored him with a look of bleak and sour bafflement.

'Have you come to deliver my breakfast?' Valentine asked.

'We have come,' said the taller one, 'to conduct you to Inner Temple.'

11

He insisted that they feed him first – a wise move, for the trip proved to be a lengthy one, all the rest of the day by swift mount-drawn floater-wagon.

The hierarchs sat flanking him in chilly silence throughout. When he asked a question – the name of some terrace through which they were passing, for example – they would reply in the fewest possible words; otherwise they offered no chatter.

Third Cliff had many terraces – Valentine lost count after about seven – and they were much closer together than those of the outer cliffs, with only token strips of forest separating them. This central zone of the Isle seemed a busy and populous place.

At twilight they came to the Terrace of Adoration, a domain of serene gardens and rambling low buildings of whitewashed stone. Like all the other terraces it was circular in outline, but it was much smaller than the others, here at the innermost part of the island, a mere ringlet that probably could be walked in all its circumference in an hour or two, whereas it might take months to complete the circuit of a First Cliff terrace. Ancient gnarled trees with close-set oval leaves rose at regular intervals along its rampart. Bowers of richly blossoming vines coiled between the buildings; small courtyards were everywhere, decorated with slender pillars of polished black stone and bedecked with flowering shrubs. In twos and threes the servants of the Lady moved quietly through these peaceful precincts. Valentine was conducted to a chamber far more gracious than his last, with a broad sunken bath, an inviting bed, windows facing into a garden, baskets of fruit on the table. The hierarchs left him here. He bathed, nibbled fruit, waited for the next event. That was some time in arriving, an hour or more: a knock on the door, a soft voice asking if he wished dinner, a cart rolled into the room bearing more substantial fare than he had had since coming to the Isle – grilled meats, blue gourds artfully stuffed with minced fish, a beaker of something cold that might almost have been wine. Valentine ate eagerly. Afterward he stood by his windows a long time, studying the darkness. He saw nothing; he heard no one. He tested his door: locked. So he was still a prisoner, although in far more pleasing surroundings than before.

He slept a dreamless sleep. A flood of golden sunlight cascading into his room awakened him. He bathed; the same discreet servitor appeared outside, with a breakfast of sausages and stewed pink fruit; and a short while after he was done the two somber hierarchs came to him, saying, 'The Lady has summoned you this morning.'

They led him through a garden of marvelous beauty and across a slender bridge of pure white stone that rose in a gentle arch above a dark pond in which golden fish swam in sparkling patterns. Ahead lay a wondrously manicured greensward. At the center of it was a one-story building of great size, extraordinarily delicate in form, with long narrow wings radiating in the form of starbeams from the circular center.

This could only be Inner Temple, Valentine thought.

Now he trembled. He had journeyed, for more months than he could remember, toward this very spot, toward the threshold of the mysterious woman whose realm this was, whom he fancied to be his mother. At last he was here; and what if it proved all to be foolishness, or fantasy, or terrible error, what if he was no one in particular, a yellow-haired idler from Zimroel, bereft of his memory through some stupidity and filled by trifling companions with nonsensical ambitions? The thought was unbearable. If the Lady repudiated him now, if she denied him—

He entered the temple.

The hierarchs still close at his sides, Valentine marched endlessly down an impossibly elongated entrance hall that was guarded every twenty feet by a grim-faced rigid warrior, and into an interior room, octagonal in shape, with walls of the finest white stone and a pool, octagonal also, at its center. Morning light entered through an open eight-sided skylight. At each corner of the room stood a stern figure in hierarchical robes. Valentine, a little dazed, looked from one to the next and saw no welcome on their faces, only a sort of pursed-lip disapproval.

There was a single note of music, softly swelling, then dying away, and when it was gone the Lady of the Isle was in the room.

She seemed much like the figure Valentine had seen so often in dreams: a woman of middle years and ordinary height, dusky of skin, with glossy black hair, warm soft eyes, a full mouth that hovered always at the edge of a smile, a silver band at her brow, and, yes, a flower behind one ear, with many thick green petals. It seemed, though, that there was an aura about her, a nimbus, a radiance of force and authority and majesty, such as befitted the Power of Majipoor that she was, and he had not been prepared for that, expecting as he had been only the warm motherly woman, and forgetting that she was a queen, a priestess, almost a goddess, as well. He stood speechless before her, and for a long moment she studied him from the far side of the pool, her gaze resting lightly but penetratingly on his face. Then she waved one hand sharply in an unmistakable gesture of dismissal. Not of him: of the hierarchs. Their glacial calm was broken by that. They looked to one another, obviously confused. The Lady repeated the gesture, a mere shallow snap of the wrist, and something imperious flashed in her eyes, a look of almost terrifying strength. Three or four of the hierarchs left the room; the others dawdled, as if not believing that the Lady proposed to be left alone with the prisoner. For an instant it seemed that a third wave of her hand might be necessary, as one of the oldest and most imposing of the hierarchs extended a quivering arm toward her in a motion of obvious protest. But at a glance from the Lady the hierarch's arm dropped back to his side. Slowly the last of them went out of the room.

Valentine fought the impulse to fall to his knees.

He said in a barely audible voice, 'I have no idea of the proper obeisance to make. Nor do I know, Lady, how I should address you, without giving offense.'

Calmly she replied, 'It will be enough, Valentine, if you call me mother.'

The quiet words stunned him. He took a faltering few steps toward her, halted, stared.

'Is it so?' he asked in a whisper.

'There can be no doubt of it.'

He felt his cheeks ablaze. He stood helpless, numbed by her grace. She beckoned to him, the tiniest movement of her fingertips, and he shook as though he were caught in an ocean gale.

'Come close,' she said. 'Are you afraid? Come to me, Valentine!'

He crossed the room, went round the pool, drew near her. She put her hands into his. Instantly he felt a jolt of energy, a tangible, palpable throbbing, somewhat akin to what he had felt when Deliamber touched him to do wizardry-work, but enormously more powerful, enormously more awesome. He would have withdrawn his hands at that first throb of force, but she held him, and he could not, and her eyes close by his seemed to be seeing through him, entering all his mysteries.

'Yes,' she said finally. 'By the Divine, yes, Valentine, your body is strange but your soul is of my own making! Oh, Valentine, Valentine, what have they done to you? What have they done to Majipoor?' She tugged at his hands, and pulled him close to her, and then he was in her arms, the Lady straining upward to embrace him, and he felt her trembling now, no goddess but only a woman, a mother holding her troubled son. In her grasp he felt such peace as he had not known since his awakening in Pidruid, and he clung to her, praying she would never release him.

Then she stood back and surveyed him, smiling. 'You were given a handsome body, at least. Nothing like what you once were, but pleasing to the eye, and strong as well, and healthy. They could have done much worse. They could have made you something weak and sickly and deformed, but I suppose they lacked the courage, knowing that eventually they would be repaid tenfold for all their crimes.'

'Who, mother?'

She seemed surprised at his question. 'Why, Barjazid and his brood!'

Valentine said, 'I know nothing, mother, except what has come to me in dreams, and even that has been befogged and muddled.'

'And what is it that you know?'

'That my body has been taken from me, that in some witchery of the King of Dreams I was left outside Pidruid as you see me, that someone else, I think it may be Dominin Barjazid, rules now from Castle Mount. But I know all this only in the most untrustworthy of ways.'

'It is all true,' the Lady replied.

'When was it that this happened?'

'In early summer,' she said. 'When you made the grand processional in Zimroel. I have no knowledge of how it was done; but one night as I lay sleeping I felt a wrenching, a tearing, as of the heart of the planet being ripped loose, and I awakened knowing that something evil and monstrous had occurred, and I sent out my soul toward you and was unable to reach you. There was only a silence where you had been, a void. Yet it was different from the silence that struck me when Voriax was slain, for I still felt your presence, but beyond my reach, as if behind a thick sheet of glass. I asked at once for news of the Coronal. He is in Til-omon, my people told me. And is he well? I asked. Yes, they said, he is well, he sails today toward Pidruid. But I could make no contact, Valentine. I sent forth my soul as I had not done in years, to every part of the world, and you were nowhere and somewhere, both at once. I was frightened and confused, Valentine, but I could do nothing but seek and wait, and news came to me that Lord Valentine had reached Pidruid, that he was guest in the mayor's grand house, and I had a vision of him across all this distance and his face was the face of my son. But his mind was other, and it was closed to me. I attempted a sending, and I could not send to him. And at last I began to understand.'

'Did you know where I was?'

'Not at first. They had switched your mind so well it was altogether changed. Night after night I cast my soul forth into Zimroel in search of you – neglecting everything else here, but this was no trifling matter, this substitution of Coronals – and I thought I felt glimmers, a shard of your true self, a fragment – and after a time I was able to determine that you were alive, that you were in northwestern Zimroel, but there was still no reaching you. I had to wait until you had awakened more to yourself, until their witcheries had faded a bit and your true mind was restored at least in part.'

'It is still far from whole, mother.'

'I know that. But that can be remedied, I believe.'

'When did you finally reach me?'

She paused a moment in thought. 'It was near the Ghayrog city, I think, Dulorn, and I saw you first through the minds of others who were dreaming the truth about you. And I touched their minds, I refined and clarified what was in them, and I saw that your soul had imprinted its stamp on them and that they knew better than you did yourself what had befallen you. I circled about you in this way, and then I was able to enter you. And from that moment on you have gained in knowledge of your former self, as I have labored across so many thousands of miles to heal you and to draw you to me. But none of it was easy. The world of dreams, Valentine, is a difficult and shifting place, even for me, and to attempt to control it is like writing a book in the sand beside an ocean: the tide returns and obliterates nearly everything, and you just write it again, and again and again. But at last you are here.'

'Did you know it when I reached the Isle?'

'I knew it, yes. I could feel your closeness.'

'And yet you let me drift for months from terrace to terrace!'

She laughed. 'There are millions of pilgrims in the outer terraces. Sensing you was one thing, actually locating you another, far more difficult. Besides, you were not ready to come to me, nor I to receive you. I was testing you, Valentine. Watching you from afar, studying to see how much of your soul had survived, whether there still was any of the Coronal remaining in you. Before I acknowledged you I had to know these things.'

'And does much of Lord Valentine remain in me, then?'

'A great deal. Far more than your enemies could ever suspect. Their scheme was faulty: they thought they had expunged you, when they only fuddled and disordered you.'

'Would it not have been wiser for them to have killed me outright, than to have put my soul in some other body?'

'Wiser, yes,' the Lady replied. 'But they did not dare. Yours is an anointed spirit, Valentine. These Barjazids are superstitious beasts; they will risk overthrowing a Coronal, it seems, but not destroying him altogether, for fear of your spirit's vengeance. And their cowardly hesitation now will bring about the ruin of their scheme.'

Valentine said softly, 'Do you think I can ever regain my place?'

'Do you doubt it?'

'Barjazid wears the face of Lord Valentine. The people accept him as Coronal. He controls the power of Castle Mount. I have perhaps a dozen followers and am unknown. If I proclaim myself rightful Coronal, who will believe me? And how long then before Dominin Barjazid deals with me the way he should have dealt with me in Til-omon?'

'You have the support of the Lady your mother.'

'And have you an army, mother?'

The Lady smiled gently. 'I have no army, no. But I am a Power of Majipoor, which is not a small thing. I have the strength of righteousness and love, Valentine. I also have this.'

She touched the silver circlet at her brow.

'Through which you make your sendings?' Valentine asked.

'Yes. Through which I can reach the minds of all Majipoor. I lack the ability of the Barjazids to control and direct, which their devices are capable of doing. But I can communicate, I can guide, I can influence. You will have one of these circlets before you leave the Isle.'

'And I'll go quietly through Alhanroel, beaming messages of love to the citizens, until Dominin Barjazid descends from the Mount and gives me back the throne?'

The Lady's eyes flashed with the kind of anger Valentine had seen in them when she was sending the hierarchs from the room.

'What sort of talk is that?' she snapped.

'Mother—'

'Oh, they *have* changed you! The Valentine I bore and reared accepted no thought of defeat.'

'Nor do I, mother. But it all seems so immense, and I'm so weary. And to make war against citizens of Majipoor – even against a usurper – Mother, there's been no war on Majipoor since earliest times. Am I the one to break the peace?'

Her eyes were merciless. 'The peace is already broken, Valentine. It falls to you to restore the order of the realm. A false Coronal has reigned nearly a year now. Cruel and foolish laws are proclaimed daily. The innocent are punished, the guilty flourish. Balances constructed thousands of years ago are being destroyed. When our people came here from Old Earth, fourteen thousand years past, many mistakes were made, much suffering was endured, before we found our way of government, but since the time of the first Pontifex we have lived without major upheaval, and since the time of Lord Stiamot there has been peace on this world. Now there has been a rupture of that peace, and it falls to you to put things to rights.'

'And if I accept what Dominin Barjazid has done? If I decline to embroil Majipoor in civil war? Would the consequences be so evil?'

'You know the answers to those questions already.'

'I would hear them from you, because my resolve wavers.'

'It shames me to hear you speak those words.'

'Mother, I have undergone strange things on this journey and they have taken much of my strength. Am I not allowed a moment of fatigue?'

'You are a king, Valentine.'

'I was, perhaps, and perhaps will be again. But much of my kingliness was stolen from me in Til-omon. I am an ordinary man now. And not even kings are immune to weariness and discouragement, mother.'

In a tone more gentle than the one she had been using, the Lady said, 'The Barjazid does not yet rule as an absolute tyrant, for that might turn the people against him, and he is still insecure in his power – while you live. But he rules for himself and for his family, not for Majipoor. He lacks a sense of right, and does only what seems useful and expedient. As his confidence grows, so too will his crimes, until Majipoor groans under the whip of a monster.'

Valentine nodded. 'When I am not so weary, I see that, yes.'

'Think, too, of what will happen when the Pontifex Tyeveras dies, which must sooner or later happen, and more probably sooner than later.'

'Barjazid goes to the Labyrinth then, and becomes a powerless recluse. Is that what you mean?'

'The Pontifex is not powerless, and he does not need to be a recluse. In your lifetime there has been only Tyeveras, growing older and older and steadily more strange. But a Pontifex in full vigor is a very different entity. What if Barjazid is Pontifex five years from now? Do you think he'll be content to sit in that underground hole the way Tyeveras now does? He'll rule with force, Valentine.' She looked at him intently. 'And who do you think will become Coronal?'

Valentine shook his head.

She said, 'The King of Dreams has three sons. Minax is the oldest, who will have the throne in Suvrael one of these days. Dominin is now Coronal and will be Pontifex, if you choose to let him. Whom will he select as new Coronal but his younger brother, Cristoph?'

'But it goes against all nature for a Pontifex to give Castle Mount to his own brother!'

'It goes against all nature for a son of the King of Dreams to overthrow a rightful Coronal, too,' said the Lady. Once more her eyes flashed. 'Consider this, also: when there is a change in Coronals, there is a change in the Lady of the Isle! I go to live out my days in the palace for retired Ladies in the Terrace of Shadows, and who comes to Inner Temple? The mother of the Barjazids! Do you see, Valentine, they will have everything, they will control all of Majipoor!'

'This must not be,' Valentine said.

'This will not be.'

'What shall I do?'

'You will take ship from my port of Numinor to Alhanroel, with all your people and others I will provide for you. You will land in the Stoienzar, and journey to the Labyrinth for the blessing of Tyeveras.'

'But if Tyeveras is a madman—'

'Not entirely mad. He lives in a perpetual dream, and a strange one, but I have touched his spirit lately, and the old Tyeveras still exists somewhere within. He has been Pontifex forty years, Valentine, and was Coronal a long while before that, and he knows the way our realm was meant to be governed. If you can reach him, if you can demonstrate to him that you are the true Lord Valentine, he will give you aid. Then you must march on Castle Mount. Do you shrink from that task?'

'I shrink only from bringing chaos upon Majipoor.'

'The chaos is already at hand. What you bring is order and justice.' She moved close to him, so that all the frightening power of her personality was exposed to him, and touched his hand, and said in a low, vehement tone, 'I bore two sons, and from the moment one looked at them in their cradles, one knew they were meant to be kings. The first was Voriax – do you remember him? I suppose not, not yet – and he was magnificent, a splendid man, a hero, a demigod, and even in his childhood they said of him on Castle Mount, This is the one, this will be Coronal when Lord Malibor becomes Pontifex. Voriax was a marvel, but there was a second son, Valentine, as strong and as splendid as Voriax, not so much given to sport and exploits as he, but a warmer soul, and a wiser one, one who understood without being told what was right and what was wrong, one who had no cruelty in his spirit whatever, one who was of even and balanced and sunny temperament, so that everyone loved him and respected him, and it was said of Valentine that he would be an even finer king than Voriax, but of course Voriax was older and would be chosen, with Valentine fated to be nothing more than a high minister. And Malibor did not become Pontifex, but died before his time hunting dragons, and emissaries of Tyeveras came to Voriax and said, you are Coronal of Majipoor, and the first to fall before him and make the starburst was his brother Valentine. And so Lord Voriax ruled on Castle Mount, and ruled well, and I came to the Isle of Sleep as I had always known I would, and for eight years all was well on Majipoor. And then what happened was something no one could have foretold, that Lord Voriax would perish before his time as Lord Malibor had, hunting in the forest and struck down by a stray bolt. Yet there still was Valentine, and though it was rare for the brother of a Coronal to become Coronal after him, there was little debate, for everyone recognized his high qualifications. Thus Lord Valentine came to the Castle and I who was mother to two kings remained at Inner Temple, satisfied with the sons I had given to Majipoor and confident that the reign of Lord Valentine would be one of Majipoor's glories. Do you think I can allow Barjazids to sit for long where my sons once sat? Do you think I can endure the sight of Lord Valentine's face masking the Barjazid's shabby soul? Oh, Valentine, Valentine, you are only half what you once were, less than half, but you will be yourself again, and Castle Mount will be yours and the destinies of Majipoor will not be altered to something evil, and talk no more of shrinking from bringing chaos into the world. The chaos is upon us. You are the deliverer. Do you understand?'

'I understand, mother.'

'Then come with me, and I will make you whole.'

12

She led him from the octagonal chamber, down one of the spokes of Inner Temple, past rigid guards and a group of frowning, bewildered hierarchs, into a small bright room bedecked with brilliant flowers of a dozen colors. Here was a desk fashioned of a single slab of gleaming darbelion, and a low couch, and a few small pieces of furniture; this was the Lady's study, it seemed. She beckoned Valentine to a seat and took from the desk two small ornate flasks. 'Drink this wine in a single draught,' she told him, handing him one flask.

'Wine, mother? On the Isle?'

'You and I are not pilgrims here. Drink it.'

He uncorked the flask and put it to his lips. The flavor was familiar to him, dark and spicy and sweet, but it was a moment before he could identify it: the wine dream-speakers used, that contained the drug that made minds open to minds. The Lady downed the contents of the second flask.

Valentine said, 'Are we then to do a speaking?'

'No. This must be done while awake. I have thought long about how to manage this.' From her desk she withdrew a shimmering silver circlet, identical to her own, and gave it to him. 'Let it rest on your brow,' she said. 'From this time until you ascend Castle Mount, wear it constantly, for it will be the center of your power.'

Cautiously he slipped the circlet over his head. It fit snugly at his temples, a strange close sensation, not entirely to his liking, although the metal band was so fine he was surprised to notice it at all. The Lady drew near him and smoothed his thick long hair over it.

'Golden hair,' she said lightly. 'I never thought to have a son with golden hair! What do you feel, with the circlet on you?'

'The tightness of it.'

'Nothing else?'

'Nothing else, mother.'

'The tightness will soon cease to matter, as you get used to it. Do you feel the drug yet?'

'A slight cloudiness in my mind, only. I think I could sleep, if I were allowed.'

'Sleep will soon be the last thing you crave,' said the Lady. She extended both her hands to him. 'Are you a good juggler, my son?' she asked unexpectedly.

He grinned. 'So they tell me.'

'Good. Tomorrow you must show me some of your skills. I would find that amusing. But now give me your hands. Both. Here.'

She held her fine-boned strong-looking hands over his for an instant. Then she interlaced her fingers with his in a quick, decisive gesture.

It was as though a switch had been thrown, a circuit had been closed. Valentine staggered with shock. He stumbled, almost fell, and felt the Lady grasping him tightly, steadying him as he lurched about the room. There was a sensation in his mind as of a spike being driven through the base of his skull. The universe reeled about him; he was unable to control his eyes or to focus them, and he saw only fragmentary blurred images: the face of his mother, the shining surface of the desk, the blazing hues of the flowers, everything pulsing and throbbing and whirling.

His heart pounded. His throat was dry. His lungs felt empty. This was more terrifying than being drawn into the vortex of the sea-dragon and disappearing into the deep waters. Now his legs betrayed him entirely, and, unable any longer to stand, he sagged to the floor, kneeling there, somehow aware of the Lady kneeling before him, her face close to him, her fingers still locked between his, the terrible searing contact of their souls unbroken.

Memories flooded him.

He saw the vast gigantic splendor that was Castle Mount and the sprawling unthinkable enormity of the Coronal's Castle at its impossible summit. His mind roved with lightning speed through rooms of state with gilded walls and soaring arched ceilings, through banquet-halls and council-chambers, through corridors wide as plazas. Brilliant lights flashed and sparkled and dazed him. He sensed a male presence beside him, tall, powerful, confident, strong, holding one of his hands, and a woman equally strong and self-assured holding the other, and knew them to be his father and mother, and saw a boy just ahead who was his brother Voriax.

—What is this room, father?

—The Confalume throne-room, it is called.

—And that man with the long red hair? Sitting on the big chair?

—He is the Coronal Lord Malibor.

—What does that mean?

—Silly Valentine! He doesn't know what the Coronal is!

—Quiet, Voriax. The Coronal is the king, Valentine, one of the two kings, the younger one. The other is the Pontifex, who once was Coronal himself.

—Which one is he?

—The tall thin one, with the very dark beard.

—His name is Pontifex?

—His name is Tyeveras. Pontifex is what he is called as our king. He lives near the Stoienzar, but he is here today because Lord Malibor the Coronal is going to be married.

—And will Lord Malibor's children be Coronals too, mother?

—No, Valentine.

—Who will be Coronal next?

—No one knows that yet, son.

—Will I? Will Voriax?

—It could happen, if you grow up wise and strong.

—Oh, I will, father, I will, I will!

The room dissolved. Valentine saw himself in another room, similarly magnificent but not quite as large, and he was older now, not a boy but a young man, and there was Voriax with the starburst crown on his head, looking somewhat befuddled by it.

—Voriax! Lord Voriax!

Valentine dropped to his knees and raised his hands, spreading his fingers wide. And Voriax smiled and gestured at him.

—Get up, brother, get up. It is not fitting that you crawl like this in front of me.

—You will be the most splendid Coronal in the history of Majipoor, Lord Voriax.

—Call me brother, Valentine. I am Coronal, but I am still your brother.

—Long life to you, brother. Long life to the Coronal!

And others were shouting it about him:

—Long life to the Coronal! Long life to the Coronal!

But something had changed, though the room was the same, for Lord Voriax was nowhere in view, and it was Valentine who wore the strange crown now, and the others who were shouting to him, and kneeling before him, and waving their fingers in the air, crying his name. He looked at them in wonder.

—Long life to Lord Valentine!

—I thank you, my friends. I will try to be worthy of my brother's memory.

—Long life to Lord Valentine!

'Long life to Lord Valentine,' said the Lady softly.

Valentine blinked and gaped. For a moment he was entirely disoriented, wondering why he was kneeling like this, and what room he was in, and who this woman was with her face so close to his. Then the shadows cleared from his mind.

He rose to his feet.

He felt altogether transformed. Through his mind coursed turbulent memories: the years on Castle Mount, the studies, all that dry history, the roster of the Coronals, the list of the Pontifexes, the volumes of constitutional lore, the economic surveys of the provinces of Majipoor, the long sessions with his tutors, with his constantly probing father, with his mother – and the other, less dedicated moments: the games, the river-journeys, the tournaments, his friends, Elidath and Stasilaine and Tunigorn, the free-flowing wine, the hunts, the good times with Voriax, the two of them the center of all eyes, the princes of princes. And the terrible moment of the death of Lord Malibor at sea, and Voriax's look of fright and joy at being named Coronal, and then the time eight years later when the delegation of high princes came to Valentine to offer him his brother's crown—

He remembered.

He remembered everything, up to a night in Til-omon, when all recollection ceased. And after that he knew only the sunshine of Pidruid, pebbles tumbling past him from a ridge, the boy Shanamir standing above him with his mounts. He looked at himself in his mind and it seemed to him that he cast a double shadow, one bright and one dark; and he looked through the insubstantial haze of false memories that they had given him in Til-omon, looked back over an impenetrable gap of darkness to the time when he was Coronal. He knew that his mind now was as whole as it was ever likely to be.

Again the Lady said, 'Long life to Lord Valentine.'

'Yes,' he said in wonder. 'Yes, I am Lord Valentine, and will be again. Mother, give me ships. The Barjazid has already had too much time on the throne.'

'Ships are waiting in Numinor, and people loyal to me who will enter your service.'

'Good. There are people here who must be gathered. I don't know from which terraces, but they'll have to be found swiftly. A little Vroon, some Skandars, a Hjort, a blue-skinned stranger from another world, and several humans. I'll give you the names.'

'We will find them,' said the Lady.

Valentine said, 'And I thank you, mother, for returning me to myself.'

'Thanks? Why thanks? I gave you to yourself originally. No thanks were required for that. Now you are brought forth again, Valentine, and if needs be I'll do it a third time. But let needs not be. Your fortunes now resume their upward path.' Her eyes were bright with merriment. 'Will I see you juggle this evening, Valentine? How many balls can you keep in the air at once?'

'Twelve,' he said.

'And blaves can dance. Speak the truth!'

'Less than twelve,' he admitted. 'But more than two. I'll stage a performance after we dine. And – mother?'

'Yes?'

'When I regain Castle Mount I'll hold a grand festival, and you'll come from the Isle, and you'll see me juggle again, from the steps of the Confalume Throne. I promise you that, mother. From the steps of the throne.'

PART IV

The Book of
the Labyrinth

1

From Nunimor port the ships of the Lady departed, seven of them, with broad sails and high splendid prows, under the command of the Hjort Asenhart, chief of the Lady's admirals, and bearing as passengers Lord Valentine the Coronal, his chief minister Autifon Deliamber the Vroon, his aides-de-camp Carabella of Til-omon and Sleet of Narabal, his military adjutant Lisamon Hultin, his ministers-at-large Zalzan Kavol the Skandar and Shanamir of Falkynkip, and various others. The fleet's destination was Stoien at the tip of Alhanroel's Stoienzar Peninsula, at the far side of the Inner Sea. Already the ships had been at sea for weeks, scudding ahead of the brisk westerlies that blew in late spring in these waters, but there was no sign yet of land, nor would there be for many days.

Valentine found the long journey comforting. He was not at all fearful of the tasks ahead, but neither was he impatient to begin them; rather, he needed a time to sort through his newly regained mind, and discover who he had been and what he had hoped to become. Where better than on the great bosom of the ocean, where nothing altered from day to day except the patterns of the clouds, and time seemed to stand still? And so he stood for hours at a time at the rail of his flagship, the *Lady Thiin*, apart from his friends, visiting with himself.

The person who he had been pleased him: stronger and more forceful of character than Valentine the juggler, but with no uglinesses of soul as sometimes are found among persons of power. To Valentine his former self seemed reasonable, judicious, calm, and moderate, a man of serious demeanor but not without playfulness, one who understood the nature of responsibility and obligation. He was well educated, as might be supposed of one whose entire life had been spent in training for high office, with a thorough grounding in history, the law, government, and economics, somewhat less thorough in literature and philosophy, and, so far as Valentine could tell, only the merest smattering of mathematics and the physical sciences, which were much in eclipse on Majipoor.

The gift of his former self was like the finding of a treasure trove. Valentine was still not fully united to that other self, and tended to think of 'him' and 'me', or of 'us', instead of viewing himself as a single integrated personality; but the split grew less apparent every day. There had been enough damage to the Coronal's mind in the overthrow at Til-omon that a cleavage now marked the discontinuity between Lord Valentine the Coronal and Valentine the juggler, and perhaps there would always be scar tissue along that cleft, the Lady's ministrations notwithstanding. But Valentine could cross the place of discontinuity at will, could travel to any point along his previous time-line, into his childhood or young manhood or his brief period of rule, and wherever he looked was such a wealth of knowledge, of experience, of maturity, as in his simple wandering days he had never hoped to master. If at the moment he must enter those memories as one might enter an encyclopedia, or a library, so be it; he was sure that a fuller joining of self and self would occur in time.

In the ninth week of the voyage a thin green line of land appeared at the horizon.

'Stoienzar,' said Admiral Asenhart. 'See, there, to the side, that darker place? Stoien harbor.'

Through his double vision Valentine studied the shore of the approaching continent. As Valentine he knew next to nothing of Alhanroel, only that it was the largest of Majipoor's continents and the first to be settled by humans, a place of enormous population and tremendous natural wonders, and the seat of the planetary government, home to Coronal and Pontifex both. But out of Lord Valentine's memory came much more. To him Alhanroel meant Castle Mount, almost a world in itself, on whose vast slopes one could spend one's entire life among the Fifty Cities and not exhaust their marvels. Alhanroel was Lord Malibor's Castle crowning the Mount – for so he had called it through all his boyhood, and the habit had persisted even into his own reign. He saw the Castle now in the eye of his mind, enfolding the summit of the Mount like some many-armed creature spreading over crags and peaks and alpine meadows, and down into the great terminal valleys and folds, a single structure of so many thousands of rooms that it was impossible to count them, a building that seemingly had a life of its own, and added annexes and outbuildings at the far perimeters of itself by authority of itself alone. And Alhanroel was, also, the great hump mounded up over the Labyrinth of the Pontifex, and the subterranean Labyrinth itself, reverse counterpart of the Lady's Isle, for where the Lady dwelled at Inner Temple on a sun-splashed wind-washed height surrounded by ring upon ring of open terraces, the Pontifex laired like a mole deep underground, at the lowest place in his realm, surrounded by the coils of his Labyrinth. Valentine had been to the Labyrinth only once, on a mission from Lord Voriax, years ago, but the memory of those winding caverns still glowed darkly in him.

Alhanroel, too, meant the Six Rivers that spilled down from the slopes of Castle Mount, and the creature-plants of the Stoienzar that he soon would see again, and the tree-houses of Treymone, and the stone ruins of Velalisier Plain, said to be older than the advent of humankind on Majipoor.

Looking eastward at that faint line, growing larger but still barely percep-tible, Valentine sensed all the vastness of Alhanroel unrolling like a titanic scroll before him, and the tranquillity that had governed his frame of mind during the voyage melted at once. He was eager to be ashore, to commence his march to the Labyrinth.

To Asenhart he said, 'When will we reach land?'

'Tomorrow evening, my lord.'

'We'll have feasting and games tonight, then. The best wines broken out, all hands to share. And afterward a performance deckside, a small jubilee.'

Asenhart regarded him gravely. The admiral was an aristocrat among Hjorts, more slender than most of his kind, though with the coarse and peb-bled skin that was their mark, and he had an odd sobriety of manner that Valentine found a bit offputting. The Lady held him in the highest regard.

'A performance, my lord?'

'A little jugglery,' said Valentine. 'My friends feel a nostalgic need to prac-tice their art again, and what better moment than to celebrate the safe con-clusion of our long voyage?'

'Of course,' said Asenhart with a formal nod. But obviously the admiral disapproved of such goings-on aboard his flagship.

Zalzan Kavol had suggested it. The Skandar was plainly restless aboard ship; he could often be seen moving his four arms rhythmically in the ges-tures of juggling, though no objects were in his hands. More than anyone he had had to adapt to circumstances in this trek across the face of Majipoor. A year ago Zalzan Kavol had been a prince of his profession, master among masters of the juggling art, traveling in splendor from city to city in his wondrous wagon. Now all that was gone from him. The wagon was ashes somewhere in the forests of Piurifayne; two of his five brothers lay dead there too, and a third at the bottom of the sea; no longer did he growl orders to his employees and have them leap to obey; and instead of performing nightly before wonder-struck audiences that filled his pouch with crowns, he wandered now from place to place in Valentine's wake, a mere subsidiary. Unused strengths and drives were accumulating in Zalzan Kavol. His face and demeanor showed it, for in the old days his temper had been churlish and he vented it freely, but now he seemed repressed, almost meek, and Val-entine knew that must be a sign of severe inner distress. The agents of the Lady had found Zalzan Kavol still at the Terrace of Assessment at the outer rim of the Isle, at work at his menial pilgrim-tasks in a shambling, sleep-walking way, as if he had resigned himself to spending the rest of his life pulling weeds and pointing masonry.

'Can you do the routine with torches and knives?' Valentine asked him.

Zalzan Kavol brightened instantly. 'Of course. And do you see those pins there?' He pointed to some huge wooden clubs, nearly four feet long, stowed in a rack near the mast. 'Last night Erfon and I practiced with those, when everyone slept. If your admiral has no objections, we'll use them tonight.'

'Those? How can you juggle anything so long?'

'Get me the admiral's permission, my lord, and tonight I'll show you!'

All afternoon the troupe rehearsed in a large vacant chamber down in the hold. It was the first time they had done such a thing since Ilirivoyne, what seemed like half a lifetime ago. But, using the improvised array of objects that the Skandars had quietly gathered, they fell swiftly into the rhythm of it.

Valentine, watching, felt a warm glow at the sight of them – Sleet and Carabella furiously passing clubs back and forth, Zalzan Kavol and Rovorn and Erfon devising intricate new patterns of interchange to replace those that had been destroyed with the death of their three brothers. For a moment it was like the innocent old times in Falkynkip or Dulorn, when nothing mattered except getting hired on at the festival or the circus, and the only challenge life offered was the one of keeping hand and eye coordinated. There was no going back to those days. Now that they had been swept up into high intrigue, the making and unmaking of Powers, none of them would ever be as they had been before. These five had dined with the Lady, had shared lodgings with the Coronal, were sailing onward toward a rendezvous with the Pontifex; they were already a part of history, even if Valentine's campaign came to nothing. Yet here they were juggling again as though juggling were all there was in life.

It had taken many days to bring his people together at Inner Temple. Valentine had imagined that the Lady or her hierarchs had merely to close their eyes and they could reach any mind on Majipoor, but it was not that simple; communication was imprecise and limited. They had located the Skandars first, in the outermost terrace. Shanamir had reached Second Cliff and in his youthful guileless way was advancing swiftly inward; Sleet, neither youthful nor guileless, had likewise wangled advancement to Second Cliff, and so had Vinorkis; Carabella was just behind them, at the Terrace of Mirrors, but through an error she was sought elsewhere at first; finding Khun and Lisamon Hultin had been no great task, since they were so much unlike all other pilgrims in appearance, but Gorzval's three former crewmen, Pandelon, Cordeine, and Thesme, had vanished into the population of the island as though they were invisible, so that Valentine would have had to abandon them had they not turned up at the last moment. Hardest of all to track down was Autifon Deliamber. The Isle had many Vroons, some of them as diminutive as the little wizard, and all efforts at tracing him led to mistakes of identity. With the fleet ready to sail, Deliamber had still been unfound, but on the eve of departure, Valentine, desperately torn between the need to move onward and the unwillingness to part from his most useful counselor, the Vroon appeared at Numinor, offering no explanations of where he had been or how he had crossed the Isle undetected. So all were united, those who had survived the long trek from Pidruid.

On Castle Mount, Valentine knew, Lord Valentine had had his own ring of intimates, whose faces and names now had been restored to his knowledge, princes and courtiers and officials close to him since childhood, Elidath, Stasilaine, Tunigorn, the dearest comrades he had; and yet, though he still felt loyalty to those people, they had become terribly distant from his soul, and this random assortment of companions acquired during his time of wanderings now stood nearest to him. He wondered how it would be when he returned to Castle Mount and had to reconcile one group with the other.

On one score, at least, he had reassured himself out of his newly regained memories. No wife awaited him at the Castle, nor intended bride, nor even an important lover to contest Carabella's place at his side. As prince and as young Coronal he had lived a carefree and unattached life, the Divine be thanked. It would be difficult enough, imposing on the court the notion that the Coronal's beloved was a commoner, a woman of the lowland cities, a wandering juggler; but it would be altogether impossible if his heart had already been given, and now he were to claim to have given it again.

'Valentine!' Carabella called.

Her voice broke him free of reverie. He looked toward her and she giggled and tossed him a club. He caught it as they had taught him so long ago, between thumb and fingers with the club's head pointing at an angle. An instant later came a second one from Sleet, and then a third from Carabella. He laughed and sent the clubs whirling above his head in the old familiar pattern, throw and throw and catch, and Carabella clapped her hands and sent another one his way. It was good to be juggling again. Lord Valentine – a superb athlete, quick of eye and skilled at many games, though hampered somewhat by a slight limp from an old riding injury – had not known juggling. Juggling was the art of the simpler Valentine. Aboard this ship, wearing now the aura of authority that had come upon him by his mother's healing of his mind, Valentine had felt his companions holding him at arm's length, try as they might to regard him as the old Valentine of the Zimroel days. So it gave him special pleasure to have Carabella so irreverently fling a club his way.

And it gave him pleasure, too, to be handling the clubs – even when he dropped one, and, stooping for it, was hit on the head by another, provoking a snort of contempt out of Zalzan Kavol.

'Do that tonight,' the Skandar called, 'and you'll forfeit your wine for a week!'

'Have no fear,' Valentine retorted. 'I drop the clubs now only for practice in recovering them. You'll see no such blunders this evening.'

Nor were there any. The ship's entire company gathered at sundown on the deck for the entertainment. To one side, Asenhart and his officers occupied a platform where they would have the best view; but when the admiral beckoned to Valentine, offering him the chair of honor, he declined with a smile. Asenhart looked puzzled at that, but his expression was not nearly so strained as it became a few moments later, when Shanamir and Vinorkis and Lisamon Hultin began to pound on drums and tootle on coilpipes, and the jugglers emerged from a hatch in a gleeful sprint, and as they began to perform their wonders the figure of Lord Valentine the Coronal appeared among them, blithely hurling clubs and dishes and pieces of fruit like any vulgar entertainer.

2

If Admiral Asenhart had had his way, there would have been a grand celebration in Stoien to mark Valentine's arrival, something at least as splendid as the festival held in Pidruid at the time of the visit of the false Coronal. But Valentine, as soon as he got word of Asenhart's plan, put a stop to it. He was not yet ready to claim the throne, to make public accusations against the individual who called himself Lord Valentine, or to ask for any sort of homage from the citizenry at large. 'Until I have the support of the Pontifex,' Valentine told Asenhart sternly, 'I mean to move quietly and gather strength without attracting attention. There will be no festivals for me in Stoien.'

So it was that the *Lady Thiin* made a relatively inconspicuous landfall at that great port at the southwestern tip of Alhanroel. Even though there were seven ships in the fleet – and ships of the Lady, though common enough in the harbor at Stoien, did not generally arrive in such numbers – they came in quietly, flying no fancy banners. The port officials asked few questions: obviously they traveled on the business of the Lady of the Isle, and her doings were beyond the purview of customs-clerks.

To reinforce this, Asenhart sent purchasing agents through the wharfside district the first day, buying quantities of glue and sailcloth and spices and tools and the like. Meanwhile Valentine and his company covertly took lodgings in an unassuming commercial hotel.

Stoien was predominantly a maritime city – export-import, warehousing, shipbuilding, all the occupations and enterprises that go with a prime coastal location and a superb harbor. The city, of some fourteen million souls, spread for hundreds of miles along the rim of the great promontory that divided the Gulf of Stoien from the main body of the Inner Sea. It was not the mainland port closest to the Isle – that was Alaisor, far up Alhanroel's coast, thousands of miles to the north – but at this season, prevailing winds and currents being what they were, it was quicker to make the long journey down to Stoien than to brave the shorter but rougher crossing due east to Alaisor.

After pausing here to restock the ships, they would sail the placid Gulf, going along the north shore of the huge Stoienzar Peninsula in tropic ease to Kircidane and then up to Treymone, the coastal city nearest the Labyrinth. It would be a relatively short overland trek from there to the abode of the Pontifex.

Valentine found Stoien strikingly beautiful. The entire peninsula was altogether flat, hardly twenty feet above sea level at its highest point, but the city-dwellers had devised a wondrous arrangement of platforms of brick faced with white stone to provide the illusion of hills. No two of these platforms were of identical height, some providing an elevation of no more than a dozen feet, others looming hundreds of feet in the air. Whole neighborhoods rose atop giant pedestals several dozen feet high and more than a square mile in area; certain significant buildings had platforms of their own, standing as if on stilts above their surroundings; alternations of high platforms and low ones created eye-jiggling vistas of startling contour.

What might have been an effect of sheerly mechanical whimsy, rapidly coming to seem brutal or arbitrary or fatiguing to behold, was softened and mellowed by tropical plantings unrivaled in Valentine's experience. At the base of every platform grew dense beds of broad-crowned trees, interlaced branch by branch to form impenetrable cloaks. Leafy vines cascaded over the platform walls. The wide ramps that led from street level to the higher platforms were bordered by generous concrete tubs housing clusters of bushes whose narrow tapered leaves were marked with astonishing splashes of color, claret and cobalt and vermilion and scarlet and indigo and topaz and sapphire and amber and jade hues all mixed together in irregular patterns. And in the great public places of the city were the most startling displays of all, gardens of the famous animate plants that grew wild a few hundred miles to the south, on the torrid coast that looked toward the distant desert continent of Suvrael. These plants – and plants they were, for they manufactured their food by photosynthesis and lived their lives rooted to a single place – had a fleshy look to them, with arms that moved and coiled and grasped, eyes that stared, tubular bodies that undulated and swayed, and though they derived nourishment enough from sunlight and water they were quite willing and able to devour and digest any small creature rash enough to come within their reach. Elegantly arranged groups of them, bordered by low stone walls that served as warnings as well as decorations, were planted everywhere in Stoien. Some were as tall as small trees, others short and globular, still others bushy and angular. All were in constant motion, reacting to breezes, odors, sudden shouts, the voices of their keepers, and other stimuli. Valentine found them sinister but fascinating. He wondered if a collection of them might not be brought to Castle Mount.

'Why not?' Carabella said. 'They can be kept alive as sideshow displays in Pidruid. There ought to be a way to keep them in good health at Lord Valentine's Castle.'

Valentine nodded. 'We'll hire a staff of keepers out of Stoien. We'll find out what they eat and have it shipped up to the Mount regularly.'

Sleet shuddered. 'These creatures give me a creepy feeling, my lord. Do you find them so lovely?'

'Not exactly lovely,' said Valentine. 'Interesting.'

'As I suppose you found the mouthplants, eh?'

'The mouthplants, yes!' Valentine cried. 'We'll bring some of them to the Castle too!'

Sleet groaned.

Valentine paid little notice. His face glowed with sudden enthusiasm. Taking Sleet and Carabella by the hands, he said, 'Each Coronal had added something to the Castle: an observatory, a library, a parapet, a battlement of prisms and shields, an armory, a feasting-hall, a trophy-room, reign by reign the Castle growing, changing, becoming richer and more complex. In my short time I had no chance even to think about what I would contribute. But listen: what Coronal has seen Majipoor the way I have? Who has traveled so far, in so turbulent a fashion? To commemorate my adventures I'll collect the weirdities I've seen, the mouthplants and these animate plants and the bladdertrees and a good-sized dwikka or two and a grove of fire-shower palms and sensitivos and those singing ferns, all the wonders of our journey. There's nothing like that at the Castle now, only the little glassed-in plant-houses that Lord Confalume built. I'll do it grandly! Lord Valentine's garden! How do you like the sound of that?'

'It will be a marvel, my lord,' said Carabella.

Sleet said sourly, 'I would not care to stroll among the mouthplants of Lord Valentine's garden, not for three dukedoms and the revenues of Ni-moya and Piliplok.'

'We excuse you from garden tours,' said Valentine laughing.

But there would be no garden tours, nor any garden, until Valentine dwelled again in Lord Valentine's Castle. For an interminable week he idled in Stoien, waiting for Asenhart to complete his provisioning. Three of the ships were going to return to the Isle, bearing the goods bought here for island use; the other four would continue on as Valentine's surreptitious escort. The Lady had provided him with more than a hundred of her sturdiest bodyguards, under the command of the formidable hierarch Lorivade: not warriors, exactly, for there had not been violence on the Isle of Sleep since the Metamorphs last invaded it thousands of years ago, but these were competent and fearless men and women, loyal to the Lady and ready to give their lives if need be to restore the harmony of the realm. They were the nucleus of a private army – the first such military force, so far as Valentine knew, organized on Majipoor since ancient times.

At last the fleet was ready to depart. The Isle-bound ships left first, early on a warm Twoday morning, heading north northwest. The others waited until Seaday afternoon, when they sailed on the same course, but swung about after dark to head due east into the Gulf of Stoien.

The Stoienzar Peninsula, long and narrow, jutted like a colossal thumb out of the central mass of Alhanroel. On its southern, or ocean, side it was intolerably hot. There were few settlements on that jungled insect-ridden coast. Most of the peninsula's considerable population was clustered along the Gulf coast, which had a major city every hundred miles or so and a virtually unbroken line of fishing villages and farming districts and resort towns between. It was early summer now, and a heavy haze of heat lay over the tepid, virtually motionless waters of the Gulf. The fleet paused a day for further provisioning at Kircidane, where the coast began its sweeping northward curve, and then began the crossing to Treymone.

Valentine spent many of the quiet seaward hours alone in his cabin, practicing the use of the circlet the Lady had given him. In a week he mastered the art of entering a light dozing trance – he could slide his mind instantly below the threshold of sleep now, and just as readily emerge from it, all the while staying aware of ongoing events. In the trance-state he was able, although spottily and without much force, to make contact with other minds, to wander out aboard ship and locate the aura of a sleeping soul, sleepers being far more vulnerable to such intrusions than those who were awake. He could lightly touch Carabella's mind, or Sleet's, or Shanamir's, and transmit his own image, or some genial message of good will. Reaching a less familiar mind – that of Pandelon the carpenter, say, or the hierarch Lorivade – was still too hard for him except in the briefest, most fragmentary bursts, and he had no success at all entering minds of non-human origin, even ones so well known to him as those of Zalzan Kavol or Khun or Deliamber. But he was still learning. He felt his skills growing day by day, as they had when he first had taken up juggling; and this was juggling of a sort, for to use the circlet he had to occupy a position at the very center of his soul, undistracted by irrelevant thought, and coordinate all aspects of his being toward the single thrust of making contact. By the time the *Lady Thiin* was in view of Treymone, Valentine had advanced to the level where he could plant the beginnings of dreams, with events and incidents and images, in the minds of his subjects. To Shanamir he sent a dream of Falkynkip, and mounts grazing in a field, and a great gihorna-bird circling overhead, descending in a foolish flapping of mighty wings. At table the next morning the boy described the dream in all details, except only that the bird was a milufta, a carrion-feeder, with bright orange beak and ugly blue claws. 'What does it mean, that I would dream of miluftas swooping down?' Shanamir asked, and Valentine said, 'Could it be that you misremember the dream, and it was another bird you saw, a gihorna, perhaps, a bird of good omen?' But Shanamir, in that straightforward and innocent way of his, merely shook his head and said, 'If I can't tell a gihorna from a milufta, my lord, even in my sleep, I ought to be back in Falkynkip cleaning out the stables.' Valentine looked away, hiding a smile, and resolved to work more diligently on his image-sending technique.

To Carabella he sent a dream of juggling crystal goblets filled with golden wine, and she reported it accurately, down to the tapered shape of the gob-lets. To Sleet he sent a dream of Lord Valentine's garden, a wonderland of glistening feathery-leaved white bushes and solemn spherical prickly things on long stems and little three-forked plants with winking playful eyes at their tips, all of them imaginary and not a mouthplant among them, and Sleet described that imaginary garden in delight, saying that if only the Coronal would plant a garden like that on Castle Mount he would be well pleased to stroll in it.

Dreams came to him as well. Almost nightly the Lady his mother touched his soul from afar. Her serene presence passed through his sleeping spirit like a cool shaft of moonlight, calming and reassuring him. He dreamed, too, of old times on Castle Mount, memories of his early days upwelling, tournaments and races and games, his friends Tunigorn and Elidath and Stasilaine by his side, and his brother Voriax teaching him to use sword and bow, and Lord Malibor the Coronal traveling from city to city on the Mount like some grand and shining demigod, and much more of the same, a flood of images released from the depths of his mind.

Not all the dreams were agreeable. The night before the *Lady Thiin* reached the mainland he saw himself going ashore, landing on some forlorn, wind-swept beach of low and twisted scrub that had a dull, weary look in the late afternoon light. And he began to walk inland toward Castle Mount, rising in the distance, a jagged and sharp-tipped spire. But there was a wall in his way, a wall higher than the white cliffs of the Isle of Sleep, and that wall was a band of iron, more metal than existed on all of Majipoor, a dark and terrible iron girdle that seemed to span the world from pole to pole, and he was on one side of it and Castle Mount on the other. As he drew near he perceived that the wall crackled as if with electricity, and a low humming sound came from it, and when he looked closely at it he saw his reflection in the shining metal, and the face that peered back at him out of that frightful iron band was the face of the son of the King of Dreams.

3

Treymone was the city of the celebrated tree-houses, famed throughout Majipoor. His second day ashore, Valentine went to visit them, in the coastal district just south of the mouth of the River Trey.

Nowhere else but in the Trey's alluvial plain did the tree-houses live. They had short stout trunks a little like those of dwikkas, though not nearly so thick, and their bark was a handsome pale green, with a high gloss to it. From these barrel-like boles rose sturdy flattened branches that curved upward and outward like the fingers of two hands pressed together at the heels, and viny twigs wandered from branch to branch, adhering in many places, creating a snug cup-shaped enclosure.

The tree-folk of Treymore shaped their dwellings to suit their whims by pulling the pliant branches into the forms of rooms and corridors and fastening them into place until the natural adhesion of bark to bark made the join permanent. From the trees came leaves tender and sweet for salads, fragrant cream-colored flowers whose pollen was a mild euphoric, tart bluish fruits that had many uses, and a sweet pale sap, easily tapped, that served in place of wine. Each tree lived a thousand years or more; families maintained jealous control over them; ten thousand trees filled the plain, all mature and inhabited. Valentine saw a few skinny saplings at the edge of the district. 'These,' he was told, 'are newly planted, to replace some that died in recent years.'

'Where does a family go when its tree dies?'

'Into town,' said the guide, 'to what we call houses of mourning, until the new tree is grown. That may be twenty years. We dread such a thing, but it happens only one generation out of ten.'

'And there's no way to grow the trees elsewhere?'

'Not an inch beyond where you see them. Only in our climate will they thrive, and only in the soil on which you stand can they grow to fullness. Elsewhere they live a year or two, small stunted things.'

Quietly to Carabella Valentine said, 'We can make the experiment anyway. I wonder if they can spare some of their precious soil for Lord Valentine's garden.'

She smiled. 'Even a small tree-house – a place where you can go when the cares of government grow too heavy, and sit hidden in the leaves, and breathe the perfume of the flowers, and pluck the fruits – oh, if you could have such a thing!'

'Someday I will,' said Valentine. 'And you'll sit beside me in it.'

Carabella gave him a startled look. 'I, my lord?'

'If not you, then who? Dominin Barjazid?' Lightly he touched her hand. 'Do you think our travels together end when we reach Castle Mount?'

'We should not talk of such things now,' she told him severely. To the guide she said in a louder tone, 'And these young trees – how do you care for them? Are they watered often?'

From Treymone it was several weeks' journey by fast floater-car to the Labyrinth, which lay in south-central Alhanroel. The countryside here was mainly a lowland, with rich red soil in the river valley and thin, gray sandy stuff beyond it, and settlements grew more sparse as Valentine and his party moved inland. There was occasional rain, but it seemed to sink immediately into the porous soil. The weather was warm and sometimes there was an oppressive weight to the heat. Day after day slipped by in bland, monotonous driving. To Valentine this sort of travel wholly lacked the magic and mystery – now enhanced by nostalgia – of the months he had spent crossing Zimroel in Zalzan Kavol's elegant wagon. Then, every day had seemed a venture into the unknown, with fresh challenges at each turn, and always the excitement of performing, of stopping in strange towns to put on shows. Now? Everything was done for him by adjutants and aides-de-camp. He was becoming a prince again – though a prince of very modest puissance indeed, with hardly more than a hundred followers – and he was not at all certain he cared for it.

Late in the second week the landscape abruptly changed, turning rough and broken, with black flat-topped hills rising now from a dry, deeply ridged tableland. The only plants that grew here were small scraggly bushes, dark twisted things with tiny waxen leaves, and, on the higher slopes, thorny candelabra-like growths of moon-cactus, ghostly white, twice as tall as a man. Little long-legged animals with red fur and puffy yellow tails skittered about nervously, vanishing into holes whenever a floater came too close.

Deliamber said, 'This is the beginning of the Desert of the Labyrinth. Soon we will see the stone cities of the ancients.'

Valentine had approached the Labyrinth from the other side, the north-west, the time he had been to it in his former life. There was desert there too, and the great haunted ruined city of Velalisier; but he had come down from Castle Mount by riverboat, bypassing all the unlucky dead lands that surrounded the Labyrinth, and the texture of this bleak and forbidding zone was new to him. He found it absorbingly strange at first, especially at sunset, when the vast cloudless sky was streaked with grotesque bands of violent color and the parched soil took on an eerie metallic look. But after a few days the starkness and austerity ceased to give him pleasure, and became disturbing, unsettling, menacing. Something about this sharp desert air, perhaps, was working unfavorably on his sensibilities. He had never experienced desert before, for there was none in Zimroel and none except this interior pocket of dryness in well-watered Alhanroel. Desert conditions were something he associated with Suvrael, which he had visited often enough in dreams, all of them troublesome ones; and he could not escape the notion, irrational and bizarre, that he was riding toward a rendezvous with the King of Dreams.

After a time Deliamber said, 'There are the ruins.'

It was difficult at first to distinguish them from the rocks of the desert. All Valentine saw were tumbled dark monoliths, scattered as though by a giant's contemptuous hand, in little patches every mile or two. But gradually he discerned form: this was a bit of wall, this the foundation of some cyclopean palace, this perhaps an altar. Everything was built to titanic scale, although the individual groups of ruins, half covered by drifting sand, were unimpressive isolated outposts.

Valentine called the caravan to a halt at one particularly broad strew of ruins and led an inspection party to the site. He touched the rocks cautiously, fearing he might be committing some sort of sacrilege. The stone was cool, smooth to the touch, faintly encrusted by leathery growths of yellow lichen.

'And are these the work of the Metamorphs?' he asked.

Deliamber shrugged. 'So we think, but no one knows.'

'I have heard it said,' remarked Admiral Asenhart, 'that the first human settlers built these cities soon after the Landing-time, and that they were overthrown in the civil wars before the Pontifex Dvorn established government.'

'Of course, few records survive of those days,' said Deliamber.

Asenhart squinted at the Vroon. 'Are you of a contrary opinion, then?'

'I? I? I hold no opinion at all of events of fourteen thousand years ago. I am not as old as you suspect, admiral.'

The hierarch Lorivade said in a dry deep tone, 'It seems unlikely to me that the early settlers would build so far from the sea. Or that they would trouble themselves to haul such huge blocks of stone about.'

'Then you too think these were Metamorph cities?' said Valentine.

'The Metamorphs are wild savages who live in the jungles and dance to bring rain,' Asenhart said.

Lorivade, looking bothered at the admiral's interruption, said with testy precision, 'I think it altogether likely.' To Asenhart she added, 'Not savages, admiral, but refugees. They may well have fallen from a higher estate.'

'Pushed, rather,' said Carabella.

Valentine said, 'The government should organize studies of these ruins, if it hasn't already been done. We need to know more about pre-human civilizations on Majipoor, and if these are Metamorph places, we might consider giving them a kind of custodianship of them. We—'

'The ruins need no custodians other than the ones they already have,' said a new voice suddenly.

Valentine turned, startled. A bizarre figure had emerged from behind a monolith – a gaunt, almost fleshless man of sixty or seventy, with fierce blazing eyes set in jutting bony rims and a thin, wide, virtually toothless mouth now curved in a mocking grin. He was armed with a long narrow sword and was clad in a strange garment made entirely from the red fur of the desert-animals. Atop his head was a cap of thick yellow tail-fur, which he swept off in a grand gesture as he made a deep, sweeping bow. When he straightened, his hand rested on the pommel of his sword.

Valentine said courteously, 'And are we in the presence of one of those custodians?'

'More than one,' the other replied. And from the rocks there quietly came eight or ten similar fantasticos, as angular and bony as the first, and like the first all clad in scruffy fur leggings and jackets and wearing absurd furry caps. All carried swords, and all seemed ready to use them. A second group appeared behind them, materializing as though out of the air, and then a third, a good-sized troop, thirty or forty in all.

There were eleven in Valentine's party, mostly unarmed. The others were back in the floater-cars, two hundred yards away on the main highway. While they had stood here debating nice points of ancient history, they had allowed themselves to be surrounded.

The leader said, 'By what right do you trespass here?'

Valentine heard a faint clearing of the throat from Lisamon Hultin. He saw a stiffening also of Asenhart's posture. But Valentine signaled them to be calm.

He said, 'May I know who it is that addresses me?'

'I am Duke Nascimonte of Vornek Crag, Overlord of the Western Marches. About me you see the chief nobles of my realm, who serve me loyally in all things.'

Valentine had no recollection of a province known as the Western Marches, nor of any such duke. Possibly he had forgotten some of his geography when his mind was meddled with; but not, he suspected, quite so much. Yet he did not choose to trifle with Duke Nascimonte.

Solemnly he said, 'We meant no trespass, your grace, in passing through your domain. We are travelers bound for the Labyrinth on business with the Pontifex, and this seemed the most direct route between Treymone and there.'

'So it is. You would have done better to approach the Pontifex by a less direct route.'

Lisamon Hultin roared suddenly, 'Give us no trouble! Have you any idea who this man is?'

Annoyed, Valentine snapped his fingers at the giantess to silence her.

Nascimonte said blandly, 'Not in the least. But he could be Lord Valentine himself and he would not pass here lightly. Lord Valentine less than any other, in fact.'

'Have you some special quarrel with Lord Valentine, then?' Valentine asked.

The bandit laughed harshly. 'The Coronal is my most hated enemy.'

'Why, then, your hand must be set against all of civilization, for everyone owes allegiance to the Coronal and must for order's sake oppose his enemies. Can you truly be a duke, and not accept the Coronal's authority?'

'Not *this* Coronal's,' Nascimonte replied. He sauntered coolly across the open space that separated him from Valentine, hand still resting on his sword, and peered closely at him. 'You wear fine clothes. You smell of city comforts. You must be rich, and live in a great house somewhere high up on the Mount, and have servants to meet your every need. What would you say, if one day all that were stripped from you, eh? If by the whim of another you were cast down into poverty?'

'I have had that experience,' said Valentine evenly.

'Have you, now? You, traveling in that cavalcade of floater-cars, with your retinue about you? Who are you, anyway?'

'Lord Valentine the Coronal,' Valentine answered without hesitation.

Nascimonte's fiery eyes flared with rage. For an instant it appeared as if be would draw his sword; then, as if seeing a jest much to his own ferocious humor, he relaxed and said, 'Yes, you are Coronal the way I am a duke. Well, Lord Valentine, your kindness will repay me for my earlier losses. The fee for crossing the zone of ruins today is one thousand royals.'

'We have no such sum,' Valentine said mildly.

'Then you'll make camp with us until your lackeys fetch it.' He gestured to his men. 'Seize them and bind them. Turn one loose – this one, the Vroon – to be the messenger.' To Deliamber he said, 'Vroon, carry word to those in the floaters that we hold these folk here for payment of a thousand royals, to be delivered within a month. And if you return with militia instead of money, why, bear in mind that we know these hills, and the officers of the law do not. You'll never see any of your people alive again.'

'Wait,' Valentine said, as Nascimonte's men stepped forward. 'Tell me your quarrel with the Coronal.'

Nascimonte scowled. 'He came through this part of Alhanroel last year, returning from Zimroel where he made the grand processional. I lived then in the foothills of Mount Ebersinul, looking out on Lake Ivory, and I raised ricca and thuyol and milaile, and my plantation was the finest in the province, for my family has spent sixteen generations cultivating it. The Coronal and his party were billeted on me, as best able to meet the needs of hospitality for him, and at the height of thuyol-harvest he came to me with all his hundreds of hangers-on and lackeys, his myriad courtiers, enough mounts to graze half a continent bare, and between one Starday and the next they drank my cellars dry, they made festival in the fields and spoiled the crops, they torched the manor-house in drunken play, they shattered the dam and drowned my fields, they ruined me entirely for their own sport, and then they marched away, not even knowing what they had done to me, or caring. The moneylenders have it all now, and I live in the rocks of Vornek Crag courtesy of Lord Valentine and his friends, and where is justice? It will cost you a thousand royals to leave these ancient ruins, stranger, and though I hold you no malice I will slit your throat as coolly as Lord Valentine's men opened my dam, and with as little concern, if the money fails to come.' He turned away and said again, 'Bind them.'

Valentine drew breath deep into his lungs and closed his eyes, and, as the Lady had taught him, let himself slip into waking sleep, into the trance that brought his circlet to life. And sent his mind out toward the dark and bitter soul of the Overlord of the Western Marches, and flooded it with love.

The effort called forth all the strength that was in him. He swayed and braced his legs, and leaned against Carabella, one hand on her shoulder, drawing further energy and vitality from her and pumping it toward Nascimonte. He understood now what price Sleet paid for his blind juggling, for this was draining him of all the stuff of life. Yet he sustained the outpouring of spirit for moment after long moment.

Nascimonte stood frozen, facing half away from him with his body twisted around, his eyes locked on Valentine's. Valentine held his grip unrelentingly on the other's soul, and bathed it with compassion until Nascimonte's iron resentments softened and loosened and dropped from him like a shell, and then into the suddenly vulnerable man Valentine poured a vision of all that had befallen him since his overthrow in Til-omon so long ago, everything compressed into a single dazzling point of illumination.

He broke the contact and, staggering, lurched hard against Carabella, who supported him unflinchingly.

Nascimonte stared at Valentine like one who has been touched by the Divine.

Then he dropped to his knees and made the starburst sign.

'My lord—' he said thickly, deep in his throat, a barely audible sound. 'My lord – forgive me – forgive—'

4

That there should be bandits at large in this desert surprised and dismayed Valentine, for there was little history of such anarchy on well-mannered Majipoor. That the bandits should be well-to-do farming folk made paupers by the callousness of the present Coronal dismayed him also. It was not the custom on Majipoor for the ruling class so carelessly to exploit its position. Dominin Barjazid, if he thought he could conduct himself that way and hold his throne for long, was not merely a villain but a fool.

'Will you put down the usurper?' Nascimonte asked.

'In time,' replied Valentine. 'But there is much to do before that day arrives.'

'I am yours to command, if I can be of service.'

'Are there other bandits between here and the mouth of the Labyrinth?'

Nascimonte nodded. 'Many. It becomes the fashion in this province to run wild in the hills.'

'And have you influence over them, or is your title of duke only irony?'

'They obey me.'

'Good,' said Valentine. 'I ask you then to conduct us through these lands to the Labyrinth, and to keep your marauding friends from delaying us in our journey.'

'I will, my lord.'

'But not a word to anyone of what I've shown you. Regard me simply as an official of the Lady, on embassy to the Pontifex.'

The faintest glint of suspicion flickered momentarily in Nascimonte's eyes. Uneasily he said, 'I may not proclaim you as true Coronal? Why is that?'

Valentine smiled. 'This is my entire army you see here in these few floater-cars. I would not announce war against the usurper until my forces are larger. Hence this secrecy; and hence my visit to the Labyrinth. The sooner I win the support of the Pontifex the sooner the true campaign begins. How quickly can you be ready to depart?'

'Within the hour, my lord.'

Nascimonte and a few of his men rode with Valentine in the lead floater. The landscape grew steadily more barren: now it was a brown and almost lifeless wasteland, where swirls of dust rose under the harsh hot wind. Occasionally men in rough clothes could be seen riding in bands of three or four, far from the main highway, pausing to peer at the travelers, but there were no incidents. On the third day Nascimonte proposed a shortcut that would save several days in reaching the Labyrinth. Unhesitatingly Valentine agreed, and the caravan plunged off to the northeast over an enormous dry lakebed and then down a tortured land of steep gullies and flat-topped eroded hills, past a range of blunt mountains of a red sandy rock, and finally out into a vast windy tableland that seemed altogether featureless, a mere expanse of grit and pebbles filling the entire horizon. Valentine saw Sleet and Zalzan Kavol exchanging troubled glances as the floaters entered this bleak useless place, and he supposed they were muttering privately about treachery and betrayal, but his own faith in Nascimonte was unshaken. He had touched the bandit chieftain's mind with his own, through the circlet of the Lady, and what he had sensed in it was not the soul of a traitor.

Another day, and another, and another, on this track through the midst of nowhere, and now Carabella was frowning, and the hierarch Lorivade looked more grim than usual, and Lisamon Hultin at last drew Valentine aside and said, as quietly as she could say anything, 'What if this man Nascimonte is a hireling of the false Coronal, who has been paid to lose you in a place where no one will ever find you?'

'Then we are lost and our bones will lie here forever,' said Valentine. 'But I give no weight to such fears.'

All the same, a certain edginess grew in him. He remained confident of Nascimonte's good faith – it seemed unlikely that any agent of Dominin Barjazid would choose so dreary and drawn-out a method of getting rid of him, when a single sword-stroke back at the Metamorph ruins would have accomplished it – but he had no real assurance that Nascimonte knew where he was going. There was no water out here, and even the mounts, able to transform any sort of organic matter into fuel, were – so said Shanamir – growing thin and slack-muscled on the scattered scrawny weeds that now were their entire fare. If anything went wrong in this place there would be no hope of rescue. But Valentine's touchstone was Autifon Deliamber: the wizard had a hearty and expert skill at self-preservation, and Deliamber looked unworried, altogether tranquil, as the drab days passed.

And at length Nascimonte halted the caravan at a place where two lines of steep bare hills converged to confine them in a high-walled narrow canyon. He said to Valentine, 'Do you think we have lost our way, my lord? Come, let me show you something.'

Valentine and some of the others followed him to the head of the canyon, a distance of some fifty paces. Nascimonte stretched his arms toward the immense valley that began where the canyon opened.

'Look,' he said.

The valley was more desert, a giant fan-shaped expanse of pale tawny sand, spreading outward and extending northward and southward for at least a hundred miles. And precisely in the middle of that valley Valentine saw a darker circle, itself of colossal size, that rose a short way above the flat valley floor. He recognized it from an earlier time, when he had seen it from the far side: it was the giant mound of brown earth that covered the Labyrinth of the Pontifex.

'We will be at the Mouth of Blades the day after tomorrow,' said Nascimonte.

There were seven mouths all told, Valentine remembered, arranged equidistantly around the enormous structure. When he had come as emissary from Voriax he had entered by way of the Mouth of Waters, on the opposite side, where the River Glayge descended through the fertile northeastern provinces from Castle Mount. That was the genteel way to reach the Labyrinth, used by high officials when they had dealings with the ministers of the Pontifex; on all other sides the Labyrinth was surrounded by far less agreeable country, the least agreeable of all being the desert through which Valentine now advanced. But there was comfort in knowing that even if he must approach through this land of deadness he would leave the Labyrinth by its happier side.

The area covered by the Labyrinth was huge, and since it was constructed on many levels, spiraling down and down and piling tier upon tier in the bowels of the planet, its actual population was incalculable. The Pontifex himself occupied only the innermost sector, to which scarcely anyone ever gained admission. In the zone surrounding that was the domain of the governmental ministers, a multitude of mysterious dedicated souls who spent all their lives toiling underground at tasks that defied Valentine's understanding, record-keeping and tax-decreeing and census-taking and such. And around the governmental zone there had developed, over thousands of years, the protective outer skin of the Labyrinth, a maze of circular passageways inhabited by millions of shadowy figures, bureaucrats and merchants and beggars and clerks and cutpurses and who knew what else, a world unto itself, where the kindly warmth of the sun was never felt, where the cool clean shafts of the moon could not penetrate, where all the beauty and wonder and joy of giant Majipoor had been exchanged for the pallid pleasures of a life underground.

The floater-cars followed the line of the outer mound for an hour or so, and came at last to the Mouth of Blades.

This was no more than a timber-roofed opening giving access to a tunnel disappearing into the earth. A line of ancient rusty swords was set in concrete across its front, forming a barrier more symbolic than actual, since they were spaced far apart. How long, Valentine wondered, does it take to turn swords rusty in this dry desert climate?

The guardians of the Labyrinth waited just within the entrance.

There were seven of them – two Hjorts, a Ghayrog, a Skandar, a Liiman, and two humans – and all were masked after the universal manner of the officials of the Pontifex. The mask too was mainly symbolic, a mere strip of some glossy yellow stuff angled across the eyes and bridge of the nose of the humans and in equivalent places on the others; but it created an effect of great strangeness about these people, as it was meant to do.

The guardians stolidly confronted Valentine and his party in silence. Deliamber said quietly to him, 'They will ask a price for admission. All this is traditional. Go up to them and state your business.'

To the guardians Valentine said, 'I am Valentine, brother to the late Voriax, son of the Lady of the Isle, and I have come to seek audience with the Pontifex.'

Not even so bizarre and provocative an announcement as that stirred much reaction from the masked ones. The Ghayrog said only, 'The Pontifex admits no one to his presence.'

'Then I would have audience with his high ministers, who can bear my message to the Pontifex.'

'They will not see you either,' replied one of the Hjorts.

Valentine said, 'In that case I will make application to the ministers of the ministers. Or to the ministers of the ministers of the ministers, if I must. All I ask of you is that you grant admission to the Labyrinth for my companions and me.'

The guardians conferred solemnly among themselves, in low droning tones, evidently going through some ritual of a purely mechanical sort, since they barely seemed to be listening to one another. When their mutterings died away the Ghayrog spokesman swung about to face Valentine and said, 'What is your offering?'

'Offering?'

'The entry-price.'

'Name it and I'll pay it.' Valentine signaled to Shanamir, who carried a purse of coins. But the guardians looked displeased, shaking their heads, several of them actually turning away as Shanamir produced some half-royal pieces.

'Not money,' the Ghayrog said disdainfully. 'An *offering.*'

Valentine was baffled. In confusion he looked toward Deliamber, who moved his tentacles, waving several of them up and down, in a rhythmic tossing gesture. Valentine frowned. Then he understood. Juggling!

'Sleet – Zalzan Kavol—'

From one of the cars they brought clubs and balls. Sleet, Carabella, and Zalzan Kavol stationed themselves before the guardians and, at a signal from the Skandar, began to juggle. Motionless as statues, the seven masked ones watched. The entire proceeding seemed so preposterous to Valentine that he was hard put to keep a straight face, and several times had to choke back giggles; but the three jugglers performed their routines austerely and with the utmost dignity, as though this were some crucial religious rite. They went through three complete patterns of interchange and stopped with one accord, bowing stiffly to the guardians. The Ghayrog nodded almost imperceptibly – the only acknowledgment of the performance.

'You may enter,' he said.

5

They drove the floaters between the blades and into a sort of vestibule, dark and musty, that opened into a wide sloping roadway. A short distance down that and they intersected a curving tunnel, the first of the rings of the Labyrinth.

It was high-roofed and brightly lit, and could well have been a market street in any busy city, with stalls and shops and pedestrian traffic and vehicles of all shapes and sizes floating along. But a moment's careful inspection made it clear that this was no Pidruid, no Piliplok, no Ni-moya. The people in the streets were eerily pale, with a ghostly look that told of lifetimes spent away from the rays of the sun. Their clothing was curiously archaic in style, and of dull, dark colors. There were many masked individuals, servants of the pontifical bureaucracy, unremarkable in the context of the Labyrinth and moving in the crowds without attracting the slightest attention for their maskedness. And, thought Valentine, everyone, masked and maskless alike, had a tense and drawn expression, a strange haunted look about the eyes and mouth. Out in the world of fresh air, under the warm and cheerful sun, people on Majipoor smiled freely and easily, not only with their mouths but with their eyes, their cheeks, their entire faces, their whole souls. Down in this catacomb souls were of a different sort.

Valentine turned to Deliamber. 'Do you know your way around in this place?'

'Not at all. But guides should be easily come by.'

'How?'

'Halt the cars, get out, stand around, look befuddled,' the Vroon said. 'You'll have guides aplenty in a minute.'

It took less than that. Valentine, Sleet, and Carabella left their car, and instantly a boy no more than ten, who had been running along the street with some younger children, whirled about and called, 'Show you the Labyrinth? One crown, all day!'

'Do you have an older brother?' Sleet asked.

The boy glared at him. 'You think I'm too young? Go on, then! Find your own way around! You'll be lost in five minutes!'

Valentine laughed. 'What's your name?'

'Hissune.'

'How many levels must we go, Hissune, before we reach the government sector?'

'You want to go *there*?'

'Why not?'

'They're all crazy, there,' the boy said, grinning, 'Work, work, shuffle papers all day long, mumble and mutter, work hard and hope you'll get promoted even deeper down. Talk to them and they don't even answer you. Minds all mumbly from too much work. It's seven levels under. Courts of Columns first, Hall of Winds, Place of Masks, Court of Pyramids, Court of Globes, the Arena, and then you get to the House of Records. I'll take you there. Not for one crown, though.'

'How much?'

'Half a royal.'

Valentine whistled. 'What would you do with so much money?'

'Buy my mother a cloak, and light five candles to the Lady, and get my sister the medicine she needs.' The boy winked. 'And maybe a treat or two for myself.'

During this exchange a goodly crowd had gathered – at least fifteen or twenty children no older than Hissune, some younger ones, and some adults, all clustered together in a tight semicircle and watching tensely to see if Hissune got the job. None of them called out, but out of the corner of his eye Valentine saw them straining for his attention, standing on tiptoes, trying to look knowledgeable and responsible. If he refused the boy's offer, he would have fifty more the next moment, a wild clamor of voices and a forest of waving hands. But Hissune seemed to know his business, and his blunt, coolly cynical approach had charm.

'All right,' Valentine said. 'Take us to the House of Records.'

'All these cars yours?'

'That one, that, that – yes, all.'

Hissune whistled. 'Are you important? Where are you from?'

'Castle Mount.'

'I guess you're important,' the boy conceded. 'But if you come from Castle Mount, what are you doing on the Blades side of the Labyrinth?'

The boy was clever. Valentine said, 'We've been traveling. We've just come from the Isle.'

'Ah.' Hissune's eyes widened just for an instant, the first breach in his jaunty street-wise coolness. Doubtless the Isle was a virtually mythical place to him, as far off as the farthest stars, and despite himself he showed awe at finding himself in the presence of someone who had actually been there. He moistened his lips. 'And how shall I call you?' he asked after a moment.

'Valentine.'

'Valentine,' the boy repeated. 'Valentine from Castle Mount. Very nice name.' He clambered into the first floater-car. As Valentine got in beside him Hissune said, 'Really? *Valentine?*'

'Really.'

'Very nice name,' he said again. 'Pay me half a royal, Valentine, and I'll show you the Labyrinth.'

Half a royal, Valentine knew, was outrageous, several days' pay for a skilled artisan, and yet he made no objection: it seemed improper for someone of his station to be haggling with a child over money. Hissune, perhaps, had calculated the same thing. In any event the fee turned out to be a worthwhile investment, for the boy proved expert in the twists and turns of the Labyrinth, guiding them with surprising swiftness toward the lower and inner coils of the place. Down they went, down and around, making unexpected turns and shortcuts through narrow, barely manageable alleyways, descending on hidden ramps that seemed to make transit across implausible gulfs of space.

The Labyrinth grew darker and more intricate as they went downward. Only the outermost level was well lit. The circles within it were shadowy and sinister, with dim corridors radiating in unlikely directions from the main ones, and hints of strange statuary and architectural ornamentation vaguely visible in the musty, dismal corners. Valentine found the place disturbing. It reeked of mildew and history; it had the chill clamminess of unimaginable antiquity; it was sunless and airless and joyless, a giant cavern of forlorn dreary gloom, through which scowling harsh-eyed figures moved on errands as mysterious as their own somber selves.

Down – down – down—

The boy maintained a constant flow of chatter. He was marvelously articulate, lively and funny, somehow not at all a proper product of this morbid place. He told of tourists from Ni-moya who had been lost between the Hall of Winds and Place of Masks for a month, living on scraps provided by lower-level dwellers, but too proud to admit they were unable to find their way out. He told of the architect of the Court of Globes who had aligned every spheroid in that elaborate chamber with regard to some monumentally complex numerological system, only to find that the workmen, having lost the key to his charts, had installed everything according to an improvised system of their own: he had bankrupted himself to rebuild the whole thing in the right deployment at his own expense, discovering in the end that his computations were wrong and the pattern was impossible. 'They buried him right where he fell,' said Hissune. And the boy told the tale of the Pontifex Arioc, he who had, when a vacancy developed in the Ladyship, proclaimed himself female, appointed himself to the Isle, and abdicated his throne: barefoot and clad in loose flowing robes, the boy said, Arioc marched publicly out of the depths of the Labyrinth, followed by a cluster of his highest ministers, who frantically tried to dissuade him from his course. 'On this spot,' said Hissune, 'he called the people together and told them he was now their Lady, and ordered up a chariot to take him to Stoien. And the ministers could do nothing. Nothing! I wish I had seen their faces.'

Down—

All day the caravan descended. They passed through the Court of Columns, where thousands of huge gray pillars sprouted like titanic toad-stools, and sluggish pools of oily black water covered the stone floor to a depth of three or four feet. They crossed the Hall of Winds, a terrifying place where cold gusts of air streamed inexplicably from finely carved stone grids in the walls. They saw the Place of Masks, a twisting corridor in which giant bodiless faces, with blind empty slits for eyes, stood mounted on marble plinths. They viewed the Court of Pyramids, a forest of stark white polyhedral figures set so close together that it was impossible to move between them, a spiky-tipped maze of monoliths, some perfectly tetra-hedral but most weirdly elongated, spindly, ominous. A level below it they wandered in the celebrated Court of Globes, an even more complex struc-ture a mile and and half long, where spherical objects, some no larger than a fist and others as big as great sea-dragons, hung eerily and invisibly sus-pended, illuminated from below. Hissune took care to point out the archi-tect's grave – unmarked, a slab of black stone beneath the greatest of the globes.

Down – down—

Valentine had seen nothing of this on his earlier visit. From the Mouth of Waters one descended swiftly, through passageways used only by the Coro-nal and Pontifex, to the imperial lair at the heart of the Labyrinth.

Someday, thought Valentine, if I am Coronal again, it will happen that I must succeed Tyeveras as Pontifex. And when that day comes I will let the people know that I do not choose to live in the Labyrinth, but will build a palace for myself in some more cheering place.

He smiled. He wondered how many Coronals before him, seeing the hid-eous enormity of the Labyrinth, had vowed the same vow. And yet somehow they all, sooner or later, withdrew from the world and took up residence down here. It was easy enough now, when he was young and full of vitality, to make such resolutions – easy enough to think of taking the Pontificate out of Alhanroel altogether, off to some congenial spot on the younger con-tinent, Ni-moya, perhaps, or Dulorn, and live among beauty and delight.

He found it hard to imagine himself voluntarily walling himself up in this fantastic and repellent Labyrinth. But yet, but yet, they had all done it before him, Dekkeret and Confalume and Prestimion and Stiamot and Kinniken and the others of times gone by, they had moved from Castle Mount to this dark hole when their moment came. Perhaps it was not as bad as it seemed. Perhaps when one is Coronal long enough one is glad to retire from the heights of Castle Mount. I will think more of these matters, Valentine told himself, when the appropriate time is at hand.

The caravan of floater-cars executed a hairpin turn and entered yet a lower level.

'The Arena,' Hissune announced grandly.

Valentine stared into a huge hollow chamber, so great in length and width that he was unable to see its walls, only the twinkling of distant lights in the shadowed corners. There were no visible supports to its ceiling. It was astonishing to think of the massive weight of the upper levels, those millions of people, those endless winding streets and alleyways, those buildings and statues and vehicles and all, pressing down on the roof of the Arena, and this vast nothingness resisting the colossal pressure.

'Listen,' said Hissune. He scrambled out of the car, put his hands to his mouth, and unleashed a piercing cry. And echoes returned, sharp stabbing sounds bouncing from this wall and that, the first few magnified in sound, the rest diminished until they were no more than the twittering chirping sounds of droles. He sent forth another cry, and another on its heels, so that sounds crashed and reverberated all about them for more than a minute. Then, with a self-satisfied smirk, the boy returned to the car.

'What purpose does this place serve?' Valentine asked.

'None.'

'None? None at all?'

'It's just an emptiness. The Pontifex Dizimaule wanted a large empty space here. Nothing ever happens in it. No one's allowed to build in it, not that anyone would want to. It just sits. It makes good echoes, don't you think? That's the only use it has. Go on, Valentine, make an echo.'

Valentine smiled and shook his head. 'Another time,' he said.

Crossing the Arena seemed to take all day. On and on they went, never once seeing a wall or a column; it was like traversing an open plain, except for the vaguely visible ceiling far above. Nor was Valentine able to discern the moment when they began to leave the Arena. He realized after a time that the floor of the place had turned somehow into a ramp, and that they had made an imperceptible transition to a lower level that returned to the familiar claustrophobic closeness of the Labyrinth's coils. As they proceeded down this new semicircular corridor it grew gradually more brightly lit, until soon it was nearly as well illuminated as that level close to the mouth where the shops and markets were. Ahead, rising to an extraordinary height directly before them, was a screen of some sort on which inscriptions in brilliant luminous colors could be seen.

Hissune said, 'We are coming to the House of Records. I can go with you no farther.'

Indeed the road terminated in a five-sided plaza in front of the great screen – which, Valentine now saw, was a kind of chronicle of Majipoor. Down its left-hand side were the names of the Coronals, a list so long that he could scarcely read its upper reaches. Down the right was the corresponding list of Pontifexes. Beside each name was the date of reign.

His eyes searched the lists. Hundreds, hundreds of names, some the familiar ones, the great resonant names of the planet's history, Stiamot, Thimin, Confalume, Dekkeret, Prestimion, and some that were only meaningless arrangements of letters, names that Valentine had seen when as a boy he had whiled away rainy afternoons reading the lists of the Powers, but that had no significance other than that they were on the list – Prankipin and Hunzimar and Meyk and Struin and Scaul and Spurifon, men who had held power on Castle Mount and then in the Labyrinth a thousand years ago, three thousand, five, had been the center of all conversation, the object of all homage, had danced across the imperial stage and done their little show and vanished into history. Lord Spurifon, he thought. Lord Scaul. Who were they? What color was their hair, what games did they enjoy, what laws had they decreed, how calmly and bravely had they met their deaths? What impact had they had on the lives of the billions of Majipoor, or had they none? Some, Valentine saw, had ruled only a few years as Coronal, carried off quickly to the Labyrinth by the death of a Pontifex. And some had occupied the summit of Castle Mount for a generation. This Lord Meyk, Coronal for thirty years, and Pontifex for – Valentine scanned the dizzying lists – Pontifex for twenty more. Fifty years of supreme power, and who knew anything of Lord Meyk and Meyk the Pontifex today?

He looked toward the bottom of the lists, where they trailed off into blankness. Lord Tyeveras – Lord Malibor – Lord Voriax – Lord Valentine—

That was where the left-hand list ended, of course. Lord Valentine, reign three years old and unfinished—

Lord Valentine, at least, would be remembered. Not for him the oblivion of the Spurifons and Scauls; for they would tell the tale on Majipoor, for generations to come, of the dark-haired young Coronal who was cast by treachery into a fair-haired body, and lost his throne to the son of the King of Dreams. But what would they say of him? That he was a guileless fool, as comic a figure as Arioc who made himself Lady of the Isle? That he was a weakling who had failed to guard himself against evil? That he had suffered an astounding fall, and had valiantly regained his place? How would the history of Lord Valentine be told, a thousand years hence? One thing he prayed, as he stood before the great list of the House of Records: let it not be said of Lord Valentine that he regained his throne with magnificent heroism, and then ruled feebly and aimlessly for fifty years. Better to abandon the Castle to the Barjazid than to be known for that.

Hissune tugged at his hand.

'Valentine?'

He looked down, startled.

The boy said, 'I leave you here. The people of the Pontifex will come for you soon.'

'Thank you, Hissune, for all you've done. But how will you get back by yourself?'

Hissune winked. 'It won't be by walking, I promise you that.'

He peered solemnly up and said, after a pause, 'Valentine?'

'Yes?'

'Aren't you supposed to have dark hair and a beard?'

Valentine laughed. 'You think I'm the Coronal?'

'Oh, I know you are! It's written all over your face. Only – only your face is wrong.'

'It's not a bad face,' said Valentine lightly. 'A little more kindly than my old one, and maybe more handsome. I think I'm going to keep it. I suppose whoever had it first has no more need for it now.'

The boy's eyes were wide. 'Are you in disguise, then?'

'You might say that.'

'I thought so.' He put his small hand in Valentine's. 'Well, good luck, Valentine. If you ever come back to the Labyrinth, ask for me and I'll be your guide again, and the next time for free. Remember my name: Hissune.'

'Goodbye, Hissune.'

The boy winked again, and was gone.

Valentine looked toward the great screen of history.

Lord Tyeveras – Lord Malibor – Lord Voriax – Lord Valentine—

And perhaps someday Lord Hissune, he thought. Why not? The boy seemed at least as qualified as many who had ruled, and probably would have had sense enough not to drink Dominin Barjazid's drugged wine. I must remember him, he told himself. I must remember him.

6

From a gateway at the far side of the plaza of the House of Records now came three figures, a Hjort and two humans, in the masks of Labyrinthine officialdom. Unhurriedly they advanced toward the place where Valentine stood with Deliamber, Sleet, and a few others.

The Hjort gave Valentine careful scrutiny and did not seem awed.

'Your business here?' he asked.

'To apply for an audience with the Pontifex.'

'An audience with the Pontifex,' the Hjort repeated in wonder, as if Valentine had said, To apply for a pair of wings, To apply for permission to drink the ocean dry. 'An audience with the Pontifex!' She laughed. 'The Pontifex grants no audiences.'

'Are you his chief ministers?'

The laughter was louder. 'This is the House of Records, not the Court of Thrones. There are no ministers of state here.'

The three officials turned and started back toward the gateway.

'Wait!' Valentine called.

He slipped into the dream-state and sent an urgent vision toward them. There was no specific content to it, only a broad and general sense that the stability of things was in peril, that the bureaucracy itself was sorely threatened, and that only they could stave off the forces of chaos. They walked on, and Valentine redoubled the intensity of his sending, until he began to sweat and tremble with the effort of it. They halted. The Hjort looked around.

'What do you want here?' she asked.

'Admit us to the ministers of the Pontifex.'

There was a whispered conference.

'What do we do?' Valentine asked Deliamber. 'Juggle for them?'

'Try to be patient,' the Vroon murmured.

Valentine found that difficult; but he held his tongue, and after some moments the officials returned to say that he could enter, and five of his companions. The others must take lodgings on an upper level. Valentine scowled. But there seemed no arguing with these masked ones. He chose Deliamber, Carabella, Sleet, Asenhart, and Zalzan Kavol to continue on with him.

'How will the rest find lodgings?' he asked.

The Hjort shrugged. That was none of her affair.

From the shadows to Valentine's left came a high clear voice. 'Does someone need a guide to the upper levels?'

Valentine chuckled. 'Hissune? Still here?'

'I thought I might be needed.'

'You are. Find a decent place for my people to stay, in the outer ring, near the Mouth of Waters, where they can wait for me until I've finished down here.'

Hissune nodded. 'I ask only three crowns.'

'What? You need a ride up to the top anyway! And five minutes ago you said that the next time you were my guide, you wouldn't charge anything!'

'That's next time,' replied Hissune gravely. 'This is still this time. Would you deprive a poor boy of his livelihood?'

Sighing, Valentine said to Zalzan Kavol, 'Give him three crowns.'

The boy hopped into the first car. Shortly the entire caravan swung around and departed. Valentine and his five companions passed through the gateway of the House of Records.

Corridors went in all directions. In poorly lit cubicles clerks bent low over mounds of documents. The air was musty and dry here; the general feel of the place was even more repellent than that of the earlier levels. This, Valentine realized, was the administrative core of Majipoor, the place where the real business of governing twenty billion beings was carried on. The awareness that these scurrying gnomes, these burrowers in the earth, held the actual power of the world chilled him.

He had tended to think it was the Coronal who was the true king, and the Pontifex a mere figurehead, since it was the Coronal who was seen actively commanding the forces of order whenever chaos threatened, the vigorous dynamic Coronal, whereas the Pontifex remained immured down below, emerging from the Labyrinth only on the highest occasions of state.

But now he was not so certain.

The Pontifex himself might be merely a crazy old man, but the minions of the Pontifex, these hundreds of thousands of drab bureaucrats in their odd little masks, might collectively wield more authority on Majipoor than the dashing Coronal and all his princely aides. Down here the tax rolls were determined, here the balances of trade between province and province were adjusted, here the maintenance of highways and parks and educational establishments and all the other functions under provincial control were coordinated. Valentine was not at all convinced that true central government was possible on a world as big as Majipoor, but at least the basic forms of it existed, the structural outlines, and he saw, as he moved through the inner maze of the Labyrinth, that government on Majipoor was not altogether a matter of grand processionals and dream-sendings. The mighty hidden bureaucracy down here did most of the work.

And he was caught in its toils. There were lodgings several levels down from the House of Records for provincial officials who were visiting the

Labyrinth on governmental business; there he was given a suite of modest rooms, and there he stayed, ignored, for the next few days. There seemed to be no way to move beyond this point. As Coronal he would have the right of immediate access to the Pontifex, of course; but he was not Coronal, not in any effective sense, and to claim that he was would probably make it impossible for him to proceed at all.

He recalled, after some rooting about in his memory, the names of the chief ministers of the Pontifex. Unless things had changed lately, Tyeveras kept five plenipotentiary officials close by him – Hornkast, his high spokesman; Dilifon, his private secretary; Shinaam, a Ghayrog, his minister of external affairs; Sepulthrove, his minister of scientific matters and personal physician; and Narrameer, his dream-speaker, who was rumored to be the most powerful of all, the adviser who had chosen Voriax and then Valentine to be Coronal.

But to reach any of these five seemed as hard as to reach the Pontifex himself. Like Tyeveras they were buried in the depths, remote, inaccessible. Valentine's skill with the circlet his mother had given him did not extend to making contact with the mind of someone unknown to him, at an unknown distance.

He learned shortly that two lesser, but still significant, officials served as the guardians of the central levels of the Labyrinth. These were the imperial major-domos, Dondak-Sajamir of the Su-Suheris stock and Gitamorn Suul, a human. 'But,' said Sleet, who had been talking with the keepers of the hostelry, 'these two have been feuding for a year or more. They cooperate with one another as little as possible. And you must have the approval of both in order to see the higher ministers.'

Carabella snorted in annoyance. 'We'll spend the rest of our lives gathering dust down here! Valentine, why are we bothering with the Labyrinth at all? Why not clear out of here and march straight for Castle Mount?'

'My idea exactly,' said Sleet.

Valentine shook his head. 'The support of the Pontifex is essential. So the Lady told me, and I agree.'

'Essential for what?' Sleet demanded. 'The Pontifex sleeps far below the ground. He knows nothing of anything. Does the Pontifex have any army to lend you? Does the Pontifex even exist?'

'The Pontifex has an army of petty clerks and officials,' Deliamber pointed out mildly. 'We will find them extremely useful. They, not warriors, control the balance of power in our world.'

Sleet was unconvinced. 'I say hoist the starburst banner and sound the trumpets and bang the drums and set out across Alhanroel, proclaiming you as Coronal and letting the whole world know of Dominin Barjazid's little trick. In each city along the way, you meet with the key people and win their support with your warmth and sincerity, and maybe a little help from the Lady's circlet. By the time you're at Castle Mount, ten million people are marching behind you, and the Barjazid will surrender without a fight!'

'A pretty vision,' said Valentine. 'But I think we still must have the instrumentalities of the Pontifex working for us before we try to make any open challenge. I will pay calls on these two major-domos.'

In the afternoon he was conducted to the headquarters of Dondak-Sajamir – a surprisingly bleak little office deep in a tangle of tiny clerkish cubicles. For more than an hour Valentine was kept waiting in a cramped and cluttered vestibule, before at last being admitted to the major-domo's presence.

Valentine was not entirely sure how to manage things with a Su-Suheris. Was one head Dondak and the other Sajamir? Did you address both at once, or speak only to the head that spoke to you? Was it proper to keep your attention moving from one head to the other while talking?

Dondak-Sajamir regarded Valentine as though from a great height. There was tense silence in the office as the four cool green eyes of the alien dispassionately surveyed the visitor. The Su-Suheris was a slender, elongated creature, hairless and smooth-skinned, tubular and shoulderless in form, with a rod-shaped neck that rose like a pedestal to a height of ten or twelve inches and forked to provide support for the two narrow spindle-shaped heads. He bore himself with such an air of superiority that one could easily think that the office of major-domo to the Pontifex was far more important than that of the Pontifex himself. But some of that frosty hauteur, Valentine knew, was simply a function of the major-domo's race: a Su-Suheris could not help looking naturally imperious and disdainful.

Eventually Dondak-Sajamir's left-hand head said, 'Why have you come here?'

'To apply for an audience with the chief ministers of the Pontifex.'

'So it says in your letter. But what business do you have with them?'

'A matter of the greatest urgency, an affair of state.'

'Yes?'

'You hardly expect me to discuss it with anyone below the highest levels of authority, surely.'

Dondak-Sajamir considered that point interminably. When he spoke again, it was from the right-hand head. The second voice was much deeper than the first. 'If I waste the time of the chief ministers, it will go hard for me.'

'If you place obstacles between me and my seeing them, it will also go hard for you, ultimately.'

'A threat?'

'Not at all. I can tell you only that the consequences of their not receiving the information I bear will be very serious for all of us – and no doubt they will be distressed to learn that it was you who kept that information from reaching them.'

'Not I alone,' said the Su-Suheris. 'There is a second major-domo, and we must act jointly in approving applications of this sort. You have not spoken to my colleague yet.'

'No.'

'She is insane. She has deliberately and malevolently withheld her co-operation from me for many months.' Now Dondak-Sajamir spoke from both heads simultaneously, in tones not quite an octave apart. The effect was weirdly disconcerting. 'Even if I gave you approval, she would refuse. You will never get to see the chief ministers.'

'But this is impossible! Can't we go around her somehow?'

'It would be illegal.'

'If she blocks all legitimate business, though—'

The Su-Suheris looked indifferent. 'The responsibility is hers.'

'No,' Valentine said. 'You both share it! You can't simply say that because she won't cooperate, I can't go forward, when the survival of the government itself is at stake!'

'Do you think so?' asked Dondak-Sajamir.

The question left Valentine baffled. Was it the idea of a threat to the realm that he was challenging, or merely the notion that he bore equal responsibilty for blocking Valentine?

Valentine said, after a moment, 'What do you suggest I do?'

'Return to your home,' said the major-domo, 'and live a fruitful and happy life, and leave the problems of government to those of us whose fate it is to wrestle with them.'

7

He had no better satisfaction from Gitamorn Suul. The other major-domo was less supercilious than the Su-Suheris, but hardly more cooperative.

She was a woman ten or twelve years older than Valentine, tall and dark-haired, with a businesslike, competent air about her. She did not appear at all insane. On her desk, in an office notably more cheerful and attractive, though no larger, than Dondak-Sajamir's, was a file containing Valentine's application. She tapped it several times and said, 'You can't see them, you know.'

'May I ask why not?'

'Because no one sees them.'

'No one?'

'No one from outside. It is no longer done.'

'Is that because of the friction between you and Dondak-Sajamir?'

Gitamorn Suul's lips quirked testily. 'That idiot! But no – even if he were performing his duties properly, it still wouldn't be possible for you to reach the ministers. They don't want to be bothered. They have heavy responsibilities. The Pontifex is old, you know. He gives little time to matters of government, and therefore the burdens on those about him have increased. Do you understand?'

'I *must* see them,' said Valentine.

'I can't help that. Not even for the most urgent reason can they be disturbed.'

'Suppose,' Valentine said slowly, 'the Coronal had been overthrown, and a false ruler held possession of the Castle?'

She pushed up her mask and looked at him in astonishment. 'Is that what you want to tell them? Here. Application dismissed.' Rising, she made brisk shooing gestures at him. 'We have madmen enough in the Labyrinth already, without new ones coming down out of—'

'Wait,' said Valentine.

He let the trance-state possess him, and summoned the power of the circlet. Desperately he reached toward her soul with his, touched it, enfolded it. It had not been part of his plan to reveal much to these minor officials, but there seemed no alternative but to take her into his confidence. He sustained the contact until he felt himself growing dizzy and weak; then he broke it off and returned hurriedly to full wakefulness. She was staring at him, dazed; her cheeks were flushed, her eyes were wild, her breasts heaved in agitation. It was a moment before she could speak.

Finally she said, 'What kind of trick is that?'

'No trick. I am the Lady's son, and she herself taught me the art of sendings.'

'Lord Valentine is a dark-haired man.'

'So he was. Not any longer.'

'You ask me to believe—'

'Please,' he said. He threw all the intensity of his spirit into the word. 'Please. Believe me. Everything depends on my telling the Pontifex what has happened.'

But her suspicions ran deep. From Gitamorn Suul came no kneelings, no homages, no starburst gesticulations, only a kind of sullen bewilderment, as if she might be inclined to think his bizarre story was true, but wished he had inflicted it on some other functionary.

She said, 'The Su-Suheris would veto anything I proposed.'

'Even if I showed him what I've shown you?'

She shrugged. 'His obstinacy is legendary. Not even to save the life of the Pontifex would he approve one of my recommendations.'

'But this is madness!'

'Exactly so. You've talked to him?'

'Yes,' Valentine said. 'He seemed unfriendly and puffed up with pride. But not mad.'

'Deal with him a little longer,' Gitamorn Suul advised, 'before you form your final judgment of him.'

'What if we were to forge his approval, so that I could go in without his knowing?'

She looked shocked. 'You want me to commit a crime?'

Valentine struggled to maintain his even temper. 'A crime has already been committed, and not a trifling one,' he said in a low, steady voice. 'I am Coronal of Majipoor, deposed through treachery. Your help is vital to my restoration. Doesn't that override all these petty regulations? Can't you see that I have the power to pardon you for breaking those regulations?' He leaned toward her. 'Time is wasting. Castle Mount houses a usurper. I run back and forth between subordinates of the Pontifex, when I should be leading an army of liberation across Alhanroel. Give me your approval, and let me be on my way, and there'll be rewards for you when everything's again as it should be on Majipoor.'

Her eyes were cold and suddenly bleak. 'Your story makes great demands on my powers of belief. What if it is all false? What if you are in the pay of Dondak-Sajamir?'

Valentine groaned. 'I beg you—'

'No. It's entirely likely. This is a trap, perhaps. You, your fantastic story, some sort of hypnosis, all designed to destroy me, to leave the Su-Suheris unchallenged here, to give him the supreme power he has long desired—'

'I swear by the Lady my mother I have not lied to you.'

'A true criminal would swear by anybody's mother, but what is that?'

Valentine hesitated, then boldly reached forth and took Gitamorn Suul's hands in his. Intently he stared into her eyes. What he was about to do was disagreeable to him, but so was all that these petty bureaucrats had been doing to him. The time had come for a little shamelessness, or he would be forever entangled down here.

He said, peering close, 'Even if I were in Dondak-Sajamir's pay, I could never betray a woman as beautiful as you.'

She looked scornful. But color flared again in her cheeks.

He went on, 'Trust me. Believe me. I am Lord Valentine, and you will be one of the heroes of my return. I know the thing you want most in the world, and it will be yours when I have regained the Castle.'

'You know it?'

'Yes,' he whispered, gently stroking the hands that now lay limply in his. 'To have sole authority over the inner Labyrinth, is that not it? To be the only major-domo?'

She nodded as though in a dream.

'It will be done,' he said. 'Ally yourself with me, and Dondak-Sajamir will be stripped of his rank, for making himself an obstacle to me. Will you do that? Will you help me reach the chief ministers, Gitamorn Suul?'

'It will be – difficult—'

'But it can be done! Anything can be done! And when I am Coronal again, the Su-Suheris loses his post! I promise you that.'

'Swear it!'

'I swear it,' Valentine said passionately, feeling foul and depraved. 'I swear it on my mother's name. I swear it by all that's holy. Is it agreed?'

'Agreed,' she said in a small faltering voice. 'But how is it to be done? You need both signatures on the pass, and if mine is on it, he'll refuse to add his.'

Valentine said, 'Write me out a pass and sign it. I'll go back to him and talk him into countersigning it.'

'He will never do it.'

'Let me work on him. I can be persuasive. Once I have his signature, I can enter the inner Labyrinth and achieve what I must achieve. When I emerge, it will be with the full authority of the Coronal – and I will have Dondak-Sajamir removed from office, that I promise you.'

'But how will you get his signature? He's refused all countersignatures for months!'

'Leave that to me,' said Valentine.

She drew from her desk a dark green cube of some sleek glistening material and placed it briefly in a machine that cast an incandescent yellow glow over it. When she removed it, the surface of the cube was infused with a new brightness. 'Here. This is your pass. But I warn you that without his countersignature it is worthless.'

'I'll get it,' Valentine said.

He returned to Dondak-Sajamir. The Su-Suheris was reluctant to see him, but Valentine persevered.

'I understand now your loathing of Gitamorn Suul,' he said.

Dondak-Sajamir smiled coolly. 'Is she not hateful? I suppose she refused your application.'

'Oh, no,' said Valentine, taking the cube from his cloak and placing it before the major-domo. 'She granted that willingly enough, knowing that you had refused me and her permission would be worthless. It was her other rejection that wounded me so deeply.'

'And which was that?'

Serenely Valentine said, 'This may sound foolish to you, or even repellent, but I was powerfully overcome by her beauty. To human eyes, I must tell you, that woman has extraordinarily physical presence, a nobility of bearing, a luminous erotic force, that – well, no matter. I threw myself before her in an embarrassingly naïve way. I made myself open and vulnerable. And she mocked me cruelly. She scorned me in a way that was like a blade twisting in my vitals. Can you understand that, that she would be so merciless, so contemptuous, toward a stranger who had only the warmest and most profoundly passionate feelings for her?'

'Her beauty escapes me,' said Dondak-Sajamir. 'But I know her coldness and arrogance quite well.'

'Now I share your enmity for her,' Valentine said. 'If you will have me, I offer myself to your service, so that we can work together to destroy her.'

Dondak-Sajamir said thoughtfully, 'Yes, this would be a fine moment to bring about her downfall. But how?'

Valentine tapped the cube that rested on the major-domo's desk. 'Add your countersignature to this pass. I'll then be free to enter the inner Labyrinth. While I'm there, you launch an official inquiry into the circumstances under which I was admitted, claiming that you gave no such permission. When I've returned from my business with the Pontifex, summon me to testify. I'll say you rejected my application, and that I got the pass, already fully countersigned, from Gitamorn Suul, never suspecting it might be forged by someone meaning to spite you by admitting me. Your accusation of forgery, coupled with my testimony that you had declined to approve my application, will be her ruination. What do you say?'

'A magnificent plan,' replied Dondak-Sajamir. 'I could have devised nothing better!'

The Su-Suheris slipped the cube into a machine that gave it a brilliant pink glow superimposed over Gitamorn Suul's yellow one. The pass now was valid. All this intrigue, Valentine thought, was nearly as much of a strain on the mind as the intricacies of the Labyrinth itself; but it was done, and done successfully. Now let these two plot and scheme against each other as they wished, while he made his way unimpeded toward the ministers of the Pontifex. They were apt to be disappointed with the way he fulfilled his promises to them, for he intended, if he could, to sweep both the bickering rivals from power. But he did not ask pure and total saintliness of himself in his dealings with those whose chief role in the government appeared to be to impede and obstruct.

He took the cube from Dondak-Sajamir and inclined his head in gratitude.

'May you come to have all the power and prestige you deserve,' said Valentine unctuously, and departed.

8

The guardians of the innermost Labyrinth seemed astounded that anyone from outside had contrived to gain entry to their realm. But though they subjected the pass-cube to a thorough scanning, they grudgingly conceded that it was legitimate and sent Valentine and his companions forward.

A narrow, snub-snouted car carried them silently and swiftly down the passages of this interior universe. The masked officials who accompanied them did not seem to be guiding it themselves, nor would that have been an easy task, for in these levels the Labyrinth branched and rebranched, curved and recurved. Any intruder would quickly become hopelessly bewildered amid these thousand twistings, twinings, sinuosities and tangles. The car, though, appeared to be floating over a concealed guidance track that controlled its journey, along a swift if not particularly straightforward route, deeper and deeper into the coils of sequestered alleys.

At checkpoint after checkpoint Valentine was interrogated by disbelieving functionaries almost unable to comprehend the notion that an outlander had come calling on the ministers of the Pontifex. Their endless thrusts were wearying but futile. He waved his pass-cube at them as though it were a magic wand. 'I am on a mission of the highest urgency,' he said again and again, 'and will speak only with the supreme members of the Pontifical court.' Arming himself with all the dignity and presence at his command, Valentine brushed aside every objection, every quibble. 'It will not go well for you,' he warned, 'if you delay me further.'

And finally – it felt as though a hundred years had passed since Valentine had juggled his way into the Labyrinth at the Mouth of Blades – he found himself standing before Shinaam, Dilifon, and Narrameer, three of the five great ministers of the Pontifex.

They received him in a somber and clammy chamber made of huge blocks of black stone, with a lofty ceiling and ornamentation of pointed arches. It was a heavy, oppressive place more suitable as a dungeon than a council-chamber. Entering it, Valentine felt all the weight of the Labyrinth bearing down on him level upon level, Arena and House of Records and Court of Globes and Hall of Winds and all the rest, the dark corridors, the cluttered cubicles, the multitudes of toiling clerks. Somewhere far above, the sun was shining, the air was fresh and crisp, a breeze blew out of the south, bearing the perfume of alabandinas and eldirons and tanigales. And he was here pinned beneath a giant mound of earth and miles of tortuous passageways, in a kingdom of eternal night. His journey downward and inward in the Labyrinth had left him feverish and drawn, as though he had not slept for weeks.

He touched his hand to Deliamber and the Vroon gave him a tingling jolt of energy, shoring up his ebbing strength. He looked to Carabella, who smiled and blew him a kiss. He looked to Sleet, who nodded and grinned grimly. He looked to Zalzan Kavol, and the fierce grizzled Skandar made a quick juggling motion with all his hands by way of encouragement. His companions, his friends, his bulwarks throughout all this long and strange travail.

He looked toward the ministers.

Maskless, they sat side by side on chairs majestic enough to be thrones. Shinaam was in the center, the minister of external affairs, of Ghayrog birth, reptilian-looking, with chilly lidless eyes and busily flicking forked red tongue and hair of a coarse snaky appearance that moved in slow wriggles. To his right was Dilifon, private secretary to Tyeveras, a frail and spectral figure, hair as white as Sleet's, skin parched and withered, eyes blazing like jets of fire out of the ancient face. And on the other side of the Ghayrog was Narrameer, the imperial dream-speaker, a slender and elegant woman who must surely be of great age, for her association with Tyeveras went back as far as the long-ago era when he was Coronal. Yet she seemed to be barely of middle years. Her skin was smooth and unlined, her auburn hair was lustrous and full. Only by the remote and enigmatic expression of her eyes could Valentine detect any hint of the wisdom, the experience, the accumulated power of many decades, that was hers. Some sorcery at work, he decided.

'We have read your petition,' said Shinaam. His voice was deep and crisp, with the merest trace of a hiss in it. 'The story you bring strains our credulity.'

'Have you spoken with the Lady my mother?'

'We have spoken with the Lady, yes,' the Ghayrog replied coolly. 'She accepts you as her son.'

'She urges us to cooperate with you,' said Dilifon in a cracked and scratchy voice.

'In sendings she appeared to us,' said Narrameer, softly, musically, 'and commended you to us, asking that we give you such aid as you require.'

'Well, then?' Valentine demanded.

Shinaam said, 'The possibility exists that the Lady is capable of being deceived.'

'You think I'm an impostor?'

'You ask us to believe,' said the Ghayrog, 'that the Coronal of Majipoor was taken unawares by a younger son of the King of Dreams and evicted from his own body, that he was stripped of his memory and placed – such fragment of him as remained – in quite another body that conveniently happened to be available, and that the usurper successfully entered the empty husk of the Coronal and imposed his own consciousness on it. We find it strenuous to believe such things.'

'The skills exist to move bodies from mind to mind,' said Valentine. 'There is precedent.'

'No precedent,' Dilifon said, 'for the displacement of a Coronal in that fashion.'

'Nevertheless it happened,' Valentine replied. 'I am Lord Valentine, restored to my memory by the kindness of the Lady, and I ask the backing of the Pontifex in regaining the responsibilities to which he called me upon my brother's death.'

'Yes,' said Shinaam. 'If you are who you claim to be, it would be fitting for you to return to Castle Mount. But how are we to know that? These are serious matters. They portend civil war. Shall we advise the Pontifex to plunge the world into agony on the mere assertion of some young stranger who—'

'I've already convinced my mother of my authenticity,' Valentine pointed out. 'My mind lay open to her at the Isle, and she saw me to be who I am.' He touched the silver circlet at his brow. 'How do you think I came by this device? It was her gift, by her own hands, as we stood together in Inner Temple.'

Quietly Shinaam said, 'That the Lady accepts you and supports you is not in doubt.'

'But you question her judgment?'

'We require deeper proof of your claims,' said Narrameer.

'Then allow me to cast forth a sending here and now, so that I can convince you that I speak the truth.'

'As you wish,' said Dilifon.

Valentine closed his eyes and let the trance-state come upon him.

From him, with passion and conviction, came the radiant stream of his being, flooding forth as it had when he had needed to gain the trust of Nascimonte in that bleak ruin-strewn wilderness beyond Treymone, and when he had swayed the minds of the three officials at the gateway to the House of Records, and when he had revealed himself to the major-domo Gitamorn Suul. With varying degrees of success he had accomplished what had to be accomplished with all of those.

But now he felt himself unable to surmount the impenetrable skepticism of the ministers of the Pontifex.

The mind of the Ghayrog was altogether opaque to him, a wall as blank and inaccessible as the towering white cliffs of the Isle of Sleep. Valentine sensed only the most cloudy flickerings of a consciousness behind Shinaam's mental shield, and could not break through, though he poured against it everything at his command. The mind of shriveled old Dilifon was an equally remote thing, not because it was shielded but because it seemed porous, open, a honeycomb that offered no resistance: he went through it, air passing through air, encountering nothing tangible. Only with the mind of the dream-speaker Narrameer did Valentine sense contact, but that too was unsatisfactory. She seemed to be drinking in his soul, absorbing all that he was giving and letting it drain into some fathomless cavern of her being, so that he could send and send and send and never reach the center of her spirit.

Yet he refused to give up. With furious intensity he hurled forth the fullness of his soul, proclaiming himself to be Lord Valentine of Castle Mount and urging them to give proof that he was anything else. He reached deep for memories – of his mother, his royal brother, his princely education, his overthrow in Til-omon, his wanderings in Zimroel, everything that had gone into the shaping of the man who had battled his way to the bowels of the Labyrinth to gain their aid. He offered himself totally, recklessly, ferociously, until he could send no more, until he was reeling and numb with exhaustion, hanging between Sleet and Carabella like some limp and useless garment that its owner had discarded.

He brought himself up from the trance-like state, fearing that he had failed.

He was trembling and weak. Sweat bathed his body. His vision was blurred and there was a savage pain in his temples.

He fought to recover his strength, closing his eyes, sucking air deep into his lungs. Then he looked up at the trio of ministers.

Their faces were harsh and somber. Their eyes were cold and unmoved. Their expressions were aloof, disdainful, even hostile. Valentine was suddenly terrified. Could these three be in league with Dominin Barjazid himself? Was he pleading before his own enemies?

But that was unthinkable and impossible, a phantom of his exhausted mind, he told himself desperately. He could not let himself believe that the plot against him had reached as far as the Labyrinth.

In a hoarse, ragged voice he said, 'Well? What do you say now?'

'I experienced nothing,' said Shinaam.

'I am unconvinced,' said Dilifon. 'Any wizard can make sendings of this sort. Your sincerity and passion can be feigned.'

Narrameer said, 'I agree. Through sendings can come lies as well as truth.'

'No!' Valentine cried. 'You had me wide open before you, you can't possibly have failed to see—'

'Not wide enough,' said Narrameer.

'What do you mean?'

She said, 'Let us do a dream-speaking, you and I. Here, now, in this chamber, before these people. Let our minds truly become one. And then I can evaluate the plausibility of your story. Are you willing? Will you drink the drug with me?'

In alarm Valentine looked to his companions – and saw alarm reflected on their faces, all but that of Deliamber, whose expression was as bland and neutral as though he were someplace entirely else. Risk a speaking? Did he dare? The drug would render him unconscious, utterly transparent, wholly vulnerable. If these three were allied with the Barjazid and sought to render him helpless, there would be no easier way. Nor was this any ordinary village speaker who proposed to enter his mind; this was the speaker of the Pontifex, a woman of at least a hundred years, wily and powerful, reputed to be the true master of the Labyrinth, controlling all others, including old Tyeveras himself. Deliamber studiously was giving him no clue. This was entirely his decision to make.

'Yes,' he said, his eyes directly on hers. 'If nothing else avails, let it be a speaking. Here. Now.'

9

They seemed to be prepared for it. At a signal, aides brought in the paraphernalia of a speaking: a thick rug of rich glowing colors, dark gold edged with scarlet and green; a slim tall decanter of polished white stone; two delicate porcelain cups. Narrameer stepped down from her lofty chair and poured the dream-wine with her own hands, offering Valentine the first cup.

He held it a moment without drinking it. He had had wine from the hands of Dominin Barjazid in Til-omon, and all had changed for him in a single draught. Was he to drink this, now, without fear of consequences? Who knew what fresh enchantment was being prepared for him? Where would he awaken, in what altered guise?

Narrameer watched him in silence. The dream-speaker's eyes were unreadable, mysterious, penetrating. She was smiling, an altogether ambiguous smile, whether one of encouragement or of triumph Valentine could not tell. He raised the cup in brief salute and put it to his lips.

The effect of the wine was instantaneous and unexpectedly powerful. Valentine swayed dizzily. Fogs and cobwebs assailed his mind. Was this stuff stronger than what the dream-speaker Tisana had given him in Falkynkip so long ago – some special demon-brew of Narrameer's? Or was it simply that he was more susceptible at this moment, weakened and drained as he was by his using of the circlet? Through eyes that were becoming unwilling to focus he saw Narrameer down her own wine, toss the empty cup to an aide, and slide swiftly out of her robe. Her naked body was supple, smooth, youthful – flat belly, slender thighs, high round breasts. A sorcery, he thought. A sorcery, yes. Her skin was a deep shade of brown. Her nipples, almost black, stared at him like blind eyes.

He was already too deeply drugged to manage his own disrobing. The hands of his friends plucked at the catches and hasps of his clothing. He felt cold air about him and knew he was naked.

Narrameer beckoned him to the dream-rug.

On wobbly legs Valentine went to her, and she drew him down. He closed his eyes, imagining he was with Carabella, but Narrameer was nothing at all like Carabella. Her embrace was dry and cold, her flesh hard, unresilient. She had no warmth, no vibrance. That youthfulness of hers was only a cunning projection. Lying in her arms was like lying on a bed of smooth chilly stone.

An all-engulfing pool of darkness was rising about him, a thick warm oily fluid growing deeper and deeper, and Valentine let himself slip easily into it, feeling it slide up comfortingly about his legs, his waist, his chest.

It was much like the time the great sea-dragon had smashed Gorzval's ship, and he had found himself being sucked down by the whirlpool. Not resisting was so easy, so much easier than fighting. To yield all will, to relax, to accept whatever might befall, to allow himself to be swept under – so tempting, so very appealing. He was tired. He had struggled a long time. Now he could rest and allow the black tide to cover him. Let others battle valiantly for honor and power and acclaim. Let others—

No.

That was what they wanted: to ensnare him in his own weaknesses. He was too trusting, too guileless; he had supped with an enemy, unknowingly, and had been undone; he would be undone once more if he abandoned the effort now. This was not the moment for slipping into warm dark pools.

He began to swim. At first the going was difficult, for the pool was deep and the black fluid, viscous and heavy, tugged at his arms. But after a few strokes Valentine found a way to make his body more angular, a blade slicing deep. He moved rapidly and more rapidly yet, arms and legs pistoning in smooth coordination. The pool that had tempted him with oblivion now offered him support. Buoyant, firm, it bore him up as he swam swiftly toward the distant shore. The sun, bright, immense, a great purple-yellow globe, cast dazzling rays, a track of fire over the sea.

'Valentine.'

The voice was deep, rolling, a sound like thunder. He did not recognize it.

'Valentine, why are you swimming so hard?'

'To reach the shore.'

'But why do that?'

Valentine shrugged and kept swimming. He saw an island, a broad white beach, a jungle of tall slender trees growing one up against the next, with tangled vines binding their crowns into a dense canopy. But though he swam and swam and swam he came no closer to it.

'You see?' the great voice said. 'There's no sense in bothering!'

'Who are you?' Valentine asked.

'I am Lord Spurifon,' came the majestic resonant reply.

'Who?'

'Lord Spurifon the Coronal, successor to Lord Scaul now Pontifex, and I tell you to give up this folly. Where can you hope to get?'

'Castle Mount,' answered Valentine, swimming harder.

'But I am Coronal!'

'Never – heard of – you—'

Lord Spurifon made a shrill shrieking sound. The smooth oily surface of the sea rippled and then grew puckered, as though a million needles were piercing it from below. Valentine forced himself onward, no longer trying to be angular, but rather now transforming himself into something blunt and obstinate, a log with arms, battering through the turbulence.

Now the shore was within reach. He lowered his feet and felt sand below, hot, squirming, writhing sand that ran in trickles away from him wherever he touched it, making walking a chore, but not so grave a chore that he was unable to push himself to land. He scrambled up on the beach and knelt a moment. When he looked up, a pale, thin man with worried blue eyes was studying him.

'I am Lord Hunzimar,' he said mildly. 'Coronal of Coronals, never to be forgotten. And these are my immortal companions.' He gestured, and the beach was filled with men much like himself, insignificant, diffident, trifling. 'This is Lord Struin,' declared Lord Hunzimar, 'and this Lord Prankipin, and Lord Meyk, and Lord Scaul, and Lord Spurifon. Coronals of grandeur and puissance. Bow down before us!'

Valentine laughed. 'You're all completely forgotten!'

'No! No!'

'Such a squeaking!' He pointed at the last in the row. 'You – Spurifon! No one remembers you.'

'*Lord* Spurifon, if you please.'

'And you – Lord Scaul. Three thousand years have entirely evaporated your fame.'

'You are mistaken in this. My name is inscribed on the roster of the Powers.'

Valentine shrugged. 'So it is. But what does that matter? Lord Prankipin,

Lord Meyk, Lord Hunzimar, Lord Struin – nothing but names, now – nothing – but – names—'

'Nothing – but – names—' they echoed, in high thin wailing tones, and began to dwindle and shrink, until they were drole-high on the beach, small and scurrying things that ran about pitifully, crying out their names in sharp little squeaks. Then they were gone, and in their place were small white spheres, no bigger than juggling-balls, which, Valentine realized, as he bent down to inspect them, were skulls. He scooped them up and tossed them blithely in the air, and caught them as they descended and threw them again, arraying them in a gleaming cascade. Their jaws clicked and chattered as they soared and fell. Valentine grinned. How many could he juggle at once? Spurifon, Struin, Hunzimar, Meyk, Prankipin, Scaul – that was only six. There had been hundreds of Coronals, one every ten or twenty or thirty years for the past eleven thousand years or thereabouts. He would juggle them all. From the air he plucked more of them, greater ones, Confalume, Prestimion, Stiamot, Dekkeret, Pinitor, a dozen, a hundred, filling the air with them, hurling and catching, hurling and catching. Never since the days of the first settlement had there been such a display of juggling skill on Majipoor! No longer was he throwing skulls; they had become glittering many-faceted diadems, orbs, indeed a thousand imperial orbs that cast sparkling light in every direction. He juggled them flawlessly, knowing each for the Power that it represented, now Lord Confalume, now Lord Spurifon, now Lord Dekkeret, now Lord Scaul, keeping them all aloft, spreading them out through the air so that they formed a great inverted pyramid of light, all the royal persons of Majipoor dancing above him, all converging toward the fair-haired smiling man who stood with legs planted firmly in the warm sand of that golden beach. He supported them all. The entire history of the world was in his hands, and he sustained it in its flight.

The dazzling diadems formed a great starburst of radiance overhead.

Without missing a beat, Valentine began to walk inland, over the smoothly rising dunes toward the dense jungle wall. The trees parted as he approached, bowing to left and right, clearing a track for him, a scarlet-paved way leading to the unknown interior of the island. He looked ahead and saw foothills before him, low gray hills that rose in slow ascent to become steeply rising granite flanks, beyond which lay jagged peaks, a formidable sharp-tipped cordillera stretching on and on and on to the heart of a continent. And on the highest peak of all, on a summit so lofty that the air about it shimmered with a pale luminous glow seen only in dreams, sprawled the buttressed walls of the Castle. Valentine marched toward it, juggling as he went. Figures passed him along the path, coming the other way, waving, smiling, bowing. Lord Voriax was one, and his mother the Lady another, and the tall solemn figure of the Pontifex Tyeveras, all greeting him cordially, and Valentine waved back to them without dropping a diadem, without breaking the smooth serene flow of his juggling. He was on the foothill trail now, and effortlessly moving upward, with a crowd growing about him, Carabella, and Sleet close at hand, Zalzan Kavol and the whole juggling band of Skandars, Lisamon Hultin the giantess and Khun of Kianimot, Shanamir, Vinorkis, Gorzval, Lorivade, Asenhart, hundreds of others, Hjorts and Ghayrogs and Liimen and Vroons, merchants, farmers, fishers, acrobats, musicians, Duke Nascimonte the bandit chieftain, Tisana the dream-speaker, Gitamorn Suul and Dondak-Sajamir arm in arm, a horde of dancing Metamorphs, a phalanx of dragon-captains merrily brandishing harpoons, a skittering cavorting troop of forest-brethren swinging hand over hand through the trees alongside the path, everyone singing, laughing, prancing, followed him toward the Castle, Lord Malibor's Castle, Lord Spurifon's Castle, Lord Confalume's Castle, Lord Stiamot's Castle, Lord Valentine's Castle—

—Lord Valentine's Castle—

He was nearly there. Though the mountain road led virtually straight upward, though mists thick as wool hung low over the trail, he went onward, faster now, skipping and running, gloriously juggling his hundreds of gleaming baubles. Just ahead he saw three great pillars of fire, which as he drew closer resolved themselves into faces – Shinaam, Dilifon, Narrameer, side by side in his path.

They spoke in a single voice: 'Where are you going?'

'To the Castle.'

'Whose Castle?'

'Lord Valentine's Castle.'

'And who are you?'

'Ask them,' said Valentine, gesturing to those who danced behind him. 'Let them tell you my name!'

'Lord Valentine!' cried Shanamir, first to hail him.

'He is Lord Valentine!' cried Sleet and Carabella and Zalzan Kavol.

'Lord Valentine the Coronal!' cried the Metamorphs and the dragon-captains and the forest-brethren.

'Is this so?' asked the ministers of the Pontifex.

'I am Lord Valentine,' said Valentine gently, and threw the thousand diadems high overhead, and they rose until they were lost to sight in the darkness that dwells between the worlds, and out of that darkness they came floating silently down, twinkling, sparkling like snowflakes on the slopes of the mountains of the north, and when they touched the figures of Shinaam and Dilifon and Narrameer the three ministers vanished instantly, leaving only a silver gleam behind, and the gates of the Castle lay open.

10

Valentine woke.

He felt the wool of the rug against his bare skin, and saw the pointed arches of the gloomy stone ceiling far above. For a moment the world of the dream remained so vivid in his mind that he sought to return to it, not wanting at all to be in this place of musty air and dark corners. Then he sat up and looked about, shaking the fog from his mind.

He saw his companions Sleet and Carabella and Deliamber and Zalzan Kavol and Asenhart huddled together strangely against the far wall, tense, apprehensive.

He turned the other way, expecting to see the three ministers of the Pontifex once more enthroned. As indeed they were, but two more of the magnificent chairs had been brought to the room, and now five seated figures confronted him. Narrameer, robed again, sat at the left. Beside her was Dilifon. At the center of the group was a round-faced man with a blunt broad nose and dark solemn eyes, whom Valentine recognized, after a moment's thought, as Hornkast, high spokesman of the Pontificate. Next to him sat Shinaam, and in the rightmost chair was a person Valentine did not know, a sharp-featured man, thin-lipped, gray-skinned, strange. The five were watching him sternly, in a distant, preoccupied way, as though they were judges of a secret court, gathered to pass a verdict that was long overdue in rendering.

Valentine stood. He made no attempt to retrieve his clothing. That he was naked before this tribunal seemed somehow appropriate.

Narrameer said, 'Is your mind clear?'

'I believe it is.'

'You have slept more than an hour past the end of your dream. We have waited for you.' She indicated the gray-skinned man at the far side of the group and said, 'This is Sepulthrove, physician to the Pontifex.'

'So I suspected,' Valentine said.

'And this man' – she indicated the one in the center – 'I think you already know.'

Valentine nodded. 'Hornkast, yes. We have met.' And then the import of Narrameer's choice of words reached him. He smiled broadly and said, 'We have met, but I was in another body then. You accept my claim?'

'We accept your claim, Lord Valentine,' said Hornkast in a rich, melodious voice. 'A great strangeness has been perpetrated upon this world, but it will be set to rights. Come: clothe yourself. It is hardly fit that you go before the Pontifex naked like this.'

Hornkast led the procession to the imperial throne-room. Narrameer and Dilifon walked behind him, with Valentine between; Sepulthrove and Shinaam brought up the rear. Valentine's companions were not permitted to come.

The passageway was a narrow high-vaulted tunnel of a glimmering greenish glassy stuff, in the depths of which strange reflections, elusive and distorted, sparkled and swam. It coiled round and round, spiraling inward on a slight downward grade. Every fifty paces there was a bronze door that entirely sealed the tunnel: at each, Hornkast touched his fingers to a hidden panel, and the door slid noiselessly aside to admit them to the next segment of the passage, until at last they came to a door more ornate than the others, richly embellished with the symbol of the Labyrinth in chasings of gold, and the imperial monogram of Tyeveras superimposed on it. This was the very heart of the Labyrinth, Valentine knew, its deepest and most central point. And when this final door slipped aside at Hornkast's touch it revealed a huge bright chamber of spherical form, a great glassy-walled globe of a room, in which the Pontifex of Majipoor sat enthroned in splendor.

Valentine had beheld the Pontifex Tyeveras on five occasions. The first had been when Valentine was a child, and the Pontifex had come to Castle Mount to attend Lord Malibor's wedding; then again years later, at the coronation of Lord Voriax, and again a year afterward at the marriage of Voriax, and a fourth time when Valentine had visited the Labyrinth as emissary from his brother, and one last meeting just three years ago – though it felt now more like thirty – when Tyeveras had attended Valentine's own coronation. The Pontifex had already been old at the first of these events, an enormously tall, gaunt, forbidding-looking man with harsh angular features, a beard of midnight black, deep-set mournful eyes; and as he grew even older those characteristics became greatly accentuated, so that there came to be something cadaverous about him, a stiff, slow-moving, wintry old dry stalk of a man, but nevertheless alert, aware, still vigorous in his fashion, still projecting an aura of immense power and majesty. But now—

But now—

The throne on which Tyeveras sat was the one he had occupied on Valentine's earlier visit to the Labyrinth, a splendid high-backed golden seat atop three wide low steps; but now it was wholly enclosed in a sphere of lightly tinted blue glass, into which ran a vast and intricate network of life-support conduits that formed a complex, almost unfathomable cocoon. Those clear pipes bubbling with colored fluids, those meters and dials, those measuring plaques mounted on the Pontifex's cheeks and forehead, those wires and nodes and connectors and clamps, had a weird and frightening aspect, for plainly they said that the life of the Pontifex resided not in the Pontifex but in the machinery surrounding him.

'How long has he been like this?' Valentine murmured.

'The system has been developing for twenty years,' said the physician Sepulthrove with obvious pride. 'But only in the last two have we kept him constantly in it.'

'Is he conscious?'

'Oh, yes, yes, definitely conscious!' Sepulthrove replied. 'Go closer. Look at him.'

Uneasily Valentine advanced until he stood at the foot of the throne, peering up at the eerie old man within the glass bubble. Yes, he saw the light still aglow in the eyes of Tyeveras, saw the fleshless lips still clamped in a look of resolve. Now the skin of the Pontifex was like parchment over his skull, and his long beard, though still strangely black, was sparse and wispy.

Valentine glanced at Hornkast. 'Does he recognize people? Does he speak?'

'Of course. Give him a moment.'

Valentine's eyes met those of Tyeveras. There was a terrible silence. The old man frowned, stirred vaguely, let his tongue flicker briefly over his lips.

From the Pontifex came an unintelligible quavering sound, a kind of whining moan, soft and strange.

Hornkast said, 'The Pontifex gives greeting to his beloved son Lord Valentine the Coronal.'

Valentine repressed a shudder. 'Tell his majesty – tell him – tell him that his son Lord Valentine the Coronal comes to him in love and respect, as always.'

That was the convention: that one did not ever speak directly to the Pontifex, that one phrased one's sentences as though the high spokesman would repeat everything, although in fact the spokesman did not do so.

The Pontifex spoke again, as indistinctly as before.

Hornkast said, 'The Pontifex expresses his concern for the disturbance that has occurred in the realm. He asks what plans Lord Valentine the Coronal has for restoring the proper system of things.'

'Tell the Pontifex,' said Valentine, 'that I plan to march toward Castle Mount, calling upon all citizens to give me their allegiance. I ask from him a general directive branding Dominin Barjazid a usurper and denouncing all those who support him.'

From the Pontifex now came more animated sounds, sharp and high of pitch, with weird compelling energy behind them.

Hornkast said, 'The Pontifex wishes to be assured that you will avoid battle and the destruction of lives, if at all possible.'

'Tell him that I would prefer to regain Castle Mount without the loss of a single life on either side. But I have no idea whether that can be achieved.'

Odd gurgling sounds. Hornkast looked puzzled. He stood with his head cocked, listening intently.

'What does he say?' Valentine whispered.

The high spokesman shook his head. 'Not everything his majesty says can be interpreted. Sometimes he moves in realms too remote for our experience.'

Valentine nodded. He looked with pity and even with love on the grotesque old man, caged within the globe that sustained his life, able to communicate only in this dreamlike moaning. More than a century old, for decade after decade supreme monarch of the world, now drooling and babbling like a child – and yet somewhere within that decaying softening brain still ticked the mind of the Tyeveras that had been, trapped in the breakdown of the flesh. To behold him now was to understand the ultimate meaninglessness of supreme rank: a Coronal lived in the world of deeds and moral responsibility, only to succeed to the Pontificate and finally to vanish into the Labyrinth and crazy senility. Valentine wondered how often a Pontifex had become the captive of his spokesman and his doctor and his dream-speaker, and finally had had to be eased from the world so that the grand rotation of the Powers could bring a more vital man to the throne. Valentine comprehended now why the system separated the doer and the ruler, why the Pontifex eventually hid himself away from the world in this Labyrinth. His own time would come, down here: but, the Divine willing, it would not be soon.

He said, 'Tell the Pontifex that Lord Valentine the Coronal, his worshipful son, will do his utmost to repair the rift in the fabric of society. Tell the Pontifex that Lord Valentine counts on his majesty's support, without which there can be no swift restoration.'

There was silence from the throne, and then a long painful outwelling of incomprehensibility, a jumble of fluting gurgling sounds that wandered up and down the scale like the eerie melodies of the Ghayrog mode. Hornkast appeared to be straining to catch even a syllable of sense here and there. The Pontifex ceased speaking, and Hornkast, troubled, tugged at his jowls, chewed at his lip.

'What was all that?' Valentine asked.

'He thinks you are Lord Malibor,' said Hornkast dejectedly. 'He cautions you against the risks of going to sea to hunt dragons.'

'Wise counsel,' said Valentine. 'But it comes too late.'

'He says the Coronal is too precious to gamble his life in such amusements.'

'Tell him that I agree, that if I regain Castle Mount I'll cling closely to my tasks, and avoid any such diversions.'

The physician Sepulthrove came forward and said quietly, 'We are tiring him. This audience must end, I fear.'

'One moment more,' Valentine said.

Sepulthrove frowned. But Valentine, with a smile, advanced again to the foot of the throne, and knelt there, and held his outspread hands up toward the ancient creature within the glass bubble, and, slipping into the trance-state, sent forth his spirit toward Tyeveras, bearing impulses of reverence and affection. Had anyone ever shown affection toward the formidable Tyeveras before? Very likely not. But for decades this man had been the center and soul of Majipoor, and now, sitting here lost in a timeless dream of governance, aware only intermittently of the responsibilities that once had been his, he deserved such love as his adoptive son and someday successor could bestow, and Valentine gave as fully as the powers of the circlet would permit.

And Tyeveras seemed to grow stronger, his eyes to brighten, his cheeks to take on a ruddy tint. Was that a smile on those shriveled lips? Did the left hand of the Pontifex lift, ever so slightly, in a gesture of blessing? Yes. Yes. Yes. Beyond doubt the Pontifex felt the flow of warmth from Valentine, and welcomed it, and was responding.

Tyeveras spoke briefly, and almost coherently.

Hornkast said, 'He says he grants you his full support, Lord Valentine.'

Live long, old man, Valentine thought, getting to his feet and bowing. Probably you would rather sleep forever, but I must wish upon you a longer life even than you have already had, for there is work for me to do on Castle Mount.

He turned away.

'Let's go,' he told the five ministers. 'I have what I need.'

They marched soberly from the throne-room. As the door swung shut behind them Valentine glanced at Sepulthrove and said, 'How long can he survive like that?'

The physician shrugged. 'Almost indefinitely. The system sustains him perfectly. We could keep him going, with some repairs every now and then, another hundred years.'

'That won't be necessary. But he may have to stay with us another twelve or fifteen. Can you do that?'

'Count on it,' said Sepulthrove.

'Good. Good.' Valentine stared at the shining winding passageway that sloped upward before him. He had been in the Labyrinth long enough. The time had come to return to the world of sun and wind and living things, and to settle matters with Dominin Barjazid. To Hornkast he said, 'Return me to my people and prepare transportation for us to the outer world. And before my departure I'll want a detailed study of the military forces and supporting personnel you'll be able to place at my disposal.'

'Of course, my lord,' the high spokesman said.

My lord. It was the first indication of submission that he had had from the ministers of the Pontifex. The main battle was yet to come; but Valentine felt, hearing those two small words, almost as though he had already regained Castle Mount.

PART V

The Book of
the Castle

1

The ascent from the depths of the Labyrinth was far more swiftly accomplished than the descent had been; for on the interminable downward spiral Valentine had been an unknown adventurer, clawing his way past a stolidly uncaring bureaucracy, and on the upward journey he was a Power of the realm.

Not for him, now, the tortuous climb through level after level, ring after ring, back up through all the intricacies of the Pontifical lair, House of Records and Arena and Place of Masks and Hall of Winds and all the rest. Now he and his followers rose, quickly and without hindrance, using the passage reserved for Powers alone.

In just a few hours he attained the outer ring, that brightly lit and populous halfway house on the rim of the underground city. For all the speed of his climb, the news of his identity had traveled even faster. Word somehow had spread through the Labyrinth that the Coronal was here, a Coronal mysteriously transformed but Coronal none the less, and as he emerged from the imperial passageway a great crowd stood assembled, staring as if some creature with nine heads and thirty legs had come forth.

It was a silent crowd. Some made the sign of the starburst, a few called out his name. But most were content simply to gape. The Labyrinth was the domain of the Pontifex, after all, and Valentine knew that the adulation a Coronal would receive elsewhere in Majipoor was not likely here. Awe, yes. Respect, yes. Curiosity, above all. But none of the cheering and waving that Valentine had seen bestowed on the counterfeit Lord Valentine when he rode in grand processional through the streets of Pidruid. Just as well, thought Valentine. He was out of practice at being the object of adulation, and he had never cared much for it, anyway. It was enough – more than enough – that they accepted him, now, as the personage he claimed to be.

'Will it all be that easy?' he asked Deliamber. 'Simply ride across Alhanroel proclaiming myself the real Lord Valentine, and have everything fall into my hands?'

'I doubt it mightily. Barjazid still wears the Coronal's countenance. He still holds the seals of power. Down here, if the ministers of the Pontifex say you are the Coronal, the citizens will hail you as Coronal. If they had said you were Lady of the Isle, they probably would hail you as Lady of the Isle. I think it will be different outside.'

'I want no bloodshed, Deliamber.'

'No one does. But blood will flow before you mount the Confalume Throne once more. There's no avoiding it, Valentine.'

Gloomily Valentine said, 'I would almost rather abandon power to the Barjazid than plunge this land into some convulsion of violence. Peace is what I love, Deliamber.'

'And peace is what there will be,' said the little wizard. 'But the road to peace is not always peaceful. See, there – your army is gathering already, Valentine!'

Valentine saw, not far ahead, a knot of people, some familiar, some unknown to him. All those who had gone into the Labyrinth with him were there, the band he had accumulated in his journey across the world, Skandars, Lisamon Hultin, Vinorkis, Khun, Shanamir, Lorivade and the bodyguard of the Lady, and the rest. But also there were several hundred in the colors of the Pontifex, already assembled, the first detachment of – what? Not troops; the Pontifex had no troops. A civilian militia, then? Lord Valentine's army, at any rate.

'My army,' Valentine said. The word had a bitter taste. 'Armies are something out of Lord Stiamot's time, Deliamber. How many thousands of years has it been since there has been war on Majipoor?'

'Things have been quiet a long while,' the Vroon said. 'But nevertheless there are small armies in existence. The bodyguards of the Lady, the servitors of the Pontifex – and what about the knights of the Coronal, eh? What do you call them, if not an army? Carrying weapons, drilling on the fields of Castle Mount – what are they, Valentine? Lords and ladies amusing themselves in games?'

'So I thought. Deliamber, when I was one of them.'

'Time to think otherwise, my lord. The knights of the Coronal form the nucleus of a military force, and only an innocent would believe anything else. As you will discover quite inescapably, Valentine, when you come closer to Castle Mount.'

'Can Dominin Barjazid bring my own knights out in battle against me?' Valentine asked in horror.

The Vroon gave him a long cool stare. 'The man you call Dominin Barjazid is, at the moment, Lord Valentine the Coronal, to whom the knights of Castle Mount are bound by oath. Or have you forgotten that? With luck and craft you may be able to convince them that their oath is to the soul and spirit of Lord Valentine, and not to his face and beard. But some will remain loyal to the man they think is you, and they will lift swords against you in his name.'

The thought was sickening. Since the restoration of his memory Valentine had thought more than once of the companions of his earlier life, those noble men and women with whom he had grown up, with whom he had learned the princely arts in happier days, whose love and friendship had been central to his life until the day the usurper had shattered that life. That bold huntsman Elidath of Morvole, and the fair-haired and agile Stasilaine, and Tunigorn, who was so quick with the bow, and so many more – only names to him now, shadowy figures out of a distant past, and yet in a moment those shadows could be given life and color and vigor. Would they now come forth against him in war? His friends, his beloved companions of long ago – if he had to do battle with them for Majipoor's sake, so be it, but the prospect was dismaying.

He shook his head. 'Perhaps we can avoid that. Come,' he said. 'The time for leaving this place is at hand.'

Near the gateway known as the Mouth of Waters Valentine held a jubilant reunion with his followers and met the officers that had been provided for him by the ministers of the Pontifex. They seemed a capable crew, perceptibly quickened in spirit by this chance to leave the dreary depths of the Labyrinth. Their leader was a short, tight-coiled man named Ermanar, with close-cropped reddish hair and a short sharp-pointed beard, who in his size and movements and straightforwardness might well have been brother to Sleet. Valentine liked him at once. Ermanar made the starburst at Valentine in a quick, perfunctory way, smiled warmly, and said, 'I will be at your side, my lord, until the Castle is yours again.'

'May the journey north be an easy one,' Valentine said.

'Have you chosen a route?'

'By riverboat up the Glayge would be swiftest, would it not?'

Ermanar nodded. 'At any other time of year, yes. But the autumn rains have come, and they have been unusually heavy.' He drew forth a small map of central Alhanroel, showing the districts from the Labyrinth to Castle Mount in glowing red on some bit of dark fabric. 'See, my lord, the Glayge descending from the Mount, and pouring into Lake Roghoiz, and its remnant emerging here to continue on to the Mouth of Waters before us? Just now the river is swollen and dangerous from Pendiwane to the lake – that is, for hundreds of miles. I propose a land route at least as far as Pendiwane. There we can arrange shipping for ourselves nearly to the source of the Glayge.'

'It sounds wise. Do you know the roads?'

'Fairly well, my lord.' He poked his finger at the map. 'Much depends on whether the plain of the Glayge is flooded as badly as reports have it. I would prefer to move through the Glayge Valley, in this fashion, simply skirting the northern side of Lake Roghoiz, never getting too far from the river as we proceed.'

'And if the valley's flooded?'

'Then there are roads farther north we can use. But the land there is dry, unpleasant, almost a desert. We would have trouble finding provisions. And we would swing much too close to this place for my comfort.'

He tapped the map at a point just northwest of Lake Roghoiz.

'Velalisier?' Valentine said. 'The ruins? Why do you look so troubled, Ermanar?'

'An unhealthy place, my lord, a place of foul luck. Spirits wander there. Unavenged crimes stain the air. The stories told of Velalisier are not to my liking.'

'Floods to one side of us, haunted ruins to the other, eh?' Valentine smiled. 'Why not go south of the river entirely, then?'

'South? No, my lord. You recall the desert through which you came on your journey from Treymone? It's worse down there, much worse; not a drop of water, nothing to eat but stones and sand. I'd rather march straight through the middle of Velalisier than attempt the southern desert.'

'Then we have no choice, do we? The Glayge Valley route it is, then, and let's hope the flooding isn't too bad. When do we leave?'

'When do you wish to leave?' Ermanar asked.

'Two hours ago,' said Valentine.

2

In early afternoon the forces of Lord Valentine came forth from the Labyrinth through the Mouth of Waters. This gateway was broad and splendidly ornamented, as was fitting for the chief entrance to the Pontifical city, through which Powers traditionally passed. A horde of Labyrinth-dwellers assembled to watch Valentine and his companions ride out.

It was good to see the sun again. It was good to breathe fresh true air once more – and not dry cruel desert air, but the mild sweet soft air of the lower Glayge Valley. Valentine rode in the first of a long procession of floater-cars. He ordered the windows swung open wide. 'Like young wine!' he cried, breathing deep. 'Ermanar, how can you bear living in the Labyrinth, knowing there's this just outside?'

'I was born in the Labyrinth,' said the officer quietly. 'My people have served the Pontifex for fifty generations. We are accustomed to the conditions.'

'Do you find the fresh air offensive, then?'

'Offensive?' Ermanar looked startled. 'No, no, hardly offensive! I appreciate its qualities, my lord. It seems merely – how shall I say it? – it seems *unnecessary* to me.'

'Not to me,' Valentine said, laughing. 'And look how green everything looks, how fresh, how new!'

'The autumn rains,' said Ermanar. 'They bring life to this valley.'

'Rather too much life this year, I understand,' Carabella said. 'Do you know yet how bad the flooding is?'

'I have sent scouts forward,' Ermanar replied. 'We'll soon have word.'

Onward the caravan rolled, through a placid and gentle countryside just north of the river. The Glayge did not look particularly unruly here, Valentine thought – a quiet meandering stream, silvery in the late sunlight. But of course this was not the true river, only a sort of canal, built thousands of years ago to link Lake Roghoiz and the Labyrinth. The Glayge itself, he remembered, was far more impressive, swift and wide, a noble river, though hardly more than a rivulet by comparison with the titanic Zimr on the other continent. His other time at the Labyrinth, Valentine had ridden the Glayge by summer, and a dry summer at that, and it had seemed calm enough; but this was a different season, and Valentine wanted no more taste of rivers in flood, for his memories of the roaring Steiche were still keen. If they had to go north a bit, that was all right; even if they had to go through the Velalisier ruins, it would not be so bad, though the superstitious Ermanar might need comforting.

That night Valentine felt the first direct counterthrust of the usurper. As he lay sleeping there came upon him a sending of the King, baleful and stark.

He felt first a warmth in his brain, a quickly gathering heat that became a raging conflagration and pressed with furious intensity against the throbbing walls of his skull. He felt a needle of brilliant light probing his soul. He felt the pounding of agonizing pulsations behind his forehead. And with these sensations came something even more painful, a spreading sense of guilt and shame pervading his spirit, an awareness of failure, of defeat, accusations of having betrayed and cheated the people he had been chosen to govern.

Valentine accepted the sending until he could take no more. At last he cried out and woke, bathed in sweat, shivering, shaken, as bruised by a dream as he had ever been.

'My lord?' Carabella whispered.

He sat up, covered his face with his hands. For a moment, he was unable to speak, Carabella cradled him against her, stroking his head.

'Sending,' he managed to say at last. 'Of the King.'

'It's gone, love, it's over, it's all over.' She rocked back and forth, embracing him, and gradually the terror and panic ebbed from him. He looked up.

'The worst,' he said. 'Worse than that one in Pidruid, our first night.'

'Can I do anything for you?'

'No. I don't think so.' Valentine shook his head. 'They've found me,' he whispered. 'The King has a reading on me, and he'll never leave me alone now.'

'It was only a nightmare, Valentine—'

'No. No. A sending of the King. The first of many.'

'I'll get Deliamber,' she said. 'He'll know what to do.'

'Stay here, Carabella. Don't leave me.'

'It's all right now. You can't have a sending while you're awake.'

'Don't leave me,' he murmured.

But she soothed him and coaxed him into lying down again; and then she went for the wizard, who looked grave and troubled, and touched Valentine to put him into a sleep without dreams.

The next night he feared to sleep at all. But sleep finally came, and with it a sending again, more terrifying than the last. Images danced in his mind – bubbles of light with hideous faces, and blobs of color that mocked and jeered and accused, and darting slivers of hot radiance that held a stabbing impact. And then Metamorphs, fluid, eerie, circling around him, waving long thin fingers at him, laughing in shrill hollow tones, calling him coward, weakling, fool, babe. And loathsome oily voices singing in distorted echoes the little children's song:

> *The old King of Dreams*
> *Has a heart made of stone.*
> *He's never asleep*
> *He's never alone.*

Laughter, discordant music, whispers just beyond the threshold of his hearing – skeletons in long rows, dancing – the dead Skandar brothers, ghastly and mutilated, calling his name—

Valentine forced himself to wake, and paced, haggard and drained, for hours in the cramped floater.

And a night later came a third sending, worse than the other two.

'Am I never to sleep again?' he demanded.

Deliamber visited him with the hierarch Lorivade as he sat slumped, white-faced, exhausted. 'I have heard of your troubles,' Lorivade said. 'Has the Lady not shown you how to defend yourself with your circlet?'

Valentine looked at her blankly. 'What do you mean?'

'One Power may not assail another, my lord.' She touched the silver band at his forehead. 'This will ward off attack, if you use it properly.'

'And how is that?'

'As you prepare yourself for sleep,' she said, 'weave about yourself a wall of force. Project your identity; fill the air around you with your spirit. No sending can harm you then.'

'Will you train me?'

'I will try, my lord.'

In his sapped and wearied condition it was all he could do to project a shadow of strength, let alone the full potency of a Coronal; and even though Lorivade drilled him for an hour in the exercise of using the circlet, the fourth sending came to him that night. But it was weaker than the others, and he was able to escape its worst effects, and sleep of a restful kind finally embraced him. By day he felt nearly restored to himself; and he drilled with the circlet for hours.

Other sendings came to him on the nights that followed – faint, probing ones, testing for some opening in his armor. With growing confidence Valentine warded them off. He felt the strain of constant vigilance, and it weakened him; and there were few nights when he did not sense the tendrils of the King of Dreams attempting to steal into his sleeping soul; but he maintained his guard and went unharmed.

For five days more they made their way north along the lower Glayge, and on the sixth Ermanar's scouts returned with news of the territories ahead.

'The flooding is not as severe as we had heard,' Ermanar said.

Valentine nodded. 'Excellent. We'll continue on to the lake, then, and take ship there?'

'There are hostile forces between us and the lake.'

'The Coronal's?'

'One would assume so, my lord. The scouts said only that they ascended Lumanzar Ridge, which gives a view of the lake and the surrounding plain, and saw troops camped there, and a considerable force of mollitors.'

'War at last!' Lisamon Hultin cried. She sounded far from displeased.

'No,' Valentine said somberly. 'This is too early. We are thousands of miles from Castle Mount. We can hardly begin battling so far south. Besides, it's still my hope to avoid warfare altogether – or at least to delay it until the last.'

'What will you do, my lord?'

'Proceed north through the Glayge Valley, as we've been doing, but begin moving northwest if there's any movement toward us by that army. I mean to go around them, if I can, and sail up the river behind them, leaving them sitting down at Roghoiz still waiting for us to appear.'

Ermanar blinked. 'Go *around*?'

'Unless I miss my guess, the Barjazid has put them there to guard the approach to the lake. They won't follow us very far inland.'

'But inland—'

'Yes, I know.' Valentine let his hand rest lightly on Ermanar's shoulder and said softly, with all the warmth and sympathy at his command, 'Forgive me, friend, but I think we may have to detour as far from the river as Velalisier.'

'Those ruins frighten me, my lord, and I am not the only one.'

'Indeed. But we have a powerful wizard in our company, and many brave folk. What can a ghost or two do against the likes of Lisamon Hultin, or Khun of Kianimot, or Sleet, or Carabella? Or Zalzan Kavol? We'll just let the Skandar roar at them a bit, and they'll run all the way to Stoien!'

'My lord, your word is law. But since I was a boy I have heard dark tales of Velalisier.'

'Have you ever been there?'

'Naturally not.'

'Do you know anyone who has?'

'No, my lord.'

'Can you say, then, that you have knowledge, certain knowledge, of the perils of the place?'

Ermanar toyed with the coils of his beard. 'No, my lord.'

'But ahead of us lies an army of our enemy, and a horde of ugly mollitors of war, eh? We have no idea what ghosts can do to us, but we're quite sure of the troubles warfare can bring. I say sidestep the fighting, and take our chances with the ghosts.'

'I would prefer it the other way round,' said Ermanar, managing a smile. 'But I will be at your side, my lord, even if you ask me to go on foot through Velalisier on a night of no moon. You may rely on that.'

'I will,' said Valentine. 'And we will come forth from Velalisier unharmed by its phantoms, Ermanar. You may rely on that.'

For the time being they continued on the road they had been traveling, keeping the Glayge to their right. The land gradually rose as they moved north – not yet the great surge that marked the foothills of Castle Mount, Valentine knew, but only a minor step-stage, an outer ripple of that vast upthrusting of the planet's skin. Soon the river lay a hundred feet below in the valley, a narrow bright thread bordered by thick wild brush. And now the road wound by switchbacks up the side of a long tilted block of terrain that Ermanar said was Lumanzar Ridge, from the summit of which one could see for an extraordinary distance.

With Deliamber, Sleet, and Ermanar, Valentine went to the rim of the ridge to take stock of the situation. Below, the land swept away in natural terraced contours, level after level descending the ridge to the broad huge plain in which Lake Roghoiz was the centerpiece.

The lake looked enormous, almost an ocean. Valentine remembered it as large, as well it should be, for the Glayge drained the entire southwestern slope of Castle Mount and fed virtually all its waters into this lake; but the size he remembered was nothing like this. Now he knew why the towns at the lake's margin all were built high on pilings: those towns now were no longer at the lake's margin, but deep within its bounds, and the water must be lapping at the lower stories of the stilt-bottomed buildings. 'It is much swollen,' he said to Ermanar.

'Yes, amost twice its usual area, I think. Still, the tales we heard made it even worse.'

'As is often the case,' Valentine said. 'And where is the army your scouts saw?'

Ermanar scanned the horizon a long moment with his seeing tube. Perhaps, Valentine thought eagerly, they have packed up and gone back to the Mount, or maybe it was an error of the scouts, no army here at all, or possibly—

'There, my lord.' Ermanar said finally.

Valentine took the tube and peered down the ridge. At first he saw only trees and meadows and stray outfloodings of the lake; but Ermanar directed the tube, and suddenly Valentine saw. To the naked eye the soldiers had seemed like a congregation of ants near the edge of the lake.

But these were no ants.

Camped by the lake were perhaps a thousand troops, perhaps fifteen hundred – not a gigantic army, but large enough on a world where the concept of war was all but forgotten. They outnumbered Valentine's forces several times over. Grazing nearby were eighty or a hundred mollitors – massive armorplated creatures, of synthetic origins from the ancient days. In the knightly games on Castle Mount mollitors often were used as instruments of combat. They moved with surprising swiftness on their short thick legs, and were capable of great feats of destruction, poking their heavy black-jawed heads out of their impervious carapaces to snap and crush and rend. Valentine had seen them rip up an entire field with their fierce curved claws as they lumbered back and forth, crashing up against one another and butting heads in dull-witted rage. A dozen of them, blocking a road, would be as effective a barrier as a wall.

Sleet said, 'We could take them by surprise, and send one squad down to drive the mollitors into confusion, and swing around on them from the other side when—'

'No,' Valentine said. 'It would be a mistake to fight.'

'If you think,' Sleet persisted, 'that you're going to regain Castle Mount without anybody's suffering so much as a cut finger, my lord, you—'

'I expect there to be bloodshed,' said Valentine crisply. 'But I intend to min-imize it. Those troops down there are the troops of the Coronal; remember that, and remember who is truly Coronal. They are not the enemy. Dominin Barjazid is the only enemy. We will fight only when we must, Sleet.'

'Change routes as planned, then?' Ermanar asked glumly.

'Yes. We go northwest, out toward Velalisier. Then swing around the far side of the lake, and up the valley toward Pendiwane, if there are no more armies waiting for us between here and there. Do you have maps?'

'Just of the valley and the road to Velalisier, perhaps halfway. The rest's only wasteland, my lord, and the maps show very little.'

'Then we'll manage without maps,' said Valentine.

As the caravan moved back down Lumanzar Ridge to the crossroads that would take them away from the lake, Valentine summoned the brigand duke Nascimonte to his car. 'We are heading toward Velalisier,' he said, 'and may need to go right through it. Are you familiar with that area?'

'I was there once, my lord, when I was much younger.'

'Looking for ghosts?'

'Looking for treasures of the ancients, to decorate my mansion-house. I found very little. The place must have been well plundered when it fell.'

'You had no fears, then, of looting a haunted city?'

Nascimonte shrugged. 'I knew the legends. I was younger, and not very timid.'

'Speak with Ermanar,' Valentine said, 'and introduce yourself as one who has been to Velalisier and lived to tell the tale. Can you guide us through it?'

'My memories of the place are forty years old, my lord. But I'll do my best.'

Studying the patchy, incomplete maps Ermanar provided, Valentine concluded that the only road that would not take them perilously near the army waiting by the lake would in fact bring them almost to the edge of the ruined city, if not actually into it. He would not regret that. The Velalisier ruins, however much they terrified the credulous, were by all reports a noble sight; and besides, Dominin Barjazid was unlikely to have troops waiting for him out there. The detour could be turned to advantage, if the false Coronal expected Valentine to take the predictable route up the Glayge: perhaps, if desert travel did not prove too taxing, they might be able to keep away from the river much of the way north, and gain the benefit of some surprise as they turned at last toward Castle Mount.

Let Velalisier produce what ghosts it may, Valentine thought. Better to dine with phantoms than to march down Lumanzar Ridge into the jaws of Barjazid's mollitors.

3

The road away from the lake led through increasingly more arid terrain. The thick dark alluvial soil of the flood-plain gave way to light, gritty, brick-red stuff that supported a skimpy population of gnarled and thorny plants. The road grew rougher here, no longer paved, just an irregular gravel-strewn track winding gradually upward into the low hills that divided the Roghoiz district from the desert of Velalisier Plain.

Ermanar sent out scouts, hoping to find a passable road on the lakeward side of the hills and thus avoid having to approach the ruined city. There was none, nothing but a few hunters' trails crossing country too rugged for their vehicles. Over the hills it was, then, and down into the haunted regions beyond.

In late afternoon they began the descent of the far side. Heavy clouds were gathering – the trailing edge, perhaps, of some storm system now buffeting the upper Glayge Valley – and sunset, when it came, spread over the western sky like a great bloody stain. Just before darkness a rift appeared in the overcast and a triple beam of dark red light burst through, illuminating the plain, bathing in strange dreamlike radiance the sprawling immensity of the Velalisier ruins.

Great blocks of blue stone littered the landscape. A mighty wall of shaped monoliths, two and in some places three courses high, ran for more than a mile at the western edge of the city, ending abruptly in a heap of tumbled stone cubes. Closer at hand the outlines of vast shattered buildings still were visible, a whole forum of palaces and courtyards and basilicas and temples, half buried in the drifting sands of the plain. To the east rose a row of six colossal narrow-based sharp-topped pyramids set close together in a straight line, and the stump of a seventh, which had been dismantled apparently with furious energy, for its fragments lay strewn across a wide arc around it. Just ahead, where the mountain road made its entry into the city, were two broad stone platforms, eight or ten feet above the surface of the plain and wide enough for the maneuvers of a substantial army. In the distance Valentine saw the huge oval form of what might have been an arena, high-walled, many-windowed, breached at one end by a rough ragged gap. The scale of everything was astonishing, that and the enormous area. This place made the nameless ruins on the other side of the Labyrinth, where Duke Nascimonte had first found them, seem trivial indeed.

The rift in the clouds suddenly closed. The last daylight disappeared; the destroyed city became a place of mere formless confusion, chaotic humps against the desert skyline, as night descended.

Nascimonte said, 'The road, my lord, runs between those platforms, through the group of buildings just behind them, and around the six pyramids, going out by the northeast side. It will be difficult to follow in the dark, even by moonlight.'

'We won't try to follow it in the dark. We'll camp here and go through in the morning. I plan to explore the ruins tonight, as long as we're here.' That brought a grunt and a muffled cough from Ermanar. Valentine glanced at the little officer, whose face was drawn and bleak. 'Courage,' he murmured. 'I think the ghosts will let us be, this evening.'

'My lord, this is not a joking matter for me.'

'I mean no mockery, Ermanar.'

'You will go into the ruins alone?'

'Alone? No, I don't think so. Deliamber, will you accompany me? Sleet? Carabella? Zalzan Kavol? And you, Nascimonte – you've survived them once; you have less to fear in there than any of us. What do you say?'

The bandit chieftain smiled. 'I am yours to command, Lord Valentine.'

'Good. And you, Lisamon?'

'Of course, my lord.'

'Then we have a party of seven explorers. We'll set out after dinner.'

'Eight explorers, my lord,' said Ermanar quietly.

Valentine frowned. 'There's scarcely any need for—'

'My lord, I swore to remain at your side until the Castle is yours again. If you go into the dead city, I go into the dead city with you. If the dangers are unreal, there is nothing to fear, and if they are real, my place is with you. Please, my lord.'

Ermanar seemed entirely sincere. His face was tense, his expression strained, but more, Valentine thought, out of concern that he might be excluded from the expedition than out of fear of what might lurk in the ruins.

'Very well,' said Valentine. 'A party of eight.'

The moon was nearly full that evening, and its cold brilliant light illuminated the city in fine detail, mercilessly revealing the effects of thousands of years of abandonment in a way that the softer, more fantastical red glow of twilight had not. At the entrance, a worn and nearly illegible marker proclaimed Velalisier to be a royal historic preserve, by order of Lord Siminave the Coronal and the Pontifex Calintane. But they had ruled some five thousand years ago, and it did not seem as though much maintenance had been practiced here since their day. The stones of the two great platforms that flanked the road were cracked and uneven. In the furrows between them grew small ropy-stemmed weeds that with irresistible patience were prying the huge blocks apart: already in some places canyons were opening between block and block, wide enough for sizable shrubs to have taken root. Conceivably in another century or two a forest of twisted woody vegetation would hold possession of these platforms and the mighty square blocks would be wholly lost to view.

Valentine said, 'All this must be cleared away. I'll have the ruins restored to the way they were before this overgrowth began to sprout. How could such neglect have been permitted?'

'No one cares about this place,' said Ermanar. 'No one will lift a finger for this place.'

'Because of the ghosts?' Valentine asked.

'Because it's Metamorph,' Nascimonte said, 'That makes it doubly accursed.'

'Doubly?'

'You don't know the story, my lord?'

'Tell me.'

Nascimonte said, 'This is the legend I was raised on, at any rate. When the Metamorphs ruled Majipoor, Velalisier was their capital, oh, twenty, twenty-five thousand years ago. It was the greatest city on the planet. Two or three million of them lived here, and from all over Alhanroel came people of the outlying tribes, bringing tribute. They held Shapeshifter festivals on top of these platforms, and every thousand years they held a special festival, a superfestival, and to mark each of those they built a pyramid, so the city was at least seven thousand years old. But evil took hold here. I don't know what sort of things a Metamorph would regard as evil, but whatever they were, they were practiced here. This was the capital city of all abominations. And the Metamorphs of the provinces grew disgusted, and then they grew outraged, and one day they marched in here and smashed the temples and pulled down most of the city walls and destroyed the places where the evils were practiced and drove the citizens into exile and slavery. We know they weren't massacred, because there's been plenty of treasure-digging here – I've done a little of it myself, as you know – and if there were a few million skeletons buried here, they'd have been found. So the place was torn apart and abandoned, long before the first humans came here, and a curse was put on it. The rivers that fed the city were dammed and diverted. The entire plain became a desert. And for fifteen thousand years no one has lived here except the ghosts of those who died when the city was destroyed.'

'Tell the rest of it,' said Ermanar.

Nascimonte shrugged. 'That's all I know, mate.'

'The ghosts,' Ermanar said. 'Those who haunt here. Do you know how long they're fated to wander the ruins? Until Metamorphs rule Majipoor again. Until the planet is returned to them, and the last of us are made into slaves. And then Velalisier will be rebuilt on the old site, grander ever than it was before, and it'll be reconsecrated as the Shapeshifter capital, and the spirits of the dead finally will be released from the stones that hold them trapped there.'

'They'll cling to the stones a long time, then,' said Sleet. 'Twenty billion of us and just a handful of them, living in the jungles – what kind of a threat is that?'

Ermanar said, 'They've waited eight thousand years already, since Lord Stiamot broke their power. They'll wait eight thousand more, if they have to. But they dream of Velalisier reborn, and they won't give up that dream. Sometimes in sleep I've listened to them, planning for the day when the towers of Velalisier rise again, and it frightens me. That's why I don't like to be here. I feel them watching over the place – I can feel their hatred all around us, like something in the air, something invisible but real—'

'So this city is accursed by them and holy to them both at once,' Carabella said. 'Small wonder we have trouble comprehending how their minds work!'

Valentine wandered off down the path. The city awed him. He tried to imagine it as it had been, a kind of prehistoric Ni-moya, a place of majesty and opulence. And now? Lizards with beady clicking eyes scuttered from rock to rock. Weeds grew thick in the grand ceremonial boulevards. Twenty thousand years! What would Ni-moya look like in twenty thousand years? Or Pidriud, or Piliplok, or the fifty great cities on the slopes of Castle Mount? Were they building here on Majipoor a civilization that would endure forever, as the civilization of the old mother-world Earth was said to endure? Or, he wondered, would wide-eyed tourists someday prowl the shattered ruins of the Castle and the Labyrinth and the Isle, trying to guess what significance they had had to the ancients? We have done well enough so far, Valentine told himself, thinking back over the thousands of years of peace and stability. But now dissonances were breaking through; the ordered pattern of things had been disrupted; there was no telling what might befall. The Metamorphs, the defeated and evicted Metamorphs whose misfortune it had been to possess a world desired by other and stronger folk, might yet have the last laugh.

Suddenly he halted. What was that sound ahead? A footfall? And a flicker of a shadow against the rocks? Valentine peered tensely into the darkness before him. An animal, he thought. Something nocturnal slithering around in search of a meal. Ghosts don't have shadows, do they? Do they? There are no ghosts here, Valentine thought. There are no ghosts anywhere.

But all the same—

Cautiously he edged forward a few steps. Too dark here, too many avenues of tumbledown structures leading off to every side. He had laughed at Ermanar, but Ermanar's fears had somehow insinuated themselves into his imagination. He had fantasies of austere mysterious Metamorphs gliding between the fallen buildings just beyond his vision – phantoms half as old as time – forms without bodies, shapes without substance—

And then footsteps, unmistakable footsteps, behind him—

Valentine whirled. Ermanar was trotting after him, that was all.

'Wait, my lord!'

Valentine allowed him to catch up. He forced himself to relax, though his fingers, strangely, were trembling. He put his hands behind his back.

'You ought not go off by yourself,' Ermanar said. 'I know you make light of the dangers I imagine here, but those dangers might yet exist. You owe it to us all to take more care of your safety, my lord.'

The others rejoined him, and they continued on, slowly and in silence, through the moonlit ruins. Valentine said nothing of what he had thought he had seen and heard. Surely it had been only some animal. And shortly animals appeared: some sort of small apes, perhaps akin to forest-brethren, that nested in the fallen buildings and several times caused startlement as they went scrambling over the stones. And nocturnal mammals of a lower kind, mintuns or droles, darted swiftly through the shadows. But did apes and droles, Valentine wondered, make sounds like footfalls?

For more than an hour the eight moved deeper into the ruins. Valentine stared warily into the recesses and caverns, studying the pools of blackness with care.

As they passed through the fragments of a collapsed basilica, Sleet, who had gone off a short way by himself, jogged back in distress to tell Valentine, 'I heard something strange to one side, in there.'

'A ghost, Sleet?'

'It might be, for all I know. Or simply a bandit.'

'Or a rock-monkey,' Valentine said lightly. 'I've heard all kinds of noises.'

'My lord—'

'Are you catching Ermanar's terrors now?'

'I think we have wandered here long enough, my lord,' said Sleet in a low, taut voice.

Valentine shook his head. 'We'll keep close watch on dark corners. But there's more to see here.'

'I wish we would turn back now, my lord.'

'Courage, Sleet.'

The juggler shrugged and turned away. Valentine peered into the darkness. He did not underestimate the acuteness of Sleet's hearing, he who juggled blindfolded by sheer sound alone. But to flee this place of marvels because they heard odd rustlings and footsteps in the distance – no, not so soon, not so hastily.

Yet, without communicating his uneasiness to the others, he moved still more cautiously. Ermanar's ghosts might not exist, yet it was folly to be too rash in this strange city.

And as they were exploring one of the most ornate of the buildings in the central area of palaces and temples, Zalzan Kavol, who was leading the way, stopped short abruptly when a slab of rock, dislodged from above, came clattering down practically at his feet. He cursed and growled, 'Those stinking apes—'

'No, not apes, I think,' said Deliamber quietly. 'There's something bigger up there.'

Ermanar flashed a light toward the overhanging ledge of an adjoining structure. For an instant a silhouette that might have been human was in view; then it vanished. Without hesitating, Lisamon Hultin began to run to the far side of the building, followed by Zalzan Kavol, who brandished his energy-thrower. Sleet and Carabella went the other way. Valentine would have gone with them, but Ermanar caught him by the arm and held him with surprising strength, saying apologetically, 'I may not permit you to place yourself in risk, my lord, when we have no idea—'

'Halt!' came the mighty booming voice of Lisamon Hultin.

There was the sound of a scuffle in the distance, and then that of someone clambering over the mounds of fallen masonry in no very ghostlike way. Valentine longed to know what was happening, but Ermanar was right: to go darting off after an unknown enemy in the darkness of an unfamiliar place was a privilege denied to the Coronal of Majipoor.

He heard grunts and cries, and a high-pitched sound of pain. Moments later Lisamon Hultin reappeared, dragging a figure who wore the starburst emblem of the Coronal on his shoulder. She had her arm locked about his chest and his feet were dangling six inches off the ground.

'Spies,' she said. 'Skulking around up there, keeping watch on us. There were two of them, I think.'

'Where's the other?' Valentine asked.

'Might have gotten away,' said the giantess. 'Zalzan Kavol went after him.' She dumped her prisoner down before Valentine, and held him to the ground with a foot pressed against his middle.

'Let him up,' Valentine said.

The man rose. He looked terrified. Brusquely Ermanar and Nascimonte checked him for weapons and found none.

'Who are you?' Valentine asked. 'What are you doing here?'

No reply.

'You can speak. We won't harm you. You have the starburst on your arm. Are you part of the Coronal's forces?'

A nod.

'Sent out here to trail us?'

Again a nod.

'Do you know who I am?'

The man stared silently at Valentine.

'Are you able to speak?' Valentine asked. 'Do you have a voice? Say something. Anything.'

'I – if I—'

'Good. You can talk. Again: do you know who I am?'

In a thin whisper the captive replied, 'They say you would steal the throne from the Coronal.'

'No,' Valentine said. 'You have it wrong, fellow. The thief is he who sits now on Castle Mount. I am Lord Valentine, and I demand your allegiance.'

The man stared, bewildered, uncomprehending.

'How many of you were up there?' Valentine asked.

'Please, sir—'

'How many?'

Sullen silence.

'Let me twist his arm a little,' Lisamon Hultin begged.

'That won't be necessary.' Valentine moved closer to the cowering man and said gently, 'You understand nothing of this, but all will be made clear in time. I am the true Coronal, and by the oath that you swore to serve me, I ask you now to answer. How many of you were up there?'

Conflicts raged in the man's face. Slowly, reluctantly, bewilderedly, he replied, 'Just two of us, sir.'

'Can I believe that?'

'By the Lady, sir!'

'Two of you. All right. How long were you following us?'

'Since – since Lumanzar.'

'Under what orders?'

Hesitation again. 'To – to observe your movements and report to camp in the morning.'

Ermanar scowled. 'Which means that other one is probably halfway to the lake by now.'

'You think so?'

It was the rough, harsh voice of Zalzan Kavol. The Skandar strode into their midst and dumped down before Valentine, as though it were a sack of vegetables, the body of a second figure wearing the starburst emblem. Zalzan Kavol's energy-thrower had seared a hole through him from back to front. 'I chased him about half a mile, my lord. A quick devil he was, too! He was moving more easily than I over the heaps of stones, and starting to pull away from me. I ordered him to stop, but he kept going, and so—'

'Bury him somewhere off the path,' Valentine said curtly.

'My lord? Did I do wrong to kill him?'

'You had no choice,' Valentine said in a softer tone. 'I wish you had managed to catch him. But you couldn't, so you had no choice. Very well, Zalzan Kavol.'

Valentine turned away. The slaying had shaken him, and he could hardly pretend otherwise. This man had died only because he was loyal to the Coronal, or to the person he believed to be the Coronal.

The civil war had had its first casualty. The bloodshed had begun, here in this city of the dead.

4

There was no thought of continuing the tour now. They returned with the prisoner to their camp. And in the morning Valentine gave orders to move on through Velalisier and begin the northeastward swing.

By day the ruined city seemed not as magical, although no less impressive. It was hard to understand how so frail and unmechanical a folk as the Metamorphs had ever moved these gigantic blocks of stone about; but perhaps twenty thousand years ago they had not been quite so unmechanical. The glowering Shapeshifters of the Piurifayne forests, those people of wicker huts and muddy streets, were only the broken remnant of the race that once had ruled Majipoor.

Valentine vowed to return here, once this business with Dominin Barjazid was settled, and explore the ancient capital in detail, clearing underbrush and excavating and reconstructing. If possible, he thought, he would invite Metamorph leaders to take part in that work – though he doubted they would care to cooperate. Something was needed to reopen lines of communication between the two populations of the planet.

'If I am Coronal again,' he said to Carabella as the cavalcade rode past the pyramids and headed out of Velalisier, 'I intend—'

'*When* you are Coronal again,' she said.

Valentine smiled. 'When I am Coronal again, yes. I intend to examine the entire problem of the Metamorphs. Bring them back into the mainstream of Majipooran life, if that can be done. Give them a place in the government, even.'

'If they'll have it.'

'I mean to overcome that anger of theirs,' said Valentine. 'I'll dedicate my reign to it. Our entire society, our wonderful and harmonious and loving realm, was founded on an act of theft and injustice, Carabella, and we've succeeded in teaching ourselves to overlook that.'

Sleet glanced up. 'The Shapeshifters weren't making full use of this planet. There weren't twenty million of them on the entire enormous place when our ancestors came here.'

'But it was *theirs!*' Carabella cried. 'By what right—'

'Easily, easily,' Valentine said. 'There's no use fighting over the deeds of the first settlers. What's done is done, and we must live with it. But it's within our power to change the way we've been living with it, and if I'm Coronal again, I—'

'*When*,' said Carabella.

'When,' Valentine echoed.

Deliamber said mildly, in that far-off way of his that gained the immediate attention of all listeners, 'It may be that the present troubles of the realm are the beginning of the retribution for the suppression of the Metamorphs.'

Valentine stared at him. 'What do you mean by that?'

'Only that we have gone a long way, here on Majipoor, without paying any sort of price for the original sin of the conquerors. The account accumulates interest, you know. And now this usurpation, the evils of the new Coronal, the prospect facing us of war, death and destruction, chaos – perhaps the past is starting to send us its reckoning at last.'

'But Valentine had nothing to do with the oppression of the Metamorphs,' Carabella protested. 'Why should he be the one to suffer? Why was he chosen to be cast down from power, and not some high-handed Coronal of long ago?'

Deliamber shrugged. 'Such things are never fairly distributed. What makes you think that only the guilty are punished?'

'The Divine—'

'Why do you think the Divine is fair? In the long run, all wrongs are righted, every minus is balanced with a plus, the columns are totaled and the totals are found correct. But that's in the long run. We must live in the short run, and matters are often unjust there. The compensating forces of the universe make all the accounts come out even, but they grind down the good as well as the wicked in the process.'

'More than that,' said Valentine suddenly. 'It may be that I was chosen to be an instrument of Deliamber's compensating forces, and it was necessary for me to suffer in order to be effective.'

'How so?'

'If nothing unusual had ever happened to me, I might have ruled like all the others before me on Castle Mount, self-satisfied, amiable, accepting things as they were because from where I sat I saw no wrong in them. But these adventures of mine have given me a view of the world I'd never have had if I had remained snug in the Castle. And perhaps now I'm ready to play the role that needs to be played, whereas otherwise—' Valentine let his voice trail away. After a moment he said, 'All this talk is mere vapor. The first thing to do is regain the Castle. Then we can debate the nature of the compensating forces of the universe and the tactics of the Divine.'

He looked back at fallen Velalisier, the accursed city of the ancients, chaotic but yet magnificent on the forlorn desert plain and then he turned away to sit in silence and contemplate the changing countryside ahead.

The road now curved about sharply, toward the northeast, passing up and over the range of hills they had crossed to the south, and descending into the fertile flood-plain of the Glayge near the northernmost limb of Lake Roghoiz. They were emerging hundreds of miles north of the field where the Coronal's army had been camped.

Ermanar, bothered by the presence of the two spies in Velalisier, had sent out scouts to ascertain that the army had not moved north to meet them. Valentine judged that a sensible move; but he did scouting of his own, by way of Deliamber.

'Cast me a spell,' he ordered the wizard, 'that will tell me where enemy armies lie in wait. Can you do that?'

The Vroon's great shining golden eyes flickered in amusement. 'Can I do that? Can a mount eat grass? Can a sea-dragon swim?'

'Then do it,' said Valentine.

Deliamber withdrew and muttered words and waved his tentacles about, coiling and intertwining them in the most intricate of patterns. Valentine suspected that much of Deliamber's sorcery was staged for the benefit of onlookers, that the real transactions did not involve the waving of tentacles or the muttering of formulas at all, but only the casting forth of Deliamber's shrewd and sensitive consciousness to pick up the vibrations of outlying realities. But that was all right. Let the Vroon stage his little show. A certain amount of show-business, Valentine recognized, was an essential lubricant in many civilized activities, not only those of wizards and jugglers, but those also of the Coronal, the Pontifex, the Lady, the King of Dreams, the speakers of dreams, the teachers of holy mysteries, perhaps even the customs-officials at the provincial boundaries and the sellers of sausages in streetside booths. In plying one's trade one could not be too bald and blunt; one had to cloak one's doing in magic, in theater.

Deliamber said, 'The troops of the Coronal appear to remain where they were camped.'

Valentine nodded. 'Good. May they camp there a long while, waiting for us to return from our Velalisier excursion. Can you locate other armies north of here?'

'Not for a great distance,' said Deliamber. 'I feel the presence of knightly forces gathered on Castle Mount. But there always are. I detect minor detachments here and there in the Fifty Cities. But nothing unusual about that either. The Coronal has plenty of time. He'll simply sit at the Castle and wait for your approach. And then will come the grand mobilization. What will you do, Valentine, when a million warriors march down Castle Mount toward you?'

'Do you think I've given that no thought?'

'I know you've thought of little else. But it needs some heavy thinking about – our hundreds against their millions.'

'A million is a clumsy size for an army,' said Valentine easily. 'Far simpler to do one's juggling with clubs than with the trunks of dwikka-trees. Are you frightened of what lies ahead, Deliamber?'

'Not at all.'

'Neither am I,' Valentine said.

But of course there was show-business bravado, Valentine knew, in talk of that sort. Was he frightened? No, not really: death comes to all, sooner or later, and to fear it is folly. Valentine knew he had little fear of death, for he had faced it in the forest near Avendroyne, and in the turbulent rapids of the Steiche, and in the belly of the sea-dragon and when wrestling with Farssal on the Isle, and on none of those occasions had he felt anything he could identify as fear. If the army that waited for him on Castle Mount overwhelmed his little force and cut him down, it would be regrettable – as being tumbled to pieces on the rocks of the Steiche would have been regrettable – but the prospect caused him no dread. What he did feel, and it was a more significant thing than fear for his own life, was a degree of fear for Majipoor. If he failed, through hesitation or foolishness or mere inadequacy of strength, the Castle would remain in the hands of the Barjazids, and the course of history would forever change, and ultimately billions of innocent beings would suffer. Preventing that was a high responsibility, and he felt the weight of it. If he died valiantly trying to scale Castle Mount, his hardships at least would be over; but the agonies of Majipoor would only just be beginning.

5

Now they traveled through placid rural districts, the perimeter of the great agricultural belt that flanked Castle Mount and supplied the Fifty Cities with produce. Valentine chose main highways at all times. The moment for secrecy was past; so conspicuous a caravan as this could hardly be concealed, and the time was at hand when the world had to learn that a struggle for possession of Lord Valentine's Castle was about to commence.

The world was starting to learn it, in any case. Ermanar's scouts, returning from the city of Pendiwane farther up the Glayge, brought news of the usurper's first countermeasures.

'No armies lie between us and Pendiwane,' Ermanar reported. 'But posters are up in the city, branding you a rebel and a subversive, an enemy of society. The proclamations of the Pontifex in your favor have not yet been announced, it seems. Citizens of Pendiwane are being urged to band together in militias to defend their rightful Coronal and the true order of things against your uprising. And sendings are widespread.'

Valentine frowned. 'Sendings? What sort of sendings?'

'Of the King. Apparently you can scarcely fall asleep at night but the King is in your dreams, buzzing to you about loyalty and warning of terrible consequences if the Coronal is overthrown.'

'Naturally,' Valentine muttered. 'He'd have the King working for him with all the energy at his command. They must be sending night and day in Suvrael. But we'll turn that against him, eh?' He looked at Deliamber. 'The King of Dreams is telling the people how dreadful it is to overthrow a Coronal. Good. I want them to believe exactly that. I want them to realize that a terrifying thing *has already happened* to Majipoor, and that it's up to the people to put things to rights.'

'Nor is the King of Dreams precisely a disinterested party in this war,' Deliamber said. 'We should make them aware of that too – that he stands to gain from his son's treachery.'

'We will,' said the hierarch Lorivade vehemently. 'Out of the Isle now are coming the sendings of the Lady with redoubled force. They'll counteract the King's poisonous dreams. Last night as I slept she came to me and showed me what kind of message will go forth. It is the vision of the drugging at Til-omon, the changing of the Coronal. She will show them your new face, Lord Valentine, and will surround you with the radiance of the Coronal, the starburst of authority. And will portray the false Coronal as a traitor, mean and dark of spirit.'

'When will this begin?' Valentine asked.

'She waits for your approval.'

'Then open your mind to the Lady today,' he told the hierarch, 'and tell her that the sendings must start.'

Khun of Kianimot said quietly, 'How strange this seems to me! A war of dreams! If ever I doubted I was on an alien world, these strategies would make it certain to me.'

Valentine said, with a smile, 'Better to fight with dreams than with swords and energy-throwers, friend. What we seek is best won by persuasion, not by killing.'

'A war of dreams,' Khun repeated, bemused. 'We do things differently on Kianimot. Who's to say which way makes more sense? But I think there'll be fighting as well as sendings before this is done, Lord Valentine.'

Valentine looked somberly at the blue-skinned being. 'I fear you are right,' he said.

Five days more and they were in the outlying suburbs of Pendiwane. By now news of their advance had spread throughout the countryside; farmers stopped in their fields to stare as the cavalcade of vehicles floated by, the crowds thronged the highway in the more thickly populated sectors.

Valentine found this all to the good. Thus far no hands were being lifted against them. They were regarded as curiosities, not as menaces. More than that he could not ask.

But when they were a day's journey outside of Pendiwane, the advance party returned with news that a force was gathered to meet them near the city's western gate.

'Soldiers?' Valentine asked.

'Citizen-militia,' said Ermanar. 'Hastily organized, from the looks of them. They wear no uniforms, only ribbons round their arms, with the starburst emblem on it.'

'Excellent. The starburst is consecrated to my favor. I'll go to them and ask their allegiance.'

Vinorkis said, 'What will you wear, my lord?'

Puzzled, Valentine indicated the simple clothes in which he had been traveling since the Isle of Sleep, a white belted tunic and a light overblouse.

'Why, these, I suppose,' he said.

The Hjort shook his head. 'You should wear finery, and a crown, I think. I think it very strongly.'

'My thought was not to appear overly ostentatious. If they see a man in a crown, whose face is not the face they know as Lord Valentine, *usurper* will be the first thought to come to their minds, will it not?'

'I think otherwise,' Vinorkis replied. 'You come to them and say, I am your rightful king. But you don't *look* like a king. A simple costume and easy manners may win you friends in quiet conversation, but not when large forces are assembled. You would do well to dress more awesomely.'

Valentine said, 'My hope was to rely on simplicity and sincerity, as I have done ever since Pidruid.'

'Simplicity and sincerity, by all means,' said Vinorkis. 'But also a crown.'

'Carabella? Deliamber? Advise me!'

'A little ostentation might not be harmful,' said the Vroon.

'And this will be your first public appearance as claimant to the Castle,'

Carabella said. 'Some look of regal splendor, I think, may serve you well.'

Valentine laughed. 'I've grown away from such costumes in these many months of wandering, I fear. The idea of a crown now seems only comic to me. A thing of twisted metal, poking up from my scalp, a bit of jewelry—'

He stopped. He saw them all gaping at him.

'A crown,' he said in a less lighthearted tone, 'is only an outward thing, a trinket, an ornament. Children might be impressed by such toys, but adult citizens who—'

He stopped again.

Deliamber said, 'My lord, can you remember how you felt, the first time they came to you at the Castle and put the starburst upon your brow?'

'There was a chill down my back, I do confess.'

'Yes. A crown may be a child's ornament, a silly trinket, true. But it is also a symbol of power, that sets the Coronal apart from all others, and transforms mere Valentine into *Lord* Valentine the heir of Lord Prestimion and Lord Confalume and Lord Stiamot and Lord Dekkeret. We live by such symbols. My lord, your mother the Lady did much to restore you to the person you were before Til-omon, but there is still a good deal of Valentine the juggler about you, even now. And that is not a bad thing. Still, more impressiveness and less simplicity is called for here, I suspect.'

Valentine was silent, thinking of Deliamber's mumbling and waving his tentacles, and his own realization that sometimes one had to indulge in theatrics to achieve one's proper effects. They were right and he was wrong.

He said, 'Very well. I will wear a crown, if one can be fashioned for me in time.'

One of Ermanar's men quickly assembled one for him out of scraps of a defective floater-engine, the only spare metal that was at hand. Considering its hastily improvised nature, it was a decent job of crown-making, Valentine thought, the joinings not too rough, the spokes of the starburst reasonably equally spaced, the inner orbits of the armature smoothly coiled. Of course it was nothing to compare with the authentic crown, with its inlays and chasings of seven different precious metals, its finials of rare gems, its three gleaming diniaba-stones mounted on the brow-band. But that crown – made in the great reign of Lord Confalume, who must have taken a hearty joy in all the trappings of imperial pomp – was elsewhere at the moment, and this one, once it took its place upon his consecrated brow, would most likely magically invest itself with the proper grandeur. Valentine held it in his hands a long moment. Despite the scorn for such things he had expressed the day before, he felt a little awed by it himself.

Deliamber said mildly, 'The militia of Pendiwane are waiting, my lord.'

Valentine nodded. He was garbed in borrowed finery, a green doublet that belonged to one of Ermanar's comrades, a yellow cloak that Asenhart had produced, a heavy golden chain belonging to the hierarch Lorivade, high glossy boots lined with the white fur of the northern steetmoy, that were contributed by Nascimonte. Not since the ill-fated banquet in Tilomon, when he had worn another body entirely, had he dressed with such gaudiness. It was a strange feeling to be clad so pretentiously. He lacked only the crown.

He started to put it on, and stopped abruptly, realizing that there was history in this moment, whether he liked the idea or not: the first time he donned the starburst in this his second incarnation. Suddenly this event began to seem less like a masquerade and more like a coronation. Valentine looked around uneasily.

'I should not put this on my head myself,' he said. 'Deliamber, you're my chief minister. You do it.'

'My lord, I am not tall enough.'

'I could kneel.'

'That would not be fitting,' said the Vroon, a little sharply.

Plainly Deliamber did not want to do it. Valentine looked next toward Carabella. But she recoiled, horrified, whispering, 'I am a commoner, my lord!'

'What does that have to do with—' Valentine shook his head. This was becoming an annoyance. They were making too much of an occasion out of it. He glanced around the group and saw the hierarch Lorivade, that cool-eyed and stately woman, and said, 'You are the representative of the Lady my mother in this group, and you are a woman of rank. May I ask you—'

But Lorivade said gravely, 'The crown, my lord, descends to the Coronal by authority of the Pontifex. It seems more fitting that Ermanar place it on you, as the highest official of the Pontifex among us today.'

Valentine sighed and turned to Ermanar. 'I suppose that's right. Will you do it?'

'It will be a great honor, my lord.'

Valentine handed the crown to Ermanar and moved the silver circlet of his mother as far down his scalp as it would go. Ermanar, who was not a man of great height, took the crown in both hands, trembling a little, and reached up, straining to extend his arms. With great care he lowered the crown over Valentine's head and slipped it into place. It fit perfectly.

'There,' Valentine said. 'I'm glad that's—'

'Valentine! Lord Valentine! Hail, Lord Valentine! Long life to Lord Valentine!'

They were kneeling to him, making the starburst to him, shouting out his name, all of them, Sleet, Carabella, Vinorkis, Lorivade, Zalzan Kavol, Shanamir, everyone, Nascimonte, Asenhart Ermanar, even – surprisingly – the offworlder Khun of Kianimot.

Valentine gestured in protest, embarrassed at all this, wanting to tell them that this was no true ceremony, that it was done only for the sake of impressing the citizens of Pendiwane. But the words did not leave his throat, for he knew that they were untrue, that this improvised affair was in fact his second crowning. And he felt the chill down his spine, the shiver of wonder.

He stood with arms outspread, accepting their homage.

Then he said, 'Come. On your feet, all of you. Pendiwane is waiting for us.'

The scouts' report had it that the militia and the high personages of the city had been camped outside Pendiwane's western gate for some days, awaiting his arrival. Valentine wondered what the condition of the towns-people's nerves might be, after so long and uncertain a vigil, and what sort of reception they planned to give him.

It was only an hour's ride to Pendiwane now. They moved quickly through a region of pleasant forests and broad, rolling, rain-sleekened meadows that soon gave way to agreeable residential districts, small stone houses with conical red-tiled roofs of the predominant style. The city ahead was a major one, capital of its province, with a population of twelve or thirteen million; it was chiefly a trade depot, Valentine recalled, through which the agricultural produce of the lower Glayge Valley was funneled on its way upriver to the Fifty Cities.

At least ten thousand militia waited at the gate.

They filled the road, and spilled over into the lanes of the market-place that nestled against the outer wall of Pendiwane. They were armed with energy-throwers, though not a great many, and with simpler weapons, and those in the front line were standing in a tense, stiff manner, holding themselves self-consciously in soldierlike poses that surely were altogether unfamiliar to them. Valentine ordered the floater-cars to halt a few hundred yards from the nearest of them, so that the roadway between formed a wide clear space, a kind of buffer zone.

He stepped forth, crowned and robed and cloaked. The hierarch Lorivade walked just to his right, clad in the glowing vestments of the Lady's high ministry, and Ermanar was to his left, wearing on his breast the glittering Labyrinth emblem of the Pontifex. At Valentine's rear were Zalzan Kavol and his formidable brothers, glowering and massive, followed by Lisamon Hultin in full battle regalia, with Sleet and Carabella flanking her. Autifon Deliamber rode on the arm of the giantess.

In a slow, easy, unmistakably majestic way, Valentine advanced into the open space before him. He saw the citizens of Pendiwane stirring, exchanging troubled glances, moistening their lips, shifting their feet, rubbing their hands over their chests or arms. A terrible silence had fallen.

He paused twenty yards from the front line and said, 'Good people of Pendiwane, I am the rightful Coronal of Majipoor, and I ask your aid in regaining that which was granted to me by the will of the Divine and the decree of the Pontifex Tyeveras.'

Thousands of wide eyes stared rigidly at him. He felt wholly calm.

Valentine said, 'I call forth from among you Duke Holmstorg of Glayge. I call forth from among you Redvard Haligorn, Mayor of Pendiwane.'

There were movements in the crowd. Then came a parting, and out from the midst emerged a rotund man in a blue tunic trimmed with orange, whose heavy-fleshed face seemed gray with fear or tension. The black sash of mayoralty lay across his broad chest. He took a few steps toward Valentine, hesitated, signaled furiously behind his back in what was meant to be a gesture unseen by those facing him; and after a moment five or six lesser municipal officials, looking as abashed and reluctant as children commanded to sing at a school assembly, came warily out behind the mayor.

The plump man said, 'I am Redvard Haligorn. Duke Holmstorg has been summoned to Lord Valentine's Castle.'

'We have met before, Mayor Haligorn,' said Valentine amiably. 'Do you recall? It was some years ago, when my brother Lord Voriax was Coronal, and I journeyed to the Labyrinth as emissary to the Pontifex. I stopped in Pendiwane and you gave me a banquet, in the high palace at river's edge. Do you recall. Mayor Haligorn? It was summer, a year of drought, the river was very much shrunken, nothing at all like it is today.'

Haligorn's tongue traversed his lips. He tugged at a jowl.

Hoarsely he said, 'Indeed he who became Lord Valentine was here in the dry year. But he was a dark man, and bearded.'

'True. There has been a witchery of fearful nature, Mayor Haligorn. A traitor now holds Castle Mount and I have been transformed and cast out. But I am Lord Valentine and by the power of the starburst you wear on your sleeve I call upon you to accept me as Coronal.'

Haligorn looked bewildered. Clearly he would prefer to be almost anywhere else at this moment, even in the trackless corridors of the Labyrinth, or the burning wastes of Suvrael.

Valentine continued, 'Beside me is the hierarch Lorivade of the Isle of Sleep, closest of the companions of my mother your Lady. Do you think she deceives you?'

The hierarch said icily, 'This is the true Coronal, and the Lady will withdraw her sublime love from those who oppose him.'

Valentine said, 'And here stands Ermanar, high servitor of the Pontifex Tyeveras.'

In his blunt straightforward way Ermanar said, 'You have all heard the decree of the Pontifex that the fair-haired man must be hailed as Lord Valentine the Coronal. Who among you will stand up against the decree of the Pontifex?'

Haligorn's face showed terror. Dealing with Duke Holmstorg might have been harder for Valentine, for he was of high blood and great haughtiness, and might not have been so easily intimidated by one who came before him wearing a homemade crown and leading a little band of such oddly assorted followers. But Redvard Haligorn, a mere elected official, who for years had dealt with nothing more challenging than state banquets and debates over flood-control taxes, was far beyond his depth.

He said, almost mumbling it, 'The command has come down from Lord Valentine's Castle that you are to be apprehended and bound over for trial.'

'Many commands lately have come down from Lord Valentine's Castle,' said Valentine, 'and not a few have been unwise, unjust, or ill-timed, eh, Mayor Haligorn? They are the commands of the usurper, and worthless. You have heard the voices of the Lady and the Pontifex. You have had sendings urging you to give allegiance to me.'

'And sendings of the other kind,' said Haligorn feebly.

'From the King of Dreams, yes!' Valentine laughed. 'And who is the usurper? Who is it that has stolen the throne of the Coronal? Dominin Barjazid is the one! The son of the King of Dreams! Now do you comprehend those sendings out of Suvrael? Now do you see what has been done to Majipoor?'

Valentine let the trance-state come over him, and flooded the hapless Redvard Haligorn with the full force of his soul, the full impact of a waking sending from the Coronal.

Haligorn tottered. His face reddened and grew blotchy. He reeled and clutched at his comrades for support, but they had received the outflow from Valentine as well, and were barely able to sustain themselves.

Valentine said, 'Give me your support, friends. Open your city to me. From here I will launch the reconquest of Castle Mount, and great will be the fame of Pendiwane, as the first city of Majipoor to turn against the usurper!'

6

So Pendiwane fell, without a blow being struck. Redvard Haligorn, wearing the expression of a man who has just swallowed a Stoienzar oyster and feels it squirming in his gullet, dropped down and offered Valentine the starburst gesture, and then two of his vice-mayors did the same, and suddenly there was a contagion of it, thousands of people giving homage, and crying out, first without much conviction, then more lustily as they decided to commit themselves to the idea: 'Valentine! Lord Valentine! Long life to the Coronal!' And the gates of Pendiwane were opened.

'Too easy,' Valentine muttered to Carabella. 'Can it continue this way right up Castle Mount? Browbeat a fat mayor or two and win back the throne by acclamation?'

'If only you could,' she said. 'But the Barjazid waits up there with his bodyguards, and browbeating him will take more than words and fine dramatic effects. There will be battles, Valentine.'

'Let there be no more than one, then.'

She touched his arm lightly. 'For your sake I hope no more than one, and that one just a small one.'

'Not for my sake,' he said. 'For the sake of all the world. I want none of my people to perish in repairing what Dominin Barjazid has brought upon us.'

'I had not thought kings would be so gentle, my love,' Carabella said.

'Carabella—'

'You look so sad just now!'

'I fear what comes.'

'What comes,' she said, 'is a necessary struggle, and joyous triumph, and the restoration of order. And if you would be a proper king, my lord, wave to your people, and smile, and put that tragic look from your face. Yes?'

Valentine nodded. 'You speak the truth,' he said, and catching up her hand, brushed his lips quickly but tenderly across her small sharp knuckles. And turned to stare at the multitudes who shouted his name, and lifted his arms to them and acknowledged their greeting.

It seemed wondrously familiar to be riding into a great city down boulevards lined with cheering throngs. Valentine remembered, though it seemed like the memory of a dream, the beginnings of his abortive grand processional, when in the springtime of his reign he had gone by river to Alaisor on the western coast, and across to the Isle to kneel beside his mother at Inner Temple, and then on the great sea-journey westward to Zimroel, and crowds hailing him in Piliplok and Velathys and Narabal, down there in the lush leafy tropics. Those parades, those banquets, the excitement, the splendor, and then on to Til-omon, once more the crowds, once more the cries, 'Valentine! Lord Valentine!' He remembered too in Til-omon a surprise, that Dominin Barjazid the son of the King of Dreams had come up from Suvrael to greet him and honor him in a feast, for the Barjazids customarily stayed down there in their sunswept kingdom, dwelling apart from humanity, tending their dream-machines, sending forth their nightly messages to instruct and command and chastise. And the banquet at Til-omon, and the flask of wine from the hand of Barjazid, and the next thing Valentine knew he was staring down at the city of Pidruid from a limestone ridge, with muddled memories in his mind of having grown up in eastern Zimroel and somehow having wandered across the entire continent to its western shore. Now, so many months later, they were shouting his name again in the streets of a mighty city, after the long and strange interruption.

In the royal suite at the mayoral palace Valentine summoned Mayor Haligorn, who still had a stunned and dazed look about him, and said, 'I'll need from you a flotilla of riverboats to take me up the Glayge to its rising. The costs will be met by the imperial treasury after the restoration.'

'Yes, my lord.'

'And how many troops can you supply me?'

'Troops?'

'Troops, militia, warriors, bearers of arms. Do you follow my meaning, Mayor Haligorn?'

The mayor showed dismay. 'We of Pendiwane are not known for our skills in warfare, my lord.'

Valentine smiled. 'We are not known for our skills in warfare anywhere on Majipoor, the Divine be thanked. Nevertheless, peaceful though we are, we fight when we are threatened. The usurper threatens us all. Haven't you felt the sting of strange new taxes and unfamiliar decrees in this year just past?'

'Of course, but—'

'But what?' Valentine asked sharply.

'We assumed it was only a new Coronal, feeling his power.'

'And you would blandly let yourselves be oppressed by the one whose role it is to serve you?'

'My lord—'

'Never mind. You have as much to gain as I in putting things to rights, do you see? Give me an army, Mayor Haligorn, and for thousands of years the bravery of the people of Pendiwane will be sung in our ballads.'

'I am responsible for the lives of my people, my lord. I would not have them slain or—'

'*I* am responsible for the lives of your people, and twenty billion others besides,' said Valentine briskly. 'And if five drops of anyone's blood are shed as I move toward Castle Mount, that will be six drops too many to suit me. But without an army I'm too vulnerable. With an army I become a royal presence, an imperial force moving toward a reckoning with the enemy. Do you understand, Haligorn? Call your people together, tell them what must be done, call for volunteers.'

'Yes, my lord,' said Haligorn, trembling.

'And see to it that the volunteers are willing to volunteer!'

'It will be done, my lord,' the mayor murmured.

Assembling the army went faster than Valentine expected – a matter of days for choosing, equipping, and provisioning. Haligorn was cooperative indeed – as though he were eager to see Valentine rapidly on his way to some other region.

The citizen-militia that had been scraped together to defend Pendiwane against an invading pretender now became the nucleus of the hastily constructed loyalist army – some twenty thousand men and women. A city of thirteen million might well have produced a larger force; but Valentine had no wish to disrupt Pendiwane to any greater extent. Nor had he forgotten his own axiom about juggling with clubs rather than with dwikka-trunks. Twenty thousand troops provided him with something that looked decently military, and it was his strategy, as it had been for a long while, to gain his purpose by gradual accumulation of support. Even the colossal Zimr, he reasoned, begins as mere trickles and rivulets somewhere in the northern mountains.

They set forth on the Glayge on a day that was rainy before dawn, gloriously bright and sunny afterward. Every riverboat for fifty miles on either side of Pendiwane had been commandeered for army transport. Serenely the great flotilla moved northward, the green-and-gold banners of the Coronal waving in the breeze.

Valentine stood near the prow of his flagship. Carabella was beside him, and Deliamber, and Admiral Asenhart of the Isle. The rain-washed air smelled sweet and clean: the good fresh air of Alhanroel, blowing toward him from Castle Mount. It was a fine feeling to be on his way home at last.

These riverboats of eastern Alhanroel were more streamlined, less fancifully baroque, than the ones Valentine had known on the Zimr. They were big, simple vessels, high of draft and narrow of beam, with powerful engines designed to drive them against the strong flow of the Glayge.

'The river is swift against us,' said Asenhart.

'As well it should be,' Valentine said. He pointed toward some invisible summit far to the north and high in the sky. 'It rises on the lower slopes of the Mount. In its few thousand miles it drops almost ten, and all the weight of the water comes rushing against us as we go toward the source.'

The Hjort seaman smiled. 'It makes ocean sailing seem like child's play, to think of coping with such a force. Rivers always were strange to me – so narrow, so quick. Give me the open sea, dragons and all, and I'm happy.'

But the Glayge, though swift, was tame. Long ago it had been a thing of rapids and waterfalls, ferocious and all but innavigable for hundreds of miles. Fourteen thousand years of human settlement on Majipoor had changed all that. By dams, locks, bypass canals, and other devices, the Glayge, like all the Six Rivers that descended from the Mount, had been made to serve the needs of its masters through nearly all its course. Only in the lower stretches, where the flatness of the surrounding valley made flood-control an ongoing challenge, was there any difficulty, and that merely during seasons of heavy rain.

And the provinces along the Glayge were tame as well: lush green farming country, interrupted by great urban centers. Valentine stared into the distance, narrowing his eyes against the brightness of the morning light and searching for the gray bulk of Castle Mount somewhere ahead; but, immense as it was, not even the Mount could be seen from two thousand miles away.

The first important city upriver from Pendiwane was Makroprosopos, famed for its weavers and artists. As Valentine's ship approached, he saw that the waterfront of Makroprosopos was bedecked with mammoth Coronal-ensigns, probably hastily woven, and even more were still being hung.

Sleet said thoughtfully, 'Do those flags mean defiant expression of loyalty to the dark Coronal, I wonder, or capitulation to your claim?'

'Surely they pay homage to you, my lord,' Carabella said. 'They know you're advancing up the river – therefore they put out flags to welcome you!'

Valentine shook his head. 'I think these folk are merely being cautious. If things go badly for me on Castle Mount, they can always claim that those were ensigns of loyalty to the other. And if he is the one who falls, they can say they were second only to Pendiwane in recognizing me. I think we ought not to allow them the luxury of such ambiguities. Asenhart?'

'My lord?'

'Take us to harbor at Makroprosopos.'

For Valentine it was something of a gamble. There was no real need to land here, and the last thing he wanted was a battle at some irrelevant city far from the Mount. But to test the effectiveness of his strategy was important.

That test was passed almost at once. He heard the cheering when he was still far from shore: 'Long life to Lord Valentine! Long life to the Coronal!'

The Mayor of Makroprosopos came scurrying to the pier to greet him, bearing gifts, great generous bales of his city's finest fabrics. He fell all over himself bowing and scraping, and was pleased to arrange a levy of eight thousand of his citizens to join the army of restoration.

'What is happening?' Carabella asked quietly. 'Will they accept anyone as Coronal who claims the throne loudly enough and waves a few energy-throwers around?'

Valentine shrugged. 'These are peaceful folk, comfortable, luxury-loving, timid. They've known only prosperity for thousands of years, and they want nothing but thousands more of it. The idea of armed resistance is foreign to them, so they yield quickly when we come sailing in.'

'Aye,' said Sleet, 'and if the Barjazid comes here next week, they'll bow down just as willingly to him.'

'Perhaps. Perhaps. But I'm gaining momentum. As these cities join me, others farther up will fear to hold back their allegiance. Let it come to be a stampede, eh?'

Sleet scowled. 'All the same, what you're doing now, someone else can do another time, and I don't like it. What if a red-haired Lord Valentine appears next year, and says *he's* the true Coronal? What if some Liiman shows up, insisting that everyone kneel to him, that the rivals are mere sorcerers? This world will dissolve into madness.'

'There is only one anointed Coronal,' said Valentine calmly, 'and the people of these cities, whatever their motives, are simply bowing to the will of the Divine. Once I've returned to Castle Mount there'll be no further usurpers and no further pretenders, I promise you that!'

Yet privately he recognized the wisdom of what Sleet had said. How frail, he thought, is the compact that holds our government together! Good will alone is all that sustains it. Now Dominin Barjazid had shown that treachery could undo good will, and Valentine was discovering – thus far – that intimidation could counter treachery. But would Majipoor ever be the same again, Valentine wondered, when all this conflict was ended?

7

After Makroprosopos was Apocrune, and then Stangard Falls, and Nimivan, Threiz, South Gayles, and Mitripond. All of these cities, with some fifty million people among them, lost no time in accepting the sovereignty of the fair-haired Lord Valentine.

It was as Lord Valentine had expected. These river-dwellers lacked the taste for warfare, and no one city cared to make a stand in battle for the sake of determining which of the rivals might be the true Coronal. Now that Pendiwane and Makroprosopos had yielded, the rest were eagerly falling into line; but these victories were trivial, he knew, for the river-cities would change allegiance again just as readily if they saw the tides of fortune swinging toward the darker overlord. Legitimacy, anointedness, the will of the Divine, all these things meant far less in the real world than one raised in the courts of Castle Mount might believe.

Still, better to have the nominal support of the river-cities than to have them scoff at his claim. At each, he decreed a new troop-levy – but a minor one, only a thousand per city, for his army was growing too large too soon, and he feared unwieldiness. He wished he knew what Dominin Barjazid thought of the events along the Glayge. Did he cower in the Castle, fearing that all the billions of Majipoor were marching angrily toward him? Or was he only biding his time, preparing his inner line of defense, ready to bring the entire realm down in chaos before he yielded possession of the Mount?

The river-journey continued.

Now the land was rising steeply. They were on the fringes of the great plateau, where the planet swelled and puckered into its mighty upjutting limb, and there were days when the Glayge seemed to rise before them like a vertical wall of water.

This now was familiar territory to Valentine, for in his youth on the Mount he had gone often to the headwaters of each of the Six Rivers, hunting and fishing with Voriax or Elidath or merely escaping a bit from the complexities of his education. His memory was nearly totally restored to him, the healing process having continued steadily ever since his stay on the Isle, and the sight of these well-known places sharpened and brightened his images of that past which Dominin Barjazid had tried to snatch from him. In the city of Jerrik, here in the narrower reaches of the upper Glayge, Valentine had gambled all night with an old Vroon not much unlike Autifon Deliamber, though he remembered him as less dwarfish, and in that endless rolling of the dice he had lost his purse, his sword, his mount, his title of nobility, and all his lands except one small bit of swamp, and then had won it all back before dawn – though he always suspected his companion had prudently chosen to reverse his flow of success rather than try to make good his winnings. It had been a useful lesson, at any rate. And at Ghiseldorn, where people dwelled in tents of black felt, he and Voriax had enjoyed a night of pleasure with a dark-haired witch at least thirty years old, who had awed them in the morning by casting their futures with pingla-seeds and proclaiming that they both were destined to be kings. Voriax had been greatly troubled by that prophecy, Valentine recalled, for it seemed to say that they would rule jointly as Coronal, in the way that they had jointly embraced the witch, and that was unheard of in the history of Majipoor. It had not occurred to either of them that she was saying that Valentine would be the successor of Voriax. And in Amblemorn, the most southwesterly of the Fifty Cities, an even younger Valentine had fallen heavily while racing through the forest of pygmy trees with Elidath of Morvole, and had cracked the big bone in his left leg with frightful pain, so that the jagged end stuck through the skin, and Elidath, though half sick with shock himself, had to adjust the fracture before they could go for help. Ever after there had been a slight limp in that leg – but leg and limp as well, Valentine thought with some strange delight, now belonged to Dominin Barjazid, and this body they had given him was whole and flawless.

All those cities, and a good many more, surrendered to him as he arrived at them. Some fifty thousand troops now followed his banner, here at the edge of Castle Mount.

Amblemorn was as far as the army could travel by water. The river here became a maze of tributaries, shallow of channel and impossibly steep of grade. Valentine had sent Ermanar and ten thousand warriors ahead to arrange for land-vehicles. So potent now was the gathering force of Valentine's name that Ermanar, without opposition, had been able to requisition virtually every floater-car in three provinces, and an ocean of vehicles waited in Amblemorn by the time the main body of troops arrived.

Commanding an army so large was no longer a task Valentine alone could handle. His orders descended through Ermanar, his field marshal, to five high officers, each of whom was given charge of a division: Carabella, Sleet, Zalzan Kavol, Lisamon Hultin, and Asenhart. Deliamber was ever at Valentine's side with advice; and Shanamir, now not at all boyish, but much toughened and grown since his days herding mounts in Falkynkip, served as chief liaison officer, keeping communications channels open.

Three days were needed to complete the mobilization. 'We are ready to begin moving, my lord,' Shanamir reported. 'Shall I give the order?'

Valentine nodded. 'Tell the first column to get going. We'll be past Bimbak by noon, if we start now.'

'Yes, sir.'

'And – Shanamir?'

'Sir?'

'I know this is war, but you don't have to look so serious all the time. Eh?'

'Do I look too serious, my lord?' Shanamir reddened. 'But this is a serious matter! This is the soil of Castle Mount beneath our feet!' Simply saying that seemed to awe him, this farmboy from far-off Falkynkip.

Valentine understood how he must feel. Zimroel seemed a million miles away.

He smiled and said, 'Tell me, Shanamir, do I have it right? A hundred weights make a crown, ten crowns make a royal, and the price of these sausages is—'

Shanamir looked puzzled; then he smirked and fought to hold back laughter, and finally let the laughter come. 'My lord!' he cried, tears at the edge of his eyes.

'Remember, there in Pidruid? When I would have bought sausages with a fifty-royal piece? Remember when you thought I was a simpleton? "Easy of mind", that's the phrase you used. Easy of mind. I suppose I *was* a simpleton, those first days in Pidruid.'

'A long time ago, my lord.'

'Indeed. And perhaps I'm a simpleton still, clambering up Castle Mount like this to try to snatch back that grinding, wearying job of governing. But perhaps not. I hope not, Shanamir. Remember to smile more often, that's all. Tell the first column to start moving out.'

The boy ran off. Valentine watched him go. So far away, Pidruid, so remote in time and space, a million miles, a million years. So it seemed. And yet it was only a year and some months ago that he had perched on that ledge of white stone on that hot sticky day, looking down into Pidruid and wondering what to do next. Shanamir, Sleet, Carabella, Zalzan Kavol! All those months of juggling in provincial arenas, and sleeping on straw mattresses in flea-infested country inns! What a wonderful time that had been, Valentine thought – how free, how light a life. Nothing more important to do than get hired in the next town down the road, and make sure that you didn't drop your clubs on your foot. He had never been happier. How good it had been of Zalzan Kavol to take him into the troupe, how kind of Sleet and Carabella to train him in their art. A Coronal of Majipoor among them, and they never knew! Who among them could have imagined then that before they were much older they would be jugglers no longer, but rather generals, leading an army of liberation against Castle Mount?

The first column was moving now. The floater-cars were getting under way, forward up the endless vast slopes that lay between Amblemorn and the Castle.

The Fifty Cities of Castle Mount were distributed like raisins in a pudding, in roughly concentric circles radiating outward from the peak of the Castle. There were a dozen in the outermost ring – Amblemorn, Perimor, Morvole, Canzilaine, Bimbak East, Bimbak West, Furible, Deepenhow Vale, Normork, Kazkas, Stipool, and Dundilmir. These, the so-called Slope Cities, were centers of manufacturing and commerce, and the smallest of them, Deepenhow Vale, had a population of seven million. The Slope Cities, founded ten to twelve thousand years ago, tended to be archaic in design, with street plans that might once have been rational but had long since become congested and confused by random modification. Each had its special beauties, famed throughout the world. Valentine had not visited them all – in a lifetime on Castle Mount, there was not time enough to get to know all of the Fifty Cities – but he had seen a good many, Bimbak East and Bimbak West with their twin mile-high towers of lustrous crystalline brick, Furible and its fabled garden of stone birds, Canzilaine where statues talked, Dundilmir of the fiery Valley. Between these cities were royal parks, preserves for flora and fauna, hunting zones, and sacred groves, everything broad and spacious, for there were thousands of square miles, room enough for an uncrowded and unhurried civilization to develop.

A hundred miles higher on the Mount lay the ring of nine Free Cities – Sikkal, Huyn, Bibiroon, Stee, Upper Sunbreak, Lower Sunbreak, Castlethorn, Gimkandale, and Vugel. There was debate among scholars as to the origin of the term Free Cities, for no city on Majipoor was more free, or less, than any other; but the most widely accepted notion was that somewhere around the reign of Lord Stiamot these nine had been exempted from a tax levied on the others, in recompense for special favors rendered the Coronal. To this day the Free Cities were known to claim such exemptions, often with success. Of the Free Cities the largest was Stee on the river of the same name, with thirty million people – that is, a city the size of Ni-moya, and, according to rumor, even more grand. Valentine found it hard to conceive a place that so much as equaled Ni-moya in splendor; but he had never managed to visit Stee in his years on Castle Mount, and would pass nowhere near it now, for it lay on the far side entirely.

Higher yet were the eleven Guardian Cities – Sterinmor, Kowani, Greel, Minimool, Strave, Hoikmar, Ertsud Grand, Rennosk, Fa, Sigla Lower, Sigla Higher. All of these were large, seven to thirteen million people. Because the circumference of the Mount was not as great at their altitude, the Guardian Cities were closer together than those below, and it was thought that in another few centuries they might form a continuous band of urban occupation encircling the Mount's middle reaches.

Within that band lay the nine Inner Cities – Gabell, Chi, Haplior, Khresm, Banglecode, Bombifale, Guand, Peritole, and Tentag – and the nine High Cities – Muldemar, Huine, Gossif, Tidias, Low Morpin, High Morpin, Sipermit, Frangior, and Halanx. These were the metropolises best known to Valentine from his youth. Halanx, a city of noble estates, was the place of his birth; Sipermit was where he had lived during the reign of Voriax, for it was close by the Castle; High Morpin was his favorite holiday resort, where he had often gone to play on the mirror-slides and to ride the juggernauts. So long ago, so long ago! Often now, as his invading force floated up the roadways of the Mount, he looked into the sun-dappled distance, into the cloud-shrouded heights, hoping for a glimpse of the high country, a quick view of Sipermit, of Halanx, of High Morpin somewhere far ahead.

But it was still too soon to expect such things. From Amblemorn the road took them between Bimbak East and Bimbak West, and then on a dogleg detour around the impossibly steep and jagged Normork Crest to Normork itself, of the celebrated stone outer wall built – so legend had it – in imitation of the great wall of Velalisier. Bimbak East welcomed Valentine as legitimate monarch and liberator. The reception at Bimbak West was distinctly less cordial, although there was no show of resistance: its people plainly had not made up their minds where their advantage lay in the strange struggle now unfolding. And at Normork the great Dekkeret Gate was closed and sealed, perhaps for the first time since it had been erected. That seemed unfriendly, but Valentine chose to interpret it as a declaration of neutrality, and passed Normork by without making any attempt to enter. The last thing he cared to do now was divert his energies by laying siege to an impregnable city. Easier by far, he thought, simply not to regard it as his enemy.

Beyond Normork the route crossed Tolingar Barrier, which was no barrier at all, but only an immense park, forty miles of manicured elegance for the amusement of the citizens of Kazkas, Stipool, and Dundilmir. Here it was as if every tree, every bush, had been clipped and wired and pruned into the most shapely of shapes. There was not a branch askew, not a limb out of proportion. If all the billion people who dwelled on Castle Mount had served as gardeners in Tolingar Barrier, they could not have achieved such perfection with round-the-clock toil. It had been accomplished, Valentine knew, by a program of controlled breeding, four thousand years and more in the past, beginning in the reign of Lord Havilbove and continuing through the reigns of three of his successors: these plants were self-shaping, self-pruning, unendingly monitoring themselves for symmetry of form. The secret of such horticultural wizardry had been lost.

And now the army of restoration was entering the level of the Free Cities.

It was possible here, at Bibiroon Sweep atop Tolingar Barrier, to look back down the slopes for a view that was still comprehensible, though already unimaginably mighty. Lord Havilbove's wondrous park coiled like a tongue of green just below, curving off toward the east, and beyond it, mere gray dots, lay Dundilmir and Stipool, with just the finest suggestion of the secretive bulk of walled Normork visible at the side. Then there was the stupefying downward glide of the land toward Amblemorn and the sources of the Glayge. And, hazy as dream-fog on the horizon, the outlines, more likely than not painted by the imagination alone, of the river and its teeming cities, Nimivan, Mitripond, Threiz, South Gayles. Of Makroprosopos and Pendiwane there was not even a hint, though Valentine saw the natives of those cities staring long and hard, and pointing with vehemence, telling one another that that hummock or this nub was their home.

Shanamir said, standing beside Valentine, 'I imagined that you could see all the way to Pidruid from Castle Mount! But we can't even see the Labyrinth. Is there a longer view from higher up?'

'No,' Valentine said. 'Clouds conceal everything below the Guardian Cities. Sometimes, up there, one can forget that the rest of Majipoor exists.'

'Is it very cold up there?' the boy asked.

'Cold? No, not cold at all. As mild as it is here. Milder, even. A perpetual springtime. The air is soft and easy, and flowers always bloom.'

'But it reaches so far into the sky! The mountains of the Khyntor Marches are not nearly so high as this – they're not even a patch on Castle Mount – and yet I've been told that snow falls on the March peaks, and sometimes remains all summer long. It should be black as night at the Castle, Valentine, and cold, cold as death!'

'No,' Valentine said. 'The machines of the ancients create an unending springtime. They have roots deep in the Mount, and suck out energy – I have no idea how – and transform it into warmth, light, good sweet air. I've seen the machines, in the depths of the Castle, huge things of metal, enough metal to build a city with, and giant pumps, and enormous brass tubes and pipes—'

'When will we be there, Valentine? Are we close?'

Valentine shook his head. 'Not even halfway.'

8

The most direct route upward through the Free Cities lay between Bibiroon and Upper Sunbreak. That was a wide, gently rising shoulder of the Mount, where the slope was so easy that little time would be wasted on switchbacks. As they neared Bibiroon, Valentine learned from Gorzval the Skandar, who was serving as quartermaster, that the army was running low on fresh fruit and meat. It seemed wisest to reprovision at this level, before tackling the ascent to the Guardian Cities.

Bibiroon was a city of twelve million, arrayed in spectacular fashion along a hundred-mile ridge that seemed to hang suspended over the face of the Mount. There was only one approach to it – from the Upper Sunbreak side, through a gorge so steep and narrow that a hundred warriors could defend it against a million. Not at all to Valentine's surprise, the gorge was occupied when he came to it, and by somewhat more than a hundred warriors.

Ermanar and Deliamber went forward to parley. A short while later they returned with the news that Duke Heitluig of Chorg, of whose province Bibiroon was the capital, was in command of the troops in the gorge and was willing to speak with Lord Valentine.

Carabella said, 'Who is this Heitluig? Do you know him?'

Valentine nodded. 'Distantly. He belongs to the family of Tyeveras. I hope he holds no grudge against me.'

'He could win much grace with Dominin Barjazid,' said Sleet darkly, 'by striking you down in this pass.'

'And suffer for it in all his sleeping hours?' Valentine asked, laughing. 'A drunkard he may be, but not a murderer, Sleet. He is a noble of the realm.'

'As is Dominin Barjazid, my lord.'

'Barjazid himself did not dare to slay me when he had the chance. Am I to expect assassins wherever I parley? Come: we waste time in this.'

On foot Valentine went to the mouth of the gorge, accompanied by Ermanar, Asenhart, and Deliamber. The duke and three of his followers were waiting.

Heitluig was a broad-shouldered, powerful-looking man with thick, coarsely curling white hair and a florid, fleshy face. He stared intently at Valentine, as though searching the features of this fair-haired stranger for some hint of the presence of the soul of the true Coronal. Valentine saluted him as was fitting for a Coronal greeting a provincial duke, bland stare and outturned palm, and immediately Heitluig was in difficulties, obviously unsure of the proper form of response. He said after a moment, 'The report is that you are Lord Valentine, changed by witchery. If that is so, I bid you welcome, my lord.'

'Believe me, Heitluig, it is so.'

'There have been sendings to that effect. And also contrary ones.'

Valentine smiled. 'The sendings of the Lady are the trustworthy ones. Those of the King are worth about as much as you might expect, considering what his son has done. Have you had instructions from the Labyrinth?'

'That we are to recognize you, yes. But these are strange times. If I am to mistrust what I hear from the Castle, why should I give faith to orders out of the Labyrinth? They might be forgeries or deceptions.'

'Here we have Ermanar, high servitor to your great-uncle the Pontifex. He is not here as my captive,' said Valentine. 'He can show you the Pontifical seals that give him authority.'

The duke shrugged. His eyes continued to probe Valentine's. 'This is a mysterious thing, that a Coronal should be changed this way. If such a thing can be true, anything can be true. What is it you want in Bibiroon – my lord?'

'We need fruit and meat. We have hundreds of miles yet to go, and hungry soldiers are not the best kind.'

With a twitch of his cheek, Heitluig said, 'Surely you know you are at a Free City.'

'I know that. But what of that?'

'The tradition is ancient, and perhaps forgotten by others. But we of the Free Cities hold that we are not required to provide goods for the government, beyond the legally specified taxes. The cost of provisions for an army the size of yours—'

'—will be borne entirely by the imperial treasury,' said Valentine crisply. 'We are asking nothing from Bibiroon that will cost Bibiroon as much as a five-weight piece.'

'And the imperial treasury marches with you?'

Valentine let a flicker of anger show. 'The imperial treasury resides at Castle Mount, as it has since Lord Stiamot's day, and when I have reached it and have hurled down the usurper I'll make full payment for what we purchase here. Or is the credit of the Coronal no longer acceptable in Bibiroon?'

'The credit of the *Coronal* still is, yes,' said Heitluig carefully. 'But there are doubts, my lord. We are thrifty people here, and great shame would come upon us if it developed that we had extended credit to – to one who made false claims upon us.'

Valentine struggled for patience.

'You call me "my lord", and yet you talk of doubts.'

'I am uncertain, yes. I admit that.'

'Heitluig, come off and talk alone with me a moment.'

'Eh?'

'Come off ten steps! Do you think I'll slit your throat the moment you leave your bodyguard? I want to whisper something to you that you might not want me to say in front of others.'

The duke, looking baffled and uneasy, nodded grudgingly and let Valentine lead him away. In a low voice Valentine said, 'When you came to Castle Mount for my coronation, Heitluig, you sat at the table of the kin of the Pontifex, and you drank four or five flasks of Muldemar wine, do you remember? And when you were properly sozzled you stood up to dance, and tripped over the leg of your cousin Elzandir, and went sprawling on your face, and would have fought Elzandir on the spot if I had not put my arm around you and drawn you aside. Eh? Does any of that strike an echo in you? And would I know any of that if I were some upstart out of Zimroel trying to seize Lord Valentine's Castle?'

Heitluig's face was scarlet. 'My lord—'

'Now you say it with some conviction!' Valentine clasped the duke warmly by the shoulder. 'All right, Heitluig. Give me your aid, and when you come to the Castle to celebrate my restoration, you'll have five flasks more of good Muldemar. And I hope you'll be more temperate than the last time.'

'My lord, how can I serve you?'

'I told you. We need fruit and fresh meat, and we'll settle the bill when I'm Coronal again.'

'So be it. But will you be Coronal?'

'What do you mean?'

'The army that waits above is not a small one, my lord. Lord Valentine – I mean, he who claims to be Lord Valentine – is summoning citizens by the hundreds of thousands to the defense of the Castle.'

Valentine frowned. 'And where is this army assembling?'

'Between Ertsud Grand and Bombifale. He's drawing on all the Guardian Cities and every city above them. Rivers of blood will run down the Mount, my lord.'

Valentine turned away and closed his eyes a moment. Pain and dismay lashed his spirit. It was inevitable, it was not in the least surprising, it was entirely as he had expected from the start. Dominin Barjazid would allow him to march freely through the lower slopes, then would make a fierce defense in the upper reaches, using against him his own royal bodyguard, the knights of high birth with whom he had been reared. In the front lines against him – Stasilaine, Tunigorn, Mirigant his cousin, Elidath, Divvis his brother's son—

For an instant Valentine's resolve wavered once more. Was it worth the turmoil, the bloodshed, the agony of his people, to make himself Coronal a second time? Perhaps it had been the will of the Divine that he be cast down. If he thwarted that will, perhaps, he would accomplish only some terrible cataclysm on the plains above Ertsud Grand, and leave scars on the souls of all people, that would fill his nights with dark accusing dreams of lacerating guilt and make his name accursed forever.

He could turn back now, he could resign from the confrontation with the forces of the Barjazid, he could accept the verdict of destiny, he could—

No.

This was a struggle he had fought and won within himself before, and he would not fight it again. A false Coronal, mean and petty and dangerous, held the highest seat of the land, and ruled rashly and illegitimately. This must not be allowed to remain the case. Nothing else mattered.

'My lord?' Heitluig said.

Valentine looked back at the duke. 'The idea of war makes me ache, Heitluig.'

'There is no one who relishes it, my lord.'

'Yet a time comes when war must happen, lest even worse things befall. I think we are at such a time now.'

'So it seems.'

'Do you accept me as Coronal, Heitluig?'

'No pretender would have known of my drunkenness at the coronation, I think.'

'And will you fight beside me above Ertsud Grand?'

Heitluig regarded him steadily. 'Of course, my lord. How many troops of Bibiroon will you require?'

'Say, five thousand. I want no enormous army up there – merely a loyal and brave one.'

'Five thousand warriors are yours, my lord. More if you ask for them.'

'Five thousand will do, Heitluig, and I thank you for your faith in me. Now let's see about the fresh fruit and meat!'

9

The stay at Bibiroon was brief, just long enough for Heitluig to gather his forces and supply Valentine with the necessary provisions, and then it was on upward, upward, upward. Valentine rode in the vanguard, with his dear friends of Pidruid close at his side. It delighted him to see the look of awe and wonder in their eyes, to see Shanamir's face aglow with excitement, to hear Carabella's little indrawn gasp of ecstasy, to notice even gruff Zalzan Kavol muttering and rumbling in astonishment, as the splendors of Castle Mount unrolled before them.

And he – how radiant he felt at the thought of coming home!

The higher they went, the sweeter and more pure became the air, for they were drawing ever closer to the great engines that sustained the eternal springtime of the Mount. Soon the outlying districts belonging to the Guardian Cities were in view.

'So much—' Shanamir murmured in a thickened voice. 'So grand a sight—'

Here the Mount was a great gray shield of granite that rolled heavenward in a gentle but inexorable sweep, disappearing into the white billow of clouds that cloaked the upper slopes. The sky was a dazzling electric blue, deeper in tone than in Majipoor's lowlands. Valentine remembered that sky, how he had loved it, how he had loathed going down into the ordinary world of ordinary colors beyond the Mount. His breast tightened at the sight of it now. Every hill and ridge seemed outlined with a sparkling halo of mysterious brightness. The dust itself, blowing along the edge of the highway, appeared to glitter and shine. Satellite towns and lesser cities could be seen dotting the distant landscape, shimmering like places of awesome magic, and, high above, several of the major urban centers now came in view. Ertsud Grand lay straight ahead, its huge black towers just visible on the horizon, and to the east was a darkness that probably was the city of Minimool; Hoikmar, famed for its quiet canals and byways, could barely be perceived at the extreme westernmost edge of the landscape.

Valentine blinked away the unexpected and troublesome moistness that suddenly was welling in his eyes. He tapped Carabella's pocket-harp and said, 'Sing to me.'

She smiled and took up the little harp. 'We sang this in Til-omon, where Castle Mount was only a storybook place, a romantic dream—'

There is a land in the far-off east

That we shall never see,
Where marvels sprout on mighty peaks,
Bright cities three by three.

On Castle Mount where Powers dwell,
And heroes sport all day—

She halted, strummed a quick fretful discord, put down the harp. She turned her face from him.

'What is it, love?' Valentine asked.

Carabella shook her head. 'Nothing. I forget the words.'

'Carabella?'

'It's nothing, I said!'

'Please—'

She looked toward him, biting at her lip, her eyes tear-flooded. 'It's so wondrous here, Valentine,' she whispered. 'And so strange – so frightening—'

'Wondrous, yes. Frightening, no.'

'It's beautiful, I know. And bigger than I ever imagined, all these cities, these mountains that are part of the big mountain, everything marvelous. But – but—'

'Tell me.'

'You're coming home, Valentine! All your friends, your family, your – your lovers, I suppose – Once we've won the war, you'll have them around you, they'll sweep you away for banquets and celebrations, and—' She paused. 'I promised myself I would not say any of this.'

'Say it.'

'My lord—'

'Not so formal, Carabella.' He took her hands. Shanamir and Zalzan Kavol, he noticed, had moved to another part of the floater-car and sat with their backs to them.

She said in a rush of words, 'My lord, what happens to the little juggler-girl from Til-omon when you are back among the princes and ladies of Castle Mount?'

'Have I given you reason to think I'll abandon you?'

'No, my lord. But—'

'Call me Valentine, if you will. But what?'

Her cheeks colored. She drew her hand from him and ran it tensely through her dark glossy hair. 'Your Duke Heitluig, yesterday, saw us together, saw your arm around me – Valentine, you didn't notice his smile! As though I were some pretty toy of yours, some pet, some little trinket to be discarded when the time comes.'

'You read too much into Heitluig's smile, I think,' said Valentine slowly, although he had noticed it too, and had been troubled by it. To Heitluig, he knew, and to others of his rank, Carabella would seem only an upstart concubine of unimaginable lower-class origins, to be treated at best with scorn. In his former life on Castle Mount such distinctions of class had been an unchallengeable assumption of the nature of things; but he had been down from the Mount a long time, and saw things differently these days. Carabella's fears were real. Yet it was a problem that could be conquered only in its proper moment. There were other conquests to deal with first. He said gently, 'Heitluig is too fond of wine, and his soul is a coarse one. Ignore him. You will find a place among the high ones of the Castle, and no one will dare slight you when I am Coronal again. Come now, finish the song.'

'You love me, Valentine?'

'I love you, yes. But I love you less when your eyes are red and puffy, Carabella.'

She snorted. 'That's the sort of thing one would say to a child! Do you see me as a child, then?'

With a shrug Valentine replied, 'I see you as a woman, and a shrewd and lovely one. But what am I supposed to answer, when you ask me if I love you?'

'That you love me. And nothing more by way of decoration.'

'I'm sorry, then. I must rehearse these things more carefully. Will you sing again?'

'If you wish,' she said, and took up her pocket-harp.

All morning they rode higher, into the open spaces beyond the Free Cities. Valentine chose the Pinitor Highway, that wound between Ertsud Grand and Hoikmar through an empty countryside of rocky plateaus broken only by sparse copses of ghazan-trees, with stout ashen-colored trunks and gnarled convoluted arms – trees that lived ten thousand years and made a soft sighing sound when their time was come. This was stark and silent land, where Valentine and his forces could gather their souls for the effort that lay before them.

All this while their climb went unopposed. 'They will not try to stop you,' Heitluig said, 'until you are above the Guardian Cities. The world is narrower up there. The land is folded and wrinkled. There will be places to trap you.'

'There will be room enough,' said Valentine.

In a barren valley rimmed with jagged spires, beyond which the city of Ertsud Grand could be seen only some twenty miles to the east, he drew his army to a halt and conferred with his commanders. Scouts had already gone forward to inspect the enemy force, bringing back news that weighed on Valentine like a leaden cloak: an immense army, they reported, a sea of warriors filling the broad flat plain that occupied hundreds of square miles below the

Inner City of Bombifale. Most were foot-soldiers, but there were floater-cars gathered as well, and a regiment of mounted troops, and a corps of great thundering mollitors, at least ten times as many of the massive tanklike war-beasts as had been camped in wait for them by the banks of the Glayge. But he let no hint of disheartenment show. 'We are outnumbered twenty to one,' Valentine said. 'I find that encouraging. Too bad there aren't even more of them – but an army that size ought to be unwieldy enough to make life easy for us.' He tapped the chart before him. 'They camp here, on Bombifale Plain, and surely they can see that we are marching straight toward that plain. They'll expect us to attempt to make our ascent via the Peritole Pass, west of the plain, and that will have the heaviest guard. We will indeed go toward Peritole Pass.' Valentine heard a gasp of dismay from Heitluig, and Ermanar looked at him with sudden pained surprise. Untroubled, Valentine went on, 'And as we do, they'll send reinforcements in that direction. Once they've begun to move into the pass it should be difficult for them to regroup and redirect themselves. As they start into motion, we'll swing back toward the plain, ride straight into the heart of their camp, and go through them and on to Bombifale itself. Above Bombifale is the High Morpin road that will take us unhindered to the Castle. Are there questions?'

Ermanar said, 'What if they have a second army waiting for us between Bombifale and High Morpin?'

'Ask me that again,' Valentine replied, 'when we get beyond Bombifale. Any other questions?'

He glanced around. No one spoke.

'Good. Onward, then!'

Another day and the terrain grew more fertile, as they entered the great green apron that encircled the Inner Cities. They were in the cloud zone now, cool and moist, where the sun could be seen, but only indistinctly, through the coiling strands of mist that never lifted. In this humid region plants that, below, were merely knee-high grew to giant size, with leaves like platters and stems like tree-trunks, and everything glittered with a coating of shining droplets of water.

The landscape here was a broken one, with steep-sided mountain ranges rising abruptly out of deep-cut valleys, and roads that wound precariously around fierce conical peaks. Choices of route became fewer: to the west were the Banglecode Pinnacles, a region of impassable fanglike mountains that had scarcely ever been explored, to the east was the wide and easy slope of Bombifale Plain, and straight ahead, bordered on both sides by sheer rock walls, was the series of gigantic natural steps known as Peritole Pass, where – unless Valentine entirely missed his guess – the usurper's finest troops lay in wait.

In an unhurried way Valentine led his forces toward the pass. Four hours forward, camp for two, travel five hours more, make camp for the night, late start in the morning. In the exhilarating air of Castle Mount it would have been easy enough to travel much faster. But beyond doubt the enemy was watching his progress from on high, and he wanted to give them plenty of time to observe his route and take the necessary countermeasures.

The next day he stepped up the pace, for now the first of the huge deep steps of the pass was in sight. Deliamber, sending forth his spirit through wizardry, returned with word that the defending army was indeed in possession of the pass, and that secondary troops were streaming westward out of Bombifale Plain to give support.

Valentine smiled. 'It won't be long now. They're falling into our hands.'

Two hours before twilight he gave the order to make camp, at a pleasant meadow beside a cold, plunging stream. The wagons were drawn up in defensive formation, foragers went out to collect timber for fires, the quartermasters began distributing dinner – and, as night came on, word suddenly circulated through the camp that they were to pull up and take to the road again, leaving all fires burning and many of the wagons still in formation.

Valentine felt excitement rising thunderously within him. He saw a renewed gleam in Carabella's eyes, and Sleet's old scar stood out angrily against his cheek as his heart pumped faster. And there was Shanamir, going this way and that but never foolishly, handling many small responsibilities and large ones with sober-faced expertness, at once comic and admirable. These were unforgettable hours, taut with the potential of great events about to be born.

Carabella said, 'In the old days on the Mount, you must have studied the art of war deeply, to have devised a maneuver such as this.'

With a laugh Valentine said, 'Art of war? Whatever art of war was once known on Majipoor was forgotten before Lord Stiamot was a hundred years dead. I don't know a thing about war, Carabella.'

'But how—'

'Guesswork. Luck. A gigantic kind of juggle. I'm making it up as I go along.' He winked. 'But don't tell the others that. Let them think their general's a genius, and they may make him into one!'

In the cloud-shrouded sky no stars could be seen and the light of the moon was only the faintest of reddish glows. Valentine's army moved along the road to Bombifale Plain by the illumination of light-globes at their dimmest intensity, and Deliamber sat beside Valentine and Ermanar in deep trance, roving forward to search for barriers and obstacles ahead. Valentine was silent, still, feeling strangely calm. This was indeed a sort of gigantic juggle, he thought. And now, as he had done so many times with the troupe, he was moving toward that quiet place at the center of his consciousness, where he could process the information of a constantly changing pattern of events without being in any overt way aware of processing, or of information, or even of events: everything done in its proper time, with serene awareness of the only effective sequence of things.

It was an hour before dawn when they reached the place where the road swung uphill toward the entrance to the plain. Again Valentine summoned his commanders.

'Three things only,' he told them. 'Stay in tight formation. Take no lives needlessly. Keep pressing forward.' He went to each of them in turn with a word, a handclasp, a smile. 'We'll have lunch today in Bombifale,' he said. 'And dinner tomorrow night in Lord Valentine's Castle, I promise you!'

10

This was the moment Valentine had dreaded for months, when he must lead citizens of Majipoor into war against citizens of Majipoor, when he must stake the blood of the companions of his wanderings against the blood of the companions of his boyhood. Yet now that the moment was at hand he felt firm and quiet of spirit.

By the gray light of dawn the invading army rolled out across the rim of the plain, and in the mists of morning Valentine had his first glimpse of the legions that confronted him. The plain seemed to be filled with black tents. Soldiers were everywhere, vehicles, mounts, mollitors – a confused and chaotic tide of humanity.

Valentine's forces were arrayed in the form of a wedge, with his bravest and most dedicated followers in the lead wagons of the phalanx, Duke Heitluig's troops forming the middle body of the army, and the thousands of unwarlike militia from Pendiwane, Makroprosopos, and the other cities of the Glayge forming a rear guard more significant for its mass than for its prowess. All the races of Majipoor were represented in the forces of liberation – a platoon of Skandars, a detachment of Vroons, a whole horde of burning-eyed Liimen, a great many Hjorts and Ghayrogs, even a small elite corps of Su-Suheris. Valentine himself rode at one of the triple points of the wedge's front face, but not the central point: Ermanar was there, prepared to bear the brunt of the usurper's counteroffensive. Valentine's car was on the right wing, Asenhart's on the left, and the columns led by Sleet, Carabella, Zalzan Kavol, and Lisamon Hultin just to their rear.

'Now!' Valentine cried, and the battle was begun.

Ermanar's car plunged forward, horns blowing, lights flashing. A moment later Valentine followed, and, looking across to the far side of the battlefield, he saw Asenhart keeping pace. In tight formation they charged into the plain, and at once the huge mass of defenders was thrown into disarray. The front line of the usurper's forces collapsed with startling abruptness, almost as though it were a deliberate strategy. Panicky troops ran this way and that, colliding, entangling, scrambling for weapons or merely heading for safety. The great open space of the plain became an ocean of desperate surging figures, without leadership, without plan. Onward through them the invading phalanx rode. There was little exchange of fire; an occasional energy-bolt cast its lurid glare over the landscape, but chiefly the enemy seemed too bewildered for any coherent pattern of defense, and the attacking wedge, cutting forward at will, had no need to take lives.

Deliamber, at Valentine's side, said quietly, 'They are strung out across an enormous front, a hundred miles or more. It will take them time to concentrate their strength. But after the first panic they will regroup, and things will become less easy for us.'

Indeed that was happening already.

The inexperienced citizen-militia that Dominin Barjazid had levied out of the Guardian Cities might be in disarray, but the nucleus of the defending army consisted of knights of Castle Mount, trained in warlike games if not in the techniques of war itself, and they were rallying now, closing in on all sides around the small wedges of invaders that had thrust deep among them. A platoon of mollitors had somehow been rounded up and was advancing on Asenhart's flank, jaws snapping, huge clawed limbs seeking to do harm. On the other side a cavalry detachment had found its mounts and was striving to get into some kind of formation; and Ermanar had run into a steady barrage of fire from energy-throwers.

'Hold your formation!' Valentine cried. 'Keep moving forward!'

They were still making progress, but the pace was slowing perceptibly. If at the outset Valentine's forces had cut through the enemy like a hot blade through butter, now it was more like trying to push through a wall of thick mud. Many of the vehicles were surrounded and some were altogether stopped. Valentine had a glimpse of Lisamon Hultin on foot, striding through a mob of defenders and hurling them like twigs to left and right. Three gigantic Skandars were out on the field also – they could only be Zalzan Kavol and his brothers – doing terrible carnage with their many arms, each wielding a weapon of some sort.

Then Valentine's own vehicle was engulfed, but his driver pulled it into reverse and swung it sharply around, knocking the enemy soldiers aside.

Onward – onward—

There were bodies everywhere. It had been folly for Valentine to hope that the reconquest of the Mount could be achieved bloodlessly. Already it seemed hundreds must be dead, thousands injured. He scowled and aimed his own energy-thrower at a tall hard-faced man who was bearing down on his car, and sent him sprawling. Valentine blinked as the air crackled about him in the wake of his own energy discharge, and fired again, again, again.

'Valentine! Lord Valentine!'

The cry was universal. But it was coming from the throats of warriors on both sides of the fray, and each side had its own Lord Valentine in mind.

Now the advance seemed altogether blocked. The tide had definitely shifted; the defenders were launching a counter attack. It was as though they had not quite been ready for the first onslaught, and had merely allowed Valentine's army to come crashing through; but now they were regrouping, gathering strength, adopting a semblance of strategy.

'They appear to have new leadership, my lord,' Ermanar reported. 'The general who guides them now holds powerful control, and spurs them fiercely toward us.'

A line of mollitors had formed, leading the counterthrust with the usurper's troops coming in great numbers behind them. But the dull-witted unruly beasts were causing more difficulty from sheer bulk than with their claws and jaws: simply getting past their mammoth humpbacked forms was a challenge. Many of Valentine's officers were out of their vehicles now – he caught sight again of Lisamon Hultin, and of Sleet, and Carabella fighting furiously, all with knots of their own troops doing their best to protect them. Valentine himself would have left the wagon, but Deliamber ordered him to stay off the field. 'Your person is sacred and indispensable,' the Vroon said brusquely. 'The hand-to-hand warriors will have to make do without you.'

'But—'

'It is essential.'

Valentine scowled, He saw the logic of what Deliamber said, but he despised it. Nevertheless he yielded.

'Forward!' he roared in frustration into the dark ivory horn of his field communicator.

But they could not go forward. Clouds of defending warriors were coming now from all sides, driving Valentine's forces back. The new strength of the usurper's army appeared to be centered not far from Valentine, just beyond a rise in the plain, and radiated outward from there in bands of virtually visible power. Yes, some new general, Valentine thought, some powerful field commander providing inspiration and strength, rallying the troops that had been so dispirited. As I should be doing, he thought, down on the field among them. As I should be doing.

Ermanar's voice came to him. 'My lord, do you see that low knoll to your right? Beyond it is the enemy command post – their general is there, in the midst of the battle.'

'I want a look at him,' Valentine said, signaling his driver to move to higher ground.

'My lord,' Ermanar went on, 'we must concentrate our attack there, and remove him before he gains greater advantage.'

'Certainly,' Valentine murmured remotely. He stared, narrowing his eyes. The scene seemed all confusion down there. But gradually he discerned a form to the flow. Yes, that must be he. A tall man, taller than Valentine, with a strong wide-mouthed face, piercing dark eyes, a heavy shock of glossy black hair braided in back. He looked oddly familiar – so very familiar, beyond question familiar, one whom Valentine had known, and known well, in his days on Castle Mount, but his mind was so muddled by the chaos of the battle that for a moment he found it hard to reach into his store of renewed memory and identify—

Yes. Of course.

Elidath of Morvole.

How could he have forgotten, even for an instant, even amidst all this madness, the companion of his youth, Elidath, at times closer even to him than his brother Voriax, Elidath, the dearest of all his friends, the sharer of so many of his boldest early exploits, the nearest to him in abilities and temperament, Elidath whom all considered, even Valentine himself, to be next in line to be Coronal—

Elidath leading the enemy army. Elidath the dangerous general who must be removed.

'My lord?' Ermanar said. 'We await your instructions, my lord.'

Valentine faltered. 'Surround him,' he replied. 'Neutralize him. Take him prisoner, if you can.'

'We could center our fire on—'

'He is to be unharmed,' Valentine ordered bluntly.

'My lord—'

'*Unharmed*, I said.'

'Yes, my lord.' But there was not much conviction in Ermanar's reply. To Ermanar, Valentine knew, an enemy was merely an enemy, and this general would do least damage if he were quickly slain. But Elidath—!

In tension and distress Valentine watched as Ermanar swung his forces about and guided them toward Elidath's camp. Simple enough to order that Elidath not be harmed; but how could that be controlled, in the heat of battle? This was what Valentine had feared most of all, that some beloved companion of his would lead the opposing troops – but to know that it was Elidath, that Elidath was in jeopardy on the field, that Elidath must fall if the army of liberation was to go forward – what agony that was!

Valentine stood up. Deliamber said, 'You must not—'

'I must,' he said, and rushed from the wagon before the Vroon could place some wizardry on him.

Out here in the midst of things all was incomprehensible: figures rushing to and fro, enemies indistinguishable from friends, all noise, tumult, shouting, alarms, dust, and insanity. The patterns of battle that Valentine had been able to discern from his floater-car were not visible here. He thought he perceived Ermanar's troops closing in on one side, and a muddled and chaotic struggle going on somewhere in the direction of Elidath's camp.

'My lord,' Shanamir called to him, 'you should not be in plain view! You—'

Valentine waved him off and moved toward the thickest part of the battle.

The tide had shifted again, so it seemed, with Ermanar's concerted attack on Elidath's camp. The invaders were breaking through and once more casting the enemy into disorder. They were falling back, knights and citizens alike, running in random circles, trying to flee the merciless oncoming attackers, while somewhere far ahead a knot of defenders held firm round Elidath, a single sturdy rock in the raging torrent.

Let Elidath not be harmed, Valentine prayed. Let him be taken, and taken swiftly, but let him not be harmed.

He pressed forward, all but unnoticed on the battlefield. Once again victory seemed to be within his grasp: but at too high a cost, much too high, if bought with the death of Elidath.

Valentine saw Lisamon Hultin and Khun of Kianimot just ahead, side by side, hacking a path through which the others could follow, and they were driving all before them. Khun was laughing, as if he had waited all his life for this moment of fierce commitment.

Then an enemy bolt struck the blue-skinned alien in the chest. Khun staggered and swung around. Lisamon Hultin, seeing him beginning to fall, caught him and steadied him, and lowered him gently to the ground.

'Khun!' Valentine cried, and rushed toward him.

Even from twenty yards away he could see that the alien had been terribly wounded. Khun was gasping; his lean, sharp-featured face looked mottled, almost gray; his eyes were dull. At the sight of Valentine he brightened a little and tried to sit up.

'My lord,' the giantess said, 'this is no place for you.'

He ignored her and bent to the alien. 'Khun? Khun?' he whispered urgently.

'It's all right, my lord. I knew – there was a reason – why I had come to your world—'

'Khun!'

'Too bad – I'll miss the victory banquet—'

Helpless, Valentine grasped the alien's sharp-boned shoulders and held him, but Khun's life slipped swiftly and quietly away. His long strange journey was at its end. He had found purpose at last, and peace.

Valentine rose and looked about, perceiving the madness of the battlefield as though in a dream. A cordon of his people surrounded him, and someone – Sleet, he realized – was pulling at him, trying to get him to a safer place.

'No,' Valentine muttered. 'Let me fight—'

'Not out here, my lord. Would you share Khun's fate? What of all of us, if you perish? The enemy troops are streaming toward us from Peritole Pass. Soon the fighting will grow even more furious. You should not be on the field.'

Valentine understood that. Dominin Barjazid was nowhere on the scene, after all, and probably neither should he be. But how could he sit snug in a floater-car, when others were dying for him, when Khun, who was not even a creature of this world, had already given his life for him, when his beloved Elidath, just beyond that rise in the plain, was perhaps in grave peril from Valentine's own troops? He swayed in indecision. Sleet, bleak-faced, released him, but only to summon Zalzan Kavol: the giant Skandar, swinging swords in three arms and wielding an energy-thrower with the fourth, was not far away. Valentine saw Sleet conferring sternly with him, and Zalzan Kavol, holding defenders at bay almost disdainfully, began to fight his way toward Valentine. In a moment, Valentine suspected, the Skandar might haul him forcibly, crowned Power or not, from the field.

'Wait,' Valentine said. 'The heir presumptive is in danger. I command you to follow me!'

Sleet and Zalzan Kavol looked baffled by the unfamiliar title.

'The heir presumptive?' Sleet repeated. 'Who's—'

'Come with me,' Valentine said. 'An order.'

Zalzan Kavol rumbled, 'Your safety, my lord, is—'

'—not the only important thing. Sleet, at my left! Zalzan Kavol, at my right!'

They were too bewildered to disobey. Valentine summoned Lisamon Hultin also; and, guarded by his friends, he moved rapidly over the rise toward the front line of the enemy.

'*Elidath!*' Valentine cried, bellowing it with all his strength.

His voice carried across half a league, so it seemed, and the sound of that mighty roar caused all action about him to cease for an instant. Past an avenue of motionless warriors Valentine looked toward Elidath, and as their eyes met he saw the dark-haired man pause, return the look, frown, shrug.

To Sleet and Zalzan Kavol Valentine shouted, 'Capture that man! Bring him to me – unharmed!'

The instant of stasis ended; with redoubled intensity the tumult of battle resumed. Valentine's forces swarmed once more toward the hard-pressed and yielding enemy, and for a second he caught sight of Elidath, surrounded by a shield of his own people, fiercely holding his ground. Then he could see no more, for everything became chaotic again. Someone was tugging at him – Sleet, perhaps? Carabella? – urging him again to return to the safety of his car, but he grunted and pulled himself free.

'Elidath of Morvole!' Valentine called. 'Elidath, come to parley!'

'Who calls my name?' was the reply.

Again the surging mob opened between him and Elidath. Valentine stretched his arms toward the frowning figure and began to make answer. But words would be too slow, too clumsy, Valentine knew. Abruptly he dropped into the trance-state, putting all his strength of will into his mother's silver circlet, and casting forth across the space that separated him from Elidath of Morvole the full intensity of his soul in a single compressed fraction of an instant of dream-images, dream-force—

—two young men, boys really, riding sleek fast mounts through a forest of stunted dwarfish trees—

—a thick twisted root rising like a serpent out of the ground across the path, a mount stumbling, a boy flung headlong—

—a terrible cracking sound, a white shaft of jagged bone jutting horridly through torn skin—

—the other boy reining in, riding back, whistling in astonishment and fright as he saw the extent of the injury—

Valentine could sustain the dream-pictures no longer. The moment of contact ended. Drained, exhausted, he slipped back into waking reality.

Elidath stared at him, bewildered. It was as though the two of them alone were on the battlefield, and all that was going on about them was mere noise and vapor.

'Yes,' Valentine said. 'You know me, Elidath. But not by this face I wear today.'

'Valentine?'

'No other.'

They moved toward each other. A ring of troops of both armies surrounded them, silent, mystified. When they were a few feet apart they halted and squared off uncertainly, as if they were about to launch into a duel. Elidath studied Valentine's features in a stunned, astounded way.

'Can it be?' he asked finally. 'Such a witchery, is it possible?'

'We rode together in the pygmy forest under Amblemorn,' said Valentine. 'I never felt such pain as on that day. Remember, when you moved the bone with your hands, putting it in its place, and you cried out as if the leg were your own?'

'How could you know such things?'

'And then the months I spent sitting and fuming, while you and Tunigorn and Stasilaine roamed the Mount without me? And the limp I had, that stayed with me even after I was healed?' Valentine laughed. 'Dominin Barjazid stole that limp when he took my body from me! Who would have expected such a favor from the likes of him?'

Elidath seemed like one who walked in dreams. He shook his head, as though to rid it of cobwebs.

'This is witchery,' he said.

'Yes. And I am Valentine!'

'Valentine is in the Castle. I saw him but yesterday, and he wished me well, and spoke of the old times, the pleasures we shared—'

'Stolen memories, Elidath. He fishes in my brain, and finds the old scenes embedded there. Have you noticed nothing strange about him, this past year?' Valentine's eyes looked deep into Elidath's and the other man flinched, as if fearing sorcery. 'Have you not thought your Valentine oddly withdrawn and brooding and mysterious lately, Elidath?'

'Yes, but I thought – it was the cares of the throne that made him so.'

'You noticed a difference, then! A change!'

'A slight one, yes. A certain coldness – a distance, a chill about him—'

'And still you deny me?'

Elidath stared. 'Valentine?' he murmured, not yet believing. 'You, really you, in that strange guise?'

'None other. And he up there in the Castle has deceived you, you and all the world.'

'This is so strange.'

'Come, give me your embrace, and cease your mumbling, Elidath!' Smiling broadly, Valentine seized the other man and pulled him close, and held him as friend holds friend. Elidath stiffened. His body was as rigid as wood. After a moment be pushed Valentine away and stepped back a pace, shivering.

'You need not fear me, Elidath.'

'You ask too much of me. To believe such—'

'Believe it.'

'I do, at least by half. The warmth of your eyes – the smile – the things you remember—'

'Believe the other half,' Valentine urged passionately. 'The Lady my mother sends you her love, Elidath. You will see her again, at the Castle, the day we hold festival to mark my restoration. Turn your troops around, dear friend, and join us as we march up the Mount.'

There was warfare on Elidath's face. His lips moved, a muscle in his cheek twitched violently. In silence he confronted Valentine.

Then at last he said, 'This may be madness, but I accept you as what you claim.'

'Elidath!'

'And I will join you, and may the Divine help you if I am misled.'

'I promise you there will be no regretting this.'

Elidath nodded. 'I'll send messengers to Tunigorn—'

'Where is he?'

'He holds Peritole Pass against the thrust we expected from you. Stasilaine is there too. I was bitter, being left in command here in the plain, for I thought I'd miss all the action. Oh, Valentine, is it really you? With golden hair, and that sweet innocent look to your face?'

'The true Valentine, yes. I who slipped off with you to High Morpin when we were ten, borrowing the chariot of Voriax, and rode the juggernaut all day and half the night, and afterward had the same punishment as you—'

'—crusts of old stajja-bread for three days, indeed—'

'—and Stasilaine brought us a platter of meat secretly, and was caught, and he ate crusts with us too the next day—'

'—I had forgotten that part. And do you remember Voriax making us polish every part of the chariot where we had muddied it—'

'Elidath!'

'Valentine!'

They laughed and pounded each other joyously with their fists.

Then Elidath grew somber and said, 'But where have you been? What has befallen you all this year? Have you suffered, Valentine? Have you—'

'It is a very long story,' Valentine said gravely, 'and this is not the place to tell it. We must halt this battle, Elidath. Innocent citizens are dying for Dominin Barjazid's sake, and we cannot allow that. Rally your troops, turn them around.'

'In this madhouse it won't be easy.'

'Give the orders. Get the word to the other commanders. The killing has to stop. And then ride with us, Elidath, onward to Bombifale, and then past High Morpin to the Castle.'

11

Valentine returned to his car, and Elidath vanished into the confused and ragged line of the defenders. During the parley, Valentine discovered now from Ermanar, his people had made strong advances, keeping their wedge tight and pushing deep into the plain, throwing the vast but formless army of the false Coronal into nearly complete disarray. Now that relentless wedge continued to roll on, through helpless troops that had neither the will nor the desire to hold them back. With Elidath's leadership and formidable battlefield presence negated, the defenders were spiritless and disorganized.

But it was that very pandemonium and tumult among the defenders that made halting the wasteful battle almost impossible. With hundreds of thousands of warriors moving in patternless streams over Bombifale Plain, and thousands more rushing in from the pass as news spread of Valentine's attack, there was no way of exercising command over the entire mass. Valentine saw Elidath's starburst banner flying in the midst of the madness, halfway across the field, and knew that he was striving to make contact with his fellow officers and tell them of the switch in loyalties; but the army was out of control, and soldiers were dying needlessly. Every casualty brought a stab of pain to Valentine.

He could do nothing about that. He signaled Ermanar to keep pressing forward.

Over the next hour a bizarre transformation of the battle began. Valentine's wedge sliced forward almost without opposition, and a second phalanx now moved parallel to his, off to the east, led by Elidath, advancing with equal ease. The rest of the gigantic army that had occupied the plain was divided and confounded, and in a muddled way was fighting against itself, breaking into small groups that clung vociferously to tiny sectors of the plain and beat off anyone who approached.

Soon these feckless hordes lay far to Valentine's rear, and the double column of invaders was entering the upper half of the plain, where the land began to curve bowl-fashion toward the crest on which Bombifale, oldest and most beautiful of the Inner Cities, stood. It was early afternoon, and as they ascended the slope the sky grew ever more clear and bright and the air warmer, for they were beginning to leave the Mount-girdling cloud belt behind and emerge into the lower flanks of the summit zone, that lay bathed forever in shimmering sunlight.

And now Bombifale came into view, rising above them like a vision of antique splendor: great scalloped walls of burnt-orange sandstone set with huge diamond-shaped slabs of blue seaspar fetched from the shores of the Great Sea in Lord Pinitor's time, and lofty needle-sharp towers sprouting on the battlements at meticulously regular intervals, slender and graceful, casting long shadows into the plain.

Valentine's spirit throbbed with gathering joy and delight. Hundreds of miles of Castle Mount lay behind him, ring after ring of grand bustling cities, Slope Cities and Free Cities and Guardian Cities far below. The Castle itself was less than a day's journey above, and the army that would have thwarted his climb had crumbled into pathetic turmoil behind him. And though he still felt the distant threatening twinges of the King of Dreams's sendings at night, they were becoming only the merest tickle at the edges of his soul, and his beloved friend Elidath was ascending the Mount by his side, with Stasilaine and Tunigorn riding now to join him.

How good it was to behold the spires of Bombifale, and know what lay beyond! These hills, that towered city ahead, the dark thick grass of the meadows, the red stones of the mountain road from Bombifale to High Morpin, the dazzling flower-strewn fields that linked the Grand Calintane Highway from High Morpin to the southern wing of the Castle – he knew these places better than the sturdy but still somewhat unfamiliar body he now wore. He was almost home.

And then?

Deal with the usurper, yes, and set things to order – but the task was so awesome he scarcely knew where he would begin. He had been absent from Castle Mount almost two years, and deprived of power most of that time. The laws promulgated by Dominin Barjazid would have to be examined, and very likely repealed by blanket ordinance. And there was also the problem, which he had barely considered before this moment, of integrating the companions of his long wanderings into the former imperial officialdom, for surely he must find posts of power for Deliamber and Sleet and Zalzan Kavol and the rest, but there was Elidath to think of, and the others who had been central in his court. He could hardly discard them merely because he was coming home from exile with new favorites. That was perplexing, but he hoped he would find some way of handling it that would breed no resentments and would cause no—

Deliamber said abruptly, 'I fear new troubles heading in our direction, and not small ones.'

'What do you mean?'

'Do you see any changes in the sky?'

'Yes,' Valentine said. 'It grows brighter and a deeper blue as we escape from the cloud-belt.'

'Look more closely,' said Deliamber.

Valentine peered upslope. Indeed he had spoken carelessly and too soon, for the brightening of the sky that he had noticed a short while ago was altered now, in a strange manner: there was a faint tinge of darkness overhead, as though a storm were coming on. No clouds were in sight, but an odd and sinister gray tint was moving in behind the blue. And the banners mounted on the floater-cars, which had been fluttering in a mild western breeze, had shifted and stood out stiffly to the south, blown by winds of sudden strength coming down from the summit.

'A change in the weather,' Valentine said. 'Rain, perhaps? But why are you concerned?'

'Have you ever known sudden changes in the weather to occur this high on Castle Mount?'

Valentine frowned. 'Not commonly, no.'

'Not ever,' said Deliamber. 'My lord, why is the climate of this region so benign?'

'Why, because it's controlled from the Castle, artificially generated and governed by the great machines that—'

He broke off, staring in horror.

'Exactly,' Deliamber said.

'No! It's unthinkable!'

'Think it, my lord,' said the Vroon. 'The Mount pierces high into the cold night of space. Above us in the Castle hides a terrified man who holds his throne by treachery, and who has just seen his most trusted generals desert to the side of his enemy. Now an invincible army climbs the summit of the Mount unhindered. How can he keep them from reaching him? Why, shut down the weather-machines and let this sweet air freeze in our lungs, let night fall in an afternoon and the darkness of the void come sweeping over us, turn this Mount back into the lifeless tooth of rock it was ten thousand years ago. Look at the sky, Valentine! Look at the banners in the wind!'

'But a billion people live on the Mount!' Valentine cried. 'If he shuts down the weather-machines he destroys them along with us! Himself as well – unless he's found some way to seal the Castle against the cold.'

'Do you think he cares about his own survival now? He's doomed in any event. But this way he can bring you down with him – you and everyone else on Castle Mount. Look at the sky, Valentine! Look at it darkening!'

Valentine found himself trembling, not out of fear but in anger that Dominin Barjazid should be willing to destroy all the cities of the Mount in this monstrous final cataclysm, to murder children and babes and mothers with child, and farmers in the fields and merchants in their shops, millions upon millions of the innocent who had no part in this struggle for the Castle. And why this slaughter? Why, merely to vent his rage at having lost what was never rightfully his! Valentine looked toward the sky, hoping to find some sign that this was only some natural phenomenon after all. But that was foolishness. Deliamber was right: on Castle Mount the weather was *never* a natural phenomenon.

In anguish Valentine said, 'We are still far from the Castle. How long will it be before the freezing begins?'

Deliamber shrugged. 'When the weather-machines first were constructed, my lord, it took many months before there was air dense enough to support life at these altitudes. Night and day the machines labored, yet it took months. Undoing that work will probably be faster than the doing of it was; but it will need more than an instant, I think.'

'Can we reach the Castle in time to halt it?'

'It will be a close business, my lord,' said the Vroon.

Grim-faced, scowling, Valentine ordered the car to halt and summoned his officers. Elidath's vehicle, he saw, was already making its way laterally across the plain toward him in advance of the summons: plainly Elidath too had noticed that something was awry. As Valentine stepped from his car he shivered at the first touch of the air – though it was a shiver more of apprehension than of chill, for there was only the lightest hint of cooling thus far. Yet that was sufficiently ominous.

Elidath came running to his side. His expression was bleak. He pointed toward the darkening sky and said, 'My lord, the madman is doing the worst!'

'I know. We also see the change beginning.'

'Tunigorn is close below us now, and Stasilaine coming across by the Banglecode side. We must go on toward the Castle as fast as possible.'

'Do you think we'll have time?' Valentine asked.

Elidath managed a frosty grin. 'Little enough to spare. But it'll be the quickest homeward journey I'll ever have made.'

Sleet, Carabella, Lisamon Hultin, Asenhart, Ermanar, all were gathered close now, looking wholly mystified. These strangers to Castle Mount perhaps had noted the change in the weather, but had not drawn from it Elidath's conclusions. They glanced from Valentine to Elidath and back again, troubled, dismayed, knowing that something was amiss but unable to comprehend the nature of it.

Crisply Valentine explained. Their looks of confusion gave way to disbelief, shock, rage, consternation.

'There will be no halt in Bombifale,' Valentine said. 'We go straight on to the Castle, via the High Morpin road, and no stopping of any kind between here and there.' He looked toward Ermanar. 'There is, I suppose, the possibility of panic among our forces. This must not happen. Assure your troops that we will be safe if only we reach the Castle in time, that panic is fatal and swift action the only hope. Understood? A billion lives depend on how fast we travel now – a billion lives and our own.'

12

This was not the joyous ascent of the Mount that Valentine had imagined. With the victory of Bombifale Plain he had felt a great burden lift from him, for he saw no further barriers standing between him and what he sought. He had envisioned a serene journey to the Inner Cities, a triumphant banquet in Bombifale while the Barjazid cowered in fearful anticipation above, then the climactic entry into the Castle, the seizure of the usurper, the proclamation of restoration, everything unfolding with grand inevitability. But that pleasant fantasy was blasted now. Upward they sped in desperate haste, and the sky grew darker moment by moment, and the wind down from the summit gained in force, and the air became raw and biting. What did they make of these changes, in Bombifale and Peritole and Banglecode, and higher yet in Halanx and the Morpins, and in the Castle itself? Certainly they must realize something hideous was in the making, as all the fair land of Castle Mount suffered under unfamiliar frigid blasts and the balmy afternoon turned into mysterious night. Did they understand the doom that was rushing upon them? What of the Castle folk – were they frantically trying to reach the weather-machines that their mad Coronal had shut down, or did the usurper have them barricaded and guarded, so that death might strike everyone impartially?

Bombifale now was close at hand. Valentine regretted passing it by, for his people had fought hard and were weary; but if they rested now in Bombifale they would rest there forever.

So it was upward and upward through the gathering night. However fast they moved, it was too slow for Valentine, who imagined the terrified crowds gathering in the grand plazas of the cities – vast chaotic hordes of the frightened, weeping, turning to one another, staring at the sky, crying out, 'Lord Valentine, save us!' and not even knowing that the dark man to whom they sent their prayers was the instrument of their destruction. In his mind's eye he saw the people of Castle Mount streaming out by the millions into the roads, beginning a dreadful panicky migration to the lower levels, hopeless, doomed, a frantic useless effort to outrace death. Valentine imagined, too, tongues of piercing wintry air sliding down the slopes, licking at the flawless plants of Tolingar Barrier, chilling the stone birds of Furible, blackening the elegant gardens of Stee and Minimool, turning the canals of Hoikmar to sheets of ice. Eight thousand years in the making, this miracle that was Castle Mount, and it might be destroyed in the twinkling of an eye by the folly of one cold and treacherous soul.

Valentine could reach out and touch Bombifale, so it seemed. Its walls and towers, perfect and heartachingly beautiful even in this strange failing light, beckoned to him. But he went on, and on and on, hastening now on the steep mountain road paved with ancient blocks of red stone. That was Elidath's car close beside his on the left, and Carabella's on the right, and not far away rode Sleet, Zalzan Kavol, Ermanar, Lisamon Hultin, and all the hordes of troops he had accumulated on his long journey. All hurried after their lord, not understanding the doom that was coming upon the world but aware that this was a moment of apocalypse when monumental evil stood near to triumph, and only courage, courage and haste, could block its victory.

Onward, Valentine clenched his fists and through sheer power of will tried to force the car higher. Deliamber, beside him, urged him to be calm, to be patient. But how? How, when the very air of Castle Mount was being stripped away molecule by molecule, and the darkest of nights was taking hold?

'Look,' Valentine said. 'Those trees that flank the road – the ones that bear the crimson-and-gold flowers? Those are halatingas, planted four hundred years ago. A festival is held at High Morpin when they come into bloom, and thousands of people dance down the road beneath them. And see, see? The leaves are shriveling already, turning black at the edges. They have never known temperatures so low, and the cold has only begun. What will happen to them in eight more hours? And what will happen to the people who loved to dance beneath them? If a mere chill withers the leaves, Deliamber, what will true frost do, and snow? Snow, on Castle Mount! Snow, and worse than snow, when the air is gone, when everything stands naked to the stars, Deliamber—'

'We are not yet lost, my lord. What city is that, now, above us?'

Valentine peered through the deepening shadows. 'High Morpin – the pleasure-city, where the games are held.'

'Think of the games that will be held there next month, my lord, to celebrate your restoration.'

Valentine nodded. 'Yes,' he said, without irony. 'Yes. I will think of the games next month, the laughter, the wine, the flowers on the trees, the songs of the birds. Is there no way to make this thing go faster, Deliamber?'

'It floats,' said the Vroon, 'but it will not fly. Be patient. The Castle is near.'

'Hours, yet,' Valentine said sullenly.

He struggled to regain his balance of soul. He reminded himself of Valentine the juggler, that innocent young man buried somewhere within him, standing in the stadium at Pidruid and reducing himself to nothing more than hand and eye, hand and eye, to perform the tricks he had only just learned. Steady, steady, steady, keep to the center of your soul, remember that life is merely a game, a voyage, a brief amusement, that Coronals can be gobbled by sea-dragons and tumbled about in rivers and mocked by panto-miming Metamorphs in a drizzly forest, and what of it? But those were poor consolations now. This was not a matter of one man's misfortunes, which under the eye of the Divine were trivial enough, though that man had been a king. A billion innocent lives were threatened here, and a work of splendid art, this Mount, that might be unique in all the cosmos. Valentine stared at the deep reaches of the darkening sky, where, he feared, the stars would soon be shining through in afternoon. Stars out there, multitudes of worlds, and in all those worlds was there anything to compare with Castle Mount and the Fifty Cities? And would it all perish in an afternoon?

'High Morpin,' said Valentine. 'I had hoped my return to it would be happier.'

'Peace,' Deliamber whispered. 'Today we pass it by. Another day you'll come to it in joy.'

Yes. The shining airy webwork that was High Morpin rose to view on the right, that fantasy-city, that city of play, all wonder and dream, a city spun from wires of gold, or so Valentine had often thought as a boy, looking at its marvelous buildings. He glanced at it now and quickly away. It was ten miles from High Morpin to the perimeter of the Castle – a moment, an eye-blink.

'Does this road have a name?' asked Deliamber.

'The Grand Calintane Highway,' Valentine replied. 'A thousand times I traveled it, Deliamber, back and forth to the pleasure-city. The fields beside it are so arranged that something is in bloom on every day of the year, and always in pleasing patterns of color, the yellows beside the blues, the reds far from the oranges, the whites and pinks in the borders, and look now, look at the flowers turning away from us, drooping on their stems—'

'They can be planted again, if the cold destroys them,' said Deliamber. 'But there's time yet. These plants may not be as tender as you think.'

'I feel the cold on them as though it were on my own skin.'

Now they were in the highest reaches of Castle Mount, so far above the plains of Alhanroel that it was almost as though they had attained some other world, or some moon that hovered motionless in the sky of Majipoor.

Everything came to an end here in a fantastic upsweep of sharp-tipped peaks and crags. The summit aimed itself at the stars like a hundred spears, and in the midst of those strangely delicate stony spikes rose the odd rounded hump of the highest place of all, where Lord Stiamot had boldly planted his imperial residence eight thousand years ago in celebration of his conquest of the Metamorphs, and where, ever since, Coronal after Coronal had commemorated his own reign by adding rooms and outbuildings and spires and battlements and parapets. The Castle sprawled incomprehensibly over thousands of acres, a city in itself, a labyrinth more bewildering even than the lairs of the Pontifex. And the Castle lay just ahead.

It was dark now. The cold pitiless splendor of the stars blazed overhead.

'The air must be gone,' Valentine murmured. 'The death will come soon, will it not?'

'This is true night, not the calamity,' Deliamber answered. 'We have journeyed all day without rest, and you've had no sense of the passing of time. The hour is late, Valentine.'

'And the air?'

'Growing colder. Growing thinner. But not yet gone.'

'And there is time?'

'There is time.'

They came around the last stupefying turn in the Calintane Highway. Valentine remembered it well: the turn that whipped at a sharp curve around the neck of the mountain and presented stunned travelers with their first view of the Castle.

Valentine had never seen Deliamber amazed before.

In a hushed voice the wizard said, 'What are those buildings, Valentine?'

'The Castle,' he replied.

The Castle, yes. Lord Malibor's Castle, Lord Voriax's Castle, Lord Valentine's Castle. Nowhere could one see the whole structure, or even any significant part of it, but from here, at least, one beheld an awesome segment of it, a great pile of masonry and brick rising in level upon level, in maze upon maze, spiraling round and round upon itself, dancing up the peak in eye-dazzling fashion, sparkling with the glow of a million lights.

Valentine's fears dissolved, his morbid gloom lifted. At Lord Valentine's Castle, Lord Valentine could feel no sorrow. He was coming home, and whatever wound had been inflicted upon the world would soon be healed.

The Calintane Highway reached its end at the Dizimaule Plaza, which lay before the Castle's southern wing, a huge open space paved with cobblestones of green porcelain, with a golden starburst at its center. Here Valentine halted and descended from his car to assemble his officers.

A cold bleak wind was blowing, biting and brisk.

Carabella said, 'Are there gates? Will we have to lay siege?'

Valentine smiled and shook his head. 'No gates. Who would ever invade the Castle of the Coronal? We simply ride in, through the Dizimaule Arch yonder. But once we're inside, we may face enemy troops again.'

'The guards of the Castle are in my command,' said Elidath. 'I'll deal with them.'

'Good. Keep moving, keep in touch, trust in the Divine. By morning we'll gather to celebrate our victory, I swear you that.'

'Long life to Lord Valentine!' Sleet called out.

'Long life! Long life!'

Valentine lifted his arms, both as an acknowledgment and to silence their uproar.

'We celebrate tomorrow,' he said. 'Tonight we give battle, and may it be the last!'

13

How strange it felt, finally to be passing under the Dizimaule Arch, and to see the baffling myriad splendors of the Castle before him!

As a boy he had played in these boulevards and avenues, had lost himself in the wonders of the endlessly intertangling passageways and corridors, had stared in awe at the mighty walls and towers and enclosures and vaults. As a young man in the service of Lord Voriax his brother he had dwelled within the Castle, over yonder in the Pinitor Court, where high officials had their residences, and many a time he had strolled on the parapet of Lord Ossier, with its stupendous view of the Morpin Plunge and the High Cities. And as Coronal, that brief time he had occupied the innermost zones of the Castle, he had with delight touched the ancient weatherbeaten stones of Stiamot Keep, and walked alone through the vast echoing chamber of the Confalume throne-room, and studied the patterns of the stars from Lord Kinniken's Observatory, and pondered what additions he would make to the Castle himself in years to come. Now that he was back, he realized how much he loved this place, and not merely because it was a symbol of power and imperial grandeur that had been his, but mainly because it was such a fabric of the ages, such as a living, breathing weave of history.

'The Castle is ours!' cried Elidath jubilantly as Valentine's army burst through the unguarded gate.

But what good was that, Valentine thought, if death for all the Mount and its squabbling mortals lay just a few hours away? Already too much time had elapsed since the thinning of the atmosphere had begun. Valentine wanted to reach out, to claw the fleeing air and hold it back.

The deepening chill that now lay like a terrible weight on Castle Mount was nowhere more manifest than in the Castle itself, and those within it, already dazed and bewildered by the events of the civil war, stood like waxen figures, unblinking and numb, shivering and immobile while the invading parties rushed inward. Some, shrewder or quicker of wit than the others, managed to croak, 'Long live Lord Valentine!' as the unfamiliar golden-haired figure rode by; but most behaved as though their minds had already begun to freeze.

The hordes of attackers, flowing inward, moved swiftly and precisely toward the tasks Valentine had assigned. Duke Heitluig and his Bibiroon warriors had charge of seizing control of the Castle perimeter, flushing out and neutralizing any hostile forces. Asenhart and six detachments of valley people had the work of sealing all of the Castle's many gates, so none of the usurper's followers might escape. Sleet and Carabella and their troops went upward, toward the imperial halls of the inner sector to take possession of the seat of government. Valentine himself, with Elidath and Ermanar and their combined forces, set out on the spiraling lower causeway to the vaults where the weather-machines were housed. The rest, under command of Nascimonte, Zalzan Kavol, Shanamir, Lisamon Hultin, and Gorzval, went forth in random streams, spreading out over the Castle in search of Dominin Barjazid, who might be hiding in any of the thousands of rooms, even the meanest.

Down the causeway Valentine raced, until in the murky depths of the cobbled passage, the floater-car could go no farther; and then on foot he sped toward the vaults. The cold was numbing against his nose and lips and ears. His heart pounded, his lungs worked fiercely in the thin air. These vaults were all but unknown to him. He had been down here only once or twice, long ago. Elidath, though, seemed to know the way.

Through corridors, down endless flights of wide stone stairs, into a high-roofed arcade lit by twinkling points far overhead – and all the time the air grew perceptibly more chilly, the unnatural night gripped the Mount more tightly—

A great arched wooden door, banded with thick metal inlays, loomed up before them.

'Force it,' Valentine ordered. 'Burn through it, if we must!'

'Wait, my lord,' a mild quavering voice said.

Valentine whirled. An ancient Ghayrog, ashen-skinned, his serpent hair limp in the cold, had stepped from a doorway in the wall and came shambling uncertainly toward them.

'The keeper of the weather-machines,' Elidath muttered.

The Ghayrog looked half dead. Bewilderedly he glanced from Elidath to Ermanar, from Ermanar to Valentine; and then he threw himself to the ground before Valentine, plucking at the Coronal's boots.

'My lord – Lord Valentine—' He stared up in torment. 'Save us, Lord Valentine! The machines – they have turned off the machines—'

'Can you open the gate?'

'Yes, my lord. The control-house is in this alley. But they have seized the vaults – his troops are in command, they forced me out – what damage are they doing in there, my lord? What will become of us all?'

Valentine pulled the quivering old Ghayrog to his feet. 'Open the gate,' he said.

'Yes, my lord. It will be only a moment—'

An eternity, rather, Valentine thought. But there came the sound of awesome subterranean machinery and gradually the sturdy wooden barrier, creaking and groaning, began to move aside.

Valentine would have been the first to dart through the opening, but Elidath caught him ungently by the arm and pulled him back. Valentine slapped at the hand that held him as though it were some bothersome vermin, some dhiim of the jungles. Elidath held firm.

'No, my lord,' he said crisply.

'Let go, Elidath.'

'If it costs me my head, Valentine, I will not let you go in there. Stand aside.'

'Elidath!'

Valentine glanced toward Ermanar. But he found no support there. 'The Mount freezes, my lord, while you delay us,' Ermanar said.

'I will not allow—'

'Stand aside!' Elidath commanded.

'I am Coronal, Elidath.'

'And I am responsible for your safety. You may direct the offensive from the outside, my lord. But there are enemy soldiers in there, desperate men, defending the last place of power the usurper controls. Let one sharp-eyed sniper see you, and all our struggle has been in vain. Will you stand aside, Valentine, or must I commit treason on your body to push you out of the way?'

Fuming, Valentine yielded, and watched in anger and frustration as Elidath and a band of picked warriors slipped past him into the inner vault. There was the sound of fighting almost at once within; Valentine heard shouts, energy-bolts, cries, moans. Though guarded by Ermanar's watchful men, he was a dozen times at the brink of pulling away from them and entering the vault himself, but held back. Then a messenger came from Elidath to say that the immediate resistance was wiped out, that they were penetrating deeper, that there were barricades, traps, pockets of enemy soldiers every few hundred yards. Valentine clenched his fists. It was an impossible business, this thing of being too sacred to risk his skin, of standing about in an antechamber while the war of restoration raged all about him. He resolved to go in, and let Elidath bluster all he liked.

'My lord?' A messenger from the other direction, breathless, came running up.

Valentine hovered at the entrance to the vault. 'What is it?' he snapped.

'My lord, I am sent by Duke Nascimonte. We have found Dominin Barjazid barricaded in the Kinniken Observatory, and he asks you to come quickly to direct the capture.'

Valentine nodded. Better that than standing about idly here. To an aide-de-camp he said, 'Tell Elidath I'm going back up. He has full authority to reach the weather-machines any way he can.'

But Valentine was only a short distance up the passageways when

Gorzval's aide arrived, to say that the usurper was rumored to be in the Pinitor Court. And a few minutes later came word from Lisamon Hultin, that she was pursuing him swiftly down a spiraling passageway leading to Lord Siminave's reflecting-pool.

In the main concourse Valentine found Deliamber, watching the action with a look of bemused fascination. Telling the Vroon of the conflicting reports, he asked, 'Can he be in all three places?'

'None, more likely,' the wizard replied. 'Unless there are three of him. Which I doubt, though I feel his presence in this place, dark and strong.'

'In any particular area?'

'Hard to tell. Your enemy's vitality is such that he radiates himself from every stone of the Castle, and the echoes confuse me. But I will not be confused much longer, I think.'

'Lord Valentine?'

A new messenger – and a familiar face, deep coarse brows meeting in the center, a jutting chin, an easy confident smile. Another unit of the vanished past fitting itself back into place, for this man was Tunigorn, second closest of all Valentine's boyhood friends, now one of the high ministers of the realm, and now looking at the stranger before him with bright penetrating eyes, as if trying to find the Valentine behind the strangeness. Shanamir was with him.

'Tunigorn!' Valentine cried.

'My lord! Elidath said you were altered, but I had no idea—'

'Am I too strange to you with this face?'

Tunigorn smiled. 'It will take some getting used to, my lord. But that can come in time. I bring you good news.'

'Seeing you again is good news enough.'

'But I bring you better. The traitor has been found.'

'I have been told already three times in half an hour that he is in three different places.'

'I know nothing of those reports. We have him.'

'Where?'

'Barricaded in the inner chambers. The last to see him was his valet, old Kanzimar, loyal to the end, who finally saw him gibbering with terror and understood at last that this was no Coronal before him. He has locked off the entire suite, from the throne-room to the robing-halls, and is alone in there.'

'Good news indeed!' To Deliamber Valentine said, 'Do your wizardries confirm any of this?'

Deliamber's tentacles stirred. 'I feel a sour, malign presence in that lofty building.'

'The imperial chambers,' said Valentine. 'Good.' He turned to Shanamir and said, 'Send out the word to Sleet, Carabella, Zalzan Kavol, Lisamon Hultin. I want them with me as we close in.'

'Yes, my lord!' The boy's eyes gleamed with excitement.

Tunigorn said, 'Who are those people you named?'

'Companions of my wanderings, old friend. In my time of exile they became very dear to me.'

'Then they will be dear to me as well, my lord. Whoever they may be, those who love you are those I love.' Tunigorn drew his cloak close about him. 'But what of this chill? When will it begin to lift? I heard from Elidath that the weather-machines—'

'Yes.'

'And can they be repaired?'

'Elidath has gone to them. Who knows what damage the Barjazid has done? But have faith in Elidath.' Valentine looked toward the inner palace high above him, narrowing his eyes as though he could in that manner see through the noble stone walls to the frightened shameless creature hiding behind them.

'This coldness gives me great grief, Tunigorn,' he said somberly. 'But curing it now is in the hands of the Divine – and Elidath. Come. Let's see if we can pluck that insect from its nest.'

14

The moment of final reckoning with Dominin Barjazid was close at hand now. Valentine moved swiftly, onward and inward and upward through all the familiar wonderful places.

This vaulted building was the archive of Lord Prestimion, where that great Coronal had assembled a museum of the history of Majipoor. Valentine smiled at the thought of installing his juggling clubs alongside the sword of Lord Stiamot and the jewel-studded cape of Lord Confalume. There, rising in amazing swoops, was the slender, fragile-looking watchtower built by Lord Arioc, a strange construction indeed, giving indication perhaps of the greater strangeness that Arioc would perpetrate when he moved on to the Pontificate. That, a double atrium with an elevated pool in its center, was the chapel of Lord Kinniken, adjoining the lovely white-tiled hall that was the residence of the Lady whenever she came to visit her son. And there, sloping glass roofs gleaming in the starlight, was Lord Confalume's garden-house, the cherished private indulgence of that grandeur-loving pompous monarch, a place where tender plants from every part of Majipoor had been collected. Valentine prayed they would survive this night of wintry blasts, for he longed to go among them soon, with eyes made wiser by his travels, and revisit the wonders he had seen in the forests of Zimroel and on the Stoienzar shores.

Upward—

Through a seemingly endless maze of hallways and staircases and galleries and tunnels and outbuildings, onward, onward. 'We will die of old age, not cold, before we reach the Barjazid!' Valentine muttered.

'It will not be long now, my lord,' Shanamir said.

'Not soon enough to please me.'

'How will you punish him, my lord?'

Valentine glanced at the boy. 'Punish? Punish? What punishment can there be for what he's done? A whipping? Three days on stajja-crusts? Might as well punish the Steiche for having jostled us on the rocks.'

Shanamir looked puzzled. 'No punishment at all?'

'Not as you understand punishment, no.'

'Turn him loose to do more mischief?'

'Not that either,' said Valentine. 'But first we must catch him, and then we can talk about what to do with him.'

Half an hour more – it seemed forever – and Valentine stood before the core of the Castle, the walled imperial chambers, not nearly the oldest but by far the most sacrosanct of all its precincts. Early Coronals had had their governing-halls here, but they had long since been replaced by the finer and more awesome rooms of the great rulers of the past thousand years, and now constituted a glittering palatial seat of power, apart from all the other tangled intricacies of the Castle. The highest ceremonies of state took place in those high-vaulted splendid chambers; but now one single miserable being lurked in there, behind the ancient massive doors, protected by heavy ornate bolts of enormous size and weighty symbolic significance.

'Poison gas,' Lisamon Hultin said. 'Pump one canister of gas through the walls and drop him wherever he is.'

Zalzan Kavol nodded vehemently. 'Yes! Yes! See, a thin pipe slipped through these cracks – there is a gas they use in Piliplok for killing fish, that would do the job in—'

'No,' Valentine said. 'He will be brought out alive.'

'Can it be done, my lord?' Carabella asked.

'We could smash the doors,' rumbled Zalzan Kavol.

'Ruin Lord Prestimion's doors, that were thirty years making, to fetch one rascal out of hiding?' Tunigorn asked. 'My lord, this talk of poison gas does not seem so foolish to me. We should not waste time—'

Valentine said, 'We must take care not to act like barbarians. There will be no poisonings here.' He caught Carabella's hand, and Sleet's, and raised them. 'You are jugglers, with quick fingers. And you, Zalzan Kavol. Have you no experience at using those fingers for other things?'

'Picking locks, my lord?' Sleet asked.

'And things of that order, yes. There are many entrances to these chambers, and perhaps not all are secured by bolts. Go, try to find a way past the barriers. And while you do that I'll seek another way.'

He stepped forward to the giant gilded door, twice the height of the tallest of Skandars, carved over every square inch with images in high relief of the reign of Lord Prestimion and his celebrated predecessor Lord Confalume. He put his hands to the heavy bronze handles as though he meant to open the door with a single hearty heave.

For a long moment Valentine stood that way, casting from his mind all awareness of the tension that swirled about him. He attempted to move to the quiet place at the center of his soul. But a powerful obstacle blocked him:

His mind was filled suddenly with overwhelming hatred for Dominin Barjazid.

Behind that great door was the man who had thrust him from his throne, who had sent him forth as a hapless wanderer, who had ruled rashly and unjustly in his name, and – worst of all, wholly monstrous and unforgivable – who had chosen to destroy a billion blameless and unsuspecting people when his own schemes began to falter.

Valentine loathed him for that. For that, Valentine ached to destroy Dominin Barjazid.

As he stood clinging to the handles of the door, fierce violent images assailed his mind. He saw Dominin Barjazid flayed alive, cloaked in his own blood, screaming screams that could be heard from there to Pidruid. He saw Dominin Barjazid nailed to a tree with barbed arrows. He saw Dominin Barjazid crushed beneath a hail of stones. He saw—

Valentine trembled with the force of his own terrible rage.

But one did not flay one's enemies alive in a civilized society, and one did not freely vent one's anger in violence – not even upon a Dominin Barjazid. How, Valentine wondered, can I claim the right to rule a world, when I can't even rule my own emotions? So long as this rage roiled his soul he was as unfit to govern, he knew, as Dominin Barjazid himself. He must do battle with it. That pounding in the temples, that rush of blood, that savage hunger for vengeance – all must be purged before he made any move toward Dominin Barjazid.

Valentine struggled. He let the clenched muscles of his back and shoulders relax, and filled his lungs with the sharp chill air, and moment by moment allowed the tension to drain from his body. He searched his soul where the hot fiery vengeance-lust had so suddenly flared in it, and swept it clean. And then he was able to move at last to the quiet place at the center of his soul and hold himself there, so that he felt himself alone in the Castle but for Dominin Barjazid somewhere on the far side of the door, only the two of them and a single barrier between. Conquest over self was the finest of victories: all else must follow, Valentine knew.

He yielded himself up to the power of the silver circlet of the Lady his mother, and entered into the dream-state, and sent forth the strength of his mind toward his enemy.

It was no dream of vengeance and punishment that Valentine sent. That would be too obvious, too cheap, too easy. He sent a gentle dream, a dream of love and friendship, of sadness for what had befallen. Dominin Barjazid could only be astounded by such a message. Valentine showed Dominin Barjazid the dazzling glittering pleasure-city of High Morpin, and the two of them walking side by side down the Avenue of Clouds, talking amiably, smiling, discussing the differences that separated them, trying to resolve frictions and apprehensions. It was a risky way to begin these dealings, for it exposed him to derision and contempt, if Dominin Barjazid chose to misunderstand Valentine's motives. Yet there was no hope of defeating him through threats and rage; perhaps a softer way might win. It was a dream that took vast reserves of spirit, for it was naïve to expect Barjazid to be seduced by guile, and unless the love that radiated from Valentine was genuine, and made itself felt to be genuine, the dream was a foolishness. Valentine had not known he could find love in him for this man who had worked so much harm. But he found it; he spun it forth; he sent it through the great door.

When he had done, he clung to the door-handles, recouping his strength, and waited for some sign from within.

Unexpectedly what came was a sending: a powerful blast of mental energy, startling and overwhelming, that roared out of the imperial chambers like the fury of a hot Suvrael wind. Valentine felt the searing blast of Dominin Barjazid's mocking rejection. Barjazid wanted no love, no friendship. He sent defiance, hatred, anger, contempt, belligerence: a declaration of perpetual war.

The impact was intense. How did it come to pass, Valentine wondered, that the Barjazid was capable of sendings? Some machine of his father, no doubt, some witchery of the King of Dreams. He realized that he should have anticipated something like that. But no matter, Valentine stood fast in the withering force of the dream-energy Dominin Barjazid hurled at him.

And afterward sent back another dream, as easy and trusting as Dominin Barjazid's had been harsh and hostile. He sent a dream of pardon, of total forgiveness. He showed Dominin Barjazid a harbor, a fleet of Suvraelu ships waiting to return him to his father's land, and even a grand parade, Valentine and Barjazid side by side in a chariot, riding down to the waterfront for the ceremonies of departure, standing together on the quay, laughing as they exchanged their farewells, two good enemies who had had at each other with all the power at their command and now were parting pleasantly.

From Dominin Barjazid came an answering dream of death and destruction, of loathing, of abomination, of scorn.

Valentine shook his head slowly, heavily, trying to clear it of the muck of poison coming toward him. A third time he gathered his strength and readied a sending for his foe. Still he would not descend to Barjazid's level; still he hoped to overwhelm him with warmth and kindness, though another might say it was folly even to make the attempt. Valentine shut his eyes and centered his consciousness in the silver circlet.

'My lord?'

A woman's voice, cutting through his concentration just as he was slipping into trance.

The interruption was jarring and painful. Valentine spun around, ablaze with unaccustomed fury, so shaken by surprise that it was a moment before he could recognize the woman as Carabella, and she drew back from him, gasping, momentarily afraid.

'My lord—' she said in a tiny voice. 'I didn't know—'

He struggled to control himself. 'What is it?'

'We – we have found a way to open a door.'

Valentine closed his eyes and felt his rigid body going slack with relief. He smiled and drew her to him, and held her a moment, trembling as tension discharged itself in him. Then he said, 'Take me there!'

Carabella led him down corridors rich with antique draperies and thick well-worn carpets. She moved with a sureness of direction surprising in one who had never walked these halls before. They came to a part of the imperial chambers that Valentine did not remember, a service access somewhere beyond the throne-room, a simple and humble place. Sleet, riding on Zalzan Kavol's shoulders, had the upper half of his body poked deep within some transom, and was reaching down to perform delicate manipulations on the inner side of a plain door. Carabella said, 'We've opened three doors this way and now Sleet's infiltrating the fourth. In another moment—'

Sleet pulled his head out and looked around, dusty, grimy, wondrously pleased with himself.

'It's open, my lord.'

'Well done!'

'We'll go in and get him,' Zalzan Kavol growled. 'Do you want him in three pieces or five, my lord?'

'No,' Valentine said. 'I'll go in. Alone.'

'You, my lord?' Zalzan Kavol asked in an incredulous tone.

'Alone?' said Carabella.

Sleet, looking outraged, cried, 'My lord, I forbid you—' and stopped, bewildered by the sacrilege of his own words.

Mildly Valentine said, 'Have no fears for me. This is something I must do without help. Sleet, step aside. Zalzan Kavol – Carabella – stand back. I order you not to enter until you're summoned.'

They stared at one another in confusion. Carabella began to say something, faltered, closed her mouth. Sleet's scar throbbed and blazed. Zalzan Kavol made odd rumbling sounds and swung his four arms impotently.

Valentine pulled open the door and strode through.

He was in a vestibule of some kind, perhaps a kitchen passageway, nothing a Coronal was likely to be familiar with. He walked warily through it and emerged into a richly brocaded hall, which after a moment's disorientation he recognized as the robing-room; beyond it was the Dekkeret Chapel, and that led to the judgment-hall of Lord Prestimion, a grand vaulted chamber with splendid windows of frosted glass and magnificent chandeliers manufactured by the finest craftsmen of Ni-moya. And beyond that was the throne-room, with the Confalume Throne of supreme grandeur dominating everything. Somewhere in that suite Valentine would find Dominin Barjazid.

He moved forward into the robing-room. It was empty, and looked as though no one had made use of it for months. The stone archway of the Dekkeret Chapel was uncurtained; Valentine peered through it, saw no one there, and continued through the short curving passage, decorated with brilliant mosaic ornaments in green and gold, that connected with the judgment-hall.

He drew in his breath deeply and laid hands on the judgment-hall door and flung it open.

At first he thought that that vast space also was empty. Only one of the great chandeliers was lit, and that one at the far end, casting but a dim glow. Valentine looked to left and right, down the rows of polished wooden benches, past the curtained alcoves in which dukes and princes were permitted to conceal themselves while judgment was passed upon them, toward the high seat of the Coronal—

And saw a figure in imperial robes standing in the shadows at the council-table below the high seat.

15

Of all the strangenesses of his time of exile, this was the most strange of all, to stand less than a hundred feet from one who wore what once had been his own visage. Twice before, Valentine had seen the false Coronal, on that day of festival in Pidruid, and he had felt soiled and drained of energy when he had looked upon him, without knowing why. But that was before he had regained his memory. Now, in the dimness, he beheld a tall, strong man, fierce-eyed, black-bearded, the Lord Valentine of old, princely in bearing, not at all cowering or gibbering or terrified, confronting him with cold calm menace. Was that how I looked? Valentine wondered. So bleak, so icy, so forbidding? He supposed that during all these months when Dominin Barjazid had been in possession of his body, the darkness of the usurper's soul had leaked out through the face, and changed the Coronal's cast of features to this morbid hateful expression. Valentine had grown used to his own amiable sunny new face, and now, seeing the one he had worn so many years, he felt no wish to have it back.

Dominin Barjazid said, 'I made you pretty, didn't I?'

'And made yourself less so,' said Valentine cordially. 'Why do you scowl, Dominin? That face was better known for its smile.'

'You smiled too much, Valentine. You were too easy, too mild, too light of soul to rule.'

'Is that how you saw me?'

'I and many others. I understand you've become a wandering juggler these days.'

Valentine nodded. 'I needed a trade, after you took away the one I had. Juggling suited me.'

'It would have,' Barjazid said. His voice echoed in the long empty chamber. 'You were always best at giving amusement to others. I invite you to return to juggling, Valentine. The seals of power are mine.'

'The seals are yours, but not the power. Your guards have deserted you. The Castle is secure against you. Come, give yourself up, Dominin, and we will return you to your father's land.'

'What of the weather-machines, Valentine?'

'Those have been turned back on.'

'A lie! A silly lie!' Barjazid whirled and threw open one of the tall arching windows. A blast of frigid air rushed in so swiftly that Valentine, at the other end of the room, could feel it almost at once. 'The machines are guarded by the people I most trust,' said Barjazid. 'Not your people, but my own, that I brought from Suvrael. They will keep them off until the order comes from me to turn them on, and if all of Castle Mount turns black and perishes before that order comes, so be it, Valentine. So be it! Will you let that happen?'

'It will not happen.'

'It will,' said Barjazid, 'if you remain in the Castle. Go. I grant you safe conduct down the Mount, and free passage to Zimroel. Juggle in the western towns, as you did a year ago, and forget this foolishness of claiming the throne. I am Lord Valentine the Coronal.'

'Dominin—'

'Lord Valentine is my name! And you are the wandering juggler Valentine of Zimroel! Go, take up your trade.'

Lightly Valentine said, 'It's a powerful temptation, Dominin. I enjoyed performing, perhaps more than anything I've done in my life. Nevertheless, destiny requires me to carry the burdens of government, regardless of my private wishes. Come, now.' He took a step toward Barjazid, another, another. 'Come with me, out to the antechamber, so we can show the knights of the Castle that this rebellion is over and the world returns to its true pattern.'

'Stay back!'

'I mean no harm to you, Dominin. In a way I feel grateful to you, for some extraordinary experiences, things that would surely never have befallen me but for—'

'Back! Not another step!'

Valentine continued to advance. 'And grateful, too, for ridding me of that annoying little limp, which interfered with some of the pleasures of—'

'Not – another – step—'

Barely a dozen feet separated them now. Beside Dominin Barjazid was a table laden with the paraphernalia of the judgment-hall: three heavy brazen candlesticks, an imperial orb, and next to it a scepter. Uttering a strangled cry of rage, Barjazid seized a candlestick with both hands and hurled it savagely at Valentine's head. But Valentine stepped deftly aside and with a neat snap of his hand caught the massive metal implement as it went by. Barjazid hurled another. Valentine caught that too.

'One more,' Valentine said. 'Let me show you how it's done!'

Barjazid's face was mottled with fury; he choked, he hissed, he snorted in anger. The third candlestick flew toward Valentine. Valentine already had the first two in motion, spinning easily end over end from hand to hand, and it was no task at all for him to snatch the third and fit it into sequence, forming a gleaming cascade in the air before him. Blithely he juggled them, laughing, tossing them ever higher, and how good it felt to be juggling again, to be using the old skills after so long, hand and eye, hand and eye.

'See?' he said. 'Like this. We can teach you, Dominin. You only need to learn to relax. Here, throw me the scepter as well, and the orb. I can do five, and maybe even more than that. A pity the audience is so small, but—'

Still juggling, he walked toward Barjazid, who backed away, eyes wide, chin flecked with spittle.

And abruptly Valentine was rocked and swayed by a sending of some sort, a waking dream that hit him with the force of a blow. He halted, stunned, and the candlesticks tumbled clangorously to the dark wooden floor. There came a second blow, dizzying him, and a third. Valentine struggled to keep from falling. The game he had been playing with Barjazid was ended now, and some new encounter had begun that Valentine did not comprehend at all.

He rushed forward, meaning to seize his adversary before the force struck him again.

Barjazid retreated, holding his trembling hands before his face. Was this onslaught coming from him, or did he have an ally hidden in the room? Valentine recoiled as that inexorable unseen power thrust against his mind once more, even more numbingly. He shook. He pressed his hands to his temples and tried to collect his senses. Catch Barjazid, he told himself, get him down, sit on him, yell for assistance—

He sprang forward, lunged, seized the false Coronal's arm. Barjazid yelled and pulled free. Advancing, Valentine sought to corner him, and nearly did, but abruptly, with a wild shriek of fear and frustration, Dominin Barjazid darted past him and went scrambling across the room. He dived into one of the curtained alcoves on the far side, crying, 'Help me! Father, help me!'

Valentine followed and ripped away the curtain.

And stood back in astonishment. Concealed in the alcove was a powerfully built, fleshy old man, dark-eyed, glowering, wearing on his forehead a glittering golden circlet, and grasping in one hand some device of ivory and gold some thing of straps and hasps and levers. Simonan Barjazid he was, the King of Dreams, the terrifying old haunter out of Suvrael, skulking here in the judgment-hall of the Coronal! It was he who had sent the mind-numbing dream-commands that nearly had felled Valentine; and he struggled now to send another, but was prevented by the distraction of his own son, who clung hysterically to him, begging for help.

Valentine knew this was more than he could handle alone.

'Sleet!' he called. 'Carabella! Zalzan Kavol!'

Dominin Barjazid sobbed and moaned. The King of Dreams kicked at him as if he were some bothersome dog nipping at his heels. Valentine edged cautiously into the alcove, hoping to snatch that dread dream-machine from old Simonan Barjazid before he could work more damage with it.

And as Valentine reached for it, something more astounding yet occurred.

The outlines of Simonan Barjazid's face and body began to waver, to blur—

To change—

To turn into something monstrously strange, to become angular and slender, with eyes that sloped inward and a nose that was a mere bump and lips that could scarcely be seen—

A Metamorph.

Not the King of Dreams at all, but a counterfeit, a masquerade King, a Shapeshifter, a Piurivar, a Metamorph—

Dominin Barjazid screamed in horror and let go of the bizarre figure, recoiling and throwing himself down, quivering and whimpering, against the wall. The Metamorph glared at Valentine in what surely was unalloyed hatred and hurled the dream-device at him with ferocious violence. Valentine could only partly shield himself; the machine caught him in the chest and knocked him awry, and in that moment the Metamorph rushed past him, dashed frantically to the far side of the room, and in a wild scramble leaped over the sill of the window that Dominin Barjazid had opened, flinging himself out into the night.

16

Pale, shaken, Valentine turned and saw the room full of people: Sleet, Zalzan Kavol, Deliamber, Carabella, Tunigorn, and he could not tell how many others, hastily pressing in through the narrow vestibule. He pointed toward Dominin Barjazid, who lay huddled in a pitiful state of shock and collapse.

'Tunigorn, I give you charge of him. Take him to a secure place and see that no harm comes to him.'

'The Pinitor Court, my lord, is safest. And a dozen picked men will guard him every instant.'

Valentine nodded. 'Good. I don't want him left alone. And get a doctor to him: he's had a monstrous fright, and I think it's done him harm.' He looked toward Sleet. 'Friend, are you carrying a wine-flask? I've had some strange moments here myself.' Sleet reached a flask to him! Valentine's hand quivered, and he nearly spilled the wine before he got it to his lips.

Calmer now, he walked to the window through which the Metamorph had leaped. Lanterns gleamed somewhere far below. It was a fall of a hundred feet, or more, and in the courtyard there he saw figures surrounding something that lay covered with a cloak. Valentine turned away.

'A Metamorph,' he said in bewilderment. 'Was it only a dream? I saw the

King of Dreams standing there – and then it was a Metamorph – and then it rushed to the window—'

Carabella touched his arm. 'My lord, will you rest now? The Castle is won.'

'A Metamorph,' Valentine said again, with wonder in his voice. 'What could it have—'

'There were Metamorphs also in the hall of the weather-machines,' said Tunigorn.'

'What?' Valentine stared. 'What did you say?'

'My lord, Elidath has just come up from the vaults with a strange story.' Tunigorn gestured; and out of the crowd at the back of the room stepped Elidath himself, looking battle-weary, his cloak stained and his doublet torn.

'My lord?'

'The weather-machines—'

'They are unharmed, and the air and warmth go forth again, my lord,'

Valentine let out a long sigh. 'Well done! And there were Shapeshifters, you say?'

'The hall was guarded by troops in the uniform of the Coronal's own guard,' said Elidath. 'We challenged them, we ordered them to yield, and they would not, even to me. Whereupon we fought them, and we – slew them, my lord—'

'There was no other way?'

'No other way,' Elidath said. 'We slew them, and as they died they – changed—'

'Every one?'

'All were Metamorphs, yes.'

Valentine shivered. Strangeness upon strangeness in this nightmare revolution! He felt exhaustion rushing upon him. The engines of life turned again; the Castle was his, and the false Coronal a prisoner; the world was redeemed, order restored, the threat of tyranny averted. And yet – and yet – there was this new mystery, and he was so terribly tired—

'My lord,' said Carabella, 'come with me.'

'Yes,' he said hollowy. 'Yes, I'll rest a little while.' He smiled faintly. 'See me to the couch in the robing-room, will you, my love? I think I will rest, an hour or so. When was it that I last slept, do you recall?'

Carabella slipped her arm through his. 'It seems like days, doesn't it?'

'Weeks. Months. Just an hour – don't let me sleep more than that—'

'Of course, my lord,'

He sank to the couch like one who had been drugged, Carabella drew a coverlet over him and darkened the room, and he curled up, letting his weary body go limp. But through his mind darted luminous images: Dominin Barjazid clinging to that old man's knees, and the King of Dreams angrily trying to shake him off, all the while waving that strange machine about, and then the shifting of shapes, the eerie Piurivar face glaring at him – Dominin Barjazid's terrifying cry – the Metamorph rushing toward the open window – again and again, again and again, scenes beyond comprehension acting themselves out in Valentine's tormented mind—

And sleep came over him gently, slipping up on him as he lay wrestling with the demons of the judgment-hall.

He slept the hour he had asked, and something more than that, for when he woke it was because the bright golden light of morning was in his eyes. He sat up, blinking and stretching. His body ached. A dream, he thought, a wild and bewildering dream of – no, no dream. No dream.

'My lord, are you rested?'

Carabella, Sleet, Deliamber. Watching him. Standing guard over his slumber.

Valentine smiled. 'I'm rested, yes. And the night is gone. What has been happening?'

'Little enough,' said Carabella, 'except that the air grows warm again, and the Castle rejoices, and word is spreading down the Mount of the change that has come upon the world.'

'The Metamorph who sprang from the window – was it killed?'

'Indeed, my lord,' said Sleet.

'It wore the robes and regalia of the King of Dreams, and carried one of his devices. How was that, do you think?'

Deliamber said, 'I can make guesses, my lord. I have spoken with Dominin Barjazid – he is the next thing to a madman now, and will be a long time healing, if ever – and he told me certain things. Last year, my lord, his father the King of Dreams fell gravely ill and was thought close to death. This was while you still held the throne.'

'I recall nothing of that.'

'No,' said the Vroon, 'they made no advertisement of it. But it looked perilous, and then a new physician came to Suvrael, someone of Zimroel who claimed great skills, and indeed the King of Dreams made a miraculous recovery, like one who had risen from the dead. It was then, my lord, that the King of Dreams placed into his son's mind the notion of trapping you in Til-omon, and displacing you from the throne.'

Valentine gasped. 'The physician – a Metamorph?'

'Indeed,' said Deliamber. 'Masquerading, by his art, as a man of your race. And masquerading afterward as Simonan Barjazid, I think, until undone by the frenzy and confusion of that struggle in the judgment-hall, which caused the metamorphosis to waver and fail.'

'And Dominin? Is he also—'

'No, my lord, he is the true Dominin, and the sight of the thing that pretended to be his father has wrecked his mind. But do you see, it was the

Metamorph that put him up to the usurpation, and one might suppose another Metamorph would have replaced Dominin, by and by, as Coronal.'

'And Metamorphs guarding the weather-machines – obeying not Dominin's orders, but the false King's! A secret revolution, is it, Deliamber? Not at all a seizure of power by the Barjazid family, but the beginning of a rebellion by the Shapeshifters?'

'So I fear, my lord.'

Valentine stared into emptiness. 'Much is explained now. And much more is cast into disorder.'

Sleet said, 'My lord, we must search them out and destroy them wherever they hide among us, and bottle the rest up in Piurifayne where they can do us no harm!'

'Easy, friend,' Valentine said. 'Your hatred of Metamorphs still lives, eh?'

'And with reason!'

'Yes, perhaps so. Well, we will search them out, and have no secret Metamorphs pretending to be Pontifex or Lady or even the keeper of the stables. But I think also we must reach toward those people, and heal them of their anger if we can, or Majipoor will be thrown into endless war.' He rose and fastened his cloak and held his arms high. 'Friends, we have work to do, I fear, and no small measure of it. But first comes celebration! Sleet, I name you the chancellor of my restoration festivities, to plan the banquet and arrange the entertainments and summon the guests. Let the word go forth to Majipoor that all is well, or nearly so, and Valentine's on his throne again!'

17

The Confalume throne-room was the largest and grandest of the rooms of the Castle, with glittering gilded beams and fine tapestries and a floor of smooth gurna-wood from the Khyntor peaks, a hall of splendor and majesty in which the most significant of imperial ceremonies took place. But rarely had the Confalume throne-room beheld a spectacle such as this.

For high on the great many-stepped Confalume Throne sat Lord Valentine the Coronal, and on a throne to his left, nearly as lofty, sat the Lady, his mother, resplendent in a gown all of white, and to his right, on a throne of the same height as the Lady's, was Hornkast the high spokesman of the Pontifex, for Tyeveras had sent his regrets and Hornkast in his place. And arrayed before them, virtually filling the room, were the dukes and princes and knights of the realm, such an assembly as had not been seen in one place since the days of Lord Confalume himself – overlords out of far Zimroel, from Pidruid and Til-omon and Narabal, and the Ghayrog duke from Dulorn, and the great ones of Piliplok and Ni-moya and fifty other cities of Zimroel, and a hundred more of Alhanroel, beyond the fifty of Castle Mount. But not all this throng were dukes and princes, for there were humbler people also, Gorzval the stump-armed Skandar and Cordeine who had been his sailmender and Pandelon his carpenter, and Vinorkis the Hjort dealer in haigus hides, and the boy Hissune of the Labyrinth, and Tisana the old dream-speaker of Falkynkip, and many more of no rank higher than that, standing among these grandees with faces shining in awe.

Lord Valentine rose and saluted his mother, and rendered a salute to Hornkast, and bowed as the cries went up, 'Long live the Coronal!' And when silence fell he said quietly, 'Today we hold grand festival, to celebrate the restoration of the commonwealth and the making whole of the order of things. We have entertainment for you this day.'

He clapped his hands and there was music: horns, drums, pipes, a lively and lilting outburst of melody, a dozen players striding into the room, Shanamir leading them. And behind them came the jugglers, in costumes of surpassing beauty, costumes worthy of great princes: Carabella first, and little scar faced white-haired Sleet just back of her, and then gruff shaggy Zalzan Kavol and the two brothers who remained to him. They carried juggling gear of many kinds, swords and knives and sickles, torches ready to be lit, eggs, plates, gaily painted clubs, and a host of other things. When they reached the center of the room they took up their positions facing one another along the points of an imaginary star, and stood straight-shouldered and poised.

'Wait,' said Lord Valentine. 'There's room for one more!'

Step by step down the Confalume Throne he came, until he was three steps from the bottom. He grinned at the Lady, and winked at young Hissune, and gestured to Carabella, who flung a blade at him. He caught it neatly and she threw another, and a third, and he began to juggle them on the steps of the throne, as he had vowed to do so long ago on the Isle of Sleep.

It was the signal, and the juggling commenced, and the air glistened with the multitude of strange objects that seemed to fly of their own accord. Never had juggling of such quality been seen in the known universe, Lord Valentine was sure of that. He threw from the throne another few moments, and then he came down into the group, laughing, in high joy, interchanging sickles and torches with Sleet and the Skandars and Carabella. 'As in the old days!' Zalzan Kavol called. 'But you're even better now, my lord!'

'The audience inspires me,' replied Lord Valentine.

'And can you juggle as a Skandar can?' said Zalzan Kavol. 'Here, my lord! Catch! Catch! Catch! Catch!' Seemingly from out of the air Zalzan Kavol plucked eggs and plates and clubs, his four arms never ceasing to weave and seize, and each thing he caught he sent toward Lord Valentine, who tirelessly received and juggled and passed off to Sleet or Carabella, while the cheers of the audience – no mere flattery, that was certain – resounded in his ears. Yes! This was the life! As in the old days, yes, but even better now! He laughed and caught a shimmering sword and sent it high. Elidath had thought it might be unseemly for a Coronal to do such a thing as juggle before the princes of the realm, and Tunigorn had felt the same, but Lord Valentine had overruled them, telling them with kindness and love that he cared not at all for protocol. And now he saw them watching open-mouthed from their places of honor, stupefied by the skill of this amazing exhibition.

And yet he knew his time had come to quit the juggling-floor. One by one he emptied his hands of the objects he had caught, and gradually he retreated. When he had reached the first step of the throne he halted and beckoned to Carabella.

'Come,' he said. 'Join me up here, and now we become spectators.'

Her cheeks deepened in color, but without faltering she rid herself of the clubs and knives and eggs, and moved toward the throne. Lord Valentine took her by the hand and together they ascended.

'My lord—' she whispered.

'Shhh. This is very serious business. Careful you don't trip on the steps.'

'I trip? I, a juggler?'

'Pardon me, Carabella.'

She laughed. 'I pardon you, Valentine.'

'*Lord* Valentine.'

'Is that how it is to be, my lord?'

'Not really,' he said 'Not between the two of us.' They reached the highest step. The double seat, gleaming in green and gold velvet, awaited them. Lord Valentine stood a moment, looking out at the throng, at the dukes and princes and the common folk. 'Where's Deliamber?' he whispered. 'I don't see him!'

'He had no taste for this event,' said Carabella, 'and has gone off to Zimroel, I think, on holiday. Wizards are bored by such festivities. And the Vroon was never fond of juggling, you know.'

'He should be here,' Lord Valentine murmured.

'When you need him again, he'll return.'

'I hope so. Come: let's sit now.'

They took their places on the throne. Below, the remaining jugglers were engaged in their most dazzling routines, which seemed miraculous even to Lord Valentine who knew the secrets of timing that underlay them; and as he watched, he felt a strange sadness come over him, for he had withdrawn himself from the company of the jugglers now, he had drawn apart to mount the throne, and that was a grave and solemn alteration of his life. He knew beyond doubt that his time as a wandering juggler, the freest and in some ways the most joyful time of his life, was ended now, and the responsibilities of power, which he had not sought but which he had not been able to refuse, were descending on him in their full weight once again. He could not deny the sorrow of that. To Carabella he said, 'Perhaps privately – when the court is looking the other way – we can all get together now and then, and throw the clubs, eh, Carabella?'

'I think so, my lord. I would like that.'

'And we can pretend – that we're somewhere between Falkynkip and Dulorn, wondering if the Perpetual Circus will hire us, wondering if we can find an inn, if – if—'

'My lord, look at what the Skandars are doing! Can you believe the skill of it! So many arms, and every one busy!'

Lord Valentine smiled. 'I must ask Zalzan Kavol to tell me how that one is done,' he said. 'Someday soon. When I have time.'

Acknowledgements for *Lord Valentine's Castle*

For assistance with the technical aspects of juggling in this novel I am indebted to Catherine Crowell of San Francisco and to those extraordinary performers the Flying Karamazov Brothers, who may not be aware until this moment of just how much help they rendered. However, the concepts of the theory and practice of juggling as expressed herein are primarily my own, especially as regards the capabilities of four-armed jugglers, and neither Ms Crowell nor the Karamazovs should be held responsible for any implausibilities or impossibilities in these pages.

Invaluable assistance in other aspects of writing this book was provided by Marta Randall. Among Ms Randall's contributions are the texts of some of the songs found herein.

For additional criticism of the manuscript in its troublesome early stages I am grateful to Barbara Silverberg and Susanne L. Houfek, and I owe thanks to Ted Chichak of the Scott Meredith Literary Agency for his support and encouragement and professional acumen.

Robert Silverberg

If you've enjoyed these books and would
like to read more, you'll find literally thousands
of classic Science Fiction & Fantasy titles
through the **SF Gateway**

*For the new home of
Science Fiction & Fantasy . . .*

✴

*For the most comprehensive collection
of classic SF on the internet . . .*

✴

Visit the SF Gateway

www.sfgateway.com

Robert Silverberg (1935–)

Robert Silverberg was born in Brooklyn, New York, in 1935, and is one of the most prolific authors of all time, writing not just SF & Fantasy, but extensive non-fiction and a large number of pseudonymously published erotica novels. In his first years as a professional writer, his output regularly exceeded a million words per year.

He has won and been nominated for the Hugo and Nebula awards dozens of times as both writer and editor, and in 2004 received the SFWA Grand Master Award. Among his many acclaimed and bestselling novels are *A Time of Changes*, *The Book of Skulls*, *Dying Inside* and *Lord Valentine's Castle*.

Robert Silverberg lives on the West Coast of the United States with his wife, author, editor and art critic, Karen Haber.